# The Sun Sister

Also by Lucinda Riley

*The Orchid House*
*The Girl on the Cliff*
*The Lavender Garden*
*The Midnight Rose*
*The Royal Secret*

The Seven Sisters Series

*The Seven Sisters*
*The Storm Sister*
*The Shadow Sister*
*The Pearl Sister*
*The Moon Sister*

# THE
# SUN
# SISTER

*Electra's Story*

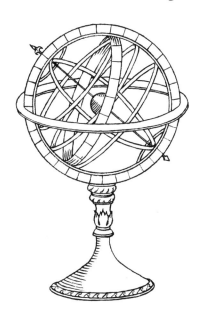

## LUCINDA RILEY

**ATRIA** BOOKS

New York   London   Toronto   Sydney   New Delhi

ATRIA
BOOKS

An Imprint of Simon & Schuster, Inc.
1230 Avenue of the Americas
New York, NY 10020

First Atria Books hardcover edition May 2020

**ATRIA** B O O K S and colophon are trademarks of Simon & Schuster, Inc.

For information about special discounts for bulk purchases, please contact
Simon & Schuster Special Sales at 1-866-506-1949 or business@simonandschuster.com.

The Simon & Schuster Speakers Bureau can bring authors to your live event.
For more information or to book an event contact the Simon & Schuster Speakers
Bureau at 1-866-248-3049 or visit our website at www.simonspeakers.com.

Manufactured in the United States of America

1   3   5   7   9   10   8   6   4   2

Library of Congress Cataloging-in-Publication Data

Riley, Lucinda, author.
The sun sister : a novel / Lucinda Riley.
New York : Atria Books, 2020.
pages   cm
ISBN: 9781982110642 (hardcover)
9781982110659 (paperback) (ebook)
LC record available at https://lccn.loc.gov/2020931825

ISBN 978-1-9821-1064-2
ISBN 978-1-9821-1066-6 (ebook)

*For Ella Micheler*

Some women fear the fire,
Some women simply become it . . .

—R. H. Sin

# List of Characters

**ATLANTIS**

Pa Salt—the sisters' adoptive father (deceased)

Marina (Ma)—the sisters' guardian

Claudia—housekeeper at Atlantis

Georg Hoffman—Pa Salt's lawyer

Christian—the skipper

**THE D'APLIÈSE SISTERS**

Maia

Ally (Alcyone)

Star (Asterope)

CeCe (Celaeno)

Tiggy (Taygete)

Electra

Merope (missing)

# ELECTRA

*New York*
*March 2008*

# I

"I don't remember where I was or what I was doing when I heard my father had died."

"Okay. Do you want to explore that?"

I stared at Theresa, sitting in her leather wingback chair. She reminded me of the sleepy dormouse at Alice in Wonderland's tea party or one of his ratty friends. She blinked a lot behind her little round glasses, and her lips were permanently pursed. She had great legs under the knee-length tweed skirt she was wearing and good hair, too. I decided she could be pretty if she wanted to be, but I knew she wasn't interested in anything but looking intelligent.

"Electra? I'm losing you again."

"Yeah, sorry, I was miles away."

"Were you thinking about how you felt when your father died?"

As I couldn't exactly tell her what I *had* been thinking, I nodded earnestly. "Yeah, I was."

"And?"

"I really can't remember. Sorry."

"You seem angry about his death, Electra. Why were you angry?"

"I'm not . . . I wasn't. I mean, I honestly can't remember."

"You can't remember how you felt at that moment?"

"No."

"Okay."

I watched her scribble something onto her notepad, which probably went along the lines of "refusing to deal with father's death." It was what the last shrink had said to me, and I was *so* totally dealing with it. As I'd learned over the years, they liked to find a reason for me being a screw-up, and then they'd take hold of it, just like a mouse with a piece of cheese, and nibble away at me until I agreed with them and talked shit just to keep them happy.

3

"So how are you feeling about Mitch?"

The phrases that came to mind to describe my ex would probably have Theresa reaching for her cell to warn the cops that there was a crazy woman on the loose, who wanted to blast away the balls of one of the world's most famous rock stars. Instead, I smiled sweetly.

"I'm good. I've moved on now."

"You were very angry with him the last time you came to see me, Electra."

"Yeah, but I'm fine now. Really."

"Well, that's good news. And how about the drinking? Under control a little more?"

"Yes," I lied again. "Listen, I'm gonna have to run to a meeting."

"But we're only halfway through the session, Electra."

"I know, it's a shame, but hey, that's life." I stood up and walked toward the door.

"Maybe I can fit you in again later this week? Speak to Marcia on your way out."

"I will, thanks." I was already closing the door behind me. I walked straight past Marcia, the receptionist, and headed for the elevator. It came almost immediately, and as I was whooshed downward, I closed my eyes— I hated any confined spaces—and laid my hot forehead against the cool marble interior.

*Jeez,* I thought, *what is it with me? I'm so messed up that I can't even tell my therapist the truth!*

*You're too ashamed to tell anyone the truth . . . and how could she understand even if you did?* I argued back to myself. *She probably lives in a neat brownstone with her lawyer husband, has two kids and a refrigerator covered in cute magnets showing off their artwork. Oh,* I added to myself as I climbed into the back of my limo, *and one of those vomit-inducing photos of Mom and Dad with the kids, all wearing matching denim shirts, that they've blown up huge and hung behind their couch.*

"Where to, ma'am?" the driver asked me over the intercom.

"Home," I barked before grabbing a bottle of water from the minifridge, shutting it fast before I was tempted to explore the alcoholic options. I had the mother of all headaches, which no amount of painkillers had eased, and it was past five in the evening. It had been a great party the night before, though, from what I could remember, anyway. Maurice, my new best designer friend, had been in town and had dropped by for a few drinks with some of his New York playmates, who had then called others . . . I couldn't remember going to bed and had been surprised to find a stranger in it with me when I'd woken up this morning. He was a beautiful stranger, at least, and after we'd gotten to know each other physically again, I'd asked him his name. Fernando had been a delivery driver for Walmart in Philly up until a few months back, when one of the fashion buyers had noticed him and told him to call a friend at a New York modeling agency. He said he'd be happy to walk me down a red carpet sometime soon—I'd learned the hard way that a shot of me on his arm would send Mr. Walmart's career skyrocketing—so I'd gotten rid of him as soon as I could.

*So what if you had told Mrs. Dormouse the truth, Electra? So what if you'd admitted that last night you were so off your face with liquor and coke that you could have slept with Santa and you wouldn't have known about it? That the reason you couldn't even begin to think about your father wasn't because of his death but because you knew how ashamed he'd be of you . . . how ashamed he'd been of you?*

At least when Pa Salt had been alive, I'd known he couldn't see what I was doing, but now he was dead, he'd somehow become omnipresent; he could have been in the bedroom with me last night or even here in the limo right now . . .

I cracked and reached for a minivodka, then poured it down my throat, trying to forget the look of disappointment on Pa's face the last time I'd seen him before he'd died. He'd come to New York to visit me, saying he had something to tell me. I'd avoided him until the last possible evening, when I had reluctantly agreed to have dinner with him. I'd arrived at Asiate, a restaurant just across Central Park, already tanked on vodka and uppers. I'd sat numbly opposite him throughout the meal, excusing myself to go to the ladies' room to do a few bumps of coke whenever he tried to start conversations I didn't want to pursue.

Once dessert had arrived, Pa had crossed his arms and regarded me calmly. "I'm extremely worried for you, Electra. You seem to be completely absent."

"Well, you don't understand the kind of pressure I'm under," I'd snapped at him. "What it takes to be me!" To my shame, I had only vague memories of what had happened next or what he'd said, but I knew I'd stood up and walked out on him. So now I'd never even know what it was he'd wanted to tell me.

"Why do you give a shit, Electra?" I asked myself as I wiped my mouth and stuck the empty bottle in a pocket—my driver was new, and all I needed was a story in a newspaper saying I'd drunk the minibar dry. "He's not even your real father, anyway."

Besides, there was nothing I could do about it now. Pa was gone—like everyone else I'd loved in my life—and I had to get on with it. I didn't need him, I didn't need anybody . . .

"We're here, ma'am," said the driver through the intercom.

"Thanks. I'll jump out," I added, then did so, closing the limo door behind me. It was best to make my arrival at any place as inconspicuous as possible; other celebrities could wear disguises and get away with going to a local diner, but I was over six feet tall and pretty hard to miss in a crowd, even if I hadn't been famous.

"Hi there, Electra!"

"Tommy," I said, managing a smile as I walked beneath the canopy toward the entrance to my apartment building, "how are you today?"

"All the better for seeing you, ma'am. Did you have a good day?"

"Yeah, great, thank you." I nodded as I looked down—and I mean *down*—at my number one fan. "See you tomorrow, Tommy."

"You sure will, Electra. Not going out tonight?"

"No, it's a quiet one in. Bye, now," I said as I gave him a wave and walked inside.

*At least* he *loves me*, I mused as I collected my mail from the concierge and headed for the elevator. As the porter rode up with me simply because it was his job (I considered offering him my keys and mail to hold, as that was all I was carrying), I thought about Tommy. He stood sentinel outside the building most days and had done so for the past few months. At first it had freaked me out and I'd asked the concierge to get rid of him. Tommy had stood his ground—literally—and said that he had every right to stand on the sidewalk, that he wasn't bothering anyone, and that all he wanted to do was to protect me. The concierge had encouraged me to call the cops and have him charged with stalking, but one morning I'd asked him his full name, then gone to do a bit of internet stalking myself. I'd discovered on Facebook that he was an army vet who'd won medals for bravery out in Afghanistan and that he had a wife and daughter in Queens. Now, rather than making me feel threatened, Tommy made me feel safe. Besides that, he was always respectful and polite, so I'd told the concierge to back off.

The porter stepped out of the elevator and let me pass. Then we did a kind of dance in which I needed to step back so that he could go ahead and lead the way to my penthouse apartment to open the door for me with his own master key.

"There we go, Miss D'Aplièse. Have a nice day, now."

He nodded at me, and I saw zero warmth in his eyes. I knew that the staff here wished that I would disappear in a puff of smoke up a non-existent chimney. Most of the other residents had been here since they were fetuses in their mothers' stomachs, back when a woman of color, like me, would have been "privileged" to be their maid. They were all owner-occupiers, whereas I was a peasant: a tenant, albeit a rich one, allowed in on a lease because the old lady who'd lived here had died and her son had renovated the place, then tried to sell it at an exorbitant price. Due to something called the subprime crisis, he'd apparently failed to do so. Instead, he'd been reduced to selling the lease to the highest bidder—me. The price was crazy, but then so was the apartment, stuffed with modern artwork and every kind of electronic gadget you could imagine (I didn't know how to work most of them), and the view from the terrace over Central Park was stunning.

If I needed a reminder of my success, this apartment was it. *But what it reminds me of more than anything*, I thought as I sank down into the couch that could provide a comfortable bed for at least two full-grown guys, *is how lonely I am*. Its size made even me feel small and delicate—and up here, right at the top of the building, very, very isolated.

My cell phone piped up from somewhere in the apartment, playing the song that had made Mitch a worldwide superstar; I'd tried to change the ringtone, but it hadn't worked. *If CeCe is dyslexic with words, then I sure am dyslexic with electronics*, I thought as I went into the bedroom to grab it. I was relieved to see that the maid had changed the sheets on the enormous bed and everything was hotel-room perfect again. I liked the new maid my PA had found me; she'd signed a nondisclosure agreement like all the others to stop her blabbing to the media about any of my nastier habits. Even so, I shuddered to think what she—was it Lisbet?—had thought when she'd walked into my apartment this morning.

I sat on the bed and listened to my voice mails. Five were from my agent asking me to call her back urgently about tomorrow's shoot for *Vanity Fair*, and the last message was from Amy, my new PA. She'd been with me for only three months, but I liked her.

"*Hi, Electra, it's Amy. I . . . well, I just wanted to say that I've really enjoyed working for you, but I don't think it's gonna work out long term. I've handed my resignation letter in today to your agent, and I wish you luck in the future, and . . ."*

"*SHIT!*" I screamed as I pressed "delete" and threw the cell across the room. "What the hell did I do to her?" I asked the ceiling, wondering why I felt so upset that a two-bit nobody, who had gone down on bended knee and begged me to give her a chance, had walked out on me three months later.

" 'It's been my dream to be in the fashion business since I was a little kid. Please, Miss D'Aplièse, I'll work for you night and day, your life will be mine, and I swear I'll never let you down.' " I mimicked Amy's whiny Brooklyn accent as I dialed my agent. There were only three things I couldn't live without: vodka, cocaine, and a PA.

"Hi, Susie, I just heard Amy's resigned."

"Yes, it's not great. She was shaping up well." Susie's British accent sounded crisp and businesslike.

"Yeah, I thought she was, too. Do you know why she's gone?"

There was a pause on the line before she replied. "No. Anyway, I'll get Rebekah on the case, and I'm sure we'll have you a new one by the end of the week. Did you get my messages?"

"Yup, I did."

"Well, don't be late tomorrow. They want to shoot as the sun is coming up. A car will pick you up at four a.m., okay?"

"Sure."

"I heard you had quite a party last night."

"It was fun, yeah."

"Well, no partying tonight, Electra. You need to be fresh for tomorrow. It's the cover shot."

"Don't worry, I'll be in bed by nine like a good little girl."

"Okay. Sorry, I've got Lagerfeld on the other line. Rebekah will be in touch with a list of suitable PAs. Ciao."

"Ciao," I mimicked into the cell as the line went dead. Susie was one of the only people on the planet who would dare hang up on me. She was the most powerful modeling agent in New York and ran all the big names in the industry. She'd spotted me when I was sixteen. At the time, I'd been working in Paris as a waitress, having been expelled from my third school in about as many years. I'd told Pa that it was pointless his trying to find me another school because I'd only end up getting expelled from there, too. To my surprise, he hadn't made a fuss.

I remembered how astonished I'd been that he hadn't been angrier at yet another of my failures. Just kind of disappointed, I suppose, which had taken the wind out of my sails.

"I thought I'd go traveling or something," I'd suggested to him. "Learn through life experience."

"I agree that most of what you need to know to be a success in life doesn't necessarily come through the academic process," he'd said, "but because you're so bright, I'd hoped you'd at least get some qualifications. You're a little young to be off by yourself. It's a big wide world out there, Electra."

"I can take care of myself, Pa," I'd said firmly.

"I'm sure you can, but what will you do to fund your travels?"

"I'll get a job, of course," I'd said with a shrug. "I thought I'd head for Paris first."

Pa had nodded. "Excellent choice. It's an incredible city."

As I'd watched him across his big desk in the study, I'd thought he'd looked almost dreamy and sad. Yup, definitely sad.

"Well, now," he'd continued, "why don't we compromise? You want to leave school, which I understand, but I'm concerned about my youngest daughter heading off into the world at such a tender age. Marina has some contacts in Paris. I'm sure she could help you sort out a safe place to stay. Take the summer there; then we'll regroup and decide where you go next."

"Okay, sounds like a plan," I'd agreed, still amazed that he hadn't fought harder for me to finish my education. As I'd stood up to leave, I'd decided that he'd either washed his hands of me or was giving me just enough rope to hang myself with. Anyway, Ma had called some contacts, and I'd ended up in a sweet little studio overlooking the rooftops of Montmartre. It had been miniscule, and I'd had to share the bathroom with a load of foreign exchange kids who were in town to improve their French, but it had been *mine*.

I remembered that first delicious taste of independence as I'd stood in my tiny room the night I arrived and realized there was no one to tell me what to do. There was also no one to cook for me, so I'd taken myself off to a café just along the street, sat down at a table outside, and lit up a cigarette as I studied the menu. I'd ordered French onion soup and a glass of wine, and the waiter hadn't even batted an eyelid at me smoking or ordering alcohol. Three glasses of wine later, I'd had the confidence to go up to the manager and ask him if he had any vacancies for a waitress. Twenty minutes after that, I'd walked the few hundred yards back to my studio with a job. One of my proudest moments had been the call to Pa on the pay phone along the hall the next morning. To give him credit, he'd sounded just as thrilled as when my sister Maia had won a place at the Sorbonne.

Four weeks later, I'd served Susie, now my modeling agent, a croque monsieur, and the rest was history . . .

*Why am I looking back all the time?* I asked myself as I retrieved my cell to listen to the rest of my messages. *And why do I keep thinking about Pa?*

"Mitch . . . Pa . . ." I muttered as I waited for the voice mail to spill its beans. "They're gone, Electra, along with Amy as of today, and you just have to move on."

"My dearest Electra! How are you? I am back in New York again . . . What are you doing tonight? Fancy sharing a bottle of Cristal and some chow mein *dans ton lit avec moi?* I'm yearning for you. Give me a call back as soon as you can."

Despite my low mood, I couldn't help but smile. Zed Eszu was an enigma in my life. He was hugely wealthy, well connected, and—despite his lack of height and the fact that he wasn't my usual type at all—incredible in bed; we'd been hooking up regularly for three years. It had all stopped when I had gotten serious with Mitch, but I'd reinstated him a few weeks ago, and there was no doubt he'd given my ego the boost it had needed.

Were we in love? It was a total no, for me anyway, but we ran with the same crowd in New York and, best of all, when we were alone together we spoke in French. Like Mitch, he wasn't impressed by who I was, which was rare these days and somehow comforting.

I stared at the phone, debating whether to ignore Zed and follow Susie's instructions for an early night or whether to call him and enjoy some company. It was a no-brainer, so I called Zed and told him to come on over. While I was waiting for him, I took a shower, then dressed in my favorite silk kimono, which had been designed especially for me by an up-and-coming Japanese atelier. I then drank what felt like a gallon of water to counteract any drinking or bad stuff I might do when he arrived.

The concierge phone beeped to announce Zed's presence, and I told the concierge to send him right up. He arrived at my door with a giant bouquet of my favorite white roses and the promised bottle of Cristal champagne.

"*Bonsoir, ma belle Electra,*" he said in his strange clipped French as he unloaded the flowers and champagne and kissed me on both cheeks. "*Comment tu vas?*"

"I'm good," I answered as I eyed the champagne greedily. "Shall I open it?"

"I think that is my job. Can I take my jacket off first?"

"Of course."

"But before that," he said, dipping into his jacket pocket and handing me a velvet box, "I saw this and thought of you."

"Thanks," I said, sitting down on the couch and tucking my irritatingly long legs underneath me as I stared at the box in my hands like an excited child. Zed often bought me presents; ironically, given his vast wealth, they were rarely flashy but always something thoughtful and interesting. I lifted the lid and saw a ring nestling inside. The stone was oval-shaped and of a soft buttery yellow hue.

"It is amber," he said as he watched me studying the way it caught the light of the chandelier above us. "Try it on."

"Which finger should I put it on?" I teased as I looked up at him.

"Whichever you prefer, *ma chère*, but if I was going to make you my wife, I think I might do a little better than that. I am sure that you know your Greek namesake has an association with amber."

"Really? No, I don't." I watched him as he popped the cork on the champagne. "Like what?"

"Well, the Greek word for 'amber' was *electron*, and legend has it that the sun's rays were trapped within the stone. A Greek philosopher noticed that if two pieces were rubbed together, they created friction, which created an energy . . . Your name couldn't suit you better." He smiled as he placed a glass of champagne in front of me.

"Are you saying I create friction?" I smiled back. "The question is, did I grow into my name, or did it grow into me? *Santé*."

"*Santé*." We clinked our glasses, and he sat down next to me.

"Um . . ."

"You are thinking to yourself, did I bring another gift?"

"Yup."

"Then look underneath the lining of the box."

I did so, and sure enough, tucked underneath the slim slice of velvet that had held the ring was a small plastic packet.

"Thanks, Zed," I said as I pulled the packet open, then dipped a finger into its contents like a child with a honey pot and rubbed some on my gums.

"Good, eh?" he asked as I tipped a little out onto the table, detached the short straw from the packet, and took up a noseful.

"Mmm, very," I agreed. "Want some?"

"You know I don't. So how have you been?"

"Oh . . . okay."

"You do not sound sure, Electra, and you look tired."

"It's been busy," I said as I took a large gulp of my champagne. "I was on a shoot in Fiji last week, and I'm flying to Paris next week."

"Maybe you need to slow down a little. Take a break."

"Says the guy who told me he spends more nights sleeping on his private jet than he does in his bed," I teased him.

"Then maybe we should both slow down. Can I tempt you to a week on my yacht? It's moored in Saint Lucia for the next couple of months before I have it sailed to the Med for the summer."

I sighed. "I wish. I have a packed schedule until June."

"June, then. We can sail around the Greek islands."

"Maybe." I shrugged, not taking him seriously. He often discussed plans when we were together that never came to anything, and more to the point, nor would I want them to. Zed was just great for a night's company and some physical action, but any more than that and he'd begin to irritate me with his fastidiousness and unbelievable arrogance.

The concierge phone beeped again, and Zed stood up to answer it. "Send it up immediately, thank you." He poured us both some more champagne. "We are having Chinese, and I promise you, it will be the best chow mein you have ever tasted." He smiled. "So how are your sisters?"

"I don't know. I've been too busy lately to call them. Ally did have a baby, though—a little boy. She's named him Bear, which is really cute. Come to think of it, I'm meant to be seeing them all in June back at Atlantis; we're taking Pa's boat out to the Greek islands to lay a wreath where Ally thinks his coffin was dropped into the sea. Your dad was found on a beach close by, wasn't he?"

"Yes, but like you, I do not want to think of my father's death because it upsets me," Zed replied sharply. "I only think to the future."

"I know, but it is a coincidence—"

The buzzer rang, and Zed went to answer the door.

"Now, Electra," he said as he carried two boxes through to the kitchen. "Come and help me with these."

# 2

I arrived home from the shoot the following day, took a hot shower, and got into bed with a vodka. I felt utterly wrecked—anyone who thinks models just float around in pretty clothes and get paid a fortune for it should try a day being me. A 4:00 a.m. start with six changes of hair, clothes, and makeup in a freezing warehouse somewhere downtown was *not* easy. I never complained publicly—I mean, I was hardly working in a sweatshop in China, and I got paid a ton for doing it—but everyone has their own reality and occasionally, even if it is a first-world problem, people are allowed to complain to themselves, aren't they?

Enjoying feeling warm for the first time that day, I lay back on my pillows and checked my voice mails. Rebekah, Susie's PA, had left me four, telling me she'd emailed me some résumés of suitable PAs and that I should look at them as soon as I could. I was scrolling through them on my laptop when my cell rang, and I saw it was Rebekah again.

"I'm looking at them right now," I said before she could speak.

"Great, thanks, Electra. I was actually calling because there's a girl I think would be the perfect fit for you, but she's been offered another position and has to give her answer by tomorrow. Would it be okay if she swung by early evening and you two had a chat?"

"I've just got in from the *Vanity Fair* shoot, Rebekah, and—"

"I really think you should see her, Electra. She comes with great references. She used to work as PA to Bardin, and you know how difficult he is. I mean," Rebekah continued hurriedly, "that she's used to working under pressure for high-profile fashion clients. Can I send her around?"

"Okay," I sighed, not wanting to sound as "difficult" as she obviously thought I was.

"Great, I'll tell her. I know she'll be thrilled—she's one of your biggest fans."

"Right. Good. Tell her to come by at six."

Promptly at six, the concierge phone beeped to indicate that my guest had arrived.

"Send her up," I said wearily. I wasn't looking forward to this—since Susie had suggested I needed help organizing my life, I'd seen a stream of eager young women arrive, full of enthusiasm, only to leave weeks later.

"Am I difficult?" I asked my reflection in the mirror as I made sure I didn't have anything stuck between my teeth. "Maybe. But it's nothing new, is it?" I added as I finished off my vodka, then smoothed down my hair. Stefano, my hairstylist, had only recently braided it tightly against my scalp in order to stitch in long extensions. My whole head always ached after a new weave had been put in.

There was a knock, and I went to answer the door, wondering what was waiting for me on the other side of it. Whatever I'd been expecting, it was certainly not the small, trim figure dressed in a plain brown suit with a skirt that fell at an unfashionable length to just below her knees. My eyes wandered down to her feet, which were enclosed in a pair of what Ma would call "sensible" brown brogues. The most surprising thing about her was that she was wearing a head scarf wrapped tightly across her forehead and around her neck. I saw that she had an exquisite face: tiny nose, high cheekbones, full pink lips, and a clear latte-colored complexion.

"Hello." She smiled at me, and her lovely deep brown eyes lit up as she did so. "My name is Mariam Kazemi, and I am very pleased to meet you, Miss D'Aplièse."

I loved the tone of her voice—in fact, if it was for sale, I'd buy it because it was deep and modulated, pouring gently like honey from her throat.

"Hi, Mariam, come in."

"Thank you."

As I took long strides toward the couch, Mariam Kazemi took her time. She paused to look at the expensive splashes and squiggles on canvas, and I could just tell from her expression that she thought as much of them as I did.

"They're not mine, they're the landlord's choice," I felt inexplicably bound to explain. "Can I get you anything? Water, coffee, tea—something stronger?"

"Oh, no, I don't drink. I mean, I do, but not alcohol. I'd love some water, if it's not too much trouble."

"Sure," I said as I changed direction and headed for the kitchen. I was just pulling a bottle of Evian out of the refrigerator when she appeared beside me.

"I would have thought you had staff to do that kind of thing?"

"I have a maid, but it's just little ol' me here most of the time. Here." I handed her the water; then she walked to the window and gazed out of it.

"You're a long way up."

"I am, yes," I said, realizing I was completely blindsided by this woman, who exuded calm like a perfume and seemed totally unimpressed by meeting me or by the grand apartment I lived in. Normally, possible candidates were bouncing off the walls with excitement and promises.

"Shall we go sit down?" I suggested.

"Yes, thank you."

"So," I said when we were settled in the living room, "I hear you worked for Bardin?"

"I did, yes."

"Why did you leave?"

"I've been offered a position that might suit me better."

"Not because he was difficult?"

Mariam chuckled. "Oh, no. He wasn't difficult at all, but he recently moved back to Paris full-time and I am still based here. We remain the best of friends."

"Good. Well, that's great. So why are you interested in working for me?"

"Because I've always admired your work."

*Wow*, I thought. *It isn't often I hear someone calling my job "work."*

"Thanks."

"It is a real gift to be able to create a personality that complements the products one is advertising, I think."

I watched as she opened her plain brown satchel, which was definitely more "school" than it was "designer," and handed me her résumé.

"I guessed you wouldn't have had time to glance through it before I arrived."

"No, I didn't," I agreed as I skimmed the details of her life, which were unusually brief and to the point. "So you didn't go to college?"

"No, my family didn't have the funds. Or more truthfully"—one of her small, delicate hands reached toward her face, and a finger rubbed her nose—"they probably did, but there are six of us and it wouldn't have been fair to the rest if I'd have gone and the others couldn't."

"I'm one of six, too! And I didn't go to college or university."

"Well, we have something in common at least."

"I am the youngest."

Mariam smiled. "And I am the eldest."

"You're twenty-six?"

"Yes."

"Then we're the same age," I said, for some unknown reason feeling pleased to find parallels with this unusual human being. "So what did you do when you left school?"

"I worked in a florist's during the day and went to business school at night. I can obtain a copy of my qualification certificate if you need it. I'm fully computer literate, can produce spreadsheets, and my typing is . . . well, I'm not sure of the exact speed, actually, but it's fast."

"That's not really one of the main requirements, and neither are spreadsheets. My accountant looks after all the financials."

"Oh, but they can be very useful in an organizational role, too. I could plan in detail your entire month for you at a glance."

"If you did that, I think I might run away," I joked. "I go on a day-to-day basis. It's the only way I can cope."

"I completely understand, Miss D'Aplièse, but it's my job to organize beyond that. With Bardin, I even had a spreadsheet for his dry cleaning and we'd work out what he'd wear to each event, right down to the color of his socks—which were often deliberately mismatched." Mariam let out a small giggle, and I joined her.

"You say he's a nice person?"

"He is wonderful, yes."

Whether he was or he wasn't, this girl had integrity. So many times I'd had prospective PAs dishing the dirt to me on former employers. Maybe they thought it was cool to explain in depth why they'd left, but I just thought of the fact that it could be me they would be talking about in the future.

"Before you ask, I am very discreet." Mariam had obviously read my mind. "I have often found the stories that circulate about celebrities in our business to be untrue. It's interesting . . ."

"What?"

"No, it's nothing."

"Please, say it."

"Well, I find it fascinating that so much of the world craves fame, yet in my experience, it often brings only misery. People believe that it will grant them the right to do or be anything they choose, but in fact they lose the most precious commodity we humans have, and that is their freedom. *Your* freedom," she added.

I looked at her in surprise. I got the feeling that despite everything I had, she felt sorry for me. Not in a patronizing way, but sympathetic and warm.

"Yup, I've lost my freedom. In fact," I declared to this total stranger, "I'm beyond paranoid that someone will see me doing the simplest thing and twist it into a story to sell more of their newspapers."

"It is not a good way to live, Miss D'Aplièse." Mariam shook her head solemnly. "Now I am afraid I must go. I swore to my mother I would babysit my little brother while she and Papa go out."

"Right. This babysitting . . . I mean, is it a regular thing you do?"

"Oh, no, not at all, which is why it is important I am there on time tonight. It is Mama's birthday, you see, and the family joke is that the last time Papa took her out to dinner was when he proposed to her twenty-eight years ago! I understand that if you employ me, you will need me twenty-four hours a day."

"And that there will be a lot of overseas travel?"

"Yes, that is no problem. I have no romantic commitments, either. Now, if you'll excuse me . . ." She stood up. "It has been a pleasure to meet you, Miss D'Aplièse, even if we do not end up working together."

I watched her as she turned and walked toward the door. Even in her ugly clothes, she had a natural grace and what a photographer would call a "presence." Despite the fact that the interview had been about fifteen minutes flat and I hadn't asked her a tenth of the questions I should have done, I really, *really* wanted Mariam Kazemi and her wonderful sense of calm in my life.

"Listen, if I offer you the role now, would you consider taking it? I mean," I said as I jumped off the couch to follow her to the door, "I know you've been offered another position and need to answer by tomorrow."

She paused for a few moments, then turned to face me and smiled. "Why, of course I would consider it. I think you are a lovely person, with a good soul."

"When can you start?"

"Next week, if you wish."

"Done!" I put out my hand toward her, and after only a couple of seconds' hesitation, she offered me hers.

"Done," she repeated. "Now I really must go."

"Of course."

She opened the door, and I followed her to the elevator. "You already know the package, but I'll have Rebekah write up a formal offer of employment and bike it to you in the morning."

"Very good," she said as the elevator doors slid open.

"By the way, what is that scent you're wearing? It's gorgeous."

"Actually, it's body oil and I make it myself. Good-bye, Miss D'Aplièse."

The elevator doors closed, and Mariam Kazemi was gone.

All Mariam's references didn't just check out, they couldn't sing her praises highly enough, so the following Thursday, the two of us boarded a private jet from Teterboro Airport in New Jersey and headed for Paris. The only nod she made to the fact we were traveling, in terms of her "uniform," was that she had replaced the skirt with a pair of beige pants. I watched her as she took her seat in the cabin, then got her laptop out of her satchel.

"Have you flown by private jet before?" I asked her.

"Oh, yes, Bardin used nothing else. Now, Miss D'Aplièse—"

"Electra, please."

"Electra," she corrected herself. "I must ask you whether you would prefer to take some rest during the flight or would like to use the time to go through a few things with me?"

Given the fact that Zed had been my playmate up until four o'clock that morning, I chose the former, and as soon as we were airborne, I pressed the button that turned my seat into a bed, donned my eye mask, and fell asleep.

I woke three hours later, feeling refreshed—I'd had plenty of practice at sleeping on planes—and peeped out of a corner of the eye mask to see what my new PA was up to. She wasn't in her seat, so I supposed she must be in the bathroom. Pulling off my mask, I sat up and to my surprise saw Mariam's rear end lifted toward me in the narrow aisle between the seats. *Maybe she's practicing yoga*, I thought, as she was kneeling on all fours with her head bent to the floor in what looked like a variation of child's pose. Then I heard her muttering to herself and as she raised her hands and head slightly, I realized she was praying. Feeling uncomfortable that I was observing her in such a private act, I averted my eyes and went off to use the facilities. When I came back out, Mariam was in her seat, tapping away on her laptop.

"Sleep well?" She smiled at me.

"Yeah, and now I'm hungry."

"I asked them to ensure there was some sushi on board—Susie said it was your favorite when you were traveling."

"Thanks. It is."

The cabin attendant was already by my side. "Can I help you, Miss D'Aplièse?"

I put in my order—fresh fruit, sushi, and a half bottle of champagne—then turned to Mariam. "Are you eating?"

"I already did, thank you."

"Are you a nervous flyer?"

She frowned at me. "No, not at all. Why?"

"Because when I woke up, I saw you were praying."

"Oh," she said and laughed, "that is not because I am nervous, it is because it is midday in New York, which is when I always pray."

"Right, wow, I didn't realize you had to."

"Please don't worry, Electra, it is not often that you will see me in prayer—I usually find a discreet private space, but up here"—she gestured around the cramped cabin—"I could not fit into the toilet."

"You have to pray every day?"

"Oh, yes, five times actually."

"Wow, doesn't that cramp your style?"

"I've never thought about it like that, because it is what I have done every day since I was a child. And I always feel better for it afterward. It is just who I am."

"You mean what your religion is?"

"No, who *I* am. Now, here is your sushi. It looks delicious."

"Why don't you join me while I eat? I don't like drinking alone," I quipped as the attendant poured champagne into a flute.

"Would you like anything, ma'am?" she asked Mariam, who had slipped into the seat opposite me.

"Some water, please."

"Cheers," I toasted her. "Here's to a successful working relationship."

"Yes. I am sure it will be."

"I'm sorry if I'm ignorant of your ways."

"Please don't be," Mariam comforted me. "If I were you, I would not have known anything about them either."

"Do you come from a strict family?"

"Not really, no. Or at least, compared to others, I don't. I was born in New York, as were my siblings, so we are Americans. As my father always says, the nation gave my parents safe harbor when they needed it and we must honor its ways as well as the old ways."

"Where were your parents born?" I asked her.

"In Iran—or Persia, as we all prefer to call it at home. It is a much prettier name, don't you think?"

"Yes, I do. So your parents had to leave their country against their will?"

"Yes. They both came to America after the fall of the shah."

"The shah?"

"He was the king of Iran and very Western in his ideals. The extremists in our country didn't like this, so anyone who was related to him had to flee for their lives."

"So if he was a king, does that make you, like, royalty?"

Mariam smiled. "Well, technically, yes, but it is not like European royalty—there are many hundreds of us related to him . . . cousins, second, third, or fourth by marriage. I suppose you would say in the West that my family was high born."

"Jeez! I have a princess working for me!"

"Who knows, if things had been different? I might well have become one if I had married the right man."

I didn't like to say that I'd been joking, but as I looked at Mariam, things fell into place. Her air of containment, her self-assurance, her perfect manners . . . maybe these were things that only hundreds of years of aristocratic breeding could provide.

"What about you, Electra? Where is your family from?"

"I have no idea," I answered, draining my champagne. "I was adopted when I was a baby."

"And you've never thought to investigate your past?"

"No. What is the point in looking back when you can't change the past? I only ever look forward."

"Then you'd better not meet my father." Mariam's eyes danced with mirth. "He is always telling stories of the life he led with my grandparents in Iran. And the stories of our forebears who lived many hundreds of years ago. They are very beautiful, and I loved listening to them as a child."

"Yeah, well, all I got were *Grimm's Fairy Tales*, and the stories always had a scary witch or a troll and frightened me senseless."

"Our stories have those too, but they are called *djinn*s. They do terrible things to people." Mariam sipped her water, eyeing me over the rim of the glass. "Papa always says that our history provides the carpet on which we stand and from which we can fly. Maybe one day you will want to find out your own history. Now, would you be up to listening while I go through the Paris schedule?"

An hour later, Mariam went back to her own seat to type up the notes she'd taken during our chat. I reclined my seat and watched as the sky began to darken outside, heralding the European night. Somewhere under that darkness lay my family home—or at least, the home of us disparate kids whom Pa had collected from around the world.

I'd never really minded that we weren't blood-related, but listening to Mariam talk about her roots—and watching her continue a centuries-old culture that she still celebrated on a private jet bound for Paris—made me almost envious.

I thought of the letter from Pa sitting somewhere in my New York apartment . . . I didn't even know where it was. As I hadn't opened it and it was most likely lost, I'd probably never get the chance to find out about my past. Maybe "The Hoff"—as I'd privately nicknamed Pa's lawyer—could shed some light on it. And I remembered that there were also those numbers on the armillary sphere that Ally said could pinpoint where we had originally come from. Suddenly, it felt like the most important thing in the world to find Pa's letter, almost important enough to ask the pilot to turn back just so I could rifle through my drawers in search of it. At the time, when I'd arrived back in New York after the quasi memorial that had been arranged because Pa had apparently decided to get himself buried at sea before we arrived at Atlantis, I'd been so angry I hadn't wanted to know.

*Why were you angry, Electra?*

The therapist's words rang in my ears. The truth was, I didn't know the answer. I seemed to have been angry ever since I could walk and talk, and probably before that, too. All my sisters loved to tell me how I'd screamed the place down as a baby, and things hadn't gotten much better as I'd grown up. I certainly couldn't blame it on my upbringing, which had been pretty perfect, although odd, given the fact we were all adopted and the family pics looked spookily like a Gap ad due to our different ethnicities. If I ever questioned it, Pa's answer was always that he'd chosen us especially to be his daughters, and that had seemed to pacify my sisters, but not me. I wanted to know *why*. The chances were, now he was dead, I'd never find out.

"An hour to landing, Miss D'Aplièse," the attendant said as she refilled my glass. "Can I get you anything else?"

"No, thanks." I closed my eyes and hoped that my contact in Paris had been as good as his word and delivered what I needed to my hotel, because I was desperate for a line. When I was clean, my brain began to work and I started to think about Pa, about my sisters, my life . . . and I just wasn't comfortable doing that. Not right now, anyway.

For a change, I actually enjoyed the shoot. Spring in Paris—when the sun was out, anyway—was crazily beautiful, and if I felt I belonged in any city, it was right here. We were in the Jardin des Plantes, which was awash with cherry blossom, irises, and peonies, and everything felt new and fresh. It also helped that I liked the photographer. We finished way ahead of schedule and continued the chemistry in my hotel room that afternoon.

"What are you doing living in New York?" Maxime asked me in French as we drank tea from delicate china cups in bed, then used the tray to do a line. "You have a European soul."

I sighed. "You know, I'm not really sure. That's where Susie, my agent, is, and it made sense to be near her."

"Your modeling '*maman*,' you mean?" he teased me. "You're a big girl now, Electra, and can make your own decisions. Live here, then we can do this more often," he said as he clambered out of bed and disappeared into the bathroom to take a shower.

As I gazed out of the window across the Place Vendôme, which was packed with people sightseeing or browsing the elegant shops, I thought about what Maxime had said. He was right, I could live anywhere; it hardly mattered because I spent so much of my life traveling, anyway.

"Where is home?" I whispered, suddenly feeling deflated at the thought of returning to New York and my soulless, echoing apartment. On a whim, I reached for my cell and called Mariam.

"Am I doing anything in New York tomorrow?"

"You have a dinner at seven p.m. with Thomas Allebach, the head of marketing for your fragrance contract," Mariam responded immediately.

"Right." Thomas and I had shared some pleasant downtime over the past few months since Mitch had left me, but I wasn't enamoured. "And Sunday?"

"There's nothing on the calendar."

"Great. Cancel the dinner—tell Thomas the shoot here has run over or something—then move the flight back to Sunday evening and extend my hotel booking for another couple of nights. I want to stay in Paris a little longer."

"Perfect. It is a wonderful city. I will confirm everything as soon as it's done."

"Thank you, Mariam."

"No problem."

"I'm staying on longer," I said to Maxime as he emerged from the shower.

"That's a shame, because I'm out of town for the weekend. If I'd have known—"

"Oh." I tried not to let my disappointment show. "Well, I'll be back again sometime soon."

"Let me know when, won't you?" he said as he dressed. "I'd cancel if I could, but it's a friend's wedding. Sorry, Electra."

"I'm staying for the city, not you," I said as I forced a smile.

"And the city loves you, as do I." He dropped a kiss on my forehead. "Have a wonderful weekend, and keep in touch."

"I will."

Once he'd left, I did a line to cheer myself up and thought about what it was I wanted to do in Paris. But just like in other big cities, the moment I stepped out of the front entrance of the Ritz, I would get recognized, and then within a few minutes, someone would have alerted the press and I'd have an unwanted entourage following me.

My hand hovered over my cell to call Mariam and have her revert to plan A when, as if by magic, it rang.

"Electra? It's Mariam. Just to let you know that the flight back to New York is changed to Sunday night and your hotel suite booking extended."

"Thanks."

"Do you wish me to make you any restaurant reservations?"

"No, I—" For some reason, tears came to my eyes.

"Are you okay, Electra?"

"Yeah, I'm fine."

"Are you . . . busy right now?"

"No, not at all."

"Then can I come and see you? There are a couple of contracts Susie's sent through today that you need to sign."

"Sure, fine."

A few minutes later, Mariam arrived, wafting her lovely scent into the room with her. I signed the contracts, then stared moodily out of the window at the approaching dusk of the Paris evening.

"So what are your plans for tonight?" she asked me.

"I don't have any. You?"

"Nothing but bath, bed, and a good book," she replied.

"I mean, I'd like to go out—visit the café I used to work in as a waitress and just eat normal food like a normal person—but I'm not in the mood to be recognized."

"I understand." She stared at me for a few seconds, then stood up. "I have an idea. Wait here."

She disappeared from the room but was back within minutes holding a scarf.

"May I try it on you? See how it looks?"

"You mean, around my shoulders?"

"No, Electra, around your head like mine. People tend to keep their distance from a woman in a hijab, which is part of the reason why many women of our faith choose to wear one. Shall we give it a go?"

"Okay. It's maybe the only look I've never tried," I added with a giggle.

I sat on the end of the bed as Mariam wound the scarf deftly around my head, draped the ends over my shoulders, then pinned it in place.

"There, take a look." She indicated the mirror.

I did and could hardly believe the change. Even *I* didn't recognize me.

"It's good, real good, but there's not a lot we can do about the rest of me, is there?"

"Do you have any dark-colored pants or leggings with you?"

"Only the black sweatpants I traveled over in."

"They will do. Put them on while I go and get something else."

I did so, and soon Mariam was back with a garment over her arm. She shook it out, and I saw it was a cheap flower-printed cotton smock with long sleeves.

"I brought this in case we were going anywhere smart. I save it for special occasions, but you can borrow it."

"I doubt that it'll fit."

"I don't think we're that different up top. And although I wear it as a dress, I think it would work on you as a shift. Try it on," she urged me.

I did so, and saw that Mariam had been right. The dress fit me fine up top and fell to my midthighs.

"There! No one will recognize you now. You are a Muslim woman."

"What about my feet? I only have my Louboutins or my Chanel pumps."

"Wear the sneakers you had on to fly here," she suggested, heading for my suitcase. "May I?"

"Go ahead," I said, staring at the new me in the mirror. With the head scarf and the simple cotton dress masquerading as a top, it would take a pair of eagle eyes to spot who I was.

"There," Mariam said as I slipped on my sneakers. "The transformation is complete. Just one more thing . . . may I look in your makeup bag?"

"Okay."

"Here, we just need to put some kohl around your eyes. Close, please."

I did as I was told, my mind skidding back to when us sisters had been on Pa's boat during our annual summer cruise and going out for dinner wherever we'd docked. Deemed too young at the time for makeup myself, I'd sit on the bed and watch Maia help Ally with hers.

"Your skin is so beautiful," sighed Mariam. "It literally glows. Now I am convinced that you will not be bothered by anyone tonight."

"You think so?"

"I know so, but test out your disguise downstairs when we walk through reception. Ready to go?"

"Yeah, why not?" I made to pick up my Louis Vuitton shopper, but Mariam stopped me.

"Put whatever you need into my bag," she said as she proffered her cheap faux-leather brown shoulder bag. "Ready?"

"Ready."

In the elevator, even though three people got in with us, no one batted an eyelid at me. We walked through the lobby, and the concierge glanced at us, then turned his attention back to his computer.

"Wow, Christophe has known me for years," I whispered as we walked outside and Mariam called over the doorman.

"We need a cab to Montmartre," she told him in very passable French.

"*D'accord, mademoiselle*, but there is a line, so it may be as long as ten minutes."

"Okay, we can wait."

"I haven't stood in line for a cab in years," I muttered.

"Welcome to the real world, Electra." Mariam smiled. "Look, here we go."

Twenty minutes later, we settled ourselves at a table in the café I used to work in. It wasn't a very good table—we were squashed tightly between two others, and I could hear every word of our neighbors' conversations. I kept looking up at George, who'd given me the job as a waitress ten years ago, standing behind the bar, but his head never turned toward me.

"So how does it feel to be invisible again?" Mariam asked me after I'd ordered a half carafe of house wine.

"I'm not sure. Weird, definitely."

"But freeing?"

"Yeah, I mean, I enjoyed walking down the street unnoticed, but there are pros and cons to everything, aren't there?"

"There are, yes, but I imagine that even before you became famous, you used to get stared at."

"I suppose I did, yeah, but I could never work out whether it was friendly staring or more because, well, I resemble a black giraffe!"

"I'd guess it was because you are very beautiful, Electra. Whereas for me, especially since 9/11, I get treated with a degree of suspicion everywhere I go. Every Muslim is a terrorist, you know." She smiled sadly as she sipped her water.

"Of course, it must be difficult for you."

"It is. In any political or religious regime, all the *real* people on the streets just want to live in peace. Sadly, I'm often judged before I've even opened my mouth because of my style of dress."

"Do you ever go out without it?"

"No, although my father said I should remove my hijab when I was looking for work. He thought it might hinder my chances."

"Maybe you should try it, become someone else for a few hours, just like I have tonight. It might be freeing for you, too."

"It might, but I'm happy as I am. Now, shall we order?"

Mariam proceeded to do so in French.

"So many hidden skills," I teased her. "Where did you learn to speak French so well?"

"I learned it at school, then picked up more when I was working for Bardin—I find it is a necessity in the high-fashion world. And I suppose I have an ear for languages. I noticed that you sound quite different in French than you do in English, almost like another person."

I bristled. "How do you mean?"

"Not in a bad way," she continued hurriedly. "You're more casual in English—perhaps because your accent has an American tone to it. You sound more . . . serious in French somehow."

"My sisters would laugh so hard if they heard you say that," I said with a grin.

Over *moules marinières* and fresh, crisp bread that only the French know how to bake, I encouraged Mariam to talk about her family. She obviously adored her brothers and sisters, and I felt jealous of the love that shone out of her eyes.

"I can hardly believe that my little sister is getting married next year. My parents keep calling me an old maid." She smiled as we both tucked into *tarte Tatin* for dessert. I'd already agreed with myself that I'd run off the extra calories in the hotel gym tomorrow morning.

"Do you think you will ever get married?" I asked her.

"I don't know. I'm certainly not ready to settle down yet. Or maybe I just haven't found 'the one.' If you don't mind me asking, what about you? Have you ever been in love?"

For a change, I didn't mind someone asking. Tonight, we were just two young women out for supper and a gossip.

"Yup, and I don't think I ever want to be again."

"It ended badly?"

"It sure did," I breathed. "He broke my heart. It messed me up, but hey, shit happens, doesn't it?"

"There will be someone else for you, Electra, I know there will."

"You sound like my sister Tiggy. She's very spiritual and always saying things like that."

"Well, maybe she is right, and so am I. There is someone for everyone, I truly believe that."

"But the question is, will we ever find them? The world's a big place, you know."

"True," Mariam agreed, then stifled a yawn. "Excuse me, I did not sleep well last night. I am not good with jet lag."

"I'll get the check." I waved an arm to signal for the waiter to come over. He totally ignored me.

"How rude can you get?" I said angrily as five minutes later he was still ignoring us.

"He is busy, Electra, he will come to us when he has time. Patience is a virtue, you know."

"And one that I've never had," I muttered, trying to keep my anger under control.

"Well," she said as we finally left the restaurant after the waiter had decided to grace us with his presence, "tonight I have learned that you don't like being ignored."

"That's right. In a family of six girls, you had to shout the loudest to be heard." I chuckled. "And I did."

"Let us try to find a cab back to the hotel."

I hardly caught what she was saying, for my attention had fallen on a man sitting alone at one of the outside tables, drinking a cognac.

"Oh, my God," I whispered.

"What is it?"

"It's that guy there. I know him. He works for my family." I walked toward the table and was virtually on top of him before he looked up at me.

"Christian?"

He stared at me, and I read the confusion on his face. "*Pardon, mademoiselle*, do I know you?" he asked me in French.

I bent down to whisper in his ear. "Of course you do, you idiot! It's me, Electra!"

"*Mon Dieu!* Of course it is you, Electra! My—"

"Shh! I'm in disguise!"

"Well, it is a most excellent one, but now of course I can see that it is you."

I realized Mariam was hovering behind me.

"Mariam, this is Christian, and he is . . . well, family, I suppose." I smiled down at him. "Would we be disturbing you if we sat down and had a drink? It is *such* a coincidence to see you here."

"If you will excuse me, I will go back to the hotel," said Mariam. "Otherwise I will fall asleep where I stand. It is a pleasure to meet you, Christian.

*Bonne soirée.*" She nodded before turning and fading into the mass walking along the busy Montmartre street.

"Can I join you?" I said.

"Of course, please, sit down. I will order you a cognac."

I watched Christian as he signaled to the young waitress on duty for the outside tables. As a young girl, I'd had a huge crush on him—after all, he was the only guy under the age of thirty who I'd come into contact with at Atlantis. Ten years on, he didn't seem to have changed, and it struck me that I had absolutely no idea how old he actually was. Or, I realized guiltily, *who* he was.

"So," I said, "what are you doing here?"

"I . . . well, I was visiting an old friend of mine."

"Right." I nodded, getting the strongest vibe that he was lying. "You know, it was Ma who found me a place to stay just a few doors down from here when I first came to Paris. I used to work at this very café. It seems a long time ago now."

"It is, Electra, almost ten years. Ah, here is the cognac. *Santé.*"

"*Santé.*" I toasted with him, and we both took a large gulp.

"And may I ask what you are doing in disguise out on the streets of Montmartre?"

"Mariam—the girl you just met—is my PA, and I was complaining that I couldn't go anywhere without being recognized. So she dressed me up, and we came out for dinner together."

"And did you enjoy not being you?"

"I'm not sure, to be honest. I mean, it certainly has its advantages—you and I couldn't be sitting here chatting without being disturbed if I wasn't in disguise—but equally it's irritating to be ignored."

"Yes, I'm sure it must be. So"—Christian took another sip of his cognac—"how are you?"

"I'm okay." I shrugged. "How is Ma? And Claudia?"

"They are well, yes. They are both in good health."

"I often wonder what they do with themselves these days, now that we're gone and so is Pa."

"I wouldn't worry about that, Electra. They keep very busy."

"And what about you?"

"There is always a lot to do on the estate, and it is rare for a month to go by without a visit from one or more of your sisters. Ally is at Atlantis now with her beautiful son, Bear."

"Ma must be in heaven."

"I think she is, yes." Christian gave me a rare smile. "He is the first of the next generation. Marina feels needed again, and it is good to see her happy."

"How is Bear? My nephew," I added, surprised by the word.

"He is perfect, as all newborn babies are."

"Does he cry, scream sometimes?" I probed. Christian was another person whom I, along with my sisters, technically employed, yet tonight his deference irked me.

"Oh, he does sometimes, yes, but what baby does not?"

"Do you remember when I was at home?"

"Of course I do, yes."

"I mean, when I was a baby?"

"When you were a baby, I was only nine, Electra."

*Ah! So Christian must be about thirty-five.*

"But I'm sure I remember you driving the boat when I was very young."

"Yes, but your father was always there to make sure I was proficient before he let me skipper it alone."

"Oh, my God!" I put a hand to my mouth as a memory came flooding back to me. "Do you remember when I was about thirteen and ran away from school to Atlantis? And then Pa told me I had to go back and at least try again because I hadn't given it a chance? And I *so* didn't want to go, so I jumped off the boat in the middle of Lake Geneva and tried to swim to the shore."

Christian's warm brown eyes showed me he did. "How could I forget? You nearly drowned—you hadn't thought to take off your coat before you jumped, and you'd gone underwater. For a short time I couldn't find you." He shook his head. "It was one of the worst moments of my life. If I'd lost you . . ."

"Pa would have been mad, all right," I agreed, trying to lighten the atmosphere because Christian looked like he was about to cry.

"I would never have forgiven myself, Electra."

"Well, at least the stunt partially worked. He didn't make me go back to school for another few days."

"No."

"So how long are you in Paris for?"

"I leave tomorrow. You?"

"Sunday evening. I just changed my flight this afternoon, but then my date stood me up." I shrugged.

"Then you should come back with me to Atlantis and meet your nephew. I have the car here, so I could drive you. Everyone would be very happy to see you."

"You think so?" I shook my head. "I don't."

"Why do you say that? Marina and Claudia are always talking about you. They keep a scrapbook with all your modeling shoots in it."

"Do they? That's cute. Well, maybe some other time."

"If you change your mind, you have my number."

I smiled. "I certainly do." It's inked onto my brain. When things got bad at school, I knew you'd soon be there to rescue me."

"I should be heading back. I'm leaving early tomorrow morning." Christian signaled for the bill.

"Where are you staying?" I asked him.

"In the same building where you stayed. Marina's friend owns it."

"Really? I didn't know that." A fleeting memory of my Parisian landlady—an ancient woman whose face bore the hallmarks of a lifetime of absinthe and cigarettes—floated back to me.

"Anyway." Christian stood up. "If you change your mind, let me know. I'm leaving at seven a.m. Now let me find you a taxi."

As we walked, I enjoyed the fact that Christian was at least as tall as I was. He was also in crazily good shape, his muscled torso outlined beneath his white shirt. As he flagged down a cab, for some ridiculous reason, I felt like I had each time he'd left me at school and I'd watched him drive off, only wishing that I was in the car with him.

"Where are you staying, Electra?"

"The Ritz," I said as I climbed into the back of the cab.

"Well, it's been good to see you. Take care of yourself, won't you?"

"I will," I called through the window as the taxi sped off.

As I sank into bed half an hour later, I suddenly realized I hadn't done a line since that afternoon with Maxime, and that made me feel very good indeed.

Irritatingly, I woke the next morning at 5:00 a.m., and even though I took a sleeping pill, my brain refused to switch off. So I lay there contemplating an empty weekend in Paris while scrolling through the contacts list on my cell to find some playmates to keep me occupied. I realized that there was no one I really wanted to see, because I would have to make the effort to be Electra the Supermodel, and I wanted some downtime.

*But not by-myself downtime,* I reflected as I watched the luminous numbers on the bedside clock move agonizingly slowly toward 6:00 a.m.

Then I thought about Atlantis, with Ma and Claudia and how I could roam the house and grounds in the old sweatpants that I kept in the bottom drawer in my bedroom and how I wouldn't need to make any effort to be anyone other than me . . .

Before I could change my mind, I dialed Christian's cell phone number.

"Electra, good morning."

"Hi, Christian. I was thinking that, actually, I will drive back with you to Atlantis."

"That is good news! Marina and Claudia will be very happy. Shall I collect you at the Ritz in one hour?"

"Great, thanks."

I then texted Mariam:

Are you awake?

Yes. What do you need?

Call me.

She did, and I explained that I needed to fly back to the States from Geneva rather than Paris.

"Not a problem, Electra. Do you need me to book you a hotel?"

"No, I'm going home to see my family."

"Wonderful!" she replied with such warmth that I could totally imagine her smiling. "I will get back to you with all the confirmations."

"What about you, Mariam?" I said, suddenly aware that I was leaving her to fend for herself. "Will you be okay in Paris? You're welcome to charge a flight home today on the credit card if you'd prefer?"

"No, Electra, I am quite happy here. I was planning to see Bardin this afternoon, if it was convenient for you, so I will make my arrangements and meet you at the airport in Geneva tomorrow night."

I did a line from the packet Maxime had left me, then threw everything into my suitcase and carry-on before ordering a selection of French pastries with a side of fruit to make me feel better about the carb overload. After breakfast, I called for the bellhop to take my bags down. Donning my big black sunglasses (CeCe had once said I looked like a bluebottle in them), I followed my bags out to Christian and the comfortable Mercedes sedan. As he greeted me and opened the rear door, I shook my head. "I'll ride up front if you don't mind."

"Not at all," Christian said as he moved to open the passenger door for me.

As I settled myself in the front seat, I smelled that initial comforting aroma of leather, air freshener, and Pa's unmistakeable lemony scent. I'd been climbing into our family's cars since I was a child, and the smell had never changed, even though Pa was now gone. It indicated home and safety, and if I could bottle it, I would.

"Do you have everything you need, Electra?" Christian asked me as he started the engine.

"I do, thanks."

"The journey usually takes approximately five hours," Christian told me as we glided away from the Ritz.

"Have you told Ma I'm coming?"

"I have, yes. She asked if you had any special dietary requirements?"

"I . . ."

I realized that last time I had been home, I had been on a detox, drinking green tea by the bucketful. I'd been with Mitch, who was so clean he'd squeaked, but I'd taken an emergency bottle of vodka with me in case I lapsed. Which I had, but that was understandable because it was Atlantis without Pa for the first time—a wake without the funeral.

"Are you okay, Electra?"

"Great, thank you. Christian?"

"Yes?"

"Did you drive Pa to many places?"

"Not really, no. Mostly to Geneva airport to board his private jet."

"Did you ever know where he was going?"

"Sometimes, yes."

"And where was it?"

"Oh, many destinations around the world."

"Do you know what he actually did?"

"I have no idea, Electra. He was a very private man."

"And then some." I sighed. "Don't you think it's weird that none of us knew? Like, most kids are able to say their dad is a shopkeeper or a lawyer, but I couldn't say anything because I didn't have a clue."

Christian remained silent, keeping his eyes on the road. As the family chauffeur by both car and boat, it was impossible not to imagine that he knew more than he was saying.

"You know what?"

"Not until you tell me, Electra." Christian offered me a glimmer of a smile.

"When I was in all that trouble at school and you'd come and collect me, you and your car became my safe space."

"And what is a safe space?"

"Oh, it's therapy-speak for somewhere you can be in your imagination or in a remembered reality that makes you happy. I often dreamed about you arriving outside to take me away."

"Then I am honored." Christian gave me a genuine smile this time.

"Did you just apply for the job with Pa?" I probed again.

"Your father knew me from when I was a young boy. I lived . . . locally, and he helped me—and my mother—a lot."

"You mean he was a father figure to you?"

"Yes," Christian agreed after a pause. "He was."

"Then maybe you are the mysterious seventh sister!" I chuckled.

"Your father was a very kind man, and his loss is deep for all of us."

*Was Pa kind or controlling? Or was he both?* I pondered as we hit the outskirts of Paris and joined the expressway to Geneva. I reclined my seat and closed my eyes.

# 3

Electra, we are at the jetty," whispered a soft voice into my ear.

I came to and blinked in the bright light, which I then realized was the reflection of the sun on the glassy surface of Lake Geneva.

"I slept for four hours solid," I said in surprise as I got out of the car. "Told you you were my safe place." I grinned at him as he opened the trunk. "I just need the carry-on—you can leave the rest in there until tomorrow."

Christian locked the car, then walked ahead of me to the pontoon where the speedboat was moored. He offered me his hand to help me aboard, then went about doing whatever he needed to before we could set off, and I settled myself on the soft leather bench at the stern. I thought how, on the way to Atlantis, I always felt excited at the prospect of arriving. And then on the way back, how I normally felt relief that I was leaving.

*Maybe this time it'll be different*, I told myself, then sighed because that was *also* something I always felt.

Christian fired up the engine, and we began the short journey to my childhood home. For a late March day, it was warm, and I enjoyed the feeling of sun on my face and my hair streaming behind me.

As we approached the peninsula on which Atlantis stood, I craned my neck for an early view through the trees. It was a spectacular house—a little like a Disney château because it was so pretty. *And very unlike Pa*, I thought to myself. He'd had a minimal wardrobe; to my knowledge he'd only ever worn the same three jackets: a linen one in the summer, a tweed one in the winter, and another of indeterminate fabric that he wore in between seasons. His bedroom was so sparsely furnished it looked like something a priest would inhabit. I'd wondered whether he was secretly doing penance for some crime he'd committed in the past, but whatever . . . As we approached the jetty by Atlantis, I reflected that his wardrobe and bedroom sure were a paradox when compared to the rest of the house.

Ma was already standing waiting for me, waving excitedly. She was dressed immaculately, as always, and I noticed her bouclé skirt was one from Chanel that I'd managed to sneak from a sample rack because I knew she would love it.

"Electra! *Chérie*, what an unexpected surprise!" she said as she reached up on tiptoe, and I bent down so she could kiss me on both cheeks and put her arms around my shoulders. Then she stepped back and appraised me. "You look as beautiful as always, but I think you are too thin. Never mind, Claudia has the ingredients ready to make you your favorite blueberry pancakes, should you wish. Did you know that Ally is here with her new baby?"

"Yes, Christian said. I can't wait to meet my nephew," I said as I followed her up the path and through the gardens that fronted the house and led down to the lake. The smell of the grass and the newly budding plants was so fresh in comparison to the stench of New York. I sucked a deep breath of the pure air into my lungs.

"Come through to the kitchen," said Ma. "Claudia is already preparing brunch."

I saw Christian bringing up the rear. As he deposited my carry-on at the bottom of the stairs, I walked toward him.

"Thank you for driving me here. I'm glad I came."

"You are welcome, Electra. What time do we leave for the airport tomorrow?"

"Around ten in the evening. My PA has booked the jet for midnight."

"Okay. If anything changes, just tell Marina and she will inform me."

"I will. Have a nice weekend."

"And you." He nodded at me, then disappeared out of the front door.

"Electra!"

I turned and saw Ally coming toward me from the kitchen, her arms open wide to embrace me.

"Hi there, new mom," I said as she hugged me. "Congratulations."

"Thanks. I still can't believe I am one."

I thought, with a hint of jealousy, that she looked amazing. Her angular face had been softened by a few pregnancy pounds, and her fabulous red-gold hair shone like a halo against her porcelain skin.

"You look great," I said.

"No, I don't. I've put on eight kilos, which don't seem to be disappearing, and I'm getting about two hours' sleep a night. I have a very hungry man in my bed." She laughed.

"Where is he?"

"Sleeping off the night before, of course." Ally raised an eyebrow in mock frustration, but I thought I'd never seen her look happier. "At least it'll give us a chance to talk for a bit," she added as we walked through to the kitchen. "I was thinking today that I haven't seen you since last June when we were all here after Pa died."

"No, well, I've been busy."

"I try and keep up with you and your life in the papers and magazines, but—"

"Hello, Electra," said Claudia in the French she spoke with a strong German accent. "How are you?" She was in the process of pouring pancake mixture into a frying pan, and I heard an enticing sizzle.

"I'm well, thanks."

"Come and sit down and tell me everything that's happened since I last saw you." Ally indicated a chair at the long table.

"I will, but before I do, I'm just going upstairs to freshen up." I turned and walked out of the kitchen, suddenly feeling panicky. I knew how Ally liked to interrogate us all, and I wasn't sure I was up to it just now.

I grabbed my carry-on, then climbed the stairs up to the attic—which really wasn't an attic at all but a spacious floor where we girls had our bedrooms—and opened the door to mine. Everything looked exactly as it had when I'd left home for Paris as a teenager. I stared at the walls, painted in the soft cream color they'd always been, and sat down on my bed. Compared to the other girls' rooms, whose walls seemed to embody their occupants' personalities, mine was bare. There wasn't a clue about the person who had lived in here for the first sixteen years of her life. No posters of models or pop stars or ballet dancers or sports stars . . . nothing to indicate who I was.

Reaching down into my carry-on, I grabbed the bottle of vodka wrapped up in my cashmere sweatpants and took a deep swig. This bedroom seemed to express all there was to say about me—that I was just an empty husk. I didn't have—and never had had—a passion for anything. *And*, I thought as I stowed the bottle back in its cashmere nest, then reached for the small packet tucked into the front pocket of my carry-on to do a line, *I didn't know who I was back then, and I don't know who I am now.*

By the time I made my way back downstairs, the vodka had calmed me and the coke had cheered me up. As Ma, Ally, and I sat down to enjoy Claudia's famous brunch, I did as they wanted me to do and told them all about the glamorous parties I'd attended and the celebrities I'd met, giving them some innocuous inside gossip as I went.

"And what about you and Mitch? I read in the papers that you'd gone your separate ways. Is that true?"

I'd been waiting for that; Ally was the high priestess of getting straight to the point.

"Yeah, a few months back."

"What happened?"

"Oh, you know"—I shrugged as I drank some hot strong coffee and wished it was laced with bourbon—"he was based in LA, I was in New York, we were both traveling . . ."

"So he wasn't 'the one'?" Ally pursued.

There was a sudden screeching sound from somewhere in the kitchen, and I looked around to find where it was coming from.

Ally sighed. "That's the baby monitor. Bear's awake."

"I'll go and see to him," offered Ma, but Ally was already on her feet and pressed Ma gently back down into her chair.

"You were on duty from five this morning, darling Ma, so it's my turn."

I hadn't even met my new nephew yet, but boy, did I like him already. He'd gotten me out of the Grand Ally Inquisition.

"So how is your new apartment?" asked Ma, changing the subject. If tact had a physical form, it would look like my surrogate mom.

"It's okay," I replied, "but it's only a year's rental, so I'll probably look for someplace else soon."

"I suppose you're not there that often, with all the traveling you do."

"Too right I'm not, but at least it gives me somewhere to put my wardrobe. Oh, wow, look who's here."

Ally was approaching the table holding a baby who had an enormous pair of quizzical brown eyes. His dark red hair was already starting to curl tightly on top of his head.

"This is Bear," Ally said, that proud mom look shining in her eyes. And why shouldn't it? Anyone brave enough to give birth was a heroine in my book.

"Oh, my God! He is . . . edible! How old is he now?" I asked as Ally sat down and cradled him in her lap.

"Seven weeks."

"Wow, he looks huge!"

"That's because he has such a good appetite," Ally smiled as she unbuttoned her shirt and positioned the baby in the right place. Bear began to suckle noisily, and I winced.

"Doesn't it hurt when he's feeding?"

"It did at first, but we got into the swing of it, didn't we, darling?" she said, looking down at him like I guessed I'd sometimes looked at Mitch. In other words, with love.

"Well, now, we will leave you two girls to chat and see you later," Claudia said as, the clearing-up done, she followed Ma out of the kitchen.

"I'm real sorry about Bear's dad, Ally."

"Thanks, Electra."

"Did he . . . did the father—"

"His name was Theo."

"Did Theo know about Bear?"

"No, and nor did I until a few weeks after he died. At the time I thought the roof had fallen in on my world, but now"—Ally smiled at me, and I read genuine contentment in her clear blue eyes—"I wouldn't be without him."

"Did you consider—?"

"An abortion? The thought did run briefly through my head, yes. I mean, I had my sailing career, Bear's dad was dead, and I had no home at the time, either. I could never have gone through with it, though. I feel Bear was a gift. Sometimes when I'm up feeding him in the small hours, I really sense Theo around me."

"You mean, his spirit?"

"Yes, I do."

"I wouldn't have thought that you believed in all that shit," I said with a frown.

"Nor would I, but something amazing happened the night before Bear was born."

"Like what?"

"I flew over to Spain in search of Tiggy, who'd just been diagnosed with a heart condition but had run off to find her birth family. And she told me something, Electra, something that only Theo could have known."

I watched Ally's pale hand go to the necklace she was wearing.

"What was it?"

"Theo bought me this." Ally held up the tiny turquoise eye that sat on a chain. "The chain had broken a few weeks before, and Tiggy said that Theo wanted to know why I wasn't wearing it. Then she said he liked the name Bear, and you know what, Electra? He did!"

Tears appeared in Ally's eyes.

"Anyway, having been a cynic, I'm afraid I'm now a convert. And I just know Theo is watching over us." She shrugged and gave me a misty smile.

"I sure wish I had a belief like that. Trouble is, I don't believe much in anything. So how is Tiggy's heart now?"

"Much better, apparently. She's back in the Scottish Highlands and very happily ensconced with the doctor who looked after her when she was sick. He also happens to be the owner of the estate she works on."

"It could be wedding bells for her soon, then?"

"I doubt it; Charlie's still technically married and going through a pretty ugly divorce from what Tiggy's told me."

"And the other sisters?"

"Maia's still in Brazil with her lovely man, Floriano, and his daughter, Star is in Kent in England helping her boyfriend—who for some reason is known as Mouse—renovate his house, and CeCe's in Australia living with her grandfather and her friend Chrissie in the Outback. I've seen some photos of her paintings, and they're just amazing. She's so talented."

"So all the sisters have found a new life?" I said.

"Yes, it seems like it."

"And they each found it through searching for their past?"

"They did, yes. And I did, too. I emailed you to tell you I had a twin brother, didn't I?"

"Um . . ."

"Oh, Electra, I did, really. And a biological father who is a musical genius but a total drunkard to boot." I watched Ally smile fondly at the thought of him as she deftly moved the baby from one breast to the other.

"So," she continued, "have you done anything about your letter from Pa?"

"I've never even opened the envelope, and to be honest, I can't remember where I put it. It may be lost."

"Oh, Electra!" Ally gave me her best disapproving look. "You can't be serious?"

"Hey, it must be somewhere, I just haven't bothered to find it."

"You really don't want to know where you came from?"

"No, I just can't see the point. What does it matter? I'm who I am now."

"Well, it certainly helped me. And even if you don't want to pursue what the letter contains, Pa's written words were his last gift to all of us."

"Jesus Christ!" I'd had enough. "You and our other sisters treat Pa as though he was some freakin' god! He was just a guy who adopted us—for some weird reason that none of us actually knows!"

"Please don't shout, Electra, it upsets the baby, but I'm sorry if I—"

"I'm going out for a walk."

I stood up from the table, marched to the front door, and pulled it open. Slamming it behind me, I walked across the lawns toward the jetty, wishing, as I always did after a few hours at Atlantis, that I'd never decided to come back here in the first place.

"What is it with my sisters and Pa? He's not even our biological father, for Chrissake!"

I continued to complain to myself as I sat down, feet dangling over the jetty, and tried to take some deep breaths. They didn't work. Maybe another line would. I stood up and retraced my footsteps back to the house, tiptoeing inside and up the stairs so no one would hear me. In my room, I locked the door and took out what I needed.

A few minutes later, I was feeling far calmer. I lay back on my bed and pictured all my sisters in turn. For some reason, they appeared as Disney princesses, which was quite fun. They weren't irritating at all when they looked like that, and I did love them, all except CeCe (she appeared suddenly as the witch in *Snow White*). I giggled and decided that was cruel, even for CeCe. I knew people said you couldn't choose your family, only your friends, but Pa *had* chosen us and we were stuck with each other. Maybe the reason CeCe and I didn't get along was because she wouldn't put up with my crap like the others did. And she could shout louder than me, too. The others would do anything to keep the peace, but she didn't care. A bit like me . . .

My four older sisters had probably never thought about the fact that they all had each other—Ally and Maia, Star and CeCe—which had left me with Tiggy. It was she whom I'd been bunched with as we were growing up—there were only a few months between us—and even though I really loved her, we couldn't have been more different. It didn't help that all my older sisters made it clear that their favorite younger sibling to play with was Tiggy, not me. Tiggy didn't holler and scream and have tantrums all the time. She just sat on a lap, sucking her thumb and being perfect. As we'd grown up, I'd tried to bond with her because I was lonely, but all her spiritual shit drove me up the wall.

As the coke wore off, my sisters stopped being Disney princesses and became themselves again. What did it matter, anyway? Now that Pa was gone, we were just a bunch of disparate women who had been thrown together as kids but were now going our separate ways. I took some breaths and tried to do as all my therapists had told me to, which was to analyze why I'd gotten so angry. And for a change, I thought I knew the reason: Ally had told me that all my sisters were happy—they had found lives with people who loved them. Even CeCe, who I'd always thought was as unlovable as me, had somehow managed to get over her weird obsession with Star and move on. More to the point, she had found her passion in art, something she had always loved.

And here was I, as usual the odd one out. Since Pa had died, I'd managed to find nothing except a new and more reliable dealer. Even though I was by far the most financially successful sister—from what my accountant said, I could stop work today and never worry about money again—what was the point when I hadn't a clue what else I wanted to do?

There was a knock on my door. "Electra? Are you in there?"

It was Ally. "Yeah, come in."

She did, with Bear in the crook of her arm. "I'm so sorry if I said something to upset you, Electra," she said, hovering in the doorway.

"Listen, don't worry about it. It's not you, it's me."

"Well, whatever, I am sorry. It's so good to see you, and I'm really glad you came. Do you mind if I sit down? He weighs a ton."

"Sure," I said with a sigh. The last thing I needed was to be trapped in my bedroom being interviewed by Ally.

"I just wanted to share something with you, Electra. Something that Tiggy told me we should investigate."

"Oh yeah, what?"

"Apparently, when she was here last month, she found a cellar with a secret lift that accessed it."

"Er . . . right. So?"

"She said it was used to store wine, but she noticed there was a door hidden behind one of the racks. Maybe we should find out where it leads to."

"Okay. Why don't we just ask Ma?"

"We can, yes, but Tiggy got the feeling that she didn't want to talk about it."

"Jeez, Ally! This is *our* house, and Ma works for us! We can ask what we want and do as we please here, surely?"

"Yes, we can, but, well"—Ally breathed—"maybe we just have to tread gently out of respect. Ma's been here a long time—she's run the house with Claudia and looked after us, and I don't want her to feel we're stepping on her toes now things are . . . different."

"So what you're saying is that you want us to sneak down in this elevator in the middle of the night and find out where this door leads to?" I raised an eyebrow. "But I still don't get why we have to do this cloak and dagger shit when we could just ask her?"

"Come on, Electra, stop being so brittle. This secret lift and cellar are *there*, and Pa put them there for a reason. Whatever you think or feel about him, he was a practical man. Anyway, I'm always awake during the night because of Bear, so I'm going to investigate. I just wondered if you fancied coming with me? Tiggy said it would take a couple of us to move the rack in front of the hidden door. She also told me where the key was. Now would you mind holding Bear for a few minutes while I use the bathroom?" Ally got up and dumped Bear on my lap. To stop him falling backward, I had to grab him with both hands. He gave a large burp in retaliation.

"Brilliant!" said Ally as she stood in the doorway. "I've been trying to get that out of him for the past hour!"

The door closed behind her, and Bear and I were left alone.

I looked down at him, and he looked up at me.

"Hi," I said, praying that he wouldn't pee on me or something. It was the first time I'd ever held a baby.

He gave me a hiccup and continued to stare at me.

"What are you thinking, little guy? Are you wondering why, even though I'm your auntie, I'm, like, a totally different color from your mom? You never met him, but you had a seriously weird grandfather," I continued, because he seemed to be enjoying the chat. "I mean, he was amazing, like real clever and stuff, but I think he kept a lot of secrets from all of us. What do you think?"

I suddenly felt his little body relax in my arms, and by the time Ally came back, Bear had closed his eyes and was fast asleep.

"Wow, you've got the touch." Ally smiled at me. "I normally have to rock him for hours before he'll give in."

I shrugged. "I guess he was bored," I said as Ally gently took him from me.

"I'm going to put him in his cot and catch some rest while I can," she whispered. "See you later."

Before dinner, I made sure that I'd taken enough precautionary vodka to keep calm, then fixed myself another large one from the pantry when I got downstairs. Thankfully, the conversation didn't go much past how phenomenal Claudia's cooking was (it was her famous schnitzel, and I ate up every scrap) and the plans for our boat trip to Greece to lay a wreath on the anniversary of Pa's death.

"I thought we girls should go on the actual cruise alone, but Maia is flying over the week before with Floriano, who I can't wait to meet, and his daughter Valentina," Ally informed me. "Star, Mouse, and his son, Rory, will be flying in, as well as Tiggy, her boyfriend, Charlie, and his daughter, Zara—"

"Wow!" I cut in. "So Maia, Star, and Tiggy are all surrogate mothers to their partners' children?"

"Yes, they are," Ally agreed.

"And as your surrogate mother, I know my girls will love the children in their care no less because they are not blood," said Ma firmly.

"Is CeCe coming?"

"She said she will, yes. She hopes her grandfather and her friend Chrissie might come with her too."

"Her 'friend' Chrissie?"

Both Ma and Ally stared at me, and I wondered why I had to be the only one in the family to actually voice the truth.

"They're in a relationship, right?"

"I don't know," Ally said, "but she sounds very happy, which is the most important thing."

"But it was obvious from the get-go that CeCe was gay, right? That she was in love with Star?"

"Electra, it is not our place to pry into other people's private lives," interrupted Ma.

"But CeCe isn't 'other people,' is she? And besides, what's the problem? I'm happy for her if she's found someone she cares for."

"We really will be struggling for room," Ma continued relentlessly.

"Well, as the rest of you guys have all found families and it's just little ol' me by myself, if there isn't room, maybe I just shouldn't come."

"Oh, Electra, don't say that! You have to come, you promised." Ally looked genuinely upset.

"Yeah, well, maybe I can sleep in the secret basement Tiggy found when she was here," I replied, turning to Ma.

Ally's expression threw daggers at me across the table, but I was too drunk to care.

"Ah, the basement." Ma regarded both of us. "Yes, I did tell Tiggy it is there, and there is no mystery to it. Once we have finished Claudia's wonderful apple strudel, I shall take you down myself to see it."

I threw back a "so there!" look to Ally, who raised her eyebrows in exasperation, and once the dessert was finished, Ma rose and took out a key from the box on the wall.

"Right, shall we go down?"

There was no need for an answer, as she was already walking out of the kitchen, and Ally and I filed after her. In the hallway, Ma took hold of a brass loop and pulled back a mahogany panel to reveal a miniature elevator.

"Why was this put in?" I asked.

"As I explained to Tiggy, your father wasn't getting any younger and wanted easy access to all parts of the house." Ma opened the door, and the three of us crammed inside. I immediately felt claustrophobic and took some deep breaths as she pressed a brass button and the door closed behind us.

"Yeah, I get that, but why did he hide it?" I asked as the elevator began to move.

"Electra, shut up, will you?" Ally hissed, by now beyond irritated with me. "I'm sure Ma will explain everything."

It was a four-second ride, and I felt the bounce as we reached the bottom. The door slid open, and we all stepped into a very plain basement, which, as Ally had said, was bounded on all sides by wine racks.

"And here you are." Ma stepped out and swung her arms around the room. "Your father's wine cellar." She turned to me and smiled. "I am sorry, Electra, that there is no great mystery."

"But—"

Behind Ma, Ally's eyes sent me a message that even I realized I couldn't ignore.

"I . . . well, it's very nice." I began to wander around the shelves, looking at what Pa had stashed down here. I pulled a bottle out. "Wow, Château Margaux, 1957. This sells for over two thousand dollars in the best restaurants in New York. Pity I'm more of a vodka fan."

"Can we go back up? I need to check on Bear," said Ally, shooting me another warning glance.

"Just give me a couple more minutes," I replied, continuing to browse the racks, pulling out the odd bottle and pretending to study its label, while all the time keeping my eyes peeled for the hidden door Ally had talked about. On the right-hand side of the room, I peered at a 1972 Rothschild Burgundy and spotted the almost invisible lines of an opening in the plaster behind the racks. "Right," I said, walking back to them both. "Let's go."

As we made our way toward the elevator, I noticed it had a solid steel frame.

"What's this for, Ma?" I pointed at it.

"If you press that button"—Ma indicated one side of the frame—"it shuts the steel doors in front of the elevator."

"So you mean if we pressed it now, we'd be trapped down here?" I asked, panic rising instinctively inside me.

"No, of course you wouldn't, Electra, but anyone trying to get into the cellar from the elevator would not be able to access it. It is a strong room," she explained as we squeezed back into the tiny space. "Nothing unusual in the house of a rich family living in an isolated spot. If, God forbid, Atlantis was under attack from burglars or worse, we could seal ourselves in and call for help. And yes, *chérie*"—Ma gave me a thin smile as we ascended the one floor upward—"it does have a Wi-Fi signal down there. Now," she said as we all exited the elevator and trooped back into the kitchen, and I noted where she hung the key in the box, "please forgive me, but I am weary tonight and must go to my bed."

"That's Bear's fault—you've been up since five, Ma. I'll see to him tomorrow morning."

"No, Ally. If I sleep now, I will be fine. I wake early anyway these days. Good night." She nodded at both of us and left the kitchen.

"I'm going up to check on Bear," said Ally, about to follow Ma before I tapped her on the shoulder.

"Then why don't you take the elevator?" I picked the key back off the hook and dangled it in front of her. "It goes up to the attic floor. There was a button for it in the lift."

"No, Electra, I'll be fine, thanks."

I shrugged. "Suit yourself," I said as she left to go upstairs. I fixed myself another vodka and Coke, then wandered through to the hall and pushed open the door to Pa's study. It was like a living museum; it felt as though Pa had just popped out for a while and would be back soon. His pen and notepad were still sitting centrally on his desk, everything immaculate as always—*unlike his youngest daughter*, I thought with a smirk, sitting down in his old leather-seated captain's chair. I studied the shelves of books lined up along one wall, stood up and went to take out the big *Oxford English Dictionary* that I'd used so often when I was a girl. One day, I'd come in to find Pa sitting in his chair and doing a crossword in an English newspaper.

"Hello, Electra," he'd said with a smile as he'd looked up at me. "I'm struggling with this one."

I'd read the clue—"They go down for a sleep (7)"—and mulled it over.

"Maybe your eyelids?"

"Yes, of course, you are right! What a clever girl you are."

From then on, during school vacations and if he was home, he'd beckon me into his study, and we'd sit together and do a crossword. I'd found the pastime soothing—I still often grabbed a newspaper from a departure lounge while I was waiting to catch a flight. It had also given me a very good English vocabulary, which I knew surprised journalists who interviewed me—they all presumed that I was as thick as the makeup that was piled regularly on my skin.

Putting the dictionary back, I was about to leave the room when I was stopped in my tracks by the strongest smell of Pa's cologne. I'd know its fresh lemony scent anywhere. A shiver went up my spine as I thought of what Ally had said earlier about feeling that Theo was there with her . . .

With a shudder, I hastily left the study, slamming the door behind me.

Ally was back in the kitchen, doing stuff with bottles.

"Why is that milk in a jug?" I asked. "I thought you breastfed Bear."

"I do, but I expressed this earlier so Ma can feed Bear when he wakes tomorrow morning."

"Ugh." I shuddered again as I watched her pour the milk into a bottle.

"If I ever have a kid, which is doubtful to begin with, I couldn't go through all that."

"Never say never." Ally smiled at me. "By the way, I saw a photo of you in some magazine a few weeks ago with Zed Eszu. Are you and he an item?"

"Christ, no," I said, dipping my fingers into the cookie tin and taking out a piece of shortbread. "We go out to play together in New York sometimes. Or to be more accurate, we stay in."

"You mean you and Zed Eszu are lovers?"

"Yeah, why? Do you have a problem with that?"

"No, not at all, I mean"—Ally turned to me, looking nervous—"I—"

"What, Ally?"

"Oh, nothing. Anyway, I'm off to bed to try and sleep while I can. You?"

"Yeah, I'm gonna join you," I said.

It was only when I'd downed a tooth glass of neat vodka from my carry-on and clambered into my childhood bed, feeling nicely woozy, that I remembered the outline of the door behind the wine rack down in the basement. Maybe I should go now and investigate . . .

"Tomorrow," I promised myself as my eyes fell shut.

# 4

The next morning, I woke to the screech of Bear's crying, then reached for my earplugs, hoping to catch another couple of hours, but it was too late. I was wide awake. I threw on my old robe that still hung on the back of the door, then padded out of my room to find some company. The crying was coming from Ma's suite at the end of the hall, so I knocked gently on the closed door.

"*Entrez.*"

I went inside and had the rare sight of Ma still dressed in her robe, too.

"Close the door behind you, Electra. I don't want Ally to wake up."

"Well," I retorted as I watched her pace the room with Bear grizzling over her shoulder, "he sure woke *me*."

Ma smiled at me. "Now you know what it was like for the older girls to be woken by you every night."

"What's wrong with him?" I asked as I watched her pat Bear's back rhythmically.

"Wind, nothing more. He is not good at getting it up."

"Was that why I screamed?"

"No, you brought up your wind easily. You just enjoyed the sound of your own voice."

"Was I really that bad a baby?"

"Not at all, Electra, you just didn't like being alone. You would fall asleep in my arms, but the minute I put you down in your cot, you would wake up and cry until I picked you up again. Can you pass me that muslin, please?" Ma pointed to a white fabric square sitting on the coffee table.

"Sure," I said as I handed it to her. I glanced around me at the pretty flowered curtains, the cream damask couch, the photos on the mahogany bureau, and the occasional tables placed around the room. Pink roses sat on the coffee table, and I thought how the room mirrored who Ma was: elegant, understated, and immaculate. I walked over and picked up a framed photograph of Ma in pearls and an evening gown and Pa in a dinner jacket and bow tie.

"Where was this taken?"

"At the opera in Paris. We saw Kiri Te Kanawa singing Mimi in *La Bohème*. It was a very special evening," Ma explained, still pacing the soft cream carpet with Bear.

"Did the two of you often go out together?"

"No, but we did share a love of opera, especially Puccini."

"Ma?"

"Yes, Electra?"

Even at twenty-six, I didn't know whether I had the courage to ask the question that had been burning on my tongue since I was small.

"Were you and Pa . . . well, were you romantically involved?"

"No, *chérie*. I am only in my midsixties, you know. Your father was old enough to be mine, too."

"In my world, age doesn't stop rich men having relationships with women young enough to be their daughters."

"Maybe not, Electra, but your father would never have countenanced such a thing. He was a consummate gentleman. And besides—"

"Besides what?"

"I . . . nothing."

"Please, say what you were going to say."

"Well, there was always someone else for him."

"Really? Who?"

"Now, Electra, I have said enough."

Bear finally let out an enormous belch, and, quick as a flash, Ma caught the milky liquid that dribbled from his mouth with the muslin.

"*Bien, bien, mon petit chéri*," she whispered as she cleaned him up. "Isn't he adorable?"

"If anything can be adorable at five in the morning while vomiting, then, yeah, he is."

"I remember so vividly walking up and down with you in here trying to soothe you when you cried," said Ma as she sank into a chair and nestled Bear into the crook of her arm. He now looked as though he'd drunk too much vodka and his eyes were rolling back in their sockets. "It seems like yesterday. And here we are with the first of a new generation. Your father would have been so happy if he had known about Bear before he died. But it was not to be."

"No. Ma?"

"Yes, Electra?"

"Were you with Pa when he found me and brought me home?"

"No, I was here caring for your sisters."

"So you don't know where I came from?"

"Surely you must already know from your letter?"

"I lost it." I shrugged, then stood up before she could reproach me. "I'm gonna go downstairs and get myself some coffee. Want anything?"

"No, thank you. I will put this little one back to bed and then follow you down when I've dressed."

"Okay, see you later."

When Ally woke up at eight, I was already on my second vodka and wishing I'd arranged the jet back to New York for earlier. I had fourteen whole hours to somehow fill before I could leave. I seriously didn't know how to do "downtime"; my boredom threshold was so low it was practically non-existent.

"Fancy going out for a sail, Electra?" Ally asked me over more of Claudia's pancakes.

"You mean on your Laser?"

"Yes. The weather is beautiful, and it's perfect conditions—just enough of a breeze but not enough to make it unpleasant."

"You know that extreme sports aren't my thing."

"Honestly, Electra, I'd hardly call a gentle sail on the lake when you just have to sit there and do nothing an 'extreme sport.'" Ally rolled her eyes. "Well, Bear and I are going, so I'll see you later."

I sighed heavily as she left and ate a freshly baked muffin just because it looked lonely in the basket. Ally was back ten minutes later with Bear, who was wearing the cutest little life vest and was strapped around her in a baby carrier.

"Are you sure you don't want to come with us?"

"No, thanks," I reiterated, then wandered into the living room, deciding I should have a movie day. Switching on the screen, I looked through the piles of DVDs but couldn't find one that interested me.

"Shit," I groaned, looking at my watch. What did I do here when I was bored and antsy as a kid?

*You ran, Electra.*

"So I did," I murmured to myself. If I was upset or someone was cross with me (and it was normally both), I'd just take off into the mountains behind the house—I'd found a winding path that took me over some rough terrain but wasn't totally vertical—and run and run all the thoughts out of my head.

I paced up the stairs to my room and in my bottom drawer found my old Lycra leggings and a T-shirt with a rude slogan on it that Ma had insisted I turn inside out when I'd worn it. Beneath the clothes, I saw one of the old sketchbooks that I used to doodle in as a child. I pulled it out and leafed through the pages, which were half filled with pencil sketches I'd made of dresses with outrageous ruffled collars, jeans with a split running from thigh to hem, and shirts that looked formal at the front but had no back.

"Wow," I muttered, remembering the shirt I'd worn only recently for a photo shoot that was almost identical in style to the ones I'd drawn. I'd even attached samples of fabric I'd found, all of them brightly colored. I'd *loved* bright colors when I was younger. I slipped the book into the front pocket of my carry-on, thinking that it was the one thing I had that linked my childhood self to the adult me. Then I retrieved my old running shoes from the back of the closet, changed, and left the house through the kitchen. I jogged through the vegetable garden and opened the back gate that led upward toward the mountains.

I followed the path I'd last used ten years before, and even though I went to the gym regularly, my legs ached and the last few yards were tough. I scrambled over boulders and slipped over damp, tough grass, but finally, I got there.

Panting hard, I stepped onto the rocky outcrop that represented only the foothills of the mountains still rising behind me but had the most spectacular vista of the lake. I looked down on the rooftops of Atlantis and, with the advantage of all the therapy I'd had, realized why this view had been so special for me when I was younger: Atlantis had been my universe when I was young—all encompassing—yet up here it looked like a doll's house—tiny and insignificant.

*It gave me perspective,* I told myself as I dangled my legs over the edge of the ridge. *It even made me feel small.*

I sat there for some time, enjoying what really was a fabulous day. Out on the lake, I saw what looked like a toy boat, its sail rippling in the breeze, gliding smoothly across the water. And suddenly I didn't want to go back down to reality, I wanted to stay right up here where no one could find me. I felt free, and the thought of flying back to New York and the man-made mountains of Manhattan made my gut churn. There, everything was false and greedy and meaningless, while everything here was real and pure and clean.

"Jeez, Electra, you're starting to sound like Tiggy," I reprimanded myself. But even if I was, what did it matter? All I knew was that I was desperately unhappy and that I envied each of my sisters their new full and happy lives. When Ally had talked about all of them bringing their new partners and friends and relatives to Atlantis, I'd felt even more lonely because I had no one I'd even think of bringing.

As I stood up, knowing I had to go back down simply because I'd stupidly forgotten to bring a water bottle with me and I was thirsty, I took one last look at the view.

"How come I'm meant to have everything but feel like I have nothing?" I asked the mountains above me.

As I jumped off the ridge, I realized that somehow I needed to get myself a real life—and some love. But where I should begin to look for it, heaven—and maybe Pa within it—only knew.

# 5

In the days that followed once I was back in New York, I took the memory of how good I'd felt after my trek up the mountain at Atlantis and began to run in Central Park whenever my schedule allowed it. The good news was that even if anyone spotted me, I could outpace them, no problem. I also tried to limit my alcohol intake, and—maybe it was due to the running and the natural high I got from it—I didn't feel the need to do so much coke. If I felt panicky, I opened the book of *Telegraph* crosswords I'd had delivered and did one of those instead to calm myself.

In short, I felt a little more in control.

The only thing that was bugging me was that even though I'd searched my whole apartment, I couldn't find Pa's letter anywhere. I racked my brain to try to remember where I'd put the envelope when I'd moved into this place. I'd even had Mariam on the case, too.

"Oh, Electra, we must find it," she'd said, her expressive eyes full of sympathy as she'd knelt down to let rip on my lingerie drawers.

"Hey, I'm not saying I want to read it even if I do find it, but it would be good to know it's there."

"Of course it would. They were his last words to you, and I am sure they were words he wanted you to read. Do not worry, Electra, we will find it."

But after searching through every drawer, closet, coat pocket, and scrap of paper in the apartment, even Mariam's positivity had waned.

"Don't worry about it," I said one sunny April morning as she emptied my bedside drawers for the umpteenth time. "Maybe I wasn't meant to read it. Now I'm gonna fix myself a lunchtime drink. Want one?"

As always, Mariam refused and said she wanted water. We sat down and ran through the day's emails, which mostly consisted of invitations to the opening of a new fashion store or a film premiere or a charity ball. I remembered the days when I'd been so excited about receiving these—but now I understood they didn't want *me* at all, just column inches for themselves.

"Oh, I almost forgot." Mariam delved into her satchel. "Susie passed on a letter that was sent to the agency."

"That's your job to deal with," I said irritably. "They're normally begging letters or a request for a donation or someone pretending to be my long-lost brother."

"I know that, Electra, and usually I *would* deal with it, but Susie and I think you should read this." She passed the envelope to me, and I saw it was addressed "care of the agency" in an elegant hand. I eyed Mariam across the coffee table.

"Why? What does it say?"

"I just think you should read it, that's all," she repeated.

"Okay," I sighed, and I slid the letter out of the envelope. "It's not anything bad, is it? Like the IRS writing me personally?"

"No, Electra, it isn't, I promise."

"Okay." I unfolded the paper and saw a Brooklyn address at the top. Then I began to read.

*My dear Miss D'Aplièse—or may I call you Electra?*
*My name is Stella Jackson and I am your biological grandmother . . .*

"Jesus!" I balled the letter in my fist and threw it at Mariam playfully. "Do you know how many of these kinds of letters from 'lost relatives' I get? Susie normally puts them in the trash. What did this one want?"

"From the letter, nothing, other than to meet you."

"Okay, so what is so unusual about it that you gave it to me?"

"There's something else in the envelope, Electra." Mariam indicated where I had discarded it on the coffee table. "I really think you should take a look."

Just to shut her up, I picked up the envelope again and looked inside. There was a small photograph lodged in one corner. I drew it out and saw it was black and white, yellowing slightly at the edges. It was of a very beautiful black woman holding a baby and smiling at the camera.

"Well?"

I looked at Mariam. "Well, what?"

"Can't you see the resemblance?"

"To who?"

"You, of course! Susie noticed it immediately, and so did I."

I looked again. "Yeah, so she's black, and okay, she's definitely a beauty, but"—I shrugged—"I'm sure there are thousands of women who look like her—and me."

"As you know well, Electra, there are very *few* women who look like you. The shape of her face, the set of her eyes and the cheekbones. Seriously, she could be you. Or what I mean is . . . you could be her."

"Yeah, well, until I find that letter from Pa, I'm not adopting random people who write to me as family just 'cause they look a little like me, okay?"

"We'd better find that letter, then," said Mariam as she retrieved and un-scrunched the granny letter (which looked seriously un-unscrunchable to me), then folded it back inside the envelope together with the photograph. "I'll put this in the safe, okay?"

"Okay." My cell pinged with a text notification, and I glanced down at it.

"So I'll be here to collect you at eight tomorrow morning. You have the meeting with Thomas and Marcella to discuss the Christmas fragrance campaign. Electra?"

"Yeah. Cool. Bye." I waved to dismiss her as I studied the message that had arrived.

"And then the watch shoot tomorrow afternoon. So if there's nothing else for now, I will see you in the morning."

I wasn't listening, as I couldn't tear my eyes away from the words on the screen, so I just nodded in Mariam's direction as she walked toward the door. I reached for my vodka and took a good deep slug as I reread them.

> Hi honey, in town for a gig and wondered if you were around tomorrow? Would be good to talk. Mitch.

"*Shit! Shit! Shit!*"

I drained the vodka and stood up to pour myself another in order to calm my racing heart.

I read it again, and again, then turned to my laptop to look up whether he was telling the truth. He was. His latest tour was winding up at Madison Square Garden just two nights from now. I stood up, went to the long windows, and slid one open so I could walk onto the terrace. Somewhere close by, Mitch was in town. Tonight, wherever he was, we breathed the same air.

I looked down at my cell again and tried to decipher whether he was offering me an olive branch and what that meant if he was. But olive branches could have twigs sprouting from them, like one that said, "Hey, I miss you and love you and I've realized my mistake," and another that said, "Now we've had some time, it would be good to move on as friends."

And I had no idea which it was.

*Just say no, Electra . . . It's too dangerous to go back there.*

"Shit! Goddamn it!" I punched the glass barrier that stopped me from plunging however many hundreds of yards to my death. At that moment, I wondered if that was the easier option; I was literally in agony because I really didn't know what to do. I wished I had a close friend I could call on to ask advice. How sad was it that I had five sisters, yet there wasn't a single one of them I could say was a friend or someone I completely trusted.

"Ignore the text," I said out loud as I paced the terrace, deadheading a flower from a bush and throwing the petals over the glass wall as I went.

Back inside, I dumped my cell facing downward on my bed. Maybe I *should* leave it. After all, if I didn't reply and he didn't bother to retext me, that would tell me a lot.

Yes, that was what I would do. I fixed myself another vodka, then wandered to my walk-in closet, thinking about what I would wear if I saw him. The one thing I had in my armory was clothes. A call to any designer in town, and the look I wanted would be biked to me within a few hours. Of course, it depended on where we were meeting. If it was at my place, I had to look casual but sexy. He'd always loved my legs, so maybe the answer was simple . . .

I walked into the bathroom and stripped off before taking a white fluffy towel off the heated rail. I draped it around me, then turned on the faucet, put my hand beneath it, and trickled some drops of water onto my skin. I took hold of my hair and twirled it up into a topknot, then studied myself in the full-length mirror.

I giggled, because *this* was what I would definitely wear if Mitch was coming to visit me here. However, if I was going to see him . . . I dropped the towel on the floor and went back to my closet. I was just pulling an emerald green Versace minidress from the rack when a text made itself known with a ping and I ran to grab my cell.

It was from Mitch, and I held my breath as I opened it.

Electra. Did you get my text? Really like to hook up and talk tomorrow.

"Yesss!" I screeched. "He's desperate!"

Jumping—literally—onto my bed, I drank some more vodka for courage, then tried to form a reply.

Hi, only just seen this.

My fingers hovered over the screen as I worked out the kind of schedule he'd have tomorrow. Media interviews would take up his morning; then, after lunch, he and his band would go to the venue for rehearsals and sound checks. I figured he'd be free by eight.

Can't do tomorrow day as have meeting for fragrance campaign but should be home around eight.

I read the whole thing back to myself and felt happy enough to send it off. It was only a few seconds before his reply bounced back.

Can make nine your place. Does that work?

At that point I decided to go have a bath. I turned up the volume on my sound system and lay in a deep pool of scented water, listening to Mitch's latest CD. Climbing out and relishing that I currently (for a change) held all the power, I sauntered into the bedroom and picked up my cell.

Yup, that works. See you tomorrow.

I pressed "send" and allowed myself a smile. *And the best thing about it*, I thought as I looked at myself in the mirror, *is that I can wear my new favorite outfit.*

I hardly slept a wink that night, and—even though I'd promised myself I wouldn't because Mitch could spot a cokehead a mile off—I was so jittery that I had to do a line before I went into my morning meeting to discuss the fragrance campaign.

"Are you okay?" asked Mariam when I emerged from the restroom.

"Yeah, I'm fine. Shall we go in?"

When we came out a couple of hours later, I was glad that Mariam had been there to record what had been agreed about my schedule for the up-coming commercial shoot in Brazil, plus the actual launch in October. All I knew was that I stank like a cheap prostitute—the client had been at the meeting, and they'd obviously had someone spray the room with the per-fume before we'd all arrived.

"Wow," Mariam said as we took the elevator down. "They're sparing no expense on this one. I've never been to Rio, have you?"

"You know what, I can't remember offhand, but I don't think so, no."

"Didn't you tell me that your eldest sister lives there?"

"I must have if you know," I said, wondering if I had time to get my manicurist to drop by this afternoon.

"You can go and visit her, can't you?"

"Yup, I suppose I can," I said as Mariam led the way out of the building before we settled ourselves in the back of the waiting limo.

"Is there anything you want me to order in for lunch?"

"No, thanks, I'm sure I'll be able to find something at home."

"Electra, your refrigerator is empty, and it's important you eat. You have the photo shoot at three for the Jaeger-LeCoultre campaign."

"What?" I turned to her in horror. "You didn't mention that to me yes-terday."

"I did, Electra," she said quietly. "Remember, we had that incredible watch set with pink diamonds sent over with two security guards last week to make sure it fit you?"

Sadly, I *did* remember.

"Shit," I muttered, under my breath because I'd begun to notice Mariam wincing every time I swore. "Can we cancel? Say I'm sick or something?"

"I suppose we could, of course, but why would we?"

"Because I'd, like, totally forgotten I had something planned tonight."

"What time does it start?"

"Oh, around eight," I said, thinking I needed a good hour to prepare for Mitch's arrival.

"Well, they're looking for a sunset shot and it will be dark by seven thirty anyway, so you could just about make it if you go straight to your appoint-ment from the shoot."

"But I need awhile to get ready! Christ! Can't they delay by a week? The campaign isn't starting for months. How much time do these guys need?!"

"Electra, I'm not your keeper, but—"

"No, you're not! No one is, though everyone acts like they think they are!"

I watched her blush and lower her eyes. "I do apologize if you feel that way."

I suddenly felt terrible. This wasn't Mariam's fault, it was mine. "No, *I* should apologize. I'm just real antsy today, that's all. Anyway"—I sighed—"I guess you're right. It wouldn't look good to let them down. I'll just have to be brilliant and get the perfect shot fast."

"If anyone can do that, it's you, Electra. Okay, so you're sure you don't want anything to eat?"

"Maybe order me up some wasabi noodles with a side of kale."

"Will do. Now I have to go see Susie, but I will be back here to pick you up at two thirty. Okay?"

"Okay."

Back in my apartment, I did a couple of lines because my nerves were jangling and washed down lunch with my friend Grey Goose. Then I drank a pint of water, gargled half a bottle of mouthwash, and chewed minty gum as I sat on my bed trying to relax by practicing the breathing exercises my therapist had given me.

They didn't work. Nothing worked except the Goose and its powdery companion, which I'd nicknamed White Heaven.

"Why are the good things always so bad for you?" I complained as I took another couple of snorts of the only medicine that I knew would calm me down.

"Hi, Electra, you're looking as gorgeous as always." Tommy, my superfan, approached me as I stepped out of the building.

"Thanks."

"Is there anything I can do for you today?" he asked.

"No, but thanks for asking." I gave him a smile as I passed him before climbing into the waiting limo.

"He is such a sweet man," Mariam commented as she got into the back of the car with me. "And so protective of you. Maybe you should hire him officially as your bodyguard. Underneath those old sweatshirts he wears, you can see he's ripped."

"Mariam!" I turned to her and raised an eyebrow. "I'm shocked."

"Honestly, Electra, I might not drink or swear, but I do have a pulse, you know." She smiled as we pulled out into traffic. "So what are you doing this evening that's so important?"

"Oh, it's just a private dinner with a friend."

"Well, we will do our best to get you back to your apartment on time."

I arrived home just before eight with a shoulder that ached from having to hold my arm in exactly the right position until they got the perfect shot of the watch. I was relieved to see that Tommy wasn't in his usual spot—he normally liked to see me home and safe before he left. The last thing I needed was anyone spotting Mitch walking into my apartment building, although he was a master of disguise, with a closetful of fake beards, mustaches, and wigs. After the porter let me into the penthouse, I ran to the tub to fill it, then surveyed my postshoot makeup to decide whether it was worth keeping on. I knew Mitch preferred me au naturel, so I scrubbed it all away, then sank into the water, careful not to get my hair wet. How I longed for *real* naturally silky hair. Maybe one day I'd have mine razored off like Alek Wek—another model whom I'd met a few times on the runways—which would be so much easier.

Once out of the bath, I padded to the kitchen to add some ice to the Goose to water it down.

"Shit!" I said, seeing that Mariam had been right when she'd said my refrigerator was empty; Mitch could barely go for more than a few minutes without a shot of iced green tea.

*On the other hand, who gives a shit what he drinks?* I told myself as I went back to the bathroom and brushed my teeth. *He dumped you, remember? He broke your heart.*

"Too right!" I added aloud to my reflection in the mirror as I dabbed some Vaseline on my lips. In the living room, I looked at the clock and saw it was a quarter to nine. As I wasn't getting dressed apart from my towel, there was little else to do except fill an empty plastic water bottle with vodka so I had emergency rations at hand without him realizing what I was drinking. Grabbing my portfolio, I pulled out the best of my recent shots and arranged them haphazardly on the coffee table to make it look as though I was trying to choose one. Then I went over to the sound system but couldn't decide between Springsteen—whom Mitch idolized—or eighties pop, which I loved and he hated. So I compromised on nothing.

"Jesus! I'm stressed," I muttered as I sat down on the couch. I detected a hint of acrid sweat and immediately went back to the bathroom to wipe myself down and spray on more scent. I hadn't been this nervous since my first trip down the catwalk in Paris.

*And what if he does want you back? Will you just go to him like a lamb?*

*You know you will, Electra . . .*

I had no further time for self-illumination as the concierge phone beeped to tell me a "Mr. Mike" was downstairs in the lobby.

"Yeah, send him up," I said, then slammed down the receiver, ran back to the bathroom, and sprinkled my shoulders with some water from the bath. Checking my reflection, I waited for the doorbell to ring. It didn't for ages, and then I heard a familiar voice from the living room.

"Electra? Are you here?"

*Jesus! Mitch was in my apartment!*

"Coming!" I made loud swishing noises with the bathwater, dribbling more of the scented water over my shoulders as I did so. I checked that the white towel was positioned seductively before walking into the living room.

And there he was, as large as life—the guy who had left me heartbroken. He'd taken off his baseball cap and false beard and looked (irritatingly) as tall and sexy as I remembered him, in dirty jeans, a checked shirt, and the cowboy boots he always wore. If any man was all American male, it was Mitch. I noticed his hair was longer than the last time I'd seen him, and he obviously hadn't shaved in a while because his chin was covered in stubble. I just wanted to reach for him and tear his clothes off.

"How did you get in?"

He shrugged. "The door was wide open. You obviously hadn't closed it properly."

"Jeez, I'm always doing that. One day I'll get murdered in my bed."

"I sure hope not." His eyes briefly looked me up and down before he averted them. "I've obviously disturbed you. You wanna go get some clothes on?"

"I . . . oh, yeah, sure. I'm just out of the tub. The meeting ran over."

"It's okay, I'm in no rush. You go ahead."

"Okay," I said and walked into the bedroom, kicking myself. Somewhere inside me I'd believed that the sight of me half naked in a towel would be enough for him to grab me immediately and rip it off. But we obviously had to go through some kind of getting-to-know-each-other-again dance before we got there.

As I didn't have a plan B clothes-wise, I dropped the towel on the floor, then stood in my closet, not having a clue what to put on. In the end, I went for my favorite pair of jeans and threw on a green vest top—Mitch was a southern boy at heart, and he had a thing for a tight-fitting pair of denims.

Breathing hard and fanning myself because I was still sweating with nerves, I walked back into the living room and found him sitting on the couch looking at my shots.

"I swear you get more beautiful every time I see you. And I'm talking about the real thing, not these." He smiled at me.

"Thanks. Can I fix you something to drink?"

"Do you have a Coke by any chance?"

"I thought you only drank herbal tea."

"It's been a stressful day, and sometimes a guy needs a shot of caffeine."

"I'll take a look," I said, walking into the kitchen and seeing that there were a couple of cans of Coke in the door of the refrigerator.

"Here you go," I said, handing him the can—he never drank from a glass. It was far too girly.

"So," I said, placing myself at a distance from him on the couch and picking up my "water" bottle. "How have you been?"

"Busy with the tour. I worked out that tomorrow night will be my hundredth gig."

"Wow, right," I said as I sucked hard on the straw and filled my mouth with neat vodka. I swallowed and nodded at him. "Well, it's nearly over."

"Yeah, it sure is, and I can't wait to get back to my place in Malibu to have some downtime. And you, Electra? How have you been?"

"Good. Busy, like you, but good, yes."

"That's great to hear, and as I told you, you look fantastic."

"You look great, too."

"Well, thanks for that, but I sure don't believe it. Months of not sleeping in your own bed can really take a toll. I'm gonna step back for a few months after tomorrow night. I'm getting too old for this shit," he said, smiling lazily at me—a smile that regularly brought millions of women to their knees.

"Don't be an idiot, Mitch. Old rockers never die, you know that. Look at the Stones for starters."

"Yeah. I rest my case." He gave me a roll of his eyes. "Hey, darlin', come and give Mitch a hug."

I needed no further bidding. I sank into his outstretched arms, waiting for the moment when he would tip my head back and kiss me. Instead, he stroked my hair.

"Compared to me, you're a baby, aren't you?"

"Hey, I am *so* not. With my line of work, I had to grow up fast. I feel old, probably older than you." I looked up at him, my lips parted in readiness, but he just looked down at me with an odd expression in his eyes.

"So, no hard feelings?"

"Why would there be?"

"Because . . . I let you down big time."

"Yeah, you did, but that's all in the past. You had your reasons. I understand."

"Well, you're being mighty generous, Electra, but that sure doesn't make me feel like any less of a jerk. It wouldn't have been right to carry on when I knew it just couldn't work."

I waited for the "but," but it never came.

"I'm real glad you've moved on," he said instead. "I never wanted to hurt you."

"I told you, I'm okay."

This conversation really wasn't going the way I'd imagined it would, so I pulled out of his arms, reached for the "water" bottle, and took another swig.

"Looks like you're clean, too."

"I am," I agreed as I swallowed a large gulp of vodka. It was time to cut the crap. "So why are you here?"

"Because . . . because I have something to tell you."

"Oh, what?"

"Well, I wanted you to know before it was officially announced. I kinda felt I owed it to you."

I stared at him silently, having no idea what it was he wanted to tell me but sure that it wasn't going to be a declaration of undying love.

"I'm getting married," he announced, "to a wonderful lady I met on the tour. She's a backup singer and from the South, like me. We just fit together, y'know?"

I'd heard descriptions of blood turning to ice, but until this moment, I'd never experienced it.

"Congratulations," I managed, almost choking with the effort.

"Thanks. Now I feel stupid coming here to tell you in person, because it's obvious you're doin' just fine."

"I am, oh yes, I really am," I said, using every ounce of self-control I'd ever possessed not to pick up the heavy bronze statuette that stood on the glass coffee table and crash it onto his handsome, arrogant head.

"So I guess that's it. I'm gonna tell the fans tomorrow night onstage— pull Sharon forward and just put it out there."

I watched him nod at the rightness of the scenario he was clearly imagining. I remained silent, sucking hard on my straw, but there was nothing left to suck.

"I can get you VIP tickets for tomorrow if you'd like."

"Sorry, I'm busy tomorrow night." I gave him a nonchalant shrug.

I watched him stand up. "Well, then, I'll leave you in peace. Gotta grab some sleep tonight. It's a big day tomorrow."

"Sure sounds like it." I nodded, not moving.

He looked at me then, and maybe something in my expression gave him a hint. "Did I do the wrong thing by droppin' by? I just—"

"Mitch?"

"Yeah?"

"Will you get the hell out of my apartment? *Now!*"

I rose from the couch then and stood toe to toe with him.

"Sure, I'm going. I'm real sorry, Electra," he said as he walked toward the door. "The last thing I meant to do was upset you."

"Well, guess what? You have! Big time!"

I marched ahead of him and held open the door. "Bye, Mitch. Have a nice life with your new wife," I spat.

Luckily for him, he said nothing else, because if he had, I might well have ended up doing time for murder. As he passed through the door, I slammed it behind him so hard that the glasses rattled in the kitchen cupboard. Then I slid down the wall and burst into great heaving sobs of anger and pain.

# 6

"Can I get you anything, Miss D'Aplièse?" the cabin attendant asked.

"Yeah, a glass of tonic water with ice."

"Will you want lemon with that?"

"No, thanks."

"What about something to eat?"

I looked around my seat for the menu card.

"Don't worry, I have one here."

He handed me the card. My head was spinning so hard, I could hardly focus.

"I'll take the stir-fry noodles and a side salad."

"Perfect. Any wine to accompany that?"

"No, just the tonic water." ·

The attendant nodded and glided away down the first-class cabin. I opened up the bin in which my purse and duty-free were stored and, making sure no one was looking, screwed the top off the bottle of Grey Goose I had bought and took a swig. When the cabin attendant came back with my tonic, I'd drink half of it and fill it up with my private vodka stash. I lay back in my seat and closed my eyes, but there were weird bright lights pinging against my eyelids. I knew I'd done too much coke last night, and ecstasy didn't suit me. It had been seven in the morning before I'd begun to come down, but by then, I'd taken a couple of sleeping pills. The next thing I'd known, I'd heard someone calling my name and had pried open my eyes to see Mariam staring down at me, telling me it was time to leave for JFK.

"Hi."

*Speak of the devil*, I thought as Mariam appeared beside me from her seat in business class.

"Hi," I said, looking up at her.

"How are you feeling?" she asked me.

"I'm okay, thanks. It was a late one last night, that's all."

"Well, the flight to São Paulo takes ten hours, so hopefully you can catch some sleep before we board the private jet up to Rio. You have a full day on the commercial shoot tomorrow."

"I know. I'll be just fine, really," I assured her.

"Did you contact your sister, by the way?"

"No, I haven't yet."

"Well, you can definitely see her tomorrow night or on Thursday before we take the night flight back."

"Yup, I'll get in touch with her when we land."

Mariam smiled. "Great. Okay, well, if there's anything you need, just send the attendant to get me."

"Will do." I nodded as my tonic water arrived with some cashews.

"Thanks," I said. As soon as both of them retreated, I downed half the tonic water, then topped it off with some Goose as planned.

The past two weeks had been the worst of my life, literally, *ever*, I thought as I took two large gulps of my drink. Everywhere I'd gone, there had been photos of Mitch with his Very Plain Fiancée plastered on the front of magazines and newspapers, the TV replaying the moment he'd announced he was going to marry her onstage at Madison Square Garden. Everyone was talking about it on shoots, their voices disappearing to a hush when I appeared. Just like the news on CNN, the whole nightmare circus went round and round in a reel inside my head. And of course, I couldn't even *begin* to look as though I cared. Any hint of the sad ex-girlfriend about me would give the media what they wanted. So I'd partied: every night I'd been seen at a movie premiere, a nightclub, or a glitzy gallery opening. I'd called up any high-profile male friend I could find to accompany me—Zed had come in handy, and there'd been pics and column inches debating whether we were officially "an item." I'd done all this because there was just *no way* anyone was going to see me cry.

"No one," I mumbled as I drained my glass.

"Your noodles and salad, Miss D'Aplièse," said the cabin attendant, appearing like Tinker Bell beside me. He pulled out my table, and another attendant arranged a tablecloth and silverware on it before the food was put in front of me.

"Can I get you anything else?"

I smiled up at him. "Maybe I'll have a glass of champagne."

"Why not?" he agreed, then moved to clear away my almost empty tonic water glass.

"I'll have a refill of the tonic, too, if you don't mind."

"Of course not, Miss D'Aplièse."

Christ, I thought, it was tiring being me. Even thirty-two thousand feet above the earth, I was still pretending to be someone I wasn't. A me who was clean, sober, and in control.

After the noodles, I had another vodka tonic, then flicked through the movie selection. Halfway through the latest Harry Potter (rom-coms were definitely off the menu right now) I fell asleep and then woke up when everyone else had their lights turned out, their comforters wrapped around them, and their seat belts strapped on top. After getting up to use the restroom, I arrived back in the cabin and with the eerie blue lighting thought it resembled a flying space lab. *Sleeping humans are so vulnerable*, I mused as I climbed back into my own area, which had magically morphed into a bed while I'd been away. And the one thing I could never show was vulnerability; any sign from me that I was struggling, and the media would broadcast the sordid details around the world. People from Tallahassee to Tokyo would nod at each other across their dinner tables and say that they'd seen it coming and they'd be glad it *had* come, because, they'd say, that was the price of success.

Maybe it was, but, I thought as I looked out of the window and saw the lights of what must be South America below me, I hadn't ever asked for it. So many "celebrities" I'd met had told me that they'd dreamed since childhood of getting rich and famous. I just dreamed of a world where I didn't feel like an outsider, a world where I belonged. Because that's all I'd ever really wanted.

"Jeez, it's hot! Can we take a break now?" I asked the director. It was three in the afternoon, and I was seriously flagging.

"Just one more take, Electra, and we can wrap for today. You're doing great, honey."

Biting my tongue hard—I'd never yet broken my golden rule of doing anything more than complaining mildly on a shoot—I walked back across the soft sand of Ipanema Beach to stand on my marks. The makeup lady was ready for me, caking more powder on my face to mop up the perspiration.

"She's good to go!" she shouted above the strong, burning wind on the beach.

"Okay, Electra!" the director boomed through his megaphone. "Three paces forward, then start to raise your arms until I say cut."

I gave him a thumbs-up.

"And . . . action!"

Off I went again for maybe the twentieth time, praying it would be the last and I could strip off the white chiffon robe—with its bulging hood that shot out like a parachute behind my head, the underslip clinging wetly to me—and throw myself into the massive waves roaring behind me.

"Okay, cut!"

I stood where I was, waiting for the director to check the frame.

"People, that's a wrap for today!"

I almost tore the robe from my body and stumbled across the sand to the wardrobe tent.

"Anyone for a swim?" I asked as both the director and Mariam poked their heads inside.

"I'm not sure the insurance covers you for swimming in the sea with that kind of swell, Electra," the director cautioned me.

"Oh, come on, Ken. I can see little kids swimming further along the beach."

"How about tomorrow afternoon when we're done? Then I'll happily allow you to drown," he quipped. "Joaquim has just arrived, so it's all looking good."

"Okay. I'll go back to the hotel and take a dip in their pool. Now, if you don't mind, I need to get changed."

"Sure, honey." Ken left and Mariam stayed, handing me a bottle of water.

"Good job," she said, smiling at me. "It looked amazing on camera."

"Great. Now, let's get out of here," I murmured under my breath as I turned back to the wardrobe lady and smiled at her sweetly. "Thanks for your help today."

"It was a pleasure, Electra. See you at seven a.m. tomorrow," she said in her strongly accented English.

As I arrived back at the Copacabana Palace, there was a cluster of autograph hunters gathered by the entrance. They shouted at me as I got out of the limo, and I smiled for their cameras and signed their photos and autograph books.

Once inside, I almost ran to the elevator in my eagerness to get up to my suite.

"Would you like me to come with you?" Mariam asked me.

"No, I'm gonna take a cold shower and get some rest. It was a long day today."

"What about your swim?" she asked me as the elevator doors opened.

"Maybe later," I said as I stepped inside and pressed the button for the top floor. "I'll call you," I added as the doors closed behind me.

Back in my suite, I headed for my carry-on and poured myself a vodka. My hands were visibly shaking as I put the glass to my lips—I hadn't dared bring any chemical supplies with me on public aviation and had relied on there being someone on the shoot I knew who could share his or her supply. But this shoot was clean (so far as I knew, anyway), and I didn't know anyone well enough to trust them. Yet I was in South America, where drug trafficking probably brought in more money than any other business. If the worse came to the worst, I thought, I'd go pay a visit to the concierge. This was Brazil, after all, and I was sure he'd be able to help.

Just as I was stepping into the shower, the room telephone rang. I left it, thinking that there wasn't a person on Earth I was interested in talking to.

Standing under the water, I let out a torrent of expletives that Ma, who'd drilled it into us sisters never to swear, would have shuddered at. Still, Mitch deserved every one of them. Grabbing a towel and padding back into the living room, I saw the red light indicating a message winking on my phone. I walked over, picked up the receiver, and pressed the button to listen to the message, which was probably from housekeeping asking me what time I wanted my turn-down service.

Instead, I heard the comforting tones of my sister Maia's voice:

*"Hi, Electra, sorry I missed you. Floriano spotted a photo in a newspaper this morning of you arriving at the Copacabana Palace. I don't know how long you're here for, but obviously I'd love to see you. I only live around the corner from the hotel, and my number is . . ."*

I grabbed the pencil by the phone and wrote the number down on the notepad provided. Then I contemplated the evening ahead. There was dinner at some flashy restaurant for the cast and crew, which I had said I'd attend but could easily get out of by feigning tiredness. Maia had said she lived close by, so maybe I should skip the dinner, call my eldest sister, and go meet her new family.

The truth was, I didn't want to do *either*. In fact, I didn't want to do anything except to get off and forget I even breathed.

"Christ, I need some coke!" I shouted, thinking that the one downside of my new and brilliant PA was the fact she was so squeaky clean. At least Amy had been on hand if I'd needed to score, being partial to the stuff herself. Mariam would probably fall to the floor in a dead faint if I even asked her to order me a vodka tonic.

The bell to my suite rang, but I ignored it. Thirty seconds later, it rang again.

"Who is it?" I called.

"It is me, Joaquim," said a deep resonant voice through the door.

"Joaquim?" *Do I know a Joaquim?*

Then the penny dropped, as Pa would say; he was the new hot male model-about-town who was appearing in the commercial with me. The director had mentioned he'd flown in today, ready for tomorrow's filming.

"Hang on, I'm coming."

I grabbed my robe and put it on, then went to open the door.

"*Olá*, Electra."

He smiled lazily at me, his thick black curls falling around a face that was already almost as famous as mine for its beauty. My eyes sized up the rest of him, and I gave him a smile.

"Well, hi there."

"It is an honor to meet you at last. Do I disturb you?"

"No, come in." I opened the door wider.

"I just think to myself that, if we are to share a kiss on set tomorrow, I should introduce myself personally to you first."

"Sure." I indicated the couch. "Come and sit down." I watched him as he walked across the room and decided that yes, he really *was* hot. "Drink?"

"What you have?"

I shrugged. "The contents of a minibar or room service."

"Then we have champagne, *sim*?"

"Sure, if that's what you'd like." I called down to room service and ordered a bottle of Taittinger on ice.

"You know, this is crazy!" He smiled at me, showing off his white even teeth.

"Why is that?"

"Because only a year ago I live here in Rio. I work raking the sand just across the street." He pointed through the window to Copacabana Beach, which lay beneath us in a perfect white line. "Then some American lady approach me and tell me she will make me a star. Now here I am, sitting in best suite in the Copacabana Palace with one of the most famous women in the world."

"Yeah, a similar thing happened to me. Weird transition, isn't it?"

"*Sim*, it is. And tomorrow we stand on that beach where I used to rake, and for kissing you I get paid more than I earn in five years!"

As I studied him more closely, I realized that he was probably not older than nineteen or twenty—a boy. He made me feel like a granny in comparison.

"Electra, can I tell you something?"

"Anything you want."

"I still have pictures of you in bedroom I share before with my kid brothers. You are my—how you say?—pinup girl!"

"Hey, that's sweet, thanks," I said as the bell rang and the champagne arrived.

"So," I toasted him when room service had left, "here's to your success. I've seen your face on billboards all over New York. You're famous."

"Not as famous as you—yet." He grinned at me boyishly, then took a sip of his champagne.

"Well, it can be a pretty crazy roller coaster, and if you ever need any advice, I'd be happy to help. I've been there," I said with feeling.

"And you are still there! My agent, he tell me all the time how my candle, it can burn out as quickly as it lit. So I will try very hard to make sure it stay alight because I never want to go back to that." Joaquim indicated the beach again. "I must behave myself, yes?"

"Yeah, you're probably already learning what the deal is with fame."

"I know, it is hard; people see me on street or in bar, and I must have pictures and sign many autographs. And the schedule, wow!" He ran a hand through his hair. "I count up that I was in three continents in the past month. I wake up and do not know where I am. But I will not complain, because I know how lucky I am."

"Yeah, that's the spirit," I mumbled as I drained my glass and poured myself—and him—another.

"And I am doing more of this than I should."

I watched him put a hand into his jean pocket and bring out a small bag of white powder. "Do you mind if I—" He indicated the bag.

I suddenly believed in God, Santa Claus, and the Easter Bunny combined.

"What if I said I did mind?" I smiled at him as he tapped some powder out onto the table.

He looked horrified. "Then of course I would not, Electra, but people in our industry tell me you . . . do not mind."

It was my turn to feel horrified, though I tried not to show it. "Yeah, but I try not to make a habit of it, of course."

"But we are at the Copacabana Palace and I meet you for the first time. Want to join me?"

*Did I?* I attempted to look calm. "Why not?"

"Here, you go first. It is very good stuff. From a friend I know in Rio."

And as that oh-so-welcome sensation began to fill my senses, I laughed out loud. "It *is* good. Maybe you could give me your friend's number just in case I need some more."

"Do not worry, Electra, I have enough for both of us."

Joaquim found the sound system and cranked it up, then we went to sit on the terrace overlooking Copacabana Beach. Suddenly life was wonderful and my new friend was becoming more attractive by the moment.

"Are you going to the dinner tonight?" he asked me.

"I'm meant to be, yes, but it doesn't appeal."

"Neither to me. I am in my home city, and I want to party. I can take you to some places no one but a local knows."

"I'd love that, I really would. I rarely get a chance to see anything much in the cities I visit."

I stood up, intending to call Mariam, but he was behind me and grabbed me by the waist.

"Or we could party here together—alone."

His supple hips swayed behind me to the rhythm of the music. He turned me around to face him, then lost no time in kissing me.

Forty-five minutes later, the doorbell rang. I ignored it, then heard my cell ring, too.

"Wait there," I said, kissing Joaquim before I slipped out of bed, donned my robe, then padded into the living room to answer my cell.

"Electra, it is Mariam. I am at the door."

"Jesus!" I murmured as I went to open it, picking up an envelope that had been slid underneath it.

"Hi," I said, trying to look sleepy, though I was totally pumped.

"You are not dressed, Electra, and we must leave for the dinner in fifteen minutes."

"Sorry, but I'm not feeling too good. Can you make my excuses for me? Say I'm having an early night."

"Okay."

I could feel her eyes boring into me. I handed her the envelope. "Deal with this, will you, whatever it is? I'll see you tomorrow, bright and early."

"Okay, but don't forget to book an alarm call for six thirty."

"I won't."

"Feel better," she said.

"Thanks. Night."

I closed the door, then put the security chain on as well. Sauntering over to the coffee table, I took another line, then went back into the bedroom and Joaquim's eager arms.

# 7

Maybe because we'd gotten to know each other so well the night before, the shoot went like a dream and we wrapped by four o'clock.

"Remember I said earlier that the note the concierge put under your door was from your sister Maia?" Mariam asked as I changed in the wardrobe tent.

"Yeah, I don't have foam for a brain, you know," I said as I fastened my shorts.

"Will you call her when you get back to the hotel? Her note said she was free tonight, and we don't have to leave for the airport until ten o'clock."

"Course I will," I said, feeling irritated. Lately, I felt, Mariam had started acting like an overprotective—and bossy—parent. Nevertheless, when I got back to my suite, I dialed the number I'd written down yesterday.

"*Oi!*" Maia's gentle voice answered immediately.

"Hey, it's me, Electra."

"Electra! I just can't believe you're here in Rio. How long are you staying?"

"I fly back tonight at midnight."

"Then have you the time to come over for a couple of hours and meet Floriano and Valentina?"

"Probably not," I lied, thinking of the assignation I had with Joaquim in twenty minutes. "But I could meet you for a quick drink here around eight before I leave for the airport?"

"Oh, okay. Well, I'll be there."

"Just ask the concierge to send you up to my suite, okay? I'll let him know you're coming."

"Okay. I can't wait to see you, Electra."

"Yeah, bye."

I put the phone down, then did a line from the stash Joaquim had left me last night before taking a shower. I called down to room service for a bottle of vodka and another champagne on ice. Ten minutes later, Joaquim was in my suite, then in my bed.

"You are a gorgeous thing," he murmured in my ear. "I can't get enough of you."

Having fallen asleep afterward, we woke up and both did another couple of lines and made more love. Then when I complained I was still struggling to stay awake, he produced a couple of pills from his wallet.

"Try these, Electra; they will pull you up like nothing you ever take before."

I washed a tablet down with champagne, and he did the same. Ten minutes later, we were making love yet again; then we showered and giggled helplessly as Joaquim tried to teach me the samba naked on the terrace.

"Someone might see," I whispered as I saw the pool below me over the balustrade.

"And it will make beautiful picture." He smiled as he kissed me.

"No!"

Even in my drug-and-alcohol-fueled blur, I knew what we were doing was dangerous, so I pulled him back inside.

And found Mariam and my sister Maia standing in the living room.

"Whoops!" I said as I did my best to cover bits of me with my hands and watched Joaquim grab a cushion to preserve his modesty. I burst into hysterical laughter at the looks on my PA's and my sister's faces.

"Sorry, guys, you should have knocked."

"We tried that, and calling the room. We were worried, so in the end the manager let us in," said Mariam, and at that moment I wanted to slap her around her almost certainly virginal and nonalcoholic cheeks. "I'll go and get your robe, Electra."

"And I had better leave you," added Joaquim, disappearing behind Mariam into the bedroom.

"Please, sit down," I said to Maia as Mariam returned and handed me my robe.

"We must leave for the airport in forty minutes. I will go and pack for you," she said quietly.

"Thanks."

Joaquim reappeared fully dressed, and I gave him a big hug.

"See you at the airport?"

"No, I stay on a little longer, then fly to Mexico for *GQ*."

I nodded. "Okay. Keep in touch, won't you?"

"I call you when I am back in New York," he agreed. "*Tchau*, Electra. *Adeus, senhora*," he added to Maia as he left.

"Want some champagne?" I asked her as I took the bottle standing on the coffee table and shook it. "Whoops, there's none left. I'll order some more."

"No, thank you, Electra."

"Anything else I can get you?" I said as I poured myself some neat vodka from the bottle I'd ordered earlier.

"Really, I'm fine. And how about you?"

"Oh, I'm great. And just crazy about Rio! What a city it is."

Maia silently watched me drinking the vodka. I put the glass down and studied her.

"Y'know, you really are the beauty of the family. It should be you doing my job."

"Thank you for the compliment."

"No, seriously," I continued, taking in her glorious head of shiny dark hair, her amazing unblemished skin, and the big dark eyes that reminded me of Joaquim's. I nodded vigorously. "You are truly beautiful. I mean, even more beautiful than the last time I saw you."

"Well," Maia replied in her slow, gentle tone, "maybe it's because I'm happy. Are you happy, Electra?"

"Oh," I said as I opened my arms wide, "I'm ecstatic! Isn't Joaquim gorgeous? He's Brazilian by birth, you know. Are all Brazilians as beautiful as you two? I think I might move here permanently if they are!"

"It is time to get ready to leave for the airport, Electra." Mariam had appeared behind me. "I've laid out your usual travel clothes on the bed."

"Thanks," I said, swaying slightly as I grabbed my vodka glass from the table. "Did you remember my underwear as well?" I giggled. "Won't be long," I added to Maia and gave her a little wave as I went into the bedroom to do as I'd been told.

I could hear my sister and my PA talking in low voices as I dressed.

"Hey, Mariam! I'm sooo hungry. Can you get room service to pack me a club sandwich to go?" I called to her.

"Of course," came her reply.

I sat down on the bed and tried to lace up my sneakers before realizing I'd put them on the wrong feet, which sent me into a round of giggles. I thought how Maia and Mariam were, like, so similar. They were both really controlled, and you never knew what they were thinking, *and* . . .

"Guess what? I just worked out that you can make the name 'Maia' out of 'Mariam'!" I announced as I joined them in the living room and sat down heavily on the couch. "Isn't that cute?"

They both gave me odd smiles; then a man in uniform appeared at the door. "Have you come to take me away?" I asked him, giggling again.

Mariam went to talk to him, and he swiftly disappeared.

"I was only joking! He needs to take my bags."

"Electra, Mariam and I were just talking, and we wondered if you'd like to stay with me here in Rio for a few days," said Maia. "Especially as you said you liked it so much."

"Yeah, I do, but that's because I had a good time with Joaquim, y'know? We got along great."

"I could see," Maia agreed. "You looked as though you connected very well indeed."

"We did, we did."

"So," Maia said after a pause, "how about you stay here tonight and try to get some sleep, then we decide whether you stay on tomorrow?"

"You have nothing on your calendar until after the weekend," Mariam added.

"I . . . don't know." I shrugged, then gave a massive yawn. And the thought of sinking into the big, comfortable bed next door, rather than schlepping to the airport and boarding a plane back to . . . what?—my empty apartment?—was somehow very appealing.

"Joaquim's here tomorrow, too." I suddenly remembered with a smile. "He said so."

"He did," said Maia.

"So . . ." Mariam came to stand in front of me. "Shall we stay here? Take a little vacation?"

I nodded. "Okay."

"Right, I'm just going downstairs to sort out extending the room booking and changing the flights, okay?"

"Okay."

When she had gone, Maia came over to the couch, sat next to me, and took my hands. "Mariam is so lovely, isn't she?"

"Yup, she's an angel. Which sure can be annoying sometimes," I added, raising an eyebrow.

I felt Maia's eyes boring into me.

"What is it?"

"Oh, I was just thinking how much I love you, little sis."

"I love you, too, big sis."

As I looked at her, I saw there were tears in her eyes.

"Hey, why are you crying? Aren't you happy to see me?"

"I'm so happy, Electra, promise. Now," she said as I yawned again, "how about we go into the bedroom and I tuck you in like I used to do when you were little and tell you a story?"

A memory came drifting back to me: of Maia, aged maybe around thirteen, sitting on my bed and reading me fairy tales. She'd once told me that her name meant "mother" in Greek, and I'd decided that if I were to have one of my own, she'd be like her.

"Sure," I agreed as I stood up, still unsteady on my feet, and walked with Maia to the bedroom.

"Hey!" As I crawled into bed, I patted the sheets that were still rumpled from spending the afternoon with Joaquim. "There's room for you to lie down next to me."

Maia straightened the covers on her side of the bed, then lay on top of them. She reached out a hand to me again, and I took it and squeezed it hard, feeling the beginnings of the comedown from the ecstasy and the coke.

"You know, you were always my favorite sister," I said, turning to her.

"Was I? What a lovely thing to say, Electra. Well, I have to tell you, you were certainly the cutest baby. Even if you did scream."

"I know what you and Ally used to call me."

"Do you?" I watched a blush rise slowly up Maia's swanlike neck.

"Yeah, you used to call me 'Tricky.' I mean, I know the meaning of the word, but how did you come up with it?"

"Because you were 'Electra,' so, elec*tric*—'Tricky,' you see? I'm so sorry, darling, we weren't being serious."

"I was hurt at the time, but maybe you were right. And I don't think I've changed much." The beginnings of tears pricked my eyes.

"Well, maybe you did have a few temper tantrums, but in many ways you were the brightest of all my little sisters. When we used to play those mental math games with Pa on his boat every summer, you were always the winner."

"Was I? So how did I grow dumber rather than smarter? You know how I flunked all my exams at school."

"I don't think you cared about them, so you didn't do any work."

"True," I said. "Maia? Can I get some coffee, do you think? I'm feeling real woozy."

"Of course. With or without caffeine?"

"Definitely with," I answered as she reached for the phone. "That healthy shit I was into last time I saw you was only for Mitch. His body was a temple."

"Really?" Maia said as she waited for room service to answer. "I saw a photo of him in a magazine, and he looked more like an old wreck."

As Maia ordered the coffee, I chuckled, but then the chuckle turned into a groan, which turned into sobbing.

"Hey," she said softly, "what is it?"

"Oh, just . . . everything." I shrugged as the tears streamed down my cheeks. "Mostly Mitch, I guess. I'm not in a good place right now."

"I understand, darling. And I suppose you can never show it, can you?"

"Too right I can't. The media would have a fiesta, and I don't want anyone feeling sorry for me."

"Well, I'm not a newspaper, just your sister who loves you. Come here."

Maia pulled me into her arms, and I breathed in the lovely natural scent of her skin.

"This feels like home," I said with a smile.

"That's a nice thing to say."

"You know, I went back to Atlantis a few weeks ago and it didn't feel like home." I shook my head vehemently. "It didn't feel like home at all."

"I know, Electra. It's because Pa's gone."

"It's not just him who's gone but all you guys, too. It's kind of sad being there with just Ma and Claudia."

"But Ally said you saw her and you met Bear."

"Yeah, he's very cute. She's lucky she has something to love and to love her. I . . . don't. I don't have anyone."

I cried real hard then, right onto Maia's white shirt that smelled all fresh and calm, just like her.

"Sorry, I'm being self-indulgent, it's the . . . stuff I took."

I realized it was the first time I'd actually voiced the words to anyone close to me.

"I know."

"Also," I said, wiping my dripping nose, "I just want to say sorry for being evil to you when I came home to Atlantis after Pa had died."

"Were you? I don't remember."

"Yeah, I was. I said it didn't matter what you looked like because you never saw a person from one month to the next. I didn't mean it, Maia, really I didn't. You're so sweet and good and perfect—all the things I'm not."

The doorbell rang, and Maia went to get the coffee from the waiter.

"Here you are," she said as she handed it to me. As I sat up, my head thundered and I felt sick, so I lay back down again.

"Maybe in a minute."

"Okay. Darling Electra?"

"Yeah?"

"Do you think it would be a good idea to take a little time off and go and get some help?"

"I get plenty of help now," I sighed. "I've fired five therapists in the past few months."

"That doesn't sound good at all, but I meant more . . . formal help."

"Like what?"

"There's a very good place I know down in Arizona—Floriano's friend went there and came out a new person. I—"

Despite my head, I sat up and glared at her. "Are you trying to suggest I need to go to rehab?"

"Well, yes. Mariam said you've not been"—Maia sighed as she tried to find the right words—"all that well recently."

"Yeah, sure I haven't! The love of my life announced he was marrying someone else, and it's been plastered all over the media! What was I meant to do? Jump for joy?"

"You really loved him, didn't you?"

"Yeah, I did, but I'll get over it. It's just been a bad few weeks, that's all. And why was Mariam telling tales on me?"

"She wasn't, Electra, she cares about you—"

"She cares about her freaking job! That's what she cares about!"

"Darling Electra, please calm down . . ."

"Wow!" I exploded. "Boy, do I hate that phrase more than any other! I wonder how many times you guys and Pa and Ma said it to me!"

"I'm sorry, I'm only trying to help—"

"Well, don't. I'm gonna be just fine." I nodded fiercely. "Just fine. Now, can we talk about something else, please?"

"We can, Electra, but—"

"No! I want you to tell me a story like you used to."

"Okay." Maia looked at me. "Which story do you want?"

"I want your story. I want you to tell me how you met your guy in Rio and fell in love."

"Okay. Do you want some coffee before I start?"

"No, I'm feeling real sick just now. Tell me about you and Floriano—that's a helluva cute name, by the way—and take my mind off my own shit." I patted the bed next to me, and Maia climbed back in. I nestled my head against her breast, unable to close my eyes because when I did, my head spun, but it was soothing as she began to stroke my hair.

"Well, I actually met him when I first went up to see *Christ the Redeemer*, which, by the way, you should try to do, too, before you leave, because it is so amazing. He was the tour guide, you see, and . . ."

I listened to the story, and it was just as romantic as any fairy tale.

"And then you lived happily ever after."

"Yes, or at least, I hope we will. I mean, he isn't a prince and we have very little money, but we're happy."

"And what about the relative Floriano helped you find? Did you meet her?"

"Yes, I did, but she was very ill, and sadly she died not long after we met. At least I feel lucky that I got to spend some time with her."

"Tell me some more of the story, Maia," I urged her, desperate to take my mind off the coke that sat so close to me in the bedside drawer. I'd never sleep if I took any more, and I desperately needed to—I'd been so good at sleeping when I was with Mitch.

So Maia told me the tale of the man who had designed *Christ the Redeemer* and the young sculptor whom her great-grandmother had fallen so deeply in love with and . . .

The next thing I knew, Maia was kissing me on the forehead and turning out the light.

"Where are you going?" I grabbed her arm in the dark.

"Home, Electra. You need to sleep."

"Maia, please don't leave me. Stay for a bit longer, please. And put the light back on—I'm scared of the dark."

"You never used to be," she said, but she did as I'd asked.

"Well, I am now. I wanna find love like you and Floriano and Izabela and Laurent." I smiled up at her.

"*Chérie*, you're only twenty-six years old. Remember I'm almost thirty-four—eight years older than you. You have plenty of time to find love, I promise."

"Well, I hope I don't have to wait another eight years for it." I shrugged. "I feel so old, Maia."

"I promise you that you're not." She put a hand to my forehead, and I liked the sensation of her cool palm on my skin. "You've had to grow up so very fast, haven't you?"

"Maybe."

"You're so brave and strong, Electra."

"No, I'm not." I shook my head. "Do you wanna know a secret?"

"I think so," she said with a grin.

"You know why I think I used to scream a lot when I was younger?"

"No, why?"

"Because I hated being by myself, and I still do."

"Maybe you should get a roommate."

"Who'd want to live with me?"

"Electra, don't be so down on yourself. You're an icon to millions of women around the world. I'd love to take you out into the hills behind Rio and show you the *fazenda*—that's a farm in Portuguese—that I inherited from my grandmother. I've developed it as a center for disadvantaged children from the *favelas*. If you turned up with me, I think they would believe they were dreaming. Don't you see that you inspire them?"

"Yeah, but they don't know me, do they? Look at you, turning your inheritance into something that does good for others. I do nothing for anyone except myself."

I heard Maia give a small sigh, but the down was *so* down, I couldn't climb up, so I closed my eyes and begged for sleep to come.

I woke up the next morning with the mother of all hangovers, grabbed some Tylenol and Advil, and threw the tablets down with a bottle of water. I checked the clock and saw it was just past six. I ordered coffee and a basket of the cheesy cakes that I'd discovered came hot from the oven and were the best thing ever. As I waited for room service to arrive, my mind played over what had happened yesterday, and my heart sank to my feet as I vaguely pictured dancing naked with Joaquim on the terrace. And Mariam's and Maia's faces when we'd appeared in the living room . . .

"Jesus, Electra," I groaned as I staggered out of bed to answer the door to room service. As I drank the hot coffee, I also remembered admitting to my sister that I'd taken some stuff—which wouldn't exactly have been a surprise to her, given the fact she'd found me obviously high and stark naked with a random guy. Then the bit about her suggesting I stayed on for a couple of days here and that I should think about going into rehab . . .

Shit! That was not good news. And worse than that, Mariam had obviously snaked on me. Well, there was no way—just *no way*—I was going to a funny farm. Yesterday had been a bad day, that was all. And I certainly wasn't going to hang around with Saint Maia to be lectured. I picked up the receiver and dialed Mariam.

"Good morning, Electra, how are you feeling?"

"Great, just great," I lied, wondering if I'd ever call Mariam up and catch her half asleep. "I need you to book us back on the flights to NY as soon as possible."

There was a small pause on the line. "Right. I thought the plan was for you to stay here awhile and spend time with your sister?"

"It wasn't a plan, Mariam, it was an idea, but I think I need to get back to the Big Apple."

"As I said, you have nothing on your calendar, so you can stay on."

"And I'm telling you I want you to book us back to New York, okay? My bags are already packed, and I'm ready to leave any time from now."

Mariam took the hint that I wasn't in the mood to be argued with, and an hour later we were on our way to the airport. I sent Maia a text thanking her for last night and saying that I'd see her at Atlantis for Pa's water memorial in June.

As the jet soared upward, I felt a sense of relief that I'd escaped. No one was going to lock me away anywhere. *Ever.*

# 8

Spooked by how out of control I'd been in Rio, I was determined to make a serious effort to stay clean over the weekend. I drank tons of water and ordered in an array of smoothies laden with vitamin C. The first day back, I managed to get to lunchtime before pouring myself the tiniest vodka. Knowing I would pour another without some distraction, I stepped out across the road to take a run in Central Park.

"You okay, Electra?" Tommy asked me as I jogged toward him on my way back.

"I'm good, yeah. How are you?"

"I'm okay, thanks for asking. Y'know, when you were in Rio, a woman came by who looked a whole lot like you."

"Really?" I raised an eyebrow as I slowed to a standstill. "Well, if she comes by again, please tell her I'm out, even if you know I'm in. She's just another crackpot who's convinced she's related to me."

"Yeah, well, she sure did *look* like she could be related to you. See you tomorrow, Electra."

Up in my apartment, I peeled off my sweaty running gear and was just about to take a shower when the concierge phone beeped.

"Hi."

"Hi, Miss D'Aplièse, a couple boxes have arrived down here for you. Can we bring them up?"

"Yeah, sure, as long as you've checked them for explosives first!" I half joked.

Five minutes later, the porter and his lackey appeared pushing a trolley loaded with two large cardboard boxes, which they then dumped on my living room floor.

"Who brought these? They look like the kind of boxes you'd use to move house."

"Some delivery guy in a van dropped them off. With this." He handed me an envelope. "Want help unpacking them, ma'am?"

"No. Thanks, though."

Brimming with curiosity like a child presented with a gift, I took the lid off one of the boxes. It was full of clothes—*my* clothes. On the top of the pile sat a shoebox, which I opened to find my silk sleeping mask, lip balm, earplugs, a pair of sunglasses—*and* beneath all the crap, I glimpsed the thick cream vellum of Pa Salt's letter.

Fishing it out, I realized immediately what these boxes were: everything I'd left behind at Mitch's house in Malibu. The shoebox was the contents of the nightstand next to the bed I'd once shared with him, thinking it would be where I'd sleep forever . . .

"No, Electra! You. Will. Not. Let. Him. Hurt. You. Any. Freakin'. More!"

Calling down to the concierge, I asked him to send the trolley back up to collect the boxes.

"Anything that your wives or girlfriends want from them, it's all theirs. And send the rest to Goodwill," I instructed the porter when the trolley had been reloaded.

"Okay, Miss D'Aplièse, will do, thanks."

I stepped out onto the terrace, holding the envelope Mitch had sent with my stuff, along with a book of matches. I set fire to his note without opening it. Then I went to the drinks cabinet and fixed myself a vodka tonic with some ice. I deserved one after *that*. And even though I tried to rein back my mind from thinking about it and to concentrate on the good news—that Pa's letter had turned up—I couldn't help myself. I could only picture Mitch arriving home from his tour. Knowing his fiancée was to join him there any day soon, he'd cleaned out all of my stuff from his house and erased me from his life.

I took another great gulp, then gave myself a top-up. As long as I kept off the coke, that was okay, wasn't it? Then I stared at Pa's letter, sitting like a ticking time bomb on the coffee table.

"Do I open you?" I asked it.

Thinking how all my sisters seemed to have found the golden ticket to future happiness within theirs, I took another megaslurp of vodka, grabbed it, and peeled it open.

*Atlantis*
*Lake Geneva*
*Switzerland*

*My darling Electra . . .*

"Oh, Christ!" I gulped as tears filled my eyes before I'd even read a word.

*There is part of me that wonders whether you will ever read this; perhaps you will put it away somewhere for the future, or even burn it—I do not know, because you are the most unpredictable of all my daughters. And ironically, I believe, the most vulnerable.*

*Electra, I know we have never had the easiest of relationships—two strong and determined personalities often fight. Yet they also love the most passionately— another quality we share.*

*First of all, let me apologize for the last time we met in New York. Suffice to say that neither of us was at our best. For my part, it pained me deeply to see my extraordinary youngest daughter having to resort to substance abuse to get through a dinner with her father. You know all too well how I feel about drugs, and I can only hope and pray that you have decided—or will decide—to take the necessary steps to rid yourself of them for good. Any parent watching a beloved child destroy themselves will naturally be devastated, but there is only one person who can help you, Electra, and that is yourself.*

*Now no more of that. I also want to explain why it may have seemed that I was not as obviously proud of you as perhaps you thought I should be. Firstly, let me tell you that every time I saw your photo in a magazine, my heart would fill with pride at your beauty and elegance. And of course your talent, for I understand it takes a gift to know how to make the camera love you. As well as the kind of patience that I'm not sure I could ever possess—and that I did not think you could either, for that matter! But you have somehow learned it, and for that, I truly admire you.*

*The reason that I became so frustrated with you when you were at school is because I could see just how clever you were, perhaps the most naturally clever of all your sisters. I only hope that one day you will be able to combine the fame you have earned with the brains you were born with. If that happens, you will be a force to be reckoned with. There are no limits to what you could become—a voice for those who can't speak for themselves. Truly, my beautiful girl, you are capable of greatness.*

*I hope that this explains why I have often found it difficult to be your father; to see a child with so much potential yet to understand that she does not realize what she possesses can be very frustrating. And I do wonder if I failed you—you never did give me a proper answer as to why you hated boarding school. If you had trusted me, maybe I could have helped you, but I also know how proud you are.*

*Sadly, now, I must leave you to discover for yourself who you are and the incredible person you could become. However, I will not leave you without offering you assistance. As you will know, all your sisters have been given a letter, and in each one I have provided them with enough clues to find the path back to their birth parents if they wish to find them. With you, all I can give is the name and contact number of your grandmother, who lives not so very far from where you do. She is one of the most inspiring women I have ever had the privilege to meet, and I only wish I had known her for longer. This information I enclose separately, with a photograph. The resemblance is unquestionable, and I feel confident that she will be there to help you when I cannot.*

*My darling Electra, I beg you to know you are, and will always be, deeply loved by your father.*

*Pa Salt x*

I took another slug of vodka as I sat staring blankly at the letter. Maybe my brain wasn't clear enough to take in what Pa had said, or maybe I just didn't want to. I sighed, then pulled out something else from the envelope. It was a photo, and it was black and white and—

"Oh, my God! Oh, jeez . . ."

I studied it again, but I already knew it was the same photograph as the one I'd seen a few weeks back, sent by a woman saying she was my grandmother.

I looked closer, and yes, the female in the photo looked very like me—or maybe I looked very like her. I remembered Mariam saying she'd put the letter from my "grandmother" into the safe, so I went to get it. Tentatively, I extracted the contents and laid the photograph the woman had sent me next to the one from Pa's envelope. They were identical.

I turned over the photo from Pa and saw there was an address written on the back, along with a cell phone number. Then I looked at the creased letter that Mariam had insisted on unscrunching and read the address at the top.

Again they were identical. I then read the letter, written on obviously expensive paper and in the same beautifully scripted hand that had addressed the envelope.

*28 Sidney Place, Apartment 1*
*Brooklyn, NY 11201*

*My dear Miss D'Aplièse—or may I call you Electra?*
*My name is Stella Jackson and I am your biological grandmother. I am sure you receive many letters, and I would also guess that a portion of them are begging letters. Let me reassure you that this is not such a thing. I simply decided that it was time to introduce myself.*
*I know you are a busy woman, but I feel it would be beneficial for you and I to meet. Your adoptive father described me as a "living clue." I am not sure I appreciate the description, but for now, I enclose a photograph of myself and your mother. I can be contacted at the above address and my cell phone is on day and night.*
*I look forward to hearing from you.*

*With kind regards,*
*Stella Jackson*

Whoever "Stella" was, she had certainly been educated. I wouldn't know where to begin writing such a letter; it felt (uncomfortably) like she was trying to set up a meeting to discuss the renovation of the common parts of a condominium building with a neighbor she'd never met. Rather than introducing herself to her long-lost granddaughter, if that's what I actually was . . .

But even for me, the mistress of cynicism, it seemed impossible that this woman was not who she said she was.

"Oh, my God! I have a blood relative!" I announced to the room as I stood up and wandered around it. "So, Electra," I said, imitating Theresa's nasal intonations as I had her begin an imaginary conversation with me, "how do you feel about discovering you have a blood relative alive and living close by?"

"Well, now, Theresa, I don't know yet. I haven't met her."

"And are you planning to?"

"I haven't decided yet."

"Well, it's a pretty big deal, so take as much time as you need. And if you want to meet her, then you must prepare yourself well."

"What do you mean, Theresa? That I might not like her or something?"

"No, I only meant that it's dangerous to attach too much weight to such an occasion, in case you are disappointed."

"Please don't worry, because I *will* prepare myself well. I'll drink half a bottle of vodka and do a couple of lines beforehand, promise."

"Great idea, Electra; you need to be relaxed when you meet her."

I giggled, then went to my special pot to pull out some White Heaven. After all, I thought, it wasn't every day you discovered you had a real-life granny.

*So what are you going to do for the rest of today and tomorrow, Electra?* I asked myself. *Your calendar certainly isn't heaving in the next twenty-four hours, is it?*

*Well, it could be, but there's no one I want to see.*

*What about Joaquim?*

*He's in Mexico, remember? And he is a bad, bad boy.* I waggled a finger at my insistent alter ego.

I went back to look at the two photos of my grandmother, wondering if the child in her arms really was my mom, then took a deep breath and picked up my cell. I dialed the phone number that was written on the back of the photograph Pa had left me and listened while it rang.

"Stella Jackson speaking."

"Oh, er, hi, my name is Electra D'Aplièse and—"

"Electra! Well, well . . ." She sounded weirdly familiar, and I eventually realized it was because the intonation of her voice sounded like mine.

"Yeah, I got your messages. Thought I'd better make contact."

"I am very glad you did. When can I come and see you?"

"I . . . tomorrow maybe?"

"I can't make tomorrow—it's a Sunday. How about tonight? Besides, how can I wait another whole day before meeting my granddaughter in person?"

"Okay." I shrugged. "Come by tonight. Would seven suit?"

"It would, yes. I have your address, so I'll see you at seven. Good-bye, Electra."

"Er, right, bye." I ended the call, realizing she would be here in just over an hour.

"Okay." I nodded as I paced around the apartment in a daze. "So my grandmother—like, my blood grandmother—is coming to visit me tonight. I'm cool, it's all cool . . . Jeez, how did this happen?"

*The good news*, I thought as I frantically tidied up the living room and blew away any traces of white powder from the coffee table, *was that I hadn't gone into meltdown about Mitch and his boxes.* And that was what my therapist would have called a real breakthrough. After setting things straight as best I could, I went to stand in front of my closet. What exactly should a granddaughter wear to meet her grandmother? I took out a tweed Chanel jacket, which I thought I'd pair with some jeans to tone it down.

*But you're inside your apartment, Electra, and it's like eighty degrees with the sun shining through the windows.*

In the end, I stuck with the jeans and put on a plain white T-shirt and a pair of Chanel flats to add some class. Next stop was the kitchen—old people drank tea, didn't they? I rooted around inside the cupboards, but teapots weren't a big thing in über-chic rented New York penthouses.

"Listen, she's just gonna have to take you as she finds you, Electra," I told myself firmly. "Which means she'll get offered some water or a vodka tonic." I giggled.

I toyed with calling Mariam and asking her to rustle up a tea service and a cake, but for whatever reason, I didn't want her to know I was meeting Stella Jackson. I wanted a secret—of the positive kind.

I had no more time to ponder, because the concierge called to let me know that Miss Jackson was downstairs and asked if he could send her up.

"Yeah, sure," I agreed, and spent the next minute pacing the apartment once again, my heart banging in my chest. The doorbell rang and I took a deep breath, trying not to think what this meant to me. What if I hated her? After my sisters had found their happy endings through meeting their relatives, that would just be typical, I thought as I went to open the door.

"Hi." I smiled simply because I was used to automatically smiling for the camera or, in fact, producing whatever expression the situation required.

"Hello, Electra. I am Stella Jackson, your grandmother."

"Please come in."

"Thank you kindly."

As she walked in front of me, I felt as though I was having the hugest déjà vu of my life. Tommy hadn't been joking around when he'd said she looked like me. It was like looking at a freaking reflection of me, only older.

"You look so young!" I said, because I couldn't stop myself.

"Why, thank you. Actually, I am almost sixty-eight years old."

"Wow! I'd have put you at forty-five max. Please sit down."

"Thank you." I watched her looking around. "This is some fancy apartment you've gotten yourself here."

"Yeah, it's very convenient."

"I once lived on the other side of the park. It's a good neighborhood. It's safe, very safe."

"You used to live on the Upper East Side?" I said, staring at her.

Now she was standing in front of me, I noticed she was dressed in a shirt which I could see was well made and a pair of tailored black trousers. What looked like an Hermès scarf was tied jauntily around her slender throat, and her hair was trimmed in a short Afro. All in all, she exuded a natural elegance and beauty—and she looked rich!

"Yes, for a while, I did."

I realized she was staring at me as hard as I was at her.

"How tall are you?" she asked me.

"Just over six foot."

"I beat you, then." Stella looked pleased. "I'm six foot one and a half."

"Can I get you something to drink?"

"No, thank you."

"Okay. I'll just fix one for myself, then." I walked to the bar and acted as though I couldn't find the vodka before I poured it and added some tonic.

"You like vodka?" she asked me.

"Sometimes, yeah. You?" I responded as I took a slug.

"No, I've never developed a taste for alcohol."

"Right" was all I could manage. "So you said in your letter that you wanted to see me?"

"I did, yes."

"Why?"

She stared at me for a while before offering me a small smile. "You're probably asking yourself what I want, aren't you? Thinking I'm here to take advantage of your fame and wealth?"

I felt the heat rise to my cheeks. This lady sure didn't mess around.

*And who does that remind you of, Electra?*

"Yeah, a bit." I decided I should fight fire with fire.

"Well, now, I can assure you I'm not here to ask you for money. I have enough of my own."

"Right. Good," I said, listening to her American accent, which was very refined. In other words, she was a classy gal. "Shall we sit down?" I indicated the couch, but Stella Jackson made straight for one of the two upright chairs and settled herself in it.

"Are you going to ask me the big question?"

"Which one would that be? Like"—I shrugged—"there are so many."

"Where did you come from, maybe?" She eyed me.

"That would do for starters," I agreed, trying to take a small polite sip of my drink, then failing and taking a gulp.

"You are descended from a long line of princesses, or the equivalent of them anyway, in Kenya."

"Isn't Kenya in Africa?"

"Well done, Electra. You're right, it is."

"And were you born there yourself?"

"I was, yes."

"So how did you—or was it my mom—wind up here?"

"Now, that is a long story."

"I'd like to hear it if you're prepared to tell it."

"Yes, I am, of course I am. It's what I came here to do. Before I start, maybe I will take a glass of water."

"I'll get you one right now." As I stood up and walked to the kitchen to take some bottled water from the refrigerator and pour it into a glass, my head spun, but it wasn't from the vodka. The lady sitting on my couch was just nothing like I'd expected. The burning question in my head was how come, when she looked so well off, had I ended up being adopted? And where and who was my mother?

"Thank you," Stella said as I handed her the glass and she took a sip. "Now, why don't you sit down?"

I did so tentatively.

"You look afraid, Electra. Are you?"

"Maybe," I admitted.

"I understand. Now, it's been a long time since I recounted this tale. Bear with me, won't you?"

"Yeah, of course I will."

"So where shall I begin?"

I watched my grandmother's fingers tapping on her thigh. It was such a familiar gesture—I did it all the time when I was thinking—that the last shred of doubt I'd had about this woman's claim to be my blood vanished.

"Pa always said one should start from the beginning."

Stella smiled. "Then your dear pa is quite right, and I shall."

# CECILY

*New York*
*New Year's Eve 1938*

*Kenyan Maasai buffalo war shields*

# 9

"Cecily, honey, what on earth are you doing lying there on your bed? We're leaving for the party in half an hour."

"I'm not coming, Mama. I told you that at lunch."

"And I told you that you absolutely were. Do you want everyone who is anyone in Manhattan gossiping about the fact that you didn't show up tonight?"

"I don't give a fig for gossip, Mama. Besides, I'm sure they have more interesting things to talk about than me and my broken engagement." Cecily Huntley-Morgan cast her eyes back to *The Great Gatsby* and continued to read.

"Well, *you* might not care, missy, but I wouldn't want the indignity of everyone thinking that my daughter was hiding away at home on New Year's Eve because she was heartbroken."

"But, Mama, I *am* hiding away on New Year's Eve. And I *am* heartbroken."

"Here, drink this."

Dorothea Huntley-Morgan proffered her daughter a champagne flute filled to the brim. "Let's toast the New Year together, but you have to promise me you'll take it down in one, okay?"

"I'm not in the mood for it, Mama—"

"That is simply not the point, honey. Everyone drinks champagne on New Year's Eve, whether or not they are in the mood for it. Ready?" Dorothea raised her own glass encouragingly.

"If you promise you'll leave me alone afterward."

"Here's to 1939 and new beginnings!" Dorothea chinked her glass against her daughter's.

Reluctantly, Cecily drank down the contents of the glass as her mother had asked. The fizz made her feel nauseated—probably because she'd eaten little more than the odd spoonful of soup for the past four days.

"I just know it will be one, if you *let* it be so."

Cecily allowed herself to be embraced in a bosomy hug and, from the smell of her mother's breath, knew that it wasn't the first alcoholic beverage she'd downed that afternoon. And it was all because of her: Jack Hamblin had broken off their brief engagement two days before Christmas, while her family had been gathered for the holiday season at their house in the Hamptons. She and Jack had known each other from childhood, his family owning one of the neighboring estates in Westhampton. They had summered together, and Cecily couldn't remember a time when she had not been in love with him. Even when he'd told her on the beach at the age of six that he'd brought her a present, then handed her a crab that had immediately bitten her finger and made it bleed all over her bathing suit. But she had not let him see her cry then, and, almost seventeen years later, neither had she cried when he'd told her he couldn't marry her because he loved somebody else.

She'd heard rumors about Patricia Ogden-Forbes—who hadn't in New York society? A Chicago heiress, the only daughter of a hugely wealthy family, her beauty had been the talk of the town since she'd appeared in Manhattan for the Christmas season. Jack—who, Dorothea never tired of reminding her and anyone else who cared to listen, was a distant relative of the Vanderbilts—had apparently taken one look at Miss Ogden-Forbes and all bets had been off. Including his forthcoming nuptials with Cecily.

"Remember, honey, Patricia has no breeding," her mother whispered breathily in her ear. "When it comes down to it, she's a meatpacker's daughter."

*And you're the daughter of a toothpaste manufacturer*, Cecily thought but didn't say.

It was something she'd often pondered—that the so-called high society in America was made up of tradespeople and bankers. Nobility had been bestowed on the families with the largest fortunes, rather than those with the bluest blood. Not that there was anything wrong with that, but unlike in Europe there were no lords or dukes or princes here in the Land of the Free.

"Won't you come to the party, Cecily? Only for an hour or so if you can't face it for longer," Dorothea begged her.

"Maybe. But *she'll* be there, Mama, with him."

"I know, honey, but you're a Morgan, and we Morgans are brave and strong and face our enemies!" Dorothea tipped her daughter's chin up to meet her eyes. "You can do this, I know you can. I've had Evelyn steam your green satin gown, and I'm going to lend you my mother's Cartier necklace.

You'll be a sensation—and who knows who might be there in that ballroom, just waiting for you."

Cecily knew that what *was* waiting for her was humiliation, as her ex-fiancé paraded his rich Chicago beauty around the Waldorf-Astoria ballroom in front of the crème de la crème of New York society. But her mother was right: she might be many things, but she wasn't a coward.

"Okay, Mama." She sighed. "You win."

"That's my girl! I'll get Evelyn to bring in your gown, do your hair, and run you a bath. You smell less than fragrant, honey."

"Gee, thanks, Mama." Cecily shrugged. "I'll need some more champagne," she called as Dorothea left the bedroom. "Buckets of it!" Then she grimaced as she put her bookmark in *The Great Gatsby*, shaking her head at this ridiculous notion that love—and a big mansion—could conquer everything.

Cecily had both. And she knew it couldn't.

The good news was that the ballroom of the Waldorf-Astoria was so vast it felt like you had to walk the Oregon Trail to get to the other side. A dazzling chandelier hung from the high recessed ceiling, and lights glittered in the balconies that ringed the room. The murmur of conversation and laughter was muted by the plush red carpet, and musicians were tuning up on a bandstand that had been constructed at one end of the room, with a gleaming parquet dance floor in front of it. The adjacent dining tables were immaculately set with fine linen, bone china, sparkling crystal, and ornate flower arrangements. A waiter appeared at her side with a tray of champagne flutes, and Cecily grasped one in her sweating palm.

Everyone who was anyone in New York was there, of course. *The jewels on the women alone could surely buy a country big enough to house the hundreds of thousands of poor in this great nation*, Cecily thought as she found her place card at one of the tables and sat down. She was glad she was facing a wall rather than staring into the abyss of wealth and imminent humiliation behind her, and trying, even though she knew she shouldn't, to spot Jack and Patricia.

"Just look who's here, darling!"

Cecily glanced up and found herself staring into the limpid eyes of one of New York society's most renowned beauties, Kiki Preston. As she was embraced in a hug, Cecily noticed that her godmother's pupils seemed to be dilated, like huge dark orbs encircled by the halo of her irises.

"Sweet girl! Your mama has told me about your travails . . . But no matter, there are plenty more where *he* came from." Kiki winked at Cecily. Then, grasping the back of Cecily's chair, she swayed a little as she sank down into the one next to it, before producing an ivory cigarette holder and lighting up.

Cecily hadn't seen her godmother for years—at a guess, not since she was twelve or thirteen—and she could only gaze in admiration at the woman whom her mother confided had once had a liaison with a prince in line to the English throne. She knew Kiki had been living in Africa for many years, yet her skin was still as pale and luminous as the strands of pearls that graced her slender throat, setting off the fluid lines of the backless Chanel gown she was wearing. Her dark hair was swept up off her face, highlighting the exquisite cheekbones and high forehead that framed her mesmerizing green eyes.

"Isn't it just wonderful to see your godmother after all this time?" Dorothea enthused. "Kiki, you should have let me know you were coming to Manhattan, and I'd have held a party for you."

"More like a wake," Kiki muttered, exhaling a thin stream of smoke. "So many deaths . . . I've been here to see lawyers . . ."

"I know, my darling." Dorothea sat down on the other side of Kiki and grasped her hand. "It's been such a terrible time for you in the past few years."

As Cecily watched her mother comfort the exotic creature next to her, for the first time in days, she felt an ironic modicum of hope for her own life. She knew that Kiki had lost a number of relatives, including her husband, Jerome, in a string of tragic circumstances. Given that Cecily thought Kiki—even though she must be around forty—the most beautiful woman she'd ever seen, her godmother was the living embodiment of the fact that beauty did not necessarily bring happiness.

"Who are you sitting with for dinner?" she heard Dorothea ask Kiki.

"I have absolutely no idea, but they're bound to be bores, so maybe I'll just stay right here with you."

"We'd love you to, darling. I'll just fetch a waiter to lay another place."

As her mother hurried off, Kiki turned her eyes to Cecily, then held out her hand. Cecily took it and found that the long, tapered fingers clasping hers were icy cold, despite the heat of the room.

"You've done the right thing by having the guts to come here tonight," Kiki said, stubbing out her cigarette in an ashtray. "I don't give a damn for a single person in this room. Nothing's real, you know." She sighed, reaching for the glass of champagne that Dorothea had left on the table and draining it. "As my friend Alice says, we all end up as dust one day, no matter how many damned diamonds we own." Kiki gazed hard into the distance, as if she were trying to see through the walls of the Waldorf.

"What is Africa like?" Cecily asked eventually, feeling she should lead the conversation as her godmother seemed to be lost in another world.

"It's majestic, terrifying, mysterious, and . . . totally inexplicable. I have a house on the shores of Lake Naivasha in Kenya. When I wake up in the morning, I can see hippos swimming, giraffes parking their heads between the trees as if they're pretending to be branches." Kiki laughed in her deep throaty voice. "You should come visit, get out of this claustrophobic ghetto of a city and see what the real world is like."

"One day I'd love to," Cecily agreed.

"Honey, there is no 'one day.' The only time we have is now, in this minute, or millisecond, maybe . . ." Her voice trailed off as she reached for her evening purse, beaded with what looked like hundreds of tiny sparkling diamonds. "Now you must excuse me, I need to visit the restroom, but I'll be right back."

With a nod of her elegant head, Kiki stood up and made her way through the tables. She rather reminded Cecily of Daisy Buchanan, the woman Jay Gatsby had idolized in *The Great Gatsby*—the ultimate twenties flapper. But times had moved on now. It was no longer the Roaring Twenties, even if her mother and her friends still lived as though they were in that glorious moment of madness just after the war had ended. Outside the hallowed walls of the ballroom, the rest of America was still struggling out of the aftermath of the Great Depression. Cecily's only personal contact with its ramifications had been when she was thirteen and had seen her father crying on her mother's shoulder as he'd described how a great friend of his had jumped out of a window after the Wall Street crash. Later, she'd grabbed her father's newspaper from their housekeeper, Mary's, hands as she was throwing it away in the trash, and had done her best to keep up with what was happening. Surprisingly, the subject was never raised at Spence, the private girls' school she'd attended, even though she'd asked her teachers about it on a number of occasions. When she'd left school, Cecily had begged her father,

Walter, to let her go on to college to study economics at Vassar—citing that two of her friends with more enlightened parents had gone off to Brown. To her surprise, Walter had agreed to a college education but had questioned her choice of major.

"Economics?" He'd frowned before taking a hefty slug of the bourbon he favored. "My dear Cecily, that is a career reserved completely for men. Why don't you major in history? It won't be too taxing for you, and it will at least equip you to make conversation when entertaining your future husband's friends and colleagues."

She had done as she was told, understanding the compromise. Taking economics as one of her minors, Cecily had loved her classes in algebra and statistics and Miss Newcomer's famed Economics 105. Sitting in the wood-paneled lecture rooms and spurred on by the other brilliant women around her, she had never felt more inspired.

So how come she had found herself back in her childhood bedroom in the family's mansion on Fifth Avenue with no hope for the future? Now alone at the table, Cecily looked around the ballroom for her mother and took a gulp of champagne in an attempt to stop maudlin thoughts filling her brain.

After leaving Vassar in the summer and joining her family at their home in the Hamptons, Cecily had had to pinch herself when Jack had begun to pay her court, singling her out at the usual round of cocktail parties, insisting she partner him at tennis, and showering her with compliments and gifts that bemused and thrilled her in equal measure. Her parents had watched with predictable satisfaction from the sidelines, no doubt whispering behind their hands about a possible engagement. Jack had finally proposed in September, ironically during the dreadful hurricane that had hit Long Island with almost no warning. She recalled that terrifying afternoon, when Jack and his family and servants had turned up ashen-faced at the Huntley-Morgans' house, seeking shelter from the violent storm. The Hamblins' house in Westhampton Beach was being lashed by huge angry waves and was in danger of flooding completely, whereas her own family residence was located further inland on higher ground and had a large cellar to boot. As they'd all cowered inside it while the wind raged above them, ripping shingles from the roof and toppling trees, Jack had drawn her to one side and held her close.

"Cecily, my darling girl," he'd whispered as she'd trembled in his arms, "times like this remind us of how damned short life can be . . . Marry me?"

She had looked up at him in bewilderment. "You can't be serious, Jack!"

"I assure you I am. Please, darling, say yes."

And, of course, she had. She should have known somewhere deep inside that it was all too good to be true, but the astonishment that he had chosen *her*, coupled with the intense love she'd always felt for him, had clouded her judgment and removed all sense. Only three months later, the engagement was off, and now here she was, sitting alone on New Year's Eve, feeling utterly humiliated.

"Cecily! Why, you came! I never thought you would."

Cecily was broken out of her reverie by the sight of her youngest sister, Priscilla, standing in front of her clad in a gorgeous rose-colored silk gown, her blond hair falling in perfect coiffured ripples to her shoulders. She resembled Carole Lombard—her heroine—and made sure she adopted Miss Lombard's style. Sadly, Priscilla's husband, Robert, was no Clark Gable. In her high heels, his wife towered over him. He held out his small and rather sweaty hands toward Cecily.

"Dearest sister-in-law, commiserations on your loss"—Cecily fought the urge to tell him that Jack wasn't actually dead—"but happy New Year all the same."

Cecily let him take her by the shoulders and kiss her wetly on both cheeks. For the life of her, she couldn't understand how Priscilla could bear to get into bed every night with this ugly, thin man whose pasty complexion reminded her of day-old porridge.

*Perhaps she lies there and counts his dollars in the bank,* she thought cruelly.

Following behind Priscilla was their middle sister, Mamie. At twenty-one, she was only thirteen months younger than Cecily. She'd always had a flat chest and boyish proportions, but seven months of pregnancy had transformed her. The blue satin dress subtly emphasized her newly full breasts and the gentle swell of her soon-to-be-born baby.

"Hello, darling." Mamie kissed her on both cheeks. "You're looking quite wonderful, especially given the circumstances."

Cecily wasn't sure whether this was actually a compliment or an insult.

"Isn't she, Hunter?" Mamie turned to her husband, who, unlike Robert, towered above them all.

"She's looking just swell," Hunter agreed as he wrapped his arms around Cecily and gave her a hug that felt more like a football tackle.

Cecily liked Hunter enormously—in fact, when Mamie had first brought him home last year, she'd developed rather a crush on him. Fair-haired and hazel-eyed, with a perfect set of white teeth, he'd gotten a summa cum laude from Yale and followed his father into the family's bank. Hunter was clever and personable, and at least he worked for a living, although Mamie said that he did seem to spend an awful lot of time having lunch at the Union Club with his clients. Cecily hoped she was sitting next to him tonight at dinner; she could pick his brains on the effect that Herr Hitler's annexing of the Sudetenland was having on the American economy.

"Ladies and gentlemen, would you kindly take your seats for dinner" came a booming voice from somewhere at the front of the ballroom.

"Just in time, Papa," Cecily said as Walter Huntley-Morgan II strode toward the table.

"I got caught in the lobby by Jeremiah Swift—possibly the most boring man in Manhattan." Walter smiled at Cecily affably. "Now, where am I sitting?" he asked no one in particular.

"On the other side, next to Edith Wilberforce," Cecily told him.

"Who is possibly the most boring woman in Manhattan. Hey ho, your mother insists she likes her. You're looking quite delightful, by the way," he added with an affectionate glance at his eldest daughter. "Brave of you to come, Cecily, and I like bravery."

Cecily gave him a wan smile as he left her side to move across to his designated seat. For an older man, she thought, he was still very attractive—only a hint of gray in his blond hair and the vaguest outline of a paunch indicated the passing of the years. The Huntley-Morgans were known as a "handsome" family, even if Cecily did feel that she rather let the side down. With Priscilla's blond, blue-eyed looks mirroring their father's and Mamie having taken after their mother, sometimes she felt like a changeling with her unruly mass of midbrown curls, eyes that moved between pale blue on a good day and gray on a bad, and a smattering of freckles across her nose, which multiplied in the sunlight. At just over five feet tall, with a slender frame that Cecily thought bordered on scrawny, she often felt dwarfed by her poised and statuesque sisters.

"Have you seen Kiki, Cecily?" Dorothea asked her as she took her place three seats away from her daughter.

"Not since she went off to the restroom, Mama," Cecily replied, and as the shrimp appetizer was served, the place set for Kiki remained vacant.

*Just what I needed—an empty seat beside me.*

Hunter leaned over and whispered to her, "If she hasn't turned up in the next ten minutes, I'll shuffle along."

"Thank you," Cecily said, taking a gulp of the wine that one of the waiters had just poured and knowing it was going to be a very long night.

After Kiki had failed to show up an hour later, her place setting was removed and Hunter moved next to her. They had a lengthy chat about the situation in Europe; Hunter didn't believe there would be war, due to the British prime minister's agreement with Hitler earlier in the year.

"But then again, Mr. Hitler is unpredictable, which is making the markets volatile again, just when they'd started to settle. Of course"—Hunter bent toward her—"there are a number I know who are rubbing their hands with glee at the thought of a war in Europe."

"Really?" Cecily frowned. "Why would they be doing that?"

"Wars require guns and munitions, and America sure is good at making those. Especially when we aren't directly involved in the military confrontation."

"Are you certain America won't get involved?"

"Pretty much. Even Mr. Hitler wouldn't dare to think about annexing the United States of America."

"It's hard to believe that any human being could actually *want* war."

"Wars make people—and therefore countries—richer, Cecily. Look at America after the Great War—a whole new raft of billionaires was created. It's all a cycle. To put it crudely, what goes up must come down and vice versa."

"Isn't that rather depressing?"

"I guess, although I hope it's possible that human beings learn from their mistakes and move forward. Yet here we are with Europe on the brink of war. Well, now"—Hunter sighed—"one must always have faith in human nature, and maybe," he added as the band struck up and people began to move toward the dance floor, "New Year's Eve is the one night we should forget our cares and celebrate. Dance with me?" He stood up and offered Cecily his hand.

She smiled. "I'd love to."

Ten minutes later, Cecily was back in her chair at the deserted table. Everyone else was dancing with their partners, and to make matters worse, Cecily had seen the shimmer of a stunning silver dress, complete with a pair of long, shapely legs, flash past her on the arm of her former fiancé.

Even though she didn't smoke, Cecily picked up the pack that someone had left on the table and lit one just to give her something to do. She pondered how lonely one could feel in a room filled with hundreds of people and was just contemplating catching a cab back home when Kiki appeared in front of her, dragging an attractive man with her.

"Oh, Cecily! You can't sit here all on your lonesome. May I introduce Captain Tarquin Price? He's a great friend of mine from Kenya."

"Delighted to make your acquaintance," said the man, giving Cecily a formal bow.

"Now I'll leave you two young things to chat—I really do need to use the restroom."

As Tarquin sat down next to her and offered her another cigarette, which she refused, Cecily thought that her godmother must have a seriously weak bladder.

"So I hear you are Kiki's goddaughter?"

"Yes, I am. And you are her great friend?"

"Oh, I wouldn't go as far as that; we've met a couple of times at Muthaiga Country Club in Nairobi. I had some leave, and Kiki invited me to stay in Manhattan with her for Christmas. Your godmother is the kind of woman who makes friends very easily. She is quite something, isn't she?"

"She sure is." Cecily only wished she could close her eyes and listen to his clipped English accent all night. "So do you live in Kenya?"

"For the moment, yes. I'm a captain in the British army, and I was posted there a few months back when this whole thing with Hitler blew up."

"And do you like it there?"

"It is undoubtedly one of the most stupendously beautiful countries I've ever seen. Rather different from Blighty." His handsome face, with its tanned skin that suited his brown eyes and thick dark hair, crinkled into a smile.

"Have you seen lions and tigers since you've been there?"

"Well now, I do hate to correct you, Miss—"

"Please just call me Cecily."

"Cecily, it seems to be a common myth that there are tigers in Africa. However, there are none. But yes, I've certainly seen a few lions. Shot one only a few weeks ago out in the bush."

"Really?"

Tarquin nodded. "Yes. The blighter came sniffing round our camp, and the damned blacks had all been asleep and were caught on the hop. Good job I heard the commotion, grabbed my gun, and killed it before it had us all for supper. There were ladies present, too."

"There were ladies out camping with you?"

"Yes, and some of them were far better shots than the men. One has to be clever with a gun if one lives in Africa, whatever sex one may be."

"I've never even held a gun, let alone fired one."

"I'm sure you'd soon learn—most people do. So, Cecily, what do you do here in New York?"

"I help my mother with her charity work, mostly. I'm on a number of committees . . ." Cecily's voice trailed off. It sounded so completely feeble telling a man from the British army who had just shot a lion about her charity lunches.

"I mean, I'd like to do so much more, but—"

*Come on, Cecily, at least try to make an effort to sound a little less like the sad little wallflower you are.*

"As a matter of fact, I'm very interested in economics."

"Are you, now? Why don't we take a turn around the dance floor, and you can tell me exactly how and where I should invest my paltry army wages."

"I . . . okay," she agreed, thinking that at least her dancing had to be better than her small talk. With the music of Benny Goodman and his band blaring out, even if she'd thought of something clever and amusing to say, Tarquin wouldn't have been able to hear it. She noted with pleasure that he was a far better dancer than Jack, and it gave her a kick when they almost collided with him and his silver-clad goddess of a fiancée. Midnight came, and a host of balloons were released from their netting prison above the guests.

"Happy New Year, Cecily." Tarquin bent down to kiss her on the cheek. "Here's to old friends and new."

After "Auld Lang Syne," the band struck up again, and Tarquin didn't seem inclined to leave her side until Kiki appeared like the beautiful wraith she was and tugged on his arm.

"Would you be a darling and escort me to my suite? I've been dancing the night away, and my poor feet are killing me. I simply must get out of these shoes. I've invited some people to join me so we can continue the party upstairs. Of course you must come, too, darling Cecily."

"Thank you, Kiki, but our driver will be waiting outside by now."

Kiki laughed. "Then tell the driver to wait a little longer."

"I can't, I must go home." After several sleepless nights, Cecily felt as though she might actually fall asleep in Tarquin's arms.

"Well, if you must, but I'll see you again before I leave for Kenya. I was saying to Cecily that she should come stay with me."

"Absolutely," Tarquin agreed, looking down fondly at Cecily. "Well, now, it's been a delight to meet you." He reached for her hand and brought it up to his lips. "It would be a pleasure to show you around if you make the trip. I hope we meet again soon. Good night."

"Good night."

As Cecily watched Tarquin escort Kiki through the crowd, then searched the room for her mother and father, she thought that even if she never laid eyes on Captain Tarquin Price again, tonight he really had been her knight in shining armor.

# 10

Like the rest of New York, Cecily had never enjoyed January, but this particular one felt more miserable than any other she had lived through. Usually, the view of a snow-covered Central Park from her bedroom window cheered her up, but this year it rained a lo,t too, and the pavements were covered in gray sludge that coordinated with the murky skies.

Before Jack's abrupt departure from her life, she had filled her days with plans for the wedding and the numerous charities that her mother and her friends worked tirelessly to run. Which, in Cecily's view, meant wasting endless hours deciding on a venue for the latest fund-raiser, then further time choosing the menus. The guest list would come next—totally dependent on how many dollars the recipient of the invitation might have to spare. Dorothea relied on her eldest daughter to let her know who her debutante friends were marrying; if the fiancé or new husband was wealthy enough, Cecily would invite them along.

Even though she knew that her mother and her cronies worked hard for their good causes, Cecily had never yet seen any of them get their immaculate silk gloves dirty by actually visiting one of the charities they raised funds for. When Cecily had suggested that she go to Harlem to visit the orphanage for which a charity dinner had raised over a thousand dollars, Dorothea had looked at her as if she was crazy.

"Cecily, honey, what can you be thinking? You'd be robbed by those Negroes before you'd had a chance to get out of the car. Everything you're doing for the charities is providing funds for those poor little colored babies. Be happy with that."

Since the Harlem Riot of 1935, which had happened when she'd been a sophomore at Vassar, Cecily had been aware of the tension. On so many occasions she'd been tempted to ask Evelyn, the household's black maid of the past twenty years, what her life was like, but the golden rule was that one never exchanged personal details with one's staff. Evelyn lived in the attic with the other kitchen staff, leaving the house only on a Sunday to go to "my church," as she called it. Archer, the chauffeur, and Mary, the housekeeper, were married and lived uptown in Harlem. At Vassar, there had been a few outspoken women who were demanding social change. Her friend Theodora had often left campus on weekends to go to a civil rights rally in the notorious 19th Ward. She'd slip back in through the dormitory window just before midnight on Sunday, reeking of smoke and brimming with rage.

"The world needs to change," she'd whisper angrily as she put on her nightgown. "Slavery might be over, but we're still treating a whole race of people as if they're less than human—segregating them, keeping them down. I'm goddamned sick of it, Cecily."

January was also a very quiet time on the charity committee circuit, so Cecily was mostly stuck in the house with her thoughts. Even the radio provided little light relief as Hitler continued to make incendiary speeches, attacking British and Jewish "warmongers."

"The winter of 1939 sure is a miserable time to be alive," Cecily muttered to herself as she took a walk through the fog-swathed Central Park, just to get out of the house.

Dorothea was away visiting her mother in Chicago. That evening, as Cecily sat down with her father at the vast table in the dining room that faced onto the snowy garden, she wondered if she would ever pluck up the courage to suggest they eat supper on such occasions at the small table in the far cozier morning room.

"Do you like the new-style decor?" Walter asked her, taking a sip of wine and gesturing vaguely at the sleek, modish furniture. The Fifth Avenue house, with its imposing stone facade facing Central Park, had been recently decorated by Dorothea in the fashionable art deco style—a style that had disoriented Cecily when she'd first seen the renovations. It seemed as though she met her own reflection at every turn in the endless mirrored surfaces, and she actually missed the heavy mahogany furniture that she'd known since childhood. The only remnant of her original bedroom was Horace, her ancient teddy bear.

"Well, I liked what we had before, but Mama sure seems happy with the new look," she ventured.

"Quite, and that is a good thing."

As her father lapsed into silence, Cecily decided to introduce the topic she'd been wondering about. "I've been keeping up with the news, Papa, and I wanted to ask you about it. Why is Hitler continuing to warmonger? He got what he wanted out of the Munich Agreement, didn't he?"

"Because, my dear," Walter began, rousing himself, "the man is a psychopath, in the truest sense of the word. In other words, he feels no guilt, nor shame, and it is unlikely he will adhere to any agreement he made."

"So might there be war in Europe?"

"Who knows?" Walter shrugged. "I guess it just depends which way Hitler's psychological wind blows on any given day. You may have noticed that the German economy is booming. He turned the economy around, so they sure can afford a war if he wishes to have one."

"Everything comes down to money, doesn't it?" Cecily sighed as she toyed with her lamb cutlet.

"Many things, yes, but not everything. So what have you done today?"

"Nothing. Absolutely nothing," she replied.

"No lunches with any of your friends?"

"Papa, most of my friends are married, pregnant, or already having babies."

"I'm sure it won't be long before you are in the same boat," he comforted her.

"I'm not sure about that personally. Papa?"

"Yes, Cecily?"

"I . . . well, I was wondering whether, given the fact that marriage isn't going to happen to me any day soon, you'd reconsider about me taking up some kind of"—Cecily swallowed hard—"employment. Maybe there's an opening at your bank?"

Walter wiped his mustache with his napkin, folded it neatly, and put it by the side of his plate. "Cecily, we have been down this road many times before. And the answer is no."

"But why? Women are taking jobs all over New York City! They're not waiting for some man to come along and sweep them off their feet! I have a degree, and I want to use it. Is there nothing I could do at your bank? Whenever I meet you for lunch, I see girls coming out the entrance, so they must be doing something inside."

"You're right, they are. They're working in the typing pool, spending their days typing up the directors' letters, then licking envelopes, sticking on postage stamps, and sending them off to the mailing department. Is that what you want?"

"Yes! At least I'd be doing something useful."

"Cecily, you know as well as I do that any daughter of mine couldn't work in the typing pool at the bank. You—and I—would be a laughingstock. These girls are from a completely different background—"

"I know that, Papa, but I don't care about 'background.' I just want to . . . fill my time." Cecily could feel tears of frustration pricking at the back of her eyes.

"My dear, I understand how Jack's betrayal has hurt you and destabilized you, but I'm sure that someone else will come along soon."

"But what if I don't *want* to get married?"

"Then you will become a lonely old spinster with a heap of nieces and nephews." His eyes betrayed a flicker of kindly amusement. "Does that sound appealing?"

"No . . . yes, I mean, right now, Papa, I really don't care. But what was the point in allowing me a college education if I can never use it?"

"Cecily, that education has broadened your mind, given you insights into subjects that will allow you to speak confidently at dinner parties . . ."

"Jeez! You sound like Mama." Cecily put her head in her hands. "Why won't you let me use my degree in a more productive way?"

"Cecily, I do understand about not being able to follow a path you've set your heart on. I studied economics at Harvard simply because my grandfather did and the Lord only knows how many 'greats' before him. When I graduated, all I wanted to do was travel the world and make my living away from the world of blatant commerce. I think I fancied myself as a great white hunter or some such." He chuckled ruefully. "Of course, when I told my father what I was planning, he looked at me as if I'd gone crazy, and the answer was no. I subsequently had to follow him into the bank, then take my place on the board."

Cecily watched as her father paused to take a large gulp of his wine.

"Do you think I actually enjoy what I do?" he asked her.

"I . . . well, I thought maybe you did, Papa. At least you're working."

"If you could call it that. In reality, I meet and greet clients—take them out for lunches and dinners and make them feel loved—while it's my big brother, Victor, who makes all the deals. I'm just the charming sidekick. And don't forget, times have been harder since the crash."

"I guess the bank survived, didn't it? We still have enough money, don't we?"

"Yes, but you must understand that our household continues to run as it always has because of your mother's inherited wealth, not mine. I understand your frustration, but nothing is perfect—life is a challenge to be faced, so we must simply make the best of it. And at least when you are married and run a household, you'll be able to immediately spot any of your staff who are trying to pull the wool over your eyes." He smiled. "You are destined to be a wife, and I am destined to have to stand by Victor's side and watch as he steers our family bank toward ruin. Now, if you're finished, I shall send for Mary to bring in the dessert."

As one gray day passed into another, Cecily thought a lot about the unusually honest conversation she'd had with her father. She had subsequently realized that he felt emasculated by his far wealthier wife. Their grand house on Fifth Avenue had been inherited by Dorothea from Cecily's maternal grandfather, after whom Cecily had been named. Cecil H. Homer had been one of the first to manufacture toothpaste on an industrial scale in America and had subsequently made a fortune. His wife, Jacqueline, had divorced Cecil when Dorothea was just a child, citing "desertion" on the legal papers—which, her mother always chuckled, in reality meant her father had deserted Jacqueline for a long slim tube of minty white cream rather than another woman. Thirteen-year-old Dorothea had been the sole heir to her father's fortune when he'd died of a heart attack at his desk, and at twenty-one, she had become the legal owner of the Fifth Avenue house, plus a large estate in the Hamptons and a raft of cash deposits and overseas investments.

Marriage to Walter Huntley-Morgan had followed soon after—Walter had an excellent lineage, but it had fallen to his elder brother to run the family's bank while her father came in "a good second," as he wistfully put it.

But however much she tried to reason with herself that her father was right, that life *was* a challenge to be faced, all she knew was that she didn't *have* a challenge, and she thought she might go mad with boredom. She was also aware of the fact that even in darkest January, there was always something going on in her New York circle, yet not a single invitation for a lunch or an afternoon tea had arrived on the silver plate in the hallway. And looking through the society section of the *New York Times*, she eventually surmised why: it was unthinkable that an ex-fiancée and a current one could be invited to the same gatherings, and Patricia Ogden-Forbes had superseded her in the circle's affections. Even her closest friends seemed to have abandoned her.

One afternoon, Cecily took a nip of bourbon from the decanter on the sideboard in the living room, then put a call through to her oldest and closest friend, Charlotte Amery. Having spoken to the housekeeper, who then went away to find Charlotte, she was informed that her friend was "otherwise engaged."

"But it's urgent!" she said. "Please tell her to return my call as soon as possible."

Another two hours passed before their housekeeper, Mary, told her that Charlotte was on the line for her.

"Hi, Charlotte, how are you?"

"I'm good, honey. How are you?"

She chuckled. "Well, you know, dumped by my handsome fiancé, possible war in Europe."

"Oh, Cecily, I'm so sorry."

"Jeez! I was only making a joke, Charlotte. I'm fine, really."

"Oh, I'm so glad. It must be hard for you with Jack and all."

"Well, it's not the best situation, no, but hey, I still breathe. I was thinking I hadn't heard from you in a while. How about we get together tomorrow? Treat ourselves to high tea at the Plaza. The scones there are the best in town."

"Oh, I'm afraid I can't. Rosemary is having a little get-together at her place. Apparently, her English friend is over to stay for a while, and we're all going to learn how to play bridge!"

Cecily swallowed hard. Rosemary Ellis was without a doubt the society queen of their generation and up to now had been a friend of Cecily's.

"I see. Oh, well, maybe next week?"

"I don't have my calendar with me right now, but why don't I call you Monday and we can see how we're both fixed?"

"Good idea," Cecily said, trying not to let her voice quaver. Nothing about New York society was spontaneous. Every hair appointment, dress fitting, and manicure, let alone a get-together with a friend, was planned and documented weeks beforehand. Charlotte would not be calling her back next Monday.

"Okay, great," Cecily managed. "Bye, now." She slammed the receiver down, then burst into tears.

An hour later, she was lying on her bed staring at the ceiling, because she couldn't even contemplate reading a book, when Evelyn tapped on her door.

"Excuse me, Miss Cecily, Mary sent me up as there's a lady and a gentleman downstairs in the hallway. They were asking to see your mother, so she told them she was away. But the lady said she wanted to see you, too."

Evelyn walked across the room and handed Cecily a card.

Cecily read it and sighed. Her godmother, Kiki, was apparently downstairs. She contemplated feigning illness but knew her mother would never forgive her if she didn't receive her old friend in her stead.

"Take them into the living room, and tell them I'll be down in ten minutes. I need to freshen up."

"Oh, but the fire isn't lit, Miss Cecily."

"Well, go light it, then, Evelyn."

"Yes, miss."

Cecily rolled off her bed and checked her reflection in the mirror. After giving her annoyingly curly hair a brush and deciding she looked more like Shirley Temple than Greta Garbo, then straightening her blouse and skirt and donning her shoes, she added a touch of lipstick before walking downstairs to greet Kiki.

"Darrrling!" Kiki purred as she embraced Cecily. "How are you?"

"I'm just fine, thank you."

"Well, now, you don't look it, sweetheart. You're as drawn and pale as the Manhattan sky."

"Oh, I've been suffering with a cold, but I'm getting over it now," Cecily lied.

"I can't say I'm surprised. Why, Manhattan is a refrigerator this time of year, and an empty one, too!" Kiki laughed as she shivered and pulled her mink coat tighter around her while walking toward the newly lit fire. She pulled out a cigarette in its holder from her purse. "I must say, I can only admire your mother's bold taste in design. Art deco isn't for everyone." She gestured around the living room, one wall of which was clad entirely in mirrored glass. "You remember Tarquin, don't you?" she asked, obviously only now reminded of the presence of the handsome man Cecily had danced with on New Year's Eve two weeks ago. He was still wearing his thick tweed coat—even with the fire, the temperature in the living room wasn't much above freezing.

"I sure do." Cecily smiled. "How are you, Tarquin?"

"I'm very well, Cecily, thank you."

"Can I offer you any refreshments? Tea? Coffee?"

"You know, I think some brandy might be just the thing to warm us all up. Tarquin, would you be so kind?" Kiki indicated the decanters on the sideboard.

Tarquin nodded. "Of course. "One for you, too, Cecily?"

"I—"

"Oh, come now, brandy is medicinal, especially for a cold, wouldn't you say, Tarquin?"

"I most certainly would, yes."

*But maybe not in the middle of the afternoon,* thought Cecily.

"So where has your mother flown off to? Warmer climes, I hope?" Kiki asked.

"No, actually, she's gone to Chicago to visit her mother—that is, my grandmother."

"And what a completely ghastly woman Jacqueline is," Kiki said, perching herself on the leather-topped fender in front of the fire. "Rich as Croesus, of course," she added as Tarquin handed both her and Cecily a glass of brandy. "She's related to the Whitneys, you know."

"Means nothing to me," said Tarquin, offering the armchair by the fire to Cecily before sitting down opposite her, while Kiki held court on the fender. "Forgive me," he continued, "I'm afraid I'm not up on who's who in American society."

"Suffice to say that if we were living in England, the Vanderbilts and the Rockefellers would be fighting it out for the throne, while the Whitneys would be looking on from the sidelines debating who to back," cackled Kiki.

"So Cecily's grandmother is American royalty, then?"

"Oh, absolutely, but isn't it all just such a charade?" Kiki said, sighing dramatically as she threw the stub of her cigarette at the fireplace. "Now, Cecily, honey, it is such a dreadful shame that your mother isn't here, for I was going to suggest that she travel back to Kenya with me when I leave the States at the end of the month. And of course, bring you along, too. You would love it there; the sky is always blue, the weather is always warm, and the wildlife is simply adorable."

"Kiki, I understand you yearn to go back, but it's not quite like that, Cecily," interrupted Tarquin. "Yes, the sky is blue, but it also rains—goodness, it rains bucket loads—and the animals can be less adorable if they happen to see you as their lunch."

"My darling, that would never happen at Mundui House! Dearest Cecily, you and your mother must come out and see for yourself."

"Well, it's very kind of you, but I doubt very much if Mama would be prepared to leave my sister Mamie until after she has had her baby."

"Oh, really, women give birth to babies every day in the thousands; even I've had three! Just the other week, I was walking to the kitchen at Mundui House to give instructions for a luncheon I was hosting and found one of my maids squatting on the ground with a baby's head between her legs. Of course I called for help, but by the time they'd gotten there, the rest of the child had slithered out of her and lay in the dust, squalling loudly while still attached by its cord."

"Holy moly!" said Cecily. "And did the baby live?"

"Of course it did. One of the mother's relatives cut through the cord, took the baby up in her arms, and marched the mother off for a rest. The next day, there she was, back in my kitchen. I think that far too much fuss is made of such things these days. Don't you, Tarquin?"

"To be honest, I've never thought about it," Tarquin replied, looking rather green as he took a swig of his brandy.

"Anyway, the point is, you and your mother simply must come back with me to Kenya. I leave at the end of January, after I've been to see my late husband's lawyers in Denver, so there's plenty of time to make the arrangements. Now, where is the restroom?"

"Oh, just down the hallway to the right." Cecily stood up. "I'll show you."

"Having navigated my way through the bush, I think I can just about manage to find my way to your facilities." Kiki smiled and swept out of the room.

"So, Cecily, what have you been up to since we last met?" Tarquin asked.

"Oh, not a lot. As I said, I've been suffering from a cold."

"Well, a visit to Kenya would soon have you on the mend. Does the thought appeal to you?"

"I honestly don't know. I mean, I've been to Europe, of course, to London and Scotland and Paris and Rome, but they didn't have lions there. Even if the thought did appeal to me, I just know Mama will never leave Mamie, whatever Kiki says. Are the natives . . . friendly?" Cecily asked.

"Most I've encountered, yes. Many of them work for us in the army, and Kiki's Kikuyus are quite devoted to her."

"Kikuyus?"

"They're the local tribe in Naivasha and the surrounding area."

"So they don't carry spears and wear loincloths around their . . . middle?" Cecily blushed.

"Now, then, the Maasai certainly do, but they live out on the plains tending their cattle. They'll give you no trouble if you give them none yourself."

"So," Kiki said as she reentered the room, swinging her purse, the strings of which were laced through her elegant white fingers. "Have you managed to persuade Cecily to come along with me?"

"I don't know. Have I?" Tarquin's brown eyes twinkled at Cecily.

"Well, it definitely sounds more interesting than New York, but—"

"Honey"—Kiki put a hand on Tarquin's arm—"we must go or we'll be late for tea with the Forbeses, and you know how punctual they always are."

"I'm leaving for Africa myself tomorrow," Tarquin said as he stood up. "I must report back to base this week, but I do hope you will think about coming to Kenya and we will meet again there soon, Cecily."

"And I'll be back here to simply bully you into it!" Kiki laughed as Tarquin held the door for her and she swept through it.

Once they'd left, Cecily sat on the fender and drank the remains of her brandy, pondering Kiki's offer. On New Year's Eve, she'd thought it merely polite conversation, rather than a serious proposition.

"Africa," she mouthed slowly as she ran a finger around the rim of her glass. On a whim, she stood up, then grabbed her coat and hat from the closet in the hall. Once outside, she headed for the local library before it closed.

That evening, over dinner with her father, Cecily told him of Kiki's suggestion.

"What do you think, Papa? Would Mama allow me to travel there without her as a chaperone?"

"What do I think?" Walter set down his glass of bourbon and steepled his fingers as he considered the matter. "I think that I wish I could come with you in Mama's stead. I've always longed to see Africa. Maybe a trip to visit Kiki is just what you need to help you forget Jack and move on. You're my special girl," Walter added as he stood up and planted a kiss on top of her head. "Now I have a meeting at my club. Tell Mary I'll be back by ten. I'll talk to your mother when she gets back from Chicago. Good night, my dear."

After her father had left, Cecily went upstairs and lay on her bed as she opened the three books she'd taken out of the library. There were endless sketches, paintings, and photographs of black natives and of white men standing proudly over the corpses of lions or holding a huge ivory tusk in each hand. She shuddered at the sight, but that shudder contained a shiver of excitement at the thought of visiting what looked like the most glorious and unfettered land. A land where no one would have even *heard* of either her or her broken engagement to Jack Hamblin.

"Cecily, will you come and join me and your mother in the living room when you are ready?" her father asked as she stepped into the hallway and dusted the flakes of snow from her coat. She'd been out all day, having her hair set in the morning and then going on to see Mamie that afternoon.

"Of course, Papa. I'll be there in a moment or two."

After handing her coat to Mary, she walked to the downstairs bathroom and tidied herself up in the mirror. As she entered the living room, the fire was burning merrily. She saw that her mother looked stony-faced as her father welcomed her in.

"Sit down, my dear."

"What did you want to talk to me about?" Cecily asked as her father settled himself in a chair next to the fire.

"Kiki came by again today to beg us to go to Africa with her. I told her that I wouldn't leave Mamie so near the birth," said Dorothea, "but your father thinks you should go without me."

"I do, yes," Walter agreed. "As I explained to your mother, it's not only an opportunity for you to see more of the world, but it also means that by the time you get back, the wedding will be over and you can move on with your life."

"Jack and Patricia have announced a date?" Cecily asked as calmly as she could.

"Yes, they are to be married on the seventeenth of April. All the society columns carried the news this morning."

"So what do you think, Mama?"

"Well, now, I agree with your father that Jack and Patricia's wedding will be the talk of Manhattan for the next few months, which will be mighty hard on you. But is that any reason to run to Africa? The place sounds totally uncivilized. Half-clothed natives running around, wild animals wandering into your garden," Dorothea said with horror. "And of course, there's the risk of disease. Walter, surely we could just send Cecily to my mother's if she needs to get away?"

Cecily and her father locked eyes and shared a joint invisible shudder.

"Well, Kiki has managed to survive the past twenty years, and there is a very well established expatriate community, as you well know," said Walter.

"I do know, and their notoriety worries me more than the lions," Dorothea answered bluntly. "They all sound a little darned racy from what I've read in the newspapers. There was that friend of Kiki's—what was her name?"

"Alice de Janzé," Walter replied. "But that was many years ago now."

"What happened?" Cecily asked, then watched her parents exchange glances.

"Oh, well . . ." Dorothea shrugged. "It was quite the scandal. Alice and Kiki were part of what was known as the 'Happy Valley set' out in Kenya. There was all sorts of talk of their antics. Alice was married, but had an . . . unfortunate liaison with a man called—"

"Raymond de Trafford," Walter answered.

"That's the one. Anyway, Alice became infatuated with Raymond and was so devastated when he refused to marry her that she shot him on a train at the Gare du Nord in Paris as he was saying good-bye to her, before turning the gun on herself. Neither of them died," Dorothea added.

"Holy moly!" Cecily was agog. "Was she put in jail?"

"No. There was a trial, of course, and she spent a short spell in custody, but she eventually ended up marrying the man!"

"No!" Cecily was enraptured by the sheer romance of the tale. Africa was beginning to sound thrilling.

"But that all happened so long ago. And I'm sure Kiki doesn't behave like that," Walter said firmly. "She said she'd look after our girl like she was her own. Well, now, Cecily, the real question is, do you want to go?"

"As a matter of fact . . . yes, I think I do. And not just because of Jack's wedding—I'm a grown woman now, and I can deal with that. It's more that, well, Kenya sounds fascinating."

"Even though you'll miss the birth of your sister's child?" said Dorothea.

"Oh, Mama, you're going to be there for Mamie, and I'm not leaving forever, you know. Only for a few weeks."

"And of course, darling," Walter said, turning to his wife, "Cecily could always go stay with Audrey while she's in England on her way to Africa?"

Audrey was Dorothea's "trophy friend," having nabbed herself an English lord for a husband fifteen years ago. If anything was going to persuade Mama to let her make the trip, it was the thought of her daughter staying with Audrey and all the eligible young Englishmen she might just meet while she was there.

"True, true, but is England safe these days, Walter, what with Mr. Hitler?"

"Is Manhattan safe these days?" Walter raised an eyebrow. "If one wanted to be safe above all, one would never walk out of one's front door. So is it decided?"

"I would of course have to get in touch with Audrey to make sure she's at home when Cecily arrives in England and have her chauffeur meet her from the steamer. Kiki could go with Cecily to visit Audrey, too—the two of them knew each other when they lived in Paris," Dorothea thought out loud.

Walter cast his daughter a glance and gave a tiny wink.

"Well," said Cecily, "if you both are happy for me to go, then I will." She nodded. "Yes, I will." For the first time in weeks, her mouth formed into a natural smile.

Having just over two weeks to prepare for her journey, Cecily and Dorothea were kept busy shopping for everything she would need for her trip: formal wear for her week at Audrey's, then sundresses and blouses fashioned from cotton and muslin (which had to be especially made by a seamstress as it was deepest winter), along with skirts and even shorts, which Dorothea had baulked at.

"Oh, Lord, where are we sending you to?" She grimaced as Cecily tried them on.

"A place that is very hot, Mama. Like summer in the Hamptons."

Despite her mother's constant negativity, as Evelyn helped her fill her steamer trunk, Cecily's excitement mounted. The night before she left, her sisters and their husbands arrived for dinner. Walter presented his daughter with a Kodak Bantam Special camera, and her sisters gave her a pair of binoculars for "manspotting," as Priscilla put it.

"Do take care, darling sis," Mamie said as they stood in the hallway after dinner. "Hopefully I'll be able to present you with a new nephew or niece on your return."

"Come back happy," Hunter said as he kissed her good-bye.

"And preferably married," Priscilla called from the stoop.

"I'll do my best," Cecily called as they disappeared out of view into the snowy night.

# II

*England*
*February 1939*

Rather disappointingly, as the steamer approached Southampton port, Cecily saw that England looked as gloomy and gray as the Manhattan she'd left behind. She donned her new hat, then wrapped her fur shrug around her shoulders as her steward came to collect her luggage.

"Is anyone meeting you, miss?"

"Yes." Cecily dipped into her purse and took out a card on which was printed the name of the chauffeur who had (hopefully) been sent from Woodhead Hall to meet her.

"Thanks, miss. You stay inside your cabin for now—it's dead nippy out there—and I'll come and fetch you when the car's pulled alongside."

"Thank you, Mr. Jones. You've been very helpful."

Cecily handed him a healthy five-dollar tip, and the young man blushed and nodded at her appreciatively.

"Well, it's been a pleasure looking after you, Miss Cecily, it truly has. Maybe I'll meet you again on the return trip?"

"I sure hope so, yes."

The steward closed the cabin door behind him and Cecily went to sit in the chair by the porthole. As soon as she arrived at Woodhead Hall, she knew, she must telephone her parents to let them know she was safe. It had all been a little hectic in the twenty-four hours before she'd left New York a week ago. Kiki's maid had telephoned on the morning they were meant to leave to say her mistress had come down with bronchitis. Her doctor had warned her it could turn into pneumonia if she didn't stay in bed for a few days. Cecily had been happy to delay for as long as it took Kiki to recover, but Dorothea, having organized the visit to Woodhead Hall, had disagreed.

"Kiki says her doctor is sure that she should be well enough to travel in a week's time, which means she can meet you in England to board the flight to Kenya. You can still continue with your visit to Audrey and her family, Cecily. Audrey has made plans especially for your visit."

So Cecily had set off from New York alone and, having been trepidatious at the thought, had actually enjoyed her days aboard ship. More than anything, it had built her confidence as she had been forced to make conversation with strangers over dinner and accept invitations to play cards (at which she was rather good) afterward. There had also been at least three young men who had been keen to win her favor; it was almost as if, away from Manhattan where nobody knew who she was, she could finally be herself.

There was a knock on her cabin door, and Mr. Jones peered around it.

"Your documents have been checked, and the car's pulled up alongside," he said, handing her back her passport, "and your trunk is loaded, Miss Cecily. Are you ready to go?"

"Yes, thank you, Mr. Jones."

A biting cold wind hit her as she walked down the gangplank, the heavy fog blurring everything around her. The chauffeur helped her into the waiting Bentley and started the engine.

"Are you comfortable, miss?" he inquired as she settled herself into the plump leather seat. "There are extra blankets if you need them."

"I'm absolutely fine, thank you. How long is the drive?"

"Depends on the fog, miss, but I'd say we'll be at Woodhead Hall in two or three hours. There's a flask of hot tea if you're parched."

"Thank you," Cecily said again, wondering what on earth "parched" meant.

In reality, the drive took well over three hours and she dozed on and off, unable to see anything of the English landscape through the fog. When she'd been to England before, Audrey had received Cecily and her parents at her grand London house in Eaton Square, and then they had moved on to Paris. She only hoped the weather would clear a little so she could see something of the famed British countryside. Dorothea had visited her friend at her vast country estate in somewhere called West Sussex and pronounced it quite beautiful. But when the chauffeur pulled through a pair of large gates and announced that they'd arrived, it was almost dark and Cecily could see only the outline of an enormous gothic mansion sitting eerily against the dimming light behind it. As she approached the imposing porticoed front door, Cecily sighed in disappointment at the workmanlike redbrick facade. It wasn't like any house she'd read about in Jane Austen's books—they had all been mellow stone, whereas this looked like something out of Edgar Allan Poe's stories.

The door was opened by a stately man whom she almost took to be Audrey's husband, Lord Woodhead, but who in fact announced himself to be the butler. Cecily walked into the vast hall, its centerpiece an impressive but rather ugly mahogany staircase.

"Darling Cecily!" Audrey—who was attractive and vivacious, just as Cecily remembered her—came to greet her. She kissed Cecily on both cheeks. "How was the voyage? I do so hate traveling across the ocean, don't you? All those enormous waves—it can quite upset the digestion. Come, I will show you to your room, you must be completely exhausted. I've had the maid light the fire for you—dear Edgar can be quite frugal with the heating."

Once installed in her room, Cecily sat warming her hands by the fire, surveying the stately four-poster bed. The room was utterly freezing, and she was glad her mother had forewarned her about the temperature in English country houses, making sure that she packed long johns and undershirts to keep her warm.

Even though Audrey had insisted that Cecily must be tired after the journey, she was feeling wide awake. Once the maid had unpacked her "England' clothes and taken her gown off to be steamed for dinner that night, Cecily grabbed a woolen cardigan, then opened the bedroom door and peered out along the hallway. She turned left and walked along it, and by the time she came to the end of it, she had counted twelve doors. Walking back past her own bedroom, she then proceeded right along to the other end.

"Twenty-four doors," she sighed, wondering how the maids remembered who was in which room, as there were no numbers on the outside of them like there were in hotels. Returning to her bedroom, she found the maid restoking her fire.

"I've hung your dress in the wardrobe, miss, ready for tonight."

"Wardrobe?"

"Yes, that," said the maid, pointing to the closet. "I've also drawn you a bath next door, miss, but it's a bit nippy in there, so I'd dip in quick before the water freezes over, then get back in here to warm up by the fire."

"Okay, thanks."

"Will you be wanting any help with your hair, miss? I do 'er ladyship's most nights. I'm a dab hand, I am."

"Well, that's very kind of you, but I'm sure I can manage myself. And you are—"

"Me name's Doris, miss. I'll be back in a jiffy, once you've had your bath."

Cecily felt nonplussed as she undressed and slipped on her robe to go next door to the bathroom. Doris seemed to be speaking a foreign language, but she certainly wasn't wrong about the temperature of either the bathroom or the water. She was into and out of it as fast as she could and was just walking back to her bedroom when she saw a young man of about her age making his way down the hallway toward her.

Given her current frame of mind over Jack, Cecily was not in the mood for romanticizing any male, but as he looked up and smiled at her, her heart rate increased. Beneath the floppy bangs of shiny black hair (worn far too long for a gentleman) a pair of large brown eyes, framed by girlishly thick lashes, appraised her.

"Hello," he said as he reached her. "May I inquire to whom I am speaking?"

"I'm Cecily Huntley-Morgan."

"Are you, now? And what exactly are you doing here?"

"Oh, my mother and Lady Woodhead are old friends, and I'm staying here for a few days before I travel on to Kenya." Cecily put a hand to her décolletage, feeling exposed in the flimsy robe she had put on after her bath.

"Africa, is it?" the man said with a smile. "Well, well. I'm Julius Woodhead." He offered her a hand. "Pleased to make your acquaintance."

"Likewise." Cecily took the proffered hand and felt an odd sensation, not unlike an electric shock, shudder up her arm.

"See you at dinner," he called as he sauntered past her. "It's apparently pheasant yet again; just be careful of the shot."

"I . . . okay, I will be," she replied, not having a clue what he meant.

Julius disappeared into a bedroom just down the hallway. With a trembling hand, she opened the door to her own room, then shut it behind her and went to sit beside the fire.

"Julius Woodhead," she whispered. "Surely, he can't be one of Audrey's children?" For starters, she wasn't aware Audrey had any. For seconds, he had been wearing an old woolen sweater with holes the size of her father's signet ring.

"Oh, my," she said, fanning herself, suddenly feeling flushed. She stood up to head over to her lingerie drawer and decided she would ask Doris to style her hair for dinner after all.

"Welcome, my dear," said Audrey as Cecily entered the vast drawing room, which made the one in her parents' home look like a doll's house version. "Come, stand by the fire." Audrey drew her toward it, taking a cocktail from a tray held by a stationary manservant and handing it to her. "Glad to see you're in velvet—far warmer than satin or silk. We're having central heating put in next month—I told Edgar I simply refused to spend another winter in this house unless he did."

"I'm just fine, Audrey. And it's awful nice of you to host me here."

"Yes, well"—Audrey waved an arm vaguely around the room at the guests—"sadly, the beginning of February is not the height of the social season here. Most people are away in warmer climes or skiing in St. Moritz. And dear Edgar is up in London all week, so you won't meet him, but I did what I could. Now, let me introduce you to some of my friends and neighbors."

Cecily did the rounds with Audrey, nodding and smiling at the assembled company. Disappointingly, only the vicar's son—Tristan Somebody-or-other—was of a similar age to her. He told her he was on a brief visit to see his parents, who lived in the local village, while training at somewhere called Sandhurst as an officer for the British army.

"Do you think there will be a war?" Cecily asked him.

"I bally well hope so, Miss Huntley-Morgan. It's pointless training for something that never happens."

"You actually *want* there to be a war?"

"I doubt there's a person in England who doesn't think that Herr Hitler needs a jolly good kicking. And I for one am eager to help."

Feeling faintly queasy, whether due to the two cocktails she'd drunk or the long day of travel, Cecily eventually managed to extricate herself from Tristan and walked back toward the fire.

"Good evening, Miss Huntley-Morgan. Glad to see you've put your clothes on for dinner."

Cecily swung around to see Julius—looking utterly divine in black tie—grinning at her in undisguised amusement.

"Why, I'd just come from the bathroom!"

"Really? I thought that perhaps you were sneaking along the hallway from your lover's room."

"I—" Cecily felt a blush rising up her neck into her face.

Julius smiled. "Only teasing. I must say, you look spiffing in that dress. It matches your eyes."

"But my dress is purple!"

"Oh, yes, well"—Julius shrugged—"isn't that the kind of thing gentlemen say to ladies all the time?"

"When appropriate, yes."

"Well, that's me all over; inappropriate should be my middle name. Forgive me. I hear that good old Aunt Audrey has laid on this little bash all for you. You're the guest of honor, apparently."

"That's very kind of her. She didn't have to."

"As you're American, I presume you'll be casting your eye around the room for an eligible member of the British aristocracy. Granted there are a few here, but all over the age of fifty. Except for me, of course," he added with a smile.

"You say Audrey's your aunt?"

"Yes, but not by blood. My late father was Uncle Edgar's younger brother."

"Oh, I'm so sorry for your loss."

"Thank you for your condolences, but my father died over twenty years ago in the Great War. I was only eighteen months old at the time."

"I see. Do you have a mother?"

"I do indeed, yes. Luckily, she's not here tonight." Julius leaned in toward Cecily. "My uncle and aunt can't stand her."

"Why ever not?"

"Oh, because rather than hanging around in widow's weeds when my father shuffled off his mortal coil in Flanders, she found herself a far richer suitor than dear old Pa and married him six months later. She lives in Italy now."

"I love Italy! You were so lucky to grow up there."

"No, no, Miss Huntley-Morgan," Julius said as he lit a cigarette. "Mama didn't take me with her when she scarpered for warmer climes. She dumped me on the doorstep of this mausoleum, and I was brought up by Uncle Edgar's old nanny. Miss Naylor she was called, and what a dragon she was."

"So you live right here at Woodhead Hall?"

"I do indeed. I've done my best to dig myself out, but time and again, like the proverbial rubber ball, I find myself bouncing back."

"What do you do? I mean, for a living?"

"Well, now, what I do for a 'living' is rather a euphemism, because I hardly earn a penny from it, more's the pity. But I am in fact a poet."

"Goodness! Should I have heard of you?"

"Not yet, Miss Huntley-Morgan, unless you are an avid reader of the *Woodhead Village Gazette*, which, out of the kindness of its heart, publishes the odd scribbling of mine."

There was a loud clanging from somewhere outside the drawing room, which reverberated around it for a few seconds.

"Dinner gong, Miss Huntley-Morgan."

"Please do call me Cecily," she said as they wandered through the drafty hallway with the rest of the guests, then into the equally lofty and freezing dining room.

"Now, then, let's see where my aunt has put you," said Julius, marching along the table and staring at the beautifully handwritten names at the top of every place setting. "Thought as much!" He smiled at her. "You're here, right by the fire. Whereas I am banished to Siberia at the other end of the table. Remember about the shot," he said as he left her side and walked off.

Cecily sat down, feeling decidedly disappointed that she'd been put next to Tristan rather than Julius. All through dinner, even though she managed to make small talk with both Tristan and an elderly major to her right, her thoughts and her eyes kept flying along the table to Julius. Just as she had extracted a small hard lump of silver metal from her mouth, having taken a bite of pheasant, she glanced up at him.

"I did warn you," he mouthed with a smile, and then went back to his conversation with a bosomy matron, who was apparently the major's wife.

"So, headed for Africa, are we? Whereabouts?" boomed the major. "I was there meself a few years ago. My younger brother bought a cattle farm in Kenya, somewhere west of the Aberdare Mountains."

"Oh, well, that's where I'm headed, too; to Kenya, I mean. I'm staying at a house on the shores of Lake Naivasha. Have you heard of it?"

"Have I heard of it? Of course I've heard of it, my dear. So, joining the Happy Valley set, are you?"

"I have absolutely no idea, I'm afraid. My godmother has invited me out there to stay for a while."

"And who might your godmother be, if I may be so bold to ask?"

"Oh, a lady called Kiki Preston. She's American, like me."

"Good Lord!" Cecily watched the major's ruddy cheeks become even ruddier as he glanced at her. "Well, well, who'd have thought it, a sweet girl like you—"

"You know her?"

"Now, then, I would be telling a lie if I said I did, because I've never met her in person. But I certainly know *of* her. Everyone in Kenya does."

"Is she famous there?"

"Oh, yes, she—and her friend Alice de Trafford—are what one might call infamous. The Muthaiga Club in Nairobi was always awash with talk of their capers and, of course, that gorgeous girl Idina Sackville. If I'd been twenty years younger and not married, Idina could certainly have led me astray, and indeed, she did lead many other lucky blighters off the straight and narrow. Her and Joss Erroll's parties were the stuff of legend, you know. And . . . I say, I'm pretty sure it was your godmother, Kiki, who was known as the girl with the silver needle."

"You mean she sewed?" Cecily's head was positively spinning.

"I'm sure she had plenty of Negroes to do that for her, but—" The major stared at Cecily's nervous expression. "Well, now, m'dear, I'm sure a lot of it was merely gossip, and besides, it was almost twenty years ago when I was there. I'm sure all concerned have calmed down from their youthful shenanigans."

"It sounds like they had a lot of fun out there."

"Oh, yes, I'll say." The major wiped his mouth with his napkin. "Rather sadly, my brother wasn't part of that set—more interested in his cattle than getting up to high jinks at Muthaiga Club. We did enjoy some jolly good nights there nevertheless. Well, now, you must look up my brother while you're there. I'll leave his name and address with Audrey. Mind you, he's not hard to find—just ask for Bill, and you'll be pointed in the right direction."

"You said he runs a cattle farm?"

"Indeed. Funny old stick, my brother," the major mused. "Never married and seems to spend rather a lot of time out on the plains with the Maasai tribe. He was always a bit of a loner, even as a child. Now, Miss Huntley-Morgan, tell me a little about you."

Cecily was almost dropping with fatigue when the last guest finally left and she was able to say her good nights and walk wearily up the endless staircase. She was just about to open the door to her room when a hand was placed on her shoulder. Letting out a small scream, she turned around to find Julius grinning at her.

"I was just coming to check if all your teeth were still in place after that ghastly pheasant."

"Holy moly! You scared me half to death, creeping up on me like that!"

"My apologies, Cecily, but before you retire, I wanted to ask if by any chance you ride?"

"Why, yes, I do. We have horses on our estate in the Hamptons. I love it, even though I'm not sure my riding is terribly polite."

"I'm not sure how riding can be 'polite,' but never mind. I normally go out early for a charge across the downs. Blows away the cobwebs so I can sit down to a morning's work. If you fancy joining me, I'll be in the stables at seven tomorrow morning. If there isn't any fog, of course."

"I'd love to, Julius, but I don't have a thing to wear."

"I'll ask Doris to lay out some jodhpurs and boots. There's an entire wardrobe full of them from guests who have left them behind over the years. There's sure to be something in your size. Until tomorrow, maybe." He smiled at her.

"Yes. Good night, Julius."

Ten minutes later, although hugely relieved to be horizontal (albeit on a mattress that must have been stuffed until it was stiff with horsehair), Cecily couldn't sleep. And her damned heart began thumping every time she thought about Julius.

She just didn't understand it. She'd been sure she'd been in love with Jack for all of her life, but never had her mind *and* her body reacted like this to a man. Julius wasn't even her type—she'd always found blonds far more attractive, whereas he was dark, almost Mediterranean-looking. Never mind his easy attitude toward her . . . She definitely did not approve of his innuendo, especially given the fact that they'd met only this evening. It was as if he hadn't a care for what anyone thought of him . . .

*Why should he? And more to the point, why should I?*

Eventually, Cecily dozed fitfully, her dreams full of women wielding huge silver sewing needles against spear-holding natives and Julius being mauled by a lion . . .

Cecily woke with a jump and sat upright. Getting straight out of bed, she ran to pull back the curtains to see if it was foggy. With a clench in her stomach, she saw that it was a glorious, crisp morning. The vast parkland that ran as far as the eye could see was still white with frost, which was sure to melt soon judging by the perfect rosy sunrise that peeked out above the endless rows of chestnut trees that bounded the formal gardens.

"Someone should write an opera about this view," she murmured as there was a knock on the door and Doris arrived with a tea tray.

"Did you sleep well, miss?"

"Oh, yes, perfectly, thank you, Doris."

"Shall I pour for you?"

"No, I can do it myself."

"Right you are. Will you be going out riding? I've picked out a habit and boots that I think will fit you. You've a lovely petite figure, Miss Cecily."

"Thank you. I . . . yes, I think I might go for a ride."

"Why not on such a beautiful morning?" Doris smiled at her. "I'll be back in a tick with your outfit."

Cecily sipped her tea, which was far more watery than she was used to, and suddenly remembered that she had not yet contacted her parents to let them know she was safe and well in England. She thought about what her mother would say if she told her she was about to go riding with Audrey and Edgar's nephew. Cecily chuckled to herself. "She'd probably start organizing the engagement party before I even got back."

"What was that, miss?" asked Doris.

"Oh, I was just reminding myself that I must telephone my parents to let them know of my safe arrival."

"No need to worry about that, Miss Cecily. The butler telephoned them last night to let them know. Now, then, let's get you into your riding habit, shall we?"

Julius was already astride a magnificent black stallion when Cecily arrived at the stables.

"Hello there, wondered if you'd show up," Julius said, casting a glance at her from his great height. "Jump aboard, will you?" He indicated the pretty chestnut mare one of the grooms was leading out into the yard.

Cecily allowed the groom to help her up into the saddle. The mare whinnied and threw her head back, almost unseating her rider.

"Bonnie's a lively one, Cecily. Think you can cope?"

It wasn't so much a question as a challenge.

"I'll sure do my best," she said as she took the reins from the groom and steadied the horse.

"Right, then, let's be off."

The two of them clopped out of the yard and Cecily followed Julius along the narrow path that then led through the trees to open parkland. He waited a few seconds for her to catch up with him.

"Comfortable?" he asked.

"I guess so, but I'd prefer to go slow for a while, if that's all right with you?"

"Of course. We'll take a gentle canter across the park and see if you're up for the wide-open spaces of the downs." Julius pointed to a vague expanse on the horizon. "The views are simply stunning from there."

The two of them took off at a gentle trot, which gave Cecily time to find her seat and her confidence; then Julius broke into a canter and she followed. Bonnie's hooves kicked up the rich smell of earth, and Cecily could see the frost shimmering and melting, while occasional snowdrops—the harbingers of spring—poked their heads out of the long grass beneath the chestnut trees. Despite the cold, birds called to one another, and Cecily finally felt very much as if she was in the Jane Austen novel she'd imagined.

"Let me know if you need to go slower," Julius called to her as the stallion's tail swished from side to side in front of her. "Can't have Aunt Audrey's guest of honor breaking her neck under my watch!"

With the biting wind blowing in her face, Cecily's eyes began to stream and her nose to run, but she doggedly followed Julius's horse. Just as she was about to pull Bonnie up as she could no longer see clearly, Julius slowed in front of her and twisted around in the saddle.

"All tickety-boo?" he asked her.

"I haven't the vaguest idea what 'tickety-boo' means, but I sure am in need of a handkerchief," Cecily panted.

"Of course." Julius turned his mount and steered back toward her until they were facing each other. He then produced a clean square of white linen from the top pocket of his tweed jacket, leaned over and proceeded to dab her eyes.

"Really, I can do it," she said, trying to grab the handkerchief from him.

"It's no trouble at all, though I won't suggest I help you blow your nose," he quipped as he handed it to her, and she blew as delicately as she possibly could. "You have such very pretty eyes."

"Thank you for the compliment, but I hardly think I do at present. They're streaming."

"Perhaps we might go up onto the downs tomorrow morning, although the wind this time of year can be quite fierce. And I suppose you're used to warmer weather in America."

"No, it's far colder in New York than it is here. I just . . . perhaps I'm getting a chill."

"That would hardly surprise me. Dear Uncle Edgar does like to watch the pennies, and you can imagine that heating a house like Woodhead Hall is costly. Rather ridiculous when one thinks of the fact that one could live in a hut in the tropics and require the minimum of necessities. Now, then, we'll head back to the house and have Doris put you in front of a roaring fire with a hot cup of tea."

"Please, if you want to go off to enjoy the downs I can easily find my way back."

"Not at all. I can see them any day of the week," he said and smiled at her. "But you're only here for a short time, so I'd prefer to look at you."

Cecily turned her face away from him so he wouldn't see the blush spreading up from her neck. She gripped the reins tightly as the two of them headed back toward the hall side by side at a trot.

"So," she said and cleared her throat, "how do you spend your days here at the hall? Writing your poetry, I suppose?"

Julius sighed. "Would that was the reality." Perhaps one day I shall run away to Paris and live in a garret somewhere in Montmartre. Sadly, most of my time is taken up helping Uncle Edgar on the estate. He's grooming me to take over one day, but, like a recalcitrant horse, I find it hard to stand still as he does so. Especially the ledgers. Oh, God, the ledgers! You know what a ledger is, I presume?"

"I do, yes. My father spends a lot of his life poring over his ledgers, too."

"A life without ledgers is sublime, if only one day that life could be mine," Julius pronounced with a chuckle. "I think dear Uncle Edgar has realized that my maths and business acumen are nonexistent, but as I'm all he's got in terms of an heir, he has no choice but to hope for the best and believe that one day I will suddenly learn to add up. The problem is, I'm simply not interested."

"Oh, I rather like sums." Cecily smiled.

"How extraordinary! Goodness, Miss Huntley-Morgan, you become more perfect with every word that falls out of your pretty mouth. I've never met a woman who confesses to enjoying mathematics."

"Well, even if I sound crazy, I do," she said defensively.

"Please, what I said was certainly not meant as criticism. Rather more a wish that I could find a woman like you to marry. And rather than plighting my troth to her, whatever a troth actually is, I'd hand over the ledgers. Well, now," he said, pointing to the buildings they were approaching, "we're here and I suggest you go directly to the house, rather than walking back from the stables with me."

Cecily was about to protest, because any further precious seconds she could spend with her new companion were ones that she would treasure forever, but Julius was already off his horse and looking up at her expectantly. As he helped her to dismount, his hands remained firmly around her waist as her feet touched the floor.

"You're such a slender little thing, aren't you? Can't feel an ounce of spare flesh around those hips of yours. Now, then, hurry back to the house and I'll be in to check how you're feeling later on."

"Oh, I'm fine, really."

But Julius was already back on his horse and catching up the reins of her mare. He gave Cecily a small salute and trotted off with both animals in the direction of the stables.

Cecily was disappointed to find that Julius was not present for luncheon; she and Audrey were alone at the table. As Audrey asked after Dorothea and Cecily's sisters, plus the friends and acquaintances whom Cecily vaguely knew from her mother's circle, she could barely swallow the soup that claimed to be vegetable but tasted like warmed-up dishwater.

"My dear, you've hardly touched your lamb," Audrey commented as the maid cleared away their plates after the main course. "Perhaps you *are* catching a cold."

"Maybe I am," Cecily agreed, a piece of fatty, inedible meat still tucked inside her cheek. "I'll go upstairs and have a rest. I can't understand why I'd be sick; it's so much colder in Manhattan."

"That it may be, but here it's the damp that gets one, you see," Audrey replied in her odd part-American, part-English accent. "Julius said you might be sickening for something earlier. I'll send Doris up with a hot water bottle and some aspirin, and if you prefer a tray in your room tonight, that can easily be arranged. Unfortunately I must attend a meeting at six—I am on the local parish council—and those meetings always drag on. As I told you, Edgar is in London and I've no idea where Julius is spending the evening." She raised her eyebrows. "Not that that's unusual. Anyway, I want you fit and well for Sunday—I'm throwing a little cocktail party for your last night. Now, then, off you go to rest."

Upstairs in her room and tucked up in bed, Cecily watched the flames of the fire dance in front of her. She was definitely not sick—at worst, she had a slight chill—but there was something else that had put her off her food. She closed her eyes, desperate to sleep, but all she saw was Julius's face as he had tenderly mopped her eyes this morning . . .

She opened her palm and breathed in the smell of the handkerchief she was clutching—and the scent of *him* within it.

*Cecily, you sure are being ridiculous! For a start, you know nothing about him, and apart from recovering from a broken heart, you're off to Africa in five days' time and will never see him again,* she told herself firmly as she replaced the handkerchief in her bedside drawer. *Tonight you will have a tray in your room, and you will not give him a second thought.*

Eventually, she dozed off and awoke to a dimming sky, heralding the arrival of night. Doris appeared with yet more tea. "If you're not feeling quite right, can I suggest you don't take a bath tonight?" she asked. "It's bleedin' freezing in there. What time would you like your tray? I'd say seven o'clock, so as it gives you time for the food to digest," Doris chattered on as she restoked the fire.

"I'm sure that will all be just fine, thank you."

"Well, it's me night off, see, so Ellen the parlor maid will be seeing to you after that. Just ring the bell if you need 'er."

"I will. So there's no one here for dinner tonight?" Cecily probed.

"Not that I know of, miss. Mr. Julius comes and goes as he pleases, so I couldn't be sure of him." Doris echoed Audrey's words from earlier.

"Is there much to do around here? I mean, is there a town close by?"

"Yeah, though I'm not sure I'd call it a town. Haslemere has shops and the flicks, which is where me and Betty are off to tonight. We're seeing *The Adventures of Robin Hood* with Errol Flynn. Now, if you don't need anything else, I'll tell Ellen to fetch up your supper at seven."

"Have a nice evening, Doris."

"Oh, I will, miss, and you get better soon."

Once Doris had left, Cecily took *The Great Gatsby*—which, with her head being everywhere these past few weeks, she had still not managed to finish—and sat down to read by the fire. She would *not* think about Julius somewhere close by in the house, she would *not*.

Promptly at seven o'clock, there was a knock on her door and Ellen appeared with the promised tray. There were more soup, a boiled egg, and thin slices of buttered bread. Even if she'd had an appetite, the food looked uninviting. She tapped the egg suspiciously. It felt as solid as a rock. She was just taking a mouthful of lukewarm soup when there was another knock at her door. Before she could say "Enter," it was opened.

"Good evening, Cecily. I heard you were eating in your room, and as I was about to do the same, I thought we should join forces to moan about Cook's lack of prowess in the kitchen."

And there was Julius, holding a tray identical to hers.

"Do you mind awfully if I join you?"

"I . . . no, of course not."

"Good-oh," he said as he placed his tray on the small table in front of the fire and sat down opposite her. "Now, then, having heard you have a chill and seeing as our supper is almost certainly inedible, I've brought a little something to warm the cockles of our hearts."

With that, Julius produced a bottle of what looked like bourbon from one pocket and a tooth mug from the other.

"We'll have to share, but life's all about improvisation, isn't it?" He smiled at her as he poured a hefty amount of liquor into the mug before offering it to her. "Ladies first. For medicinal purposes only, of course."

"Really, I—"

"Right, I'll go first, then," he said, then took a deep gulp. "Ah, that's better. Nothing like a dash of whisky to keep out the cold."

Cecily's heart was fluttering all over the place, and she needed something to calm her. "Maybe a small sip won't do me any harm."

"No, it won't, and a larger one may actually do you good," Julius encouraged her as she tipped the mug tentatively between her lips.

"Right, now for the egg," he said. Cecily watched him take his teaspoon, tap the top thoroughly, then slice it off with a knife. "Hard boiled as always," he said and sighed. "I have spoken to my aunt about the standard of fare in the house and the dubious qualifications of the woman who provides it, but it seems to fall on deaf ears." He sat back in his chair. "Inedible. So, all that is left to do is drink. Cheers." He picked up the tooth mug and drained the rest of the contents. "So tell me about your life in New York," he said as he refilled the mug and handed it back to her. "I've never been myself, but everyone tells me it's a wonderful city."

"It is. The skyscrapers go up and up toward the heavens, yet there are big wide-open spaces so you never feel claustrophobic. Our house overlooks Central Park, and you can walk for what feels like miles and rarely see another human being. It's the best of both worlds, I guess. It's my home"—she shrugged—"and I love it."

"Pray tell me, if you love it so much, why are you scuttling off into the African bush in a few days' time?"

"Because my godmother invited me."

"Did she, now?" Julius's piercing brown eyes bored into hers. "Given the fact that Europe is currently in such a muddle and Kenya may well be drawn into any coming war, I'd surmise there's more to the story than that."

"I . . . was going to get married, and, well, it didn't work out."

"I see. So," Julius said, having taken a further swig from the shared tooth mug, "in short, you're running away."

"I rather hope I'm running *to* something, actually. It's a wonderful chance to be somewhere completely different, and I decided to take it."

"Good for you, and I like your positive frame of mind. Anywhere has to be better than Woodhead Hall in the depths of winter." Julius sighed. "But that is my lot. Unless of course there is war in Europe; then I shall without a doubt be traveling to distant lands in a uniform to face certain death. So one must seize the moment, mustn't one?" he added as he refilled the tooth mug again. "Perhaps I can become the Rupert Brooke of the new war, though I rather hope I don't end my days on a battlefield in Gallipoli."

"I'm sorry, but I don't know who you're talking about."

"Good grief, Miss Huntley-Morgan, did you receive an education?"

"Why, yes, I went to Vassar, one of the best women's colleges in America!" she replied, wounded.

"Then your English literature professor has failed you miserably. Rupert Brooke was a genius and the most famous war poet of all time. I shall furnish you with a book of his poems forthwith."

"Literature wasn't ever my thing, although I enjoy reading for pleasure." Cecily shrugged, feeling much more relaxed after the whisky. "As I told you, I'm far better at arithmetic."

"Then you have a logical rather than an aesthetic brain. So let's test it out: right now, how quickly can you work out, uh . . . let's see, nine hundred and seven minus two hundred and fourteen."

"Six hundred and ninety-three," Cecily said after a few seconds.

"One hundred and seventy-two divided by six?"

"Twenty-eight point six recurring."

"Five hundred and sixty multiplied by thirty-nine."

"Twenty-one thousand, eight hundred and forty." Cecily giggled. "That was positively easy; quiz me on some algebra or logarithms."

"As I hardly know the meaning of either word, I don't think I'll bother. You're a seriously clever girl, aren't you? Do you ever feel miffed that you had a college education and yet, because you're a woman, apart from whizzing through household ledgers in the blink of an eye, you can't use your gifts to earn a living?"

"To be honest, of course I do. But Papa simply won't allow a daughter of his to work. I guess it's just the way things are."

"Well, now, isn't that ironic? All I want to do is to be left alone to think of the perfect words to put into a poem and dream my days away, rather than learning the ropes of running the estate—and plowing through the ledgers, of course." He grinned at her. "And here's you, who could do all that with alacrity, yet you're denied the chance because you're female."

"Life is never fair, and I guess we just have to accept it. I mean, we're both very privileged, Julius. You will one day inherit all this land and the house, and I will get to live a comfortable life as a wife and mother. Neither of us is living in poverty, are we?"

"We're certainly not, no, but the question is, Miss Huntley-Morgan," he said as he eyed her, "does money bring one happiness? I mean, are you happy? Am I?"

*At this moment, I'm as happy as I've ever felt,* thought Cecily.

"I'm good right now, actually," she said out loud.

"But what brings true happiness, do you think?"

"Well . . . love, I guess," Cecily said, thinking that even if a blush was spreading across her cheeks, her face was probably already pink from the whisky.

"Absolutely right!" Julius thumped the arm of his chair. "So you *do* have a poetic soul somewhere underneath all that logic."

"Everyone knows love is what makes you happy."

"But it also has the capacity to bring the most acute pain, wouldn't you agree?"

"I would, yes." It was Cecily's turn to drain the tooth mug. Her head was spinning from the lack of food and the liquor, but she didn't care. This was the most deliciously truthful conversation she'd ever had with a man.

"You really are the most awfully interesting female, but given my aunt is due back any second from one of her endless meetings, I must leave you." Julius stood up, as did Cecily. "Shall we go riding again tomorrow?" he asked as he stepped toward her. "That is, if you're better, of course." Then he grabbed her hand and pulled her to him. Before she had time to protest, his mouth was on hers and she was kissing him back more passionately than she'd ever kissed Jack. Even when one of his hands slid down her front to caress her breast and the other pulled her so close that she was aware of his excitement, she didn't stop him.

"My God, you're gorgeous," he breathed into her ear.

Only when one of the hands started searching for a way inside her blouse did she—with effort—pull away. "Julius, we shouldn't . . ."

"I know we *shouldn't*," he said, his erstwhile wandering hand moving to her cheek and caressing it gently. "My apologies, Cecily. You are just . . . irresistible. And before I am tempted further, I will take my leave. Good night." He kissed her once more on the lips before sweeping out of the room with his barely touched supper tray.

# 12

Cecily definitely *had* felt well enough to go riding with Julius the morning after "the Kiss"; in fact, she'd thought as she had lain on a smelly horse blanket in his arms two days later, she had never felt healthier in her life. Once they'd seen the sunrise on the downs, he had recommended that they tether their horses so he could show her the folly—a strange square building standing in the middle of nowhere, far away from the prying eyes of the house. Inside, it had smelled dark and damp, but the minute the door was closed behind them, she had fallen into his arms. All sense had left her as she had let him pass second base. And then, the following day, third base . . .

"What am I doing?" she moaned as she looked out of her bedroom window after a near miss of the dreaded "fourth base" earlier that morning. "I have two days left before I go to Kenya. I don't want to go to Kenya," she whispered as tears came to her eyes. "I want to stay here with Julius."

Cecily walked disconsolately back toward her bed and lay down on it, closing her eyes. She was exhausted from a run of sleepless nights, her heart palpitating every time she thought of being in his arms. Yet she was also euphoric, with more energy than she'd ever had—at least when it came to being with him.

"I never felt this way about Jack, never," she told the top of the four-poster bed, remembering the fumblings that she'd endured rather than enjoyed when Jack had kissed her good night. "Goodness, what am I to do?"

They hadn't really talked about the future. In fact, they hadn't talked about anything much because Julius's lips had been mostly sealed on hers when they were alone together. But he'd told her over and over how she was the most beautiful girl in the world, that he'd never met anyone quite like her, and even that he thought he might be in love with her.

"Well, I sure love *him*," she said, more tears springing to her eyes at the thought of leaving. Still, there were two days left, two days in which he could still ask her to stay . . .

That evening, after dinner with Audrey, Cecily feigned a headache and excused herself. The pain of watching Julius across the table making small talk, knowing that every precious minute that went by was wasted when she was not in his arms, was simply too much for her. Slipping between the sheets, she turned the light out, praying for her mind to still and let her sleep. She was just dozing off when she heard a tap on the door.

"Cecily, darling, are you asleep?"

Before she knew it, he was there beside her on the bed, wrapping his arms around her.

"Julius, what are you doing? What about your aunt? I—"

"She's retired for the night. And besides, she sleeps right at the other end of the hall. Now hush, and let me kiss you."

First the covers and then her nightgown were peeled off her body.

"No! We can't, we mustn't! I'm off to Kenya soon—"

"But doesn't it feel wonderful, my darling? Naked for the first time, skin touching skin . . ." He took her hand and laid it on the satin-smooth skin of his neck, then guided it downward and she felt the slight bristle of hair on his chest, then the muscles of his stomach, and then . . .

"*No!* Please, I can't. We're not even an official couple."

"Oh, we very much are. A couple bound up in a passionate love affair. I do love you, Cecily. I love you so much."

"And I love you," she murmured as her hand was released so his own could travel across her breasts before journeying farther down her body.

"Will you wait until I'm back?" she breathed.

"Wait for what?" he said as he rolled on top of her and she felt his hardness pressing against her.

"Me, of course," she whispered, her mental faculties anesthetized by the wonderful sensations her body was experiencing.

"Of course I will, my darling, of course."

It was only as he started to ease himself inside her that her brain finally overran her body. "No, Julius! I might get pregnant. I can't, please."

"Don't worry, darling, I won't let that happen, I promise. I'll pull out before. Now just relax and trust me."

"But we're not even engaged, Julius!"

"Then we'll get engaged," he said as he began to thrust into her. "This was just meant to be, darling Cecily, wasn't it?"

For a fleeting moment, she thought how thrilled Dorothea would be if she one day became the chatelaine of Woodhead Hall. Surely, even her father might forgive her for tonight if that was the prize.

"Yes," she said.

Cecily awoke late the next morning, looked at the travel clock sitting by her bed, and saw it was past nine o'clock. She lay there, still sleepy from last night's exertions, her mind flitting from the wrongness of what she had done— immediately comforting herself with the thought that there had been a number of girls at Vassar who had lost their virginity during their college years—to thoughts of how and when they would announce their engagement. Julius hadn't actually *said* that he would marry her or when—perhaps when she came back from Africa. Of course, there was also the threat of war . . .

Eventually, she sat up and swung her legs over the edge of the bed, her whole body aching in places she didn't know could ache. As she stood up to ring the call bell, she saw a small smudge of blood on the bottom sheet. "Surely it's not time for my monthly?" she muttered to herself, confused, then remembered the whispered conversations overheard in the common room at Vassar and realized what the blood might be. Blushing at the thought of Doris noticing it, she pulled the top sheet and eiderdown across it before she rang the bell. Then she noticed an envelope that had been pushed under her door. Hurrying to pick it up before Doris arrived with her tea, she sat down on the bed and opened it.

*My dearest darling Cecily,*

*I have had to go up to London today on business for my uncle, but I hope to return to say good-bye to you before you leave. This week has been quite wonderful, don't you think? In case I don't return in time, safe travels, darling girl. And do write to me with your address in Kenya as soon as you can. We must keep in touch.*

*Julius x*

Cecily had little time to ponder the subtext of the note before Doris bustled in with the tea tray.

"Good morning, Miss Cecily, and ain't it a beauty?" she said, pulling back the curtains. "You slept in late for a change, but there ain't no harm in that, 'specially as the cocktail party is tonight, and tomorrow you're on that airplane from Southampton. Rather you than me," Doris said with a shudder as she poured Cecily's tea. "I'd be saying me prayers, I would. You all right, miss? You don't look quite yourself."

Cecily, who had been gazing out of the window, turned to Doris and gave her a smile. "Maybe I'm a little nervous about the flight, that's all."

"Well, you've got to leave bright and early, so how about we pack your trunk this afternoon? Then you can have a little rest before the party. Want me to style your hair again for tonight?"

"Why not?" Cecily smiled, desperate for the maid to leave the room so her mind could fully dissect the note Julius had left her. "Thank you, Doris. I'll be down for breakfast shortly."

"All right, miss. Ring if you need me." Bobbing a curtsey, Doris left the room.

Cecily reread the note the minute the door had clicked shut. She couldn't work out the sentiments behind it—or why on earth Julius hadn't told her he was leaving for London this morning. Perhaps he had been in a rush—yes, that could account for the coolness that seemed to permeate his written words. It was such a contrast to what he had said to her last night.

*He said he hoped to get back in time to say good-bye in person,* she told herself as she sipped her tea. *Perhaps this was just a note in case he didn't.*

Feeling very alone—Julius had been her playmate for most of the time she'd been here—Cecily then went for a walk in the park to clear her head. She had a sinking feeling in her stomach as she went over and over the words in his letter. People often wrote far more formally than they spoke, but on the other hand, Julius was a poet . . .

That afternoon, Cecily paced the bedroom while Doris folded her clothes neatly and stowed them away in the trunk; the maid talked so much that all Cecily needed to do was to add the odd "yes," "no," or "really?" until Doris finally closed the lid.

"There, all done, miss. Now you can relax and enjoy the party."

"Do you know if Julius is attending tonight?"

"Don't ask me, miss, he's a law unto himself, that one." Doris rolled her eyes to exaggerate her point. "He often stays overnight in London. That's where his fiancée lives, see."

"His fiancée?"

"Yes, Veronica, she's called. Real society girl—I'm always seeing her in the pages of some magazine or another. Gawd knows how she'll cope when they're married and she 'as to live 'ere in the middle of nowhere."

Cecily sat down on the bed abruptly, wondering whether she would faint clean away with shock. "I see. I . . . How long have they been"—Cecily swallowed hard—"engaged?"

"Oh, just over six months, I'd reckon. The wedding's all set for the summer."

"Lady Woodhead's never mentioned it to me."

"No, well, maybe she wouldn't, because I know she don't approve. 'Er Ladyship thinks Veronica's 'fast' and not suitable to be the next lady of the 'ouse. Well, we're only young once, ain't we, miss, and I'm sure she'll calm down when she's married. Besides, I reckon she's got 'er work cut out, being his wife, if you know what I mean."

"I'm afraid I don't," Cecily replied hoarsely. "Please explain."

"I've more than an inkling he sees other women, and so have the rest of the maids here. I know for certain there was a girl in the village he was after; me and Ellen are sure we saw her running from the 'ouse one morning a couple of months back when we was up at dawn lighting the fires. Men, eh? Sometimes I think I'd be better off spending me life on me own rather than trusting 'em. Right, I'll leave you to have a little rest and I'll be up to run your bath at five."

Doris left, and Cecily sat where she was, hands folded in her lap, staring out of the window. She could still feel his presence inside her, the soreness at her core a physical reminder of how she had been duped. She had previously thought how very dumb some women were to believe the sweet nothings of a man when he wanted his way, yet now she had almost certainly joined their ranks.

Never once had he mentioned Veronica or his forthcoming marriage.

Unless, of course, he was planning to call it off tonight and that was why he'd gone to London . . .

"No, Cecily," she whispered, hanging her head and moving it rhythmically from side to side. "Don't be so naive, you know he's doing nothing of the sort."

A tear left one of her eyes, but she brushed it away harshly. She wouldn't allow any self-indulgence. This situation was of her own making. She had been so very stupid, despite all her supposed cleverness. So *stupid* that she deserved not one iota of sympathy.

After a while, she stood up, walked over to her trunk, turned the brass key to lock it, then sat down on the top.

All she knew for certain was that she would never trust any man ever again.

# 13

*Lake Naivasha, Kenya*

"Welcome to Mundui House, darling girl!" Kiki said as she jumped down from the passenger seat of the white Bugatti that had brought them on the three-hour journey from Nairobi and that was now covered in a thick layer of reddish brown dirt. Cecily had kept her eyes closed for most of the drive, partly due to the dust that had coiled up around the car like the smoke from Aladdin's lamp and made them itch, but mostly because she was so completely and utterly exhausted that it was too much effort to keep them open.

"Oh!" said Kiki, raising her arms up to the heavens. "I am so very glad to be home. Come on, I want to show you around. You have to see everything, and then we'll have champagne to celebrate you being here—or maybe we'll have it before the tour—and then I might call up some friends to come for cocktails later on so they can meet you."

"Kiki, I . . . well, after the journey, I can't walk another step," Cecily said as she managed to haul herself out of the car and blink in the bright sunlight, which felt as if it was boring into her pupils. She closed her eyes against the solar onslaught, staggered a little and caught hold of the car door.

"Of course. You poor thing." Kiki was by her side in seconds, steadying her. "Aleeki!" she called. "Come help Miss Cecily into the house, she's fit to drop. Put her in the Rose suite at the other end of the hallway to me—the one where Winston stayed."

"Yes, *memsahib*."

A strong arm complete with fingers of steel was placed around her shoulders.

Cecily opened her eyes, expecting to see a great tall Negro, but instead she found herself staring into the quizzical brown eyes of an elderly, birdlike man.

"You lean on me, *memsahib*."

And Cecily did so, horribly embarrassed that the man must be at least three times her age. All she noticed as he led her inside and up the staircase was the wonderful coolness after the stifling heat of the car journey.

"This your room, *memsahib*."

Cecily walked straight toward an easy chair placed in the corner and sat down before she fell where she stood. Aleeki proceeded to pull back the white sheet and eiderdown on the bed—why on earth was there an eiderdown when it was so darned hot?—then reached up and pulled the string on the ceiling fan, which whirred into life.

"You want shutters closed, *memsahib*?"

"Yes, please."

Cecily breathed a sigh of relief as the sun that had been streaming in through the large many-paned windows was banished from the room.

"I bring you tea? Coffee?"

"No, just water will do, thanks."

"Water there," he said, pointing to a flask by the bed. "More below." He indicated the cupboard underneath. "You want help with clothes? I can call the maid."

"No, thanks, I just need to sleep."

"Okay, *memsahib*. Press bell for help, understand?" He pointed to a button on the wall next to the bed.

"I will, thank you."

Finally, the door was shut. Cecily thought she might cry with relief as she walked the few paces to the large bed and sank onto the mattress. She should undress, of course—her clothes were filthy with dust from the journey—but . . .

Her eyes closed and, with the breeze from the fan gently cooling her hot cheeks, she slept.

"My darling, it's time to wake up. You'll never sleep tonight if you don't. Besides, I have some friends coming around to meet you in an hour."

Her godmother's voice floated through Cecily's dreams.

"I've had Muratha draw your bath, and here's a glass of champagne to perk you up."

"I . . . What time is it?" Cecily murmured. Her voice sounded croaky and she swallowed hard, due to a dry and painful throat.

"It's five in the evening, sweetie. You've slept solid for the past six hours."

*And I could sleep for another six weeks*, Cecily thought as she raised her head from the pillow and stared up blearily at her godmother.

Kiki was looking as fresh as a daisy, her dark hair drawn back into a chignon, her makeup perfect. The long green silk robe she was wearing set off her emerald-and-diamond earrings and matching necklace. In short, she looked utterly beautiful and not at all like she had just crossed continents by plane, boat, and motorcar. Whatever it was that her godmother kept in her sparkly purse, Cecily thought she could do with some of it right now.

"Drink up, darling; I promise you, it's the perfect pick-me-up." Kiki proffered the glass, but Cecily shook her head, wondering why her elders continually insisted she should drink liquor.

"I can't, really, Kiki."

"Well, then, I'll leave it by your bed just in case you change your mind. I've chosen something from your trunk to wear tonight and had Muratha iron it. It's hanging up in your closet just there." Kiki pointed to an oriental-style cupboard as she wafted across the room and began to pull open the shutters. "You just have to hurry to get ready, my darling, or you'll miss your first sunset at Mundui. However blue I'm feeling, it never fails to cheer me up."

Cecily watched her godmother pause for a few seconds as she gazed out of one of the windows. A small sigh escaped her lips before she turned and smiled at her goddaughter.

"I am so glad you came, honey. We're going to have such fun together and mend that broken heart of yours. See you downstairs no later than six." Kiki left the room, leaving her signature scent—which was as unusual and exotic as she was—lingering in her wake.

Now fully awake, Cecily was aware of how incredibly thirsty she was. Pulling the top off the flask, she gulped back some lukewarm water that had a slightly sour aftertaste. There was another knock at her door, and a young Negro girl with wiry hair that looked as though a razor had been taken to it, so close did it sit next to her scalp, entered the room. She was wearing a simple cotton dress, beige in color, that hung off her slender frame. She looked to be around thirteen or fourteen . . . *Little more than a child*, Cecily thought.

*"Bwana*, your bath drawn." The girl indicated the door behind her, then beckoned to Cecily.

Reluctantly, Cecily climbed out of bed and followed her next door into a room that held a large tub and a lavatory with an enormous wooden seat. It looked rather like a throne.

Muratha indicated the bar of soap, the washcloth, and the pile of cotton towels folded neatly beside the bath. "Okay, *bwana?*"

Cecily nodded and smiled at her. "Okay, thank you."

If Cecily had ever felt she'd "luxuriated" in a bath before, she now knew she hadn't known the true meaning of the word. The journey had begun in Southampton and had taken three—or was it maybe four?—days. They had made several stops to refuel the plane, the last of which had been somewhere called Kisumu by Lake Victoria, although Cecily had lost all sense of time and direction by that point. She had staggered off the small plane, and Kiki had ushered her into a tin hut beside the airfield, where they'd merely thrown some water over themselves before boarding another flight headed (eventually) for Nairobi. Her body had not seen a bar of soap the entire time. Nor had it seen sleep or, for that matter, peace of mind since she'd left England . . .

Having soaked herself thoroughly, Cecily surveyed the water around her, which looked distinctly murky and had a layer of grit floating around the edges of the tub. She longed to climb into another bath to clean off, but there was no time and who knew how many gallons human hands had had to carry in to fill *this*—there was no faucet that she could see.

Back in her room, Cecily comforted herself with the fact that Kiki's house was certainly not the mud hut she'd been expecting. With its large square-paned windows, high ceilings, and wooden floors, it reminded Cecily of the old colonial houses she'd seen in Boston. The bedroom itself was painted white, which set off the oriental furniture. A heavy wood-framed bed sat in the center, above which hung a strange contraption made up of what looked like netting. Cecily walked to one of the windows and for the first time looked out upon her surroundings.

She put a hand to her mouth as she gasped out loud. Kiki's words had not done this landscape justice. The sun hung low in the still blue sky, casting a stream of golden light onto strange-looking trees with flat tops. The lawns of Mundui House curved gracefully down to the shores of a vast lake, the water reflecting the tones of the sky as colorful birds glided through the trees. The colors seemed more vivid than anything she had ever seen before.

"Wow!" she said softly to herself, because the view was almost "biblical," as one of her friends at Vassar (who was studying theology, of course) had liked to say.

For the first time since she'd left England's shores, her pulse—which had raced madly whenever she'd remembered what she had done with Julius, not to mention when she'd been bounced through the skies over land and sea for the past few days—began to slow slightly. She opened the window and leaned her face into the blast of warmth, hearing the calls of unknown birds and animals and thinking that England *and* America seemed so very far away right now. This was another country—another world—and Cecily had the sudden and oddest feeling that it was a place that would shape the rest of her life.

"*Bwana?*" a timid voice came from behind her and pulled Cecily out of her reverie.

"I . . . yes, hello."

"No, no, no!" Muratha, the young maid, stepped toward her. "Never, never," she said as she shut the window firmly. "Not night," she added, wagging her finger. "*Mbu.*"

"Pardon me?"

The girl flapped her fingers and made a small buzzing sound, then indicated the swathe of netting above the bed.

"Oh! You mean mosquitoes?"

"Yes, yes, *bwana*. Very bad." Muratha slid her finger across her throat and added an agonized expression, then checked the window again as if mosquitoes could open locks. "No at night. Understand?"

"I do, yes." Cecily nodded exaggeratedly, thinking of the quinine that apparently warded off malaria, which her mother had insisted on adding to the medical box their family doctor had prescribed to bring with her.

She watched as the girl went to the closet and took out her dress for tonight.

"Help you?"

"No, thank you."

"*Hakuna matata, bwana*," Muratha answered and ducked out of the room.

"Darrrling!" Kiki greeted Cecily on the terrace as she was escorted out by Aleeki. "Just in time." Kiki took her arm and led her across the terrace, then through the strange flat-topped trees that grew outward rather than upward to the water's edge. "I'm so glad no one else has arrived and we can share your first sunset alone. Isn't it just spectacular?"

"Yes," Cecily breathed, watching the sun set the sky alight with bursts of oranges and reds as it retreated after a long day. A high-pitched chorus of cicadas struck up and filled the warm air with their vibrations. The cacophony made Cecily shiver, goose bumps rising on her skin despite the heat. As the sun finally plummeted beneath the horizon, the noise intensified in the now purple dusk.

"Don't be frightened, honey, it's only all the insects, birds, and animals saying good night to each other. Or at least that's what I like to think, until we hear the growl of a lion on the terrace at three in the morning!" She tittered. "I'm only teasing you, or at least, it's only ever happened once before. And the good news is, no one got eaten. When you're recovered from the journey, we'll take you out into the bush on a safari."

A sudden ripple in the still waters of the lake caught Cecily's eye.

"Oh, that's just a hippopotamus going for his nightly swim," Kiki said with a shrug, lighting one of her endless cigarettes in its long ivory holder. "They're so very ugly and enormous, and I'm amazed they don't sink, but they're dears, really. As long as we don't disturb them, they don't disturb us." She blew the smoke out of her nose slowly. "That's the key to life in Africa: we have to respect what was here first. Both the people and the animals."

A mosquito suddenly buzzed in Cecily's ear, and she brushed it away, wondering whether she should respect it.

"And don't worry about those," said Kiki, catching her movement. "You'll inevitably get bitten—hopefully you won't die of malaria—and then you'll be a local and immune. And aloe vera works great on the bites. Champagne?" Kiki asked her as they walked back up to the terrace, where a number of Kiki's staff—all dressed in variations of beige cotton—were setting up the bar on a table. Cecily recognized Aleeki, who had helped her earlier. His clothes set him apart from the other servants. As well as a gray waistcoat, he wore a long piece of checked fabric fastened at the waist that looked more like a skirt than pants. A snug patterned cap that resembled a fez sat on his grizzled head. He regarded Cecily with his dark serious eyes and gestured to the bar.

"Or maybe a martini?" suggested Kiki. "Aleeki makes an excellent one."

"I don't think I should be drinking liquor tonight, Kiki. I'm so tired still from the journey, and—"

"Two martinis, please, Aleeki," Kiki ordered, then tucked Cecily's arm into hers. "I promise you, honey, I've been traveling between continents for many years, and the best thing you can do is to start as you mean to go on. Sit," she said as they stood in front of a number of café-style tables that had been set up on the terrace.

"You mean we should get drunk all the time?"

"I guess I'd be dishonest if I didn't say that everyone out here drinks more than they should, but it numbs the pain and makes everything just a little more pleasant. I mean, who wants to live until they're eighty, anyway? Everyone I've known who was any fun has died already!"

Kiki gave a short, hoarse laugh as Aleeki brought over the martinis. Kiki picked hers up immediately, and Cecily—not wanting to be rude—did the same.

"Cheers, sweetie, and welcome to Kenya."

They clinked glasses, and as Kiki drained hers, Cecily took a delicate sip and nearly choked on the strength of the liquor.

"Now," Kiki said, indicating to Aleeki that she needed another by tapping her glass, which was swiftly removed for a refill, "tonight you'll meet some of the characters who live around these parts. And rest assured, they're *all* characters. I suppose one has to be if one is going to travel across the world and settle in a country like this. Life here, in every way, is pretty goddamn wild. Or at least it used to be. Aleeki, darling, wind up the gramophone, why don't you? We need some music."

"Yes, *memsahib*," he said, furnishing Kiki with a further martini.

Cecily studied the woman sitting next to her, her perfect profile set against the dusky amber sky, and decided that Kiki was the most confusing human she had ever met: on the journey across to Africa, Kiki had either been euphoric—dancing down the narrow space between the aircraft seats, singing Cole Porter songs at the top of her voice as the plane bumped and dived through the clouds—or she had been passed out cold, sleeping the sleep of the dead. When they'd boarded the plane that would fly them on the final leg of their journey, she had noticed Kiki staring down below at the landscape.

"It's so beautiful, yet so brutal," her godmother had whispered, almost to herself, with tears in her eyes. Even though Cecily knew how many losses Kiki had suffered in the past few years, Kiki rarely spoke about them directly, only collectively. And although they had spent four days crammed together in a flying tin can, Cecily felt she knew no more about this woman than when they'd left Southampton. Despite her great beauty and what her mother called Kiki's "extraordinary" wealth, never mind her supreme social confidence, which Cecily could only dream of emulating, she sensed a vulnerability lying below the surface.

No trace of it was in evidence as Kiki's first guests arrived, led onto the terrace by Aleeki.

"My dears, I'm back!" Kiki stood up and went to embrace the couple in a huge hug. "You must tell me everything that's happened since I left—knowing the Valley, it'll be a lot, and after almost dying of pneumonia in New York, I can't tell you how swell it is to be home. Now come and say hello to my gorgeous goddaughter. Cecily, honey, meet Idina, one of my best friends in the whole wide world."

Cecily greeted the woman, who was wearing a long, gauzy dress that her mother would no doubt tell her was made of the finest chiffon. Idina smelled of expensive perfume, her short hair was waved neatly in a bob, and her eyebrows were perfectly arched.

"And who might this be?" Kiki asked, smiling at the tall gentleman next to Idina.

"Why, it's Lynx, of course!" said Idina in a very British accent. "You must remember, I wrote to you about him. We're engaged to be married."

"Hello, Cecily." Lynx gave a bow, then took her hand and kissed it. Cecily saw features that were perfectly arranged in his face, and the eyes that appraised her were sharp and intelligent, like those of the animal he was named after.

"What a delight to meet you, my dear," said Idina. "I hope Kiki has filled you in on every bit of scandal I've caused since I arrived in Kenya."

"Actually, she's been very discreet."

"That's not like her at all. Anyway, I'm on the straight and narrow now, aren't I, Lynx?"

"I bally well hope so, my dear," he replied as Aleeki arrived with a tray of martinis and champagne. "Although from what Idina has been telling me, I rather feel I've missed out on all the fun."

"It's not what it used to be around here, but we do our best to live up to the scandalous reputation we've garnered over the years," said Idina, giving Kiki a wink.

Content to listen rather than participate and still so tired, Cecily made an effort to sit up very straight in her chair so that she wouldn't doze off. Idina and Kiki continued to gossip about their mutual friends, while Lynx sat patiently by his fiancée's side.

Cecily watched as Aleeki placed a golden samovar on the table. Kiki removed the lid to reveal a small heap of white powder and a number of slim paper straws. Still chatting to Idina, Kiki slid the samovar so it sat in front of her, then picked up a straw and separated a small amount of powder from the rest. She stuck the straw up her nose, bent over, and sniffed hard. Removing the straw from her nose, she wiped away any remaining dust, then passed the samovar to Idina, who did the same.

"Want some, honey? It'll sure help to keep you awake a little longer tonight," Kiki said.

"I, er . . . no thanks." Since Cecily had no clue as to what the powder actually was and why one would put it up one's nose rather than into one's mouth, she decided she wasn't about to take any chances.

"Alice, my darling!" Kiki stood up once more to greet another woman who had arrived on the terrace, dressed in a midnight blue silk gown that skimmed her thin frame. She had wide brown eyes and short dark hair that framed her elegant jaw. "It's our very own wicked Madonna!" Kiki greeted the new arrival with a warm hug. "Thank you for not coming in your farm clothes, my dear. And look who you dragged with you!"

"Actually," said Alice, "I think he rather dragged me."

Cecily recognized the man immediately, even though he was looking rather different from how he had in New York—Captain Tarquin Price was fully attired in military dress, despite the heat of the evening.

"Sorry, I didn't have time to change—I came straight from Nairobi, and it was rather a detour to Alice's farm to collect her."

"I think you look very dapper, Tarquin, darling," said Kiki as she guided the two of them across to the table. "And look who *I* managed to drag all the way from Manhattan," she said, indicating Cecily.

"Good grief! Miss Huntley-Morgan, we meet again. Glad you could make it," Tarquin said with considerable understatement as Cecily stood up to be politely kissed on both cheeks. He took a glass of champagne and sat down next to her. "How was the journey?"

"Long," Cecily said as she took a sip of her martini, "and dusty."

"But you're glad you came? It is rather an extraordinary place your god-mother has here, isn't it?"

"I really couldn't say yet, because I've slept most of the day. But the sunset was just incredible, and the lake is simply marvelous. Can one swim in it?"

"As long as one is aware of the hippos, yes. And the crocodiles, of course."

"Crocodiles?"

"Only teasing, Cecily, of course you can swim in it. The water is wonder-fully cooling. I've taken a few morning dips in it myself. Anyway, welcome to Kenya. I have to admit that I'm rather surprised you came. It takes a brave heart—especially when it's a female one—to make the trip."

"I sure hope I settle here, because I really don't fancy making the journey back anytime soon."

"Give yourself some time to get used to it; it's so different to New York—a different planet, one might say. But now you're here, you must em-brace it. Cast off the Manhattan Cecily, with all her inbuilt prejudices, and enjoy every second of your time here."

"I intend to if I can stop feeling so sleepy." Cecily stifled another yawn. "Kiki said I should take some of that," she said, pointing to the samovar. "She said it would help keep me awake, but the truth is, I have no idea what it is."

"That, my dear Cecily"—Tarquin leaned toward her—"is a highly addic-tive and illegal substance called cocaine."

"Cocaine! Holy moly! I mean to say, I've heard of it, of course, but never seen it. Surely if it's illegal, the cops could come and arrest Kiki?"

"My dear girl, we *are* the 'cops' here." Tarquin chuckled. "As you will learn, anything goes in Happy Valley," he said as they both watched Kiki take another snort from the samovar.

"Have you ever tried it yourself?" she asked him.

"A gentleman is never meant to tell a lie, and I would be lying if I said no. So yes, I have on occasion, and it does give one the most amazing feeling. But I wouldn't recommend it for a young lady like yourself. As I'm sure you know, your godmother has had the most terribly difficult few years. What-ever gets you through the night, as they say. Neither you nor I are in a posi-tion to judge."

"No, of course not. I mean, I wouldn't like her to get sick on it or anything, though."

"I know what you mean, Cecily, but as I said, the normal rules do not apply to either Kiki or Kenya, and that is the best piece of advice I can give you."

Tarquin left her a few minutes later, probably to talk to someone far more interesting. Cecily was content, in between being introduced to various middle-aged friends of Kiki's, to sit and watch the gathering crowd. Aleeki and his band of servants buzzed around, keeping the guests' glasses topped up and handing around trays of canapés. Realizing she hadn't eaten anything all day, Cecily tentatively took a deviled egg and found to her surprise on biting into it that it tasted just like the ones back home. Somehow she'd expected to be eating antelope roasted over a fire rather than American-style delicacies. After she had taken two of everything that came her way, Aleeki bent down to whisper in her ear.

"I will make *memsahib* a sandwich if she would prefer? And there is soup in the kitchen."

"Oh, no, these canapés are just divine," she replied, touched that he had noticed her obvious appetite.

"All alone and forgotten about by your godmother already, my dear?"

Alice, the lady in the blue silk dress who'd arrived with Tarquin, sat down next to her. "Don't take it personally, she'll have forgotten her own name by the end of tonight," she drawled. "I think I met your mother once in New York. She lives in that sweet house surrounded by apartment blocks on Fifth Avenue, doesn't she?"

"Yes, she . . . we do," Cecily said, looking into Alice's eyes, which were very pretty but had a rather glazed appearance. "I . . . Do you live close to here?" she added, struggling to find conversation.

"I suppose that depends on how you define 'close,' doesn't it? It isn't so far away, not as the crow flies, at least. But the problem is, we're not crows, are we? Just humans, damned humans with arms and legs but no wings. You must come over to my farm someday. Meet all my animals."

"What kind of animals do you have?"

"Oh, all sorts, really; I had a pet lion cub for years, but sadly, I had to give him away when he got too large."

"A lion?"

"Yes. You don't like guns, do you?"

"I can't say, because I've never held one or used one."

"Good girl, then don't. Animals have hearts and minds too, y'know. They feel in just the same way as we do."

They both watched as the woman called Idina swept past them with Lynx, the man she had arrived with. The couple walked toward the lake, then disappeared into the darkness beyond.

Alice sighed. "Y'know, Idina was once married to the love of my life. We shared him, a long time ago . . ."

"Oh—" Cecily nearly choked on her drink. "Is he here tonight?"

"No, although he used to live just around the corner from here at the Djinn Palace, on the lake. Don't you let Joss Erroll seduce you, will you, my dear? It would be nice to know that one virgin managed to keep her virtue safe from him."

Cecily blushed heavily at Alice's words, not because they particularly shocked her—she was learning fast that the wild plains of Africa had nothing on the wildness of their human inhabitants—but because it reminded her of the fact that she no longer had a "virtue" to lose.

"Does America think war will come?" Alice asked as she glanced around dreamily at the other guests.

"I think it's just as much in the dark as everyone else," Cecily said, trying to keep up with the conversation, which seemed to bounce erratically from one subject to the next. Yet there was something about Alice that she liked, however crazy she seemed.

"I hope not, or it will be the end of everything we've known here. Joss will be involved in it, of course. And I just couldn't bear for him to die, y'know?" Alice said as she stood up. "I'm pleased to meet you, honey. Come over and see me soon."

Cecily watched her float off into the crowd on the terrace. A few of the guests had started to dance to the tinny gramophone music, and one woman was openly kissing her dance partner as his hands slid down the back of her dress.

"Time for bed," she said with a sigh and stood up. She heard a peal of laughter from down by the lake, turned, and saw the backs of two completely naked bodies running into the water. With another sigh, she headed for the sanctuary of her bedroom.

Cecily was woken by a dawn cacophony of tweets, calls, and caws of un-known birds and animals. She lay there desperate to return to sleep. She had been awake for hours last night, disturbed by the hilarity of the guests and the gramophone, which had played beneath her bedroom window until at least four in the morning. Even after that, there had been stifled screams and giggles from inside the house. If it was possible to feel exhausted when one had just woken up, Cecily did. However, as she forced her eyelids to close, the sunrise chorus only increased in volume.

"Darn it!" she swore, realizing that counting imaginary sheep—or lions—was not going to help, so she rose from the bed, taking a few seconds to extricate herself from the mosquito net, then walked over to one of the windows and pulled back the shutters.

"Oh, my goodness!" she breathed, because there, standing on the grass that led down to the lake, was a giraffe nibbling the leaves of one of the flat-topped trees.

Despite the fatigue and the anxiety that was still making her tummy clench after everything she'd witnessed last night, Cecily couldn't help but smile. She searched the room for the camera Papa had given her as a parting gift but had no idea where Muratha had stowed it after emptying her trunk. By the time she did find it, the giraffe had wandered out of sight. Still, she thought, even without the giraffe, the view was enough to make grown men weep.

It was not even 7:00 a.m., and the sky was already glowing turquoise, casting a shimmering light on the lake. Cecily walked to her closet to search for one of the cotton dresses Kiki had suggested she bring from New York. After dressing hurriedly, then giving her hair—which had become even more unruly in the heat—a cursory brush, she opened the door, walked along the silent hallway, and tiptoed downstairs.

"Good morning, *memsahib*."

Cecily's heart gave a small start as she turned around to find that Aleeki had appeared behind her.

"Did you sleep well?"

"Why, yes, I did, thank you."

"Would you like some breakfast?"

"That's most kind, but I was going to take a stroll down to the lake first."

"Then I shall set breakfast for you on the veranda, ready for when you are back. Tea or coffee, *memsahib*?"

"Oh, coffee, please. Thank you, Aleeki."

She started to walk toward the door, but Aleeki overtook her swiftly to open it for her, giving her a small bow as she walked through it. There was no sign on the terrace of last night's festivities; all traces had obviously been cleared away by the servants. As Cecily donned her sunglasses to shield her fragile eyes from a sun that felt as though it had moved miles closer overnight, she marveled at Kiki's "houseboy," as she'd heard her godmother call him, looking fresh as the proverbial daisy after what must have been a night of even less sleep than she'd had. At the water's edge, Cecily glanced to her left and saw a group of hippos sunning themselves on the bank a few hundred yards along.

"This is just surreal," she whispered to herself. "Am I really here?"

She went to the bench positioned thoughtfully at the edge of the lake and noticed a white brassiere hanging over the back of it. She thought of Idina and her fiancé swimming naked last night and wondered with a chuckle whether she should alert Aleeki to the brassiere's presence. He was so inscrutable that she could imagine him not batting an eyelid, even if she handed it to him over the breakfast table.

"Maybe it was just a homecoming party that got out of hand," Cecily said aloud to a bird with a coat of metallic blue and green feathers sitting in a tree right on the water's edge. She was pretty certain it was a kingfisher. This was confirmed as the bird suddenly plunged into the water beneath the overhanging branch and plucked a fish from it a few seconds later.

Cecily sat there for a while, feeling her shoulders relax as she watched the natural world go about its day around her. However the humans—still asleep in the house behind her—wished to behave, this landscape and what it contained had a heartbeat of its own, and that was what she must try to tap into.

Eventually the sun forced her to head for the cover of the shady veranda on one side of the house—she really must remember to wear a hat, even this early in the morning, otherwise her freckles would speckle her face like a leopard's coat. She walked through the gardens that bordered the terrace, which were full of sweet-smelling flowers and exotic-looking plants that she couldn't name. The sun had already warmed the grass under her feet, and the air hummed with insects dipping their heads into the nectar-rich blooms.

"All is ready for you, *memsahib*." Aleeki pulled a chair out for her as she arrived on the veranda. The table was set for breakfast, with all sorts of goodies sitting in baskets or on silver platters.

"Thank you," Cecily said, feeling rather dizzy from the sun.

"Here." Aleeki proffered her a glass of water and a fan. "Most helpful in the heat of the day. Shall I pour your coffee?"

"Yes, please," Cecily said as she drained the cool glass of water and began to fan herself rapidly. "Goodness, it's hot today."

"It is hot here every day, *memsahib*, but you will become used to it." With a click of his fingers, a servant arrived carrying a gigantic version of her own fan. He began wafting it, and Cecily's dizziness began to abate.

"*Memsahib* must wear a hat, it is very important," said Aleeki. "Milk in your coffee?"

"I'll take it black, thank you. And please tell him he can stop fanning me now. What time does my godmother usually rise for breakfast?"

"Oh, very rarely before midday. There is fruit, cereal, and fresh bread with homemade jam and honey. We can toast the bread for you if you wish, but we also have eggs. Sunny-side up is your preference?"

"I think I'm good for now, thank you." Cecily indicated the feast spread out on the table.

Aleeki gave his customary bow, then withdrew to the side of the veranda. As she sipped her coffee, she felt as if she were being served breakfast in a tropical version of the Waldorf-Astoria. The food so far had been tastier than anything their family's chef provided in Manhattan. *And* the staff were more attentive.

As Aleeki was pouring her a second cup of coffee and she was eating a slice of the gorgeous freshly baked bread smothered in honey, she turned to him.

"How long have you worked for my godmother?"

"Oh, ever since she arrived here and built this house. Many years, *memsahib*."

"I'd love to see what's beyond the trees," she said, indicating the boundary that had been planted around the gardens and house. "What's there?"

"On one side there is a cattle farm, and on the other the *memsahib* keep her horses. If you wish to ride after breakfast, I can arrange a good horse for you."

A sudden image jumped into Cecily's head of riding out with Julius across the frozen English parkland, then lighting a makeshift fire in the folly and warming up together in front of it.

"Maybe another time, Aleeki. I'm still a little tired today."

"Of course, *memsahib*. You wish for eggs now?"

"No, thanks," she murmured, the memory of Julius washing the beauty and calm of her first morning in Kenya clean away.

It was two in the afternoon before Cecily glimpsed her godmother strolling onto the veranda. She'd spent the past few hours alone in her room, avoiding the intense noon sun and doing her best to take photographs of the view from the vantage point of her window. She would have to find somewhere to get them developed so she could send them home to her family. She'd written them a long letter on the thick vellum paper Aleeki had provided for her, documenting (most) of her adventures so far. The process had left her tearful on occasion; home had never felt so far away as it did right now.

"Cecily, darling! Are you sleeping?" called a loud voice from beneath the window.

*Well, if I was, I'd certainly be awake now.*

She poked her head outside. "No, I was writing home to my parents."

"Then come down at once!"

"Of course." With a sigh, Cecily grabbed the letter and headed downstairs.

"Champagne?" said Kiki as Cecily approached the table on the veranda. Her godmother sat alone, a bottle in an ice bucket and a pack of Lucky Strikes apparently her only sustenance.

"No, thank you, I'm still full from lunch."

"Please accept my apologies, honey," Kiki sighed, taking a large slug of champagne and a draw on her cigarette holder. "The party went on late last night."

Cecily didn't think Kiki looked sorry at all.

"So what did you think of my friends? I hope they were nice to you. I certainly told them to be."

"Oh, they were all very kind, thank you."

"Well, you were a hit with Alice. She's asked us over to tea at Wanjohi Farm tomorrow. Did you like her?"

"Why, yes, she was certainly interesting—"

"Oh, she's that, all right. You know that a few years ago, Alice was on trial for shooting her lover in Paris at a railway station?"

"Oh, my! That was her?" Cecily remembered her mother's mention of the scandal.

"The very one. Luckily she shot him in Paris, the city that understands love, and didn't go to jail for attempted murder. She is seriously crazy, and I just adore her."

"She did tell me that she once had a pet lion cub."

"Dear little Samson, yes . . . She only let him go when he was eating two zebras a week." Kiki took another mouthful of champagne. "So Aleeki has been looking after you?"

"Oh, yes, he's marvelous," Cecily agreed. "I was wondering whether it was possible to mail this letter to my parents?"

"That's no problem at all. Give it to Aleeki, and he'll see to it for you."

"Okay. Where is the nearest town to here?"

"Depends what you want to do or buy. Gilgil is the nearest, but it's a mighty dump with a railroad that runs right through it. Then there's Nairobi, of course, where we landed yesterday, and Nyeri, which is some distance from here, on the other side of the Aberdare Mountains, but it's popular with the Wanjohi Valley lot."

"Wanjohi Valley?"

"Where most of the crowd who were here last night live, including Alice. You'll see it tomorrow when we drive up for tea with her. Now, I'm not feeling so great today—like you, I'm probably suffering from the effects of our journey on top of the bronchitis. Aleeki can show you the library if you need a book to read, and we'll meet for dinner at eight tonight, okay?"

"Okay."

As if by magic, for there was no physical gesture Cecily could discern, Aleeki appeared by his mistress's side. Kiki stood up, took his arm, and walked back into the house.

As Cecily dressed for dinner that night, she thought about all the things she knew—or had overheard—about her godmother: that she was an heiress and, more important, related to both the Vanderbilts and the Whitney family. She'd divorced her first husband, then married Jerome Preston—Cecily remembered meeting him as a young girl and being struck by his handsome looks and jovial nature. Her whole family had been shocked by his sudden and unexpected death five years ago. Then, her mother had told her, Kiki's brother-in-law had died a couple of years ago, and only recently her beloved cousin William had suffered paralysis due to an automobile accident.

Now here was Kiki lying in her bed a few yards away, alone.

"And so sad." Cecily sighed, the thought striking her out of the blue. "She is so sad."

# 14

I am afraid my mistress is feeling unwell again today," Aleeki announced as Cecily appeared on the terrace at noon the following day, ready to drive to tea at Alice's farm.

"Oh, dear, it's nothing serious, is it?"

"No, she will be quite well by tonight, I am sure, *memsahib*. But she says you are to go alone. And take this as an apology."

Aleeki was holding two wicker baskets, one full of bottles of champagne and the other covered by a linen cloth, which Cecily could only presume contained food of some kind.

She followed Aleeki around to the back of the house, and he opened the rear door of the Bugatti, which had been cleaned and polished so thoroughly that the sun glared off its white roof. The interior was burning hot, and Cecily perched close to the open window, fanning herself violently on the cream leather seat.

"This is Makena, *memsahib*. He is driver who will take you to Wanjohi Farm."

The man, dressed in spotless white, bowed to her. She vaguely remembered him from their journey here.

"I will see you later for dinner, Miss Cecily," said Aleeki as he closed the door and Makena started the engine.

The drive along the lake was a pleasant one, but it was only as they passed through a small settlement, which Cecily realized must be Gilgil as she saw the train line running right through the center of it, that it began to become interesting. She could feel the car's powerful engine straining to bump upward over the rough rutted road (which would be considered no more than a narrow pathway in America), and she smiled as she thought how typical it was of Kiki to have a stylish but fundamentally unsuitable car for the Kenyan terrain. In the distance, the scenery became increasingly lush and verdant, and she could see a range of mountains, their peaks covered in misty cloud. She only wished she could ask Makena what they were called, but after a couple of attempts to make conversation, she realized his English was limited to a few stock phrases. She noticed the temperature was growing considerably cooler, with a brisk wind that blew her hair about her face. The scents here were different from those at Mundui House; she could smell the metallic charge of future rain in the air and wood smoke emanating from the various farms they passed.

"Goodness!" she said as she saw houses that would not have been out of place in the English villages she had passed through on the way to the airfield in Southampton. Ditto the impeccably kept gardens, which were blooming with roses, trumpet lilies, and jasmine, filling the air with their rich, sweet fragrance.

Two hours after they had left, the Bugatti pulled into the drive of a U-shaped single-story house, featuring oversized roofs similar to the others she had noticed on her way. She presumed it must be to keep the sun out of the rooms, but as she stepped out of the car, she gave a small shiver in the biting wind. Dark green bushes bordered the lawn, and she saw an antelope was nibbling the grass; it glanced up at her with its large brown eyes, then calmly returned to its grazing.

"Hello, darling, you made it!"

Cecily turned to see Alice approaching her, wearing an oversized cotton shirt and a pair of khaki culottes.

"Oh, yes, hi, I mean, hello, Alice. Forgive me, I was transfixed by the view. It's . . . spectacular," said Cecily as she gazed down across the verdant valley, at the bottom of which ran a river.

"It is quite extraordinary, isn't it? When one sees it every day, one tends to ignore it."

"Last time I was in Europe with my parents, we traveled from London up to the Scottish Highlands for a few days. It reminds me a little of there," Cecily said as she realized that her hostess had a strange-looking creature nestled contentedly on her neck. It was small and furry, with a long pointed nose and round ears, and reminded Cecily of a misshapen kitten.

"What is that?" she asked Alice as she followed her toward the house, trailing a number of dogs in her wake.

"It's a mongoose, only a few days old. I found it abandoned under a bush in the garden. I haven't named it, of course, because if I do, I'll just have to adopt it; then I'll become fond of it and it'll have to sleep with me every night. Which would make the dogs jealous, and . . . Maybe you would like it?"

Alice grabbed the mongoose from her shoulder and placed it wriggling into Cecily's hands. "They make very good pets and are awfully good at killing vermin."

"I've never had a pet, Alice, and as I'm only staying for a short time, it wouldn't be right to take it on."

"Pity. Then I'll just have to release it back into the wild, and it'll surely get eaten. They're great protectors, because they're impervious to snake venom. I found a cobra in my bedroom once, and dear little Bertie, whom I'd had for years, jumped off the bed and killed it for me. Keep him for a bit, and see how you bond before deciding," she said as she led Cecily onto a wide terrace where a number of people were already sitting drinking tea at a long table.

"I . . . okay," said Cecily, trying to control the creature, which seemed to be desperate to climb over her shoulder and out of her grasp. "I forgot to say that my godmother couldn't make it today. She sends her apologies. She was feeling unwell."

"Aleeki called me earlier," Alice said breezily. "All the more champagne for us, eh? Let's break it open," she announced to the assembled group as she indicated the baskets Makena was carrying behind them. "This is—" She gestured airily toward Cecily.

"Cecily Huntley-Morgan."

As Cecily struggled to keep hold of the mongoose and greet the assembled party, she was at least relieved to see a couple of young faces sitting at the table.

"Give me that pesky creature." Alice plucked it from her and tucked it into her shoulder, where it curled up contentedly and closed its tiny pink eyes. "Go sit over there by Katherine."

Cecily sat down, feeling slightly breathless and extremely disheveled. She was also desperate to ask where the bathroom was after her long journey but felt too shy to do so.

"Hello there, I'm Katherine Stewart," said the young woman next to her, with looks that her mother would have called "homely." She was on the plump side, but no less attractive for it in Cecily's opinion, with her striking Titian-colored hair curled prettily around a pale-skinned face and a pair of bright eyes as blue as the sapphire sky above them.

"And I'm Cecily Huntley-Morgan. Pleased to make your acquaintance."

"Have you just arrived?" Katherine asked her in a soft British accent.

"Not just, no—I arrived a couple of days ago by air. It sure was a long journey, and I'm still suffering from it."

"Tea or champagne?" Katherine asked her with a smile at her, as Alice's equivalent of Aleeki offered the choice of both. Unlike the ever-pristine Aleeki, the man wore a crumpled white robe sporting several obvious stains and a battered red fez.

"Most definitely tea, thank you."

"Good choice. Even though I was originally brought up in the Valley, I can still hardly believe the way everyone drinks in the afternoon. And the morning," Katherine said, lowering her voice.

Cecily didn't know the woman well enough to comment, but she gave Katherine a quiet nod. "Tea is certainly enough for me at this time of the day."

"So, Cecily, where are you staying?"

"With my godmother, who has a house by Lake Naivasha. It's beautiful but far hotter than here."

"Well, we're another thousand feet above sea level, and we often have to light a fire in the evening. Perhaps that's why so many of the original settlers chose this area—its climate reminded them of England and home."

"I said to Alice that it reminded me of the Scottish Highlands, especially with those purple mountains in the background."

"Gosh, my father is Scottish, and I went to boarding school just outside a place called Aberdeen"—Katherine smiled—"which is where the Highlands begin."

"So you're just back here visiting family?" Cecily took a bite of a cucumber sandwich from the silver stand she was offered by the houseboy.

"Actually, I'm back for good. My father originally came over as a missionary with my mother before I was born; sadly, my mother died a few years back, but Daddy is still very much alive and my fiancé, Bobby Sinclair, lives here. After we're married, I'll move to Bobby's parents' farm—they moved back to Blighty some years ago—and together we intend to build the cattle herd back up, as well as renovate their archaic house." Katherine smiled fondly across the table at a stout man with a sun-weathered face and dark hair that had the odd thread of gray running through it.

"How did you meet?"

"I knew Bobby as a child when I lived out here. He's ten years older than me, but I always adored him from afar. You could never get rid of me when I was home from school for the holidays, could you, darling?" she called to him.

"Aye, and isn't that the truth." Bobby smiled back at his fiancée. "She was like a wee limpet, she was, always calling round to see if I'd take her swimming in the river. Who'da thought we'd end up getting wed one day?"

The affection between the two of them was obvious, and the fact they had known each other since childhood and were to marry soon brought back an image of Jack. Cecily forced herself to remember the vow she had made to herself as she'd looked down at the plains of Africa while the aircraft carried her farther away from the two men who had destroyed her faith in romance; love, with all the joy and pain it could hold, was something she was in no hurry to experience again.

"How long are you here for?" she heard Katherine asking her.

"Oh, I . . . I'm not sure. A few weeks, I should think."

"Well, if you're still in the country, you must come to our wedding. We're desperate for anyone under the age of fifty, aren't we, Bobby?"

"Oh, aye, and I hope you're including me in that category, despite my gray hairs."

"I'd be delighted to come if I'm able, thank you." Cecily lowered her voice. "Do you by any chance know where the, uh—"

"Oh, the lavatory, you mean? Of course I do. Come on, I'll take you."

Cecily followed Katherine toward the house, hearing laughter from the table as Kiki's champagne began to flow. The interior was beautifully cool, if chaotic, what with dogs running between their legs and books and papers strewn on top of what looked like some fine but dusty antique furniture.

Once she'd relieved herself and made an effort to tidy herself up, Cecily wandered along the hallway and outside into the courtyard. She could hear raised voices coming from a building to the side of the main house and walked toward it to find it was a kitchen. Katherine was speaking very firmly (and fluently) in a foreign language to a slovenly-looking Negro woman, who, from the fact she was wearing an apron, was obviously a cook or a maid. Even though Cecily couldn't understand a word of what was going on, it was clear that they were disagreeing about something. The woman was gesticulating, but Katherine seemed as though she was having none of it.

Katherine saw her standing there, said her last few words to the woman, then walked toward Cecily.

Lucinda Riley

"By golly, did you see the state of that kitchen? It's disgusting! No wonder poor Alice has had pains in her stomach."

"She's sick?"

"Yes, and has been for some time. She saw Dr. Boyle last week—only because I marched her there myself. He's sending her to the hospital in Nairobi for further tests. But of course, while the cat's away and all that—"

"Excuse me?"

"What I mean is, Alice hasn't had her eye on the domestic ball for some time, and with her old housekeeper, Noel, abandoning ship a few weeks ago, the servants are simply not doing what they should. No matter." Katherine smiled at Cecily as they walked back toward the terrace. "Alice has asked me to stay here while she's in Nairobi, so I'll soon be knocking them into shape, that's for sure."

"Have you known Alice a long time?"

"Since I was tiny, yes. My mother was a friend of hers, which, now that I look back on it, was actually odd, given the fact they were so frightfully different."

"In what way?"

"Well, Alice was a rich heiress and certainly played her part in the hedonistic lifestyle of the Valley, and my mother was a plain-speaking woman, married to a penniless Scottish missionary. I think it was their love of animals that bonded them—when Alice and her first husband were traveling abroad, my mother would come here with me to earn a little extra as a housekeeper and look after the menagerie. Well, now," Katherine said as they reached the table and sat down, "perhaps you could come and visit me here when Alice is in hospital?"

"I'd love to," Cecily said as they sat back down at the table. She was liking Katherine more and more.

"Look, little Minnie has taken a shine to you," Alice called to her as a small dachshund jumped up onto Cecily's knee. "Animals always know who the good people are," she remarked as she poured herself more champagne. Once again, Cecily refused the offer of a glass of "bubbles," as Alice called it, and turned her attention to the clouds that were settling more heavily on the tops of the mountain range behind the farm.

"Whoops!" Katherine stood up as the sapphire sky seemed to darken almost instantaneously and large drops of rain began to fall. "Under the veranda, everyone!" she said as she gathered up as much as she could from the table into one of the baskets. Like a well-oiled machine, the guests moved as one to sit at another table under the overhanging roof as the rain gathered force and began to pelt down around them.

"It's only a short shower," said Katherine. "You wait until the *real* rainy season arrives in April and the road below us here becomes a sea of red mud that washes down from the hills."

"That sounds dramatic," said Cecily, "but I'm not sure I'll still be here by then."

"Talking of leaving, lassie, we'd better be on our way," said Bobby, coming to put a protective arm around Katherine's shoulders. He was a physical beast of a man and towered over his wife-to-be.

"Do you live close by?" Cecily asked them.

"Aye, it's only ten miles or so west from here as the crow flies, but on the road it can take a long time. Do you ride, Cecily?" Bobby asked.

"Yes, I do." Cecily wondered why horses, which up until recently had made up only a small portion of her past, were suddenly featuring so heavily in her present.

"It's often the best way to get around these parts, to be honest. That's how we're getting home, anyway," said Bobby.

"It's been truly lovely to meet you, Cecily," said Katherine with a warm smile. "I'll be in touch about you coming over to keep me company while Alice is in hospital. You must stay overnight next time—it's quite a journey from here back to Naivasha."

Cecily watched Bobby and Katherine mount their horses and trot off down the drive.

An hour later the rain had stopped and the guests had ventured outside once more. Cecily hoped that it wouldn't be considered rude to take her leave.

"I'm afraid I should return home now," she said as she approached her hostess at the head of the table, the baby mongoose still settled on Alice's shoulder. "My godmother is giving a dinner tonight." Cecily didn't know this for certain, but the chances were very good that she was.

"Of course, my dear, and I'm so happy that you and Katherine seem to be hitting it off. She's a lovely girl, with far more sense than I'll ever have. Send my regards to Kiki, and come see me again soon, won't you?" Alice's delicate white hand pressed onto Cecily's. "It's so refreshing to have some young company, rather than these worn-out old codgers living on their past glories."

"I'd love to come visit again. Thank you, Alice."

Cecily didn't bother to say good-bye to the rest of the guests—they were obviously all settled in for the evening, downing champagne like water, their laughter echoing across the valley as she walked along the driveway toward the Bugatti. Makena opened the door for her and settled her into the back seat with a blanket over her knees to ward off the chill that the rain had left behind.

Even though she'd had no champagne, she felt light-headed as they pulled onto the now muddy road. At such a height above sea level, the air was thinner, so maybe that was why, she thought as she peered out of the window and saw the vast expanse of the Great Rift Valley emerge below her. It was a complete contrast to the luxuriant green vegetation above her and utterly spectacular. She knew from studying her library books about Africa that the rift extended for several thousand miles and had been formed millions of years ago by the primal forces of nature. But no amount of reading could prepare a person for the sheer awe-inspiring scale of it in reality, especially from this vantage point. The setting sun bathed the flat, largely treeless valley floor in a rich apricot glow, and if she strained her eyes, she could make out tiny dots that could be animals or people—or both— moving almost imperceptibly across the spectacular terrain.

"What an incredible country this is," she murmured as she rested her head against the windowpane. "Too much to take in," she sighed, wishing her family were here to share it with her and make sense of it; the contrast between Manhattan and here was a rift as wide as the majestic valley it- self—the two were just worlds apart. She wanted to come to grips with it, both the people and the place. It felt like trying to eat an elephant—simply overwhelming—but somehow, she vowed, she would manage to do it before she returned home.

The next thing she knew, Aleeki was gently shaking her awake.

"Welcome home, *memsahib*. Let me help you out of the car."

Cecily allowed him to do so, and they walked together across the terrace, then inside the house.

"What time is it?" she asked.

"It is half past eight."

"Oh." Cecily looked back at the deserted terrace and listened to the si- lence. "Is my godmother out tonight?"

"No, *memsahib*, she is still feeling unwell and is in her room, sleeping. You must be hungry. I can set up the table on the terrace, or send a tray to your room, whichever you prefer."

"A glass of milk will do me just fine, thanks. May I take a bath? I feel so filthy from the journey."

"Of course, *memsahib*. I will send up Muratha with your milk and to fill the bathtub for you."

"Thank you." Cecily walked toward the stairs, then stopped. "I . . . is my godmother all right? I mean, how sick is she?"

"She will be well soon. Do not worry. I will take care of her."

"Please tell her good night from me then."

"Of course," Aleeki said with a bow. "Good night, *memsahib*."

# 15

The following day, with Kiki still indisposed, Cecily felt grateful (guiltily so) for the peace that had descended on the house. For the first time since she'd arrived, she felt as though she had time to breathe and take in the beauty of her surroundings. Aleeki was on hand with suggestions to entertain her, and that afternoon, she was taken out on the lake by Kagai, a young Kikuyu boy who told her in his halting English that he had been born here. As well as teaching her some basic native phrases, he showed her how to dip a rod off the side of the boat and hold it steady until she felt a tug and then helped her pull out a wriggling fish, whose metallic skin shone rainbow-colored in the sunlight. Sitting in the center of the enormous silver lake, the water millpond still, she watched the hippos sun themselves on land, then stand and slide their bulk into the water, gliding through it as gracefully as any swan.

The next day (with still no sign of Kiki) she accompanied Aleeki into Gilgil, mailed a further letter to her parents, and took her camera roll to be developed by a German man Aleeki knew, who had a darkroom tucked away at the back of his car repair shop. Cecily wandered around the town, stopping at the stalls along the street, which sold a vast array of both strange and familiar fruits and vegetables.

"Are they bananas?" Cecily pointed to large green facsimiles as Aleeki joined her after completing his errands.

"No, *memsahib*, they are plantain. They are similar, yes. They go very good in a stew. Out here, it is called *matoki*. Maybe I can ask Cook to make you some?"

"Why not? I would certainly like to try some of the local cuisine before I leave."

"We have plenty time for you to do that, *memsahib*," he said as he negotiated a good price with the stallholder for the vegetables. "Indian food is popular here, too, very spicy. I like it very much."

"I've never eaten anything with spice in it," Cecily admitted as they walked back to the car along the hot dusty street.

"Then you must try a curry and also some stew and *yugali*—very popular with the Kikuyu."

"Are you Kikuyu?" Cecily asked, curiosity getting the better of her.

"No, *memsahib*, I am from Somaliland," he replied. "Just across the border from this country."

Before she could question Aleeki further, she was startled by a voice from behind her.

"Cecily?"

She turned around and saw Katherine hurrying toward her.

"Gosh, I thought it was you! How are you settling in?"

"Very well, I think, thank you, Katherine."

"It does take some time to adjust, but once you do, I promise it's awfully hard to leave."

"Aleeki, this is Katherine Stewart. I met her at Alice's tea party."

"Very pleased to make your acquaintance, *memsahib*," Aleeki said with a bow.

"How is Alice?" Cecily inquired.

"She's still in hospital in Nairobi—and it looks as if she may be there for a while longer. Bobby's driving me from here to visit her this afternoon."

Cecily could sense that whatever Alice's problem was, it certainly hadn't been caused by food poisoning from her dirty kitchen.

"Do send her my best, won't you?"

"Of course I will. And please come over as soon as you can to visit me at Wanjohi Farm. Bobby's busy sorting out our own farm and that wreck of a house that will become our marital home in a month's time." Katherine smiled. "I'm lonely. How about this Friday?"

Cecily automatically looked at Aleeki for confirmation.

"Certainly, *memsahib*. What time would be convenient for the visit?"

"How about Miss Cecily arrives for lunch and leaves after breakfast on Saturday?" Katherine suggested.

"Then I will arrange everything," Aleeki replied.

"I must be off to find Bobby; he's at the bank sorting out a loan to buy more cattle for the farm"—Katherine raised her eyebrows—"but I'll see you at the end of the week. Bye, Cecily."

"Good-bye, Katherine. And thank you."

"Has Katherine ever visited Mundui House?" Cecily asked as Aleeki helped her inside the car, which was the usual veritable furnace.

"No, I do not believe she has," Aleeki replied before shutting the back door firmly, then climbing into the front seat next to Makena.

Cecily rolled down the window, took out her fan, and flapped it as fast as she could, feeling the dreaded dizziness again and wondering why Aleeki had made it perfectly clear, despite his outwardly polite words, that her new friend was not welcome at Mundui House.

By the time the planned overnight stay dawned, Cecily was desperate for some company. Five more days had passed, and her godmother had still not ventured out of her room. Even though she had begged Aleeki to be allowed in to see Kiki, the answer was always "*Memsahib* is sleeping." At various points during the week, Cecily had actually wondered if her godmother was lying dead up there and Aleeki was just too frightened to tell her.

At breakfast that morning, Cecily was just about to insist that she visit Kiki before she left for Wanjohi Farm when Aleeki handed her an envelope. Opening it and pulling out a sheet of Kiki's expensive embossed notepaper, she saw her godmother's familiar elegant script.

*Darling girl,*

*Forgive me for not attending to your needs—I find myself indisposed. Rest will remedy my ailment, I am sure, and then I will be at your service for the rest of your stay.*

*For now, I do hope Aleeki is seeing to your every whim. He tells me you are to visit Katherine at Wanjohi Farm. Enjoy it!*

*A big kiss,*
*Kiki*

At least, she thought as Aleeki waved her off in the Bugatti after breakfast, her godmother was alive and she could now speed away from Mundui House and its strange muted atmosphere with a clear conscience.

"Cecily! You made it. I'm so very happy to have you here," Katherine said as Cecily climbed out of the car in the drive of Wanjohi Farm.

"And I'm real happy to be here," she replied as Makena unloaded not only her small overnight bag but more wicker baskets full of champagne and food—courtesy of Kiki.

"Goodness! Does your godmother think we're having a party tonight?" Katherine took Cecily's arm in hers as they walked toward the house.

"Maybe any visit can't be complete unless there's champagne flowing."

"I see you've already learned the ropes around here," said Katherine as she led Cecily into what was now—in the space of a week—a radically reformed interior. The piles of books and papers had disappeared, and the stench of dog and other unknown adopted wildlife was camouflaged by the sweet scent of polish and the lilies and roses placed atop a shiny mahogany table.

"Jeez! You've worked miracles here," Cecily said as Katherine showed her to her bedroom.

"Thank you, I'm afraid it's more for me than Alice—I just can't bear to live in chaos," she said. "I've even erected a temporary chicken-wire pound for Alice's dogs. Although I'm afraid the monkeys who see this as their second home are not so easily contained. Do you think I'm cruel?"

"Not at all," Cecily replied as one of the female servants hurried to transfer her overnight bag to her room. "Please tell her not to unpack it—there's nothing in there but my nightgown, toothbrush, a change of clothes, and clean undergarments."

"I'm afraid she jolly well will," Katherine said, then barked orders to the girl, who looked half terrified. "They've all forgotten that they're paid a good wage and are well looked after by Alice. In return, they actually need to do some work. Now, I'm sure you must be parched. There's some homemade lemonade ready on the terrace."

"But no champagne?" Cecily feigned horror as Katherine chuckled.

They settled down in chairs on the terrace, and Cecily took in the view of the green pastures spread out before her and the glint of the river running through them. Antelope, horses, and goats were roaming freely, and the gentle fresh breeze caressed her face.

"How is Alice?" Cecily asked as she took a sip of the delicious lemonade.

"Not terribly well, I'm afraid. She's had to have a drain inserted in her stomach. William—that is, Dr. Boyle—thinks the pains may be the result of the shooting injuries she sustained in Paris all those years ago."

"Will she be okay?"

"I hope so, though she really doesn't take care of herself."

"Jeez. What a complicated life Alice has had. She must have loved the man very much to want to shoot him and then herself."

"I've heard many versions of the tale, but apparently Raymond told her he couldn't marry her because his family had threatened to disinherit him if he did. Golly, the things people do for love, eh?" Katherine sighed. "Though I think I might shoot Bobby if he suddenly announced he couldn't marry me. I simply can't imagine life without him."

"So when—and where—will you marry?" Cecily asked.

"In terms of when: in just under a month, as I might have mentioned. But as far as where is concerned, it's all been rather complicated."

"Why?"

"Well, my father works in a mission in Tumutumu, just on the other side of the Aberdare Mountains, and he's been there for years. He speaks the local language fluently, and, as you've heard, so do I. He'd like me to be married there, but the church is a hut, and I'm not sure I can see the likes of Idina and the others round here arriving in their smart wedding frocks, especially if the rains have begun." Katherine chuckled.

"Surely it's your wedding and must be your decision?"

"Mine *and* Bobby's, yes, though he doesn't care as long as we get wed. But you have to understand that when my parents first arrived in Kenya, they lived on the mission. Then when I came along, and given that my father was so often traveling into the bush to preach the gospel, my mother insisted that he build us a small house up in the Valley, so at least I could make some friends."

"That makes sense," Cecily agreed. "So you grew up between two worlds?"

"Yes, I did, I suppose. And to be honest, I loved both of them. I was sent away to school when I was ten, but during the holidays, I'd spend most of my time with Mother and annoying Bobby up here but then at least two weeks down at the mission with Father. Which brings me back to the tricky subject of where Bobby and I should tie the knot. I think we've finally reached a compromise; Bobby and I will officially be married at the mission in Tumutumu, which will keep Father happy, then the reception will be held at Muthaiga Club the following day. Darling Alice has insisted on paying for it as our wedding gift, even though I suggested that a check to help put some sticks of furniture in our new home might be more useful. She's such an old romantic, even after the disasters of her own marriages. And of course, it's a good excuse for a party, too," she added wryly. "I just hope she'll be well enough to attend. So what do you think?"

"I think it sounds like the perfect solution. Where are you going on honeymoon?"

"Goodness, absolutely nowhere." Katherine smiled. "I'll be moving into Bobby's parents' old farmhouse, which, as I told you, the poor dear is doing his best to renovate before the big day. That will be honeymoon enough, and besides, restocking a cattle farm is a risky business. I'll be helping Bobby with the animals—at least I'll be able to put those years I spent at Dick's to some use."

"Excuse me?"

"The Dick Vet college in Edinburgh—I'm a qualified vet, Cecily, which will certainly be helpful as far as keeping the cattle healthy is concerned. Bill Forsythe, Bobby's—and soon to be my—nearest neighbor, is educating both of us about modern cattle-rearing methods and the intricacies of vaccinations, pesticide baths, and so on. There are so many diseases to worry about when you have animals in large numbers together—anthrax, rinderpest, BPP. Not to mention the lions who will try to get a free meal," Katherine added. "Actually, I've invited Bill round to join us for supper tonight—I must warn you, though, he's quite a character."

"That's okay, I'm slowly getting used to the locals. There sure are some interesting personalities around here," said Cecily.

"Bill has a special relationship with the Maasai tribe—who have plenty to teach us as well, with their natural remedies developed over centuries."

"Are the staff here Maasai?" Cecily inquired as a woman appeared from the kitchen block with a broom and started sweeping the dust from the covered veranda that edged the inner courtyard.

"No, Kikuyu. The Maasai are nomadic—they spend their lives with their cattle out on the plains. Domestic staff tend to be Kikuyu, and Ada—as she's known here—was recommended by my mother from the mission when Alice was looking for more help."

"Do you find they make good servants?"

"They certainly do, as long as they have firm leadership. They are very loyal people, on the whole. Now, enough of all that; tell me, what you do back in Manhattan?"

"I . . . nothing much. I was engaged, you see, and then, well, I wasn't."

"Ah, so you're here to mend a broken heart? May I ask how old you are?"

"I'll be twenty-three this year. An old maid."

"Hardly!" Katherine chuckled. "I'm twenty-seven this year. Did you love him?"

"I thought I did, yes, but truly, I'm done with men."

"We'll see." Katherine smiled, then stood up. "Right, I think it's time for lunch."

They ate a delicious spiced fish, which Katherine told her had been plucked from the river only this morning.

"Have you ever visited Mundui House?" Cecily probed, remembering Aleeki's discreet coldness toward her new friend.

"No, my mother and father disapproved heavily of the whole Happy Valley set. Apart from Alice, of course, because of the animals. I hear it's beautiful, though, and obviously Kiki is so very generous."

"Yes, she is, although . . . well, I'm worried about her," Cecily confided. "She hasn't been out of her room in days. I only know she's alive because she wrote me a letter this morning before I left. You don't happen to know if she suffers from any recurring illness, do you?"

"Gosh, I . . . no, I don't think so, Cecily. Now, why don't I take you to the stables, and we can go for a ride? I'll show you some of the beauty spots in the area."

Pushing down both her feeling that Katherine knew more than she was telling, plus the thought of riding again—she knew she *literally* had to get back on the horse if she was going to be in Kenya for some time—Cecily nodded.

"Thank you, I'd love to."

Luckily, the terrain was challenging, and rather than thinking about the last time she'd been out riding with Julius, Cecily concentrated on guiding the mare along the riverbank. She took in the cool, fresh air, the sounds of the birds, and the sunlight glinting off the peaceful run of the river to her side. When the horses stopped to drink, Cecily stared across the wide expanse of flat, verdant valley spread out below her.

"You know, it almost feels as though England up here has been glued to Kenya down there," she said.

"You're right, it does, rather. Now, Bobby and Bill will be arriving shortly, so we should head back."

Having washed herself as best she could in the bowl of warm water set on top of the chest of drawers, Cecily put on a clean cotton dress, tidied her hair, then went back outside to join Katherine and watch the sun set over the valley. As it disappeared below the horizon, Cecily shivered in the fresh breeze that whipped across the terrace. She pulled her wrap closer around her shoulders, relishing the feeling of being cool.

They both heard the growl of engines approaching.

"The boys are here," said Katherine, and Cecily followed her out to the driveway, where two ancient-looking open-topped pickups had just pulled to a halt. Bobby climbed out of one, followed by another man who Cecily assumed must be Bill.

"As I said, Cecily, do try not to be offended by Bill. He's rather gone native over the years and forgotten how to behave in company," Katherine whispered as the two men walked toward them.

From a distance, she was surprised at how youthful and slim Bill looked, but as he came closer, despite his plentiful head of sandy hair, she saw there were deep lines etched onto his tanned face. She revised her estimate upward, guessing he was around forty. He also looked vaguely familiar.

"Hello, darling," Katherine said as she reached up to receive a kiss from Bobby. "Bill, how are you?"

"I'm quite well, thank you." His voice was low and rather hoarse, with a clipped British accent.

"This is Cecily Huntley-Morgan, who has recently arrived from New York," Katherine informed him as they all walked toward the terrace.

Cecily felt Bill's blue eyes assessing her before he looked off into the distance.

"Poor you," he said after a few seconds. "Living there."

"I like living in Manhattan. It's a wonderful place, and it's my home," Cecily responded, suddenly feeling defensive.

"All those ridiculously high buildings, not to mention the number of people crammed tightly together on that tiny island."

"Don't mind Bill, Cecily. He's been out in the bush for too long, haven't you?" Katherine said as they all sat down and she offered champagne or beer to the men.

"And thank God that's the case," said Bill, taking a bottle of beer. "As you know, Katherine, I'm not a particular fan of humans."

Once again, Bill's strange, almost hypnotic gaze turned upon Cecily.

"How long are you here for, before you scuttle back to the claustrophobia of what you would call 'civilization'?"

"She doesn't know, Bill, do you, Cecily?" intervened Katherine.

"No, I don't," Cecily replied, reaching for her glass of champagne. This man's abrupt manner was unnerving her.

"Have you been out into the bush yet?"

"No."

"Then you have yet to truly experience Africa."

"I'm sure we'll find an opportunity to take her, won't we, Bill?" said Bobby.

Cecily noticed Bill was looking under the table at something.

"Well," he said, eventually raising his eyes and his glass to her. "At least you're not wearing those ridiculous high-heeled shoes that other Americans— such as that ghastly Preston woman—insist on."

Cecily nearly choked on her champagne. She looked at Katherine, silently begging for guidance.

"Kiki happens to be Cecily's godmother, Bill," said Katherine calmly. "Now, for goodness' sake, stop terrifying the poor girl. She's nothing like her godmother. And just because she's American, you shouldn't pigeonhole her. Never judge a book by its cover, remember? So how did you two get on today?"

Cecily listened half-heartedly as Bobby described the cattle auction they'd been to and how many "head" he'd bought.

"He did well," Bill said, which was the first positive thing she'd heard fall out of the man's mouth since he'd arrived. "Got the Boran for a good price."

"With your help, Bill. They know they can't pull the wool over your eyes. Bill's famous in the area for his knowledge o' cattle," Bobby added to Cecily.

"And what are you knowledgeable about, Miss Huntley-Morgan?" Bill asked.

"Probably nothing much," Cecily said with a shrug, still affronted by his rudeness toward her and her godmother.

"Oh, come now, Cecily. Don't let Bill get you down." Katherine gave Bill a hard stare. "He does this to everyone on first meeting them, don't you?"

"As you know, I haven't lived amongst polite society for a long time."

"Charmed, I'm sure." Bobby rolled his eyes and winked at Bill. "Now, we're both starving. What's for dinner?"

Over supper, Cecily was thankful that Bill's attention was diverted from her as the others talked over how soon Bobby could make a profit on the cattle farm versus how long he could hold off the bank from wanting its loan repaid.

"It mostly comes down to how much time you're prepared to let Bobby spend with the animals up in the hills or out on the plains during rainy season, Katherine. I was only away for a week last November, as I had business to attend to in Nairobi. I reckon I lost at least a hundred heads."

"Where to?" Cecily asked, interested for the first time.

"To the Maasai, of course."

"But I thought they cared for your cattle, worked for you."

"Some do, but there are many different clans of Maasai around these parts. The Maasai see all cows in Kenya as belonging to them. They are sacred to the tribe, you see, and even though they rarely kill the cattle themselves, they can trade them for maize and vegetables with other clans."

"But the cows belong to you?"

"Technically, yes, but money exchanging hands with *mzungu*s means little to them."

"*Mzungu* is the local term for a white person," Katherine explained.

"Can't you dismiss them and find other people to look after your cattle?" Cecily asked.

Bill stared at her. "No, Miss Huntley-Morgan, I could not. I have an excellent relationship with them—many have become my friends. And if the price I must pay is a few dozen heads of cattle per year, then so be it. The Maasai were here first, and despite various attempts by the authorities to move them on and enclose them, they continue with their traditional nomadic ways. They have a symbiotic relationship with the cows; they drain blood from them and drink it, believing it will give them strength and well-being."

"That sounds perfectly revolting," said Cecily.

"Well, at least the cows don't like the taste of human blood, unlike lions," retorted Bill.

"I have yet to see a lion, or an elephant."

Bill regarded her silently for a while, as though mulling something over. Eventually, he spoke. "I'm off to the bush tomorrow, Miss Huntley-whatever-you're-called. Are you free to come along? Or are you going to bottle out now that you've been asked?"

"Oh, Cecily, you have to go! We'll come with you, of course," said Katherine quickly. "Bill took me out when I was eleven. Do you remember you told me then that it was the age when Maasai girls became women?"

"At eleven?" said Cecily.

"Many of them are married and pregnant by twelve or thirteen, Miss Huntley-thingummy," said Bill.

"Oh, please! Call me Cecily." She sighed, now exasperated by the fact she knew he was doing his best to rile her.

"Must I? I'm afraid I loathe that name. I had a great-aunt who lived in West Sussex. Even though she was an utter dragon, my parents always sent me and my older brother to stay with her in the summer holidays. Her name was Cecily."

"Then I apologize for bringing back such bad memories, but I can hardly be blamed for it, can I?"

"Honestly, Bill," Katherine admonished him, "leave the poor girl alone."

But Bill was still staring at her. And in that stare and the mention of West Sussex, Cecily finally realized who he was.

"And your name is Bill? Bill Forsythe?"

"Yes, and a jolly good solid British name it is too."

"Your brother is a major, isn't he? And he lives where you said your great-aunt did, in West Sussex?"

"Well, yes. He is and does. How did you know?"

"I met him recently in England." Cecily was pleased that this seemed to rattle Bill momentarily.

"Did you indeed? Where and when?"

"At Woodhead Hall in Sussex, about three weeks ago. I was invited there by Lady Woodhead, and he lives nearby."

"Well, I'll be jiggered, as the major would say. My dear elder brother came to visit Kenya when I first moved out here and crawled up every skirt he could find at Muthaiga Club—even though he had a very sweet wife. Are you married?"

"No."

"And like you, Bill, she isn't interested in love," Katherine announced from the other side of the table, giving Cecily a reassuring glance.

"Well, that's quite a statement, if I may say so." Bill raised an eyebrow. "Certainly at your age. It's taken me until the age of thirty-eight to realize that love is a myth. Anyway"—Bill stood up and turned to Bobby—"as we're up early tomorrow, you and I should leave."

"Of course." Bobby nodded, then stood up and Cecily got the distinct impression that he was in complete awe of his friend. "So are you going to brave your first safari, Cecily?"

"Oh, do say yes," Katherine said as they all walked along the drive together. "The staff can manage for a night here, and it's been ages since I went out into the bush."

"You must warn your American friend that it isn't as glamorous as the game drives her godmother may have told her about." Bill ignored Cecily as they walked toward the pickup. "No canapés and champagne and servants; just a blanket, a makeshift tent, and a campfire under the stars."

"We'll sort her out, Bill. So, Cecily, is it a yes?"

Three pairs of eyes stared at her.

"I . . . okay. I'd love to come."

"Jolly good," said Bill. "Then I'll see you all at my place tomorrow morning at seven o'clock sharp. Thank you for the supper, Katherine. It's not often I get a home-cooked meal these days."

"Bye, darling." Katherine kissed Bobby as he climbed into the pickup parked next to Bill's. "See you tomorrow bright and early."

Cecily and Katherine waved the vehicles off, then walked back toward the house.

"We must get you kitted out for tomorrow," Katherine said. "Alice has lots of safari clothes, and you're around the same size."

"Thanks. I have to admit I'm a little nervous, especially about Bill. He made it plain obvious that he dislikes me," Cecily said as they entered the hallway.

"Golly, I don't think he 'dislikes' you at all. That's the most attention I've seen him give a woman in a long time."

"Well, if that's his idea of attention, no wonder he's never married. He's so darned rude!"

"Interestingly, from what I've heard, like you, he ran away to Africa to escape a broken heart. That was nearly twenty years ago, and I've never heard a hint of gossip about him since he's been here. He keeps himself to himself, if you know what I mean. He's quite attractive, don't you think?"

"I don't think so, no," Cecily said, the two glasses of champagne she'd drunk to get through the evening making her speak bluntly. "All he did was insult me."

"Well, that's Bill all over, but you couldn't be in safer hands for your first trip into the bush. He knows the territory and the dangers of it better than any other white man. Now"—Katherine stifled a yawn—"I have to put the dogs in the pen and find that pesky mongoose that Alice is so fond of. I fed it this morning, and I haven't seen it all day. I'll look for some suitable clothes for both of us, too. Good night, Cecily, see you bright and early."

"Good night, and thank you so much for this evening."

As Katherine went out into the cool night to gather the ever-present pack of dogs together, Cecily closed the bedroom door, walked over to the bed, and lay down. She wondered what heartbreak Bill had suffered to turn him into a man who seemed to have little trust in humanity itself. And most certainly not in females.

Kicking off her shoes and unbuttoning her dress, Cecily was glad of the eiderdown because she was actually cold. Snuggling beneath it, she put out her hand and felt something warm and furry. Giving a small scream, she peered under the covers and saw it was the baby mongoose she'd met on her last visit here. He'd obviously been hiding under the eiderdown. Tiny paws crept up across her chest, then came to rest in the crevice between her neck and shoulder.

Cecily smiled as she thought of her mother's reaction if she could see her now. A wild animal—probably full of fleas and lice—curled up with her in bed. Yet the animal's breathing was comforting, and Cecily was secretly pleased that the mongoose had sought out *her* bedroom as a place of refuge. As for Bill and the complexities of the evening, Cecily was too tired to think of them.

*But if I ever decided to stay, I'd definitely live up here in Wanjohi Valley.* And with that thought, she fell asleep.

# ELECTRA

*New York*
*April 2008*

# 16

I stared at my grandmother, whose hands were folded neatly in her lap. Her eyes were closed, and I guessed she was still in another world—a world so different from the one we were both sitting in now, it was tough to comprehend it. Finally she opened her eyes, and I saw her shake herself as she coaxed her body and mind back to the present.

"Wow. Africa," I said, standing up and going to pour myself a fresh glass of the Goose. "Someday, I'd like to hear how I fit into the story and why my parents had me adopted."

"I know you would, but there's a whole lot more to tell before we get to that. I have to explain to you who Cecily was and what happened to her for you to understand. Patience, Electra," she added with a sigh.

"Yeah, it's not one of my strongest qualities. Hey, Cecily sure sounds like she had a rough time. That English guy seemed like a total asshole."

"Electra, is it necessary for you to swear? There are many words in the great English language that describe what that man was far more adequately."

"Sorry."

I saw she was watching me with those gimlet eyes of hers.

"Want one?" I asked.

"As I said, I don't take liquor. Nor should you. That's the fourth enormous vodka you've poured yourself since I arrived."

"So what?" I said as I took a gulp. "And anyway, who are you to walk in here telling me what to do and say and what to drink?! How come you've suddenly appeared in my life anyway? Where were you when I got adopted?"

I watched as Stella stood up.

"Are you leaving?" I asked her.

"I am, Electra, because you're completely out of control, as your Pa told me you were. Not only have you had liquor, but when you said you needed to go to the bathroom, you came out and I could see from your eyes that you'd been doing a line or two of cocaine in there. And I've probably wasted my breath telling you all I have tonight, because you won't even remember it tomorrow. I'm here because I am your flesh and blood and because your Pa sent me to you. And along with him, I'm begging you to get help before it's too late and you destroy your young life. I doubt you'll want to see me again because you'll be so angry with me for saying this. You're in denial right now, but someday soon you'll reach the bottom, and when you do, call me and I'll be there for you. Okay? Good-bye, now." And with that, she walked across the living room, opened the apartment door, and left, shutting it with a bang.

"Wow!" I chuckled to myself. "Just *wow!*" I walked to the bar to grab some more vodka and saw the bottle was empty. Reaching for another one from the cupboard below, I poured myself a large glass and gulped it down. *Jeez! She's a seriously crazy woman! How dare she walk in here when she's never set eyes on me before and accuse me of that stuff? Who the hell does she think she is? No one has ever spoken to me like that.*

*She's your grandmother, your flesh and blood . . .*

"And what was that shit about Pa 'sending' her?" I asked the empty room. "Pa is dead, isn't he?"

I felt the anger building up inside me and went to do another line to try to brighten my mood. Anger was dangerous—it made me say and do all sorts of stupid things. Like call Mitch and tell him what I thought of him.

"Maybe I should call his fiancée instead, give her a few home truths," I spat as I stood in front of the windows, gazing out at the New York skyline. My heart was banging, and my head felt like it was going to explode.

"Christ! Why do my sisters get sweet, cuddly relations and I get the granny from hell?"

I began sobbing loudly and sank to my knees. *Why does nobody love me? And why does everybody leave me? I just need to sleep. I really need to sleep.*

Yes, that was the answer. I'd put myself to sleep. Dragging myself from the floor and taking my glass of vodka with me, I stumbled into the bedroom. I opened my bedside drawer and found the bottle of sleeping pills that a doctor had prescribed me recently when I'd had bad jet lag. I twisted the top off the bottle and tossed the contents out onto the comforter. I threw back a couple with some vodka, because one didn't work anymore, then laid my head down on the pillow and closed my eyes. But my head spun, so I had to open them again. I wished Maia were with me to tell me stories like she'd done in Rio.

"She loves me, I know she does," I whimpered. I tried closing my eyes again, but tears dribbled out of them and the room was still spinning, so I sat up and took another couple of tablets.

"I want to speak to Maia," I said and climbed off the bed to find my cell.

"Where are you? I need to call my sister!" I sobbed as I searched the apartment for it. Finally finding it on top of the bar by the vodka bottle, I grabbed both and sank to the floor because I was feeling very woozy by now. I managed to find Maia's number even though my eyesight was blurry and pressed the button to make the call. It rang a few times, then went to voice mail.

"Maia, it's Electra," I said in between sobs. "I really need you to call me back. Please call me."

I studied my cell, willing it to ring, and when it didn't, I threw it across the room.

Then it *did* ring, and I had to crawl across the floor to reach it.

"Hello?"

"It's Maia, Electra. What is it, *chérie?*"

"Jus' about everything!" I cried, tears exploding at the sound of my sister's gentle voice. "Mitch sen' back my stuff from his house 'cause he's marryin' someone else, and I jus' met my granny an' she's a witch an'"—I shook my head and wiped my running nose with my arm—"I jus' wanna go to sleep for a very long time, y'know?"

"Oh, Electra, I so wish I was there. What can I do?"

"I dunno." I shrugged. "Nothin,' there's nothin' anyone can do."

And as I said the words, I realized they were true.

"Sorry t'bother you, I'll be okay . . . Took some tablets, an' hopefully I'll go to sleep soon. Bye."

I ended the call and took the vodka bottle back to bed with me, leaving the cell where it was. I took two more pills, because I just *had* to sleep, and curled up like a fetus, wishing I'd never been born.

"Nobody wanted me anyway," I gulped, as finally my eyelids began to droop and I fell asleep.

"Electra? *Electra,* speak to me! Are you okay?"

The voice came from far away, as though it was muffled by a great black cloud hanging above me.

"Mmm," I managed, feeling the blackness descending, but then someone was slapping my face hard.

"Do you know how many she's taken?" said a male voice that I recognized but couldn't place.

"I have no idea. Should I call 911?"

I felt someone grab my wrist and press fingers against it.

"Her pulse is slow, but it's there—go grab some water from the kitchen and bring some salt. We need to get her to vomit."

"Okay."

"Electra, how many pills did you take?" the male voice boomed in my ear. "Electra!"

"A few," I mouthed.

"How many is a few?"

"Four . . . six . . ." I slurred. "Couldn't sleep, y'see . . ."

"Okay, okay."

"Shouldn't we call an ambulance, Tommy?"

"She's conscious and talking. If we can get her to vomit, she should be okay. Okay, empty that salt into the water and stir it. Right, Electra, we're gonna sit you up. And unless you want to go to the emergency room and have the whole world see you pushed in on a gurney, you're gonna do exactly as I tell you. Right, here we go."

I felt a strong pair of arms lift me upright, and the world began spinning again.

"I'm gonna puke! Shit!"

And I did, all over me and the floor.

"Grab a bowl!" the male voice shouted as I vomited again. "Hey, you're doing just great, sweetheart. We didn't even have to give you that salt water," he said as I vomited some more. And then some more again.

"I need to lie down, please let me lie down!"

"Not yet. You're gonna lean on me, and I'm gonna get you upright, then we're gonna walk, okay?"

"No, please, let me lie down."

"Mariam, get some strong black coffee. You're doing great, Electra," he said as he hauled me to standing and I bent over and was sick yet again.

"Who are you?" I asked, my head lolling forward and my body feeling as limp as a rag doll.

"I'm Tommy, the guy who stands outside your apartment building, remember? I'm your friend, okay, and I know what I'm doing, so trust me. Now let's walk, shall we? One foot in front of the other . . . That's real good, sweetheart, keep going now. You got that coffee, Mariam?"

"It's coming right up."

"Great. Now, we're gonna go out onto the terrace and take in some deep breaths of fresh air, okay? Here we go. Careful of the lip on the door . . . great! You're out."

"Can I sit down now? I feel so dizzy . . ."

"Let's walk a little more first, and then we'll sit you down and you can have a nice hot drink."

The coolness of the air began to work as Tommy paced me up and down the terrace. I opened my eyes and swayed a little as he counted our breaths in and out.

"You're doing fantastic! Feeling better?"

I nodded. "A bit."

"Okay, that's great. So let's sit you down here."

He eased me into a chair, and seconds later I smelled the strong scent of coffee wafting up my nostrils, which made me heave again.

"I don't think there's anything left inside you to throw up," he said. "Here's the coffee, sweetheart."

For the first time, I focused on his face and grasped the cup as he handed it to me.

"I'll go and clear up in the bedroom," said a female voice, which I now recognized as Mariam's.

"No! Please don't. It's disgusting!"

"Don't you worry about me, Electra. Remember, I have five brothers and sisters at home. I am used to vomit," she added cheerily as she stepped inside.

"Sip the coffee, Electra, it'll help."

I did but also managed to spill it everywhere because my hands were shaking so much.

"Hey, I'll feed it to you. Here."

Tommy lifted the cup to my lips, and I took small sips as my head began to clear.

"How come you're here?" I asked him.

"Mariam came by to check on you, 'cause your sister had called her in a panic. I was outside, and she told me your sister thought you might have

OD'd. She wanted to call 911, but I said I'd take a look at you first, because I have some medical training from my army days and I know you wouldn't have wanted the hospital, would you?"

"No, and thanks, Tommy. I feel so ashamed. That was *sooo* disgusting."

"Hey, I'm an army vet, and I've seen any number of guys turning to drink and drugs on their return to civilian life. I went there myself for a while, too."

"Okay, well, thanks again." My stomach churned with the aftermath of what I'd put inside it and what Tommy must think of me. "Not much of a goddess tonight, am I?"

"Hey, Electra, you're just flesh and blood like all of us. Human, y'know?"

I looked down at myself, at my vomit-covered jeans, and felt utter revulsion at the level I'd sunk to.

"I'm gonna go have a shower, if you don't mind."

"Course I don't. Need some help gettin' there?"

"No, thanks, I can manage." I stood up, still feeling wobbly but able to walk unaided into the living room.

"Almost done in here," Mariam said, coming out of the bedroom. "You might want to sleep in your spare room for tonight, though; the smell of disinfectant's pretty strong."

"Okay, thanks."

In the shower, I scrubbed my skin until it was almost red raw, as though the chemicals I'd taken had infected that, too. I stepped out, wrapped a towel around me, and sat down heavily on the toilet seat. And only wished I could stay in here and not face the mess I'd made of myself and the people who'd tried to help me who had seen it.

"You're a goddamn screw-up, Electra," I whispered as I rubbed my hands up and down my thighs in agitation. "They're right; you need help. You. Need. Help."

As I voiced the words, I felt a sudden sense of release or relief or *something* that felt better than where I'd been for the past few weeks. "Be honest, Electra, for the past year—"

*It was what Tommy said that did it*, I thought. "You're just flesh and blood, like all of us. Human." . . . And he was so, so right, because I was.

There was a knock on the bathroom door.

"You okay in there?" asked Mariam through the wood.

"Yeah, I'm okay."

"Maia is on the line for you. Do you want to speak to her?"

"Yes." I stood up, went to the door, and opened it. Mariam handed me my cell as I walked back into my bedroom. "Thanks, Mariam. Maia?"

"Oh, Electra!" came Maia's soft voice. "Thank God you're okay! I was so worried about you when you said you just wanted to go to sleep. I—"

"I wasn't trying to kill myself, Maia. I genuinely wanted to go to sleep. Nothing more than that, seriously."

"Mariam says you're okay now, but you weren't when she found you."

"No, I wasn't. I took too many sleeping pills by mistake, that's all."

"You sounded so terrible, so I called Mariam straight after you put the phone down on me and asked her to go and check you were okay."

"Yeah, I know. Well, thanks for doing that."

"Electra, I—"

"Before you tell me I need help, I know I do. *And*"—I swallowed, like, *really* hard—"if you can give the details of that clinic you mentioned to Mariam, she can see how soon I can get checked in."

There was a pause on the line, and I heard a couple of gulps and realized Maia was crying.

"Oh, my goodness! That's amazing! I've been so worried, we all have. It's such a brave thing to do, to admit you need help. I'm so proud of you, Electra, I really am."

"Well, I'm not saying it's gonna work, but at least I can give it a try, can't I?"

"Yes, you can." I heard Maia blowing her nose. "Are you okay for me to tell Ma and Ally? They've been worried, too."

"*Just* Ma and Ally. Yeah, sure. And I'm sorry I've worried everyone."

"Well, we wouldn't worry about you if we didn't love you, would we, little sis? And we do love you so very, very much."

"Okay, I'm gonna go now before you get me crying, too. I'll hand you over to Mariam. Bye, Maia, and thanks again."

"Maia wants to give you the details of a rehab clinic in Arizona," I said lightly as I passed over my cell to her. "I'll go as soon as they can have me."

Before I witnessed her reaction, I put on my robe, then left the bedroom, which stank of all the reasons I needed to fly down to Arizona tomorrow, and went back out onto the terrace to see Tommy.

"Hi there, Electra," he said, turning toward me from where he'd been leaning over the glass barrier. "Helluva view you got from up here."

"Yeah, it is. Could you get me some water? I'm thirsty."

"Sure, course I can."

He came back with water for both of us. "Cheers." I clinked my glass against his, and we both drank. "I need to say thank you again for your help tonight."

"Hey, you're my queen! I was glad to help and always will be."

"Actually, I was just thinking about something you said to me, about only being human. It put a lot of things into perspective. It's okay to admit weakness, isn't it?"

"Sure it is."

"I just told my sister I'm going to go to the rehab clinic she suggested as soon as I can. I'm tired of being a screw-up."

"That's the best news, Electra, though I'll miss you while you're gone."

"I hope it won't be for long, but anyway, Tommy," I hurried on, not wanting to think about the reality of my decision, "you were great."

"It's not gonna be easy—take it from one who knows—but you've just done the hardest part by admitting you need the help. If I could turn the clock back"—he shrugged—"well, I would. You haven't lost anything yet—and I swear to you, life just gets better and better once you're clean. Anyways, guess I'll be on my way."

"Okay." I watched him stand up. "See you when I get back, Tommy."

"Good luck, Electra, I'll be with you in spirit all the time, promise." He gave me one last smile and stepped back inside the apartment.

"Hi there," Mariam said as she came outside a few minutes later.

"Hi."

"Okay, so I spoke to Maia and called the clinic—they have someone on reception twenty-four-seven. And yes, they have room, so it's fine for you to fly down there tomorrow. I placed another call to the private jet company, and they can have one on the runway at Teterboro Airport at ten a.m."

"Okay. Did the clinic say how long I'd be there?"

"The lady I spoke to said the average stay is a month, so that's what I booked you in for."

"A month! Jeez, Mariam, what will we tell everyone? I mean, they can't know the truth."

"Susie does, because I called her, too—you're hardly the first model she's had who's been . . . ill. She sends her love, and she's so pleased you've taken the decision to go. She's used to dealing with these situations—she'll just tell the clients you're suffering from exhaustion and need to take a break."

"And they'll *so* believe that," I muttered morosely.

"Who cares what they believe? The most important thing is that your calendar will be as full as it always has been once you're back. You're one of the best models in the business—if not the best. You're great to work with, Electra, everyone tells me that."

"Really?" I raised an eyebrow.

"Yes! You're never late for a shoot, you're always polite on set and treat everyone around you with respect, unlike some other models I could name."

"Then why do *I* think I'm a nightmare?"

"Because you feel like one inside?" Mariam suggested softly. "The great news is that you've never let that nightmare out in public. And you're creative, too—remember that *Marie Claire* shoot when they couldn't quite find the right look that they were going for and you simply stood up and grabbed that African-print tablecloth from the catering team and wrapped it around yourself? It looked amazing, and it saved the shoot!"

The doorbell rang, and Mariam jumped to answer it. She had a weird look in her eye, almost as if she felt guilty.

I heard her talking to someone in the living room, and I stood up to go and see who the new visitor was.

"Hello, Electra," my grandmother said to me. "How are you feeling?"

"I . . . okay." I frowned, feeling the anger suddenly surging inside me again. "Why are you here?"

"I called your assistant after I left here earlier tonight," said Stella. "Remember you gave me her number?"

"Yes, but—"

"I told her that I was concerned about you, and that my visit might have destabilized you further. I asked her to let me know if you were okay. And to call me if you weren't."

"And when you weren't, I mean, when we found you unconscious, I called her." I watched a blush travel up Mariam's neck as she read the expression on my face. "Stella is your grandmother, Electra, she wants to help you."

"Electra, please." Stella walked toward me and reached out her hands. "I'm only here to support you. Not to preach. Mariam told me you've decided to get help. I'm so proud of you."

I was beginning to feel like I'd won some kind of competition at school rather than just accepted that I was an addict.

"Thanks." I nodded as I felt the press of her cool calm hands on mine. "But it's late, and we should all be in bed."

"Well, how about we let Mariam go home and I stay around awhile in case you need some company?"

I saw a look pass between Mariam and my grandmother, and I jumped on it. "You're here to make sure I don't change my mind and get on a flight to Timbuktu before tomorrow, aren't you?"

"Maybe." Stella gave me a smile that made her eyes, that were so like mine, twinkle. "It has been known to happen. More importantly, I just want you to be safe during the night."

"You mean not take any more alcohol or drugs?"

"That, too. Now, Mariam, you've done enough, and you need to get home. I'm sure Electra is very grateful to you, aren't you?"

"Of course I am! Mariam knows that."

"Okay." Mariam gave me a smile. "Well, I will see you here at eight a.m. I've packed most of what you need—which isn't much—in your suitcase, ready to go. Good night."

Stella and I stood in silence as Mariam left the apartment.

"You've got a gem there, Electra."

"I know, she's very efficient."

"She's a gem because she genuinely cares about you. And that's what really counts."

"Listen, you don't have to stay. I promise I'll behave—I'll go straight to bed like a good girl and be up bright and early to go to the airport."

"I know I don't have to stay, but I want to. Just for a while at least."

"Well, I'm gonna use the bathroom and then get into bed. And no"—my eyes flashed at her—"I'm not gonna do a line of coke while I'm in there."

A few minutes later, I was in the spare bed and thinking how tired I felt. As I turned off the light, there was a knock at my door.

"Come in."

"I just . . . well, I wanted to say good night to my granddaughter for the first time in twenty-six years. May I?"

"Of course."

She walked over to me and planted a gentle kiss on my forehead. I looked up at her, silhouetted in the light coming through the open door behind her.

"Why didn't you contact me before?"

"Because I didn't know you even existed up until quite recently."

"Oh. Why?"

"That, my dear Electra, is a long story and not one for this time of night."

"Did you . . . did you say Pa told you to come find me?"

"I did, yes."

"But he's dead."

"Yes, he is, God rest his soul."

"Then how?"

"Do you remember meeting him in New York . . . why, it must have been a year ago now?"

"Yeah, we had dinner, and it was a train wreck."

"I know, he told me. He'd actually flown over to see me, as well as you—he'd managed to trace me after all these years and wanted to meet me in person. I think he knew he was very ill by then. He told me how worried he was about you. And asked me to make contact with you if he was no longer here to do that himself. His lawyer—Mr. Hoffman—subsequently contacted me by mail in July to inform me of his death, but I was abroad for several months and didn't receive his letter until I got back in March. Which was when I wrote to your agent."

"Oh, okay." My eyes were drooping with tiredness now.

"Anyway, it's been a very difficult night for you, honey, and you have more to come. I want you to get some sleep. Do you want me to leave?"

The weird thing was that now I knew that Pa had genuinely trusted her, I *didn't* want her to leave. This woman, whom I couldn't get a handle on at all, had been sent by him to watch over me. And it actually felt comforting.

"Maybe in a while?"

"Okay," she said, walking over to the easy chair in the corner of the room, "Then how about I sing you to sleep as my *yeyo* used to do for me? Now close your eyes, and imagine the wide-open skies that hang full of stars over the plains of Africa."

*The Lion King*, which had always been my favorite Disney film, immediately popped into my head, especially as "Granny" (would I call her that one day?) began to hum, then sing words I couldn't understand. But her voice was so rich and mellow and goddamn gorgeous that I *did* close my eyes and see those vast starry skies. I smiled, feeling calmer than I had for a long, long time. And with her voice lulling me, I fell asleep.

"Electra, it's time to get up. Mariam is here."

I opened my eyes, frustrated because I hadn't slept so deeply for as long as I could remember and now someone was trying to make me wake up. I rolled over, shaking my head.

"Electra, you have to wake up, honey. The car's already downstairs waiting to take you to the airport."

As I surrendered and rose to consciousness, I remembered why I was being woken.

*Nooo . . .*

"I don't wanna go . . . Please let me stay here. I feel better already," I moaned.

The covers were lifted from me, and strong arms pulled me upright.

"You *have* to go, Electra. Now, put these on."

I stared at my grandmother, who was holding out my cashmere sweatpants, and slammed my fist into the bed. "Who are you to tell me what to do?" I spat. "I don't hear from you or see you or even know you exist for the first twenty-six years of my life, then you suddenly turn up and start ordering me around!"

"Well, somebody has to do it; look at the mess you've gotten yourself into without it."

"Get out! Get out!" I screamed at her.

"Okay, okay . . . I will. I know I have no right to tell you anything, but I'm begging you, if you don't face this moment now, it will only come again and again. And would you like to know something? I lost my precious child to addiction. So don't you lie there feeling sorry for yourself, miss! You don't know what hardship is, and I'll be damned if I'm going to lose you, too! Get your skinny behind out of that bed, and get yourself clean!"

With that, my grandmother turned tail out of the room and slammed the door behind her, leaving me shaken to the core. No one—not even Pa Salt—had ever spoken to me with such anger before. Maybe it was the shock, but I did get dressed and opened the door timidly to find Mariam sitting on the couch waiting for me.

"Ready to go?" she said.

"Yeah. Has she gone?"

"You mean your grandmother? Yes. Your carry-on is in the trunk. We need to leave now."

I followed Mariam out of the apartment, feeling exactly as I had when I was leaving Atlantis for a new term at boarding school. I could so easily turn around and go right back inside, pour myself a vodka, do a line . . .

But my grandmother's words rang in my ears, and I followed Mariam out of the apartment and down in the elevator like a lamb to the slaughter.

# 17

*The Ranch, Arizona*
*May 2008*

Electra, you're on day twenty-two of your program here with us at The Ranch; how do you feel?"

Fi's deceptively gentle gaze appraised me. When we'd begun our therapy sessions, I'd felt that it didn't matter what shit I spouted to her, because her soft voice (with traces of a European accent) and her hooded blue eyes had made her appear half asleep. How wrong I had been. That question, the "how do you feel?" trope, had haunted me since my first therapy session here.

So how *did* I feel?

Week one: In my initial forty-eight hours in the medical detox center, my response had been "Like I want to mainline vodka mixed with a couple of mollies and twenty lines of coke. And then steal a gun so I can shoot my way out of here."

I had been put on suicide watch, due to my "overdose," and pumped full of medication that was meant to ease me off the booze and drugs. I don't think I'd ever felt more rage and despair in my life than in those two days; it felt like no one would believe that it hadn't been a suicide attempt and that I wouldn't harm myself again.

Once out of detox and into the "dorm," I was horrified to find out that I was basically back at boarding school with two roommates who snored, screamed in their sleep, broke wind, or sobbed into their pillows (and sometimes a mixture of all those in one night). And why the hell didn't a place that was costing more than the most exclusive five-star hotel offer private rooms?

Week two: I spent this feeling angry that the Twelve Steps of the AA program meant I had to ask a God I didn't believe in for help and, even worse, that to get clean I must subjugate myself to this mythical figure and His greater glory. And hating Fi for being so nosy about my life and how I "felt" about it, when it was none of her goddamned business. On the plus side, I really liked one of my dorm mates, Lizzie, and the fact that there were people in group therapy who were obviously far bigger screw-ups than me.

Week three: This is when I started to feel relieved that the Twelve Steps had begun to make more sense when one of the guys in group therapy said he didn't believe in God, either, so instead he imagined a higher power— something far more powerful than we humans walking the earth could ever be. And that helped a lot. Also, I discovered that I loved the equine therapy, but I didn't want to just groom the horses, I wanted to get on the back of them and race away across the Sonoran Desert. And that Lizzie and I had "bonded," especially after the third roommate had left (she'd had serious body odor issues and slept with a cuddly rabbit she called "Bobo") and that we were getting closer all the time.

"So, Electra? How *do* you feel?" came Fi's ubiquitous prompt.

Actually, now I thought about it, I felt *proud*, yes, proud that I hadn't drunk liquor or done a line or swallowed a pill in twenty-two days.

So that's what I said, because I knew Fi liked positive feedback.

"That is just fantastic, Electra. And so you should be. Like everyone here at The Ranch, you've been on a very tough journey, but you've stuck with it. You *should* be proud of yourself." She smiled. "I am."

I shrugged. "Thanks."

"I know you've had a difficult time addressing the events that led up to you coming here," Fi said.

I knew exactly where she was going with this, and I felt the usual stab of anger and irritation.

"Have you had any more reflections on your overdose that night in New York?" she said.

"No!" I snapped. "I keep trying to tell all of you that it was an accident. I just wanted to sleep! That's all I wanted! I was having a bitch of a time getting my mind to shut up, and I just wanted it to be quiet—"

"Electra, it's not that I don't believe you, it's simply that if there's any indication that you would try to hurt yourself, it's my duty as your therapist to protect you. Even though I'm happy that you've gained a new perspective,

I want to talk about the fact that you've told me you find it difficult to open up to anyone about your feelings. As you've learned during your time here, how we feel affects everything that we do—and that includes your ability to stay clean once you leave The Ranch."

"I've told you, I'm a private person. I like to deal with stuff alone."

"And I get that, Electra, I do, but by agreeing to join us here, you were accepting that you needed help from others. And I'm concerned that once you step back out into the 'real' world, you won't ask for it when you need it."

"We've talked about my trust issues. I guess it's just that."

"Yes, and I accept that like any celebrity, it's a natural issue to have. However, you've seemed particularly reluctant to discuss your childhood."

"I've told you I was adopted along with my five siblings. That we had a privileged lifestyle . . . there's not a lot more to it than that. Besides, Pa always taught me never to look back. Even though that's what therapy seems to be all about."

"Therapy is all about *dealing* with the past, so you don't need to look back any longer, Electra. And your childhood is two-thirds of the life you've lived so far."

I gave my usual shrug and inspected my naked nails and thought how well they were growing now that I had stopped chewing on them. We then had what I termed a "battle of the silences"; it was a war that I knew I could win anytime. And I regularly did.

"So would you say that your father was the most powerful influence in your life?" Fi finally piped up.

"Maybe. Aren't all parents?"

"Often, yes, though sometimes it can be another relative or sibling who fulfills that role. You told me your father was away a lot during your childhood?"

"Yeah, he was. But all of my sisters worshipped him, and as I was the youngest, I guess I followed their lead."

"I'd bet it's a tough deal to be bottom of the pile of six girls," said Fi. "I'm one of four girls, but I was the eldest."

"Lucky you."

"Why do you say that?"

"Because . . . I don't know. My two eldest sisters have always been in charge, and the rest of them always fell into line. All except me."

"You were the rebel?"

"I guess. But not on purpose," I replied, wary of the fact that Fi was drawing me into territory I just did *not* want to talk about.

"Was that when you were a teenager?"

"No, I think I was born a rebel; they all told me I screamed the house down when I was a baby. They used to call me 'Tricky'—I heard Ally and Maia talking about me one day when I was four or five. I went and hid in the gardens and cried my eyes out."

"I can imagine."

"I got over it. No big deal. All siblings call each other names, don't they?"

"Yes, they do. So what were your other sisters' nicknames?"

"I . . . don't remember." I looked up at the clock on the wall. "I have to go now. I have equine therapy at three."

"Okay, we'll wrap for today," Fi said, even though I had ten minutes of my allotted session left. "But your task for tonight is to continue with your mood diary and focus on what your triggers were for cravings. And how about you also think back if you can remember those nicknames for your other sisters?"

"Sure. I'll see you tomorrow."

I got up from the chair and walked out of the room, irritated that we both knew that I wouldn't remember any nicknames for my sisters because there had never been any. As I walked along the therapy hallway into the main reception area and out into the blinding light of the Arizona sun, I gave that round to Fi. Oh, she was good, really good, leading me into traps of my own making. As I had a few minutes to spare, I headed for my new favorite place: the Worry Maze—a circular brick path that led you round and round in a different direction each time, depending on which way you chose to turn at any given point. It felt to me like a metaphor for life; we had talked in group therapy about how each decision we made affected the future course of our life—some small and some mighty big, but each one having an effect. Today, as I walked along the worn brick path, I thought about the decision I seemed to have made without even knowing it . . .

"Why can't you trust anyone?" I asked myself.

It was so very easy to blame it on my celebrity status. I smiled ruefully as I thought of all the billions of people in the world who wanted to be famous and how fame had come to me unexpectedly—literally overnight—at such a young age.

But I knew it wasn't that. Nor was it my sisters finding me irritating, or

Pa, though he was partly responsible because he'd put me in that situation in the first place . . .

*So why don't you tell Fi and talk it through?* I asked myself. *Because you're scared, Electra, scared of having to relive it.*

Besides, it was pathetic, I thought, to base one's whole perception of trust on one small event in one's childhood.

And the one thing I wasn't and would *never* be was a victim. And wow, had I met a lot of victims here at The Ranch.

I hadn't come here for therapy, anyway, I'd come here to get clean, and I was.

"For now," I said out loud, remembering the Twelve Steps. "One day at a time" was the mantra. The three weeks had been so hard, like, the hardest thing I'd ever done in my life, and today wasn't so great, either, because being clean meant that you had a brain again, which meant that you had to face yourself and who you were and . . . well, all that shit. Though it did feel great to wake up in the morning after an actual night's sleep and be able to *think*. So even if I didn't manage to conquer my trust issues, I'd conquered my addictions. And wasn't that the most important thing of all?

I stepped out of the Worry Maze and headed toward the stables and the field where the horses grazed, ready for all the screw-ups (which included me) to come and pat them.

"How are you, Electra?" said Marissa, the young stable hand.

"I'm good, thanks," I said, giving my stock reply. "How are you?"

"Oh, I'm okay," she said as she led me into the stable and pointed to the pile of dirty straw. "Your turn to shit shovel." She grinned at me, handing me a pair of rubber gloves and a pitchfork.

"Thanks."

She left the stable, and I wondered what she really thought about one of the world's top supermodels up to her eyes in horseshit. Whatever it was, I knew they were (technically, anyway) sworn to secrecy and only on pain of death would reveal who and what went on inside The Ranch's walls.

As I began the revolting but calming task of baling out the dirty straw, I thought about what Fi and I had discussed—i.e., my childhood—and it actually made me think of a happy memory. When I'd been six or seven, we'd been vacationing in the Med as usual on the *Titan* and Pa had taken me off on the speedboat to some stables owned by a friend of his somewhere close to Nice.

"I thought you might like to come and see the horses," he'd said. "You could maybe even ride one if you want."

At first I'd been frightened, because they'd seemed gigantic and I'd been so small, but the groom had found the smallest pony in the yard and I'd sat up on its back, feeling a million times taller than I ever had before. I'd been led around the paddock, at first bumping up and down but then letting my body adapt to the natural rhythm of the animal, and by the end of it, I'd been able to encourage the pony into a gentle canter.

"You have a natural gift with horses," Pa had said as he had pulled up beside me on a beautiful brown stallion. "Would you like to learn to ride properly?"

"I'd like to very much, Pa."

And so Pa had arranged riding lessons for me in Geneva and then again when I went to boarding school. It had been the highlight of my week, because I knew that I could tell all my secrets to my horse, love him as much as I wanted, and he would never, ever betray me.

"There, all done," I said to Marissa as I took off my gloves, having refreshed the straw from the bale in the yard.

She indicated the paddock where three of the screw-ups were leaning over the fence watching another screw-up pet Philomena, a gentle bay mare.

I went to the fence and leaned over it, nodding at the others but not engaging.

"Hi, Electra!" Hank, who ran the stables, waved at me. "You're up next!"

"Thanks," I replied, giving him a thumbs-up. I watched him from a distance, thinking how attractive he was with his muscled torso that had been honed not in the gym but by riding out in the desert every day. I enjoyed the way Hank was with the horses; even though I'd seen him kill a diamondback rattlesnake with a shovel when it had appeared in the paddock, he showed a gentleness with the horses that was endearing. I had to admit, I'd been coming down to see him as much as the animals . . .

"Okay, honey, you're on," he shouted to me a few minutes later, after I'd had him stripped naked in a stable in my imagination. The good news about my dark complexion was that blushes didn't show.

"She's all yours," he said as I approached Philomena.

"Hi, Philly," I whispered as I stroked her nose and gave her a kiss, breathing in her fresh horsey smell. "Gee, you're a lucky girl. Number one, you are an animal, and number two, you get so much love and none of the grief that goes with it. But I sure wish I could climb on your back and take you for a ride," I added, turning to see Hank watching me and shooting him a smile.

When they'd done my original psych appraisal, there had been a question mark as to whether I was a sex addict. I'd replied that I was a twenty-six-year-old woman who enjoyed sex, especially when I was high, but no way—*no way*—did I think I was addicted to it. Well, not any more than the next woman of my age.

"This is the problem with coming here," I whispered to Philly. "You come out with more possible addictions than you arrived with."

Once my "horse-hugging" session was over—there was only so much you could do with a static mare—I nodded at Hank, who ambled across to offer me a treat to feed to her.

"You okay?" he asked me as I gave Philly probably her twentieth carrot of the day.

"Yeah, I'm okay. This horse is gonna get fat if she stands here and eats all day."

"Don't worry, I'll give her a good run later."

I sighed. "I wish I could take her out."

"It's against the rules, I'm afraid. Otherwise . . ." He shrugged.

"I understand."

"Maybe when you're out of here you could come to my ranch and take a ride."

"Thanks, I'll see," I said, feeling the sweat pool under my armpits. Maybe it was just me, but as I walked away and saw out of the corner of my eye that he was watching me, I wondered whether that had been a come-on. Whatever, it cheered me up a bit to think that maybe I could still attract a man, even in rehab.

I returned to my dorm, a pastel-painted room with three double beds that were only just long enough for me to fit on. I had a narrow closet for my hoodies and track pants and a desk that I hadn't had use for so far. At first, the thought of sharing a shower and the subsequent body hair that got left behind (I had a thing about hair in drains) had been enough to make me stay sweaty and unwashed, but I'd finally given in when I realized I smelled, and actually it was just fine.

Luckily, the shower was sparkly clean today—the maid had obviously just been in—so I stripped off as fast as I could and stood beneath the blissfully cool spray, casting my eyes upward and not down to the swirl of water around my feet. When I'd emerged from the shower and dressed, I took out my old sketchbook (I'd found it in the front pocket of my carry-on, still tucked away after my trip to Atlantis), then grabbed a pencil and began to draw. I'd recently found that thinking up ideas for unusual but comfortable clothes relaxed me—so many times I'd been dressed up in basically unwearable (and often hideous) haute couture to create images that the average woman on the street couldn't even begin to emulate. But as I heard from endless designers, fashion was a modern art form. Personally, it pissed me off that they claimed this idea as their own when fashion had *always* been an art form. The Versailles courtiers, for example, or the ancient Egyptians.

I began to sketch a dress that had a detachable glittery collar and that would fall in soft folds to the ankles. Beautifully simple and very, very wearable. A few minutes later, my attention was caught by a new face appearing around the dorm door. The girl wandered over to the empty bed closest to the window. She was—as a lot of the inmates were here—anorexically thin and little more than five feet tall. She had the gorgeous skin tone that, like Maia's, indicated a mixed-race heritage and a head of lush, glossy dark curls.

"Hi," I said as I put my pencil down. "You new?"

She nodded as she sat on the bed, knees together, hands clasped in a fist on top of them. She didn't look up at me, and I was glad—normally it only took one glance for a stranger to recognize who I was and to start asking the usual questions.

I watched her release her hands and saw they were shaking as she lifted one to push a lock of hair away from her face.

"Just out of medical detox?" I asked.

She nodded.

"It's tough, but you'll get through it," I said, feeling like an old pro after my three weeks here.

She shrugged in response.

"Have they got you on the benzos? That sure helped me," I added. This girl looked so frail and now her hair wasn't covering her eyes, I could see the fear in them. "Was it coke?"

"No, junk."

As my eyes sought out the telltale track marks on the inside of her thin arms, her hands automatically covered them from view.

"I've heard that's the toughest," I said.

"Yeah."

I watched the girl as she put her arms around herself and curled up onto the bed in a fetal position, her back toward me. I could see she was shivering, so I took the blanket from the end of her bed and draped it over her.

"You can do it," I said, patting her on the shoulder. "I'm Electra, by the way."

There was no reaction, which was surprising, because there usually *was* when I said my name.

"Okay, I'm going to head to lunch. See you later."

I left her curled up under the blanket, marveling at the fact that I'd just found myself caring for her. Seeing her in the same state as I'd been in when they'd taken me out of clinical detox had obviously given me "empathy."

The canteen was busy, with many of the inmates chatting quietly at the circular tables, light pouring in through the tall windows that gave a great view of the Serenity Garden beyond. The buffet spanned the whole length of the canteen, with hatted chefs serving up surprisingly delicious food. I collected my daily intake of carbs—a piping-hot beef enchilada with golden cheese melted over it and a side of fries. I figured I would have to go on a crash diet when I left, but eating seemed to ease the craving for vodka. As I ate, I thought about the word "empathy." It was one that was used a lot at The Ranch; apparently alcohol and drug abuse made you lose any of it that you had for others, cutting off the good parts of you as well as dulling the bad things you wanted to block out, which was the reason you'd taken the booze and pills in the first place. Tomorrow, I thought, I'd tell Fi that I might just have shown some empathy to the new girl in my dorm. She'd like that.

"Hi."

I looked up as Lizzie, my roommate whose bed was next to mine, came and sat down with her soup and plate of green stuff. Her hair was as sleek as always, blond, perfectly highlighted, and styled into a bob. She reminded me of a china doll—except that she'd had so much work done, her face looked like it was made by a psychopathic sculptor who'd studied under Picasso. She was in here for food addiction, and I was amazed she came to the canteen at all; for me it would be like being in a bar with lines of coke spread across the counter.

"How are you today?" she asked me in her British accent.

"I'm doing okay, thanks, Lizzie," I responded, wondering if she remembered me rolling her onto her side last night when she was snoring fit to wake every coyote in the neighborhood.

"You look a lot better. Your eyes are brighter. Not that they were ever dull," she added quickly. "You have beautiful eyes, Electra."

"Thanks," I said, feeling guilty as I munched on my enchilada, which she stared at in a way that told me she'd kill just for a taste of it. "How about you?"

"Oh, I'm doing well," she replied. "I've lost twelve pounds since I came in—only another three weeks and Christopher will hardly recognize me!"

Christopher was Lizzie's husband. An LA producer who, so Lizzie had confided to me at length, was the usual cliché of the married man who played around. Lizzie was convinced that if she lost twenty pounds, his shenanigans would stop. The fact was, she wasn't even fat in the first place, and I wasn't sure how much of her was actually real, either. She'd been nipped and tucked and lifted so much that it looked like a pair of invisible hands were dragging the skin on her face upward. Personally, I didn't hold out much hope for Christopher's return to fidelity. In my humble opinion, Lizzie wasn't addicted to food, she was addicted to pleasing her husband.

"How much longer have you got now?" she asked.

"A week, and then I'm out of here."

"You've done so well, Electra. I've seen so many who have come in here who don't, you know. And you're far too beautiful and bright to need all that stuff," she added as she forked up a leaf of arugula salad and chewed it purposefully, as if it were a chunky piece of rib-eye steak. "I'm proud of you."

"Hey, thanks." I smiled, feeling that this was my first proper "good" day and it felt great to get compliments like that. "There's a new girl in our dorm, by the way," I added, wondering if it was okay for me to bring a slice of chocolate cheesecake back to the table in front of her.

"Oh, yes, Vanessa." Lizzie raised her eyebrows—she was always the first to know anything in here, and I soaked up her gossip. "Poor love. She's so young—only just eighteen, apparently. One of the detox nurses told me she was picked out of a gutter in New York by some wealthy person, who has sponsored the cost of getting her properly clean here. State-funded programs for juveniles do exist, but a kid gets in and by the time they've detoxed and are technically clean, they're out and back to their old life. And using again within weeks." Lizzie sighed. "And if you're legally an adult, like Vanessa is now, then forget it."

It had dawned on me only in the past few days, as my brain had started to function properly, that we in here were the privileged few. I hadn't had to even think about what it would cost to come in and get clean, just whether I wanted to or not. There were thousands of young American kids who were addicts like me, with no hope of getting the kind of proper treatment they needed.

"The nurse said Vanessa's one of the worst cases she's had in here. She was in the detox clinic for four days. Poor little thing." Lizzie, despite her desperation to be beautiful and the carnage she had wreaked on her once pretty face, had a definite motherly quality to her. "We'll look after her, won't we, Electra?"

"We'll try, Lizzie, yes."

That afternoon, to work off my lunch, I went for a run along the nature trail that looped around the perimeter of The Ranch. As I ran, I remembered my trek up the mountain behind Atlantis over a month ago and how much better I'd felt after it. Even though the dry, hot Arizona air burned in my lungs and stung my nose as I breathed, I kept going.

I came to a halt near the watercooler and poured myself a cup, which I drank down thirstily, and then another, which I dumped all over me. I plopped down on a bench and enjoyed the feeling of . . . well, *feeling*. Despite my reluctance to embrace The Ranch's spiritual approach, just sitting here with the mountains behind me, the blue sky against the red of the earth was calming. Nature *was* calming. The air carried the scents of the low green shrubs that were unfurling in the sun. Incredible flowers and cacti were dotted all across the desert's arid beauty—some over ten feet tall, their green spiky trunks filled with water to keep them sated until the next rains.

For the first time, I pictured myself back in my New York apartment and felt trapped, like an animal in a cage. Somehow, what was around me here felt like more natural territory for me, as though it suited who I was. The heat didn't bother me like it bothered Lizzie, and the open spaces made me feel alive.

As I sat there, I felt my lips form into a smile.

"Why?" I asked myself.

*Just because, Electra . . .*

As I stood up to go inside, remembering group therapy was about to start and I'd have to go in my running gear, I suddenly realized I hadn't thought about having a drink or doing a line for the past two hours. And that made me smile all over again.

When I got back to the dorm later, desperate for another shower, Vanessa was still curled up on her bed. She was now shaking violently, and Lizzie—whose bed was sandwiched between us—was sitting there watching her.

"She's not in a good way, Electra," she said and sighed. "I've called the nurse, and she's given her another injection of whatever it is she needs, but . . ."

"She doesn't look good, no," I agreed as I grabbed my towel and went in for a shower. Coming out, I dressed in a clean pair of track pants and a hoodie. "Are you coming to supper?" I asked Lizzie.

"No, I'm going to stay here and just watch Vanessa for a while. I'm worried about her."

"Okay, see you later."

Feeling low because I really didn't want to stick around to see Vanessa going through what I had, I went into the canteen. I avoided what I called the "woo-woos": those who had taken up The Ranch's spiritual ethos and spoke only in quotes, like a bunch of walking, talking self-help books—and piled my tray with steak and sides. Not wanting to go back to the dorm once I'd finished eating, I grabbed some paper and pens from the side table and thought about what we had discussed at the AA meeting that morning. I was on step number nine, the one where I had to write an apology letter to anyone I might have hurt when my substance abuse had gotten out of control.

*Okay, so who do I have to apologize to?* I thought. *Ma?*

Yes. I knew that I'd been a huge pain in the butt as a child and she had always been so patient with me. I'd definitely write her a note. But then again, I thought as I wolfed back some cheesecake, were these apologies about being a bad person or being a bad person because of my substance abuse? I'd hardly seen Ma in the past few years and rarely called her.

*Then she deserves an apology for me ignoring her*, I thought, and gave her a check on the list.

Maia? Yup, she definitely deserved an apology for my shitty behavior after Pa had died and we had been in Atlantis, and in Rio. If it hadn't been for her calling Mariam, I might have died. She'd been wonderful, and I really, really loved her. I gave her a big check.

Ally: she should get one, too. I stared out of the window, thinking back to when we'd been at Atlantis together last month and how rude I'd been to her. I wondered then why Ally had always irritated me, because she was such a good person. Maybe that was it: the fact that she *was* a good person and so together, even though she'd lost the love of her life and had a baby. It had always made my *un*togetherness more obvious.

Star: my mousy little sister, who would never say boo to a goose. I had no idea if I liked her or if I didn't, because she'd always said so little; she'd been the silence to my big noise. Ally had said that she had met some guy and was living in England with him. Maybe I'd make the effort to go see her when I got out of here. I had always felt sorry for her and the way she was overshadowed on every level by my nemesis sister, CeCe. I'd write Star a letter anyway, just to say hello, because I couldn't think of anything bad I'd actually done to her specifically.

CeCe. I ground the nib of the pen hard into the paper. She and I had never gotten along; Ma had always said we were too similar, but I wasn't so sure. I didn't like the way she'd dominated Star, and sometimes when we were younger, we'd fallen out and had physical fights that Ally had had to break up. I'd been glad when I'd heard that she'd moved to Australia.

"Basically because Star dumped her for a man," I murmured maliciously, knowing Fi and the group therapy crowd wouldn't like that negativity, but you couldn't like everyone in the world, could you? Although apparently, you could get them to forgive you.

For now, I put a question mark against CeCe's name and then moved on to Tiggy.

As an adult, she had definitely morphed into the kind of person who could probably apply for a job here. Then I metaphorically slapped myself for being bitchy about her, because she didn't deserve it. She was sweet and gentle and just wanted to make everybody happy. We were polar opposites, yet I aspired to be like her because she could see the good in everything and everybody, whereas I was wired the opposite way around. I vaguely remembered Ally telling me at Atlantis that she'd had a health issue. To my shame, I hadn't even dropped her an email to ask how she was. Tiggy was definitely going on my list of apologies.

I then sat back and wondered whether, if Pa were alive, I'd be wanting to write him an apology. No. I felt he should be writing me one, having died when I was still so young and leaving me to deal with all this stuff. Including Stella, my grandmother. Anyway, I didn't want to think about all that, so I moved on to my New York life.

Mariam: *MASSIVE APOLOGY*, I wrote. She was by far the best PA I'd ever had, although I had no idea whether she *was* still my PA. I put that on my list to ask Maia when I replied to the email she'd sent me a couple of days ago. We were allowed our laptops and cell phones for an hour each day, but everything we wrote was monitored, so I hadn't written to anyone so far.

Stella, aka "Granny." I paused and chewed the end of my pen as I navigated the brain fuzz that was the last few weeks before I'd come here. Truthfully, I couldn't remember much about our conversations, though I did remember waking up and her sitting in the easy chair by my bed. I also thought I remembered her singing, but maybe that had been a dream. Although even in the haze of my couple of meetings with her, I remembered that she was truly one of the scariest humans I'd ever met.

Before I could decide whether I should write her, my attention was caught by a supertall black guy who walked past me with a tray of food. Unlike most of the inmates who wore hoodies and track pants like me, he was dressed in a crisp white shirt and chinos. I hunched over my paper with my head down as he went to sit at the table opposite. I normally didn't give a shit who saw me looking as rough as hell, but I glanced to my left and saw he was crazily beautiful and had a certain elegance about him. Before he could spot me, I put my hood up, picked up my tray and the pen and paper, and left the canteen.

When I arrived back at my dorm, Vanessa's bed was empty and Lizzie was involved in her usual nighttime beauty regime, her desk transformed into an expensive cosmetics counter.

"Where's Vanessa?" I asked as I watched her lather cream onto her face, use a pipette to put drops of what she said contained gold flakes onto her neck, and swallow a series of pills that had been okayed by the doctor so must contain a bunch of nothing.

"The poor little mite started having a seizure, so I called the nurse and she's been taken back to the clinical detox ward." Lizzie sighed. "I just hope it's not too late."

"What do you mean?"

"Electra, surely you must know the effect that heroin and all those other drugs she'd taken can have on your vital organs? If you've been abusing them for a long time, when you try to come off them, it can cause seizures. Apparently, the boyfriend who was feeding her the drugs was also her pimp, and goodness knows what was in them."

"So she was a prostitute?"

"So I overheard a nurse saying, yes. She's HIV positive, too," Lizzie commented as she began packing away her "shop" into a Louis Vuitton suitcase. "It's so so sad, because she is only the tip of the iceberg. My husband once produced a documentary on the drug gangs of Harlem; those are the guys who are the real criminals in all this."

"Right," I said as I changed into my nightwear and climbed into bed. "It's crazy to think that Harlem is only a few blocks uptown from where I live." I took my sketchbook and pencil out of my nightstand and flipped to a new page. Now that the impulse to design had returned to me, every night before bed I'd quickly dash off a couple of fashion sketches.

"It is, yes," Lizzie agreed as she got into bed, too. "Of course, we have big gangs in LA, too; sadly, they're everywhere these days. We don't know how lucky we are, do we? We live such protected lives."

"Yes, we do," I agreed, feeling I was learning more about the world while cloistered in The Ranch in the middle of the desert than I'd ever learned in New York and all my travels around the globe. And I thought how naive I must have been, believing that I was somehow above it all. Where did I think my dealers had gotten my cocaine from in the first place? It didn't matter if you were doing a bump in an expensive hotel or on a street corner—it all came from the same place, from brutality and death and lust for money. I shivered at the thought.

"So what have you got planned for tomorrow?" Lizzie asked.

"Oh, you know, the usual. A run before breakfast, an AA meeting, then therapy with Fi."

"She's the best therapist I've ever had. And I've had a few," said Lizzie.

"So have I," I said with feeling. "But I guess I'm just not very good at the whole therapy thing."

"What do you mean?"

"I just don't like sitting there talking about myself."

"You mean you don't like having to face up to who you are," she observed shrewdly. "Until we do that, sweetheart, none of us in here get anywhere."

"They seemed to do okay in the old days. I've never heard of anyone having a therapist, like, in movies I've seen about World War I and World War II."

"No." Lizzie gave me a lopsided grimace, due to all the filler she had in her lips. "Well, remember, Electra, a lot of those men came home with shell shock—or PTSD, as we know it today—and they sorely needed help, just like soldiers did after Vietnam, but their needs were ignored. So it's a good thing that we're living in a culture where it's okay to admit you need help. I'm sure it will save many lives that would have been lost."

"Yup, you're right," I agreed.

"It's also bad that we've lost our communities. I grew up in a little village in England where everyone knew everyone. When my father died, I remember them rallying around my mum. They were all there for her and for me, but that doesn't seem to happen anymore. We're all so displaced. We don't feel we "belong" anywhere. Or to anyone. One of the downsides of globalization, I suppose. How many friends do you have that you feel you can trust?"

I thought about that question for about one second, then shrugged. "None. But maybe that's just because of who I am."

"Yes, I'm sure it's partly that, but the rest of us aren't much better off, either. It's sad, because so many of us feel alone with our problems these days."

I looked at Lizzie, with her weird face and ridiculous beauty regime and obvious snake of a husband, and wondered where it had all gone wrong. She was so thoughtful and articulate.

"What did you do before you married Christopher?" I asked.

"Oh, I was a trainee lawyer. When I met Chris, I was temporarily based in the firm's New York office. I wanted to specialize in family law, but then I was swept off my feet by him and we ended up moving to LA. Then I had the kids, and then they left home and"—Lizzie shrugged—"that's the story."

"So you got a degree in law?"

"Oh, yes, but I never did get to practice."

"Maybe you should think about it. As you say, all your kids have left now."

"Oh, Electra, I'm not far off fifty! It's too late for me now."

"But you're so clever, Lizzie. You shouldn't let your brain go to waste. That's what my father always said to me."

"Did he?"

"Yeah. I know he thought I was selling out when I became a model."

"Electra, you were only sixteen! From what you've told me, you didn't choose modeling, it chose *you*, and before you knew it, you were on a roller coaster that you couldn't get off. Goodness, just twenty-six now—only a year older than my eldest, and he's still in med school."

"At least he knew what he wanted to do. I've never known."

"Well, whatever it is, you have the luxury of choice. And someone with your profile could really make a difference."

"What do you mean?"

"You know, being an ambassador for those who don't have a voice. Like Vanessa, for example. You've experienced firsthand what drugs can do. You could help."

I shrugged. "Maybe." But models don't have voices or brains, do they?"

"Now you're being self-indulgent, and if you were Rosie, my daughter, I'd give you a good telling off. It's obvious to me—and to your pa—that you are very bright indeed. You have all the tools necessary, so use them. I mean, look at what you've drawn during our conversation just now," she said, pointing to my sketchbook as I cradled it protectively against my chest. "You're so talented, Electra. I'd buy that jacket in a heartbeat."

I looked down at my sketch of a model in a cropped leather jacket and asymmetrical dress.

"Yeah, whatever," I said. "I think I need some sleep now, Lizzie. Good night." I reached over to turn off my lamp.

"Good night," Lizzie said as she opened the book she was reading about how diets could make you fat. I snuggled down under the comforter and turned over.

"Oh, just one more thing," she said.

"Yup?"

"It takes strength to admit you've got a problem, Electra. It is not a sign of weakness—quite the opposite. Good night."

# 18

I woke up naturally with the sunrise the following day, which was a sensation that was new to me—for years I'd had to drag myself out of bed, take a handful of painkillers and uppers to stem the headache and give me a lift. I'd discussed my sunrise wakings in group therapy (it was something innocuous to make me look like I was briefly engaged without giving anything away), and a number of people had told me it was the natural rhythm of my body clock returning after years of being suppressed by booze and drugs. And now I came to think of it, I remembered that I had always been the first to wake as a child at Atlantis. I'd be bouncing around, full of energy, while all my sisters slept on, so I'd creep downstairs to the kitchen, where Claudia was the only other soul up in the house. She'd give me a slice of her newly baked bread, still warm from the oven and dripping with butter and honey, while I waited impatiently for the rest of my siblings to wake up.

I put on a pair of shorts, laced up my sneakers, and set off for a run. Nobody was around, other than the group of Buddhists who sat in the Serenity Garden with their legs crossed and eyes closed, welcoming in the new day. I reached the nature trail, and as my feet pounded the red soil beneath them, I thought about Lizzie and our conversation last night. And the fact that it wasn't a sign of weakness to admit you needed help. Well, I'd gotten this far—I was here, getting the help I needed, wasn't I? Ironically, the easy bit (comparatively, anyway) had been coming off all that shit I'd been taking. As my doctor, then Fi had explained to me, I'd been caught in time, when many others weren't. If I stayed clean from now on, I'd have made no dent on my long-term health, unlike Vanessa.

The hard bit was confronting *myself*, which would explain the why of my substance abuse. It wasn't good enough just to say I'd stop taking alcohol and drugs—it had only been three weeks, for Chrissake, and the euphoria of getting clean and the safe environment I was living in would disappear like mist once I was forced back into the never-ending circuit of my "real" life. I'd start having the odd drink, then maybe taking a line socially, and then eventually, I'd end up back here, but probably worse off, and maybe eventually wind up like Vanessa. But until I acknowledged all my angst and let it out, I knew I would always be in danger.

As I was thinking all this, I had the oddest instinct that I was being followed. Luckily, I was hanging a right around the circuit and was able to look back and see that the edible guy I'd seen in the canteen was maybe a hundred yards behind me and catching up fast. Well, he wouldn't, because I didn't want him to for all sorts of reasons I couldn't work out, so I upped my pace and stretched out the gap. But he was still closing in on me, even though I was now running as fast as I could. The end of the trail was only a couple of hundred yards away, so I put my feet down to maximum and headed full pelt for it.

Reaching the finish line, I ran for the watercooler, desperate for a drink and panting heavily.

"That's some gas you've got in your tank," a rich, well-modulated voice said from behind me. "Excuse me," it added as a large hand with long, elegant fingers—the pinkie adorned with a gold class ring—reached for a cup as I moved out of the way. "I ran the five thousand meters for my college and never got beat. You run for yours?"

"I didn't go to college," I said as I lifted my head to look up at him, which was an unusual feeling.

"Hey, that's not an all-American accent, is it?" he asked me as I took another cup of water and poured it over me. Even though it was early, the sun was already beating down.

"No, it's kind of part French. I was raised in Switzerland."

"Oh, really?" he said as he eyed me more closely. And then "Do I know you? You seem familiar somehow."

"No, we've never met before."

"I'll take your word for it." He smiled at me. "But you sure do look like I know you. I'm Miles, by the way. You?"

"Electra," I sighed, waiting for recognition to dawn on his face. Which it did.

"Wow . . . okay," he said, throwing his cup into the trash and digging his hands into his shorts pockets. "I was looking at a twenty-foot-high billboard of you when I drove to the airport last week."

"Oh," I said. "Well, I gotta get back now."

"Sure, so have I."

We walked back toward The Ranch in silence. Something about this man was making me feel shy and girly. I guessed he was in his late thirties by his confidence and the gray that peppered the tightly curled hair on his scalp.

"Is it okay to ask you what you're in for?" he said.

"Yeah, there are no secrets here, are there? Alcohol and substance abuse."

"Ditto."

"Really? I saw you in the canteen last night, and you didn't look like a guy who'd just gone through detox."

"I haven't, I've been clean for over five years now, but I just come back here every year to rest and remind myself what's at stake. It's easy to think you can handle everything when you're here with support all around you, but out there in the big, bad world, it can close in on you again."

"What do you do?"

"I'm a lawyer," he said. "The pressures build up and . . . I want to make sure I never explode and end up back where I was, but hey, you must know all about that."

"Yup," I said as we arrived at the entrance to The Ranch.

"All I can say is don't rush it, take your time. It's a disease we can never be cured of; the answer is to learn how to manage it properly. Listen to what the people here say, Electra, because they know how to save your life. See you around." He gave me a small wave and marched off along the hallway on a pair of toned legs that were even longer than my own.

"Well," I whispered to myself, feeling shell-shocked. Miles had an air of gravitas about him that reminded me of my grandmother. *In any court, I'd want that guy on my side*, I thought as I walked in for breakfast, feeling hot and bothered. And it wasn't just from the run.

"God, grant me the serenity to accept the things I cannot change, the courage to change the things I can, and the wisdom to know the difference."

I chanted the serenity prayer that signaled the end of the meeting, along with the five others in the small AA circle. I was holding hands with Ben, a bass guitar player in a band I'd never heard of, and a new woman called Sabrina on the other side of me. I could see Sabrina was still tearful—she had just shared her story with us.

"I had everything, and then I threw it away down the neck of a bottle," she'd said, her hands clenched together in front of her. She was a petite Asian woman, and her black hair hung in a shiny curtain around her thin face. "I've lost my job, my husband, my family . . . I stole from everyone I knew—even my kids' piggy banks—just to buy more liquor. It was only when I ended up in the ER because I'd passed out in my work restroom that I decided to come here." She bit her lip. "I can't mess up or take my life for granted any longer."

It struck me as I left the meeting that I, too, had taken my life for granted. I'd been so desperate for an escape, I had almost thrown it all away.

"So, Electra, how have the last twenty-four hours been?" Fi asked me later that morning.

"Interesting," I said as I rubbed my nose.

"Good, good." Fi smiled. "Can you tell me why?"

"I . . . well, I don't know exactly, but a lot of things seem to be coming into focus. It's like I've been in a dream for the past year."

"In a sense, you have. That's what substance abuse creates, except of course it all ends in a nightmare, as you know. So how does this clearer sense of reality make you feel?"

*Here we go again . . .*

"Well, um, I feel euphoric that I'm clean but ashamed because I'm remembering all the bad stuff I did to people and the way I was with them and scared of falling back into the same pattern when I leave."

"Great, that's just great, Electra!" Fi gave me a smile. "You're really making progress, and all these emotions you're feeling at this stage are completely natural. Taking accountability for yourself and your behavior toward others is a big step forward. You're no longer a victim."

"A victim? Hell, no, I was never a victim."

"You were, Electra, a victim of the abuse you were subjecting yourself to," Fi countered. "But now you're dealing with it, fighting it and not being victimized by it, do you see?"

"Yeah, I do, but I drank and took all that stuff to *help* me deal with my life, so no one would see me as a victim."

"Does the thought of being seen as a victim—as weak—scare you?"

I nodded vehemently. "Yeah, it sure does. Something my dorm mate said last night made me feel better, though."

"And what was that?"

"That I stopped being weak when I asked for help."

"Do you think she was right?"

"Yeah, but I don't want to get all needy or anything. I can take care of myself."

"Perhaps the point was that you couldn't and didn't. Would you agree with that?"

"Well, yeah, I suppose," I said.

"As the saying goes, no man—or woman, for that matter—is an island." Fi smiled. "But you're not alone. The world we live in is full of people who are too scared or embarrassed to ask for help."

"Or too proud," I added. "I'm very proud."

"I can see that," Fi said. "Do you think it's a good quality?"

"I don't know; whether it is or it isn't, it's just part of who I am. Maybe it's a bit of both."

Fi nodded and scribbled something on her pad. "You know what, Electra? I think you might be ready for a visit. What do you think?"

"I . . . I don't know."

"Would you like a member of your family or a friend to come and see you?"

"Can I think about it?"

"Of course you can. Showing off the new you and having contact with the outside world via someone close can be frightening. Do you feel frightened at the thought?"

"Yeah, I do. I mean, you know how much I didn't want to come in here, but I've met some great people and I kind of feel safe here, you know?"

"We've never discussed when you might want to leave, because both of us have known you haven't been ready to go yet. You have seven days left until your thirty-day treatment program is over. You've grown in leaps and bounds in the past few days, but would you agree you've still got issues that need to be sorted out before you go?"

"Probably," I said.

"How are the cravings at the moment?"

"Much better when I'm active, like when I'm running; then I don't think about it."

"Then one of the tools you can take out of here is that physical activity helps. How are your mood swings? You mentioned last week you were experiencing feelings of anger and 'blackness,' as you described it. Are you still experiencing those?"

"No." I swallowed. "Those negative thoughts have gotten better . . . yes, they're better."

"So how do you feel about a visit?" Fi asked again.

"Maybe next week?" I said.

"Okay. And who would that person be, do you think?"

*Aye, there's the rub*, I thought, one of Pa's favorite Shakespearean quotations floating into my brain. Sadly, the list of potential visitors reflected the low point my life had come to: there was only Ma, who was my mom of sorts, or Maia or Stella, a grandmother whom I'd met only a couple of times when I'd been completely wasted . . .

"Can I think about that one?" I said.

"Of course you can. Is the list quite small?"

"Very," I admitted.

"How many?"

"Three."

"Well, you may not think that's a lot, Electra, but I can tell you that by the time most people get here and sit in this room with me and I ask them the same question, they struggle to name anyone. They've isolated themselves— pushed people they love and who love them away. Alcohol and drugs have become their only friends. Would you agree with that?"

"Yup," I said, hearing the fear in my voice. "I would. Actually, there's probably a fourth person."

"Even better." Fi smiled. "Who would that be?"

"Mariam. She's my PA, but, well, I really, like, admire her."

"Does she like you, too, do you think?"

"I . . . I've behaved real badly to her, but yes, maybe."

"Sometimes it can be good to have someone who is not so directly emotionally attached to you as your first contact. Anyway, you think about it, Electra, and tell me tomorrow."

"Okay," I agreed.

"Great, well, keep up the good work," she said as I stood up.

"Thanks. Bye, Fi."

I walked out of her office feeling almost high and like a child who had just received a gold star from her teacher.

"Any news on Vanessa?" I asked Lizzie in the dorm later on that day.

"No, even I couldn't pry any information out of the nurse, so I guess not good. You look sparkly today, Electra," Lizzie commented as I grabbed my towel from the peg and prepared to go into the shower. "What's been going on?"

"Like, nothing," I said as I stripped off my clothes and pulled the towel around me.

"Gosh, of all the dorm mates to get in rehab," sighed Lizzie, "I get stuck with one of the world's most beautiful women. You seriously have a body to die for. And you eat like a horse and never put on an ounce of weight. I should hate you." She chuckled as I walked into the shower and shut the door behind me.

As I stood under the water, I thought about what Lizzie had said just now; I mean, it was hardly anything new, being told that I had a fantastic body. So if I did, why had I been so keen on abusing it?

Maybe it was because *I* hated it, because it had made others hate *me*. Most women didn't trust me, and if they were with a man, I could almost sense their lacquered fingernails tightening their hold on their male as I approached. Besides, I didn't even think I *did* have a beautiful face or body—it just happened to look nice in the clothes that were fashionable right now. I'd grown up with a sister who had always been known as the beauty of the family, and if I was asked to describe my image of a perfect woman, it would almost certainly be Maia with her curves, full breasts, glossy dark hair, and stunning features.

While I brushed my teeth, I looked at myself in the mirror and decided I definitely had nice eyes, great cheekbones, and a pair of lips that would never need fillers. The color of my skin would never change. And that was one of the things that marked me out as a successful model. I only hoped that a time would come soon when there were more dark-skinned models. As a little girl, I'd never given much thought to the fact that I was black and the rest of my sisters were differing shades of brown (Maia and CeCe) to white (Star, Tiggy, and Ally). Each one of us had looked different from the others, so it was just my "normal." It was only when I'd gone to boarding school, where I'd been the only black girl and also a good head and a half taller than the other girls, that I had become self-conscious about my outer self.

"Electra, have you finished in there? I'm desperate for a wee."

"Coming," I said, opening the door to let Lizzie in. She'd obviously been on one of those juice regimes that filled you up with liquid but meant you spent the rest of the day peeing.

When she reappeared, she regarded me as I sat on the bed in my track pants and hoodie.

"You know it's a Tuesday Night Out tonight, don't you?" she asked me with her arms folded. "We're all off to go bowling in town."

"Yeah, I do, but it isn't my scene."

"I didn't think it was mine, either, when I first came here, but actually it's really fun. We're going for a pizza afterward—well, for everyone other than me—and I think you'd enjoy it. It's a chance to get to know the other residents, have a chat out of school, if you know what I mean."

I shrugged. "Thanks, but no thanks. I have some letters to write."

"Okay . . . By the way," she said as she went back to the cosmetics case to set up her makeup station in preparation for tonight's outing, "did you see that hunk who arrived recently?"

"Er, did I?"

"You could hardly miss him; he's at least as tall as you are, packed with rippling muscles, and has the most seductive brown eyes ever."

"Oh, you mean Miles."

Lizzie looked up at me, her mascara brush held in midair. "You've spoken to him?"

"Yeah, he was on the trail this morning when I was out for my run."

"Now, that is a man even I could imagine doing extremely rude things with." Lizzie giggled. "He looks like a movie star. Is he?"

"No, he's a lawyer."

"Wow, you two obviously got to know each other quite well this morning. He was sitting by himself when I went into the canteen at lunchtime. So, being the friendly, welcoming person I am, I went to sit with him. Two minutes later, he picked up his tray and left." Lizzie frowned. "So much for my pulling tactics, eh?"

"I thought you were devoted to your husband?" I said.

"You know I am, but there's no harm in window-shopping occasionally, even if you can't buy the product! He looks far too fit to be in here. Why is he?"

"He says he comes back every year to make sure he doesn't relapse."

"This is my sixth time here, so I totally understand. I like it here because everyone is so friendly and you're never short of someone to talk to. Not like at home."

"Doesn't your husband miss you?"

"Oh, he's hardly ever at home, either. And now that the children have gone, well . . . Anyway, if you're sure you won't come, I'd better be off. How do I look in these jeans?" she asked, standing up and giving me a twirl. "I couldn't even get them to do up when I arrived a few weeks ago. And please don't lie, just say it how it is."

I looked at her trim figure, with a narrow waist and pert little butt that any twenty-five-year-old would be proud of, let alone a woman of forty-eight.

"Seriously, Lizzie, you look just great."

"Are you sure? My husband hates me in jeans—says I have a 'jelly belly.'"

"You don't, I swear. Now you go off and have a great evening, okay?"

"Thanks, Electra, see you later."

As Lizzie left the room in a cloud of her expensive perfume, I suddenly realized that she wasn't just here to lose weight; she was here because she was lonely.

I pulled the chair out by my desk, retrieved the notepaper, envelopes, and pens from the drawer, and began my "apology" letters.

*Dear Maia,*

*I am doing well here. I've been off the shit for three weeks and going to AA meetings every day. Being in here has given me time to think about how badly I've behaved toward you in the past . . .*

*Month? Year?* I thought.

*. . . year. And especially in Rio. I can see now that you were only trying to help me. If it wasn't for you calling Mariam that night, I literally wouldn't be here anymore. I hope you can forgive me, and I look forward to seeing you in June.*

*Thanks again.*

*Love,*
*Electra*

As I folded the letter and stuck it in an envelope, I wished that I could simply email her, because God only knew how long my note would take to get to Rio. But Margot, the AA leader, had said it was better if it was written, because letters were more meaningful. Maybe I'd send Maia an email anyway, to tell her the letter was on its way. Or if she was to come visit next week, I could give it to her then.

I addressed the envelope and stuck it in my drawer.

Then I wrote to Ma, using mainly the same words but altering it a little to suit. I had a sudden urge to write "I love you" at the bottom. I couldn't even remember whether I had ever said those words to her. Well, I *did* love her, I realized, a whole lot. She was the kindest person I'd ever met, and she had put up with me and my behavior for a long time, so I finished the letter with words to that effect.

Feeling suddenly tearful, I thought about Atlantis and how safe I'd felt there and how much I'd always wanted to go back when I'd been away at school because it was "home" . . .

"Now I need to find my own," I muttered, a tear splashing onto the envelope as I wrote Ma's name and address on the front.

I was feeling low now, which wasn't good, so I put the paper and pens away, stretched, and decided to go outside and get some air. Just down the hallway there was a kitchenette with coffee, tea, and cookies, so I fixed myself a ginger tea—the zing as it went down my throat was the nearest I could get to a hit these days—then wandered outside. The night was noticeably cooler, and I could smell the scent of the large saguaro flowers that grew on the cacti in the garden. The sky was just incredible—inky black and wide open above me. As always when I looked up to the stars, I searched for the Seven Sisters, and there they were, twinkling away. As usual, I counted six—it was only very rarely I got to see the seventh. Pa had once told me that some cultures said that Electra—i.e., me—was the lost sister of the Pleiades. He'd even given me an old black-and-white print of a scene from a ballet called *Electra, or the Lost Pleiad* that had been on once in London. I walked toward the bench that sat amid the pretty Serenity Garden, full of herbs nestled among the bright flowers, which gave off a delicate scent. A little fountain played soothingly in the background, and I closed my eyes and thought about how I'd always felt like the "lost" sister out of the six of us. Even though Pa had never found the seventh.

"Hi there," a voice said from the bench on the other side of the garden.

I opened my eyes, and as they readjusted to the low lighting, I saw it was Miles, smoking a cigarette.

"Hi. Am I disturbing you?" I asked him across the fountain.

"No, to be honest, I could use some company." He stood up from his bench and walked over to mine. "If that's okay?"

Sitting down as I was, he rose above me and I had to crane my neck to make eye contact.

"Yeah, take a seat," I said.

He sat down next to me. "Want one?" He offered me the packet from the pocket in his shirt.

"No, thanks. It's one addiction I've never started, and I don't wanna come out of here with a new one."

"For me it was the first of many, and the one I've fallen back on as the rest aren't available," he said as he dragged on the cigarette, then stubbed it out with his foot. "A few years ago, around this time of night in New York, I'd have been out at a bar, hearing the clink of ice going into that glass and the Grey Goose pouring over it like a mountain stream."

I chuckled. "That sure is poetic." The Goose and I were great pals as well. Now it's some dried ginger in hot water."

"I haven't been to that bar in about five years now," he said as he lit another cigarette. "My old dealer probably still hangs out there."

"How long were you on all the stuff?"

"I did my first line nineteen years ago at Harvard."

"Wow! You went to Harvard? You must be real smart."

He shrugged. "I guess I was once. I was a total geek—you know, debate club and all that. I was on an academic scholarship; even though I'm tall and black, I sucked at basketball, which I think the WASPs at that place found tough to wrap their minds around. I felt like a total alien, you know? Still . . . I got a law degree, then started with one of the biggest firms in New York. And that's where I really became dependent on liquor and drugs."

"It's interesting you felt like you stuck out at college. I was raised in a multicultural family. We were all adopted from various countries in the world, so because we were all 'different,' I never thought about it. Then I went to boarding school, and, well, things changed. I've been thinking about that time a lot—you know, they like to take you back into your past here."

"I do, Electra. Clearing out the debris you have stuck in your mind is as important as clearing out the stuff from your body. Go on, sorry, I interrupted."

"Well, what I've been mulling over is that because I didn't feel any different from the rest of my sisters, I wasn't aware that I was 'black,' so when I got to boarding school and bad things happened, I never associated them with that. Like you, I was in a predominantly white school, and yeah, some stuff happened, but I don't know whether it came from that or just being a pain in the butt."

"Maybe it just came from being different from them. Kids can be so cruel."

"Yeah, they can, and they were, but what's the point of talking about it now? It's done."

"Seriously?" Miles gave a deep chuckle. "You can't have been in here for long if you're asking me that. Sounds like I'm the other way around from you; I always had trouble with the physical withdrawal, whereas you've gotta get your head around the mental aspects and find the reason you became an addict in the first place."

There was a silence between us as Miles finished his cigarette.

"You got someone?" he asked after a while. "A significant other?"

"Nope, and no insignificant ones either," I joked as I sipped my tea. "I thought I did awhile back, but he dumped me."

"Yeah, I think I read about it. Sorry." Miles looked embarrassed. "Did that set you back?"

"Big time! Can you imagine how humiliating it is to have the whole world know you've gotten thrown over and the love of your life is engaged to someone else?"

"The love of your life up to now, Electra," Miles put in. "You can't be much older than most college kids. But no, in answer to your question, I can't imagine. I've gone a few rounds in court with the media for some high-profile clients, but that's the extent of my brushes with the paparazzi."

"Did you win?"

He grinned. "Nope."

"Were you high in court?"

"Probably. You been high when you've been modeling?"

"Probably." I looked at him, and we shared a wry smile.

"Well, there are a heap of lawyers I know who rely on a quick line of cocaine before entering the courtroom and giving their summation. But don't tell anyone I told you that." Miles grinned again.

"Oh, it's the same in my business, too. We're both giving a performance, like actors."

"The problem is, when you're feeling like you're king of the world, you just don't know when to quit. I probably lost a few cases because of it. And as I'm working in a predominantly white man's world, I can't afford to do that."

"You never know, we might just be getting ourselves our first black president," I said, having glanced at the news on the TV in the canteen earlier that day. "Obama's doing well in the primaries."

"And won't that just be something." Miles smiled. "We've still got a long way to go, but at least the world is finally changing."

"I just feel lucky I was brought up by a father who never differentiated between any of us. We were just all his girls. And if he ever had cause to reprimand us, it was because of our behavior, not our color. And I got reprimanded a lot."

"Yeah, I can imagine that, you seem like a feisty lady. Where do you come from originally?"

"I . . . don't know for certain," I said, thinking about what Stella had told me.

"Shame you don't have parents and grandmas and great-grandpas who can tell you stories of the past. Mine never stop telling me theirs."

"I told you, I was adopted."

"And you never asked your father to tell you about your birth family?"

"No."

Miles was beginning to irritate me now by asking questions I couldn't deal with. It was like having a speed dating therapy session, and my head was spinning. I stood up. "You know what? I'm real tired tonight. See you around."

Back in the safety of my room, I climbed into bed, wishing I'd never gone out to sit on that bench. My head felt screwed up, and suddenly I fully appreciated why people went to therapy—it was a safe space with someone who didn't air their own opinions, only asked you gently and slowly about yours.

For the first time since I'd arrived at The Ranch, I felt truly grateful that I had Fi to talk to the next day.

# 19

I was out on the trail again the next morning, having woken even earlier and needing the pounding of my feet on the earth to ground me. I was on my second circuit when I glimpsed Miles begin his first. The good news was, there was an entire lap between us, and it was impossible for him to catch up with me. Nevertheless, I upped my speed just in case and concentrated on clearing my mind and taking in the nature around me. A few minutes later, I saw him in front of me—not behind—and realized to my horror that I was actually catching up with *him*. I slowed down my pace, but unlike yesterday, he was traveling at the speed of the elderly joggers I always overtook whenever I ran in Central Park.

"Fuckwit!" I mumbled, using one of Lizzie's favorite words. I slowed down to a walk, but I could see that unless I left the trail, we were about to come side by side.

"Okay, you win," I murmured under my breath as I stepped over the bricks that marked the trail and headed at a jog for the main entrance of The Ranch.

"Hey!"

My jog turned into a run as I looked behind me and saw he was now sprinting toward me.

"Stop!"

Swearing under my breath, I raced to the entrance and was just about to fly through the sanctuary of the door when a strong hand landed on my shoulder.

"Get off of me!"

"Electra, whoa!"

I turned and saw his hands were up in the air like he'd just been caught by the cops.

"I didn't mean to scare you, I just wanted to apologize for last night. The last thing I want to do is screw up your head with stuff that isn't a problem. I'm so sorry; I realize that I was placing my own issues on you."

We were both panting after the race to reach the door. I bent down and put my hands on my knees. "Really, it's okay," I managed.

"No, it's not."

"Well, anyway, I gotta get to breakfast and then the—"

"Serenity prayer, I know."

I pushed the door open and walked inside, not turning back to see if he was following me. I just needed to see Fi and talk all this through.

"So let me get this straight." Fi looked down at her notes. "You want to talk about something that happened at your boarding school?"

"Yup."

I mean, I *so* didn't, but I knew I had to.

"And what was it that happened to you, Electra?"

I swallowed hard and then took some deep breaths, steeling myself to tell her. Because I had never, *ever* told anyone about this.

"So . . . I had just arrived at this new school, and there was a gang of girls who I knew were, like, the popular ones. They were all very pretty and talked about how rich their parents were. I wanted to be friendly and to, like, belong," I said, finding that I was panting nearly as hard as I had at the end of my run.

"Take your time, Electra, there's no rush. We can stop whenever you want."

"No." I was on the runway now, and this plane of shit needed to take off before it crashed and burned me up. "So I told them about our house— Atlantis—and how it was on a lake and looked like a castle and how Pa called us all his princesses and that we could have everything we wanted—which wasn't true, because we only ever got presents at Christmas and for birthdays or sometimes when he came back home from wherever he'd been. And how we went off on our superyacht every year to the south of France and—" I swallowed again and took a breath. "I did everything I could to be like them, with their big houses and their designer clothes and—"

"Here, have some water." Fi handed me a plastic cup that had sat in front of me every time I'd been in this office and I'd never needed to drink. I gulped some down.

"Anyway, I hung out with them for, like, a few weeks, and my other sisters who were there—that's Tiggy, Star, and CeCe, who were in the years above me—saw me with my group and were pleased I was settling in so well. And then—" I took another sip of water. "Well, I told this girl—Sylvie, the leader of our gang—that when I was younger, I'd gotten locked in the little toilet that was in the cabin I slept in on board the *Titan*, my father's boat. All my other sisters had been up on deck or swimming, and I was in this tiny space for what felt like hours, and I'd screamed and screamed, but there was nobody there to hear me." I gulped. "Eventually, a maid came into my cabin and heard me and let me out, but ever since I've had a fear of small spaces."

"That's understandable, Electra. So what happened after you'd told your school friend?"

"Well, it was just before a hockey match, and I was very good at hockey"— I nodded, the tears starting to gather behind my eyes—"and there was this tiny cupboard in the gym where they kept all the sports equipment. Sylvie said she couldn't find her stick, that someone had stolen it and that maybe I could help her find it. So I went to the cupboard to look for it, and the next thing I knew, I'd been pushed inside and someone had locked the door. I was in there for hours—everyone else was out on the hockey pitch, and then they had team teas and . . . Finally, Sylvie came to let me out."

"Here, Electra." Fi passed me the box of tissues that I'd sworn I'd never use. Tears were coursing down my cheeks now, and I grabbed a bunch of them. Once I'd composed myself, I looked up at Fi's gentle face.

"How did you feel when you were locked in that cupboard?"

"Like I was gonna go crazy . . . I felt like I wanted to die, that I was so scared . . . I can't relive it, I just can't."

"You *are* reliving it, Electra, and then you're going to let it go. Because guess what? You got out. And no one is ever going to put you back in there again."

"Too right they're not," I said. "Ever."

"And what did this girl, Sylvie, say to you when she let you out?"

"That I didn't belong, that I was a bragger, and that none of them wanted anything more to do with me. And if I snitched, they'd punish me again. So I didn't. Say anything, that is."

"Not even to your sisters?"

"They'd seen me happy—I'd spent weeks going around with those girls.

They would have just thought it was another story I'd made up because I'd fallen out with them."

"I don't know your sisters, but from what you've said—about Tiggy in particular—I'm not sure that's the case."

"I'd told lies before, Fi. Lots of them to get me out of trouble at home."

"So what did you do?"

"I ran away. I had my pocket money—that got me into the city—then I called Christian, our driver, and asked him to come and get me."

"And what did Ma and your father say to you when you arrived home?"

"They were confused, of course they were, because up to that point, I'd told them that I was happy at the school. So they made me go back."

"I see. And what happened then?"

"Oh, you know how it goes. More stuff. Like finding ink all over my school shirts—the teachers were very fussy about personal tidiness—no laces in my gym shoes, spiders and other creepy crawlies in my desk . . . Juvenile stuff, I guess, but it was anything to either get me into trouble or scare me witless."

"In other words, classic bullying."

"Yup. So I ran away again, and then when I got sent back, I decided the only way to get out of the place was to make sure I was expelled. Then I went to another school, and yeah, I guess I became the bully so the girls wouldn't bully me. No one was gonna mess with me, y'know? But I got expelled again for the bad stuff I did, then the same happened at the next school. That was on top of flunking my exams. So I went off to Paris, got a job as a waitress, and within a few weeks was spotted by a modeling agent." I shrugged. "The rest is history."

I watched Fi busy scribbling—she had more to write today than she'd had in all of the last three weeks put together. She looked up at me and smiled.

"Thank you for trusting me enough to tell me, Electra. I knew there was something you needed to get out, and it's brave of you to do it. How do you feel?"

"If you'll pardon my French, I have no fucking idea right now."

"No, of course you don't. But you're a bright woman, and you know without any prompting from me that this is where a lot of your trust issues have come from. Being offered the hand of friendship and then seeing that friendship so cruelly abused . . . Anyway, that's beyond enough for today.

You've done so well," she said as I stood up. "Just out of interest, what was it that finally encouraged you to tell me?"

"It was a conversation with someone in here. See you tomorrow."

After I'd walked around the Worry Maze a few times to calm down, I headed back inside to use the bathroom. I saw Vanessa was back in our dorm, looking healthier than she had last time.

"Hi, how are you feeling?" I asked her.

"Like shit," she replied. "They sent me out too soon. These *putas*, they don't know what they're doing. Don't trust 'em, will you?"

Given the conversation I'd just had, I decided it was probably best if I didn't hang out with Vanessa right now.

"I'm off to equine therapy. See you later."

It was good to smell the horses' clean and natural scent after the stink of the poisonous memories that had just poured out of me. Now that I thought about it, one of my "great escapes," as Ally had called them, had been made on horseback. I'd taken one of the horses from the school stables, ridden to the nearby farm, then explained to the farmer where the horse needed to be returned to. Then I'd walked—or, in fact, run—the five miles into Zurich before boarding the train for Geneva.

Hank wandered over to me with a carrot to signal my allotted time was at an end.

"Is it seriously impossible to take a ride sometime?" I asked him. "I could sure do with a gallop."

"Not with me while you're in here, ma'am. As I said, it's against the rules. But there's a neighbor of mine who has a ranch out here. Have a word with them at reception, say you're an experienced horsewoman and that it's good for your mental health." He winked at me.

"Thanks, I will." I walked away from the stables, now on a mission.

After a lot of wrangling, it turned out the issue was more to do with insurance than anything else; I'd have to officially leave the clinic for the time I was at the stables in case I fell off and broke my neck, then check in again on my return. Litigation in the States really was something else, I thought as I went to lunch, feeling exhausted from the stress of the morning. I sat down with Lizzie, scanning the canteen nervously for Miles, because I wasn't up for any kind of conversation with him right now.

"Hello, Electra," said Lizzie. "You look tense. What's up?"

"Oh, nothing. In fact, everything's gonna be good. You?"

"Not so good, actually," Lizzie sighed as she toyed with a cherry tomato. "Why?"

"I just saw Fi and"—Lizzie swallowed hard as tears came to her eyes— "she says it's time for me to leave. We've discussed how my overeating habit stems from trying to compensate for things I feel are missing in my life, but she thinks that I need to get back into the real world. "

"Okay. Isn't that good news?"

"Not really, no. I mean, like you and everyone else in here, I'll be okay for a few weeks, then something will happen and I'll be in back in my local bakery, bulk-buying doughnuts and double-chocolate-chip muffins for my binges."

"Oh, Lizzie, it's not like you to be negative," I soothed her. "Surely you're looking forward to showing Chris how amazing you look?"

"Electra," she said quietly, "we both know I don't. I've botched my face with all the surgery I've had—I look like a horror show! Why did I do it? All for *him*! And where is he now? Probably in bed with one of his little whores!"

Lizzie was shouting now, and the room had gone quiet around us. Clattering her fork onto the plate, she stood up and ran out of the canteen.

I sat there in a quandary, at a loss as to whether I should go after her or whether she wanted to be alone. After a few seconds, I decided I should do the former; it would show her I cared, even if she sent me away. I tried our dorm first but only saw Vanessa slouched on her bed with her headphones in, so then I set off at a run around the gardens, knowing that Lizzie's propensity for stilettoes would mean she couldn't have got far. I eventually found her in a hidden corner of the Serenity Garden, crying her eyes out behind an enormous cactus.

"Lizzie, it's me, Electra. Can I sit down?"

She shrugged, and I decided to take that as a yes. I didn't have a clue what to say—I was only just beginning to learn about comforting others (which was something else that I needed to put on my ever-growing list of things to talk to Fi about). So I just reached for her hand and held it until the sobs turned into hiccups. Her face looked as if it was collapsing as all her carefully applied makeup dribbled downward with the wetness of her tears. I took off my hoodie and handed her the sleeve to wipe it with.

"Thanks, Electra." She sniffed. "You're a lovely person."

"I don't think I am, but thanks for saying so."

"Oh, you are," she said as she blew her nose and looked up at me with a small, sorrowful smile. "I bet I must look a right state, don't I?"

"A bit," I answered honestly, "but we all do after we've bawled our eyes out."

"The truth is, I'm just dreading going back to that great empty mausoleum of a house. Cooking Chris's supper, then getting the phone call at ten to say he'll be late and I'm not to wait up for him. Then by the time I'm awake in the morning, he's gone—we have separate bedrooms, you see. I've learned it's possible to live under the same roof as someone and never see them from one week to the next."

None of what she was saying came as a surprise to me.

"Um, Lizzie?"

"Yes?"

"Have you ever thought about, well, divorcing him?"

"Yes, of course I have. And more to the point, he's thought about divorcing me, but under California law, I get half of everything he has and he's far too greedy to ever go for that. So I'm trapped in this sham marriage and . . . even though I know about his endless affairs, what hurts the most is the fact he's ashamed of me, Electra. Ashamed of his own wife! And I still bloody love him!"

"Are you sure? I mean, I'm no expert on anything much, but I did do therapy in New York when a relationship ended. The therapist asked me if I actually liked the guy, and I said no, I hated him, but I loved him, too. The therapist pointed out that I was in a codependent relationship."

"Oh, sweetie, I've been through the whole nine yards and more with therapists over the years." She sighed. "Thousands of dollars and boxes and boxes of tissues. But it still doesn't stop me loving him, even if they call it something else. Besides, there's the children. They'd be heartbroken."

"But your youngest is twenty-three, Lizzie. And they don't even live at home anymore. Besides, I don't think any child wants to see their parents unhappy."

"The two of us put on a show whenever they're around. We give Oscar-winning performances, playing the happy family to perfection. They'd be so shocked if they knew the truth."

"Surely your kids must know? I mean, where do they think you've been this whole time while you've been in here?"

"Oh, they think I'm staying with my best friend, Billie, who lives near

Tucson. I call them every week and lie about what fun the two of us have had. Pathetic, isn't it?"

Truthfully, I thought it was a bit—her kids were grown adults, for Chrissake—but obviously that wasn't the thing to say.

"I guess if you're a parent, you always want to protect your kids, however old they are," I replied, thinking that just maybe I was beginning to learn tact, a quality Pa had once told me was a necessary skill that I didn't have. I remembered replying to him that being "tactful" just felt like you were lying.

"I do, Electra. They're the one thing in my life that I'm proud of. Anyway"—Lizzie gave a big sigh—"I shouldn't be bothering you with all this stuff. You've got enough on your plate."

"Hey, you're my friend, Lizzie. And friends help each other out, don't they?"

"Yes, they do. And I don't have many of them, to be honest. Certainly none that I can trust."

"Me, neither," I agreed.

"I'd be proud if I could call you my friend." Lizzie reached out her hand to me, and I took it.

"Me, too."

For the second time that day, a great lump came to my throat. I wasn't a big crier—never had been—but I felt distinctly moved. We stood up and walked back to The Ranch together. As we did so, I saw Hank in the distance, heading in the direction of the stables.

"Hey, Lizzie, do you ride?" I said suddenly.

"I do indeed! I'll have you know I was Pony Club champion of my county when I was thirteen."

"So when do you get out of here?"

"On Saturday."

"Then how about I book both of us a ride across the desert before you go back to California?"

"You know what?" Lizzie's face lit up. "There is nothing I would enjoy more."

Having slept the sleep of the dead, exhausted from all the emotional processing of the day before, I woke at dawn the next day to find Lizzie sitting on her bed in her robe, drinking a cup of coffee.

"Morning," I said sleepily. "You're up early."

"Yes, I can't believe you managed to sleep through it with our dorm mate"—she indicated Vanessa, snoring gently—"having nightmares. Every time I dropped off, she'd wake me up with her shouting. I gave up in the end and got up. She's sleeping peacefully now, though. Poor little thing. She's obviously very traumatized."

"I didn't hear a thing," I said as I stripped off and put on my tank top, shorts, and sneakers. "I'm going for my run. I'll see you at prayers."

I jogged out of The Ranch, eager to arrive at the track before Miles and get my three circuits in. As I set off, I felt irritated that he was affecting the serenity of my morning runs. I was by the watercooler drinking a cup when he appeared at the start of the trail.

"Morning, Electra," he said as I started to walk back toward The Ranch.

"Morning."

"Listen," he said, changing direction and walking beside me, "are you avoiding me?"

"Maybe."

"I told you I was sorry yesterday. Do I need to apologize again?"

"No, no . . ." I stopped and turned to face him. "As a matter of fact, I should thank you."

"Thank me?"

"Yeah, it was partly due to you that I got some stuff out that I needed to."

"Oh, okay. Then we're cool?"

"Yeah, we're cool."

"Then why are you avoiding me?"

"I . . . I'm still working some stuff out."

"Right. And you don't want me to say anything more that could compli-cate it?"

"Yeah, sort of."

"Then I'll back off."

I watched him turn away from me toward the trail and swore under my breath. That had to be one of the most uncomfortable exchanges I'd ever had, and I had no idea why I felt so awkward around him.

After breakfast and prayers, I trotted off to see Fi.

"Good morning, Electra. How are you feeling today?"

"Lighter," I replied. Because it was true.

"That's great news. Want to talk about it some more?"

"I . . . I'm confused."

"What about?"

"I just met someone in here and he's black and he talked to me the other night about prejudice. And I think that those girls might have been mean to me because I am. Black, that is."

"And you'd never thought that before?"

"No, I honestly hadn't. Call me naive, but I'm just me: Electra the super-model."

"Exactly. Do you think that who you are is in any way defined by your racial origins?"

"No, but when I was running this morning, I was thinking that some human beings define *others* by the color of their skin." I looked up at her. "Do you think they do?"

"Off the record, of course they do. We're tribal animals, culturally. The more enlightened can move on, but—"

"Many can't." I sighed. "But I've hardly suffered, have I? My face and body have been my fortune, not my downfall."

"But, Electra, surely you can see that you *have* suffered?"

"How?"

"Because of what happened to you at school. Whatever the reason for it—and it's almost certainly a mixture of things—that event has shaped the course of your life ever since. Can you see how it has?"

"Yeah, I suppose I can. It made me stop trusting people and—"

"Go on," Fi encouraged me.

"So I suppose if you lose your trust in human nature, it makes you feel alone. I've felt alone ever since. Yup." I nodded as I thought about it some more. "I have."

"We talked about no man or woman being an island a couple of days ago, didn't we? And that is where you were, on your island. How do you feel now?"

"Better." I shrugged. "Less alone. I've made . . . well, I think I've made a friend in one of the women here. A real friend."

"That's great news, Electra. And do you feel comfortable with her joining you on your island?" Fi smiled.

"Yeah, if you put it like that, I do," I said, thinking of Lizzie reaching out her hand to me yesterday. "You know, I'm also angry about the fact that I let those girls stop me getting my diploma. I could have made Pa proud."

"Do you not think he was proud of you for what you achieved as a model?"

"He said he was, but I just got lucky; I was born with this face and body. It doesn't take brains to appear in an ad campaign, does it?"

"I've had a number of well-known models sit right where you're sitting, and many of them have said exactly the same as you. Yet from the little I know about it, it sounds like a grueling job, with the added complication of fame and money at a very young age. You've mentioned the fact that you feel you let your father down on a number of occasions. Is that because you feel on some level ashamed of what you do?"

"Maybe. I hate the thought of anyone—especially Pa—thinking I'm dumb. I was doing well at my studies before I moved to boarding school and the . . . thing happened. And now I can't tell Pa why everything changed, because he's dead."

"Are you angry about that?"

"You mean am I angry that he's dead? Yup, I guess I am. We didn't get along so well in the past few years, to be honest. I didn't go home so much."

"You were avoiding him?"

"Yeah, I was. And then the last time I saw him was in New York. I was . . . well, out of it. I can't remember much, apart from the look on his face as we said good-bye. It was like"—I gulped—"pure disappointment. And a few weeks later, he was dead."

"You told me he died last summer. Which was also the time when your substance and alcohol abuse became more frequent. Do you think these two are linked?"

"For sure. I didn't want to feel sad that he'd gone—anger felt better. But"—I gave a sudden choke as I felt the lump in my throat again—"I miss him, I miss him so much. Oh shit!" It was tissue-ville again, big time. "He was, like, my person, you know? Like, the one human being that I really did feel loved me, and even if we fell out, he was always there and . . . now he's not, and there's a big hole and I can never tell him I love him or that I'm here, getting treatment, and . . ."

"Oh, Electra, I'm so sorry," Fi said, and I realized there were tears in her eyes, too. Which made my own waterworks start all over again.

"And, like, all the sisters, they were grieving for him, too," I said, "and I guess I thought that they all felt they had more of a claim on him than I did, because they knew that we fell out and I hadn't been around, and I just felt excluded all over again."

"Your relationship with your sisters is something else we can work through if you want to?"

I nodded, blowing my nose hard. "Yeah, why not? We're covering all bases, aren't we?"

"I'd also like you to think about whether you feel there is a connection between the relationship you had with your sisters and how you gravitated toward an already established group of girls when you went to boarding school. You could have singled out a girl who might have made you a best friend, but perhaps you were used to being in a pack?"

"Hey, I never thought of it like that before, but yeah, you could be right."

"And that the natural relationship you'd had with your siblings all through your childhood made your expectations of the new group you were joining unrealistic."

"You mean I expected them to love me and accept me because my sisters did? That I was blind to who they really were?"

"Perhaps. Well, now, think that one through, and that is enough for today," said Fi, looking at the clock. I saw that, amazingly, we were three minutes over. "I'll see you tomorrow, but Electra, you're making amazing progress." Fi stood up with me, then held out her arms to give me a hug. "Seriously, I'm proud of you."

"Thanks," I said, and hurried out before I burst into tears all over again.

# 20

I'm going to miss you so much, Electra," Lizzie said as we drove out of The Ranch on Saturday (the first time I had done so since I'd arrived nearly four weeks before).

"Hey, we've only just passed the gate and we have a whole day together, remember?" I said, feeling dazed as we hit the open desert road.

"Yes, and I must enjoy it," Lizzie agreed. "I feel like we're those two women in that film—what was it called? *Thelma and Louise.* That was it! Have you ever seen it?"

"Maybe. Wasn't it about two women who stole things and then drove their car over a cliff?"

"That's the one, yes." Lizzie giggled. "Don't worry, I hope our little adventure won't come to that, although it did feel like you were making the great escape."

"It's crazy, having to check out for the day so I won't sue them if I fall off a horse!" I laughed.

"But you will go back, won't you?"

"Yeah, course I will, I'm not quite finished there yet, but I'm getting real close."

"Hopefully you'll know when you're ready, unlike me, who had to be kicked out. These places can get addictive, you know, especially to addicts."

"It's not just being at The Ranch for me; it's *this!*" I said as I opened my arms wide, embracing my surroundings. "I feel so free!"

"So do I! Woo-hoo! Let's ride!" Lizzie put her foot down, and the powerful open-topped Mercedes sped us through the incredible Arizona landscape. The air shimmered with heat, and tall cacti sat jaggedly in the orange earth, their arms reaching up to the blue sky. Brilliant golden flowers ran riot through the rough green bushes that gripped the desert sand, and I could see the odd rabbit scurrying to safety as our car approached. I'd previously pictured deserts as empty landscapes, but this was teeming with life and color.

"It's always reminded me of Africa—the red dust and the wide-open spaces," said Lizzie. "Have you ever been there?"

"No."

As Lizzie drove, I thought again about Stella and the story she had started to tell me about the woman called Cecily who had fled to Kenya when her fiancé had dumped her. I had no idea how her story was related to mine, but I had to presume that it was. That probably meant that Africa was where I had come from. Which was maybe why, if Lizzie said Arizona was like Africa, I liked it here, too.

"Electra? Which way?"

"Sorry, I zoned out there for a while." I looked down at the little map Hank had drawn for me. "We've just been through Tucson, so now we need to hang a right at the signpost for the mountain park."

A few minutes later, the sign appeared in front of us, and we turned off the main highway, heading for the mountains. Eventually, we saw a small sign for the Hacienda Orquídea and bumped down a narrow dusty track, which looked as though it was leading nowhere.

"Goodness, this really isn't the right vehicle to be in," joked Lizzie as the low-slung car scraped through the potholes. "Are you sure this is the right way?"

"Yes, look." I pointed between a couple of huge cacti at a horse grazing in a fenced-off field. A little further along, a low-roofed building came into view.

Lizzie pulled up in front of it, and we both got out of the Mercedes.

She giggled. "I hope the horses are fit, because I'm not sure this set of tires is going to get me back to LA and I might have to ride back home."

There were no signs telling us where to go, so we walked up the steps onto a wide veranda, shielded from the sun by an oversized roof and filled with huge turquoise planters of oleander. A long, rustic wooden table and chairs sat on the deck, and as I looked at the desert plain that led up to the mountains, I found myself imagining balmy nights sitting out here, eating in perfect solitude.

"Hi there!" A man opened the door before Lizzie had raised her hand to knock. "You two the friends of Hank?"

I looked up at him, wondering if all men in Arizona were built tall and handsome—this one looked Latino, with his dark skin, brown eyes, and head of shiny blue-black hair. "Yup, that's us."

"Welcome to the Hacienda Orquídea," he said, extending an arm. "I'm Manuel. Can I get you a cool drink before I take you around to the stables?" he asked as he led us both inside. The temperature dropped by several degrees, due to the air-conditioning.

"Thanks," Lizzie answered as I looked around.

If I had been expecting a rancher's shack that smelled of horses and dogs, I could not have been more wrong. I was standing in a huge square room with two walls made entirely of glass, which gave glorious views of the mountains at the back of the house. Colorful indigenous plants and flowers wrapped around the house, and I could see more horses grazing in a paddock in the distance.

The floor was made of shiny red wood, and in the center of the space there was a huge stone chimney breast with big comfortable couches on either side of it. There was a kitchen area as well, filled with sleek, shiny units, which reminded me of my apartment in New York.

"Wow! What an amazing place you have here," I said as he poured water and ice from the refrigerator into two glasses.

"Glad you like it." Manuel smiled. "My wife, she design all this. She is talented, *sí?*"

"Very," said Lizzie, joining us as we gazed out of the back window onto the mountains. There was another large veranda beyond the kitchen, and Manuel opened the glass door, indicating that we should follow him. Again, the space was covered by an oversized roof, and I could hear water playing in the background as we sat down at a curved wooden table that looked as if it had been carved whole from an ancient tree trunk.

"Is there a stream around here?" I asked him.

"No, but my wife, she says hearing water makes one feel cool, so we had that piped from the house." Manuel pointed to a rectangular stone-clad pond in which large koi carp were meandering. It was surrounded by blooms of hibiscus and oleander, and I thought it was one of the prettiest things I had ever seen.

As I lifted the glass of water to my lips, the clink of the ice made every inch of me long for the burn of alcohol. But I told myself that I was in my first social situation outside The Ranch, and it was going to be tough.

I took a deep breath and grabbed a handful of the chips Manuel had put on the table. At least they had a slightly spicy taste to them—for some reason spice helped stem the cravings—and I swallowed a mouthful fast, hoping I wouldn't end up back in here in a few months' time with a food addiction like Lizzie.

"Manuel, this is the most delightful place I think I've ever seen," Lizzie said. "How did you find it?"

"It was my father's ranch and his father's before him. He died two years ago, and I inherit it. My father, he had sold off much land by the time he died, and what's left is not enough to run as a business. My wife, Sammi, and I decide we should put in all our savings and renovate it as a private home for someone who want to keep a few horses. But so far, no luck."

"It's for sale?" I asked him.

"*Sí, señorita.* Sammi and I live in the city—she has the interior design business, and I work in construction," he explained. "Okay, you ready for a ride now?"

"Yes," I said, standing up eagerly and hoping I wouldn't decide to canter off straight back to the liquor store we'd passed in Tucson, because the craving for alcohol was now something else.

"Goodness me," said Lizzie, as we followed Manuel off the veranda in the direction of a newly built stable block. "This place is just magical, isn't it? I could so live here, couldn't you?"

The answer was an enormous yes, but I could only nod as a bottle of Grey Goose came into view in my imagination.

"You okay?" Lizzie looked at me.

"Yeah, I will be."

She grabbed my hand and gave it a squeeze. "One day at a time. The first trip out is the hardest of all. You're doing so, so well," she whispered as we reached the stable and Manuel handed us boots and riding hats.

"So you don't run this as a proper stable?" I asked.

"No, but on weekends I like to leave the city and come here to ride out."

"You won't have that option when it's sold, though, will you?" said Lizzie pragmatically.

"Oh, we will keep enough land back for a small paddock, and we will renovate the shack just behind it." Manuel pointed across the flat red plain to a tumbledown wooden building some hundred yards beyond the stables. "We wait for the sale of the big house to give us the cash to do it." He shrugged as he put on his own hat. "Now, when Hank call me to ask if I will take you out, he say you are both strong riders."

"That might be an exaggeration for me," Lizzie said, rolling her eyes. "I haven't been on a horse for almost thirty years."

"Then I will give you Jenny. She is very gentle. And you, Electra?"

"The same as Lizzie, but it hasn't quite been that long for me."

"Charmed, I'm sure." Lizzie stuck her tongue out at me as Manuel led Jenny out of the stables and handed her the reins.

"How about Hector?" Manuel beckoned me over to a huge black horse who was moving restlessly around his box.

"I'll give him a go," I said.

"He's fine once he know who is boss. And you look like a boss girl to me."

"Do I?"

"*Sí*, like my Sammi is the boss girl," Manuel clarified as he grabbed the reins and drew Hector out of the stable. "Now you climb on, okay?"

As we clopped out of the courtyard behind him, Hector did a lot of whinnying and tossing of his head, while I tried to find my seat on top of him.

"Okay, so we go slowly at first, and then we see," Manuel suggested as he pulled up next to us.

I watched Lizzie move ahead of us and thought how elegant she looked on horseback.

"She is English, your friend?"

"She is."

"Hah! I can tell from the way she sits on the horse."

"Whereas I'm a mess, I know," I said as Hector threw his head back impatiently.

"He will calm down once we are on the move. He just like to go fast."

It took a good fifteen minutes before I got the hang of Hector, and when I did, Manuel signaled to me.

"So now we can go."

Manuel and I arrived back a couple of hours later, filthy from the red dust, which I could taste on my lips. But wow, I felt euphoric. After setting off at a polite trot, I'd begun to feel the thrum of Hector's engine revving up beneath me. I'd glanced at Manuel, who'd nodded, obviously confident in my riding skills, and let Hector take the lead. We'd flown across this magnificent plain, and I thought I couldn't remember feeling happier in a very long time. I was free, yet in control, and it was incredible.

"Did you enjoy that?" Lizzie asked as I clopped back into the yard, shadowed by Manuel. She had turned back twenty minutes before us.

"Oh, wow, Lizzie, I just adored it," I said as I dismounted. "Sorry if we went too fast."

"Not at all, it was fantastic to watch you both. Sedate point-to-points were more my thing in England. You're a natural, isn't she, Manuel?"

"She is." Manuel smiled. "Now time for a cold beer."

After Lizzie and I had taken ourselves into the big, modern bathroom to wash the dust from our faces (and had a sneaky peek into the incredible master bedroom, which faced the mountains and had a plunge pool built into a small enclosed terrace just beyond the glass wall), we joined Manuel on the veranda and sat down.

He was already halfway through a beer, and there were two more on the table, along with a jug of water.

"You want?" He indicated the beers.

"Thanks," Lizzie said, taking one.

"Er—" I swallowed hard. "No, thanks. I'll stick to water."

Lizzie turned and gave me a look of approval as I poured myself a glass from the jug. I had to get used to the fact that people would be drinking around me constantly when I went back to my old life. The good news was that I was getting a soft entry, as beer was not a drink I liked. I let Lizzie's and Manuel's voices wash over me as I breathed deeply, took in the view, and enjoyed the desert breeze.

"Now, ladies, I am sorry to tell you, but I must leave," Manuel said eventually. "Sammi and I have a dinner party in the city this evening."

"Of course, and thank you so much for today," said Lizzie, draining her beer. "And your house is absolutely beautiful. I hope you sell it soon," she added as we walked back through the house toward the front door.

"We hope so, too. We borrow the money to do it when things were good and now . . . well," he said as he opened the front door, then shook both our hands. "It was a pleasure meeting both of you."

"And you," Lizzie said as she headed down the steps.

"Maybe I could come again?" I said as Manuel locked up the house and we walked to his jeep, which was parked next to Lizzie's car.

"Of course, I am always here on weekends."

"Okay, do you have a cell phone number?"

"Just ask Hank, he will have it. *Hasta luego*, Electra, Lizzie."

We followed Manuel's jeep back into the city, and I watched as the desert sky around me began to turn different shades of magenta and purple as the sun prepared to retire for the night.

"I think I need one of those cars," I said as Manuel put a hand out of his window and waved as he turned right and we continued straight.

"What for?" Lizzie asked me.

"For driving in and out of the city, of course. When I get back to The Ranch, I need to call my business manager."

"Why?"

I turned to her and smiled. "Because I'm going to buy that house."

As it was a Saturday, there were no therapists on duty, and there was another group outing to the local cinema, so The Ranch was blissfully quiet. So far, I'd liked it best on weekends because there were no therapy sessions, but tonight I found myself wanting to tell Fi, or at least someone, about my amazing day. After dinner in the almost deserted canteen, I went back to my dorm, thinking I needed to finish my apology letters and have them mailed. I'd decided there was also one to write to Susie, my agent, and another to dear, sweet Mariam.

Vanessa was lying on her bed with her headphones on, staring at the ceiling as usual. I'd seen her with Miles, sitting in the Serenity Garden, after I'd had a tearful good-bye with Lizzie and was walking back inside. I sat down in the chair and pulled paper, pen, and envelopes out of the desk drawer.

"Where'd you go today?" Vanessa asked, startling me because she spoke so rarely.

"I went out horseback riding."

"They let you outta here? Alone?"

"Yeah, but I was with Lizzie. We're not prisoners in here, you know," I reminded her. "We can walk out of the door anytime we want."

"Yeah, I so would, but I ain't got no place to go."

"You're homeless?"

"No, but I can't go back there no more. He'd kill me."

"Who's he?"

"My boy, Tyler. He ain't good news. You ever had a guy rough you up?"

"No, I haven't."

"Then you lucky, girl."

"So what will you do?"

Vanessa shrugged. "Miles said he'd help me find a place in the city and a job. But I never finished high school, and I'm never gonna get my diploma."

"Miles?"

"Yeah, he's the one who picked me up off the streets and brought me with him to this place. He's payin' for everythin', but that don't make him Jesus Christ my Savior," she muttered.

"Right," I replied neutrally. I was out of my depth with this girl, and I knew it. "You doing all right now with the detox?"

"Yeah, they pump you full of gear to get you off the gear!" A glimmer of a smile came to Vanessa's lips. "But as soon as I'm back in the city, I'll be back on it."

"If Miles says he can get you a job and someplace to live, then you have to trust him."

A "humpf" emanated from Vanessa as she rolled her eyes and stuck her headphones back on. I looked at the pen and paper, then put it all back in the drawer and left the dorm to get some fresh air. *I've never felt more like a privileged princess than I do at this moment,* I thought as I went outside to the Serenity Garden and sat down on a bench. And what made it even worse was that I had been aware of the drugs and prostitution that hummed in the background of my daily life in New York. Yet up to now, it had only ever been a hum.

"Hi there," said a familiar voice from the bench behind the fountain. "We should stop meeting like this—people will talk."

"Hi, Miles," I replied, and as he came to sit by me, I felt glad he was there.

"A little bird told me that you escaped for the day."

"I did, yes. I went horseback riding, and it was fantastic."

"I'm glad for you. We all gotta find things that make life worth living."

"I didn't know it was you who was sponsoring Vanessa."

"Yeah, well, that could have been me in the gutter, but I had people supporting me, a family. She's got no one."

"She says she can't go back to where she was living and you're going to find her a home and a job."

"I can fund somewhere for her to live, for sure—a halfway house or a hostel—then maybe get her some low-paid work. But that doesn't guarantee she won't go running back to what she knows." Miles sighed. "She has to want to do it for herself."

"Maybe when she's got all the shit out of her body and brains, then therapy will help."

"Maybe, but what I've realized since I brought her in here is that listening to a bunch of educated, entitled folks who don't even have the bones of what her life is like isn't going to cut it. I volunteer at a drop-in center back in Manhattan, advising kids on the legal side of stuff if they're in trouble and trying to keep them out of jail if I can. There's a drug epidemic building out there, and let me tell you, it's affecting all colors and creeds."

"I could help, couldn't I?" It was out of my mouth before I could stop it. "I want to do something. I was just thinking how I've seen this stuff on TV, but—"

"You don't give a damn until it directly relates to you," Miles finished for me.

"You got it. I was sitting here feeling really bad, and selfish and spoiled and—"

"Don't beat yourself up, Electra, you're not much older than Vanessa and you've lived in a different world. That's not your fault."

"But now that I have, I want to help." I rubbed my forehead hard as I pictured Vanessa's face and the dullness in her eyes. "You know, when I looked at her, it was like she was dead inside, like there was no—"

"Hope. That's the word you're looking for. Yeah, well, I'm trying to give that back to the kids I work with—that belief that it's worth carrying on the fight because there might be something better ahead, rather than sinking back into the abyss and feeling like it doesn't matter whether you live or die. And that's the hardest damn thing of all, but hey, you gotta keep trying."

"You know, I was thinking earlier about the Twelve Steps and the fact that it's all about God and how He will help us and save our souls and stuff. But why does He give some of us seriously crappy lives, while others get everything?"

"Because we suffer for our sins here on Earth before entering His glorious kingdom."

"You're saying it's better up there than it is down here?"

"Yes, ma'am, I am," he said.

"Then why don't you kill yourself now and go?"

"Oh, Electra." Miles chuckled. "Because we've got our jobs to do down here, whatever it is that He asks of us. And if you look into your heart and pray for guidance, you'll find out just what that is. I did."

I turned my whole body to look at him. "You're a believer?"

"I sure am. Jesus saved me many years ago, and I'm now down here doing His work. Or trying to, at least."

"Oh." I sat staring into the darkness for a while, not sure what to say because I was so shocked. I'd never met a devout Christian before. To me, the whole Bible thing was on the same level as fairy tales and Greek myths.

"Well"—I cleared my throat—"I really would like to help if I can. I need to call my business manager anyway—he looks after all that stuff—so I'll speak to him and see what I could offer. I guess I'm pretty rich."

It was Miles's turn to stare at me in shock. "You mean you don't know how much you're worth?"

"No. I live in a very nice apartment, and I buy whatever I need, although I get given most of my clothes for free from designers. There's not much else that I've wanted—other than drugs and alcohol. Though there is something I want now." The thought of it made me smile.

"Excuse me for saying, Electra, but shouldn't you know how much money you've got? I personally don't trust anyone but me when it comes to my dollars."

"Oh, they show me the accounts once a year and tell me about my investments, but they're just columns of figures and . . . I don't have a clue what they actually mean," I confessed.

Suddenly, Miles reached out a hand to stroke the side of my face gently with his fingers. He gave a sigh as his eyes focused on mine. "You sure act like you're a tigress, but you're just an innocent cub underneath it all, aren't you? You make me feel real old." He smiled. "Hey, and I should be getting to bed like people of my age do."

As I watched him stand up, all of me wanted to ask him to stay and stroke my face again. But I didn't, because I felt too shy—a first for me.

"Good night, sweetheart," he said as he walked away into the darkness.

That night, I didn't sleep well, even though I was physically exhausted from the horse riding. This was partly to do with Vanessa, who was having another restless night, but also because I couldn't stop thinking about Miles. I thought I was quite good at getting a handle on guys, but I seriously couldn't work him out. A Harvard-educated lawyer, former addict, savior of junkies, and a Christian . . .

Then I wondered if he was married, because he never talked about a wife, not that we'd talked that often. Besides, what did I care? He was way older than me, and we lived in different worlds.

I woke up feeling groggy, as if I'd taken stuff. When I looked at the clock by my bed, I saw it was after ten o'clock. Normally, the morning gong would sound at seven, giving us half an hour before we needed to gather together in the canteen for the serenity prayer, but today was a Sunday, so there was no gong and prayers were at ten.

"You missed breakfast an' prayers," said Vanessa as I sat up. "I got you a bowl of grits and some juice." She indicated my desk.

"Oh," I said, touched by her thoughtfulness. "Thanks."

"'S'okay. Miles wanted to take me to church in town, but I told him I had to stay an' look after you."

"Hey, I was just sleeping. You could have gone with him."

"You think I want to go to that place? They're as bad as the pushers, tryin' to get you onto all that Jesus stuff. I googled you last night," Vanessa continued. "You must be the most famous supermodel in the world, and I'm sharin' a room with you. Ain't the world a crazy place!"

"It sure is," I agreed as I reached for the grits, which I hated, but I didn't want to upset Vanessa.

"How'd you get to be a model?"

"An agent spotted me in Paris when I was sixteen." I shrugged. "It was just luck."

"It's 'cause you're as tall as a giraffe," she said, then giggled, and even though the joke was on me, it made me happy to see her smile. "You make the clothes look good. An' you're pretty, too. Where are your folks from?"

"I don't know. I was adopted. You?"

"Mom was Puerto Rican, an' Dad, hey, he was just a sperm, y'know?" Vanessa studied me. "Your hair real?"

"No. Not most of it, anyway. I wish I had hair like yours, Vanessa. It's so long and beautiful."

"You don't want nothin' that I got," she said, but her expression told me she was pleased. "You like bein' a model?"

"It's okay. I mean, I get paid well, but it can get boring being dressed up like a living doll every day, and all the hair and makeup stuff."

"Like your body ain't your own?"

"I suppose so, yes."

"Hey, I sell mine every day to anyone who wants it. So I guess we're just the same, ain't we?" With that, she got up and walked out of the dorm.

"Wow. Wow," I breathed, feeling my heart banging against my chest. Tears sprang to my eyes because somehow, a young junkie plucked from the streets of New York had made me feel about two inches high.

In a panic, because those feelings of anger were the ones that had sent me down Vodka Alley and inevitably steered me along Cocaine Walk, I put on my running gear and headed for the door. Outside on the trail, it was far busier than it ever was at sunrise, and I ran past the other joggers, trying to pound the outrage I felt out through my feet.

"How frigging dare she! Comparing me to her . . . Jesus Christ!"

By the time I came off the track and was at the watercooler, I was dripping wet, partly due to the sun that was frying everything beneath it and also because I had just completed five circuits. I gulped back the water, feeling dizzy and disoriented and wishing that Fi was around to talk to about how I was feeling.

"Hi there," said Miles, walking toward me from the parking lot as I dragged myself toward the entrance of The Ranch. He was looking even smarter than usual in a jacket, button-down shirt, and tie.

"You're late for your run today," he said as we hovered in front of the door.

"Yeah, I am. Listen, could we go talk for a moment?"

"Sure. How about the canteen? It has AC, and the sun's boiling hot today."

We went inside, me grabbing myself a bottle of water and Miles fixing himself a coffee.

"What's up?" he asked as we sat down and he loosened his tie.

"Vanessa. She told me I was no different from her; that I sold my body, too."

"I guess that struck a nerve with you." Miles sipped his coffee, then regarded me steadily. "So?"

"What do you mean, 'So?'? Jesus, Miles, can you just quit sounding like a therapist?"

"I'm honestly not trying to do that, but when you get uptight about stuff, it's normally because part of you thinks it's true."

"Gee, thanks! So you think modeling equates to prostitution?"

"I'm not saying that, Electra. I'm asking you what you think."

"I think that I get paid a shitload of money for being in promotion," I said, quoting a line from another famous model who had been quizzed on the subject. "And you know what? I'm sick of people thinking that just because I do this job, it's, like, easy." I stood up suddenly. "It's damned hard work, the hours are crazy, I rarely sleep in the same bed for more than a few days, and before coming here, I hadn't had more than a couple of days off for maybe two years. And . . . there's something else I'll tell you."

"You go for it!"

"Being famous isn't exactly a walk in the park. Like, everyone in the world is chasing fame, but they take for granted having the freedom to just walk out of their apartment on a Sunday morning and go for a run without someone recognizing them or a newspaper getting a tip-off and then getting a shot of them sweating like a pig. Every week there's gossip about me with a new man—or the fact I've dumped a man or haven't dumped him but am screwing someone else at the same time . . . Jesus! Sorry," I added hastily.

"It's okay. Thanks for the apology."

"And you know something else? I *have* earned a load of money, and I don't know how much exactly, but I'm gonna find out, and when I do, I'm gonna buy myself a real home and then start doing stuff that matters. Like helping kids like Vanessa."

"Hallelujah!" Miles said and gave me a slow round of applause.

"Please don't make fun of me. I'm being serious. Completely serious."

"I know you are. And I'm loving you for it. Sounds like you've had an epiphany."

"Maybe I have," I said, feeling suddenly exhausted and slumping into my chair. "I haven't been in control of my life for maybe . . . ever. Oh, for a few days in Paris, before I got spotted, I guess. All this booze and drugs and not knowing about my finances and letting everyone else make all the decisions for me is wrong, and I'm gonna change it, Miles, I really am. Cheers." I toasted him as I threw back the rest of my water.

"You go, girl!" he said. "And you know what?"

"What?"

"All that stuff you just said about the hard work and the fame?"

"Yes?"

"You can flip it on its head, just like an egg turned sunny side up, and use your high profile to do good. For example, bring those darned cameras along to my drop-in center and start raising awareness of what goes on out there on the streets."

"You know what? You're right," I said. "And you know something else?"

"What?"

"I think I'm ready to go home."

"You sure?"

"Yeah. I mean, I'll talk to Fi, see what she thinks, but I feel fired up, you know?"

"I can see that, but you need to be careful, Electra; the bad times, they'll roll in and—"

"I know," I cut him off. "I know."

"You're doing real well, Electra, and I'm proud of you."

"Thanks, Miles," I said and stood up. "I need to go finish writing those apology letters before tomorrow."

"Okay. And Electra?"

"What?"

"You're only twenty-six years old. You had to grow up too quick, just like Vanessa. You've got plenty of time to do some good, so cut yourself some slack, won't you?"

"Sure. Thanks." I began to walk away from the table, then I stopped and turned. "Hey, how old are you? You talk like you really are an old man."

"Thirty-seven—soon to be thirty-eight. Like you, I've seen a lot. I guess it makes you old before your time."

"Maybe we both need some fun," I said as I began to walk away.

"Maybe we do," I heard Miles mutter behind me.

# 21

So do you think I'm ready to leave?" I asked Fi the next morning, having filled her in on my weekend activities and my "epiphany," as Miles had called it.

"You're the only person who can judge that. This time last week, I would have said no, but somehow the cork got pulled and all the things that you'd bottled up for years have spilled out."

"Yeah, that's a good way of putting it," I murmured.

"I think that maybe you should see how you go in the next couple of days, because often there can be euphoria after a revelation, followed by a downer. You need to get your balance back a little, don't you think?"

"I suppose so. How about I plan to leave on Thursday, maybe? It means I'd get home for the weekend and have some time to adjust before real life begins again. And instead of having a friend come visit me, they can take me home."

"That sounds like a plan. Which friend would you like to do that?"

"Mariam," I said firmly. "Maia's so far away in Rio, and I don't think it's fair to her to ask her to come all this way. She has a family to look after."

"Well, it's up to you. Whenever she's called to see how you're doing, she's said she's happy to make the trip. Try to remember you've been ill, Electra, and when people are sick, those that love them rally around."

"No, I'd like it to be Mariam."

"Right, well, I'll recommend to your doctor that I think you're good to go on Thursday, okay?"

"Okay," I agreed. "You know, this place has been amazing. In the last week, anyway, and sometimes it's been talking to the others in here that's really helped. I hated sharing a dorm when I first got here, but now I'm glad I did. And I even contributed to group therapy this morning."

"That's great." Fi knew how much I'd struggled in the public sessions. "Do you want to share what you said?"

"Oh, it was a girl—Miranda—and she was talking about being badly bullied at school. So I shared my experiences, and afterward, she said it had helped to hear about them."

Fi smiled. "Excellent."

"And I've been thinking about whether to share my story with, well, the wider world."

"You mean in the media?"

"Yeah, because you can be damned sure that there will already be speculation about why I've pulled out of shoots and where I've been."

"Did your agent put out a statement?"

"She probably said something about going on a vacation because I was suffering from exhaustion. Maybe there's already been stuff in the papers, but I was thinking that if I'm going to get involved in the drop-in center that I told you about, it might help if I did share my story."

"That's your decision, Electra, and the power lies within your hands. Try not to think about it now; it's enough that you have to face your life again at the end of the week. Take things one day at a time, remember?"

"Yeah, of course."

"Okay, I'll see you tomorrow. Stay safe," Fi said as I left the room.

When I got my cell and laptop back that evening, I went into the Serenity Garden and placed my first call in a month to the outside world.

"Electra! How the hell are you?" Casey, my business manager and accountant, answered after the second ring.

"I'm good, Casey, very good."

"Well, I'm sure pleased to hear that."

I thought he sounded relieved, which made me suspect that he knew where I was.

"What can I do for you?" he said.

"I'd like to set up a meeting with you when I'm back in town next week. I'm thinking of buying a property."

"Okay. It's definitely a good time to buy; the market is as flat as the proverbial pancake right now. You could get a steal on a new build in the city that the construction company and their backer need to shift. The bad news is, the Dow Jones has been hit hard."

"Right," I said, deciding I needed to find out what words like "Dow Jones" actually *meant*. "But I'm not thinking about anything in New York right now. I've seen a ranch down here in Arizona."

"Okay, can you give me some figures?"

"Not at this moment, but I'll find out as soon as I'm back."

"Well, most of your wealth is tied up in bonds, which are down in value because of the market, but we can certainly liquidate whatever you need to buy the property."

"Up to how much?"

"I'd have to check on the numbers, but as you know, you're a very rich young lady."

I wanted to ask him how rich "rich" actually was, but then I just felt embarrassed because he'd know I hadn't read anything he'd sent me.

"Listen, does next Monday morning work for you? I'll come to your office and we can go through some stuff, because there's something else I want to talk to you about."

"Sure, Electra, I'd be delighted. Shall we say eleven o'clock?"

"Great, see you then. Bye."

*That wasn't too painful*, I thought as I ended the call and saw the cell was covered in the sweat from my palms. I sat there dreaming about the Hacienda Orquídea and how I could spend all my downtime—which I was determined to carve out of any schedule that Susie presented me with—there. I could make my own trail to run on, get a maid to take care of the house and a ranch hand to look after the horses I was going to buy. Maybe Manuel might even sell me Hector . . .

I went back to my dorm and sat down on the bed, thinking it was time to sleep, but I was feeling too pumped. I looked across the room and saw Vanessa's bed was empty. I sniffed, and a weird metallic smell filled my nostrils as I turned and saw that there was red liquid seeping out from under the bathroom door.

"*Shit!*" I screamed, then pressed the emergency call bell as I gathered my courage and pushed the door open. Vanessa was lying on the floor in a pool of blood. Her eyes were closed, and I could see she had deep cuts along her splayed inner arms.

"Help!" I ran out into the deserted hallway. "Somebody help!" As no one responded, I remembered I still had my cell and went back to pick it up from my bed to dial 911.

As an operator answered, I gave the address of The Ranch and tried to respond to her questions. Mercy, the night nurse on duty, came into the room, her eyes widening in horror as I pointed to the bathroom.

"It's Vanessa," I managed. "She's hurt herself . . . I don't know if she's okay . . . I don't know . . ."

Mercy ran into the bathroom, and I could see her begin to resuscitate Vanessa, whose small body looked completely limp.

"Ma'am?" came a voice from my cell. "Ma'am, an ambulance will be right with you. Please make sure someone is at the front entrance to meet the paramedics and lead them to the patient."

I dropped the cell onto the bed and ran to the bathroom, panting in shock. "The ambulance is on its way. Is she going to be okay?" I asked Mercy.

"Grab me some towels, honey," she said briskly. "We gotta stem the bleeding. A nurse from the clinical ward should be here any moment to help."

With a deep gulp—I'd always been bad with blood—we both took an arm and I did as she directed, wrapping the towels as tightly around the gaping wounds as I could. I sat there on the floor, the towel in my hands getting steadily wetter as I held it. I saw a small kitchen knife on the floor by her and picked it up.

"How in the hell did she get hold of this?"

Mercy sighed. "Where there's a will, there's a way. She probably snuck into the kitchen asking for something or other and stole it while no one was lookin'."

Another nurse appeared in the bathroom, and I let out a huge sigh of relief.

"Thanks, Electra, Vicky can take over from you now. Can you run to reception and tell them to ask security to open the gates for the ambulance?"

"Of course."

I pelted to reception and gave them the message, then went to the nearby restroom to wash my blood-soaked hands. When I got out, two paramedics were already wheeling a gurney through the glass doors. I led them to our room and watched numbly as they tended to Vanessa. They placed her on the gurney, and I followed them through the building and out into the parking lot, where the ambulance's blue lights were flashing, lighting up the night.

"Will she be okay?" I asked one of the paramedics as they lifted the gurney inside the ambulance and Mercy followed it.

"We'll do our best, ma'am," he said. "We need to leave right now, though." He made to close the ambulance door, but I instinctively put out an arm to stop it.

"I'm coming with you. Vanessa needs me," I added to Mercy.

"Electra, it's best you stay here. Vanessa is in good hands now."

"*No!* I'm coming."

"Okay, then," Mercy said, "we'll ride with Vanessa together, honey." She offered me her hand to help me up into the ambulance.

"Right, ma'am," said one of the paramedics. "You sit down just there and strap yourself in while we see to your friend. Hold on tight, now."

I'd never been in an ambulance before, and I'd always imagined they'd be the ultimate in comfort suspension. But no, as the siren went on and we set off at high speed, I hung on to the handle attached to the side as we swerved and bumped our way toward the city. I watched with a mixture of disgust and awe as the paramedics worked to insert lines into Vanessa's painfully thin and wounded arms.

"The vein is shot in this arm, I'm going for the top of her hand," I heard one say.

I winced and turned away as I saw the damage that constant needles had done to her inside elbow.

"BP dropping," said the other as a machine beeped urgently. "Heart rate slowing."

"Stay with us, Vanessa." The guy now trying to get the needle into her hand continued to talk to her.

"How far now?" I asked.

"Not far, ma'am."

"It's still dropping! Get that line in!"

"I'm doing my darnedest here!"

Five minutes later, the ambulance screeched to a halt, the back doors were flung open, and Vanessa's gurney was rushed inside.

I unstrapped myself, my heart banging against my chest as Mercy helped me climb out, and together we walked inside to the bustling emergency room. I was ashamed to admit that the only thing I was thinking about right now was where the nearest liquor store was, because I doubted I'd ever needed ten shots of the Goose more.

While Mercy was pulled aside by a nurse and disappeared with her through some swing doors, I was corralled by the nurse on reception, who then proceeded to ask me for details of Vanessa's health insurance, about which I had no clue. In the end, I signed something to say that I'd pick up the bill if she was uninsured (which I had no doubt she was), but then she asked me for my credit card.

"Listen, I just jumped into the ambulance, I didn't stop for my purse—my friend was bleeding to death, for Chrissake!"

"Yes, ma'am, but we need the number of that card. Is there anyone you can call?"

I was about to say no, but then I realized that I still had my cell on me.

"Yeah, give me a couple of minutes." I walked away from the counter, dug in my pocket for the cell, and called Mariam.

"Electra? It is wonderful to hear from you! How are you?"

The sound of Mariam's warm, rich voice calmed me slightly. "I'm good, I'm real good, but, um, a friend of mine isn't. It's a long story, but we're in the emergency room of some hospital in Tucson and they're demanding my credit card details. Could you speak to them?"

"Of course I can. Oh, Electra! You say this is a friend of yours?"

"Yeah, I just need to guarantee the payment of her treatment," I said, walking back to the counter and handing the cell over to the receptionist. I lurked nearby as they spoke; then the receptionist handed the cell phone back to me.

"She'd like a word with you, ma'am."

"Okay. Hi, Mariam, did you sort things out?"

"Yes, it was no problem. Although I must get the insurance details of your friend, because her treatment may be very costly."

I sighed. "If it is, it is. I'm paying, and that's that."

"I understand. Now, are you sure that *you* are okay?"

"I am, truly. Gotta go now, but I'll call you back later. Thanks, Mariam. Bye."

Seeing the restroom opposite, I ran to it and shut myself in a cubicle, breathing hard as I sat down on the toilet seat. Putting my head between my legs because I felt dizzy, I looked down at my track pants and saw that they were spattered with blood. I groaned, thinking of all those people sitting in reception who might or might not have recognized me. I pulled out my cell, thinking I should text Miles to tell him what had happened, but then realized it was way past cell phone hour and he wouldn't get it anyway. Instead, I called The Ranch and left a message for him at reception for them to pass on immediately. Then I sat there, staring at the ad about STDs stuck to the back of the door.

"That could have been me one day," I whispered to myself. "You can never go back there, Electra," I added as I mentally smashed the bottle of Goose that was filling the television screen in my head. I heard the door to the restroom open.

"Electra? You in here?"

"Yeah," I said, opening the door to the cubicle to see Mercy standing there. "How is she?"

"Why don't we go and have a chat outside?"

As I followed her out, I glanced around the reception area and saw ten faces staring at me in astonishment. I sighed as Mercy led me away fast around the side of the hospital and into an alley full of smelly trash containers.

"So?"

"She's alive, honey. They're stabilizing her now. They got her in time, and she's gonna be okay."

I let out a huge breath, and I felt Mercy's arm go around me.

"You helped saved her life, Electra. If you hadn't found her . . . You did good, sweetheart. Now you should get some rest. I'm calling you a cab to take you back to The Ranch while I stay on here. They can organize a different dorm for you to stay in tonight as well."

"No! I need to stay here for Vanessa. She doesn't have anyone else, she's all alone," I insisted.

"Electra, you're still in treatment, and this is all too much for you right now. You should head back—"

"No way! I'm staying here, and I'm going to be right by her side when they say I can be. If you need me to sign something so I won't sue The Ranch, I'll do that, but you can't make me leave, okay?"

"Okay, Electra, okay," Mercy said gently. "I'll let reception know that you're staying here and speak to someone inside about getting you somewhere to wait with more privacy. It's best you stay out of sight here until we do."

"Yeah." I sighed.

"You want anything to drink?"

*Vodka*, I thought, but "Coffee, thanks" was what I said.

"You wait here, an' I'll be right back."

I watched her go, at this moment hating my fame more than I ever had and not giving a shit if I got papped by every two-bit newspaper in Tucson. I just wanted to be inside with Vanessa.

Twenty minutes later, I'd been smuggled in through a back door and given a side room that contained a couple of easy chairs and a TV. A doctor with kind blue eyes was waiting for me there.

"Hi, Miss D'Aplièse, I'm Dr. Cole."

"How is she?" I asked him.

"Her stats are stable now, so we've moved her out of the emergency room and settled her for the night." He smiled. She's a tough little nut. Would you like to see her?"

"Yes, please." I stood up.

"Electra," Mercy said to me, "I'm going to head back to The Ranch now, but someone will be here in the morning to see how Vanessa is and pick you up. And remember, you saved Vanessa's life tonight." She reached out, gave me a warm hug, and smiled up at me before following us out of the room.

"Vanessa's awake but not talking much. We've given her some strong meds for the pain, so she'll be feeling sleepy," Dr. Cole said as he led me into a dimly lit hospital room. "I'll leave you to it," he said as he left.

I walked around the bed and sat down in the chair next to Vanessa. She looked so frail and young lying there. I could see her eyes were open, and her arms lay on top of the sheets, bandaged from her wrists to her inner elbows. She was attached to a drip and a monitor that beeped every so often.

"Hi there, Vanessa, it's me, Electra," I whispered as I leaned toward her. "How are you feeling?"

There was no response as she continued to stare at the ceiling.

"The doctor says you're doing real well, that you're strong," I said, searching desperately for positive things to say. I lifted a hand, not sure where I could put it on her overcrowded forearms, so I laid it on top of her head and stroked her lovely hair. "I just wanted to tell you that I'm here for you."

Still nothing.

"I came with you in the ambulance; I'd never been in one before. It was like being in an episode of *Grey's Anatomy*, but the doc says you're gonna do just fine."

There was a long pause, and then Vanessa made a noise. "My—"

It sounded like "my," anyway, I thought, as I watched her lick her cracked lips.

"My mom used to do this," she whispered.

"Do what?"

"Stroke my hair. Feels nice," she said.

"Then I'll keep right on doing it. Would you like your mom to come here?"

"Yeah, but she's dead."

I watched as two tears trickled out of Vanessa's eyes. "I'm so sorry, sweetheart," I murmured, feeling tears burn behind my own eyes. "I'm gonna stay right here with you and stroke your hair until you go to sleep, okay?"

She gave a slight nod, and slowly, her eyes began to close.

"You're safe," I added as her breathing relaxed into a rhythm, and I settled in for a long night.

A few minutes later, the door opened, and to my surprise, Miles appeared from behind it. "How is she?" he asked.

"Sleeping," I whispered, putting a finger to my lips.

"Can you come outside for a second so we can talk?"

I shook my head. "No. I said I'd stay right here until she woke up."

"Okay." Miles tiptoed into the room, took a chair, and carried it across to put it next to me.

"How did you get here?"

"When I got your message from reception, I got in my rental car, but because I had no note from the 'authorities' to say I could leave, the darned guard wouldn't open the gates! So then I had to scale the fence, call a cab, and wait for it to arrive outside."

We both stifled a giggle.

"Does this constitute a mass breakout of Ranch inmates?"

"It sure might, yes," he agreed. "How are you?"

"Oh, okay, apart from a sore arm." I indicated the one that was still stroking Vanessa's hair. "She said her mom used to do this. She told me she was dead."

"Yeah, she is."

"What happened?"

"I don't know," Miles said. "Vanessa is HIV positive, so it might have been AIDS."

Vanessa stirred, and I hushed Miles. "You'd better go. We'll talk later."

"Hey, I can do quiet. I'll just sit right here and keep you company."

And so he did, and I had the oddest sensation that we were parents watching over our kid. Despite the circumstances, it felt comforting. As the clock on the wall ticked by the hours until dawn, my head became heavy and I began to doze. I felt an arm come around my shoulders and pull me closer so I could rest my head against his warm chest.

# 22

I'm thirsty," said a voice somewhere in the distance.

I jolted awake as my pillow was taken from behind my head and I opened my eyes. Miles was pouring some water into a cup and pressing the button that made the bed rise so that Vanessa could take a drink.

"Just sips now, honey, take it slowly," he said, holding the straw for her.

When Vanessa had finished, he sat back down in the chair and she turned to look at us. "What are you two doin' here? You my mom and dad or something?"

I smiled as Vanessa voiced just how I'd felt last night.

"I can see you're feeling better, missy," Miles smiled. "You scared us."

Vanessa shrugged. "I was hopin' I'd never have to wake to see another morning, but hey, here I am."

Maybe it was me, but I thought Vanessa seemed perkier.

"Electra here has refused to leave you all night in case you woke up," said Miles, who then turned to me. "How about you go freshen up and find someone who can bring us some coffee?"

As it happened, I was bursting to go to the bathroom, so I agreed.

"Black or white?" I asked.

"You talking about the coffee, ma'am?" he said, smirking at me.

"Ha! You'll get what you're given."

"Hey, you two got a thing going on or what?" Vanessa chirped from the bed as I left the room. Heat rose up my neck as I went to the washroom and looked at myself in the mirror. My hair had untied itself from its plait and hung greasily in curtains on either side of my face, and my eyes had great pouches beneath them. I did my best to tidy myself up, but with no equipment on hand, it was impossible, so I walked down the hallway in search of coffee.

"Room service will be here shortly," I said as I reentered the room.

Vanessa eyed me. "You sure have some strange accent going on there, don't she, Miles?"

"I was brought up in Switzerland, that's why. My mother tongue is French," I added as I went to sit down and Miles stood up.

"Excuse me while I leave you girls together and go and wash up, too."

"I ain't never been outside Manhattan, apart from coming here, and this ain't like no emergency room I ever visited." Vanessa rolled her eyes as Miles left. "Do I have to screw someone to pay for it?"

"No, it's all paid for, Vanessa," I reassured her as I watched her nod and her eyes began to droop like a puppy who had woken up to play and had suddenly run out of energy. It was difficult to believe that the sullen young woman I'd slept next to in rehab had tried to take her own life last night and woken up this morning seemingly so happy . . .

Maybe it was the fact that both Miles and I were there for her. Or—my heart sank at the thought—was it more to do with the fact that she was probably on some kind of opiate for the pain and her brain was simply reacting to the stimulant?

"She's sleeping again," I said as Miles reappeared at the same time as a nurse came with the coffee. I gulped back the hot liquid after lacing it with sugar to replace my morning carbs. "What happens next, do you think?"

"When I talked to the doctor last night, he said that the psych team will come to assess her. We both know that what happened last night was no practice run."

"And after that?"

"I'm not sure, but as I said the other night, she needs more than a serenity prayer and petting some horses to steer her back. Maybe once she's recovered and out of here, the doc said, a spell in long-term rehab is the way forward. She did have a social worker back in Manhattan, though once she turned eighteen a couple months back, technically she's no longer a juvenile, but I'm going to contact her anyway. In special circumstances, the care team can apply for an extension to maintain the supervision until she's twenty-one. In basic terms, it means the state would pay for any help she needs."

"Hey, I don't know anything about all that, but I just think she needs to feel loved."

"You're right, Electra, she certainly does, and that's not something you can buy."

"I . . . what if I took her back to New York to live with me? I could take care of her."

There was a pause as Miles turned to look at me, his expression one of shock and disbelief.

"Are you crazy? You're a top model who spends her life flying around the world in private jets! You don't have the time to give her what she needs. Besides"—he lowered his voice as Vanessa shifted position—"you can't put someone into that life when they have no hope of keeping it."

"You have no idea what I may or may not want to do with my future once I get out of here," I retorted.

"I . . . Look, let's talk about this later, okay? This is no fairy tale, Electra, and Vanessa isn't Cinderella. You can't mess with her as though she's a project you can forget about when you've lost interest."

My cup clattered into the saucer as anger rose up inside me. "Jesus, Miles! I'm only trying to help! Anyway," I added, trying to control myself, "you should know that I'm checking out of The Ranch today."

"Oh, yeah?"

"Yeah. I'm about as fixed as I can be for now, and I've got stuff to get on with. A life to lead," I said as my hands clutched the coffee cup for some kind of moral support. I stood up and maneuvered past him. "I'm gonna go find the doctor."

Miles sighed. "Okay. You do what you gotta do."

"I will," I said, marching to the door.

"Just one thing before you leave, Electra."

"What?"

"I wouldn't step outside the front of the hospital right now. There's a load of paps waiting to catch a glimpse of you."

Because I was trying to be quiet for Vanessa's sake, I didn't even have the pleasure of slamming the door behind me as I walked toward the nurses' station and asked if I could see the doctor in charge.

The woman made some calls, then nodded. "He's on his rounds just now, honey. He shouldn't be too long."

With nowhere else to go, I retreated into the restroom and sat on the tiled floor to seethe. I just couldn't work Miles out. Last night, I'd felt so close to him; sitting there with my head on his shoulder and his arm around me had felt natural. And now this morning . . . I let out a howl of frustration.

I took some deep breaths to calm down and tried to get my brain into gear without the purple haze of the initial anger. I eventually realized he was trying to tell me that if I took Vanessa on, she would need all I had to give her, perhaps for a lifetime. She wasn't like a novelty toy that I could just pick up, then drop when I'd finished with it. She was a living, breathing, and seriously damaged human being . . . And I was *also* a living, breathing, damaged human being . . .

"Miss D'Aplièse?" came a voice from the other side of the door.

"Yes?"

"Do you mind coming out for a quick chat?"

I recognized Dr. Cole's gentle voice.

"Sure," I said and opened the door to step outside.

"Hello." He smiled at me. "Are you okay?"

"Yeah, I'm fine. How is she?"

"Vanessa is doing very well. Physically, anyway. She should be out of here in a couple of days, and then ideally, depending on what the psych team here and then her social worker say, she'll need to spend some time in a specialized institution that can really help her."

"Do you think Vanessa is . . . well, saveable?"

Dr. Cole sighed. "Where there's life, there's always hope. I'm sure you've been made aware that every addict is somewhere on a spectrum. Some are lucky and get caught early on, and others, like Vanessa, are right at the end and are hardest of all to turn around. The good news is that The Ranch has begun that process, but now she needs to continue in some form of medium-to long-term program that she can integrate into her life when she leaves. She will need to do that in or near Manhattan. Not least because that's where her funding is based, if her social worker can get her state care extended."

"I can help if necessary, Dr. Cole."

"And that's more than generous of you, ma'am, but the state has got the dollars to fund the help she needs. It's a case of working through the red tape and having a strong arm on your side. There's a lot of misappropriation and corruption in the various government departments, but your friend Miles seems to know what he's doing there. Anyway"—he smiled—"it's good of you to take an interest in Vanessa and be prepared to help her."

"Well, I was given help myself not so long ago," I said. "Please keep her here for as long as she needs. You have my cell number, don't you?"

"It's on the record, yes. And now, you must excuse me, I've got to get around to see other patients. Good-bye."

He nodded at me and walked away, and I went back into my "office" in the restroom and dialed Mariam's number.

"Hello, Electra. How is your friend?" Mariam asked me before I'd said a word.

"Oh, she's out of danger now, thanks. Actually, I was just wondering if you could look at flights back to New York for me?"

"For when?"

"Tomorrow morning if possible. I was coming out Thursday anyway, as you know, so it's only a day earlier."

There was a slight pause on the line. "Okay. Are we talking by private jet here?"

"Probably." I thought about the crowd of paps that were apparently stationed outside the hospital.

"What time would suit?"

"I don't know, around two? That will get me in about ten p.m."

"No problem. I . . . Are you sure you don't want me to fly down and accompany you back, Electra?"

"I have flown alone before, Mariam, and I'm not sick or anything. Besides, it's a long way for you to come."

"I'm happy to do it if you need me."

"Thanks, I appreciate that, but I'm sure I'll be fine."

"Okay, I'll check everything out and give you a call back between seven and eight when you have your cell phone."

"Oh, don't worry about that. I'm going back to The Ranch to see my therapist now, and I'm sure she'll let me have my cell for the day. Bye, Mariam."

As I walked back to Vanessa's room, I wondered whether Mariam's eagerness to accompany me home was because she cared or because she was worried I might have drunk the on-board bar dry by the time I landed in New York.

*I* wondered whether I would, too, but I had to face temptation alone sometime.

Vanessa was sitting up in bed, picking at her breakfast of juice and a pastry. I was happy to see that the line was out of her arm and only the blood pressure monitor remained on her finger. She didn't look as perky as she had earlier, so maybe grim reality was starting to set back in.

"Hi," I said. "How are you?"

"''Kay, thanks."

"She's worried about the psych team coming to evaluate her," commented Miles from the other side of the bed.

"Yeah, I ain't going to no nuthouse. I might be a junkie, but I ain't loco." Vanessa shuddered. "You won't let them lock me away somewhere like that, will you, 'Lectra?"

"Everyone is only trying to help you, Vanessa," I said, "and you're going to have to trust them, okay?"

"Yeah, but they're not gonna lock me up in an asylum or nothin', are they?" she repeated.

"Listen . . ." I could see that Vanessa was getting worked up. "I just spoke to that nice doctor who admitted you last night. We talked about trying to find you a facility nearer Manhattan that can give you the help you need. It would be like The Ranch but without the horses," I joked. "Miles and I got scared last night, and we don't want that happening to you again."

Vanessa stared at me hard. "An' why would you care what happens to me? You, with all your dollars in the bank?"

"Because I do. And so does Miles. And you have to trust us and the doctors who all want to help you."

"Why should I trust you any more than I trusted Tyler? He said he'd look after me, but he just got me hooked on the junk."

"Because I said I wouldn't leave your side last night, and I didn't. At the end of the day, you've got two choices: you trust us and the professionals who want to help you, or you go back to your old life."

"Or I end it and leave you all behind," Vanessa muttered.

"Remember, you're doing well," said Miles. "You've been off the hard stuff for almost two weeks now."

"Yeah, and it worked out so good I tried to kill myself." Vanessa rolled her eyes, pushed her breakfast tray away, and stared at the ceiling.

I looked at Miles for guidance.

"Electra and I are just gonna go out and have a chat," he said, standing up.

"Yeah, you guys had enough of me already, see?"

I opened my mouth to speak, but Miles shook his head and I followed him out of the door.

"Shit! She's so negative!"

"The doc says she's got postwithdrawal depression and she needs a shrink to prescribe her some meds that will help."

"But the doc also said that Vanessa *is* off the junk now and just needs the right help and support to keep her off. So that's got to be positive."

"Yeah. Look, I'm sorry I lost it earlier, Electra. I know you only want to help her."

"Yeah, I do, but I understand she needs more than I can give her." I felt so tired, physically and mentally, that I was swaying where I stood.

"Why don't you go back and get some sleep? I'll stay with her. One of the Ranch nurses has arrived to drive you back in their jeep. There's nothing more you can do here."

"I will. I feel totally out of it, to be honest. I'll come say good-bye to Vanessa first."

"Okay, then, I'll just use the facilities while you do." He smiled at me and walked off down the hallway.

"Vanessa? Are you awake?" I asked as I stood looking at her. I got a shrug in return. "Listen, I just wanted to tell you that the doc says you'll be out of here as soon as you're feeling better."

"An' then they send me to a funny farm, right?"

"No, Vanessa, I swear on my life I won't let that happen to you. I'm going back to New York tomorrow and—"

"So you're leavin' me after all?"

"No! I'm going back so I can sort stuff out to *help* you. And other kids like you who get into trouble. Please, Vanessa, trust me. Miles and I are gonna make sure you get the best care we can find. I won't abandon you, I swear."

"Then take me with you. I wanna get outta here now," Vanessa moaned.

"Listen to me now, and listen good," I said, my grandmother's words suddenly coming to mind. "You've had a shit time, but when you needed it most, help appeared. And now you've got it, when a lot of kids like you don't. I'm not saying I'm your fairy godmother, or Miles either—"

I watched the tiniest of smiles appear on Vanessa's lips.

"But," I continued, "we *are* here, and you are safe and we are gonna get you well, okay? And one day, you are gonna help others like you've been helped."

I don't know how I knew this, but somehow I just *did*. ("Tiggy" was becoming my middle name.)

"So, missy, you do what the docs tell you and count yourself lucky, okay? And I'll see you in New York, and when you're fixed, we'll go for a fancy dinner someplace. And everyone, including Tyler, will see you with me in a magazine and know you're a winner, not a loser."

"That'd be cool," Vanessa said eventually. "Swear on that?"

"I already did. And you know what?"

"What?"

"Your hair will always look better than mine. Love you, Vanessa. See you soon."

I kissed the top of her head and left the room. Miles was waiting in the hallway.

"All okay?"

"Yup. I'm off now. Keep me updated."

"I will."

"Thanks."

"Oh, and the jeep's parked discreetly around the back of the hospital," he called before disappearing into Vanessa's room.

As I stepped into the Ranch jeep, for the first time ever I appreciated my fame and what it could do for others. I had power. And now it was time to channel that into something positive.

"So are you sure you want to leave tomorrow morning?" said Fi later that afternoon, after I'd had some sleep and we had discussed the events of the night before. "Why not stay on? Last night was a traumatic experience for you, Electra."

"Because I need to go," I said simply. "I want to get back to my life and begin making some changes, rather than just sitting here thinking about them."

"Would you like to share with me what those changes are going to be?"

"Well, firstly, I'll be clearing the booze from my apartment and deleting my dealer's number," I joked.

"Well, that's a start. And?"

"I'll be meeting with my agent to work out a way to give me some free time. I've already arranged a meeting with my business manager to discuss my finances, because there's other stuff I want to do."

"Such as?"

"Help kids like Vanessa," I said. "And not just by giving money but by maybe becoming a kind of spokesperson for them and getting involved in the fight against drugs."

"That sounds fantastic, Electra." Fi gave me a genuine smile. "Boy, oh boy, do these kids need someone to fight for them. But just be careful that in the first few weeks, especially, you don't wear yourself out implementing all your new ideas. You need to spend time on yourself, like you have here: your morning run, *daily* AA meetings, at least for the first six months, good food, early nights . . . You're in recovery, too, Electra, and you can't afford to forget that. You're no good to anyone if you fall off the wagon. Do you have any vacations coming up?"

"Yup, actually, I do," I said. Then I explained to Fi about the planned reunion for all us sisters to sail on the *Titan* to the Greek islands to lay a wreath for Pa.

"Spending time with your family is crucial," Fi agreed. "What about at home in New York? Do you have people there to support you?"

"Mariam, the PA I've told you about, and my grandmother Stella. I didn't get around to telling you much about her, but I know she will be there for me."

"Okay, well, don't be afraid to call on them, and Maia of course, who has been so concerned for you. I'll be emailing her and your assistant a list of local AA meetings, plus the names of a couple of good therapists I know in New York. You can't forget that you need other people, Electra, and to trust them."

"I won't, but I also want to be there for Vanessa," I added.

"Well, that's a good thing, but the stronger *you* are, the more you can help her."

"She needs me," I said, "and besides, seeing what I did last night was, like, the most powerful reality check I could ever have."

"True," Fi agreed. "Is the fact you feel she needs you a good feeling?"

"Yeah, I guess it is." I watched Fi's eyes glance up to the clock and knew my time was up. "Listen, Fi, before I go, I just want to say sorry if I was difficult to begin with, but thanks for everything. You—this—has been amazing. It's changed my life."

"Don't thank me," she said as we both stood up. "You've done it all by yourself. Good luck, Electra," she said, then opened her arms wide and gave me a hug. "Keep in touch, won't you? Let me know how you're getting along."

"I will, yes." I walked toward the door, then turned back and smiled at her. "I never thought I'd say this, Fi, but I'm sure gonna miss you. Bye, now."

That evening, I spotted Miles in the canteen. "How is she?" I asked him, setting down my tray opposite his.

"Scared, negative . . . pretty much like she was when you left this morning," he said.

"What did the psych team say?"

"The shrink said he knows a good place in Long Island that specializes in dealing with kids like Vanessa. I've already contacted her social worker, and I'm going to talk to Vanessa's probation officer as well."

"She has a probation officer?"

"Yeah. Her social worker told me earlier that she's been in and out of foster homes since her mother died; then, at sixteen, she disappeared off the radar until she was arrested for soliciting in Harlem. She only got a caution, but she was classified as a delinquent, which means that up until a few months ago, when she turned eighteen, she had a 'team' that monitored her. Ida—the social worker—is gonna put things in motion fast, and if the court grants an extension until Vanessa's twenty-one, she can then make the right calls to get her into this program the shrink has recommended. And then she'll get the welfare she's due and, eventually, a place to stay. Hopefully not in one of the projects."

"What's a project?" I asked.

"Wow, Electra." Miles rolled his eyes. "You sure have lived in a different world. I thought all Americans knew about those."

"I'm technically Swiss." I blushed, but I knew it was no excuse. "What is it?"

"It's social housing, paid for by the state. Trouble is, some of them can be very rough. But anyway, let's see where we go from here."

"Please, Miles, remember I've told you both I'd help as much as I can. If she needs a place to stay, I can pay for it. I feel bad that I'm leaving her, but I just need to get out of here now."

"You gotta do what's best for you, Electra. Vanessa knows you're there for her and that you've already paid for her treatment at the hospital."

"If I gave you some cash, can you buy her a cell? Then I can call her on it direct."

"Yeah, of course, but remember, she's in a dark place just now and maybe won't want to communicate much. And you, young lady, have got to put yourself first." He wagged a finger at me. "You're no good to Vanessa if you're back on the Goose."

"I know, Miles. And what about you?"

"I'll kick around here for a while till Vanessa's sorted out, then hopefully bring her back with me to New York."

"Okay, well, I'd better go and pack. Here." I handed him an envelope. "That's got my cell phone and my PA's cell just in case you can't get hold of me. Let me know as soon as there's news on Vanessa, won't you? Bye, Miles."

"Course I will. Hey!" Miles called to me, and I turned around.

"What?"

"You're a good person, Electra. It's been my pleasure to get to know you."

"Thanks," I said and walked away from him before he could see the tears forming in my eyes.

# 23

A week later, I woke up luxuriating on the cloud of down that was the mattress in my New York penthouse. I stretched and rolled over to look at the time and saw it was 6:00 a.m. I needed to get up and get running before the park became too crowded. Putting on my track pants and hoodie and adding the wig, sunglasses, and baseball cap that had so far protected me from the paps, I left the apartment, took the elevator down, and jogged from the lobby across into the park. The magnolia trees were in full bloom, and summer flowers were adding color in the beds along the path. New York was wearing its best today—the sky was as blue as anything you'd find in the south of France—and I smiled simply because I felt happy.

When Mariam had met me at the airport, I could see the trepidation on her face. The first thing I'd done after I'd walked down the steps of the jet was to give her a big hug. She'd immediately hugged me back.

"You look amazing, Electra!" she'd said as we walked to the limo parked on the tarmac.

"No, I don't. My weave and nails are a mess, and I have all sorts of hair growing in all sorts of places." I'd laughed. "They don't allow razors at The Ranch."

In the limo on the way into Manhattan, we'd talked about my time inside and Mariam had thanked me for her letter, which she said she'd treasure forever.

"Don't thank me. I was a total bitch to you, and I apologize. You still wanna carry on working for me, don't you?" I'd shot her a worried glance.

"Of course I do, I love my job, and you, Electra," she'd added, and even if it could have just been a cheesy line, I really didn't feel it was.

Back at the apartment, I'd noticed that Mariam had decorated it with lots of sweet-smelling flowers and loaded the refrigerator with Coke and other soda and endless flavors of juice.

"I wasn't sure what you'd be drinking."

"Coke and ginger tea are good," I'd said, opening a can of the former and taking a sip.

Then we'd run through what Susie had said to the bookers about my sudden departure. "She told them you had a family crisis and had to take time out. Seriously, I don't think there's been a lot of gossip. I certainly haven't seen anything untoward in the press," Mariam had comforted me.

I'd sighed. "Well, I'm lucky no one managed to get a shot of me covered in blood in that ER in Tucson. I looked like I'd murdered someone."

As it was late, I'd told her she should go home, but she'd shaken her head. "Not me, sorry. I am staying in the spare room tonight."

"I swear, I'm off everything, Mariam," I'd said, momentarily affronted.

"I know, Electra, it's not that I don't trust you. I just want to hear about everything that has happened to you since you left. I thought we could order some takeout and you could tell me all about your friend who ended up in the hospital."

So we'd showered, gotten into our robes, and eaten take-out Chinese and I'd told her all about Vanessa.

"Oh, Electra, you are a Good Samaritan," Mariam had said, which had made me blush. "She's lucky you have taken such an interest in her."

So I'd begun to tell her about my plans to do more, and then I'd felt my eyes closing and gone to lie on my cloud of feathers and slept right through until six the next morning.

Since then, I hadn't stopped. I'd had a meeting with Susie to tell her I was cutting my schedule back, and even though she hadn't looked pleased, she'd eventually agreed and we'd worked out that I'd do only the campaigns I was already contracted for.

"But what about the fall shows?" she'd asked me.

"No," I'd said firmly, knowing that if anything could drag me back into my old ways, it was the crazy world of the catwalk.

"Oh, and I've had a couple of inquiries from designers who'd like to talk about collaborations, in the same vein as the one you did with Xavier last year."

As I'd listened to Susie, for a couple of brief seconds I'd thought back to my sketchbook and how much I'd loved designing. But then again, I'd promised myself not to take on too much.

"Maybe next year," I'd told her.

The upshot was that I had just enough work to keep me busy up until mid-June, and after that, I'd go away to Atlantis for the sisters' sailing trip. Then I hoped to go down to the Hacienda Orquídea to organize the building works I wanted done.

Excitement bubbled up inside me every time I thought about my new home-to-be. Casey, my business manager, had confirmed that I could easily afford it, so I'd called Manuel with an offer and he'd accepted. He'd also agreed to sell me Hector and said that he'd find a ranch hand to look after him and other horses I might care to add to my stable.

"But you must come to choose, *señorita*. Horses are a soul choice," he'd said.

I was buying it fully furnished, at what even Casey said looked like a good price. I was also planning on adding a pool and an extra wing to provide further bedroom accommodation; I had dreams of inviting all my sisters to come stay with me at Christmas . . .

As for Miles, he'd moved out of The Ranch and was staying in a motel near the hospital as he waited for Vanessa's team to complete the red tape needed to bring her back to New York and get her into the program the doctor had suggested. There wasn't much news on Vanessa herself; since I'd left, they'd put her on what Miles described as heavy-duty antidepressants, and she'd been sleeping a lot. I called her on her cell, but she didn't answer, so I sent her a text every night and occasionally received the odd "OK" or "thanks" in return.

Talking to Miles on the phone felt different from talking to him in person; perhaps it was because he had such a warm, rich tone to his voice and a clever sense of humor, but I'd started to see our calls as the highlight of my day. It was partly because he knew exactly what I'd been through and how the transition back to reality was one of the hardest moments of staying clean. I could talk to him freely about the way I was feeling. Which, for the main part, had been positive. Yes, it was still hard to open the fridge and take out a can of Coke or some juice when a month ago there had always been a bottle of vodka in the icebox. At night, when I was watching TV or drawing in my sketchbook (I hadn't dared venture out to any social functions—I wasn't strong enough for those just yet), I knew it would take one call to bring my dealer to my front door. Life on the level was tough; I missed the highs badly, but at least there were no lows, either.

Mariam had the list of therapists and the dates of local AA meetings sent to her by Fi for my arrival. I'd needed her to force me to go to AA the first time; she'd driven with me there, squeezed my hand, and told me that she'd be right outside. She'd even walked me to the door.

"What if people recognize me?" I'd asked her as I stood outside, abject terror filling me.

"It's anonymous, remember? No one is allowed to tell on anyone else. Now go, you'll be fine."

I did, and I had been. To my utter surprise, I'd seen other well-known faces at the meeting, and when I'd stood up and announced that my name was Electra and I was an alcoholic, everyone had clapped and I had cried.

Then the meeting leader had welcomed me and asked me if there was anything I wanted to say. When I'd done this for the first time at The Ranch, I'd shaken my head and hurriedly sat down, but to my utter shock, this time I'd nodded. "Yeah, I just wanted to say that I've just come out of rehab and at first I hated it and didn't understand the Twelve Steps or how they could help me. But . . . I held on, and then I just got it, and I want to say thank you to, well, the higher power and everyone who supported me, because people like you guys have saved my life."

There had been another round of applause (and some cheering), and I'd felt so warm and welcomed that I'd actually started to look forward to my daily meetings.

*Surely it's all too good to be true?* I thought as I pounded the pathway, which was exactly what I had said to Miles last night.

"It's anything but," he'd countered. "You're in the honeymoon phase at the moment, thinking you can deal, but it's when you're really back to reality and you've been off the stuff for a while that it gets dangerous."

Every time I felt the urge—which was like a red haze that descended, with a devil voice in my ear telling me that just one shot wouldn't hurt, would it? Because honestly, I deserved it for getting through a day without and for going to the AA meeting or taking a run—I visualized instead the redness of the blood that had poured out of Vanessa's arms as she lay on that bathroom floor. And that made me want to gag in horror and helped take away the craving.

Mariam was the perfect housemate, I thought as I ran out of the park and along Central Park West to get home. She'd insisted on staying ever since I'd come back and seemed to know instinctively when I needed company and when I didn't. I also took inspiration from the fact that she'd never taken a drink in her life and was one of the calmest people I knew. She'd proven herself to be a superb cook, especially with curries, which I lapped up because the spice was still helping the cravings. Even though I'd said we could easily order takeout, she'd refused.

"I love cooking, Electra, so it's my pleasure. Besides, I know what I am putting into the food, and that makes me happy that we are both eating well."

"Morning, Tommy," I said, giving him a big smile and coming to a halt by him. There'd been a small posy of flowers waiting for me upstairs when I'd arrived home. Mariam had said they were from Tommy—picked illegally from Central Park, she'd added.

"Morning, Electra," he greeted me. "How are you today?"

"I'm good," I said. "You?"

He shrugged. "Oh, I'm okay."

"You sure you're okay, Tommy? You look a little low."

"Oh, it's probably because I'm having to get up a whole lot earlier to see you these days," he joked weakly.

"Well, why don't you come and join me on my run sometime?" I asked him suddenly. "I could use some company."

"Hey, I just might do that. Thank you, Electra." He tipped his baseball cap to me, and I ran inside.

"Breakfast will be ready in ten," Mariam called from the kitchen.

"Okay, just gonna take a shower," I replied, giving her a wave as I passed by. Mariam got up even earlier than I did to say her morning prayers.

"Those were great," I said as I polished off the blueberry pancakes, which had been smothered in maple syrup. "Goodness, I'm having a food baby!" I added as I cradled my belly in my hands.

"Goodness" was my new go-to word. Ma and my sisters had always told me I had a "potty mouth," and what with Miles and his notable shudder every time I took his precious Lord's name in vain, as well as Mariam, I'd decided it was time to clean that up, too. The occasional "fuck" or "shit" came out automatically, but I felt proud that even the queen of England would consider having me as a guest if I carried on like this. Next thing, I thought wryly, I'd be buying myself a Bible and attending church.

"Thank you." Mariam started to clear up the dishes. "One day I'll cook you a proper Iranian feast," she said as my cell rang.

My heart gave a jolt as I saw it was Miles.

"Hi."

"Hi, Electra. Good news: Ida just called to say Vanessa's care extension has been granted and they've managed to get her into the center Dr. Cole recommended. It's on Long Island, about thirty minutes from JFK. I'm going to make the travel arrangements right now, and I hope to get on a flight back either later tonight or tomorrow morning."

"Fantastic! That's such good news!"

"Yeah, it is. I called a friend who I work with at the drop-in center, and she rates this place highly. It's a proper rehab unit, which means medium- to long-term residency, i.e., she won't be kicked out after a couple weeks. Anyway, more when I see you."

"Great. Why don't I come collect you from JFK? Give me a chance to see Vanessa?"

*And you*, I thought.

"If you have time, then that would be great."

"I do. Listen, I've got to leave for my AA meeting, but call Mariam when you know the flight details, okay?"

"Sure. See you soon, Electra. Bye, now."

"Miles will be calling you," I said to Mariam as I headed for the door.

"Okay, and by the way, your grandmother called again this morning. Your calendar's clear for the weekend, so—"

"I'll let you know later, okay?"

"Sure. See you shortly."

On my way downtown to the meeting, I pondered why, even though Stella had called a number of times on my cell (which I hadn't picked up) and on Mariam's (which she had), I felt reluctant to see her. As I climbed out of the sedan—limos were just too noticeable, and I also wanted to use my finances a bit more constructively these days—I concluded that I just didn't know the answer.

The AA meeting was held in a church hall near the Flatiron Building, at the intersection of Broadway and Fifth Avenue. I loved it because it was at a crossroads; a metaphoric melting pot of humanity. No one cared where anyone else was from, because we all had the same diagnosis: we were all on the addict spectrum somewhere.

The place smelled of sweat and dogs, with the slightest hint of alcohol, probably from years of holding meetings where the drunks came in off the street to say they'd fallen off the wagon. It was a well-attended meeting with about two dozen people already there, so I sat down on a chair at the back of the hall.

We all stood and said the serenity prayer, and then the meeting leader asked if anyone was new to the group.

I watched someone in the front row adjust his baseball cap and stand up. He looked very familiar . . .

"Hi. My name's Tommy, and I'm an alcoholic."

We all clapped for him automatically.

"Welcome, Tommy. And is there anything you'd like to say to the group?" the leader asked, as my brain finally got into gear and I drew in a deep breath.

"Yeah, I'd like to say that I didn't think I needed these meetings anymore, so I stopped coming. Then two days ago, I took a drink."

Tommy paused, then cleared his throat as we waited (me, with bated breath) for him to continue.

"I've met a girl, see, and . . . I think I love her, but we can't ever be together. She'd been away for a while, and I really missed her . . . And I need you guys . . . this . . . to help me through."

We all clapped again, but he didn't sit down, so there was obviously more.

"Some of you here might remember that when I came back from Afghanistan, I found my wife had left me and taken the kid with her. I turned to liquor, and I swore then that I'd never love anyone else. But I do, and . . . she's been away for a while, but, yep, that's all I have to say."

"Shit!" I muttered under my breath.

"We'll all be thinking about you and praying for you, Tommy, and you know we're here for you," the leader said.

I saw a number of people around Tommy clap him on the back.

"Now, is there anyone else who wants to stand up and speak?"

An actor I recognized stood up, but I zoned out. Tommy, *my* Tommy, whom I'd seen on Facebook had a wife and a kid to go home to, had no such thing. And apparently he was in love with someone he could never have— someone who had been "away for a while"—and he'd really missed her.

The rest of the meeting totally passed me by, and when the leader was doing the closing notices, I sneaked out before Tommy could see me. I didn't want him to suffer the embarrassment of knowing I'd heard his most intimate thoughts. I jumped back into the car and checked my cell. Mariam had left a voice mail, so I called her back, still breathing hard.

"Hi, it's me. You called?"

"Yes. What is it, Electra? Is everything all right?"

*Wow*, I thought, *Mariam knows me well*. This was the first time I'd ever been faced with the confidentiality issue, because I was bursting, just *bursting* to confide in my PA. I knew she, too, was fond of Tommy—it was him she'd turned to that night to help me when I'd been off my face—but I swallowed hard, remembering the AA code.

"Oh, it was nothing, just an upsetting story from one of the guys at the meeting. What did you want?"

"Oh, just to tell you I'm making tomato soup with chili for lunch. Is that okay?"

"Sounds perfect," I said.

"And also, Miles has managed to get himself and Vanessa on a flight from Tucson. They land at ten tonight at JFK."

When we pulled up in front of my apartment building, I got out and checked around the awning to make sure that Tommy wasn't going to jump out at me to say hi. He definitely wasn't there, so unless he had a twin, I knew it had been him at that meeting. However, there *was* a surprise waiting for me in the lobby. There, sitting on one of the leather chairs, was Stella, my grandmother.

"Hello, Electra," she said as she stood up to greet me. "Do forgive me for arriving like this, but if the mountain wouldn't come to Mohammed . . . I wanted to see for myself how you were."

"Of course, please come up." I ushered her toward the elevator, marveling at the way she held herself so straight and elegantly in her old-fashioned bouclé jacket and skirt.

"I won't keep you long if you have things to do," she said as we walked into the apartment.

"No problem at all," I replied, feeling a sudden warmth toward her and wondering why I'd been so frightened of seeing her. "Come in and sit down. Mariam's preparing some lunch."

"I am," Mariam said, appearing in the hallway. "It'll be ready in five minutes. Hi, Stella," she added with a smile, then went back to the kitchen.

"She is such a genuine person, Electra," Stella said as she sat down in an easy chair—I could never picture her lounging on a couch in track pants and a hoodie like me. "She called me regularly with updates while you were . . . away. How are you feeling?"

"I'm good—really good," I added, just in case she thought I was throwing her a line.

"And you're still off the liquor and drugs?"

"I totally am, yup. But as you know, it's one day at a time, so I can't get too cocky and think I'm out of the woods or anything."

"No, you shouldn't. That's the most dangerous thing of all. So tell me, what was it like in the place you went to?"

I did my best to give her a brief overview. "Y'know, I was dreading it, but actually, it was fantastic."

"You should count yourself lucky to have been able to go to such a place. It sounds like a holiday resort. Except I know that it isn't, of course," she added hurriedly.

"Lunch is served," Mariam called from the kitchen, and my grandmother and I trooped in to eat at the table, which Mariam had set using some of the flowers from the vases around the apartment as a centerpiece.

"I was saying to Mariam this morning that I need to start watching my calories," I commented as we all dug in. "I'll soon be too fat to be called a supermodel."

"I doubt it. Look at me, I am heading toward seventy, and I've never put on a pound in the whole of my life. You've got good genes."

"Your cheekbones are identical," Mariam commented. "Mine are somewhere near my jaw!"

"Nonsense! You're a very attractive young lady, if I may say so, both inside and out," said Stella. Mariam glowed at the compliment.

"By the way, I want an opinion," I said, once I'd cleaned my bowl and we were onto the fresh fruit salad that Mariam had doused in some heavenly coulis. "I've been thinking of a change of hairstyle."

"Okay," said Mariam. "Have you spoken to Susie about this?"

"No, it's my hair, isn't it? I can do what I want with it."

"Well said, Electra. Your body is your own property, and you should make the decisions about it," said Stella. "Personally, I think you could do with a decent trim. It looks far too long to me. And the upkeep must be a nightmare. How you young black girls manage to keep it under control, I just don't know."

"See these bits?" I grabbed a piece from my ponytail. "They're not my real hair, they're extensions."

My grandmother took the strand and shrugged. "It feels real to me."

"It is, except it's not mine. I was thinking how tasteless that is, especially because the girl whose hair I'm now wearing might have had to sell it just to feed her family. So I've decided that I'm going to get my extensions taken out and then I'm going to shave it off so it's short, like yours." I indicated Stella's trimmed Afro, which was about a centimeter long.

"Wow!" said Mariam, and I wanted to laugh, because she'd obviously picked the word up from me, but it sounded so wrong coming out of her mouth.

"Well, I wear mine like this just because it's sensible, but would the clothes designers and the photographers want you to look like that?"

"I don't know. And you know what? I don't give a damn, either." I then saw Stella's expression at my use of an expletive. "Sorry," I apologized, "but as you just said, it *is* my hair and maybe I literally want to go back to my roots! They can jam wigs on my head for a shoot if that's what they want to do. And . . ."

"Yes?" Stella prompted during my long pause.

"Well, it's also about being who I am, even though I'm not sure yet. I mean, Mariam's family are all Muslim and know their history from hundreds of years back. I grew up in a mixed household, as a black child with a white dad and sisters in between."

"And you're perhaps feeling confused about your identity," said Stella. "Trust me, I, too, grew up between worlds, Electra, just like you have. Some would say we were privileged, and in many ways we have been, but . . . you end up feeling you don't belong in one camp or another."

"Yup." I nodded and suddenly felt all emotional again, as if I'd finally found a real-life person who maybe understood my confusion. "Stella, you remember you began telling me the story about that girl going to Africa before I went to rehab?"

"Sure, I do. The question is, do you?"

I saw her eyes twinkle and knew she was teasing me. Partly at least.

"Some of it, yes, but I think . . . I think I need to hear more."

"Well, then, we'll take a day when you've got some time, and I'll continue the story. *Your* story."

"I've got time now, really. Miles and Vanessa's plane doesn't land until ten p.m., right, Mariam?"

"Yes," she confirmed. "Stella, if you're staying on for a while, I might head out and run some errands. Shall I bring you both coffee in the living room?"

"That would be just fine," Stella said as she rose. "Can we help you with the clearing up?"

"No, but thank you for asking. You two go through."

Chastened by the fact it had never even crossed my mind to ask Mariam if she wanted help in the kitchen, I followed my grandmother into the living room and watched as she sat down.

"I realized when I was away that I still don't know about my mom or the rest of my family. Or maybe you did tell me and I was just so out of it, I don't remember. Who was she?" I asked as I curled up on the couch.

"No, I haven't told you about her yet. All in good time, Electra, all in good time; there is a lot to explain. Do you remember I told you how Cecily, the American lady, had been jilted by her fiancé so decided to go to Africa to mend her broken heart?"

"Yeah, I do, and how she'd fallen in love with a complete bas—*idiot*," I said quickly.

"Exactly. Now, I think I'd reached the point in the story where Cecily was staying at Wanjohi Farm with Katherine . . ."

# CECILY

*Kenya*
*February 1939*

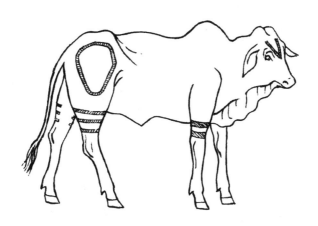

*A Kenyan Boran cow with Maasai clan brands*

# 24

"Time to get up," Katherine said when she woke Cecily at five the following morning. "I've put your safari clothes on the end of your bed. We'll drive Alice's DeSoto over to Bill's, so I'll see you outside. I'm packing some hampers with supplies, then I need to call Aleeki and let him know you'll be coming home tomorrow instead," she said as she left the bedroom.

Sleepily, Cecily put on a khaki suit and pants that fitted her almost perfectly, then pulled on the heavy lace-up boots, which didn't. They were a few sizes too big—she'd always had tiny feet—but they would have to do.

"Hop in," said Katherine, as she stowed some blankets on the back seat of the car. She started the engine and switched on the headlights as it was still pitch black.

Cecily did so, and with a last glance at Wanjohi Farm and the relative safety and comfort it offered, they were off.

She dozed fitfully during the hour-long journey until bright sunlight jolted her awake. She opened her eyes to see that they seemed to have left the main road and were bumping violently along a narrow track that appeared to go on forever, winding through acres of hot plain, with grasses and trees clinging to the orange earth. Cecily rolled down the window to search for a breeze and was assaulted by the smell of livestock, earthy and fecal. She saw a group of cattle being herded across the grasslands by very tall men in dark orange robes that matched the color of the earth beneath their bare feet. She marveled at the cows, which bore only a vague resemblance to their American cousins. They had large humps on their backs and folds of extra skin that hung almost to the ground from their scrawny necks.

"Nearly there now, darling," said Katherine. "Welcome to Bill's farm."

Cecily saw they were now approaching a low building with a timber frame sitting in the middle of the plain, the sun glaring off its tin roof.

"Hello there! You made it." Bobby had emerged from the hut and walked toward them as Katherine slowed the car to a standstill.

Cecily climbed out. "Jeez," she said, looking around her, "is this the bush?"

"It's on the edge of the Loita Plains," said Bobby, which meant nothing to Cecily. "You girls go inside and have a cool drink. Bill and I are readying the vehicles with supplies."

"The hampers and blankets are in the back of Alice's DeSoto," Katherine called as the two women walked toward the shack. Inside, Katherine poured them both a glass of water as Cecily looked around the very basic accommodation.

"Is this where Bill lives?"

"It is. As you can see, there's no woman's touch here." She smiled. "He spends so much time out in the bush, I suppose he hardly thinks it's worth doing anything about it. I must say, I'm rather excited. I do hope we find some elephants for you; out of all the creatures that inhabit these parts, I find them the most magnificent."

"Are they dangerous?"

"Like any wild animal, they can be, but you couldn't be in safer hands with Bill. Talk of the devil," Katherine said as Bill strode inside.

"Good morning, Cecily. Glad you could make it. Ready to go?"

"I am." Cecily saw he was staring at her feet again.

"Katherine, can you sort out her puttees?" Bill offered her two rolls of bandages. "Can't have her precious ankles bitten by a puff adder while she sleeps, can we? I'll see you both outside."

"Sit down, Cecily," Katherine ordered. Cecily did so, and Katherine wound the bandages around each of her ankles, tucking the hems of her pants in at the top and tying the bandages in two tight knots. "There we go. Not very attractive, but it does the job."

"Goodness, I'm sweating like a pig in all these clothes," Cecily muttered. The heat was something else, and she felt dizzy and sick.

"You'll get used to it, don't worry. Right, let's be off."

They left the shack and walked around the side of it, where Bill was sitting behind the wheel of his old pickup, with Bobby in his next to it. Cecily's eyes widened as she saw what could only be described as a real-life version of one of the drawings of a Maasai warrior she'd seen in the books she'd taken out of the library in Manhattan. The Maasai man, who was sitting at the back on the flat area loaded with supplies, nodded at her regally. He clutched a long spear by his side and was dressed in deep red robes that were knotted around his shoulders. His long neck was adorned with multicolored bead necklaces, and his ears were pierced by several large rings. His face was angular, the dark skin barely lined, and his hair was cropped closely to his scalp and dusted with a reddish powder. Cecily could only guess at his age— he might have been anywhere between twenty and forty.

"This is Nygasi, a friend of mine," said Bill. "Climb aboard, ladies." Bill indicated that Cecily should sit next to him in the front as Katherine climbed onto the rear seat with Nygasi perched just behind her. She shielded her eyes against the glare of the sun bouncing off Nygasi's spear and wondered if he had ever had cause to use it.

"All ready to go?" called Bobby from the pickup beside them. Two more Maasai men were sitting on the rear of his vehicle, also holding spears.

"Absolutely," said Katherine gaily, passing Cecily a flask of water.

"Only drink what you need. Water is precious out in the bush at this time of year," she advised, which did nothing to calm Cecily's jangling nerves.

The pickup's engine rumbled to life, and Cecily clutched the seat, praying she wouldn't be sick, as Bill pushed down on the accelerator and they set off with a lurch.

As they drove for what felt like hours through the dusty grassland, eventually the terrain began to subtly alter and grow lusher. It was a wide-open landscape, the vast blue sky skimming the tops of the fever trees on which giraffes nibbled, their tongues curling out as they pulled the branches toward them. The pickup swerved suddenly, and Cecily could see that they had narrowly avoided running over two hyenas that had dashed past their wheels.

"Bloody pests!" Bill swore above the engine noise.

"Look, Cecily, those are wildebeest—the ones with the manes on their backs. And there's Nygasi's *enkang*—his settlement—where his wives and children live." Katherine pointed to the left.

Cecily looked at what appeared to be a gray circular hedge made up of branches. Women in deep red robes were strolling toward it with bundles of wood under their arms and goats at their heels. Some had makeshift baby carriers containing babies slung over their shoulders. At the sound of the passing pickups, the women stopped to wave and smile.

"Did she say wives in the plural? You mean Nygasi has more than one?"

"It's the Maasai way," Bill answered. "The more cattle and women and children you have, the more respect you command within the tribe. And Nygasi commands quite a lot of respect."

"Look over there!" Katherine shouted to her half an hour later, pointing into the distance, where Cecily could see animals gathered around a hazy silver shimmer. "Do you see those Thomson's gazelles there, the little ones with the straight horns? They're very brave drinking the water, you never know when a croc will come out and snap at them! But that's life here on the plains."

Cecily was awfully glad when Bill eventually pulled the pickup to a halt by a copse of fever trees, and Bobby pulled up beside them. The sun was beating down on the open-topped pickup, and she'd felt horribly sick the whole journey.

"Are we stopping here?" Bobby called to them.

"Yes, Nygasi says it's the best spot for today," Bill said and climbed down from his vehicle.

"Time to set up camp," Katherine said cheerfully as she began to help Bobby unload the equipment and supplies. Cecily made a move to assist her, but Bill laid a hand on her shoulder and held her back.

"I'd like to help," she protested.

"You'd be best to stay out of the way while we set up," he said firmly. "You look flushed, Cecily. Go and sit in the shade and drink some water."

Cecily sat down on a convenient rock under a clump of trees, sipping water and watching the others ready the camp. Large rolls of canvas, the iceboxes, and the hampers were heaved from the backs of the pickups and placed next to her in the shade of the trees. The three Maasai men worked together as they laid out the ground sheets, then swung the canvas over supple bamboo poles to create tents, replete with mosquito netting. Then they packed armfuls of grass on top of the canvas until the tents seamlessly blended in with the surroundings. Katherine unpacked provisions from the iceboxes and eventually sat down beside Cecily, handing her a sandwich wrapped in wax paper.

"You'd best eat up, we'll be doing a lot of walking today. Bill doesn't believe in driving around to view the animals, then shooting them from the comfort of the pickup."

"He's planning on shooting game?" Cecily asked. She had seen the large rifles being unloaded but had thought they were for protection.

"What else are we going to eat for supper?" Katherine chuckled. "Here, have some tea, it'll keep you cool."

Cecily accepted the flask of hot, strong black tea laced with sugar and felt her nervous stomach begin to calm.

"Oh, and if you're concerned about the . . . facilities," Katherine whispered to her, "simply do your business behind a bush, no one will look. Just don't pull up any rocks; you never know if a snake or a scorpion is having a nap underneath them." Katherine patted her knee and stood up to help Bobby, while Cecily sat frozen with apprehension.

After the camp was set up and everyone had eaten, Bill and Nygasi led the march into the bush with the two other Maasai men bringing up the rear. Cecily walked closely beside Katherine and Bobby and listened as they regaled her with stories of previous safaris.

"I once heard that Lord Delamere tracked a bull elephant for a whole seven days," Bobby commented. "He was absolutely determined to get the bugger. The tusks are still hanging up at Soysambu; I've never seen such big ones."

Behind them, the other two Maasai conversed softly in their own language, and Cecily found their presence reassuring. It was now well past midday, and the sun hung high in the sky. As she looked up, she saw the shadows of vultures circling above. A soft breeze rustled through the grasses, bringing with it the humming of insects and the occasional grunts of wildebeest. Katherine pointed to their right, where a dozen zebras were standing together in the shade of some acacia trees. Cecily took out her camera and snapped as many shots as she could, only hoping that the photographs would do this incredible place justice.

Eventually, when Cecily wondered if she could walk another step in the heavy boots, Bill gestured for the women to squat in the long grass as he indicated a large watering hole a hundred yards or so away. He, Bobby, and Nygasi crept forward, Nygasi gripping his spear lightly, while Bill and Bobby carried their heavy rifles over their shoulders.

The watering hole was densely packed with wildlife, but Cecily watched as Bill pointed out a herd of large striped animals, some sporting majestic twisted horns.

"Kudu," Katherine whispered to her.

Cecily watched Bill cock the gun and look through the sight. A heartbeat later, a loud shot rang out. Startled birds took to the air, and the animals around the watering hole bolted for safety. Cecily could see the slain kudu lying on its side.

The five men walked toward the kill, Nygasi thumping the ground with his spear to scare off the jackals that were already circling, sniffing at the carcass. Despite herself, Cecily found she couldn't look away as they methodically skinned the animal, which was the size of a horse, then gutted and quartered it. Eventually, the three Maasai heaved the large parcels of meat over their shoulders, while Bobby and Bill carried the head between them, its horns the length of an adult's leg.

"Clean brain shot," Bobby said with admiration as they arrived beside Cecily and Katherine. "Bill's the best hunter I know. A full-grown kudu; look at these mighty horns!"

Now faced with the blood-spattered men and the gamey stench of the kill, Cecily turned away and tried not to vomit. Katherine helped her to her feet, and they all began the long trek back to the campsite, Cecily trying to take discreet gulps of fresh air.

"Are you all right?" Katherine asked her.

"I will be," she managed. "I've never seen an animal killed before."

Katherine nodded sympathetically. "It's quite a shock, I know. As abhorrent as I find shooting for trophies, I believe there is a raw honesty to shooting for sustenance. Every part of that kudu will be used, Cecily. And look behind us." She gestured to where the remains lay by the water's edge. Vultures, jackals, and hyenas were already fighting over the spoils. "The cycle of life continues; we are simply taking our place in the food chain."

Cecily was about to disagree, but then she remembered that every bite of meat she had ever taken had begun with the process she had just witnessed. So she shut her mouth, humbled by her naiveté.

The walk back to camp was much slower, and dusk was encroaching when they came upon a herd of elephants about half a mile away in the distance.

"I can't believe it!" Cecily gulped as she looked through her binoculars and felt a sudden lump in her throat. "They are . . . majestic!"

"We must be cautious, they have young calves with them," Katherine advised. "They're very protective and won't hesitate to charge at you."

"It's a cow herd," Cecily heard Bill say to Bobby. "No shootable bulls— I'm sure we'll get an ivory trophy sometime, mind."

Cecily felt a shaft of fury at the thought of Bill—or anyone—shooting these beautiful creatures. She watched the herd move slowly together, the young calves weaving between their mothers' legs, and she could almost feel the ground beneath her vibrating with their weight and strength.

There was a sudden tap on her shoulder, and she looked away from the elephants. Nygasi beckoned her over and crouched down, pointing to something on the ground. She looked at it and gasped. In the soft orange earth was the perfect outline of a large paw print.

"*Olgatuny*," he said. "Lion," he added for Cecily's benefit.

"Yes, a lion." Bill's voice sounded out from above her. "He was here quite recently, too, judging by the sharp outlines of the track. Nygasi can distinguish between individual cattle, and he once tracked and killed a leopard that had been prowling around his *enkang*—that's his village to you, Cecily," he said, clapping the taller man on the back. "It's too close to our camp for my liking. We need to be careful."

As the two men walked to a spot a few yards away, deep in conversation, Cecily stayed where she was, staring at the paw print in front of her. She reached out to touch it gingerly, her heart thumping at the thought of how huge the lion must be if his paw had left a mark this size.

Back at camp ten minutes later, Cecily sat down gratefully. Sipping some tea, she watched the sun slip gently below the horizon, the fever trees forming sharp black outlines in the landscape. A large fire had been lit, and Katherine appeared beside her to tuck a blanket around her shoulders as the temperature began to plummet. She watched, fascinated, as the Maasai prepared the kudu flesh on spits and the air was soon filled with the enticing aroma of roasting meat. Given the fact she'd witnessed the animal's grisly demise, Cecily was ashamed to feel her stomach growl with hunger.

Dusk turned to night, and Cecily looked up to find the heavens filled with more stars than she had ever seen. Bobby and Bill were drinking beer beside the campfire as they discussed the day's shoot and ate the proceeds of it.

"Here, darling." Katherine handed her a hunk of steaming meat folded into flatbread that had been warmed over the fire.

"Thank you." Cecily smiled gratefully and took a tentative bite. It was delicious.

After dinner, she sat back and listened to the soft murmurings of conversation around the campfire. She was glad of it; the flickering flames and the wood smoke curling up into the velvety night sky made the camp feel like a safe haven. However, as occasional cries and barks of unidentified animals came out of the darkness, Cecily was still relieved at the thought of the heavy rifle that lay casually at Bill's feet.

After they'd eaten, Bill lit up a pipe, and the comforting scent of tobacco wafted toward her.

"I'm for my bed now," Katherine said, giving a wide yawn. "Coming, Cecily?"

Even though she, too, felt exhausted, the incredible starry skies and the fact she was actually sitting in the middle of the African bush made Cecily want to hold on to the moment awhile longer.

"I'll join you in a minute."

"Okay. Night, everyone," Katherine said as she stood up and Bobby did, too.

"Aye, it's been a long day," Bobby agreed. "We'll see you in the morning, bright and early."

Bobby and Katherine retreated to their separate tents, while Nygasi and the other two Maasai left the fire and walked out into the darkness. Cecily could see them stationed around the perimeter of the camp, then suddenly realized she was all alone with Bill.

"How did you find today?" he asked her as he stirred the fire with a stick.

"I . . . well, it's been just incredible. I feel privileged, even if it was scary sometimes. My adrenaline level was sky high all day."

"Are you an adventurer, Cecily?" Bill stared at her with that deep gaze of his. "Or do you prefer to play it safe?"

"You know, I'm not sure. I mean, coming to Africa has changed me already. Maybe I'm still finding out who I am."

"Perhaps none of us ever truly find out who we are."

"You're definitely an adventurer, surely?"

"Maybe I wouldn't have been if life hadn't made me one. I was training for the law in England, and then, well, war—and love—came and my life was altered irrevocably. So, Miss Huntley-Morgan, what are you really doing here in Africa?"

"Visiting my godmother." Cecily shrugged, unable to meet his gaze.

"It's patently obvious to me that you're running away from something. You have the look."

"How do you know that?"

"Because I had the same look when I arrived here originally, too. The question is, will you run back?"

"I have absolutely no idea. Now I must get some sleep." Cecily stood up. "Thank you for including me in this, Bill. I swear, I will never forget it. Good night." She nodded at him, crossed the few yards to the tent she shared with Katherine, and crawled inside. Katherine was already snoring gently on her pallet, so Cecily removed her boots, then wriggled her toes in relief and lay down fully clothed, drawing the rough blanket across her body to ward off the chill of the night. She lay thinking that despite his brusqueness and his propensity for embarrassing her, there was something about Bill Forsythe that fascinated her. Unable to stay awake a moment longer, she made doubly sure the blanket was tucked firmly around her feet in case anything slithered in during the night, then closed her eyes and slept.

Cecily woke at dawn, her mouth dry from thirst. She took a sip of water from the canister beside her, then put on her boots, trying not to wake Katherine, who was still sound asleep.

She crawled out of the tent, then stretched and looked upward. The sky was a mass of soft hues of blues, pinks, and purples, and she felt rather as if she was standing in an impressionist painting. Turning away from the spectacle, she went quietly to find a private place to relieve herself.

Having done so in grass that was almost waist high, she walked back through it slowly, taking in the fresh smells of nature. Then she heard a soft growl, like a running engine. But there weren't any other cars around for miles . . .

Cecily stopped in her tracks as she saw a fully grown lion crouching stationary in the grass only a few yards in front of her, its golden eyes fixed upon her. It stood up and began to prowl toward her.

She stood rooted to the spot, her heart thumping in her chest. The lion charged.

"CECILY! GET DOWN!"

On instinct, she ducked, and a shot rang out into the dawn. The lion stumbled but continued undeterred. Another shot was fired, then another, and the lion went still, then collapsed onto its side.

"Good Lord, that was a close call! Cecily! Are you all right?"

She tried to reply, but her mouth didn't seem to be working properly, her legs refused to move and the world spun . . .

"*Cecily*, can you hear me?"

"Ouch!" Cecily felt a sharp slap across her cheek and opened her eyes to see Bill staring down at her.

"Sorry, it's the fastest way to bring somebody round after a faint. Here, let's prop you up and give you a dash of brandy."

Cecily felt strong arms lifting her upright; then some liquid was dribbled into her mouth. Despite the fact that she almost choked on its strength, it helped bring her senses back. Seeing Bill standing above her, she almost wished she hadn't. She immediately blushed in embarrassment.

"I'm so sorry. I don't know what came over me."

"Perhaps it was the sight of a lion heading straight for you," said Bill. "I've seen grown men vomit all over their shoes. You'll be all right. Let's get you back to the camp."

He supported her as they returned to the tents. Cecily saw Nygasi just behind them and could still smell the gunpowder in the air.

"How . . . how did you know?" she asked, her legs like jelly beneath her.

"That you'd be a silly girl and wander off?" he said, raising an eyebrow. "I didn't. Nygasi had seen the lion's tracks, and we'd been following them. We'd just spotted him when I saw you. You were lucky I was there."

Cecily blushed to the roots of her hair, only hoping he hadn't seen her squatting in the long grass just before the lion had pounced.

As they approached the camp, Katherine came running toward them and supported Cecily on her other side.

"What were those shots? What's happened?" she asked.

"Just a hungry lion," Bill replied. "He's taken care of. Right." Bill handed Cecily over to Katherine, then spoke to Nygasi, who nodded, then walked back in the direction of the lion.

"It's definitely dead?" Cecily managed.

Bill nodded. "Yes. Trust me, I've shot many a lion in my time. Now let's get you some tea."

Cecily allowed Katherine to fuss over her, wrapping her in a blanket and sitting her down by the fire with a tin cup of fresh tea that she insisted Cecily should drink in small sips.

"Honestly, I'm fine now," Cecily said as she hauled herself to standing, her pride winning over her tenuous physical strength. "What will happen to the lion?"

"They'll load it onto the back of Bill's pickup and take it back with them. Some rich American is sure to buy the head and the skin as a trophy."

"That American sure won't be me," she panted. "It was all my fault. I wandered off too far."

"Well, I promise that Bill will be secretly thrilled. He had an excuse to win another trophy. Are you able to walk to the pickup? I think you've had quite enough excitement for today—I'll fetch Bobby to drive us back. He was just filling up our water canisters."

Katherine left her side, and, clutching her mug, Cecily walked to the edge of the camp and saw Bill and Nygasi carrying the lion on a canvas sheet. She followed them to Bill's pickup, where they and the other two Maasai unceremoniously hauled the animal onto the back and began fastening it in place with ropes.

Up close, the lion was simply huge, and even in death he had not lost his dignity. His mane shone a rich dark gold in the sun and his mouth hung open, baring his yellow fangs. She could see what looked like scars across his face.

"He's an old one," Bill said. "Been through some battles, by the looks of him, and he'd been going hungry, too—see his ribs? Most likely he was already injured and hadn't been able to hunt decent prey. Good job he didn't get you, Cecily."

Cecily nodded wordlessly and walked back to the camp, where Bobby was dismantling the tents and Katherine was packing up their hampers.

"Have you ever shot a wild animal, Katherine?" Cecily asked her.

"Yes. Lord forgive me, I have. If you're brought up out here, you're taught to shoot from an early age. As you've just seen, it's a skill that can save your life. I've never done it for sport, only for self-preservation, but you have to remember it's a very different life out here, Cecily. Danger is real."

"I'm beginning to realize that."

"Ready to go?" asked Bobby as he got into the driver's seat.

"Yes," said Katherine firmly as she helped Cecily into the back and climbed in next to Bobby.

"Good-bye, Cecily. I'm sorry your first safari was so . . . eventful." Bill had appeared by the pickup and was looking down at her.

"Oh, no, Bill. I'm sorry to have been such a bother. Thank you for saving my life," Cecily said.

"I aim to please. Safe journey home."

"Are you not coming with us?"

"No. Nygasi and I and the others have work to do out here. Good-bye, now."

Cecily looked behind her as Bobby hit the accelerator pedal and they drove away from the camp. As she watched Bill—now standing with Nygasi over his trophy—she could see he was in another world and had forgotten all about her.

Having dropped off Bobby and swapped to the far more comfortable DeSoto at Bill's farm, as she and Katherine approached Wanjohi Farm, Cecily could see Kiki's gleaming white Bugatti parked in the front drive.

"Are you sure you're up to making the journey back to Naivasha tonight?" asked Katherine as she switched off the engine and they got out. "You're welcome to stay another night with me here."

"Thank you, but the car's here and I feel I must go back. I worry about my godmother."

"I know you do." Katherine put a comforting arm on Cecily's shoulder. "But you have to remember that she is not your responsibility."

"Yes, but—" Cecily shrugged. "Thank you for everything," she said as they embraced. "It's definitely been an adventure."

"You did very well to cope, Cecily, and if you need me, I'll be up here staying at Alice's until the wedding. I can hardly believe it's only just over a month away," said Katherine as the silent Makena stowed Cecily's overnight case into the Bugatti's trunk.

"Well, anything I can do to help, just ask," she said as she slid into the rear seat.

"I will. Good-bye, now."

"Good-bye, Katherine, and thank you so very much," she called through the window as the Bugatti began to drive along the rutted track.

Waving good-bye to her friend, Cecily wondered if being threatened by a hungry lion was actually better than returning to the strange atmosphere that hung like a gray cloud over Mundui House . . .

# 25

Sweetheart! Is that really you?"

"Yes, Mama, it is. I—"

The sound of her mother's voice at the other end of the crackly line brought unbidden tears to Cecily's eyes.

"How are you? How's Papa? And Mamie, of course? Has she had the baby?"

"One question at a time, Cecily," her mother chuckled. "I've been trying to get through to you for days, to tell you that yes, Mamie has had a sweet little girl whom she's named Christabel. Papa isn't happy because he was so hoping for a boy to help 'fight his corner,' as he put it, but oh, Cecily, she is the most beautiful little thing."

"And are they both well?"

"Sure, they are. The birth was a breeze according to Mamie—she keeps asking why so many women complain about it."

"It must be all those calisthenics classes she took," said Cecily. "Please send her my love and tell her I can't wait to see my new niece. You will send me a photo of her, Mama, won't you?"

"Of course I will. How is Kenya?"

"I . . . It's good, Mama."

*And so hot that I can't breathe sometimes, and it's so very weird and lonely here at Mundui House and I nearly got eaten by a hungry lion and I'm missing you so much . . .*

"So when are you coming home? Papa says everyone here is getting concerned about the war. Some are saying that it's inevitable now."

"I know, Mama, I've heard that, too, but—"

"Well, now, I was wondering whether it might be an idea for you to fly to England as soon as you can, honey. Then at least if anything does happen, you're only a steamer's trip across the Atlantic away. Audrey says she's happy to have you back at Woodhead Hall until—"

"After Jack and Patricia's wedding is over," Cecily finished for her. Her body gave a small shudder, not only at the fact that her mother would put the embarrassment of the wedding of her ex-fiancé above her daughter's safety but also at the thought of ever setting foot in Woodhead Hall again.

"Really, Mama, even though I'm desperate to come home as soon as I can, I'm fine right here. If war does break out, my friend Tarquin swears it won't affect Kenya immediately. So how about you book me a ticket for the middle of April?"

*In other words, just after the nuptials have taken place.*

"Are you sure you don't want to go stay with Audrey in England?"

"Totally," Cecily replied firmly.

"Okay, I'll tell Papa to look into making the reservation. Oh, I've missed you so much, honey, and we all—"

Dorothea's voice disappeared into the ether as the crackling grew louder. Cecily replaced the old-fashioned receiver onto its cradle and, arms folded, walked out onto the terrace and surveyed the view.

Maybe she should just return home next week, and to hell with Jack's wedding.

"Who cares?" she whispered to a baboon, who was staring at her, wondering whether he should risk making the leap onto the table on the veranda to steal the breakfast that had just been set up by Chege, the junior houseboy who was second in command to Aleeki.

"Boo!" She clapped her hands as she walked toward the baboon, who sat where he was, regarding her slyly. "Off with you!" she shouted, and eventually, he retreated. Sitting down at the table and drinking the hot, strong coffee, Cecily listened to the now familiar caws, cackles, and calls that heralded the start of the day here at Mundui House. She'd breakfasted alone here every day for almost three weeks now. On her return from the safari, she'd been handed a letter by Chege.

"From *memsahib* to *memsahib*," he had said.

The letter from Kiki had informed her that she had gone to Nairobi to support Alice through her illness and had taken Aleeki with her. She'd added that she would "return in a trice," but a few days later, Aleeki had come back to collect a trunk of his mistress's clothes. He'd explained that Kiki was staying in Nairobi for longer and had disappeared off back to her soon after.

Cecily knew full well that what Aleeki had told her was a lie; she'd met

Katherine only last week, when she'd joined Makena and Chege on a trip into Gilgil.

"I'm so sorry I haven't been in touch," Katherine had apologized, "but the wedding has rather taken over, amongst other things."

When Cecily had asked her how Alice was and when she might be leaving hospital, Katherine had looked surprised.

"Oh, she's been back home for the past two weeks. She insisted she couldn't stay in hospital a moment longer, so I've been taking care of her at Wanjohi Farm. She's much better now and talking about going off on safari in the Congo, although, of course, she's concerned, as we all are, about the situation in Europe and how that might affect things in Africa . . . Gosh, I'm amazed Kiki didn't tell you Alice was back."

"I haven't seen Kiki for weeks," Cecily had explained. "Aleeki told me she was in Nairobi."

"Well, maybe she is—probably staying at Muthaiga Club, although I must say that it's pretty bad form to abandon her goddaughter. Anyway, once this wedding of mine is over and I've finally moved into our new home, you'll be terribly welcome to come and stay with me and Bobby. You must be lonely at Mundui all by yourself, poor darling."

"Oh, I'm okay, Katherine. I'm sure Kiki will be home soon."

"Well, now, darling, I'm afraid I must fly—I have the order of service cards to take to the printer's, and they close at noon. See you at the wedding next week."

"Yes, and good luck!" Cecily had called after her.

Two days after meeting Katherine in Gilgil, and Cecily had still not heard a word from Kiki. None of the staff at the house spoke much English, and besides, it wouldn't be right to ask them where her own godmother had gone . . .

On top of all this, she'd obviously picked up some kind of virus, for every morning after breakfast she felt nauseous, and by two in the afternoon, she could hardly lift her feet up the stairs to go take a nap. She'd expected it to pass, but, she thought with a sigh as she picked up a piece of bread and eyed it, feeling bile rise to her throat, it had only gotten worse.

Realizing there was every chance that she might actually vomit up her coffee, Cecily rose and walked swiftly across the terrace. Aware that she wouldn't make it to the restroom in time, she darted behind some bushes and was sick into a flower bed.

"Oh my, oh my," she moaned, wiping her streaming eyes. "You sure are in a state, Cecily." She made her way slowly into the cool interior of the house and staggered up the stairs to drink some water, then lie down for a while until the nausea eased.

"Oh, Cecily," she muttered, "what are you to do?"

Muratha arrived a few minutes later to tidy her room, then stopped in surprise as she saw Cecily lying down on her unmade bed.

"You sick, *bwana*?"

"I'm afraid I might be, yes," she admitted, feeling too terrible to continue lying.

"Maybe malaria." Muratha put down her pile of fresh sheets and walked over to Cecily. She tentatively reached out a cool palm to feel her forehead, snatching it back quickly.

"No hot, *bwana*, so okay. We call doctor, yes?"

"No, not yet. Maybe tomorrow, if I'm not better."

"Okay, you rest." Muratha nodded and left the room.

Cecily dozed off and by lunchtime felt well enough to get up and eat a little soup and some bread. Choosing another book from the library and comforted that she hadn't brought up her lunch, Cecily took up her usual spot on the sunbed beneath the shade of a sycamore tree. A few minutes later, she heard the tinkling laugh of her godmother as she appeared on the terrace, Captain Tarquin Price and Aleeki bringing up the rear.

"I'm home, my darling!" she shouted across the lawn, spying Cecily. "Forgive me for leaving you alone for so long, but we're back now, aren't we, Tarquin?"

"We are, my love, yes," Tarquin said as he smiled fondly at her.

"Come give me a hug, Cecily." Kiki threw her arms wide open, and Cecily went into them. "My, you're looking a little peaky. Are you quite well?"

"I seem to have had a virus of some kind, but I'm all better now."

"Why, you should have told one of the servants, and I'd have come running home and sent for Dr. Boyle. Aleeki, let's have champagne to celebrate! Tarquin has a few days' leave, so we've come away from the city for some fresh air."

It was only then that the penny dropped—Kiki was looking up adoringly at Tarquin, who must be, *had* to be, a good ten or fifteen years younger than she was.

Ten minutes later, they were sitting around the table on the veranda, Kiki smoking and downing champagne with Tarquin, Cecily sticking firmly to tea. Kiki recounted tales of high jinks at what Cecily now thought of as the infamous Muthaiga Club and the fun they'd all had at some polo match.

*And there was me, worried to distraction about your health, when you were almost certainly love-nesting with your young British officer and living it up in Nairobi,* Cecily thought, suddenly feeling nauseous again. Whether it was from the small slice of cake she'd nibbled or her godmother's selfish behavior, she didn't know.

"Excuse me, Kiki, Tarquin, I'm still not feeling so good. I'm going to go take a rest in my room."

"Of course," Tarquin replied. "Do let us know if you need us to call Dr. Boyle, won't you?"

Upstairs, she lay down, the hum of conversation continuing below her. Even though there was no reason Kiki shouldn't take comfort in the arms of another man—after all, she was a widow with no attachments—Cecily couldn't help thinking about how Kiki had introduced her to Tarquin on New Year's Eve. In those precious minutes in his arms on the dance floor, Cecily had wondered whether this handsome, charming Englishman might have designs on her. But no; almost certainly, Tarquin had already been Kiki's lover, dispatched as a favor that night to keep her goddaughter from social embarrassment.

Jack, Julius, and Tarquin . . . within the space of a few weeks, they'd all played their part in reducing Cecily's self-confidence to a nonexistent status. New York, England, Kenya . . . Holy moly! She was a female failure across the globe. And she hated herself even more for leaving her Kenya address with Doris to give to Julius just before she'd left Woodhead Hall . . .

"You are so *pathetic*, Cecily," she muttered miserably. *And even* more *pathetic,* she thought, *for asking the servants every day if any letters have arrived for me from England.*

Cecily rolled restlessly off the bed and walked to the window, just in time to see Kiki, now clad in a chic striped bathing suit, walking hand in hand toward the lake with Tarquin, whose tanned and supple physique was on show in a pair of trunks.

She watched them splash into the water, laughing together, then Tarquin took Kiki in his arms and kissed her in what Cecily could only describe as a very thorough way. She thought of Bill Forsythe and his self-professed claim not to like human beings.

And wondered if she was right there with him.

Thankfully, over the next few days, Cecily's sickness abated. By cutting out her usual cup of strong coffee in the morning, she found she could eat a little bread and cereal. Any kind of alcohol was off the menu, a fact that seemed to irritate Kiki intensely.

"Goodness, you sure have lost your zest for life since I've been away. Won't you please try a sip?" Kiki said for the umpteenth time as Aleeki proffered a martini.

"Kiki, darling, leave the poor girl alone, won't you?" Tarquin said, giving Cecily an apologetic look. "She's obviously still getting over her illness."

Even if Cecily was grateful to Tarquin for tempering Kiki, she kept out of their way as much as she could, which was really quite easy, given that they rarely rose until lunchtime, when she'd meet them briefly on the veranda before scuttling upstairs for an afternoon nap. The window seat in her bedroom had become her favorite place in the house. Sitting curled up on it, with a cool breeze from the overhead fan alleviating the heat outside, she'd use binoculars to study the comings and goings of the wildlife both in and around the lake.

Today, the pod of hippos, whom she had all named in her head, were taking their customary afternoon naps, sprawled together on their sides. Around them, small horned antelopes were nibbling at the dense water lily pads at the lake's edge, not perturbed at all by the huge creatures snoring beside them. Farther out in the water, the trunks of dead trees reached up into the sky and provided convenient perches for all manner of birds, from tiny kingfishers to heavy pelicans.

"How can I sit here and watch this and feel so blue?" Cecily berated herself. "If Mamie was here, she'd be out there, swimming in the lake, rowing a boat, *living*! 'You're in a funk,' she'd say and—"

The thought of her sister and her newborn baby so far away sent her desperately searching for positive thoughts, which spiraled away from her mental grasp as quickly as they had arrived.

There was a sharp knock on her door, and Muratha appeared, cradling the green silk dress she would be wearing at Katherine and Bobby's wedding party in a couple of days' time.

"It beautiful, *bwana*," Muratha said as she hung it carefully in the closet. "Tomorrow we pack trunk, yes?"

"Yes, thank you, Muratha."

"Never see Nairobi, big city," said Muratha. "You lucky. I run bath, yes?"

Before Cecily could reply, Muratha had disappeared, leaving Cecily to berate herself further for her inability to stop wallowing in her own misery like one of the hippos. She knew that Muratha would swap lives with her instantly.

She walked over to the mirror and gazed at her own reflection. "You *will* go to this wedding, and you will darned well enjoy yourself, do you hear me?" With that, she turned away and headed for the bathroom.

"Just be sure they give you my usual room at the club, won't you? It faces the garden, not the road," Kiki said as Cecily climbed into the back of the Bugatti. "You did call ahead to tell them, didn't you?" Kiki turned to Aleeki, who was standing beside her.

"Yes, *memsahib*."

"Now, you send my best love to Alice and anyone else there who doesn't hate me," Kiki said to Cecily, forcing a harsh chuckle. It was obvious that she was hurt by her lack of an invitation to the wedding. "And just have the best fun, okay?"

"I will, I promise," Cecily agreed.

"In the meantime, we'll make our own party here, won't we, Tarquers?"

"We will indeed, darling," Tarquin said as he walked up and kissed Kiki on the top of her dark head. "Good-bye, Cecily, and tell any of the chaps you meet in khaki that I'll be back soon to sort them out."

"I will. Bye." Cecily waved gaily, then let out a sigh of relief as the Bugatti pulled smoothly out of the drive.

Even though she was anxious about going to the wedding party alone to face a sea of strangers, as they headed along the lake toward Nairobi, she felt excited, too. After weeks of being cooped up by herself at Mundui House, it might perk her up to be in a bustling city. She was also intrigued to see the Muthaiga Club for herself, having heard so much about it. She had given her reflection a last glance in the mirror before she'd left, and, in the emerald green silk gown, as well as a matching hat with a white satin band fashioned into a starched bow, she thought she looked presentable at least. She removed her long white satin gloves and put them on the leather seat next to her and, as the journey progressed, wished she could remove her dress, which seemed to have grown awfully tight since she'd last worn it for dinner at Woodhead Hall.

"What do you expect, Cecily? Apart from the safari, you've hardly stirred from your room," she muttered, promising herself that when she returned to Mundui House, she'd take a dip in the lake every morning.

As they approached the city, Cecily glanced eagerly out of the window but could only glimpse the buildings of central Nairobi spread out to her left, interspersed by endless shacks built haphazardly along the road.

"Manhattan it is obviously not." She chuckled as Makena steered the Bugatti off the dusty main road. Stopping at a set of gates, he stuck out his head to speak to the security guard on duty. The gates were opened, and they drove past pristine green lawns planted with oak, chestnut, and fever trees, which reminded Cecily of an English parkland. They pulled to a halt in front of a two-story salmon pink building with a smart red-tiled roof, its windows edged by clean white shutters. Palm trees and neat hedges lined the walls, and small Doric columns graced the entrance. Cecily had not seen a building in Kenya that seemed to insist more on its own civility. She stepped out of the car and was greeted at the double doors by a man who resembled a younger version of Aleeki.

"Good afternoon, *memsahib*. May I inquire as to your name?"

"I am Cecily Huntley-Morgan."

"You are here for the wedding of Mr. and Mrs. Sinclair?"

"I am," Cecily said as the man ran a fountain pen down a long list of names.

"Mrs. Sinclair has already signed you in. Ali!" The man turned inside the shadowy interior and clicked his fingers. A servant appeared immediately by his side. "Please see Miss Huntley-Morgan to her room."

Ali took her cases from Makena, who gave her a salute, then stepped back into the Bugatti. As she followed the man through the wooden-floored reception area and along a couple of narrow hallways, Cecily could already hear the hum of voices coming from somewhere in the building.

"Here, *memsahib*. Room number ten," said Ali.

Cecily walked into a spartan cell with only a narrow single bed, a chest of drawers with a washbasin atop it, and a closet that resembled an upturned coffin wedged into the corner.

"Okay, *memsahib*?"

"Perfect, thank you."

As Ali left, shutting the door softly behind him, she shook her head in disbelief; she'd imagined that the Muthaiga Club would be the Kenyan version of the Waldorf-Astoria. Not that she cared—it was simply a place to lay her head for the night—but she could hardly imagine Kiki sleeping in a room like this.

Refastening her hat in the mirror, then applying some fresh lipstick, Cecily surveyed the door that would lead her out to the party. Taking a deep breath, she opened it, then, with absolutely no idea of which way to turn down the hallway, decided to follow the hum of the crowd. Eventually, she found herself in a deserted dining room, the many tables set with creamy roses and garlands, the silver cutlery polished to a high shine. The tables flowed out into a veranda, beyond which stood a large crowd of guests sipping champagne. She felt rather like she was walking through a beautiful garden filled with exotic birds of paradise. Well, that was the women at least, she thought, because they all seemed to be dressed in colorful silks and their jewels sparkled in the late-afternoon sun. As for the men, they looked like a flock of penguins in their white tie and tails. She emerged at the other side of the crowd and saw Bobby and Katherine, who was wearing a simple but beautiful lace gown that hugged her generous figure and showed off her creamy bare shoulders. Ivory roses adorned her lovely red hair, and Cecily smiled, thinking she looked the picture of happiness.

"Champagne, madam?" asked a passing waiter.

"Do you have water?" Cecily wasn't taking any chances; she wasn't going to throw up in the bushes among the crème de la crème of local society.

"Cecily, darling!" Katherine waved at her as a flashbulb popped in front of her. "Just a couple more photographs, and I'll be over to introduce you to everyone."

"No problem!" she shouted back, content to cast her eyes around the crowd while she waited. There was Alice, attired in a long, beaded sapphire gown that skimmed her too-slim figure. And Idina (whom she'd last seen running naked into the lake at Mundui House) fully clothed in a purple shot-silk dress and matching turban. Standing between the women was a tall, debonair man with blond hair and blue eyes. From a distance, he reminded her—or at least his coloring did—of Jack. For an older man, he was extremely handsome, and the two women seemed to be hanging on his every word.

"Darling Cecily! Thank you so much for coming." Katherine had arrived by her side, dragging Bobby with her.

"You look beautiful, Katherine."

"She does, doesn't she?" Bobby put an arm around his new wife's shoulder and kissed her on the top of her head.

Katherine held out her left hand and indicated her wedding finger. "Look, Cecily, it's really happened. After all those years of loving him from afar, my dream came true."

"I'm so happy for both of you," Cecily said, meaning it. If this wasn't a genuine love match, then she didn't know what was. "How was the ceremony yesterday?"

"About as different as it could be from this," Katherine said. "I wore a cotton dress, and all Daddy's Kikuyus came in their ceremonial clothes—you've never seen such extravagant jewelry! It was quite perfect, actually, and at the end of the service, they sang their traditional wedding song for us."

"Which I enjoyed far more than 'Amazing Grace,'" Bobby interrupted with a smile.

"Is your father here?"

"No, he said it was too far to travel, and as you know, this kind of event isn't his cup of tea." Katherine smiled. "Now come with me, and I shall introduce you to the rest of the Valley whom you haven't yet met."

By the time she had shaken at least twenty hands, Cecily had lost track of everyone's names. There had been Lord this and the Earl of that and women with names like Bubbles and Flossy and Tattie.

"And of course, you know darling Alice, who has staggered out of her sickbed to be here today," said Katherine, leading her into another circle. "You remember Cecily, don't you, Alice?"

"Of course I do. You look beautiful, Cecily. Doesn't she, Joss?"

Cecily watched Alice gaze up adoringly at the handsome blond man she'd noticed earlier. His hawklike eyes focused first on her face, then swept up and down her body as though assessing her worth.

"Indeed," he said in a rich English tone. "And who might you be?"

"Kiki Preston's goddaughter, of course!" Idina spoke from the other side of Joss. "I'm amazed the jungle drums haven't already informed you of the exact statistics of the newest—and youngest—arrival to our ranks," she drawled. "Cecily, darling, meet Josslyn Hay, Earl of Erroll—my ex-husband."

*So this is the man Katherine has told me about,* Cecily thought as Joss took her hand and put it to his lips to kiss it.

"Delighted, Cecily. So you're staying at Mundui House?"

"I am, yes," Cecily managed to splutter. Because, despite their difference in age, he really was a "dreamboat," as Priscilla would say.

"It's a dreadful shame that I'm no longer living at the Djinn Palace by the lake, or I could have invited you—and your godmother, of course—to come for lunch or dinner. Sadly, my wife, Molly, is very ill and we must be near the hospital."

"Oh, I'm so sorry to hear that," Cecily said, unable despite herself to drag her eyes away from his gaze.

"Will you be staying long in Kenya?" he asked her.

"Well, I—"

"Come along, Cecily, you have plenty more friends of mine to meet, and I can't let Joss monopolize you all evening." Katherine firmly took her arm and more or less frog-marched her away. Cecily could not help but cast a glance backward for one last look and found his eyes were still upon her.

"Honestly, Cecily, I was counting on you to be impervious to Joss's charms. Look at you, a perfect wreck!" Katherine rolled her eyes. "I just don't know what it is that he does to women, but they all go weak at the knees when they're around him. He's a tad too old for you anyway." Katherine reached for a glass of water that the waiter had found for Cecily. "Drink this, and recover your senses. He's thirty-seven, for goodness' sake!"

"The same age as your Bobby!" Cecily found her voice. "Anyway, I see what everyone means about him. He is devastatingly handsome and so very charming."

"Darling," Alice cut into their conversation. "May I steal you away for a moment? The kitchen needs to know how long a pause you'd like between courses."

"Sorry, Cecily, back in a tick. Just behave yourself while I'm gone," Katherine called as she followed Alice through the crowd.

Cecily sipped her water and, feeling the heat of the sun beating down on the top of her silk hat, stepped into the shade of a large bush covered in glorious pink flowers.

"Wonderful, aren't they?" came a voice from the depths of the bushes.

"They're hibiscus, you know. I often think if I had time to plant a garden, I'd have them growing everywhere."

Bill appeared by her side, looking very unlike himself in formal dress. "Sorry to creep up on you—I was just quietly relieving myself, if I'm honest."

"Oh, I see," said Cecily, feeling a blush spread up her cheeks and wondering if he actively enjoyed shocking her.

"If I may say so, you scrub up rather well." Bill indicated her gown.

"So do you," she retorted.

"Got over the shock of missing being a lion's breakfast by a hair's breadth?"

"I have, yes. And thank you again for saving me."

"My pleasure, madam."

There was a pause in conversation as both of them stared at the crowd.

"They rather remind me of the flamingos on Lake Nakuru, gathering together to gossip then migrating off again, back to their eyries in the hills, sated with booze and food," said Bill. "Not my scene, as you might have guessed, but I am rather fond of Katherine and Bobby, so I felt I should break the habit of a lifetime, stifle my contempt, and come along. At least for an hour or so."

"You haven't brought Nygasi along with you today?"

"As a matter of fact, I have. He's guarding the pickup, ready to make a quick exit."

"You didn't invite him in then?"

"Would that I could, Miss Huntley-Morgan, would that I could. There's a strict no-blacks policy here for members. Which is faintly ridiculous, don't you think? Given the fact that they work here and that there are a hundred thousand times as many of them in this country as there are of us. Colonialism, eh? From where does it get its arrogance, I wonder?"

"Your British Queen Victoria might have had something to do with it."

"Indeed she might." Bill looked down at her. "Didn't take you for a history buff, I must say."

"I majored in the subject at Vassar," said Cecily and for the first time mentally thanked her father for suggesting it would be a far more useful subject to study than economics.

"Did you, indeed? Well, now, isn't that a thing?" Bill reached out a hand to grasp a glass of champagne from a waiter. "What do you intend to do with your education, might I ask?"

"Nothing much." Cecily shrugged. "What can women 'do' with their knowledge?"

"You yourself have just pointed out that all this—the British Empire—was created by a woman," he countered.

"Sadly, I am not an empress. And I don't wish to be one, either."

"Well, let me tell you, there are many 'empresses' standing in front of you—in their own minds, anyway. And some emperors, too. But it's easy to be a big fish in a small pond, as long as there are tiddlers—that's small fish to you, my dear—swimming around them, prepared to take second place. Look over there, for example." Bill pointed at Joss Erroll, with Idina and Alice on either side of him. "They've all had to learn to share, if you know what I mean."

"Yes, I think I do."

"Now, then, I mustn't keep you on the grandest social occasion of the year. Although I doubt there'll be many more to come. I've just heard that Germany has invaded Czechoslovakia. We're on the brink of another world war. If I were you, I'd scuttle off home to America before it's too late."

"Oh, my goodness!" Cecily looked up at Bill in horror. "When did you hear that?"

"Joss Erroll is a friend of mine, and in fact, it was he who convinced me to come over here and settle in Africa. He told me in confidence earlier. He's the deputy director of the Central Manpower Committee and is responsible for planning the distribution of military and civilian personnel. I'm sworn to secrecy, of course—he doesn't want a word of it getting out to the happy couple on their special day—but . . . I'm afraid all bets are off. Chamberlain's 'peace for our time' declaration has just been well and truly trounced. So, having shown my face here, I'm going to take my leave and return to my farm to work out how many head of cattle the British army are likely to requisition for the forthcoming war effort, because I'm more certain than not that war is on its way. Good night, Cecily."

Bill gave her a small bow, then left the way he had arrived—through the hibiscus hedge.

At dinner an hour later, Cecily found she could hardly eat a thing. She had been placed at a table next to a man called Percy, who managed the Shell

Oil Company in East Africa. On her other side was Sir Joseph Somebody, who had apparently been the governor-general of Kenya up until a couple of years ago. It was obvious that word had somehow spread about what Bill had told her in secrecy, for after a few minutes of polite formalities, the two men talked in hushed voices over Cecily's head. At least Joss Erroll sat opposite her, so she had something pleasant to look at while she was ignored, but he seemed entranced by his neighbor Phyllis, who had been introduced as the wife of Percy, the Shell Oil man. Not normally prone to being rude about the looks of other women, Cecily couldn't help but wonder why the heavenly Joss found this woman so fascinating. His hands constantly wandered over parts of her body, yet she was really quite plain and dumpy.

"How are you settling in, my dear?"

A younger woman—or younger, at least, than most of the guests—turned to her as the band struck up and half their table left for the dance floor.

"Oh, I'm doing well, thank you," Cecily lied.

"I'm Ethnie Boyle, and I'm married to William; you may have heard of him—he's the local doctor."

"Oh yes, of course. He has been looking after Alice, hasn't he?"

"Trying to, yes, but as I'm sure you know, she's rather difficult to look after. May I?" Ethnie indicated the seat vacated by the Shell Oil man.

"Why, of course."

"Katherine told me to look out for you tonight. It can be jolly tough facing this crowd, especially when one is alone."

"Yes, I'm doing my best to remember who everyone is, but—"

"It can be awfully confusing, especially as so many of us have intermarried." She chuckled. "How is your godmother? I saw her here a few days ago, and she looked full of her usual high spirits. She's had such a rotten time of it, one way and another."

"She has, yes."

Maybe it was the cloying heat of the night or the small glass of champagne Cecily had drunk to toast the happy couple, not to mention the terrible news about Czechoslovakia, but she was feeling extremely unwell. As her head spun, she grasped for her purse to extract a fan.

"Are you quite well, my dear?"

"Yes, it's just so darned hot and—"

"Let's get you inside, shall we? William," Ethnie called across the table to her husband, "this is Kiki's goddaughter, Cecily, and the heat is rather getting to her. Give me a hand, will you, darling?"

To Cecily's humiliation, husband and wife helped her up from her chair and supported her as they walked into the relative cool of the lounge. A ceiling fan was blowing a cool breeze above her as they sat her in a leather armchair and Dr. Boyle fetched her a glass of water.

*They probably think I've drunk too much liquor,* Cecily thought in embarrassment as Ethnie fanned her and Dr. Boyle fed her sips of water.

"Feeling a little better, dear?" he asked.

"A little, yes. I'm so sorry for the trouble."

"Don't be silly, it's perfectly understandable. Now, are you staying here for the night, or should we call you a driver to take you home?"

"I'm staying here."

"Your pulse has calmed down a little now," Dr. Boyle said as he removed his fingers from her wrist. "And I'm sure a good night's sleep will sort you out, if that is possible with this racket." He smiled as the band struck up 'Ain't She Sweet.' "I'll leave my wife to take you to your room, and I'll drop in on you tomorrow morning."

"Oh, I'm sure there's no need," she said as Ethnie appeared beside her with her room key. She helped Cecily to stand, and they walked slowly out of the dining room, the bursts of music and laughter gradually subsiding as they moved farther away down the hallway.

"Have you had other instances of dizziness recently?" Ethnie asked.

Cecily was feeling too sick and miserable to lie. "A few, yes, but I'm sure it's just the heat."

"Well, my husband will be back in the morning, just to double-check. Better to be safe than sorry, isn't it? Now, good night, Cecily dear," she said as they stopped in front of her bedroom door and Ethnie opened it.

"Good night, and thank you so very much for your kindness."

Sitting down on her bed and drawing down the zipper at the side of her dress, Cecily sighed in relief, feeling she could finally breathe for the first time that evening. Once she had slipped into her nightdress, she lay down under the sheet and closed her eyes. Even though the band played on well into the night, she didn't stir.

She was woken by a knock at the door. With a great deal of effort, she pulled herself into consciousness.

"Who's there?"

"It's Dr. Boyle. May I come in?"

Before Cecily had even answered, the door was opened and there was Dr. Boyle with his medical bag.

"Good morning, Cecily. Feeling any better?"

"I sure slept well, thank you."

"Jolly good. Best cure of all, sleep. Now, then, I thought I'd just pop in and take a look at you before I leave."

"Honestly, Doctor, I'm fine, and—"

"I saw Captain Tarquin Price a few minutes ago—after yesterday's news about Hitler, there's a powwow going on in the Gentlemen's Bar. He asked whether I'd seen you at last night's shindig, and I told him I had and that you'd felt unwell. Captain Price said that this ailment has been going on for quite some time. So let's have a look at you, shall we?"

With a sigh of embarrassment, Cecily submitted herself to being poked and prodded and answered endless questions. Dr. Boyle took his stethoscope out of his ears and looked down at her. "My dear, are you married?"

"Why, no, I was engaged up until Christmas, but it was broken off."

"Before Christmas, you say?"

"Yes."

"And when did you have your last monthly?"

"Why, I—" Cecily felt herself blushing. Never once in her life had she talked about *those* to a man. "I'm not sure."

"Try to think back."

Cecily, who had never been "regular" anyway, did so. "I believe it would have been just before I left to travel here."

"And how long ago was that?"

"It was the last week of January. So my . . . monthly was about two weeks before."

"And here we find ourselves on the sixteenth of March. Cecily dear"— Dr. Boyle reached for her hand—"given your symptoms and having had a good feel of your tummy, I would normally be fairly certain that you are expecting."

"Expecting what?" Cecily stared up at him.

"A baby." Dr. Boyle gave her a wry smile. "However, given the fact that your engagement to your young man was broken off before Christmas, I am now confused. I will put this as delicately as I can . . . is there a possibility that you *could* be pregnant?"

"Oh, my." Cecily put her hands to her face as shock resonated through her body, and she wondered if one could faint clean away while lying down.

"My dear, it is none of my business to ask you about the whys and wherefores, but I would stake my career on the fact that you are a couple of months pregnant. I can see this news has obviously come as a huge shock to you."

"Yes," Cecily whispered, her hands still over her face, too horrified and ashamed to meet the doctor's eyes.

"The good news is that you are most definitely not ill. Captain Price was concerned you might have malaria."

"Malaria would have been preferable, Doctor," Cecily muttered. "I beg you," she said, finally taking her hands from her face and looking up at him, "please, do you swear never to tell a soul about this?"

"Patient–doctor confidentiality is guaranteed, my dear. However, I do think it is important you tell someone about your . . . current state of health."

"I'd rather die!"

"I do understand, but let me tell you, living out here and treating my many patients, it is impossible to shock either me or most other people around here, too. I would advise you to tell your godmother. Mrs. Preston may be many things, but she is a woman of the world and has a kind heart to boot."

Cecily lay there silently. No words could express her horror and shame.

"What about the father? Am I to presume he is local to here?"

"I . . . no, he isn't. I met him in England. And no, he wouldn't be . . . willing to take responsibility. He's engaged to someone else. I only found out after—" Cecily could hardly bear to look up into Dr. Boyle's sympathetic eyes.

"I can understand how shocked you are," Dr. Boyle said eventually, "but you're not the first and certainly won't be the last young lady to find herself in this predicament. I'm sure that you will find a solution; most usually do."

"Is there any way I could, well . . . stop the baby coming?"

"If you are asking me about an abortion, then I would tell you that it is not only illegal but very dangerous. I think you must accept that your baby is coming in about seven months' time and make your plans accordingly. Do you have family?"

"Yes, in New York."

"Then maybe you should think about returning to America sooner rather than later, especially given what is happening in Europe."

Cecily remained silent; her brain was fogged with shock, and it was impossible to think of anything at all, let alone a plan for the future.

"I'll leave you to it now, my dear, but as I said, I'd certainly advise confiding in your godmother. She is *in loco parentis* while you're here, after all. And not to put too fine a point on it, she's bound to notice in the next few weeks. Here's my card. Please call me if you need any help, medical or personal."

Cecily watched him put the card on the bedside table next to her. "Thank you. Surely I must owe you some money for this morning's . . . consultation?"

"Consider it on the house. And of course, if you do decide to stay here, I'll be delighted to look after you during your pregnancy. Good day, my dear."

Cecily watched him leave the room. She stared at the wall in front of her, on which hung a dreadful painting of a Maasai warrior standing over the body of a dead lion, his spear piercing the animal's side.

Her hands were freezing cold, despite the heat of the room. Pulling back the sheet, then tugging up her nightdress, Cecily tentatively placed her hands on her stomach. What was she meant to feel? She just didn't know. Perhaps she could ask Mamie . . .

*No! No, no . . .*

"Oh, my dear Lord, my God . . ." She shook her head as she curled her body up into a ball and turned away from the door as if to avoid any more bad news coming through it. "What have I done?"

There was another knock on her door, and Cecily, her sight blurred with tears, remained silent.

"Cecily, it's Kiki. Can I come in?"

"No," Cecily whispered to herself, shaking her head from side to side as she heard the door behind her open and then close again softly.

"Oh, my poor darling, my angel . . . What is it?"

"Please, Kiki, I'm begging you, just leave me alone . . ."

"What is it that Dr. Boyle told you? Is it terminal? Why, I just saw him in the hallway when I arrived here for breakfast . . . I'll go fetch him now and ask him myself."

"*No!*" Cecily sat upright, wiping her eyes. "Please, Kiki, there's no need to do that. The problem I have is not"—Cecily swallowed hard—"terminal or life-threatening."

"Okay." Kiki took another step toward her. "So you don't have malaria?"

"No."

"Or cholera?"

"No."

"Or cancer?"

"No, Kiki. I promise you, Dr. Boyle confirmed that I'm not sick. Please don't worry about me, I'll be fine."

"Of course I worry about you, sweetie, you're my beloved goddaughter. And I'm responsible for you while you're here. I haven't been very good at looking after you recently, have I?"

Cecily, who still had her eyes firmly shut, could hear Kiki breathing above her and smell her perfume, which made her feel immediately sick.

"So what did Dr. Boyle say to upset you so?"

Again Cecily gave a shake of her head and remained silent. Which engendered silence from above.

"So the symptoms you have are dizziness and nausea," Kiki said after a pause. "Along with exhaustion, right?"

"Really, Kiki, I'm feeling much better. I—"

Kiki laid a gentle hand on Cecily's arm, and Cecily felt her sit down on the bed behind her.

"He's told you you're pregnant, hasn't he?"

Cecily squeezed her eyes shut even tighter so the tears couldn't dribble out. Maybe if she played dead, Kiki would just go away and leave her alone.

"Sweetie, I know you must be in a terrible state of shock, but you know what? I've been where you are at this moment. It's mighty scary, but we're going to find a way through this together. You hear me? Cecily?"

She felt Kiki shake her gently, and she managed a miserable nod.

"So let's get you out of here. Aleeki is outside with the car. Tarquin was called back to Nairobi last night after the terrible news about Hitler and has to stay on to do whatever an army captain does in these situations. So you and I will go back to Mundui House together. Okay?"

Cecily shrugged, feeling like a spoiled child, when she really wasn't. She heard Kiki moving around the room.

"Come on, sweetie, I have your day clothes here. You need to put them on, and then we can go home."

"I'm so ashamed, Kiki," she moaned. "What if Dr. Boyle has told all those people out there? Everyone who is anyone around here could know already."

"I swear to you that Dr. Boyle is the soul of discretion. Some of the things he could have told everyone about me, he never did. Come on now. Let's get you up and dressed."

Common sense prevailed, and with Kiki's help, Cecily put on her blouse and skirt, packed her case, and, while Kiki spoke to Ali, Aleeki met her at the door, then escorted her to the Bugatti. Cecily slid down the back seat, just in case anyone decided to come peering in through the windows.

"We're all set, now let's go," Kiki said, getting into the front with Aleeki.

Cecily dozed on and off on the journey to Mundui House, shock acting like a drug to dull her senses. When they arrived, Aleeki handed her over to Muratha, who helped her up the stairs and into bed.

Having fastened the shutters, Muratha left. Cecily closed her eyes once more and slept.

# 26

Cecily woke with a start and, for a few blissful seconds, didn't remember what had happened earlier that day. Then, as reality dawned, she climbed out of bed, walked to the window, and opened a shutter to see what she now recognized as a soft afternoon sun lighting the perfectly manicured lawn between the fever trees. She turned her back on the view and moved to sit on the end of her bed.

"What on earth am I to do?" she whispered, her hands instinctively going to her stomach once more. Was it really possible that one coupling with Julius could have produced a tiny, fledgling life inside her? Perhaps the doctor had been wrong—he couldn't see inside her, couldn't prove that she was pregnant, she thought suddenly. Perhaps it *was* some form of malaria (which would be infinitely preferable at this stage) or food poisoning or in fact *anything* that wasn't what he'd said it was.

But Cecily realized from talking to Mamie that she had every symptom there was to have; she'd noticed in the last week that her breasts had become heavier and tingled oddly. That her waist had filled out, which was why her dress last night had been so uncomfortable. Then there was the absence of her monthly since she'd left New York, plus the sickness . . .

There was a soft tap on her bedroom door.

"*Bwana?* You awake?" Muratha's bright eyes appeared around the door.

"Yes, come in."

"I get you dressed, then you downstairs for tea with mistress, okay?"

"I can dress myself, thank you. Tell Kiki I'll be down in fifteen minutes." Cecily was now paranoid about anyone seeing her developing body.

Kiki was waiting for her in the living room, a lofty space with a polished wood floor, filled with objets d'art and comfortable armchairs placed in front of a fireplace, which Cecily could not imagine was ever needed.

"Come in, sweetie, and close the door behind you," Kiki said from one of the armchairs. "I'm sure we can manage to serve ourselves some tea, can't we? I guess you'd prefer complete privacy while we have our little chat."

"Yes, thank you," said Cecily, looking at the tiered silver cake stand filled with delicate sandwiches, scones, and cake. She felt queasy at the sight of them.

"I've had some ginger tea prepared for you. It's very good for morning sickness. Come sit down." Kiki indicated the chair opposite her, then proceeded to pour some pale orange liquid into a bone china cup. "Try it; it saved my life when I was pregnant."

Despite Cecily's current feelings of misery and shame, it was interesting to hear Kiki talk about that moment in her life. She was aware her godmother had children, who were around the same age as her, yet Kiki almost never mentioned them. She took a tentative sip of the liquid, which burned her throat as she swallowed, but found she liked the taste.

"Now, my darling, let's talk about what is best for you to do." Kiki put down her teacup and lit a cigarette. "Dare I ask who the father is? The ex-fiancé, maybe?"

"No, he—" Cecily gulped. "I—"

"Listen to me, Cecily, and listen good. I've had many things happen to me in my life, and anything you say to me will not only be in complete confidence, but I will not be shocked. I've been around more blocks than most people living in Manhattan will ever walk in their lifetime. And then some. Do you understand?"

"Yes, I do."

"So who is the father?"

"His name is Julius Woodhead. He's the nephew of Audrey, Lady Woodhead, Mama's friend."

"Well, now, I know Audrey from the old days. She would have done anything to get a coronet on that head of hers," Kiki said rather bitchily. "Of course she hated me because . . . well, I'll save that story for another time. So you met this Julius while you were staying at Audrey's house in England?"

"Yes, he . . . I, well, I thought that he was in love with me. I was sure in love with him. He told me we'd get engaged, and—"

"Then he seduced you?"

"Yes. Please, Kiki, don't tell me I shouldn't have believed him, that I was being dumb . . . I know all that now. But at the time, he was so loving and maybe because of my fiancé breaking our engagement off for another woman, I was—"

"Vulnerable," Kiki finished for her. "We've all been there, Cecily. It's Englishmen who are so goddamned charming and funny and they manage to entice us into bed with just a whisper of that wonderful accent." Kiki sighed. "In many ways, I feel responsible. If I'd have been with you at Wood-head Hall, I could have seen the signs and made sure that this didn't happen. But no matter, it did. Now that I know the facts, which are so very similar to when I was in my own . . . predicament, we can work out a way forward for you. I guess there is no chance that this Julius will stand by you?"

"Hah!" Cecily gave a bitter chuckle. "I discovered just before I left that he was engaged to another woman."

"Honey, you're facing this situation alone, but at least you have me, who knows the ropes, so to speak." Kiki gave her a wry smile, then stood up. "I think this calls for something a little stronger than tea." Kiki walked over to a corner cabinet and poured herself a healthy measure of bourbon from a decanter atop it. "I'm presuming you don't want any?"

"No, thank you."

"I guess your mother knows nothing of this relationship with Julius?"

"Oh, no, nothing! If it had been for real, of course, she'd have been over the moon. Julius is set to inherit the title and Woodhead Hall from his uncle."

"And wouldn't she just have loved that!" Kiki cackled as she drained the bourbon. "You could of course write to him and tell him what has happened to you. Or even better, I could write to Audrey and tell her."

"No! Please, I'd rather die than go groveling back to him. Besides, there's no way of proving who the father of a child is, anyway, is there?"

"No, otherwise half the marriages in the world would end in divorce." Kiki gave a husky chuckle as she refilled her glass and sat down. "You're right, of course; he'd only deny it, and you'd end up feeling like a fool. Which you are most definitely not, I might add. Cecily, honey, I'm going to let you in on a secret, which may make you feel just a little better. Once upon a time, there was a young girl of around your age who met a prince—a real-life prince; a prince of England, too, who was fourth in line to the throne. She fell head over heels in love with him but then, sadly, found herself in the same position as you do now. She believed that he'd be there for her—look after her and help her; maybe they'd marry, and she would become his prin-cess. So she called him up and told him she needed to speak to him because she was carrying his child. He told her he'd help her, but that telephone call was the last time they ever spoke. Next thing she knew, an equerry—that's a royal servant, by the way—appeared at her home. The young lady was told she must go to a clinic in Switzerland and wait out her pregnancy so she could give birth there. And she did. Right afterward, when she hadn't even held the baby in her arms, the child was whisked away from her. And she never saw it again."

Cecily watched Kiki's eyes brimming with tears as she took a deep drink of her bourbon.

"I think we both know who that young girl was, don't we, honey?"

Cecily nodded.

"So when I say I've been where you are now, I truly have. The good news is that no one on the planet knows about your condition, apart from Dr. Boyle, you, and me. And if we're clever, we can keep it that way. No one need ever know about this."

"But how, Kiki? Where will I go?"

"To Switzerland, just like I did. Whatever happens with the hostilities in Europe, Switzerland is neutral, so you'll be perfectly safe there. We'll just write your mother and say you want to stay on in Kenya for a while longer, while everyone here will think you've gone back to America. Don't you see? It's perfect!" Kiki clapped her hands, obviously pleased with her own cleverness.

"But what about after I've given birth to it?"

"Why, you have it adopted. The clinic will find a nice family—probably American—who will give your baby a wonderful home and a new life. And then you can be free to carry on with yours. That is what you want, isn't it?"

"I . . . I think so, Kiki. I don't know. I'm still in shock."

"I know you are, my darling, but it's very important to make plans as soon as you can. We don't want any gossip coming out this end and spreading itself across to Manhattan, do we?"

"No, of course not."

"I mean, I can't see another alternative, can you?"

"No." Cecily shook her head, despair filling her once more. "I can't."

"And of course I'll come with you to the clinic, settle you in—some fresh mountain air will do me good. But we'll have to leave soon. Borders are changing regularly across Europe just now, and we don't want Mr. Hitler ruining our plan, do we?"

"Are you sure Switzerland will be safe? I mean, it's awful near Germany."

"Oh, yes, honey, it'll be safe, because it holds most of the fortunes of its close neighbor in its banks and the Nazis won't ever put those at risk," explained Kiki. "Now, should I telephone your mother and tell her you'll be staying on here for a while longer? She called me earlier while you were resting. She and your father have heard the news and are obviously concerned about the situation in Europe. They were talking about booking you a passage back home right away, so we need to stop them."

"But what excuse will I use?" Cecily bit her lip, desperate at the thought of being separated from them for months on end. *Just when I need my family the most . . .*

"Oh, I'll think of something, honey, don't worry," said Kiki. "I'm good at that."

Cecily studied her godmother, thinking that even though Kiki could not have been kinder to her, it felt a little as though all of this was a game to her.

"Maybe leave it a couple days? I just need to, well, take time to think," said Cecily.

"Okay, honey, but time is not something you have on your side just now. I mean, what other option is there? Unless you can find a man to marry you tomorrow." Kiki chuckled dismissively.

"Well, thank you so much for being prepared to help me. It's real kind of you, but as I said, I just want a little time to think it all through." Cecily stood up. "I'm going to take a walk now, if that's okay?"

"Of course. I know it's a lot to take on board, but you will cope. Trust me, you are stronger than you think you are."

"I hope so. See you later."

Cecily walked out of the room and headed for the front door.

"Your hat, *memsahib*!" Aleeki came running behind her with it. "Too hot for you outside."

It was only a split-second glance down at her stomach as he spoke the words, but it was enough for Cecily to realize that he knew.

"Thank you, Aleeki." She nodded at him and walked off across the lawn to sit on her favorite bench by the lake and try to get her head around everything that had happened in such a few short hours.

Of course she could not, so she simply sat there, watching the hippos slowly rouse themselves from their sunbathing and slip into the water for their sunset dip. The fact that they did the very same thing every day and at such a leisurely pace was hypnotic and calmed her frazzled senses. Never had she thought she'd sit wishing to be a hippopotamus—quite the ugliest of animals on God's great earth—yet here she was.

Eventually, she gave up trying to make sense of everything and wandered back inside the house. Upstairs, Muratha prepared her a bath and she lay in it, wondering whether the tiny bump she saw in her stomach was real or imagined . . .

"Madame asking if you take dinner downstairs with her?" Muratha appeared in her room.

"Not tonight, no. Please send my apologies, but I'll take a tray up here instead," Cecily said firmly, feeling guilty for avoiding Kiki after the kindness she'd shown her but not able to face the almost jovial way in which Kiki was treating the situation. Like Hitler annexing Czechoslovakia, she, too, had been annexed by a tiny human being, and the situation was grave, very grave indeed.

Having managed to drain the soup Muratha had brought her, Cecily found herself reaching for the Bible that her mother had given her on her departure.

She had never questioned the faith that she had been brought up in—up to now, it had simply meant an outing to church, dressed in her best, on Sundays. But as she skimmed through the pages, she began to.

Did Christians dispose of their babies as if they were a mere inconvenience? Cecily thought of her sister Mamie: a self-confessed nonmaternal type, who by all accounts had taken to motherhood like a duck to water.

"How will I feel after carrying you for the next seven months?" Cecily whispered to her stomach. "I mean, Mary got pregnant by God before she and Joseph had even been married . . . holy moly! That means the whole New Testament is based on a woman who had been unfaithful to her husband-to-be!"

It was such a huge thought that Cecily had to lie back on her pillows, only wishing she'd paid more attention to the sermons of the preacher at her local church.

Later, when she finally turned out the light and settled herself for what she hoped would be a few hours of respite from her scrambled brain, she knew she didn't have any answers but equally that she must find the right one for herself.

Even though she'd slept, Cecily woke feeling wearier than when she'd gone to bed. As a wave of nausea swept over her, she ran to the bathroom and vomited nothing more than bile into the lavatory.

"*Bwana* sick again?" Muratha led Cecily back to bed and helped her into it. Again Cecily noticed the glance at her stomach, and when Muratha had left her alone, she rolled onto her side and groaned. It was patently obvious that the entire household staff was aware of her condition.

*Kiki's right, I just need to do what she says before everyone else around here finds out, too*, she thought.

With effort, Cecily dressed and went down for breakfast. Ginger tea rather than coffee was put in front of her, and she did her best to pick miserably at the copious food spread out on the table.

"Good morning, honey. How did you sleep?"

"Okay, thank you." Cecily was surprised to see Kiki up so early, clad in a magenta robe.

"Good. I'm going for a swim—it's too darned hot to sleep," she said as she walked toward the lake. "You should come in with me, the mud in the water does wonders for one's complexion."

For want of anything better to do, Cecily followed her godmother down to the water's edge and watched as Kiki stripped off her robe to reveal a striped bathing suit. For an older woman who'd had children, Kiki had a fabulous figure. As Cecily sat down on the bench, she only hoped her own would survive the travails of childbirth as well . . .

Kiki splashed around for a while, then took the towel Aleeki handed her as she stepped out of the water. "I'll stay down here with Cecily and dry off in the sun," she said to Aleeki, who nodded, handed Kiki her cigarette holder and left the two women alone.

"Any more thoughts?" Kiki asked as she dragged on her cigarette, the plumes of smoke making Cecily feel nauseous again.

"Only that you're right. I can't see any alternative, even though I can hardly bear to think of my baby being adopted. I'll have to live a lie to everyone around me for the rest of my life."

"I know, honey. But you have to remember that you're doing it for the baby as well; as an unmarried mother, you would both be social outcasts.

Not to mention the disgrace it would bring on your family. You'll have other kids, I swear you will. When you've found the right man, this will just be a horrible dream you can put behind you. Now, I need some coffee after all that exertion. Join me?"

"I'll just sit here awhile longer, thank you."

Cecily watched Kiki don her robe, then wander off back up to the house. She then stood up and walked along the shoreline of the lake until Mundui House was out of sight. Looking down at the lapping water in front of her, a part of her was tempted to grab a bottle of Kiki's bourbon, down it, then walk into the still waters and just keep on walking until she and the terrible mess she had made of her life no longer existed.

"Oh, Mama, if only I could talk to you, but I can't, I can't."

Cecily put her head in her hands as her shoulders began to shake, and her body slid down the trunk of an acacia tree behind her. She was so busy crying, she didn't notice the footsteps approaching until they were almost upon her.

"Cecily, darling! Your godmother said you were down here by the lake. What on earth is wrong?"

Katherine stood above her, concern written on her kind face.

"Oh, nothing, nothing." Cecily wiped away her tears harshly. "What are you doing here?"

"Bill heard from Dr. Boyle that you hadn't been well when he dropped in to Muthaiga Club yesterday. He told me this morning, and I was so worried that he insisted he drive me over here to see you."

"Bill's here, too?" Cecily was horrified how fast word of her indisposition had already spread through the community. "Why, it's awfully sweet of both of you, but really, I'm fine."

"Cecily." Katherine crouched down next to her and took Cecily's hands. "I have never seen anyone who looks less 'fine.' What on earth has happened? And please don't lie to me; after our two-and-a-half-hour journey to get here, I deserve the truth at least."

A hundred different answers came to mind, but Cecily was just too exhausted and frightened to lie any longer. "I'm pregnant! That's what's wrong with me, Katherine. Dr. Boyle says I'll be giving birth to a baby in just over seven months. There!"

Cecily stood up and began to march along the lake, desperate to get as far away from the house and Katherine as she could. Perhaps someone could run a headline in the local newspaper, she thought bitterly. It would probably sell more copies than Hitler's invasion of Czechoslovakia.

"Oh, Cecily, wait! Please!" Katherine ran to catch up with her, but she continued to scramble along the bank.

"No! And I won't be at all offended if you never want to see me or speak to me again. I'm a disgrace! And it seems everyone around here knows it already!"

"Please, will you calm down? Nobody knows anything about it. And of course I still want to speak to you . . . Cecily, will you please stand still for a while so we can talk?"

"There's nothing to talk about, nothing." She was sobbing again now. "Kiki's organizing for me to go to a clinic in Switzerland where I can stay until I've had the baby; then I have to give it up for adoption the moment I have it and then carry on with my life as though nothing's ever happened. You see? Everything's decided."

"Cecily, I know you're upset, but—"

Cecily had reached the end of the walkable ground as the lake curved around, and the foliage became impenetrable. She turned to Katherine and shook her head. "Please, I just need to be alone, okay?"

"From the look of you, that's the very last thing you need. Could we just sit down and talk this over calmly?"

"As I said, there is nothing to discuss, nothing!"

"Cecily, you are behaving like a hysterical and petulant child, not the mother-to-be that you are. If you don't calm down, I'll be forced to slap you to bring you to your senses."

Cecily was breathing heavily now and felt light-headed and faint. She staggered a little, and Katherine steadied her. "Goodness, what a state you're in. Come on, hold on to me, and we'll get you back to the house and into bed."

"I don't want to go back to the house. I don't want to go anywhere, Katherine. I simply want to die!"

"I do understand that you're in rather a bind, my dear, but there are always solutions," Katherine replied calmly as she wrapped an arm around Cecily's waist and virtually carried her along the lake back toward the house.

"But there aren't! I mean, I can't keep the baby even if I wanted to, can I? Maybe I *do* want to, but, oh . . . I think I'm going to—"

Katherine felt the full weight of Cecily's body slump against her. She was just about to shout for help when she saw Bill in front of her, a few yards away from them.

"Bill, thank God! Cecily's fainted!" she said as Bill ran toward her, took Cecily's weight, and lifted her up in his strong arms. "What are you doing here?"

"I followed you down to the lake—I simply couldn't tolerate another moment in that woman's company," he panted as they emerged back in the gardens of the house. "You run ahead and get some water. She's out for the count."

"Will do," Katherine replied as Bill laid Cecily gently down on the bench in the shade of an acacia tree.

"Before you go, I gather that Cecily is . . . pregnant? I overheard the end of your conversation as I was coming to find you both."

"Then you must swear never to tell another living soul," Katherine said fiercely. "Cecily's reputation relies on your discretion."

Bill watched Katherine run up to the house, then looked down at the young woman lying on the bench. He took off his hat and began to fan her with it.

"Feeling better?" asked Katherine as Cecily lay in her bedroom half an hour later.

"Lots, yes. And I'm so, so sorry for being rude and ungrateful, when you've made the effort to drive up here with Bill to see me."

"Oh, don't worry about that, Cecily. It's quite natural under the circumstances. Shock does funny things to people."

"It made me shoot my mouth off to you, and you didn't deserve it. Please, Katherine, forgive me."

"I forgive you, I promise."

"And seriously, I'm going to be fine. Kiki's right, I just have to face my problem—after all, I have no one to blame for it except my own stupid self," Cecily said as she took a sip of ginger tea.

"So whoever it was didn't . . . force himself on you?"

"No, but in some ways I wish he had; then I wouldn't be feeling quite so guilty."

"Please don't ever say that." Katherine shuddered. "My father had to take

THE SUN SISTER

care of a number of young women who had been taken by force by their so-called husbands at the age of eleven or twelve. Nothing could ever be as bad as that."

"You're right, of course you are," Cecily agreed. "I'm going to stop feeling sorry for myself and get on with doing what I have to do. Even though the thought of giving up my baby is so terrible."

"For now, all I can say is *don't* think about it," Katherine advised. "The main thing is to look after yourself and the baby. Now, I know Bill is eager to get off; you know how difficult he finds your godmother."

"Yes, of course, and please tell him a huge thank you from me for bringing you here to see me."

"He said he wanted to pop up and say good-bye himself, so you can thank him then. Right." Katherine stood up from beside the bed. "Please, Cecily, promise me you'll come and say good-bye before you leave for Switzerland."

"Of course I will. Do you think . . . it's the right thing to do?"

"No, I can't say it's 'right,' but in practice, until this world of ours rids itself of the ridiculous stigma surrounding unmarried mothers, with no blame or responsibility directed at the fathers, I really can't see what choice you have. I'm so very sorry. Keep in touch, won't you?" Katherine squeezed Cecily's hand.

"I will, and send my love to Bobby."

Cecily watched Katherine leave and thought that she would be the person she would miss most when she left here.

A few minutes later, there was another knock on her bedroom door.

"Come in."

Bill appeared, taking off his hat as he entered and standing uncomfortably near the door.

"Hi, Bill. Please, come sit down." Cecily indicated the chair by her bed.

Bill ignored her, walked to the end of the bed, and stared down at her. "Glad to see you have a little more color in your cheeks now."

"Yes, thank you for rescuing me. For the second time."

"Today was just a happy coincidence. Or not, as the case may be."

Cecily watched as Bill began to pace up and down. "Are you okay, Bill?"

"Yes, I'm very well indeed. As a matter of fact, Cecily, there was something I wanted to ask you."

"Then ask away. I'll do anything to repay you for your kindness since I've been here in Kenya."

"Well, the thing is that—" Bill fiddled with some loose change in his pocket. "It transpires that I've become rather fond of you since you arrived here."

"Oh, really?" Cecily waited for the insult to follow the compliment, as it usually did with Bill.

"Yes, really. So I was wondering whether, well, you would consider, well, marrying me."

"I—" Cecily looked up at him, stunned. "Please, Bill, don't tease me. I'm all out of humor just now. What is it you actually want to say?"

"Exactly that. I mean, it really is time that I took a wife to run the homestead, so to speak, and you and I seem to rub along together quite well, don't we?"

"I . . . well, yes, I suppose we do."

"And I did hear a little of your current . . . predicament when I was searching for you along the lakeside. So as you were lying there on the bench, dead to the world, I thought that it might be possible to come to some sort of an arrangement which would be beneficial for both of us. If you see what I mean."

Cecily could only stare at him in shocked silence. The fact he was telling her that he knew she was pregnant and was still offering his hand in marriage was beyond her scope of understanding. Besides which, this was Bill, the eternal bachelor.

"I do understand that I am a good few years older than you—I'm thirty-eight—and that my home is, well, basic to say the least. If you were to say yes, I would make sure to build a proper one for you and the child. It would be *our* child, of course. As far as anyone else need know, that is."

"Oh. I see. I think."

"There's no reason why we couldn't have more if we wanted, I suppose. People do, don't they?"

"Yes, but—"

"I'm sure you have lots of 'buts,' and this can hardly be the proposal a young woman like yourself would have expected when she was dreaming of her future. But"—Bill sighed—"we are where we are, and I rather did feel that I might miss your presence if you were to scurry off to Switzerland and then back to America. It's not a declaration of love, but it's certainly the nearest I've got to one in a very long time. We've both been scarred by our past experiences, and we should go into this . . . arrangement with our eyes wide open. That is, if you were to agree to it. Now I will leave you alone to think about it, but if you did feel it was a possible solution to your quandary, then I would suggest that we announce our engagement sooner rather than later, which will stop tongues wagging and salvage your reputation. I'll drop in again tomorrow to see how you are, by which time I hope you will have had the chance to consider my proposal. For now"— Bill strode over to the bed, took Cecily's hand in his, and kissed it—"I will say good-bye."

And with that, he turned on his heel and left the bedroom.

Cecily kept what Bill had said to herself—she'd learned enough to know that Kiki was an impulsive person; parties were planned on the spur of the moment and decisions made in the blink of an eye. And if Cecily knew one thing, it was that she needed time to think alone. Whatever she decided, that decision would alter the course of her life irrevocably.

But at least she *had* a choice now, which made everything better, yet at the same time more complicated.

When she heard Kiki's footsteps pass her door, heading for her afternoon "siesta," as she called it, Cecily went downstairs to sit on the bench by the lake and commune with her hippos.

"Could I live here permanently?" she asked them as she stared across the calm water. "It is so very beautiful, after all. But more importantly"—she sighed—"could I live with Bill?"

She cast her mind back to his tin shack and tried to imagine herself there. At least he'd promised to build her a new house, and it might be fun to create a wonderful garden like this one around it . . . The thought of being in charge of her own home was a mighty tempting one. And Katherine and Bobby would be her near neighbors . . .

Her parents would be thrilled to hear that she was marrying an Englishman from a good background—Bill's brother, the major, was a friend of Audrey's, after all. But most important of all, she wouldn't have to give up her baby, because Bill had told her he would bring the child up as his own. Yes, she was sure there would be local gossip about their shotgun wedding and the subsequent early birth of their baby, yet that was nothing compared to having to relinquish her child for adoption.

"But what about Bill?" she asked the hippos. "He's made it plain that this is a marriage of convenience."

On the other hand, weren't all marriages "convenient" in some way? A simple contract?

*Besides, Cecily, you said you were done with love and would never trust a man again,* she told herself firmly. *So you've just got to stop hankering after it once and for all.*

At the very least, she knew she could trust Bill to take care of her—he had saved her life, after all—and to her surprise, after their first awkward meeting, she had recently begun to enjoy his company.

She wished she could ask him whether he'd want to consummate the marriage, so they could truly become man and wife, but of course that was out of the question. Cecily squeezed her eyes shut to try to imagine what it would be like to have him kiss her. The thought really wasn't so bad. He certainly wasn't unattractive, even if he was fifteen years older than she was.

Or she could go to Switzerland and have the baby, then return to America to resume her life there . . . In truth, she knew it would be impossible to look her parents in the eyes and keep her dreadful secret from them for the rest of her life.

She stood up and walked to the water's edge. "You know what, hippos? I don't think there is a choice at all."

That evening, Cecily sat with Kiki on the terrace, Kiki drinking a martini and Cecily a cup of ginger tea.

"You look a lot better, honey."

"I feel it," Cecily replied.

"Good, you're being a brave girl, and I like bravery. Now, we absolutely must call your mother and let her know you're not going home. And then make plans to leave for Switzerland as soon as possible. Tarquin says that war is now inevitable; it's just a question of when it becomes official. But please don't worry, honey, you'll be tucked up safe and sound in Switzerland, which really is the most beautiful place."

"As a matter of fact, Kiki, it won't be necessary for me to travel to Switzerland."

"Why ever not? We agreed that it's the only solution."

"Yes, but another solution has appeared since we talked yesterday."

"Has it? How can that be?"

"Bill Forsythe has asked me to marry him."

Cecily couldn't help but enjoy the look of total incomprehension on her godmother's face.

"Why, I . . . Bill Forsythe wants to marry you?" Kiki repeated, parrotlike.

"Yes, he does. I'm to give him my answer tomorrow morning."

"Well, I'll be damned!" Kiki threw back her head and laughed. "You dark horse, you. How long has this been going on?"

"I—"

Cecily realized suddenly that she would have to play the game from here on in and hide the true nature of the arrangement. Even if she knew the truth about the pregnancy, at least it was still possible to pretend that she and Bill had feelings for each other. Kiki was very much part of this community, and she couldn't risk her gossiping after a few cocktails.

"Oh, since I went on the game drive with him a few weeks ago."

"Then why didn't you tell me about this, honey?"

"Because I thought that Bill wouldn't want anything more to do with me once I told him about the baby. What man would, knowing his . . . girlfriend was pregnant with another man's baby?"

"A very special one, obviously. Bill must love you very much to be prepared to do this. I thought only yesterday how odd it was that he'd driven over to see how you were. Presumably the two of you will tell the world it's his?"

"Yes."

"And Bill is comfortable with that?" Kiki eyed her.

"Yes. I mean, if he wasn't, I'm sure he would never have asked me to marry him."

"No. Well, now, I can't say I've ever been his biggest fan, and nor has he been mine. But I take my hat off to him for being so . . . open-minded. I hope you realize what a lucky girl you are, Cecily. You have a knight in shining armor who has come to your rescue."

"I know. So you think I should accept his proposal? I said I had to discuss it with you first."

"I think that if I was you, I'd be biting his hand off. Seriously, honey, I am thrilled for you! And what's more, it means I get to keep you here in Kenya. Shall we telephone your mother right now? She'll be over the moon that you've gotten yourself an English husband and an aristocratic one, too. Bill's mother is an 'Hon,' you know."

"What's an 'Hon'?"

"It means she was a lady before her marriage. Now, shall we call?"

"If you don't mind, Kiki, I'd prefer to speak to Bill tomorrow and say yes first."

"Of course, and let's just hope he hasn't changed his mind by then. Now, this calls for champagne!"

An hour later, when Cecily had managed to extricate herself by feigning exhaustion, she walked upstairs, pausing on the landing to look out of the big picture window at the descending dusk.

"Hello there, Africa," she whispered. "Looks like I'm here to stay."

# 27

Well, Cecily?"

She and Bill stood by the lake. She was touched that he had made an effort to look smart; in a freshly ironed white shirt and spotless khaki pants, Cecily thought how attractive—and nervous—he looked, standing in front of her.

"Did you give some thought to my proposal?"

"I did. And . . . the answer is yes. I accept your kind proposal."

"Good Lord. Right, then." He smiled. "Perhaps I should kiss you or something? I'm sure we're being watched by prying eyes from the windows behind us."

"Of course," Cecily agreed.

Bill leaned in and kissed her tentatively on the lips. To her surprise, Cecily did not mind it at all; in fact, she almost wished it had gone on longer when he pulled away.

"Thank you," she said shyly.

"There's nothing to thank me for, my dear. This is a mutually beneficial arrangement, and I'm sure it will work out very well indeed."

"Hello there!"

They both turned to see Kiki waving at them from the terrace with a bottle of champagne.

"Are congratulations in order?"

"I think they are, Kiki, yes."

Bill rolled his eyes and gave Cecily a grimace. "So," he said as he offered her his elbow and Cecily tucked her arm into his, "the charade begins."

"You're getting . . . *what?*"

"Married, Mama," Cecily shouted into the receiver. The crackling was worse than ever, and they could hardly hear each other. "I'm getting married."

"Oh, my! Did I hear you right? You're getting married?" Dorothea repeated.

"Yes!" Cecily giggled at the absurdity of the moment. "I am."

"But who to?"

"I'll write you with all the details, but he's called Bill and he's English! His family knows Audrey's very well. I met his brother, who's a major, at dinner at Woodhead Hall." The crackling on the line reached fever pitch. "Can you hear me, Mama?"

There was no reply, so with a sigh, Cecily hung up. She decided the best thing to do was to go to Gilgil and send a telegram to her parents with the details. Earlier, over the champagne that Kiki had popped, the three of them had discussed when and where the wedding should be held.

"Of course, it must be here, surely? And as soon as possible, don't you think?" Kiki had insisted.

"Whatever Cecily would like," Bill had said, looking at her askance.

Cecily could hardly believe how very patient he was being with Kiki. She'd felt a sudden wave of tenderness because he was trying to make it easy for her, despite his misgivings about her godmother.

"I . . . In truth, I haven't had time to think about. Whatever you think is best."

"To be frank, I don't think either of us wants any kind of grand bash, do we, Cecily?"

"Not at all, Bill. Something low key would suit me just fine."

Kiki had smiled. "I'm not sure 'low key' is in the Valley's dictionary. We all love to celebrate here, don't we, Bill?"

"Some of us, yes," Bill had replied before standing up. "Well, I must get back to my cattle. I'll leave you girls to work out the details of the nuptials, but it would certainly be best to hold it before the rains arrive."

"Wait a moment!" Kiki had said, staring down at Cecily's hand. "Why, Bill, Cecily has no engagement ring on her finger?"

Bill had nodded. "Ah, yes, of course. I've been staying at Muthaiga Club for the past few days and haven't had a chance to sort that one out, but rest assured I will." Bill had kissed Cecily's hand, nodded to Kiki, and left.

She hadn't seen him for a few days now, as he'd been busy with his cattle. They'd communicated by the crackly telephone, Cecily reporting in verbal shorthand that Kiki had suggested the third Friday in April (which just happened to be the same day as Cecily's ex-fiancé's, a coincidence that gave her a healthy modicum of satisfaction). This would allow everyone time to organize whatever it was that one needed to organize for a wedding. Her godmother was eager to hold the reception here at the house, but equally, Cecily was acutely aware of Bill's feelings toward Kiki.

She walked upstairs to tidy herself up. Bill was due for supper here in an hour. At least Kiki was in Nairobi visiting Tarquin tonight, so she and her husband-to-be could discuss the situation openly. It was sad that her family wouldn't be with her for the wedding, Cecily thought as she surveyed her wardrobe, wondering which dress would still zip up around her already expanding waist, but at the very least she'd make sure there was a photographer on hand to record the event. Perhaps it was her godmother's infectious enthusiasm for the wedding, but even Cecily felt a tingle of excitement at the thought of her fiancé arriving for dinner tonight to discuss the plans.

"My fiancé." She laughed out loud at the absurdity of it, but then all romantic notions of the union were swept away as she tried to zip up her favorite blue dress and failed miserably.

*You have to remember, Cecily,* she told herself, *this is just an arrangement. Bill doesn't love you. And how could he, anyway, when you are expecting a baby by someone else?*

Eventually, dressed in a cream muslin blouse and a skirt with an elastic waist, Cecily walked downstairs. She went into the library to collect the notes she'd made with Kiki.

"*Sahib* is just arrived. Ginger tea, *memsahib*?" Aleeki said.

"I'll stick to water tonight, thank you," she said as she stepped outside onto the terrace.

"Good evening, Cecily. My apologies if I'm a little late."

"No, you're not at all." Cecily smiled as Bill came to join her.

"And I probably stink of cattle, too; there's been a problem—six of them have got sleeping sickness, so I've spent the past three days checking on the rest."

"I see."

"You almost certainly don't and probably never will." Bill sighed, striding to the table set for two under the veranda, then reaching for the champagne and pouring himself a glass before Aleeki could do it for him. "The damned animals rule my life—they'll be on the move down from the mountains when the rains come, and we want them in good health for the journey. So how has your week been?"

"Good, thank you. I obviously have a few questions for you," replied Cecily as she sat down opposite him.

"Of course you do." Bill took a slug of his champagne. "And I have some for you, too." He placed a cardboard tube on the table, then unrolled a sheet of paper from it. "These are the original plans for the farmhouse that I intended to build when I first came to Kenya. Up to now they've never come to fruition and the tin hut has sufficed. I'd like you to have a look over them and see if there's anything you want to change. Then I'll get a team going on the building of it."

"Why, I'd be delighted to look at them."

"You'll be there a lot more than I will, so you might as well have a say," Bill said, pouring himself another glass of champagne. "God, I hate this stuff! Have you any beer, Aleeki?"

"Yes, *sahib*." As Aleeki scuttled away to get it, Cecily could read the tension on Bill's face.

"So," he said as Aleeki reappeared with the bottle of beer, "have you decided when we're going to make the announcement?"

"Well, as soon as we have a date for the wedding, I suppose. Kiki has suggested the third Friday in April."

Bill nodded. "That sounds about right. Hopefully just before the rains arrive. And what about the ceremony itself?"

"Kiki wants to hold it here."

"Whatever *you* want, Cecily, is fine by me. All that is your concern; I'll just turn up wherever and whenever."

"The only thing I'd like is a minister to marry us. In the eyes of God and all that," Cecily said tentatively. "It just won't feel the same if it's a civil ceremony. Kiki says she knows a pastor in Nairobi who would conduct the service."

"Good, fine. If that's important to you, then go ahead," Bill answered abruptly.

"So you don't believe in God?" Cecily asked him.

"Not in a traditional god per se, no. Haven't you noticed how every god is made in the culture's image? Jesus was a Jew from Israel—dark-skinned, yet in every painting we see, his skin is as white as the average Christian's idea of snow. However, I do believe in a magnificent maker, as I call it. In other words, something that created all we see in front of us." Bill swept his arms around. "Because it is a miracle that we can live in such beauty, don't you think?"

"Magnificent maker." Cecily repeated Bill's words, pleasantly surprised by his uncharacteristic eloquence. "I like that."

"Well, thank you. Despite being a humble farmer, I do have my moments," Bill replied.

"I . . . I was wondering where you were educated?"

"I suppose your parents are asking for my credentials?" He gave her a wry glance as Aleeki arrived with their supper.

"No, it's just that there are lots of things I feel I don't know about you and I should."

"Well, I went to Eton, which, as you may know, is a school where the British aristocracy are beaten into submission and made ready to go and run an empire. A hideous place." Bill shuddered. "I cried like a baby at night for months on end. Strange as it may seem, it was Joss Erroll who saved me. He was in the same year and house as me. On the surface not at all my type of chap, but for some reason we hit it off and we've remained good friends ever since. Sadly, Joss was expelled from Eton—you can imagine he never played by the rules. I went to Oxford to study law, but then I was drafted into the army at the age of eighteen, toward the end of the Great War. I was lucky because by then it was all over, bar the shouting. I stayed in the army for a couple of years, having no idea what exactly I wanted to do with my life. Then my fiancée left me, and"—Bill took a gulp of his beer—"I rather lost the plot."

"I'm so sorry, Bill."

"Please don't be, Cecily. You've suffered from the same malady recently, and in fact, it was a blessing in disguise. I'd given up thoughts of going back to the law by then, so Joss tipped me the wink that the British government was looking for young men to come out to Kenya and establish a community—as well as impose some sort of order on the locals, of course. They were offering land by way of a bribe. I signed up, got my thousand acres, and out here I came. That's not far off twenty years ago now." He sighed. "Can't believe I've been here so long. So that's a little more about me, now what about you? Perhaps you should at least tell me who the father is," he added, lowering his voice. "So I'm prepared in the future. I'm guessing it's someone from round here?"

"Oh, no, it isn't."

"Your fiancé, then?" He raised his eyebrows as he forked up the goat curry and rice.

"No, it wasn't him."

"Well, who was it, then? If it's England or America, it'll mean nothing to me anyway."

"Actually, I'm afraid it might. It was when I was at Woodhead Hall, and I met your brother at dinner. Lord and Lady Woodhead have a nephew called Julius—"

"Good Lord." Bill looked shocked. "That's closer to home than I thought. My brother wouldn't have got wind of it, would he?"

"Oh, no, Julius is due to marry someone else. It was only a"—Cecily gulped, blushing to the roots of her hair—"quick fling."

"And he broke your heart?" Bill asked her, his tone softening slightly.

"Yes, he did. I . . . believed his intentions were pure."

"Never trust an Englishman, eh? Well, I can't promise you much more than a few thousand head of cattle, but I can promise you that I am an honorable man. Well, well, we really are quite the pair, aren't we?"

"I suppose we are."

"Now, then." Bill searched in his pocket and brought out a small velvet box. "Here's the ring. Try it on, why don't you? I've had it made, but I fear it may be a little too large."

Cecily opened the box and found a pretty diamond band with a reddish pink stone at its center.

"Oh, it's beautiful!"

"It's a star ruby. My grandfather brought it back from Burma for my grandmother. And now here it is in Kenya—about to go on your all-American finger. Do you like it? When the light is shining directly on it, you can see a perfect star on the top."

"I think it's . . . magical," Cecily said as she placed it underneath the lantern that sat on the table and saw the shape of a shimmering star. "Thank you, Bill."

As Bill made no move to put it on her finger himself, Cecily took it from its velvet nest and placed it on the fourth finger of her left hand.

"As I thought, slightly too big, but the jeweler in Gilgil can fix that in a trice. So now that we're officially affianced, I'll send a telegram to my brother and ask him to put a notice of our engagement in *The Times*."

"What about here?"

"Oh, the jungle drums will announce it for us," said Bill. "Although perhaps it would be better for us both if you kept quiet for now about your . . . condition. When it becomes public knowledge, as it inevitably will, I shall of course take full responsibility."

"Thank you."

"Not at all. And you needn't worry, Cecily, when we are married, I'll be out of your hair most of the time. The blasted cattle demand my constant attention."

"Don't you have a manager?"

"I do indeed, and the Maasai to help me, but it takes all of us to do the job properly. In truth, I rather like being nomadic. There's been nothing much to come home for up until now. Anyway," Bill said as Aleeki and the staff cleared away the supper dishes, "why don't we look at these plans so we can get started on the house?"

An hour later, when they had made some alterations to the layout, Cecily adding extra bedrooms as she one day imagined her family coming out to join them, she followed Bill toward his pickup. Nygasi, the Maasai man, was sitting patiently waiting for him. Bill gave her a chaste kiss on the cheek and said good night.

"I'll be away on the plains for the next ten days, but please feel free to add to the house plans and organize the wedding as you wish," he said as he climbed into his pickup. "Good-bye, Cecily."

"Bye, Bill."

As Cecily walked back to the house, she decided she was liking Bill more and more. Even if he was uncomfortably honest, his complete lack of pretension was endearing. Upstairs, she undressed, musing that she had only three weeks left before she would be sharing a bed with her new husband . . . or at least, she presumed that would be what he wanted. To her surprise, the thought excited her rather than horrified her.

*Stop it, Cecily*, she berated herself firmly as she slipped into bed. *You have to keep remembering this is a marriage of convenience and love isn't involved.*

Even so, she went to sleep feeling calmer and happier than she had for many, many weeks.

# 28

Cecily was to become Mrs. William Forsythe on April 17 at midday. As promised, Kiki had arranged for the pastor from the church in Nairobi to officiate. In fact, her godmother had truly outdone herself with all the wedding preparations: chairs covered in white silk had been placed on the lawn, and a canopy adorned with white roses had been erected at the edge of the lake, under which Cecily and Bill would stand to take their vows.

She stood at the window of her room, looking down at the lawn where Kiki was greeting the arriving guests—a lot of whom Cecily had never met. She spied Bill sitting on what she now thought of as "her" bench at the water's edge with Joss Erroll, who was acting as his best man.

"Are you feeling nervous?" asked Katherine as she pinned Cecily's veil into place and then handed her the bridal bouquet of blush pink roses. "It's perfectly natural. I could barely eat the week before I married Bobby."

Cecily gulped. "I guess I am. It's all happened so quickly."

"When it's meant to be, time doesn't matter," Katherine said kindly. "You look a picture! Come and see." She guided Cecily to the full-length mirror.

A dressmaker had been called in to make her a pretty gown in an empire style, so the folds of creamy satin fell from beneath her breasts and hid any sign of a bump. The sun had lightened her hair to a soft blond, and Katherine had fixed roses to one side, just above her ear. She'd applied a little makeup, but even without it, she thought that her skin had never looked better. It glowed, and her eyes sparkled.

"Now let's get you married," said Katherine.

Throughout her life, Cecily had entertained many fantasies of what her wedding day would be like. Never had she imagined that it would be without her family in the humid heat of Kenya, in the company of a pod of hippos.

Bobby was waiting for her at the bottom of the stairs. In place of her father, Bobby had agreed to give her away.

"You look beautiful," he said as he offered the crook of his arm. Cecily tucked her own into his, then heard the band start up the wedding march.

"Ready?"

She smiled. "Ready." With a deep breath in, she and Bobby stepped out onto the terrace and made their way onto the lawn and through the congregation.

Bill stood under the canopy; his only objection to the proceedings was that he hadn't wanted to wear morning dress but had settled on black tie for himself and the guests. Cecily thought he looked very handsome indeed; his normally unruly sandy hair had been combed down, he was clean shaven, and his blue eyes reflected the sky against his deeply tanned skin. Despite the more dashing Joss standing beside him, she found she could not take her eyes from her husband-to-be.

Bobby passed her hand to Bill, who towered above her, and as the pastor began to speak, all Cecily could focus on was Bill's eyes. She heard the sounds of the birds calling to each other across the lake as if they, too, were celebrating with her.

"I now pronounce you man and wife. You may kiss the bride," the pastor announced, to a resounding whoop from Alice, sitting in the front row beside Kiki—who'd obviously been at the champagne before the ceremony—and a round of applause from the rest of the guests.

Bill did so. "Hello, Mrs. Forsythe," he whispered in her ear.

"Hello," she said shyly as she looked up at him, and they walked through the guests standing on either side of them.

Even though Cecily had been dreading the wedding breakfast, she was relieved at the fact that her morning sickness seemed to have eased and she could at least enjoy the wonderful spread that Kiki had provided. Katherine, who, as maid of honor, was sitting next to her at one of the circular tables laid out on the terrace, gave her a hug.

"I'm so happy for you, Cecily. You look utterly radiant, and so does your husband," she whispered, indicating Bill sitting on the other side of her.

And Cecily realized that she *did* feel radiant; despite the subterfuge on which the marriage had originally been based, she was enjoying the day. A few minutes later, Joss stood up and made a humorous best man's speech, referencing the way in which Cecily had appeared from nowhere and stolen the heart of "Happy Valley's eternal bachelor."

"Really, Cecily, my dear," Joss drawled, "you have me to thank for your wedded bliss—since it was I who originally convinced Bill to come to Kenya. So I do hope you'll be showing your gratitude to me in years to come." He winked at her, and she heard Idina giggle at his joke.

His tone then became more heartfelt as he read out telegrams from her family in New York. Cecily found her eyes full of tears but knew that at least she had done the right thing today and saved them from further shame.

She had no time to feel homesick, though, because the band struck up "Begin the Beguine" and Bill swept her onto the wooden dance floor set up on the lawns down by the lake. She was surprised at how skillfully he led her, and as dusk approached, she did indeed feel as though she'd won the hand of a very eligible bachelor.

It was midnight when Katherine arrived by her side as she was dancing with Lord John Carberry, another handsome man around the same age as Bill, whose wandering hands she was struggling to keep under control.

"Time to change and set off for the Norfolk Hotel, my dear," Katherine said, almost wrenching her out of the man's arms. Upstairs, Katherine helped her out of her wedding gown and into her going-away suit, fashioned out of pistachio-colored silk and with a matching pillbox hat.

"There we are, all set to go," said Katherine.

"Holy moly, I'm nervous about tonight. I mean, I'm just not sure what Bill will . . . expect."

"Don't be, darling. If nothing else, Bill is a gentleman. And he'll treat you accordingly, I promise."

"Are you sure it's okay for us to live with you while the new house is being built?" Cecily asked as she stood up from the dressing table and turned to her friend.

"Darling, of course it is. What are guest rooms for, after all? Both you and Bill are welcome there, even though it's hardly Mundui House. And you'll be surprised how quickly your own house gets finished. Hopefully in time for the baby."

"Yes. And remember—"

"I promise you, Cecily, I won't say a word."

"Do you think anyone else knows?"

"If they do, they're keeping very quiet about it. I've not heard a whisper of gossip so far."

"Thank goodness. Right, then." Cecily pulled the jacket—the bottom button of which was straining a little across her ever-extending belly—back into place. "Off I go."

"Off you go, Mrs. Forsythe."

Downstairs, the guests had gathered around the front door. As Cecily emerged with Bill next to her, they clapped and cheered.

"Throw your bouquet, Mrs. Forsythe," shouted Alice. "I need a new husband, don't I, Joss?" She smiled up at him.

Cecily did so, but it was Joss who caught it.

"Spoilsport," said Alice, sulking as the rest of the crowd gave nervous chuckles. Joss's wife, Molly, was apparently very near death.

"Come on then, my dear, off we go," said Bill.

Bill's pickup had been decorated by Joss and his cronies. Nygasi sat regally on the back of it, surrounded by balloons. Trailing tin cans had been attached to the rear fender.

"He's not coming with you into the bedroom at the Norfolk Hotel, is he, Bill?" shouted someone from the crowd.

"Very funny," Bill replied as he climbed into the driver's seat.

"Congratulations, my darling," said Kiki, coming forward and embracing her goddaughter. "Your mother would have been so proud of you today. Welcome to Happy Valley, sweetie, you're truly one of us now."

As Cecily climbed up next to Bill, she felt a sudden splash land on top of her head, then another on her suit.

"Good grief! The rains have arrived!" shouted someone else from the crowd.

"Inside, everyone!" called yet another voice.

As the crowd retreated and the rain began to pelt down, Cecily sat there feeling as though she was in a warm bath as Bill and Nygasi worked swiftly to attach the canvas hood to the pickup.

Nygasi muttered something to Bill as he started the engine.

"What did he say?" Cecily asked him.

"He said that the rain coming on our wedding day is auspicious."

"In a good or a bad way?" Cecily inquired.

"Oh, good, definitely good." Bill smiled at her as they drove off.

Cecily dozed on the journey to Nairobi, exhausted not only from the day but also from the preparations leading up to it. Before she knew it, Bill was gently shaking her awake. "We're here, my dear. Have you the energy to go inside, or shall we all just sleep in the pickup?"

"I'm fine, thank you, Bill."

The hotel lobby was deserted, as it was past two in the morning, and a night porter showed them up to their room. As the door closed behind them, Cecily looked at the bed and then at Bill and thought it seemed awfully small to accommodate the both of them.

"God, that entire carnival has exhausted me more than a day out shooting game in the bush," Bill said as he stripped off his jacket and shirt, followed by his pants.

Cecily sat down on the other side of the bed with her back to him and primly removed her hat and then her jacket.

A hand was placed on her shoulder. "Listen, if this is too uncomfortable for you, I can always sleep in the pickup."

"Oh, no, I'm fine."

Cecily stood up to open her case and find her nightgown. She heard the creak of the bed behind her as Bill climbed beneath the sheets.

"I won't look, I promise," he said, turning away.

Blushing profusely, Cecily removed her dress, slip, and brassiere and hurriedly pulled the long muslin nightgown over her head.

"Good Lord! You look like something out of a Jane Austen novel," he said as she slipped into bed next to him. The bed was so small she could feel the heat from his body next to her.

"Look here, Cecily," he said as he turned her head toward him. "Given your current . . . condition, I don't feel it's appropriate to do what one would normally do on one's wedding night. So I'll simply say good night, Mrs. Forsythe, and sleep well."

Bill kissed her on the forehead, then rolled over onto his side away from her. Within a few seconds, she heard him snoring gently. She lay there listening to the rain beat on the roof of the hotel and the panes of the window.

And only wished that she *could* do what people normally did . . .

Cecily stirred the next morning as a hand was placed on her shoulder. She blinked, and in a sudden flash, the events of the previous day came back to her. She looked up at Bill and could see the pink glow of dawn creeping through a gap in the curtains behind him.

"Good morning," he said in a low voice. "I ordered room service. Have some breakfast."

Cecily sat up as Bill placed a tray gently on her lap.

"I know you like your coffee black," he said, indicating the steaming cup, which was accompanied by triangles of toast and small pots of jam. "Eat up, and then get dressed. Then we'll head out."

"Out?" she asked, picking up the coffee. "Where are we going?"

"It's a surprise," he said, then went into the bathroom. Cecily heard the faucet running and took a bite of her toast, feeling as hungry as she ever had.

Once she was dressed, Bill, now attired in his habitual khaki, led her out of the hotel and into the pickup, where Nygasi was stationed at the back. She wondered where he had slept and thought that she might as well become accustomed to his presence, as it was so rare to see Bill without him.

Bill opened the door and helped her up, then climbed in beside her and started the engine. He gave no hint of where they were going, but Cecily was content to enjoy the morning breeze on her face as they drove through bustling Nairobi, happy that the rains of last night had not yet returned and the sun was once more radiant in the sky. An hour later, they arrived at the edge of an airfield, and Cecily looked at him quizzically.

"As there won't be a honeymoon, especially now the rains have come and the cattle will be on the move, I thought that you deserved a wedding present. And I wondered what could I give you—I've been a bachelor for so long, all I know of is Kenya and its nature. So come along, I have something to show you. And I do hope you aren't afraid of heights," he added.

He helped her out of the pickup and led her toward a small biplane that was sitting on the runway, with a man in overalls standing next to it.

"All right there, Bill?" said the man cheerfully as they reached him. "And this is your young wife, is it? Pleased to make your acquaintance, Mrs. Forsythe."

"It's nice to meet you, too," she responded automatically.

"She's all fueled up, and she's been serviced," the man said. "That's the plane, not you, Mrs. Forsythe," he joked.

"Put these on, please." Bill handed her a thick leather flying jacket and a pair of goggles, which he helped her with, then stepped up onto the lower wing of the aircraft and held out a hand to Cecily. "Come on, then," he said.

She took his hand, and he helped her up onto the wing, then into one of two scooped-out cockpits, where he strapped her in. He then climbed into the rear cockpit himself, so he was sitting just behind her.

"You know how to fly this thing?" she asked.

"It would be your bad luck if I didn't," he said wryly. "Now, don't worry, there's an ejector seat in case something goes wrong."

"Are you serious?" She twisted around in her seat to look at him, and he gave her a smile.

"Cecily, you're perfectly safe. Just trust me, and enjoy the views."

With that, the plane's engine roared to life, and the propeller started to whir. Bill guided the plane down the runway, and a minute later they were up in the air, Cecily's stomach turning somersaults.

As they climbed higher and she became used to the sensation, Cecily stared down beneath her in fascination. She could make out the tops of the gray buildings and the streets of Nairobi, cars and people crawling along them like ants, but after a few minutes, all she could see was undulating countryside, gentle greens and flashes of orange earth and the occasional sparkle of a lazy river.

After a half hour's flight, Bill tapped her shoulder and pointed to a spot below them, and Cecily gasped. There was Mundui House, like a perfect little doll's house on the edge of the shimmering lake.

Then Bill swung the plane north, and Cecily recognized the train tracks that ran through Gilgil and saw the dark expanse of the Aberdare Mountains to their right. A glimmer of pink and blue appeared in the distance, and Cecily squinted through her goggles to try to see what it was.

"Lake Nakuru," Bill shouted to her, barely audible over the noise of the engine.

Cecily gasped as he swooped the plane downward and the pink cloud she had seen crystallized in front of her eyes: thousands upon thousands of densely packed flamingos stood peacefully together in the water. As the plane flew overhead, they began to open their wings in a ripple effect, their bright coats reflected in the blue water so they appeared like a single gigantic organism, moving as one.

When Bill finally headed south again, Cecily looked down at Kenya spread out below her, marveling at the new perspective her husband had so thoughtfully given her. This was now her home, and right now, she could not imagine being anywhere more beautiful.

When they landed, Bill helped her out of the plane and Cecily felt her legs wobble beneath her. She stripped off her goggles, shook back her wind-swept hair and looked up at him, hardly knowing how to put into words the beauty of what she had seen.

"Thank you," she managed. "I will never, ever forget this moment and what I just saw."

"Glad you enjoyed it. I'll take you up again after the rains. Now," he said curtly, as he handed her into the pickup, "I'm afraid it's back to business."

As they drove away from Nairobi, toward the Aberdare Mountains and their temporary marital home with Bobby and Katherine (Bill had point-blank refused to stay under Kiki's roof until their own home was built), Cecily couldn't help but cast a glance at him. Whatever their marriage was based on, he not only made her feel safe and protected, but his self-containment fascinated her. He—and the life she would now begin to live—might not have been what she would have naturally chosen, but as they entered Katherine and Bobby's farmland and bumped through the surrounding red plains, which would soon be filled with the cattle coming back down from the hills, she felt she wanted to do everything to embrace it. She'd do her best to be a good wife to the man who had saved not only her life but also her reputation.

*My husband is a special man*, she thought as a little bubble of unexpected longing popped in her stomach.

"Hello there!" Katherine waved at them from the veranda as they made their way up the muddy drive to the small but newly renovated cottage. "How was the flight?" she asked Cecily as she put her arm through hers and led her toward it.

"It was truly the most incredible experience of my life." Cecily smiled as Katherine ushered her into a chair on the veranda.

"Oh, I'm so glad." Katherine smiled, sitting down next to her. "Bill asked me whether I thought you'd be up for it, and of course I said yes. It's the only way to see just how magical Kenya is," she said as Bill brought Cecily's suitcase from the pickup. "He took me up once and decided to show off with his new tricks. I admit, I vomited all over the cockpit." She chuckled.

"Shall I put this in the spare room, Katherine?"

"Do, yes, Bill."

"Aleeki said he'd send Kiki's chauffeur over with the rest of my things tomorrow," Cecily said as she watched Bill walk inside the cottage.

"Well, it's a shame that you don't have your own home to go to, but we'll do our best to make you comfortable here."

"Oh, don't worry about that; I'm just so grateful I don't have to stay down at Mundui House any longer. The atmosphere is awful strange. And besides, this is quite lovely, Katherine." Cecily swept her hand around the veranda, on which stood a table that Bobby himself had made out of discarded timber and had polished to a high shine. Katherine had planted bushes of hibiscus along the borders, along with bright orange and blue bird-of-paradise flowers. The cottage was cozy and inviting, with pretty flowered curtains Katherine had sewn for the windows and clean white shutters. "It feels very homely."

"Well, Inverness Cottage is certainly not grand, but it's all ours and that's what matters. Now," Katherine said as Bill came out of the front door, "can I get you both a drink of some sort?"

"Not for me, Katherine. I'm afraid I must be off back to the farm."

"Yes, Bobby left this morning."

"Then I'm sure I'll see him up there. Real life begins again, and I need to get those cattle safely down onto the plains."

Cecily did her best to hide her disappointment. "When will you be back?"

"Not sure, to be honest. Sometime next week, I should think."

"Oh." Cecily swallowed the lump in her throat. "Well, I'll be just fine here with Katherine."

"She will indeed," Katherine agreed, seeing Cecily's distress and coming to her rescue. "And"—Katherine looked up at Bill expectantly—"you have another gift for your new wife, don't you? How about I go and get it while you two say your good-byes?"

Bill nodded, so Katherine walked off the veranda and disappeared around the side of the cottage as Cecily stood up.

"Thank you again for everything, Bill. I'm very grateful."

"As I said originally, I'm sure we'll rub along together well. I'd appreciate it if you would keep an eye on our house-building project while I'm gone. While the cat's away and all that."

"Of course I will, I'll enjoy it."

"And here's your transport!" Katherine reappeared, leading a glossy chestnut mare toward them. "Come and meet her."

"The horse is for me?"

"She is, yes," said Bill. "The easiest way of visiting your neighbors, that's for sure."

"Why, she's beautiful, aren't you?" Cecily stroked the mare's nose, which looked as though someone had dropped a large splotch of white paint all over it.

"She should be the perfect size for you and seems very even-tempered," added Bill.

"I love her! Is she really mine?"

"She is, yes, although you'll have to take care of yourself for the next few months." Bill indicated her stomach. "We wouldn't want any accidents, would we?"

"No," Cecily said with a blush, "we wouldn't."

Even though Katherine knew about the baby, it was the first time Bill had mentioned it openly in front of her.

"The horse doesn't have a name yet." Katherine stepped into the breach once more. "You'll have to think of one for her, Cecily."

"Yes, she must. Right, I'll be off then."

"I'll walk you to your pickup," said Cecily.

"No, stay here with Katherine—you've had a tiring couple of days. Bye, Cecily," he said, and, with a short wave and a nod, strode off toward the ever-patient Nygasi waiting for him in the pickup.

*He didn't even kiss me good-bye,* Cecily thought as she followed Katherine disconsolately back onto the veranda. She'd been so encouraged by Bill's perfect wedding gift and the wonderful smile he'd given her before taking off in the plane, but now . . .

"Are you all right, darling?" Katherine asked.

"Yes, I'm just a little tired is all."

"Of course you are. It's a shame that Bill has to go away so soon, but I'm sure he'll be back here to you as soon as he can."

"Yes, and I shouldn't feel bad or make him feel guilty, because I knew when he asked me to marry him that this was the deal."

"Oh, darling, you really care about him, don't you?"

"I guess I do, but I truly have no idea how he feels about me."

"I always knew that Bill harbored feelings for you, Cecily. It was obvious when we were out on that safari. It was you I wasn't sure of."

"I'm sure you're wrong. I thought he asked me to marry him out of the kindness of his heart." Cecily could feel the tears pressing at the back of her eyes as she saw Bill's pickup finally disappear from sight.

"I wasn't aware until recently that Bill *had* a heart, let alone a kind one." Katherine smiled. "But you've changed him, Cecily, you truly have. And the fact he's prepared to take on your . . . situation must be evidence of his feelings for you?"

"I . . . just don't know."

"Well, everything will be better once you're settled in your new home together. Hopefully it won't be too long, but we'll try and have a lovely time while you're here. Now sit with me in the kitchen while I peel the vegetables. Remember, Bobby has gone, too, so we can keep each other company."

Cecily followed Katherine into the entrance hall, which doubled as a living room. To her left was a narrow hallway, housing a room the size of a closet that was a study for Bobby to use, and beyond that, a small kitchen with a scrubbed pine table and two chairs. It was, of course, as neat as a pin. Everything about Katherine was.

"I'm surprised you didn't put your kitchen in a separate block like all the other houses around here," Cecily commented as she watched Katherine expertly peel some potatoes.

"Given I have no staff to cook for me, it seemed absurd to do that. One of my favorite moments of the day is when Bobby sits down right where you're sitting and we eat and chat over where we've been and what we've done."

"I'm afraid I have never learned to cook," Cecily confessed. "Do you think you could teach me?"

"Of course I could, but I'm sure that Bill will employ someone to do it for you."

"Still, I should know what to do so I can direct them."

"Yes, you're right, although I doubt the likes of Kiki or Idina have ever put together toast and jam, let alone a beef casserole," said Katherine.

"Well, there's no harm in learning, is there? I'd like to."

"All right, then," Katherine agreed, handing Cecily some carrots and a knife. She grinned. "Lesson one."

# 29

*925 Fifth Avenue*
*New York, New York*

*April 30, 1939*

*My darling Cecily,*

*Your Papa, your sisters, and I were overjoyed to receive the photographs of your wedding ceremony. You looked beautiful, honey, and I must say that your Bill is very handsome indeed. Although your dear Papa was somewhat surprised at his age, I assured him that it was a good thing you have chosen a husband who is more mature.*

*As you may know, Jack and Patricia are now on their honeymoon on Cape Cod. Junie DuPont attended, and she told me that Patricia looked nowhere near as beautiful as you and her hair was very unfortunate. She said the reception was like Mardi Gras and rather crass. (There has also been gossip recently that Jack's family bank is on the verge of collapse. As Mamie said, it looks like you had a lucky escape!)*

*Baby Christabel is a delight, and Mamie has been a perfectly serene mother. And I must tell you the big news: Priscilla is expecting, too! Your Papa and I are so very happy that all of our three daughters are married, and maybe it won't be so long before you, too, have some baby news for us.*

*Cecily, even though you say you are safe from any war that may happen in Europe, we do worry about you, honey. I only wish that you and Bill would come stay out here until things are more certain, but I understand his livelihood is in Kenya.*

*Write me soon, and send my best to Kiki and to your new husband.*

*All my love,*
*Mama xx*

Cecily sighed heavily as she read her mother's letter and tried to summon up joy at Priscilla's news, but all she felt was a cold lump of anxiety as she wrote back to her mother telling her of her own pregnancy.

"I am due in December," she wrote, although she knew she would be sending them a telegram far earlier to announce the birth.

"I'll deal with that when the time comes," she murmured as she folded the letter into an envelope.

The good news was that the days at Inverness Cottage passed far faster than they had at Mundui House. She was kept busy helping Katherine plant a vegetable garden at the back of the cottage and learning how to prepare dinners and to make cakes (which, after a number of failed attempts, convinced Cecily that baking was never going to be her forte). If she woke early, she would ride Belle, her beautiful chestnut mare, over to Bill's farm five miles away to check that the builders were doing what they should.

Subsequently, Cecily fell into bed exhausted each night. She found the rain that pounded on the roof above her comforting somehow but worried about Bill out there on the plains, with the rivers swelling and the risk of mudslides from the mountains. When it rained too hard to sit outside, Katherine would light a fire in the small grate and they would play cards or listen on the crackly wireless to the BBC World Service. This was often a sobering experience, as the news continued to report the political situation in Europe; many commentators believed that war was inevitable, despite the various pacts and alliances that had been formed.

While the tensions in Europe were never far from Cecily's mind, Katherine could not have done any more to make her feel welcome. Bobby was away, too, with his cattle but somehow always managed to return every few days to see his wife.

At least, Cecily thought, as she bathed in the tin tub that sat in an outhouse at the back alongside the lavatory, Bill was due back here tomorrow. She couldn't believe how eager she was to see her new husband. The following morning, she drove with Katherine into Gilgil and went into what claimed to be a hair salon but was actually a spare room at the back of a shack. Cecily winced with nerves as the Kikuyu woman chopped away at her hair.

"There, *bwana*, is okay?"

Cecily tried to view her reflection in the small piece of cracked, faded mirror the woman had offered her.

"Why, yes, I'm sure it's fine."

"What do you think? Do I look terrible?" she asked Katherine, who had recommended the woman.

"Not at all," Katherine comforted her.

"It feels so short."

"The good news is that it will grow again. Come on, we have to get home to prepare supper for our boys."

When Cecily was back at the cottage and was able to view herself properly in a mirror on the wall, she covered her face and let out a little scream. Her curls had been chopped into submission, and now what was left of them clung tightly to her head in ringlets.

"I hate it! I absolutely hate it," Cecily said, her eyes full of tears.

"I think it rather suits you."

"I look like a boy, Katherine! Bill will loathe it, I know he will."

"I'm sure he won't even notice," said Katherine, handing her a couple of barrettes. "Bobby certainly doesn't. Here, try these."

Bobby arrived home at seven that night and indeed didn't notice that either of the women had had their hair cut.

"I saw Bill out on the plains briefly yesterday, Cecily. He sends his apologies, but he'll be delayed by a few days, I'm afraid. It's taken longer than expected to round up the cattle for vaccination, what with the rains."

"Oh." Cecily didn't know whether she was relieved that he wouldn't see her hair in the state it was in or disappointed. Disappointment won.

"Let's have a drink, shall we?" Katherine poured them all a gin from the bottle Cecily had bought in Gilgil at great expense to celebrate Bill's return. "Let's toast to your husband's imminent arrival. Cheers!"

It was another week before Bill arrived unexpectedly on the threshold of Inverness Cottage.

"Hello, Cecily," he said as she rose hurriedly, throwing the ball of wool and knitting needles into a basket beside her.

"Bill! We weren't expecting you," she said as she walked toward him.

He put out his hands. "Please don't come near me, Cecily. I stink of cow and mud. I'll go round the back and have Nygasi throw some buckets of water over me while I have a good scrub."

"There is a bath, you know," Cecily called after him.

"Baths are for girls," he said, winking at her as Nygasi joined him, carrying a pail.

"Bill's back," she said to Katherine, who was preparing supper in the kitchen.

"Good. Better get out that gin, then, eh?"

Having done so, Cecily ran to her room to brush her hideous hair and apply a little lipstick. Fifteen minutes later, Bill was back in a fresh linen shirt and pants, looking more like himself.

"Gin?" she offered him.

"Thank you. Tchin tchin," he said and downed half the delicate crystal glass's contents in one. "Back to civilization," he said as he eyed her. "You've had your hair cut."

"Yes, and it was all a terrible mistake. The woman in Gilgil butchered it."

"I rather like it. And it'll save you having to go back into town for a while, at least."

"If I'd known you were expected, I'd have made some . . . well, arrangements."

"My dear Cecily, I've never been 'expected' in my life. There's certainly no need to stand on ceremony every time I come back."

"Hello, Bill." Katherine smiled as she came out onto the veranda. "Any spare gin going, Cecily?"

Over supper that night, Bill and Bobby discussed all things to do with cattle and Cecily wished only that she and Bill could be alone. She had lots to tell him, too.

"Right, I'm going to turn in for the night. Excuse me, won't you?" he said as he yawned and patted Cecily on the shoulder. "Good night, my dear."

Cecily followed him to the guest bedroom only ten minutes later, but Bill was already snoring gently in one of the twin beds. Slipping on her nightgown even though she'd recently been sleeping naked because it was more comfortable, Cecily climbed into her own bed, switched out the light, then laid her head on the pillow and did her best to sleep.

When she woke up the next morning, Bill had already left.

"Where has he gone?" she asked Katherine, who was always up far earlier than she.

"Not sure, to be honest. He and Nygasi took off in the pickup about half an hour ago."

"Did he say when he'd be back?"

"No, I'm afraid he didn't. Look, I think you're going to have to accept that Bill has lived by himself for the whole of his adult life. He's used to coming and going as he pleases and to not pleasing anyone else for that matter. You must have known that when you married him."

"Oh, yes, I did, of course I did. And you're right," Cecily said. "I just have to accept it."

"It's no reflection on his feelings for you, I'm sure. He's simply not used to having a wife yet, that's all. Plus it's the rainy season, which is always busy for the farmers."

"He was so wonderful to me when we got married. I'd just"—Cecily sighed—"like to have a little more time with him."

"Nothing in life is ever perfect, Cecily, and as my father always drummed into me, patience is a virtue. He's married you, darling, much to the surprise of everyone round here. *And* despite your situation. Given where you were a few weeks ago, I think you should count your blessings and not be too demanding. Now, then, I'm off to plant some cabbages in the garden before the heavens open again."

Katherine left the kitchen, and Cecily sat down, chastened by her friend's words. She was right, of course: Bill was his own man, and she had to accept that.

This proved very difficult when Bill didn't show up until three days later, a dead leopard sprawled across the rear of his pickup, the huge paws tied by rope to the undercarriage. Cecily looked away, hating the sight of the majestic creature lying lifeless in front of her.

"Sorry I've been AWOL, Cecily," Bill said as he arrived in the living room, driven inside by the pelting rain. "I needed to let off a little steam. I'll go and dry myself off."

*Obviously, letting off steam means shooting wild animals dead,* Cecily thought but didn't dare say.

"So how's the house coming along?" he asked her over the supper table an hour later.

"Well, I think. The foreman is a good guy—"

"He should be, he's a friend of mine," Bobby said. "He'll see you right, so he will. Or he'll have me to deal with."

"Maybe we could go over there tomorrow and take a look for ourselves, Bill?" suggested Cecily.

"Yes, I'm sure we can," he agreed. "I have some things to do in town first thing, but I could go along with you tomorrow afternoon."

"Well, the roof has gone on since you last saw it, so at least we don't have to worry about keeping dry," encouraged Cecily.

"How exciting," Katherine said. "With all these ideas Cecily's got, the farmhouse is going to be wonderful."

"Let's hope so, although on the budget I've got, it's hardly going to be the Ritz."

When Bill said he was retiring to bed, Cecily immediately said she'd come, too. The bedroom door closed behind them, and Bill proceeded to strip down to his undergarments and climb into his bed.

"You're getting bigger, aren't you?" Bill said as he surveyed her in her nightgown.

"I seem to be, yes. Bill—" she said as he was about to switch off the lamp on his nightstand.

"Yes?"

"I just wanted to tell you that my parents have wired some money as a wedding gift. For both of us, that is. So I can at least contribute to furnishing the house and any extra costs that come along."

"You mean they've provided you with a dowry?" Bill smiled at her. "How very generous of them. Well, I won't say it won't come in helpful, because it will. I sometimes wonder why I run a cattle farm for a living; it gives me continual grief, and I earn little from it, given the amount of hours I put in."

"Maybe because you love it?"

"Maybe," he agreed. "I certainly can't see myself working nine to five in an office, that's for sure. Joss was saying that if war does come, they'll be wanting as many men as possible to help out. He's got an idea to join the Kenya Regiment himself, and I think I should do the same if and when the time comes."

"Surely you're too old to fight?" Cecily was horrified.

"Not so much of the 'old,' young lady," Bill chided her.

"Do you really have to do it?"

"I rather think I do, yes. I can hardly sit out in the plains chewing the cud with the local elders while Blighty and my fellow countrymen are under attack, can I? Anyway, it hasn't happened yet, so let's wait and see." Bill rolled over. "Good night, Cecily."

# 30

Cecily and Bill finally moved into their new home at the end of June. Perhaps it was the nesting instinct that had taken hold of Cecily, but she had spent the past few weeks choosing paint colors for the walls, as well as curtain fabric (albeit from the paltry selection in the haberdashery shop in Nairobi). She was elated when Bill arrived home in early June to tell her a shipment of furniture from America had arrived in Mombasa and would be brought out by truck to the farmhouse in the next week.

At least with everything to do for the house, Cecily had noticed Bill's regular absences less; he was either away checking on his cattle and moving them back up the mountains now the rainy season was over, on a game drive, or disappearing to commune with his Maasai friends.

"I must bring a couple of them up to the house at some point to meet you, Cecily," he'd said in passing. "The way they live is fascinating. They go where their cattle go and simply rebuild their homes each time they settle."

"Then they'll find Paradise Farm very strange, I'm sure," Cecily had said.

The name for the farmhouse had come about one evening when Bill had arrived back unexpectedly and they'd taken a trip out to see their soon-to-be-finished home. Cecily had sat on the steps leading up to the front veranda and sighed as she gazed down at the valley laid out beneath her.

"It's paradise here, it really is," she'd said.

"Like *Paradise Lost*," Bill had said, coming to sit next to her. "My favorite poem; it's by John Milton. Heard of it?"

"No, I'm afraid I'm just not very good with English literature."

"Well, the poem is actually in twelve books and contains ten thousand lines of verse."

"Wow, that isn't a poem, that's a story!"

"It's actually a biblical epic, reimagined by Milton. It follows the story of

Satan, who is determined to destroy God's favorite new creatures: humans. Perhaps we should name the farmhouse 'Paradise'? It can mean different things to both of us."

"Umm, okay, but I hope you won't feel that paradise *has* been lost when we finally move in here," Cecily had said.

"Oh, don't worry about that—the poem that comes after is called *Paradise Regained*." Bill had smiled. "Come on." He'd offered her his hand and pulled her up from the stoop. "Let's leave paradise and go back to our temporary digs."

Cecily had subsequently had a carpenter fashion a sign that said "Paradise Farm" to hang on the gate, just in case anyone came to visit them.

"And I remain optimistic about that," Cecily said to Katherine, who was helping her hang curtains in the living room.

"Of course people will come and visit you, darling; they're all far too nosy to stay away."

Cecily rolled her eyes. "Then they might also notice that I'm awful large for what's supposed to be less than three months of pregnancy."

Katherine shrugged. "Perhaps, but they'll just assume that the two of you simply couldn't keep your hands off each other before you got married. Seriously, if you're going to live here in the Valley, or at least on the edge of it, you absolutely can't be worrying about what people say. Anyway, it's certainly stopped the rumor that Bill batted for the other side."

"What does that mean?"

"Oh, you know," Katherine said, lowering her voice. "That he is a homosexual."

"No! Just because he never married, they thought that?"

"Cecily, the women round here in particular have far too much time *to* think. Now, that's the sitting room done," said Katherine as she climbed down from the stepladder and surveyed her handiwork. "And isn't it starting to look lovely?"

The curtains swayed in the breeze from the fan that had been installed in the center of the high-ceilinged living room, and Cecily looked around at the surprisingly pleasing mix of Kenya and New York she had created. She had asked her parents to send over all their old furniture that had been gathering dust in the basement of the Fifth Avenue house, and the sturdy mahogany pieces gave the farmhouse a certain gravitas. Cecily had arranged the chaise longue and leather armchairs around the fireplace, with a large oriental rug between them. She had stowed Bill's books in the bookcases that lined the room, and the air was filled with the smell of polish.

She tried her best not to look at the leopard-skin rug in the entrance hall—Bill's contribution to the proceedings, fashioned from the animal he'd brought home a few weeks ago.

She pushed one of the leather chairs closer to the fireplace and imagined herself sitting opposite Bill beside the fire, drinking gin and talking about their day.

"Cecily!" Katherine laid a firm hand on her arm. "You're in no condition to push anything at the moment, let alone that heavy chair."

"Exercise is good for pregnant women, and I've managed so far." Cecily shrugged. "I hope Bill will like it, though it might just be too civilized for him."

"I'm sure he'll love it, darling. I certainly do, and how I envy you your indoor bathroom—Bobby has promised me that we should be able to afford the plumbing for one next spring."

"Come and use mine whenever you want," Cecily suggested.

"I'd love to, but I'd only get hot and dusty riding back!"

A few days later, Bill returned home. The plan was for him to go to Inverness Cottage, as usual, where Katherine would tell him that Cecily was up at Paradise Farm, sorting out the shipment from America. Cecily peeped through the curtains as she saw Bill's pickup approach and swerve to a halt in front of the house. Picking up two champagne glasses, she walked to the front door and waited for him to enter.

"Hello?" he called as he opened the door.

"I'm here, Bill, right here."

"Thank God!" Bill's forehead was creased with worry. "I couldn't understand what you were doing at the farm alone so late in the day."

"I'm absolutely fine," she said, handing Bill the glass of champagne. "Welcome home to Paradise Farm."

"What?" Bill looked around the newly furnished hallway. "Are you saying that you've moved in?"

"*We* have, yes! Come and see the living room first."

Bill accepted the champagne and allowed Cecily to give him a guided tour of the house. She had arranged fresh flowers in vases in each of the four bedrooms and placed photographs and paintings, so that it truly felt lived in.

"This is where Mama and Papa and my sisters can stay," she said to him as they went into the two guest rooms, where the beds were already made up. The main bathroom was sparkling and featured a claw-footed tub with a polished brass faucet, while the kitchen at the end of the house had already been stocked with food.

"Goodness, this is a real home now." Bill seemed bemused as he followed her around. "I have to say that you have done the most remarkable job here. The only problem is, I'll be scared to enter in my filthy clothes in case I spread dust on all the polished surfaces."

"Oh, don't worry about that." Cecily smiled as she led him back into the living room and topped up their champagne. "All this furniture is very old; my mother was about to throw it away before I asked them to ship it over. Now, are you hungry?"

"You know I'm always hungry, Cecily," Bill said as he admired the pictures on the walls. "Who is that?" he asked, glancing at a small oil painting of a young girl.

"Why, it's me! I think I was about four at the time. Mama had an artist come paint all her girls for posterity."

"It looks nothing like you at all; you're far prettier than that. Right, are we heading back for supper at Katherine and Bobby's?"

"Of course not! This is our home now. And I've made supper for both of us. Why don't you go wash up, and I'll bring it through to the living room."

"Good idea," Bill said, and Cecily smiled as she walked through to the kitchen. Bill looked mesmerized, and she hoped it was a good sign.

"No more wandering around in my long johns, then," Bill said as she served the roast beef at the highly polished round table she'd placed in an alcove in a corner of the living room. "I think I'll have to go to town and have the tailor make me some more formal clothes if we're going to dine in here regularly. This looks awfully good, Cecily. I had no idea you could cook."

"There's plenty you don't know about me, Bill," she said, smiling at him coquettishly. Her euphoria at finally moving into her own home, combined with the glass of champagne, had made her brave.

"I'm absolutely sure you're right about that," he agreed. "And this is delicious. Here's to you." Bill raised his glass. "You truly have created something lovely. I might be tempted to come home more often in the future."

"I'd like that," she said. "Oh, and I forgot to show you the study just off the hall. It's not a big room, but I've put Papa's old desk in there, along with a bookcase, so you have somewhere to go and have some peace and quiet when you're working."

"I don't think there's anything you haven't thought of," Bill said. "Where will the nursery be?"

Cecily blushed as she always did when Bill mentioned the baby. The nursery was a compact room just next to the master bedroom, which she had omitted to show him on purpose.

"Really, Cecily, please don't be embarrassed. I knew what I was doing when I asked you to marry me."

"I know, but . . . you've just been so darned good about it and it must be horrible for you."

"Not at all. I see it as a bonus; at the very least, he or she will be company for you when I'm away. Cecily, please don't cry." Bill put his knife and fork down as he watched his wife's eyes fill with tears.

"Pardon me, I'm just exhausted from doing all this."

"And I'm now thoroughly ashamed that I wasn't here to help you more. Here"—Bill rooted inside his trouser pocket and produced a white handkerchief—"use this."

Bill's action immediately took Cecily sailing back to a moment when Julius had done the exact same thing, which then brought further tears to her eyes.

"Come now, Cecily, you shouldn't be crying on our first night at Paradise Farm," he said gently.

"No, but—" She blew her nose and shook her head. "Just ignore me, I'm fine now. Tell me where you've been in the past few days?"

Later, after Bill had helped her pile the used plates into the sink and they had discussed finding a Kikuyu maid to help her around the house, Cecily wandered around her new home, switching off the lights. She stood in the darkened living room, looking out of the window at the moonlit plains.

"Please," she whispered, "let us both be happy here."

Throughout a balmy July, Cecily felt the baby kicking inside her, the force of it rippling across her belly. Despite the dramatic effect on her life that the baby had wrought, she found herself becoming more and more excited to meet the child. And to become a mother. At least it would mean she would have some company, someone to whom she belonged and who belonged to her. She had so much love to give, and for the first time in her adult life, she felt it could be given freely, without fear.

Kiki had recently telephoned her to ask her to come on a safari. "The wildebeest will be crossing the Mara River in their thousands—and the crocs will be waiting just below to get their dinners. It's quite the spectacle," she'd said.

Cecily had gently reminded her that she was now six months pregnant.

"Oh, honey, pregnancy is such a killjoy," Kiki had drawled and hung up.

Bill had been making an effort to be home more often, but she still went days without seeing him; he was even busier than normal, spending most of his limited spare time in Nairobi, attending meetings with Joss and various military staff. The rumblings of war in Europe had escalated to a roar that could be heard as far as the Wanjohi Valley, and she secretly fretted about Bill's previous assertion that he would follow Joss into the Kenya Regiment if war became a reality.

As Cecily spent days alone, cleaning an already clean house, knitting matinée jackets, booties, and little hats for the new arrival, she'd attempted to come to terms with the fact that Bill regarded her as a companion rather than a wife or lover. Since they'd moved into Paradise Farm, Bill had been sleeping in one of the guest rooms, rather than beside her in the master bedroom. Cecily had tried to comfort herself that this arrangement was to do with her pregnancy and that he was merely being gallant, but she never managed to fully convince herself.

*We're just two acquaintances who share a house*, she thought one night as she put out the light and crawled into her bed.

After all, he had never tried to kiss any other part of her except her hand, aside from the brief brushes of his lips against hers at their engagement and on their wedding day. Cecily had grown used to pushing down the very human desire to be touched, telling herself she should be grateful as they got along very well indeed. She rarely ran out of things to say or questions to ask him. He was knowledgeable on a whole host of different topics, especially when it came to her new homeland and the war.

"My parents so want to come out and visit us after the baby is born," Cecily said one night over supper.

"Well, they shouldn't hold their breath, and nor should you. British intelligence says that the Germans have been cozying up to the Russkis—that's Russians to you, Cecily. There's something going on there, mark my words.

They're probably deciding how they'll carve up the rest of Europe between them."

"When do you think it's all going to start happening for real?" she asked.

He sighed. "Who knows? All the governments in Europe are doing their best to prevent it, but there's already been a noticeable buildup of troops along the German border with Poland."

"I miss my parents so." She sighed, then realized she'd never asked Bill about his.

"Oh, they're tucked up safe and sound in an English county called Gloucestershire. For now, anyway."

"But what if there's war and England is invaded?"

"Let's hope it won't come to that, old girl, but as my father was a colonel in the army last time round, I'm sure there's nothing he'd like more than to feel important again."

"I don't understand why men seem to love war so much."

"The majority of men don't when it comes to the ghastly reality, but the thought of it certainly brings out one's inner patriot. I have asked Ma and Pa if they'd like to come out here and stay with us. We're relatively safe here, although we are beginning to station troops along the Abyssinian border. The trouble is, we have no idea where the blighters will turn their attention next. Seems as though Hitler's been recruiting his army for years in preparation and the rest of us are having to play catch-up."

"You make it sound as though we've lost before we've even begun!"

"Do I? I'm sorry to be so negative, but all the military intelligence that's coming into the HQ in Nairobi indicates that Hitler is almost ready to execute his master plan of world domination."

"We could always leave here and go stay with my family in New York?" Cecily suggested again. "Get out while the going is good."

"Cecily, you know very well I can't just jump ship, so to speak. And you are in no condition to fly," Bill reminded her. "How are you feeling?"

"Oh, I'm fine, thank you," Cecily said, although in truth, in the past few days, she'd been suffering from a series of headaches and her ankles looked more like an elephant's than a human being's. "Can I get you dessert?"

August in Kenya brought with it a dry, stifling heat that had Cecily begging for the rains to arrive. She was also becoming less mobile, which meant she was stuck in the house by herself much of the time.

Bill arrived back one afternoon unexpectedly to find his wife lying in bed fast asleep with the shutters closed to keep out the bright sunshine.

"There you are. I tried telephoning, but you can't have heard the ringing. I've brought guests," he said unceremoniously and walked out of the bedroom to leave her to struggle to wakefulness.

When she emerged into the living room, she was startled by what she saw there. Three impossibly tall and regal Maasai men were perched on the edge of the couch.

"Ah, Cecily! Meet Leshan." Bill gestured to one of the men bedecked in silver and beaded jewelry, his earlobes stretched and adorned with what looked like large fangs. "He is the chief of the Ilmolean clan and a dear friend of mine," Bill continued. "And these are his trusted *moran*s," Bill said, gesturing to the two other men sitting on the couch, their spears leaning against the wall beside them. "The most famed warriors in Kenya. Any chance of something to eat? I'll make a round of gin for everyone."

"Of course." Cecily left the room, and Bill followed her into the kitchen where she rounded on him. "Bill, I do wish you'd warned me we were having guests."

"I did try to telephone, as I said, but you were sleeping. Don't worry, Leshan and his men aren't expecting much. It is an absolute honor that they wanted to visit our new home."

"Of course." She sighed, and set to making sandwiches for their strange guests, while Bill went back into the living room with a bottle of gin and their finest crystal glasses.

Holding the tray of sandwiches, Cecily went to join them, feeling a headache beginning to form just behind her eyes.

Five days later, Katherine arrived at the front door of Paradise Farm but received no reply to her knock.

"Cecily?" she called as she opened the front door and went into the hall.

"Yes, in here" came a weak reply from Cecily's bedroom.

Katherine walked along the hallway, gave a peremptory knock on the door, then opened it. The room was in complete darkness, the shutters closing off the brightness of the day. She moved to open one.

"Please don't! I have the most dreadful headache right now."

"You poor darling. Did it start today?"

"I've had it on and off for the past week or so, and it's just gotten worse and worse . . . Oh, Katherine, I feel so ill."

"Where's Bill?"

"I don't know, he went out yesterday, or was it this morning? I just wish my head would stop pounding so."

"Right, I'll go and telephone Dr. Boyle immediately. Get him to come over and take a look at you."

"Please don't make a fuss—I've taken more aspirin, and I'm sure it'll start to work soon . . ."

Katherine ignored her and went into the hall to dial Dr. Boyle's number. His wife, Ethnie, answered after a couple of rings. Katherine explained the situation and heard a long sigh at the other end of the line.

"Do you think it's something serious?" Katherine asked.

"Severe headaches can be a sign of high blood pressure, which is very worrying in a woman only a few weeks from giving birth. Has she had any swelling around her ankles, do you know?" Ethnie said.

"Yes, she has. She had them in a bowl of cool water only last time I was here."

"I can certainly ask William to come out to see her, but in truth, Katherine, it would be far better if you could bring her to Nairobi. She may well need urgent hospital treatment."

"I'm not sure how we'd get her there." Katherine bit her lip. "I rode over here, you see, and Bill's got the pickup."

"Well, see if there's anyone else around who would lend you their vehicle, and let me know. I'll speak to William and have him on standby to meet you at the hospital."

"Thank you, Ethnie."

Katherine immediately picked up the receiver again to dial Alice's number; she'd recently returned home from a safari in the Congo.

"Oh, Alice, thank goodness," Katherine said, breathing hard. "Dr. Boyle wants Cecily in the hospital in Nairobi as soon as possible, and we don't have transport. Is your DeSoto at home?"

"It is, and I'll send Arap, my driver, over immediately. Anything else I can do, just give me a call."

"Thank you, Alice."

"The poor lamb. Send her my love."

"I will."

Katherine headed back into the bedroom, where she could hear Cecily's erratic breathing. Opening the shutter so she could at least see her, Katherine tiptoed toward the bed and saw that Cecily's eyes were closed. Tentatively peeling back what felt like a soaking sheet, Katherine took another look at Cecily's ankles. Without a doubt, they were hugely swollen. Swallowing hard to try to stem her panic, Katherine went to the wardrobe in the corner of the room to collect one of Cecily's cotton maternity shifts and a pair of shoes, then moved toward the chest of drawers to find some clean underwear.

The top drawer was full of tiny knitted hats, matinée jackets and booties, all wrapped in tissue paper. And all made by Cecily. The sight of them brought a lump to Katherine's throat as she collected undergarments from the drawer below and looked across at her friend, who was restlessly shifting on her pillow.

"Dear Lord," Katherine whispered as she dragged Cecily's overnight case from beneath the bed, "please let her and the baby be all right."

# 31

I'm afraid her condition is very serious," said Dr. Boyle, coming to find Katherine in the waiting room at the hospital a long three hours later. "Shall we go and talk elsewhere?"

Dr. Boyle led Katherine down a narrow hallway. The heat was stifling, and she was relieved when he opened the door to an office, where a fan was blowing cool air full blast.

"Oh, Lord," Katherine said, tears bubbling in her eyes. Not that the doctor's words were a surprise; Cecily had screamed in pain when Katherine had tried to move her from her bed to get her dressed and then into the DeSoto. In the end, she'd had the driver lift Cecily out of bed as she was and fold her as carefully as he could into the back seat, where Katherine had laid a blanket and a pillow.

"My eyes, my eyes . . . the light is so bright . . ." Cecily had moaned as she'd rested her forearm limply over them. "Where are we? What's happening? Where is Bill?" she had asked as the car began to bump down the track to the road that would eventually take them to Nairobi.

Katherine had never been so grateful to arrive anywhere in her life. Cecily had groaned in agony most of the way, telling Katherine that her head was about to explode, that she couldn't see properly, and that the pains in her abdomen were unbearable.

"What's wrong with her?" she asked.

"We believe she has a condition known as preeclampsia. Have you tried to contact Bill?" Dr. Boyle asked her.

"I rang Muthaiga Club and the British army HQ before I left, but both of them said they hadn't seen him today. He could be anywhere out on the plains, Dr. Boyle. He may not be back for days."

"I see. Then I'm afraid it's down to you to make a decision for your friend. In order to save Cecily, we must operate immediately to remove the baby. As you know," he said, lowering his voice, "Cecily has almost eight weeks left of her pregnancy, so it is a huge risk to the child's life to remove it so early. However, if we don't, then—"

"I understand what you're saying." Katherine put her head in her hands, feeling as though the Sword of Damocles was hanging over it. "If you didn't operate to remove the baby, what are the chances of its survival?"

"Both mother and baby will most certainly die. At least this way, there's a chance to save one of them. But there are no guarantees, and it's important you know the risks."

"Then . . . of course you must operate."

Katherine looked up as another man entered the office, attired in the green that indicated a surgeon.

"Good. Now, this is Dr. Stevens, who only recently arrived from Guy's Hospital in London and is well versed in this particular procedure."

"Delighted to make your acquaintance," Dr. Stevens said, stepping forward and shaking Katherine's hand. "I'll do my best for both of them."

"Thank you."

"Now I must set to work." He gave her a short smile and walked back out of the room.

"Oh, Lord." Katherine shook her head. "What a choice to have to make."

"I know, my dear. Time to trust in that God your father is so keen on. I'd try to contact Bobby if I were you. It might be some time until there's further news."

And indeed it was. Katherine paced the claustrophobic room up and down, side to side, and diagonally a few hundred times before Bobby finally arrived.

"Oh, my God!" she said, running to him and feeling his arms go about her. "I'm so glad you're here."

"There, there. I came as soon as I got word. How is she?"

"No one's told me anything," said Katherine. "I've heard nothing for hours now."

"Come on, let's sit you down."

Bobby led his wife to a chair as she sobbed onto his shoulder. "She's so ill, Bobby, you've no idea. And where is Bill? How could he leave her alone in such a state? And without means of transport?"

"Maybe he didn't realize she was ill; I saw her wi' my own eyes only a couple of days ago, and she looked fine."

"But still, Bill's aware that she's close enough to her time; the very least he could have done was to leave a note saying where he'd gone!"

"Aye, but we both know that Bill is not in the habit o' telling anyone where he is. Besides, the bairn isn't—"

"Does it make that child's life any less valuable because he or she is illegitimate? I don't think so, Bobby, I really don't."

"Now, then, Katherine, you know I didn't mean that, and whatever the circumstances, young Cecily needs her husband by her side."

"God forgive me, I know you didn't, Bobby. I'm just beside myself. Cecily's been in the operating theater for almost four hours now, and there's been no word."

It was another hour before Dr. Stevens appeared in the room. He looked utterly exhausted.

"What news, Doctor?" Katherine stood up, her heart in her mouth. Bobby stood and reached for his wife's hand, squeezing it tight.

"It was touch and go, but I'm pleased to inform you that I did manage to save one of them."

"Which one, Doctor?" Katherine was in an agony of suspense.

"The mother is still in a serious condition—she lost a lot of blood—but she is alive. As for the baby, I—" Dr. Stevens gave a sad shrug. "We got her out and did our best, but I'm afraid she only lived for half an hour before she slipped away."

"It was a girl?" Katherine asked, gulping back the tears. "God rest her little soul."

"Yes, it was. The next twenty-four hours will be crucial for Mrs. Forsythe, but with a fair wind, she should pull through."

"Does she . . . know?" Katherine asked him. "About the baby?"

"Lord, no, she's still heavily sedated and will be for some time. I wouldn't recommend telling her until she's passed the worst."

"I understand. Is it possible to see her?"

Dr. Stevens sighed. "Not tonight, no. We'll be keeping her under sedation until tomorrow. I'm so very sorry, we did all that we could for the little one."

"I'm sure you did. Thank you, Doctor."

"I suggest that you two go home; there's nothing you can do for either of them here." He nodded at them sadly. "Good-bye, now."

When the door had closed behind him, Katherine turned into her husband's arms and sobbed into his chest. "How will we ever tell her, Bobby? She'll be devastated. Everything she's done was to protect that baby, you see. And now . . . and now . . ."

"I know, hen, I know."

Cecily was dreaming that she was emerging from a pool of quicksand, but every time she managed to get her head above it and breathe, it immediately pulled her back down into a dark, terrifying world.

"Please!" she shouted. "Let me go!"

"It's all right, my dear, you're safe with us."

This was a voice Cecily didn't recognize, so she insisted her brain follow her command to open her eyes and see who it was. A blurry image appeared: that of an awful lot of white and a gentle female face with a headdress on top of her golden curls.

*Perhaps she's an angel and I've died and am up in heaven . . .*

"Where am I?" Cecily's voice came out as a hoarse whisper, and it hurt to talk.

"You're in hospital in Nairobi, Cecily. My name is Nurse Syssons, and I've been looking after you. I'm very glad to see that you're back with us."

Cecily closed her eyes again, trying to remember what had happened. Yes! She'd had that terrible, agonizing headache, which had gotten worse and worse . . . She vaguely remembered Katherine and being put in a car, but beyond that, nothing.

"There's no need to be frightened; you're going to be absolutely fine and up and about in no time," the soothing voice of the angel continued.

"I—" Cecily licked her lips, which felt cracked and numb, as if they didn't belong to her. "What has happened?"

"You were very ill when you came in here, so Dr. Stevens performed an operation to make you better," the angel replied. "Here, drink this. Fluids will help you feel more normal."

Cecily felt a straw being eased between her lips. She was desperately thirsty, so she swallowed what she could.

"What was wrong with me? I remember the headache, but—"

"Now you're awake, I'll go and see if I can find Dr. Stevens to come and tell you all about it. You rest there while I pop off to find him."

"But . . . what about my baby? Is it okay?"

Her plea was left unanswered. Perhaps she was still dreaming, she thought, or maybe a better dream would come next. She closed her eyes and let the quicksand of unconsciousness pull her back down.

When she woke again, Cecily opened her eyes almost immediately, feeling much more alert. She was in hospital, she reminded herself as she took in the whitewashed walls and the fan spinning above her. Looking down, she saw she was covered in a sheet. Lifting the arm that was not attached to a drip, she felt beneath the sheet, her fingers walking down to feel the comforting shape of the bump, which, like a deflated balloon, seemed to have shrunk in size.

"Oh, my God, oh, no, please . . ." she whimpered as she turned to her left and saw a blur of faces looking down at her.

"Good afternoon, Mrs. Forsythe, my name is Dr. Stevens, and I performed your operation yesterday," said an unfamiliar man in a white coat. "You were a very sick young lady, but thanks to your friend Katherine, you got here fast enough for us to save you."

"Hello, Cecily," said Katherine, who was standing next to the doctor. "How are you feeling?"

"Never mind how I'm feeling! Is my baby all right?"

"I'm so very sorry, Mrs. Forsythe, I'm afraid there was nothing we could do. We managed to get her out of you safely, but sadly, she died shortly afterward."

"I . . . but . . . what was wrong with her? And why am I here and she . . . it's a she? Oh, my, I so wanted a daughter . . ."

"You—and hence the baby—were suffering from a condition called preeclampsia. If we hadn't operated when we did, then we'd have lost the both of you. I do apologize for being the bearer of bad tidings, but there is no easy way to break the news. Right, I'll leave you with your friends."

Dr. Stevens gave her a sad, sympathetic look, then left the room.

"Katherine?" Cecily reached for her hand. "What does he mean? It can't be true, can it?"

"I'm so very, very sorry, darling, but it is, yes. The baby was just too small and weak to live, you see, and—"

"But why didn't they save her rather than me?"

"I don't think it works like that," said a deeper voice beside Katherine. Cecily looked up into the troubled eyes of her husband.

"Bill . . . you're here, too."

"Yes, of course I am, you're my wife. I came as soon as I heard."

"But what do you mean, it doesn't work like that? I'd have been happy to die . . . really, I would."

"Darling, the baby had to be removed to have a chance of saving both your life and hers," Katherine said. "She wasn't growing properly inside you, you see, because of the preeclampsia. There was a better chance for her to live if she came into the world early, but it was just *too* early, Cecily. You must understand that they didn't save you over your baby. If they'd have done nothing, both of you would have died," Katherine repeated. "Now, perhaps it's best if I give you and Bill some time alone."

As she left, Katherine glanced at Bill and put a finger to her lips as a message to say nothing more.

"I . . . wish . . . I'd have died . . . with her." Cecily shook her head from side to side. "I wish I'd have died, too, really I do . . . oh, Lord, Lord . . ."

"Well, I for one am awfully glad you didn't die," Bill said as he sat down beside her and took her hand in his.

"You don't mean that, Bill. You're probably glad the baby's dead, and I wouldn't blame you one bit!"

"Cecily, I . . . well, they've asked me to ask you if you . . . *we* . . . want to say good-bye to the baby?"

"Why, I haven't even said hello to her yet," Cecily scraped her forearm across her nose to stop it running. "I haven't even said hello."

"Perhaps you can think about it."

"Before they bury her in the ground?"

Tears began to course down her cheeks, and Bill bowed his head before she squeezed her eyes shut.

It was several seconds before her husband spoke again. "Cecily, please believe me, I didn't just marry you to protect your reputation. Hearing the news about . . . this . . . well, it brought it home to me how much I care for you. And I'm truly sorry that our baby didn't live. I am so very sorry, my dear.

If I'd have been there" Bill whispered, his voice quavering. "I should have been there. I . . . well, I love you."

Cecily felt a gentle sensation on her forehead. She opened her eyes and saw that Bill had bent to kiss her.

"Perhaps it's best if Mrs. Forsythe has a little rest now." The nurse with blond curls, who had been hovering outside the door, bustled in and took charge. "You can come back and visit her later."

"She's right, you need to rest now," Bill said gently to Cecily. "I'll be back tonight," he added, squeezing her hand before he stood up and left the room.

"Right, now I'm going to give you a little injection, which will help with the pain," said the nurse. "It'll also relax you a little."

Cecily closed her eyes once more. She didn't care if she was being injected with cyanide, she thought, as she felt a sharp scratch at her elbow. Her precious child was dead, and whatever Bill had said, she still imagined that part of him must be glad that the baby had gone.

# ELECTRA

*New York*
*June 2008*

# 32

I saw my grandmother's eyes were closed and wondered whether she was asleep. It had been interesting to listen to the story of Cecily in Kenya, and I felt sorry that she'd lost her baby . . . but to be honest, I didn't feel I was any closer to discovering what all this had to do with *me*.

"That's . . . real sad," I said in quite a loud voice, to see if I could wake her.

"Yes," Stella agreed, opening her eyes immediately. "The loss of that child affected the course of her life—and mine, too."

"But how? Where do you come into the story? And where was I born, and—"

There was a light tap on the living room door, and Mariam's head appeared around it. "I am so sorry to interrupt, ladies, but the car is waiting downstairs to take you to the airport, Electra."

"Okay, thanks." I turned my attention back to Stella. "Well?"

"Seems like you must be patient for a while longer. And besides," she said, standing up, "I am weary. Recounting the past is always traumatic, especially when it is your own."

"But how is it your own?" I urged her as I followed her into the hallway. "Are you even in it yet?"

"This isn't a movie we're watching, Electra; it's a real-life story, and you have to understand what came before in order to reconcile what happened next. Now you must go, and so must I."

"When can you come back again and tell me the rest?"

"I'm away in Washington, DC, this weekend, but I'll be back on Monday, so let's make a plan for that evening, shall we? Say, eight p.m.?"

"Sure," I said as we stepped into the elevator, irritated that I had to wait four more days until I discovered who I was.

"I'm very proud of you, Electra; you've come so far in such a short time.

Keep up the good work, won't you, honey?" We'd reached the lobby, and she turned to kiss me on both cheeks.

"I'll try," I said, and added a grudging "thanks," remembering just in time that I was the "new me." We stepped out of the apartment building, and the driver opened the door to the limo that was waiting outside. I hopped into the back.

"And maybe you'll tell me who this Miles is next time I see you. Bye, now," Stella said, then grinned at me rather wickedly.

"Hi! How was your journey?" I asked, leaning out of the window as Miles and Vanessa appeared from JFK arrivals and walked toward the limo. (I'd booked it especially for Vanessa because I'd hoped she would think it was cool.)

"All went smoothly," Miles called to me as he helped the driver load their luggage into the trunk.

"Hey, Vanessa, you get in next to me, and Miles, you can sit up front, okay?" I said.

Vanessa did so, and as the driver closed the door behind her, I looked at her pinched features and thought that she seemed to have lost even more weight since I'd last seen her.

"How are you?" I asked as she traced the leather seat with her long, skinny fingers.

"This ride is so cool, 'Lectra," she said, ignoring my question. "I had a joe pick me up in one once. He drove me uptown and screwed me in the parking lot under his apartment building. His wife arrived, and he had ta hide me in the trunk. It was three hours before he came back. Thought I was gonna suffocate in there."

"That must have been scary," I said with feeling. "I got locked in a cupboard by some mean girls at school, and I still can't deal with small spaces."

Vanessa nodded. "Yeah, right? It was bad, real bad, man."

I did my best to try to think of something positive to say but failed miserably, and the two of us lapsed into silence.

"Hey, is that a minibar there?" Vanessa pointed to the box that sat between the two front seats.

"It is, yeah. Want some soda?"

Vanessa gave me one of those looks as if to say "We both know what I really want." "I'll have a Coke."

I opened the little fridge, pulled out the can before I could glance at the miniatures lined up in a neat rack tucked inside the door, and handed it to her.

"Miles has told me that the place you're going to is great," I ventured.

Vanessa stared out of the window, and I didn't blame her. To her it must feel as if she was just going to a different kind of prison, but at least she seemed calmer and a little more responsive than she had at the hospital.

"How far is it, Miles?" I asked.

"About another half an hour; it's near a place called Dix Hills."

Vanessa sniggered. "I told Miles the address suited me just fine."

Thirty minutes later, having driven through what looked like a pleasant residential suburb, we arrived at a gated entrance. As Miles spoke to the guard on duty, I noticed that although from the outside all one could see was tall hedges along the perimeter, behind them stood a high fence topped with barbed wire and bright security lights shining into the distance. Even Miles would struggle to reach the top of it with his outstretched hands.

We drove through the well-kept gardens, and eventually I saw a large and very grand white house.

"Jeez," said Vanessa, staring out of the window, "looks like the president could live here."

"Actually, Landsdowne House and the grounds were bequeathed to the charity that runs the rehab center by the woman who used to live here," said Miles. "She'd lost her only son to his addiction and lived like a recluse until she died ten years ago. It sure is beautiful," he commented, looking at the Doric columns on either side of the steps leading up to the imposing front door.

"I woulda worn my evening gown if I'd known," Vanessa sneered as I saw a woman step out of a car and walk toward us.

"Shit! It's Ida!" said Vanessa, almost cowering in the seat beside me as the woman tapped on the back window. She was around the same skin color as me and dressed in a fabulous bright purple tie-dye kaftan that I wanted to own immediately.

"Vanessa's social worker," explained Miles as he got out of the limo to greet her. He'd already warned me that I should stay out of sight once we arrived and leave Ida to take her in. Turning up with a famous supermodel in tow was not going to get her stay off to a good start with the other patients.

"She looks great," I said to Vanessa, who was positively shaking. She grabbed my forearm.

"You don't know her. She's a witch! If I'da known Ida was coming, I'da stayed right back in the hospital," Vanessa joked morosely. "I ain't gettin' out, and you can't make me."

I watched her as she fumbled in her hoodie pocket, drew out a pack of cigarettes and a lighter, and lit up.

"I know this is going to be so hard for you, but—" I struggled to find the right thing to say to her. "You know what, Vanessa? I'm here for you, and so are Miles *and* Ida, who fought so hard to get you into the best place she knew. We all care. So you gotta go in and get well, and I'll come and visit the first moment I'm allowed to, okay? Once you're better, you and I are gonna start having some fun!"

"You jus' sayin' that. You'll forget all about me while I'm shut up in there and you're gettin' on with bein' rich 'n' famous."

"I haven't forgotten about you up to now, have I? Here." I dug in my bag and brought out a Burberry baseball cap a stylist had sent me a few months back. I wouldn't be seen dead or alive in it, but I'd thought Vanessa would like it.

She looked at it, feeling the fabric. "Is this real?"

"Course it is."

"Cool." She stuck it on her head backward, and for just a few seconds, I saw a flash of childlike pleasure in her eyes. "It's mine?"

"Yup."

"No one'll believe it's real, anyway—and if they do, they'll think I stole it." She shrugged as she stubbed out her cigarette.

"Well, *you* know it is, and that's all that matters. Now, time to go."

"I—" She looked up at me, and I could see there were tears in her eyes. "'Kay."

"I'll be with you every step of the way, promise." Then I opened my arms and gave her the biggest hug I could.

She opened the door, and I watched as she joined Miles and Ida, who immediately embraced her, too, which made me feel a little better. Miles caught my attention and put an imaginary phone to his ear.

"I'll call you," he mouthed as the three of them walked away and up the steps toward the front door.

"Ready to go, ma'am?" the driver asked me.

I nodded. "Yeah." As the limo reversed, I opened the window to let out the fug of cigarette smoke. At that moment, Vanessa turned back toward me, a look of pure fear on her pinched features.

"Love you," I mimed to her as the car sped down the drive. As I gulped back tears, feeling like a mom leaving her child on the first day of school, I realized I truly did.

I was thankful I had a photo shoot the following day because the whole Dix Hills experience the night before had given me déjà vu and freaked me out. But in every report I'd read on the internet, it came out with flying colors, rated by all the professionals as the best in New York state for "young, underprivileged addicts," as the *New York Times* had termed them. Miles had called to say that Vanessa had seemed calm when she'd been introduced to the other young women in her ward.

"The good news is," he'd added, "the hospital in Tucson had stabilized her, so she got to go into the midterm facility right away."

In layman's terms that meant she'd missed out on the detox unit, which I'd read online included padded rooms.

Ironically, I enjoyed the day's shoot, even though it was a good year since I'd done one without taking some form of mood enhancer first.

Xavier, known as "XX," a designer I'd worked with a number of times— including when we'd designed a capsule range of sportswear with a gold lightning bolt down the front of the hoodie, which had sold out within a week—was present at the shoot.

"Are you up for another collaboration sometime soon?" he asked me.

"Maybe," I said as I walked onto the set.

As I automatically went through the usual series of poses, my thoughts flew back to my sketchbook. I'd loved working on the designs in rehab, and it had been way more fulfilling than spending my life making faces . . .

"Wow, Electra, that vacation's sure done you good! You were on fire in front of the lens today." Miguel, the photographer (who I was positive had been born a simple "Mike"), waxed lyrical at me.

"That was amazing, Electra," said Mariam as she sought me out in the dressing room afterward. "I've never seen you look more radiant."

"Aw, shucks, Mariam." I smiled at her. "Miguel and XX have asked me if I want to get some lunch at Dell'anima as we finished so early—"

"Electra, I don't want to be a spoilsport or anything, but—"

"It's okay, I already said I couldn't. I get that it's too soon. I told them I had a meeting to attend, which I do, later. But first, there's somewhere I want to go."

As we pulled up in front of the salon on the corner of Fifth Avenue and East 57th Street, I turned to Mariam.

"Would you go see if Stefano could fit me in?"

"Oh, but . . . even for you, Electra, I doubt it. You know he's always booked up months ahead, and it takes hours to straighten your hair."

"Mariam." I rolled my eyes. "Do you not remember the conversation we had over lunch yesterday with Stella?"

"Of course, but you were only joking, weren't you?"

"I so was *not* joking. Don't worry, I'm gonna go in and speak to him."

I was out of the car before Mariam could stop me. I spoke to the receptionist, who said that Stefano was at lunch, but as it was me, he might see me to say hello.

Stefano and I had met way back when I'd first arrived in New York and Susie had sent me to him before my first ever photo shoot. Being a mix of African American and Italian blood himself, he was used to dealing with my kind of hair. I regarded our sessions as a necessary torture, but I liked him a lot.

"Is he out back?" I asked her.

"Yeah, but—"

I marched through the salon and pushed open the door marked "Private" where Stefano and I had shared countless illicit lines during the very long and boring process of straightening my frizz into submission.

Sure enough, there he was, "powdering" his nose.

"Electra! *Cara*, what are you doing here?" he said as he stood up and kissed me on both cheeks. "We do not have an appointment today, do we?"

"No, we don't, but I was just wondering if you have hair clippers on hand . . ."

Half an hour later, I walked out of the back door with perhaps, if I was being generous, a centimeter of hair left on my head. At first Stefano had refused to do what I wanted, but after threatening to do it myself, he had given me a fantastic fade. He'd tried to fuss over it with creams and a special comb, but I had batted him away—I just wanted it to be natural.

"Oh, my!" Mariam said as I got into the back of the car next to her, and she put her hand to her mouth. She was a terrible actress—every emotion was written on her face.

"So apart from the shock factor, what do you think of the new me?"

"I . . . seriously?"

"Seriously."

Mariam appraised me with her perceptive and critical eye. Eventually she nodded and gave me a big smile. "I think it looks amazing!" We gave each other a high five.

"Can you imagine how many hours of my life I'm going to save having my hair like this? Wasted hours, Mariam. We'll just tell Susie that from now on, if necessary, it's wigs all the way. Now, there's an AA meeting in thirty minutes in Chelsea, so let's head there and stop off at a deli to get some lunch on our way."

In the car on the way home after the meeting, Mariam turned to me. "Electra, would you feel okay if I went home tonight? I . . . need to see my family."

"Of course! I don't want to keep you from them."

"You know that I'll be on my cell if you need me, and it won't take long to come uptown. It's just for the weekend."

I nodded, feeling guilty that I had kept her from her family. When we arrived back at my apartment building, I was pleased to see that Tommy was at his usual post again. As Mariam headed straight inside with no more than a "hello," I stopped for a chat.

"Hi, Tommy. I haven't had the chance to tell you again how grateful I was for you helping me and Mariam that night when I got so . . . sick."

"Electra, you know there's nothing I wouldn't do for you." Tommy's lips made a smile, but I could see sadness in his eyes.

"Listen, if there is anything—*anything*—I can ever do for you, Tommy, please just say the word, okay?"

"Okay, thanks. And by the way, I really dig your new haircut."

"Thanks, Tommy."

As I rode up in the elevator, I decided that I'd attend all my AA meetings in Chelsea from now on. The last thing I wanted was to lose Tommy as a friend, and I knew it would embarrass him if he ever found out I'd heard his confession.

Sitting down on the couch in the living room, I saw I had a missed call from Miles on my cell, so I called him back.

"Hi, everything okay with Vanessa?" I asked him.

"Ida called earlier—Vanessa's settling in okay."

"Great. And how are you?"

"I'm okay. It's kinda weird being back at work and not being able to talk to anyone about all the crazy shit that I—*we*—have been through recently."

"I know, right? I did my first photo shoot today, and it was odd being so . . . *present*, without all the stuff I used to take to mask it."

"Yeah, listen, I gotta go. I have a client calling any moment and I'm playing catch-up here at the office right now."

Miles ended the call, and I stood up and wandered outside onto the terrace. I leaned over the glass railing and looked down on New York; for the first time since I'd arrived home, I felt low. Perhaps it was because the weekend was yawning out in front of me. Normally, I'd be in transit to somewhere, which suited me fine, because weekends were the time when successful people left the city to head to their country homes and spend quality time with their family and friends.

"Hi, Electra," said Mariam behind me. "There's some lentil soup that I made earlier and some salad in the refrigerator for your dinner tonight."

"Thanks."

"Oh, and did you call back that therapist Fi recommended?"

"Yup."

"And?"

"After Fi, she just doesn't sound right."

"I understand, Electra, but you do have to find someone here in Manhattan. That's the third one you've contacted who you've said is a no. Maybe you should just go and meet one of them? See how they are?"

"Maybe, but I just don't want to risk choosing the wrong person and them screwing up my head, you know? I'm in a good place right now, Mariam. And I have plenty of people to talk to if I need them."

"Okay. I don't want to be a nag; it's only because I care, Electra."

"I know, and you've been amazing, Mariam."

"Is there anything else you need before I go?"

"No. You get home now and see your family."

"If you're sure, because—"

"I am. I've gotta learn to live without a babysitter sometime, don't I?"

"If you need me, day or night, just call. Promise?"

"I promise. Please, Mariam, go home!"

"I will. Thanks, Electra, bye."

"Bye."

The door closed behind Mariam, and for the first time in over five weeks, I was alone. "You're going to go down to the gym and lift some weights, have some supper, then get into bed and watch a movie," I told myself, trying to stem the panic. So I went to the gym, had a shower, ate what Mariam had left me for my supper, then got into bed and switched on the TV. It seemed like there was only stuff on about gang warfare or shows set in hospitals, neither of which I felt was suitable for my first night alone. I did my best to concentrate on a rom-com, then a French movie, which normally I would have liked but was *so* noir that I zoned out and started checking my emails on my laptop. I was thrilled to see that there was a long, juicy one from Tiggy. It was also written in French, which made me glad that I had just watched forty minutes of the noir film as a warm-up.

Chère Electra,

How wonderful to get a letter from you (or, in fact, a letter from anyone these days), especially up here in the middle of nowhere. What with the internet signal being so unreliable, I do feel very cut off, which has both its pros and cons. But that's like everything in life, isn't it?

Anyway, today is a good signal day, and so I am sitting outside at a picnic table and looking across a valley (or "glen," as it's called here) that is turning a glorious purple with heather as we speak.

The first thing I wanted to say to you is that I am your sister and even though it was sweet of you to apologize to me, it was totally unnecessary. I can't think of one thing you've ever done or said to me that would warrant an apology—everyone calls me a "snowflake," so that really isn't a problem!—but it was just so lovely to hear from you.

Ma told me awhile ago that you'd decided to get help for your problems and honestly, Electra, I'm so proud of you. It's incredibly difficult to ask for help, isn't it? But making that leap is the important thing. I'm not sure if you're out yet—I haven't spoken to Ma or Maia in a while as I've been so busy—but wherever you are, I just want to send you the biggest hug and tell you that I've been thinking about you every day and praying for you in my own "Tiggy" way. I know you're not a great one for "woo-woo," as you always used to call it, but all I can say is I feel that you're massively protected and will come out of what must have been such a difficult experience better and stronger and more beautiful than you ever were.

As for me, I don't think that I've ever been so happy! Maybe Ma told you that I'd had some health problems recently, and although I won't be swimming the length of Lake Geneva anytime soon, as long as I take care of myself and don't overdo it, I should live a long while yet.

Isn't it amazing how something good often seems to come from the bad? Well, out of my difficult health (and a shooting incident that sounds much more dramatic than it was, but I'll tell you about that some other time), I have met The Love Of My Life. It's a bit of a cliché, because he's a doctor and he specializes in hearts, which is the part of me that's had the problem. His name is Charlie Kinnaird, and I'm ashamed to say that he is still a married man just now, with a wife who you would say was from hell! She's certainly a very difficult character anyway, but the good news is they also have a daughter called Zara, who is from heaven! She's seventeen and is currently at agricultural college, because one day she will take over forty thousand acres of the most spectacular Scottish land you've ever seen (Charlie is actually a laird, which in Scotland means he's a lord, but he never bothers with his title). He's just moved hospitals so that he can be closer to me and Zara and to sort out the estate, which really does need a lot of time and even more money invested in it. Anyway, it's all a bit of a mess at the moment, one way and another, but ironically, as I sit here gazing across the glen, I feel totally content, because I know that I have found the person I want to spend the rest of my life with. And I'm lucky enough to be doing that in the most beautiful surroundings I could ever wish for.

Also, I don't know whether you ever opened your letter from Pa Salt? I opened mine, and it sent me down a rabbit hole into my past. And, well, put it this way, if you think I'm a little "woo-woo," you should meet Angelina, who is my seventy-year-old cousin! It turns out that I am descended from Romany gypsies in Andalusia, which goes a long way to explaining who I am and the weird things I've always seen and felt. When it's all calmed down a little here, I intend to explore that side of me further, and I'm already working alongside the local vet, putting to use what Angelina has taught me about natural healing and treating animals. Eventually, I've decided that I'd like to help humans, too, with my gift, but for now, one step at a time.

Anyway, darling sis, I do hope you haven't forgotten our trip on the *Titan* to lay a wreath on the anniversary of Pa's death; everyone else has said they can come, even CeCe, who you might have heard has moved to Australia. I feel instinctively that it's terribly important we're all there—above and beyond laying the wreath. Could you let me/Ma/Maia know that you can definitely make it? I can't believe it's happening this month!

Well, that's about all for now, though I'd love to hear more of your news, if you get the chance to drop me an email. I'm going to send this off now before the signal disappears.

All my love to you, Electra, and I can't wait to see you at Atlantis.

Tiggy xxx

I smiled as I reread the email just to make sure I hadn't missed anything and felt genuinely happy that Tiggy had found a life that so obviously suited her. Given that I had the whole weekend to reply to her, I decided I'd save writing it until tomorrow morning, when my head would be clearer. I wasn't good at chatty letters—or anything much writing-wise at the best of times— but her long email deserved a decent response.

Thinking of the approaching anniversary reminded me of the armillary sphere that had mysteriously arrived in the garden at Atlantis after Pa's death. The bands had been engraved with our names and some numbers that Ally had said were coordinates of where we were all born, and there was also a quote in Greek for each of us. Ally had handed my details to me in an envelope, but for the life of me, I couldn't remember where it was.

Before I could think about it further, I decided to call Ally. Then, just as I realized it must be something like 2:00 a.m. in Europe, she picked up.

"Electra? Are you all right?"

"Hi, Ally. Yeah, I'm good, really good. I was just about to hang up when I remembered what time it is in Norway."

"Oh, don't worry about that. Night and day have blurred into one recently. Bear's now in full teething mode, and even my legendary energy is being drained."

"I'm sorry, Ally. It must be hard bringing up a kid by yourself."

"Yeah, it is actually," Ally admitted. "And lonely, especially at this time of night."

*Wow*, I thought, raising an eyebrow that she couldn't see. It was one of the few times I'd ever heard Ally admit to being anything less than superhuman.

"Well, here I am, keeping you company, and sending you and Bear a big hug."

"And I've never been so grateful for it. Thanks, Electra. I've just been thinking that I might go home to Atlantis before the rest of you arrive. Maia called to say she's going to arrive early, and I also need some Bear support from Ma, aka 'Grand-Mère.' I seriously can't remember the last time I had more than a few hours' sleep."

"That sounds like a great idea, Ally."

"Anyway"—she cleared her throat—"are you just phoning for a chat?"

"Partly. I got an email from Tiggy, which reminded me that I wanted to ask if you still had my coordinates from the armillary sphere?"

"Of course I do. Why?"

"I guess I must have lost the envelope you gave me and . . . well, I had some time to think in rehab and—"

"You've decided you want to know where you come from," Ally said very gently as a great squawk came from the other end of the line. "Hold on a minute," she said, as I heard some rustling and a kind of suckling noise. "Right, I'm just going to my laptop."

"Okay," I said, realizing that my heart rate was increasing as I waited.

"Soo . . . I'm opening the file now . . . Okay, here we go. Can you write these down?"

"Yeah, sure."

Ally read out the coordinates, which I scribbled down. Then I stared at the set of numbers. "Thanks. So what do I do now?"

"Okay, go onto Google Earth, and on the left-hand side there should be a little search box. Enter the numbers in there—they're in degrees, minutes, and seconds—then it should zoom in to the location the coordinates pin-point."

"Great," I said. "Thanks."

"Electra, are you actually going to look up the coordinates now?"

"Yeah, why wouldn't I?"

"Only that . . . it's a big moment, isn't it, finding out where you're from? Is anybody with you?"

"No, but—" Then a thought struck me. "Hey, Ally, do you actually know where I'm from?"

"Well, when we were first shown the armillary sphere, I looked up all the coordinates briefly to make sure they worked, but honestly, I only have a general idea of where yours lead to."

"Okay, so you're not worried about me looking at it because it's bad or anything?"

"Oh, Electra, it's not as simple as 'bad' or 'good.' I can tell you that my coordinates led me to a museum in Oslo. It now stands where an old theater once was that my ancestor performed in. It turns out that my brother Thom and I were born in a hospital in a place called Trondheim in Norway. Some-time after that, I was privately adopted by Pa."

"Right. And none of us know why he actually chose *us*? He always said he *had*—chosen us especially, I mean."

"No, it could simply have been that we were in need of adoption and he wanted to provide a home for us. Are you worried about looking up where you were found, Electra?"

"Yup." I nodded as I opened up my laptop, went to Google Earth on my browser, and began to follow the instructions Ally had given me.

"I suppose it's a fair assumption that none of us was born into a happy family scenario," Ally said. "If we had been, we wouldn't have ended up being adopted."

"True, true," I agreed as I tapped in the coordinates. "Okay, here goes . . ."

"Want me to stay on the line or leave you to do this alone?"

"Stay, if you don't mind," I said, knowing this was not the moment to be brave. I watched the spinning wheel of death on my screen and sighed. "Sorry, for some reason the internet here is always slower at night . . . Right! Here we go . . . Okay, so we've got the globe and it's closing in and it seems to be moving toward North America . . ." I trailed off, feeling bizarrely like a NASA space reporter as the picture zoomed in on New York City, then onto

Harlem. I watched with my heart in my throat as the pixels on the screen crystallized into a block of buildings on a leafy street and a red pin landed on one.

"Oh, my God!"

"What? Don't keep me in suspense here."

"Jeez!"

"Electra! Please, has it shown you yet?"

"Yup, it has." I nodded to myself. "It turns out I was born right here in New York City. To be precise, in a place called Hale House, which, according to Google Earth, is in Harlem and approximately"—I counted quickly—"fifteen blocks or so from my own front door."

"You're joking!"

"I'm really not, no. Hold on, let me just google Hale House."

I read the few words that were on the screen and sighed heavily. "*Quelle surprise!* I was born—or at least found—in a mother and baby home for addicts and AIDS victims. Get me, hey?" I said as I rolled my eyes.

"Oh, Electra, I'm sorry. Please don't let this upset you. Maia came from an orphanage, too, plus me from a hospital and . . . that's how Pa found us, remember?"

"I know, but . . . Anyway, it's late, Ally, and you need to get some rest. I'm going to go now. Thanks so much for being there for me, and I promise I'll be absolutely fine. Night."

I ended the call before she could stop me and stared at the Wikipedia page, then closed the laptop. It wasn't so much the mother and baby part that I minded—Ally was right to expect most of us to have come from somewhere like that. It was the fact that I was pretty sure that my grandmother had mentioned to me that I came from a line of princesses. And somewhere in my head, this thought had stuck with me.

"You seem to have got that wrong, Granny." I shrugged. "The only genes I inherited are addiction ones. Oh, and maybe a side of AIDS for good measure," I added morosely, knowing that I was being overdramatic but feeling that I deserved a little self-pity right now. At least I'd been tested for HIV and knew I was clear, but that wasn't the point, was it?

Feeling distinctly unsettled, I decided to call the only sister who I knew was in a similar time zone to me and would also offer words of wisdom and comfort. Dialing Maia's number, I waited for her to answer, but her voice mail picked up instead.

"Oh, hi, Maia, it's Electra. Don't worry, I'm doing well and this isn't a panic call or anything like that. I just wanted to see how you were and have a chat, you know? Oh, and also, do you have the translation you did of my quote from the armillary sphere? I'd like to know what it said. Okay, speak soon. Bye."

I stared at the phone for a while, hoping Maia would call back, but she didn't.

I picked up the remote again and started scrolling through the channels, trying not to dwell on what I'd just discovered, but felt panic rising up inside me as I pictured a vodka bottle, which could arrive within minutes if I simply lifted the concierge phone and asked the porter to go fetch it for me. It had become obvious to me that I was definitely more dependent on the booze than I was on the drugs—but one could so easily lead to the other . . .

"*Shit!*" I said as I got out of bed, knowing I was in the danger zone and looking for something to distract me. I was in the kitchen, making a mug of ginger tea, when I heard my cell ringing from the bedroom.

I'd just pounced on it when it stopped ringing. It was Miles. I listened to the message, which said simply, "Call me." In a panic that something might have happened to Vanessa, I did so immediately.

"Hi," he answered after the first ring.

"Is everything okay with Vanessa?"

"As far as I know, yes. I've heard nothing more since this morning."

"Thank God," I said, breathlessly. "I . . . why did you call, then?"

"Because Mariam told me it was your first night by yourself."

"So you're checking up on me?"

"If you want to put it like that, then, yeah, but I'm doing it because I know that the first night alone is always tough. I've been there, remember?"

"Yeah, well, there are a heap of things I could have done tonight, but I decided to stay in," I replied, suddenly defensive.

"And how is it?"

"Oh, it's . . . okay," I lied. "Not much on TV, mind you."

"You getting the feeling that the walls are closing in on you?"

"A bit," I replied, which was the understatement of the century right now.

"That's normal, Electra. And I just wanted to say that I'm here—only a few blocks away, as it happens—so if you need some conversation, all you gotta do is call, as the song goes."

"Yeah, thanks. That's kind of you to think of me."

He chuckled. "One way and another, I've thought of little else. It was quite a ride, these last weeks, wasn't it?"

"It was, yeah."

"The other thing I wanted to ask is if you were busy tomorrow?"

"Er, no. Why?"

"Because I'd like to take you uptown to Harlem and show you around the drop-in center. It's a Saturday, and due to the lack of resources, we've had to close the doors over the weekends, but at least you can see the place itself."

"Wow," I said, struck by the coincidence.

"What?"

"Well . . . it's something I just found out . . ." I trailed off, not sure if I wanted to tell him or not.

"Right."

"Like tonight. A few moments ago."

"And?"

*Remember, you have to trust, Electra.*

"I just discovered that I was found by my adoptive dad in a place called Hale House. It's in Harlem."

"I know it. Everyone in Harlem does. Jeez, Electra, that's a big one! Who told you?"

"My sister Ally. My pa left coordinates for us all to look up if we wanted to know where he found us."

"Okay. You know what Hale House was in those days?"

"Yup, a place where a woman called Mother Hale took in babies whose moms were addicts or had AIDS," I recited from what I'd read earlier.

"And how do you feel about that?"

"I don't know right now. And stop sounding like a therapist!" I said, only half joking.

"Sorry. I'm just worried about you. It's a lot for you to deal with. Want me to swing by and we can talk?"

"No, I'm fine, but thanks for the offer."

"You're sure, Electra?"

"I'm sure."

"Then why don't I pick you up at around eleven a.m. tomorrow?"

"Okay," I agreed. "Do you need my address?"

"Your ever-efficient PA has already given me that, just in case I—"

I smiled. "Had to dash across town to save me when I was so wasted I couldn't remember where I lived?"

"Something like that, I guess, yeah. But you sound like you're doing great, Electra. Really great. And as I said, I'm here if you need me, whatever time it is. I'll keep my cell right by me."

"Thanks, Miles. I'll see you tomorrow, then."

"You sure will. Try to get some sleep. Bye, now."

"Bye."

The smile that had formed on my lips was still there as I switched off my cell. I got the feeling that Miles really cared about me, and that made me feel warm inside.

The question was, I thought, as I decided I didn't need the ginger tea anymore, would I also go and visit the place where Pa had found me tomorrow?

I just didn't know.

# 33

I slept right through until eight and staggered blearily to the bathroom. I gave a small shriek as I saw my reflection in the mirror, having forgotten about my hair transformation.

"Christ, Electra." (I'd decided it was okay to occasionally swear under the privacy of my own breath, although the purists would say that Jesus was always listening.) "What on earth is Miles gonna say? My hair is shorter than his!"

As I went to make myself some coffee, then padded back through the living room to the terrace to enjoy the glorious early June morning, I wondered why I cared.

After a very speedy run around the park, I jogged back inside, had a shower, and towel-dried the centimeter of wiry fuzz on my head. Then I went to my closet, wondering what on earth to wear that would be suitable for my date—no, "meeting"—with Miles. I'd been to Harlem only a handful of times, and that had just been passing through for a shoot on my way uptown to Washington Heights or Marble Hill.

Having tried on most things in my wardrobe that were vaguely suitable, I went back to my original choice of jeans, sneakers, and one of the hoodies with my signature gold lightning bolt zigzagging across the front. It hadn't taken a lot of imagination to come up with a design for XX, but whenever I wore it—and I had it in four different colors—I felt empowered.

I added some mascara and a dab of Vaseline to my lips, then sat down on the couch, waiting for the concierge phone to beep and tell me I had someone waiting for me downstairs.

My cell rang, and I caught a flash of an "M" briefly as I put it to my ear. I felt my stomach plunge as I braced myself for a cancellation from Miles.

"Hi."

"Electra, it's Maia!"

"Oh."

"What?"

"I just thought you were someone else—I have you both under M and you're 'Mi' for short, and . . . Oh, never mind," I gibbered.

"Right. Anyway, sorry I missed your call last night. How are you?"

"Oh, I'm really good, thanks. You?"

"Up very early to drive out to the *fazenda*. Remember I told you about the project I'd started? We run weekends there for kids in the *favelas* who've never been out to the countryside."

"Of course I remember." I looked at the clock and saw it was five past eleven. "Hey, that's a coincidence, because I'm heading to Harlem right now with a friend, to look at a drop-in center for teen addicts that he advises at. I want to do something to help."

"Electra! That sounds fantastic. I'm just so proud of you, I can't even tell you! And yes, of course I still have the quote I translated for you from the armillary sphere. Want me to tell you what it says?"

"Yeah, go for it."

"It's by a very famous Danish philosopher called Søren Kierkegaard: 'Life can be understood only backward, but it must be lived forward.' I think it's beautiful."

I paused as I took in the words and thought that Pa could not have found anything more perfect for me. Tears pricked my eyes.

The concierge phone beeped at me from across the room. I breathed an involuntary sigh of relief.

"Listen, I gotta go, but it's so good to talk to you."

"And you, Electra. Let's both speak next week in a calmer moment. We might be able to pool some ideas on our different projects."

"Yup. Bye, Maia," I said, canceling the call as I lifted the concierge phone receiver. "I'm on my way down."

"Hi."

Miles was sitting in the waiting area and rose as I emerged from the elevator.

"Hi," I said, feeling ridiculously shy.

"Your hair—"

"I know," I said as my hand went protectively toward my head.

"I really dig it," he said, giving me a wide smile. "It suits you."

"I feel, like, very exposed," I said as we walked out of the entrance.

"With cheekbones like yours, I don't think you've got any need to worry."

"Thanks. So where's the car?"

"I don't own one—who wants to drive anywhere in this city?"

"So how do you get around? By limo?"

"Nope," Miles said as he put out an arm to flag down a yellow cab. One screeched to a halt, and he opened the passenger door for me. "Your carriage awaits, m'lady," he said as I climbed in and did my best to fold my legs into the cramped space. "Welcome to my world."

Miles shouted out an address through the glass partition, and the cab set off.

"I guess it's awhile since you've been in one of these, and you're honored, honey, because I only take these on special occasions; most of the time I'm on the subway."

I turned my head away from him and stared out the window so he couldn't see the shame on my face. To be fair, I'd been only sixteen when Susie had whisked me off to New York. One of the original stipulations Pa had insisted on was that I would always have a car to take me to any meeting across town. Things had carried on from there, with the occasional yellow cab taken with the other models I'd lived with in an apartment in Chelsea. The subway remained a subterranean world that I'd never entered.

"You know, Electra, I've been using the subway for years and I'm still here to tell the tale," Miles commented.

I hated that he seemed to be able to guess everything I was thinking. But I supposed I kind of liked it as well.

"So tell me more about the drop-in center," I said as we sped uptown.

"A lot of the volunteers are either parents who have lost kids to drug addiction or ex-addicts themselves. Problem is, since we lost our funding last year, the center is struggling to pay its bills."

"Is it, um, safe here?" I asked nervously as we arrived twenty minutes later in a street full of walk-ups and brownstones.

"Better than it was, yeah," Miles said. "There's still some no-go areas, but a lot of it was rezoned by Bloomberg and gentrified. Harlem's becoming a cool and expensive address these days. Times were when you could buy a brownstone for no more than a dollar around here. I only wish I'd had that dollar." Miles grinned. "So we're here."

We stepped out of the cab, and I tried to dust the smell of stale coffee and fried food off me. Miles walked up to a battered blue door sandwiched between a bodega and a building that was boarded up and covered in graffiti. Above the blue door was a small hand-painted sign, indicating it was the Hands of Hope Drop-in Center.

Miles pressed buttons on a keypad and pushed the door open. He led me along a dark hallway, then into a long, narrow room lit only by skylights. A number of worn melamine-topped tables and plastic chairs were dotted around it.

"This is it," Miles said. "A cousin of a cousin of mine let us build this extension in his backyard for no more than the concrete it took. It's nothing special, but it's made a difference. You want a coffee?" Miles indicated the stainless-steel contraption that sat on a counter at the back of the room. "The refrigerator's broken and we've got no more money to repair it, so it's that or a warm soda."

"I'm good, thanks," I said, suddenly feeling as privileged as the spoiled little rich girl I was.

"On top of that, we got an eviction notice a couple months back—some developer has bought this brownstone, along with five others on the street." Miles sighed. "I know it doesn't look like much, but it was a safe place for the local kids to come and get support, advice, and a real bad but free cup of coffee. It's a tiny project, but even if it's saved one life, then for me, it's been worth it."

"So how much does a place like this cost to run?" I asked.

"How long is a piece of string? I give my services for free, as does everyone else who works here, but in an ideal world, we'd have trained counselors, a twenty-four-seven helpline so the kids can talk to us anonymously, a health professional, and a lawyer who's here every day to give on-the-spot advice, and enough space to house them all."

"Right, well, I want to help if I can," I said, "but I need to think about how we could raise the funds. I've got money, but I guess the kind of place you're talking about could take, like, millions of dollars."

"I'm not asking you to fund us, Electra, but to maybe use your profile to help it happen. You get what I'm saying?"

"I think so. I'm sorry, Miles, I have zero experience in this kind of stuff, so I need you to guide me."

"I was hoping you could get some network coverage for the center," he said. "I could ask some of the kids who've come through these doors over the years if they'd be prepared to be interviewed alongside you and say how it's helped them."

"That's a great idea," I agreed. "I'm up for anything."

"Good. Now, come on, let's go. This place depresses me right now."

As we walked outside, I could hear the sound of rap being played on a tinny radio in the bodega next door.

"So," he said, looking at me as we stood on the sidewalk, "you wanna go take a look at where your pa found you? We can walk to it from here."

I stood in an agony of indecision.

"Listen, let's take a stroll toward it; it's a place you should see anyway while you're here in Harlem," he said.

"Okay," I agreed, my stomach doing one of those weird plungey things and sending my heart rate up at the thought.

As we walked, I tried to stay calm and take in the streets around me. Even though some of the brownstones were crumbling away—windows filled with cardboard and overflowing trash cans—it was obvious from the hipster cafés we were passing and the scaffolding erected around a number of the conversions that this area was being gentrified. We passed a large redbrick building and had to step off the sidewalk and onto the road to pass the crowd that was standing outside. They were all dressed formally, in colorful suits and dresses with matching hats, and as I stepped back onto the sidewalk, I saw a car decorated with flowers pull up outside.

"That's Sarah and Michael getting hitched," Miles commented. "She's one of my success stories; I helped her fight to get an apartment when she was living in a women's shelter," he added as a young woman dressed in an enormous wedding gown of shiny white satin maneuvered herself out of the back seat of the old car. The crowd waiting outside what I now realized was a church clapped and cheered her and started to funnel inside.

"Let me go give her a hug," Miles said and walked back swiftly toward the bride. The woman turned and smiled at him as he embraced her.

"So you know people around here?" I asked as he came back.

"Sure, I do. I moved here five years ago, after I got clean. That's my church," he added as we watched a man who had to be the bride's father take his daughter's hand and lead her inside. "It's supernice to see a happy ending—it fires me up to keep pushing for help for these kids," he continued as he began to walk faster and I doubled my stride to keep up with him.

"So what kind of lawyering do you actually do?" I asked.

"After law school, I was recruited by a top firm to join their litigation department—that's where lawyers bill the most hours—and I made money hand over fist. Which I then spent as fast as I could, putting it up my nose and pouring it down my throat. The pressure was something else. Then I got clean, and even though it meant a big salary cut, I decided to transition to a smaller firm, where I get a lot more opportunity to take pro bono cases."

"What are they?"

"Cases like Vanessa's. In crude terms, my law firm lets me take on charity cases for free. And yeah, I wish I could do more, but even I gotta pay my bills."

"That makes you sound like a very good person, Miles," I said as the road led upward and I figured we were heading in the direction of Marble Hill.

"It makes me someone *trying* to be a good person, but I fail more often than I succeed." Miles shrugged. "But that's okay, too. Since I came back to Jesus, I understand that it's all right to fail as long as you are trying."

"What do you mean, you 'came back to Jesus'?" I asked him.

"My whole family—in fact, my whole community in Philly—was centered around the church. It was like one great happy family, and I had a whole load of aunties, uncles, and cousins who weren't related to me by blood but through Jesus. Then I went to Harvard, moved into the world of big bucks, and felt big with myself—bigger than my family, my church, and the Lord himself. I decided I didn't need any of them, that the church was some human conspiracy to keep the workingman down and in his place— I'd read some Karl Marx at Harvard." Miles gave a deep throaty chuckle. "I was a total asshole back then, Electra. Anyway, you know what happened next—eventually I found my way back to Jesus and my family. You ever sing with a choir?"

"Are you joking? I've never sung in my life."

Miles stopped right where he was in the street. "You cannot be serious."

"I am. As a kid, I used my vocal chords to scream, not sing, so my sisters told me."

"Electra"—Miles lowered his voice—"you simply cannot be a black woman who doesn't sing, even if it's not in tune. In fact, I can't think of one single guy or girl I know who doesn't. It's, like, part of our culture."

Miles began to walk again; then a mellow sound came out of his mouth. He was humming just three notes.

"You try."

"What? No way!"

He hummed the three notes again. "Come on, Electra, everyone sings. It makes them feel happy. 'Oh, happy day,'" Miles suddenly sang out very loudly and perfectly in tune. I looked around at the passersby, and they took no notice as Miles continued with a melody even I recognized.

He grinned. "I'm embarrassing you, aren't I?"

"Yup. I told you, I didn't grow up in a household that had your traditions."

"It's never too late to learn, Electra. And one day, I'm gonna take you to church and you're gonna see what you've been missing all these years. Okay." Miles's long legs stopped abruptly in front of a brownstone. "This is it, Hale House, where your pa found you."

"Oh, er, right."

"And that there," he said, pointing at a statue of a woman with a very kind face holding out a hand toward me, "is Mother Clara Hale. She's the stuff of legend around here. You were born in 1982, weren't you?"

"Yeah."

"I was just trying to work out whether Mother Hale would have been here when you were. And yes, she would have been."

I glanced at this woman, who might or might not have held me in her arms, then read the words engraved on the plaque next to the statue. Clara Hale had initially cared for her own three children, then begun taking the neighborhood children into her care. Eventually, she had started looking after babies whose parents suffered from substance abuse and later HIV. Apparently, in 1985, President Ronald Reagan himself had called her a "true American hero."

I turned to Miles. "So the fact I was found here . . . does it mean that my mom was an addict or died of AIDS? Like, did she take in regular babies, too, or what?"

"I don't know, but yes, she was known for nursing babies of addicts—especially heroin—through their inherited addiction. Having said that, no baby was ever refused entry, and I'm sure many desperate new moms beat a path to her door whether or not they were addicts."

I looked up at Miles, wondering if he was just trying to make me feel better.

"Wow, right, well . . . Should I take a picture or something? Post it on

Facebook and show all my fans the place where I was found?" I rolled my eyes at the irony, but I was suddenly feeling close to tears.

"Hey, come here." Miles pulled me close to him and gave me a hug. "You don't know anything right now, so stop second-guessing. Maybe it's time you went off and did some research on your long-lost family."

"Perhaps," I said, not really listening because I was *soo* enjoying the hug.

"The good news is, honey, that wherever you came from, you turned out to be a real success story. And that's the most important thing of all. Now," Miles said, pulling away from me and looking at his watch, "at the risk of seeming rude, how about I put you in a cab? I have a heap of work to catch up on after my three weeks of being AWOL, and it's pointless going downtown with you only to come back up again."

"I . . . okay, fine." I shrugged as one came past and Miles hailed it.

"Thanks for coming up here, Electra," he said as I got inside. "I'll be in touch about Vanessa as soon as I hear anything. Take care, now, and remember, call me anytime you need to."

With a wave, Miles was gone, and I felt my heart drop like a stone. If I was honest, I'd been imagining lunch with him at one of those intimate hipster cafés; besides anything else, I was starving.

Twenty minutes later, I walked under the canopy of my apartment building and saw that even Tommy wasn't at his post ready to greet me. I went inside and up in the elevator, feeling tearful. Seeing the miserable concrete shed that represented what little help kids like Vanessa could expect, then the truth of my own sad origins, plus the fact that I'd felt so close to Miles as we'd walked through Harlem together only for him to dump me back down to earth and shove my backside into a cab as if he didn't care about me at all . . .

Trying not to dwell on it, I got a Coke and some leftover lentil soup from the fridge and sat down to eat but immediately felt sick to my stomach as guilt ran through me like the streak of designer lightning on my chest. How could I sit here in my flashy apartment with a closet full of even flashier clothes, feeling sorry for myself, while there was so much suffering going on not more than a few miles away?

I drank the Coke can dry and grabbed another, feeling that scary black cloud beginning to descend—the one that I'd always "medicated" against with alcohol or drugs. I checked my cell and saw it was just past one thirty. My AA meeting wasn't until 5:00 p.m., which gave me three and a half hours to sit here with only the insides of my currently messed-up head for company.

"Shit," I muttered, knowing I needed to talk to someone. Picking up my cell, I saw there was a missed call from Zed. I automatically went to return the call, then stopped myself just in time. Zed was *not* good news, because he'd arrive laden with all the substances I needed to steer clear of. I switched to my address book and scrolled down to find Mariam's number. Even though the last thing I wanted to do was to bother her on her first day off since I got back, it had been drummed into me by everyone around me that if I was struggling, I had to make a call and get help.

I dialed the number and it rang, then went to voice mail.

I pressed the "end call" button; she was probably having a wonderful day, spending quality time with her family . . .

"Her family," I muttered. "And where is mine? Where do I belong? Yeah, right! In a home for unwanted babies!"

I even wished that Stella was in town so I could talk to her, find out how come she'd let her granddaughter end up there. Feeling my anger rising, I knew I needed to divert my attention urgently. I stood up and walked through the living room and onto the terrace, holding my cell and waiting for Mariam to call me back. Looking over the tops of the densely packed trees that covered Central Park, I sat down and then thought about Miles and the way he'd made it so obvious today that ours was only a business relationship. I decided I should have an imaginary conversation with Fi about the situation.

Fi: "So, Electra, how do you feel about Miles?"

Me: "I'm . . . confused," I admitted.

Fi: "And why do you think you're confused?"

Me: "Because even though he's not my type *at all*," I underlined, "I think I might have feelings for him."

Fi: "Okay. And are these feelings for a friend or a more emotional attachment, do you think?"

I paused as I considered this question.

"Initially, I guess I thought it was just friends; he's the first person I've ever met who I could identify with. I mean, he's black, brought up in a middle-class family, got a scholarship to Harvard, and has had a successful career. Oh, yeah, and of course a drug problem."

Fi: "I can imagine that was a very powerful experience. Did it make you feel less alone?"

Me: "Yeah, it did, a lot. Like, maybe because we were in rehab, I didn't have to pretend to be anyone other than myself. I was"—I searched the air for the right expression—"comfortable with him. Like I didn't have to explain anything to him."

Fi: "So when did that feeling of having a friend tip over into something romantic?"

I winced as she—or rather *I*—said that, but it *had* to be said.

Me: "It was that night of Vanessa's suicide attempt. I was at the hospital, and then Miles joined me. He put his arm around my shoulder, and I fell asleep against his chest. It felt like . . . home."

At this point, Fi would have handed me the box of tissues, but there weren't any out here on the terrace, so I swept a hand across my eyes, then grabbed my ringing cell like a lifeline.

"Hi, Mariam."

"Electra? It's me, Lizzie, from rehab, remember?"

"Of course I do! Sorry, Lizzie, I was expecting my PA to call me back. It's great to hear from you. How are you?"

"The honest answer to that question is not good. I've left Christopher."

"Oh, my God! Like, how? Why?"

"Listen, it's a long story, but I was wondering if you're busy just now?"

"No, not at all. Fire away," I said, thinking how a conversation about Lizzie's shit of a husband would fill in the time nicely before I left for AA.

"Actually, I'd prefer to tell you in person. Can I come and see you?"

"What? From LA?"

"I'm not in LA, Electra. I'm here in New York. And I've just discovered that the bastard has called the bank to cancel all my credit cards. I'm at JFK and don't have enough money to get a cab, let alone a hotel room. Oh, dear—" I heard a sudden sob on the other end of the line.

"Oh, no, Lizzie. I'm so sorry. What a vindictive prick!"

"I know. I bet he was scared that I would max out the cards. Obviously I need to see a lawyer, but . . . I'm so sorry to call, I had no one else to turn to."

"Lizzie, you go and get yourself in a cab right now. I'll tell the concierge to pay for it once you arrive here. Do you have my address?"

"Yes, you gave it to me the day I left The Ranch, remember? I'm so sorry, Electra, I—"

"Please stop saying 'sorry,' Lizzie. We'll talk when you get here, okay?"

"Okay. See you soon."

I stood up and hung over the balcony and screamed out unrepeatable words on Lizzie's behalf into the toxic Manhattan air. As I was halfway through spelling out a particularly juicy one, my cell rang again.

"Electra? It's me, Mariam," she said, panting slightly. "Are you all right?"

"Yeah, I'm fine, really."

"I'm so sorry I didn't answer my phone immediately, but I'm actually close by and can be with you within ten minutes."

"No, no, I'm good, Mariam, honestly. I'm sorry for interrupting your day."

"Oh, okay. Phew." She chuckled. "Well, I'm here if you need me."

"Sure, thanks, Mariam. See you on Monday." I ended the call, then grabbed my wallet and went down to the concierge to give him the cash to pay for Lizzie's cab. I was feeling much brighter. Simply because I had a friend—a *real* friend—and it made me feel good to think she had turned to me for help.

An hour later, I settled Lizzie on the terrace with a "nice cup of tea," as she always called it. She looked so bedraggled, it was now *me* having the maternal feelings rather than the other way around.

"Oh, Electra, it's such a cliché." She sighed and sipped her tea. "Chris has been having an affair with one of the actresses on his new film. She's young enough to be his daughter and incredibly beautiful. She's Brazilian, six feet to his five-five, and . . . Maybe it was the time in rehab that gave me some modicum of self-worth back, but I just . . . well, I blew up."

"How did you find out?"

"Apart from the stench of exotic perfume that hung in my bedroom when I arrived home?" she said. "As well as the bright red lipstick made by a brand I would never even contemplate buying still sitting on my dressing table? On *my* dressing table! Can you believe it?" Lizzie shook her head. "It was like she was marking her territory—she obviously wanted me to know, and my poor stupid husband hadn't even noticed it."

"So you confronted him?"

"I did, yes, and forgive me for saying so, Electra, but only after I downed half a bottle of one of his most expensive wines. I mean, I've known he's played away for years, but somehow that lipstick was just so blatant—like she didn't even care that she was screwing a married man with two kids—that I realized what a fool I'd been."

"Was he shocked?" I asked, *really* feeling like Fi now.

"Totally, absolutely, completely, yes." A hint of a smile appeared on Lizzie's oddly shaped lips. "He gave me the usual rubbish about how it was nothing, that they'd been on location together and I'd still been away when they'd returned, and one thing had led to another and . . . You know what? I can't even be bothered to repeat his pathetic excuses. He said he would end it immediately, blah blah blah, but I just grabbed my holdall that I'd packed before he arrived home—late for dinner as usual, of course—then drove to LAX. I got on the next flight to New York—first class, I might add," she said with a wink, "and landed to find out that he'd stopped all my credit cards."

"Have you told him you want a divorce? I mean, *do* you want a divorce?"

"Absolutely, I do. That man has played me for a fool for years, treating me like some glorified nanny and housekeeper whilst he went on a shagathon around LA!"

I had to giggle at Lizzie's unusual expletives, which still sounded very polite when spoken in her English accent.

"What about the kids?"

"As you yourself said to me, Electra, they're all grown up now, with their own lives. The worst thing is, I think they probably knew what their father was like." Lizzie sighed. "I called Curtis, my eldest, from the airport—I think I was still a bit drunk at the time, because I'd had the other half of the bottle in the cab on the way—and he asked me why it had taken me so long. I'm not sure that Rosie, my youngest, will feel the same—she's always been the apple of her daddy's eye and spoilt rotten—but at least I have one of them on my side."

I watched as Lizzie stared across the Manhattan skyline and felt an enormous wave of affection for her.

"You know what, Lizzie?"

"What?"

"I am so proud of you for what you've done. Your new life begins today."

"Well, it certainly doesn't if the rat fink is going to cut me off without a bean."

"All that can be sorted out, I'm sure. Maybe Miles—that tall black guy at the rehab clinic—could help you or knows someone who could. He's a lawyer. And you can stay here with me for as long as you want. I could use the company, to be honest."

"That's awfully kind of you, Electra. Maybe just for the weekend—I do have some money in a checking account I started when I was first living in New York before I met Chris, so I can go in on Monday to get it. It'll at least tide me over for a month or two whilst things are sorted out."

"Don't worry about money, Lizzie, I won't let you starve."

"Even though I'm in a mess, I do love New York," she said as her eyes wandered over Central Park. "That's why I decided to head for here, because it's a place where I feel at home. I thought I could maybe get some kind of a job," she continued. "I mean, I know I'm not qualified for anything much, but I am computer literate. And besides, whether the rat likes it or not, I will end up getting fifty percent of everything he has. I just hope I don't crack and run back to him."

"Lizzie, I'm not going to let you do that. You keep me off the hard stuff, and I'll keep you safe from your husband. Is that a deal?"

Lizzie smiled. "It's a deal. Electra, I just can't thank you enough for taking me in; you really are such a wonderful person."

"I'm not, but thanks anyway," I said as I saw Lizzie give a great yawn. I checked the time on my cell. "How about I show you to your room and you take a nap? I've gotta go to my AA meeting."

"Perfect," Lizzie said as we both stood up. She grabbed her carry-on from the corridor, then followed me into the bedroom recently vacated by Mariam. "This is far nicer than the hotel I was thinking of checking into," she said as she stood by the full-length windows.

I showed her the buttons to press on the remote control to bring down the blinds and left her to settle in. As I went down in the elevator, I thought how great it was to have someone who seemed to need me as much as I needed them.

# 34

Thanks so much for coming, Miles," I said as I ushered him into the living room on Monday evening.

"It's a pleasure, Electra," he said as I tried not to swoon over how god-damned handsome he looked in his suit and tie. I'd called him earlier today to ask if he had a free slot to see Lizzie. He'd said he didn't but could come after work.

"Hi, Lizzie."

"Hi." Lizzie stood up and shook his hand. "This is so kind of you, Miles."

"Don't even think about it. Any friend of Electra's is a friend of mine."

"I'll leave you two to it, shall I? Can I get you anything to drink, Miles?" I offered.

We both eyed the glass of white wine that Lizzie was cradling. It was me that had asked Mariam to put it on the list for the home delivery from the grocery store; I had to face the fact that alcohol would appear regularly in my daily life.

"If you've got Coke, I'll take one of those." He grinned at me.

"Oh, boy, do I have plenty of that." I grinned back and left the room, wondering whether that last exchange counted as a flirt.

Mariam was working on her laptop at the kitchen table. I pulled a Coke out of the refrigerator, debating whether I should offer Miles a glass or just hand him the can. The glass won because of his sharp suit.

"It's time you were going home," I said to her as I poured the Coke into the glass.

"Actually, I just need a few minutes of your time to run through your schedule for the next few days. It's been like Grand Central Station here this afternoon."

I took the Coke in to Miles and left it on the table because he and Lizzie were already deep in conversation, and gave myself a metaphorical hug. It *had* been busy in the apartment today, but nicely busy. Susie had come to see me, having heard about my new haircut, and she'd pronounced it "fabulous!" She'd then ruined it by telling me I now had a head that was ready to be covered in any way the client and the photographer chose. I'd told her I wanted Patrick, my favorite photographer, to do a shoot just for me, completely *au naturel*, and he was now booked for sometime next week.

Susie, who was originally English, and Lizzie had gotten along like a house on fire and had sat there bitching to their hearts' content about their exes while I dealt with a rail of clothes that had arrived from a designer and picked out the ones that I wanted to try on later and wear on high-profile occasions. Lizzie had then joined me and *ooh*-ed and *aah*-ed over a jacket that I'd put in my pile of yesses. Given that her carry-on had contained only her array of makeup, skin care products, and a change of underwear, her wardrobe would definitely need boosting.

"Right," said Mariam as I arrived back in the kitchen. "Hopefully, we won't be disturbed. How are you feeling about flying up to Quebec for *Marie Claire* the week after next?"

"You can confirm it."

"Great. Oh, and also XX sent me an email, asking again if you could design another capsule collection for him."

"I—"

I paused before I answered. My sketchbook was full of designs I could use for the project, but then I thought that surely my *own* name was big enough to enable me to do it by myself and not let someone else in on the profits. And *then* . . . I thought of Saturday's visit to the drop-in center, and the vaguest of ideas began to form in my mind . . .

"Tell him no, I'm not interested," I said firmly.

"Okay. Oh, and remember, your grandmother is due here at eight tonight."

"Of course, thanks."

I watched Mariam close her computer. Maybe it was because I'd been desensitized to the feelings of others for so long—certainly since I'd met Mariam—that I was now overly sensitive. But there was something about her that looked and felt different.

"Are you okay?" I asked her.

"Yes, of course. I am the same as I always am," she replied, obviously shocked by my question.

"Good, right, well, you'd better go home now. Lizzie has said she's going to take over the cooking while she's here, so at least that will relieve the burden on you."

"Oh, it really wasn't a problem, Electra. You know I love cooking."

It was probably me, but I thought I saw a slight film of water in her eyes as she stowed her laptop in her leather satchel and stood up.

"Good night, Electra," she said as she walked out of the kitchen.

"Bye, Mariam."

I sat back down at the table and opened my laptop to check my own emails. I replied to the realtor who was handling the purchase of the Hacienda Orquídea and saw that Tiggy had sent out an official round-robin email to all my sisters, reminding us about our cruise. Then I turned on the small kitchen TV to keep me company so I wouldn't think about the fact that Stella Jackson was due here in just under an hour's time. And how I felt about her after discovering where Pa had found me. CNN was doing its usual tick-tack of news bulletins and share prices; then I winced out loud as a very familiar face came onto the screen.

"Mitch Duggan announced today that he will be joining the Concert for Africa, which will be held at Madison Square Garden this Saturday. A host of musicians and celebrities are set to attend, including, it is rumored, Senator Obama, the presidential candidate for the Democratic Party."

A picture of Obama appeared; then the camera cut back to the reporter.

"Stella Jackson, the leading civil rights activist and lawyer who works with Amnesty International, has joined me in the studio to explain the continuing AIDS crisis in Africa and how the concert will help raise awareness of the problem."

And there was *my* grandmother, sitting as cool as a cucumber in the chair right next to the reporter.

"Thank you, Cynthia. I can tell you that more than awareness is needed at this point," Stella said. "We need direct action and aid from our politicians. HIV and AIDS have ravaged eastern and southern Africa, and three-quarters of all global AIDS deaths last year were recorded in those regions. The highest impact is on babies and young children, who—"

I was so shocked, I didn't really listen to what she was saying, just stared at her open-mouthed.

I went to the hallway to shout for Lizzie and Miles to come see my grandmother on TV, but the door to the living room remained closed. By the time I got back to the kitchen, the interview had finished.

"Damn it," I muttered, then, needing a distraction until the two of them finished talking, I went to my bedroom to begin to try on the clothes I'd pulled out from the rack earlier. Still, my mind refused to switch off from the person who was Stella Jackson, aka "Granny."

"Miss Uber Civil Rights activist, who still managed to lose her *own* grand-daughter to Hale House somewhere along the way," I growled as I squeezed myself into a pair of tight black leather trousers that made me feel like a predatory panther and suited my mood perfectly. "Bet the interviewer would have liked to hear *that* story!"

"Electra! We're finished! You can come in now," I heard Lizzie say from the hallway.

"Coming," I called back.

"You look amazing," Lizzie said as she ushered me through into the living room. "You going out somewhere?"

"No, just trying on the stuff I got sent today and working out what suits me."

"Well, those leather trousers are like a second skin on you. Aren't they, Miles?"

I turned to see Miles's expression, and it was fair to say that it was an extremely satisfying one. Very satisfying indeed. Which cheered me up a lot.

He saw us both staring at him and averted his eyes. "Yeah, you look great, Electra."

"Thanks. And you'll never guess who I just saw on CNN—my grandmother! I had no idea she was famous."

Miles and Lizzie looked at me nonplussed.

"Who is your grandmother?" he asked.

"Her name is Stella Jackson."

"That definitely rings a bell," said Lizzie.

"Hold it right there! You're saying *the* Stella Jackson is your grandma?" asked Miles.

"Um, yup, that's her name. Do you know of her?"

"Hah!" Miles slapped his well-muscled thigh. "In the civil rights world, Stella Jackson is an A-lister goddess! At Harvard, they speak her name in hallowed tones. She was right there when Malcolm X was shot in the Audubon Ballroom, and at the rally in Washington when Martin Luther King, Jr., made his 'I have a dream' speech. She came to talk to us law students at Harvard, and I freely admit I sat there in tears. She's your grandmother?" he asked again. "I thought you had no blood relations, Electra?"

"I kinda found her recently," I said, feeling guilty I hadn't mentioned it to him.

"Well, I'll be damned!" Miles swore, so I knew this was *big*. "Wow wow wow! And you had no idea who she was?"

"Nope, she never said," I replied, seeing what amounted to hero worship in Miles's eyes.

"It's rumored that if Obama wins the presidency, she'll have some form of role as an adviser. Those are some genes you've inherited there, girl. And actually, now I look at you, you're the living image of her, especially with your new haircut," he added.

"Well, it's nice to know your grandmother is a powerful woman, isn't it?" said Lizzie, somehow sensing my tension. "I'm off to powder my nose after that very long and stressful conversation," she added, exiting stage left to the bathroom.

"Was it a good chat with Lizzie?" I asked him, determinedly changing the subject as I tried to sit down in my tight pants.

"Yes and no." Miles shrugged. "I did my best, but she's going to need a California guy to represent her. Divorce law's very different over there, but I've given her the name of a good lawyer I know. Sounds to me as if that husband of hers will screw her to the wall if he can. The good news is, the law is on her side. And there's nothing he can do about that, apart from draw the process out. Lizzie needs some cash—and a home—fast. It's great of you to take her in, Electra. You're a good person," he added. "Mind you, knowing your heritage, I'm not surprised. I'm still in shock."

"Well, when I see Stella, I just might ask her how I ended up in Hale House." I eyed him for a few seconds, and I knew he'd gotten the implication. "Anyway, how's Vanessa?"

"Doing real well; Ida says she should be ready for a visit by the weekend. I'd better be heading home now. Work is crazy at the moment. If you see your grandmother, tell her I'm a fan. I'll call you about Vanessa when I hear. Night, Electra."

"Night, Miles, and thanks," called Lizzie, appearing in the hallway as he closed the door behind him.

I sighed heavily.

"What's up with you?" Lizzie stood there eying me, her hands on her hips.

"Nothing, nothing."

"There's obviously something. Is it to do with Miles?"

I paced restlessly around the living room. My anxiety and irritation weren't helped by the fact that Lizzie was pouring herself a fresh glass of white wine from the bottle on the table.

"Come on, Electra, what's eating you?" Lizzie asked as I watched her take a large gulp.

"Oh, this and that." I shrugged, knowing that if I wasn't careful, my anger would boil over like a volcano and I didn't want to traumatize poor old Lizzie.

"It must be to do with Miles. Are you two in a relationship?"

"What? God, no! Hah!"

"Okay, Electra, keep your hair on." Lizzie grinned at me. "It's just obvious that he thinks the sun shines out of your bottom, from the way he looks at you."

"Yeah, well, that's just peachy but . . . Listen, Lizzie, I didn't say anything to Miles earlier because I thought I'd never get rid of him, but my grandmother is due here any second. And the thing is"—I looked at her hard—"it's her I'm really pissed at."

"Right." Lizzie took another couple of large gulps of wine and nodded. "I'll go and make myself scarce, shall I? Central Park is so lovely on a summer's evening."

The concierge phone beeped, and I went to pick it up. "Yup, send her up."

"Good luck, Electra. I'll see you later, sweetheart," said Lizzie as she grabbed her bag and walked toward the door.

It banged shut behind her, and I only just managed to refrain from draining what was left in her wineglass to calm my nerves. Instead, taking some deep breaths in, I was relatively composed by the time the bell rang to announce that Stella Jackson was at my front door.

I went to open it, and there she stood, wearing the same smart tweed jacket I'd seen her in on TV earlier. She must have come straight from the studio.

"Hi, Electra, how are you?"

"Good, thanks, Stella. How are you?" I asked, smiling at her through gritted teeth.

"I'm well, thank you, dear. I've had a very busy but productive weekend."

"That's, um, good, then." I nodded as I watched her walk to her favorite chair and sit down. "Can I get you some water?"

"Thank you, honey, that would be great. Oh, my, those pants you've got on sure are tight," she commented as I poured some water into a glass and handed it to her. "I like your hair, by the way; no one would doubt now that the two of us are related."

"No," I agreed as I sat gingerly on the couch, wishing to God I'd changed out of these pants before she'd arrived.

"How has your weekend been, Electra?"

"It's been . . . interesting." I nodded. "Yup, interesting."

"May I ask in what way?"

"Oh, I discovered where I'd been found by my father."

"Did you, now?"

"Yup, I did."

"And where would that be?"

I stared at her hard then, wondering if she was simply being disingenuous or was playing some kind of weird game that I didn't know the rules of.

"Surely you must know?"

"Why, yes, I do, I was just checking to see you'd gotten your facts right."

"Oh, I've got my facts right, all right." I nodded, my teeth biting on my bottom lip to stop the anger exploding from behind them. "It was Hale House in Harlem, the place where they cared for babies of addicts and AIDS sufferers."

I kept my gaze right on her face and was pleased when she pulled her eyes away from mine first.

"So you knew that was where I was found?" I said.

"Not at the time you were actually taken there, but after the fact, yes. Your father told me."

"Okay. So you're saying you didn't know that I—your granddaughter—was actually in a home for young addicts and HIV sufferers?"

"Yes, I am saying that."

"I mean, *you*, who I saw earlier on TV talking about the AIDS crisis in Africa, *you*, the great champion for civil rights in this country, *you* didn't know that your own granddaughter was left at a place like that?" I stood up then, partly because I could no longer sit in the pants but also because it made me feel strong to tower over my grandmother, who I saw had slumped from her normal elegant posture right down into the chair. I noticed she suddenly looked old, and there was something in her eyes as she gazed past me into the distance. I realized it was fear.

"Yeah, I'm sure that the media would just lap this story up, wouldn't they?" I continued. "Especially given my profile. I bet you wouldn't like that, Granny dearest?" I almost spat.

"You're right, I wouldn't, because yes, it would destroy my reputation. But I guess if I was you, it would be what you thought I deserve. And maybe I do deserve it."

I began to pace the living room. "The burning question is, where the hell was my mother in all this? Who was she? And why, if she was in such big trouble, weren't you there for her? And for *me*? How you can sit there spouting your shit on TV, with everyone thinking you're some kind of a goddess of goodness . . . Jeez, Stella! How do you live with yourself?!"

"I—" Stella gave a long sigh. "As I said, at the time I didn't know."

"You didn't *know* that your daughter was a drug addict or an AIDS victim or had a baby girl?"

"No, I did not."

"Then where the hell were you?!"

"I was in Africa at the time, but it's a long story, and you can't begin to understand it until I've told you what happened before your mother was even born."

"Does it really matter what led up to it? It's not going to change the fact that you weren't there for me or my mom when we needed you, is it?"

"No, and you have every right to get angry, Electra, but please, I beg you, just hear me out. Because if you don't, you're never going to understand."

"To be blunt, Stella, I don't think I'll ever understand, but okay"—I sighed—"I'll try. As long as you can swear to me that I or my mother or you or some goddamned relative of mine gets into the story!"

"I can swear that, yes," she said. I saw her draw a handkerchief out of her purse—the kind that the queen of England always carried—and that her hand shook a little. I immediately felt sorry for her. She was old, after all.

"Listen, I'm going to change out of these ridiculous pants and come back in some comfy ones, okay?" I said.

"Okay. You like hot chocolate?" she asked me.

"Yeah, Ma—my sort-of mom—used to make it for me before bed."

"Well, I make the best darned hot chocolate in the whole of Brooklyn. If you have the ingredients, I'm going to make us both a mug of it."

"I do. Great, fine."

Ten minutes later, we were both sitting back in the living room, nursing what even I had to admit was a pretty good hot chocolate. I was still trying to feed the anger in my belly, but somehow it had all dissipated, which was kind of weird because normally I was good at holding grudges—too good.

"Okay, so you remember that last time I told you Cecily had just lost her baby?"

"I do, yes. Does the story get a little more relevant to me in this part?"

"Electra, I swear, this is the part of the story that you'll hardly believe."

# CECILY

*Kenya*
*September 1940*

*Traditional beaded collar of a Maasai woman*

# 35

Cecily sat back and wiped her sweating brow, stuck the trowel into the soil, then stood up and walked into the house to pour herself a glass of cool lemonade from the refrigerator. She stepped out onto the veranda to drink it and admire her handiwork. The garden was really starting to take shape now; the green lawns that swept down toward the valley were edged by beds of hibiscus and clusters of white and red poinsettias.

She heard Wolfie barking from his pen at the side of the house and left the shade of the veranda to go and release him.

"Hello, darling," she said as she knelt down and the enormous dog smothered her in wet kisses. She almost lost her balance as he reared up to place his great paws on her shoulders; she smiled as she remembered the tiny puppy that Bill had presented her with a few days after they'd buried Fleur, her daughter.

"He needed someone to take care of him," he'd said as he'd handed the squirming, furry bundle to her. "He's a cross between a husky and an Alsatian, so the owner told me. In other words, dependable and loyal—but aggressive if he needs to be."

Wolfie—who'd been named very unimaginatively for his resemblance to one—was certainly no beauty, with his strange mixture of white and black markings, not to mention one blue and one brown eye, but there was no doubting his affection for his mistress. At the time, so drowned in grief and not caring about anything at all, Cecily had found his late-night and early-morning whining irritating, until she had discovered that he slept peacefully if he was allowed into her bedroom. She'd often wake up in the morning with him sprawled belly up next to her, his head mimicking hers as it lay on the pillow. Despite her determination not to love the puppy, Wolfie had been equally determined to demand it of her. And slowly, with his endearing nature and antics that made even the sullen Cecily crack a smile, he had won.

Wolfie bounded around her as she walked with him back to the veranda to finish her lemonade. He had a horrible habit of digging up seedlings, so he had to be restrained while she was gardening, but the rest of the time, he followed at his mistress's heels.

"I'll take you for a walk in a minute," she told him. "Now sit down and be quiet."

Cecily drank the remains of the lemonade and thought that she had more conversations with Wolfie—however one-sided—than she had with any human being. War had broken out in Europe only a couple of weeks after she had lost Fleur; she'd still been in the hospital at the time. When she'd eventually returned home, the black fug of devastation had hung so thickly around her she'd barely registered the start of the conflict. All it had meant was that Bill was away even more than he had been before, though in truth, she didn't much care. Though her body had had the time to recover, her spirit had taken far longer.

She remembered the day when Kiki had driven up to see her at Paradise Farm and she'd hidden away behind the closed shutters in her bedroom, begging Bill to say she was too ill to see her godmother. Kiki's hampers of champagne and pots of caviar, let alone her enforced air of jollity, were anathema to Cecily. The only person she had been able to countenance seeing was Katherine, who had been so very kind and patient with her. With Katherine nearby, she had holed up in the comfort and safety of Paradise Farm while the rest of the world went to war. Her mother and father had been desperate for her to come home to the sanctuary of America, but by the time she'd been well enough to contemplate it, even Bill had admitted that it was just too dangerous a journey.

"Sorry, old thing, no one wants to risk you being blown to bits by either a German bomber or one of their U-boats. I'm afraid you'll just have to stick it out here until things calm down a little."

"Things" hadn't calmed down, but at least she could hide away here, gardening as well as plowing through Bill's extensive library of books. If she'd been in New York, she knew her mother would have done her best to rehabilitate her, getting her "out and about," the thought of which horrified her. However, a year on now from her loss, the numbness she'd felt had lifted just a little and she found she missed her family.

Not that she spent time focusing on them, or on anything else that went near the emotional bone—she had learned that life was simply to be endured, not enjoyed. Any loving relationship she had ever tried to forge out-side her family had gone horribly, horribly wrong.

"Except for you, Wolfie darling," she said, dropping a kiss on his head. Apart from Wolfie, Cecily knew she was alone. Even though Bill had stood by her side and held her hand when they had lowered Fleur's tiny coffin into the red earth, she thought he'd been relieved that he wasn't saddled with bringing up another man's child. Or any child, come to that; the doctors might have saved her life, but they had destroyed it again only twenty-four hours later by telling her that she would never bear further children. Bill had seemed genuinely sad about this—and to be fair to him, he had insisted on staying at home with her until war had forced him to Nairobi. Cecily was sure the gesture was borne of a guilty conscience—Dr. Boyle had let it slip that Bill had been uncontactable when she'd been taken ill. He had been on a game drive, and it was only when Bobby had finally hunted him down that he'd come to the hospital.

These days, she no longer listened to Bill's explanations of where he would be when he was away and how he could be contacted if he was needed. She was cordial to him when he was home but no longer wished that he would wrap his arms around her or join her in the marital bed. Whether she could have children or not was irrelevant, given that they had never even attempted the process of making them.

Cecily was pleased that Katherine was coming over tonight for supper and a chat. She, too, was currently husbandless, Bobby having joined up. Due to his asthma, he served in an administrative capacity in the Agricultural Office in Nairobi.

"Thank heavens for Katherine," she sighed. "Come on, Wolfie, let's go and prepare supper."

"Help yourself to casserole." Cecily indicated the steaming dish she'd placed on the table.

"Thank you. It looks delicious. At least we're not on rations like everyone in Europe is, anyway," Katherine said as she cut the freshly baked bread that Cecily had made. "By the way, Alice has asked me to invite you to a party she's having up at Wanjohi Farm. She's been so very lonely. Will you come?"

"I really don't think so."

"Cecily! You haven't been out now for a year. It might do you good to come and have some fun."

"Not the kind of fun Alice and her friends indulge in, but thank you anyway."

"Goodness, you sound prissy. Just because you've forgotten how to enjoy yourself, you shouldn't hate the rest of the world because it still tries to remember."

Hurt by her friend's words, Cecily lowered her eyes and buttered her bread in silence.

"I . . . oh, forgive me, please. I do understand that you're still grieving and that Fleur's first anniversary was so recent. It's just that . . . you're only twenty-four, for goodness' sake. You have a lot of life left to live, and I don't want to see you waste it."

"I'm perfectly happy living it the way I do. How's Bobby?" Cecily swiftly changed the subject.

"Bored with organizing his crop rotas and wishing he could get back to our cattle full-time."

"Bill said he'd be checking on them while he's out on the plains this week. He had a few days' leave."

"So I heard. Thank goodness they can look out for each other. I was wondering," Katherine added as she toyed with her food, "why didn't you go with him?"

"Because he didn't ask me."

"He's probably given up asking you, because you always say no."

"Why don't you stop nagging me and eat some of the casserole I've made?"

"Because . . . in truth, I'm feeling rather sick. Oh, Cecily, I've put off telling you now for a month, but you're my best friend, and you should hear it from me. Bobby and I are going to have a baby. It's due next May. I'm so terribly sorry, but I had to tell you." There were tears in Katherine's eyes as she reached her hand out across the table.

"I . . . That is the most wonderful news! I'm thrilled for you both," Cecily managed.

"Are you sure? I've been so worried about saying anything; I didn't want the news to upset you."

"Upset me? Why, I'm happy for both of you, really."

"Are you absolutely positive?"

"Completely. Actually, we should break out the champagne that's still left over from Kiki's hampers."

"Oh, don't waste it on me. I feel ill at the very thought of alcohol just now. The other thing I wanted to ask you is whether you would be prepared to be godmother to the little one? I can't think of anyone else I'd rather ask."

"That is so sweet of you! Of course I'd be honored, Katherine, honest I would."

"That's wonderful! And as you're my nearest neighbor, I'm sure I'll be begging to dump the baby on you quite often."

Cecile smiled. "That will be just fine by me."

Later, she waved good-bye to Katherine from the veranda. As the taillights of the pickup disappeared along the drive, Cecily sat down at the table, put her head in her hands and sobbed as if her heart were breaking all over again.

Cecily was in the middle of scrubbing the kitchen floor when Bill arrived home three days later. Even though he kept insisting she should have help, Cecily refused. She enjoyed her solitude, and besides, keeping house gave her something to do.

"Good evening," he said as he surveyed his wife on her hands and knees.

"Hi," she said, dropping the scrubbing brush into the bucket and standing up. "How were the cattle?"

"Dwindling by the day."

"Oh. I'll put the supper on. I wasn't sure what time you'd be back."

"No. Sorry. Cecily, can we have a chat?"

"Why, yes, of course. There's nothing wrong, is there?"

"No, not with me, anyway. Any gin going? I could certainly do with one."

"There's some in the cabinet in the living room."

"Then let's go and talk in there, shall we?"

Cecily followed him through the hall and into the living room, then watched him pour two fingers of gin into each glass and hand one to her.

"Tchin tchin," he toasted her.

"Cheers." Cecily took a sip. "What is it, Bill?"

"Do you remember my friend the Maasai chief Leshan, who I once brought here to visit?"

"Of course I do. Why?"

"He heard I was out on the plains and came to find me. He's run into a bit of a problem, you see, and wondered if we could help him out. As you might have gathered by now, the Maasai have a complex tribal hierarchy. Leshan is the leader of the Ilmolean clan, one of the most powerful in the area. Nygasi belongs to it, too." Bill paused and took a sip of his gin. "Leshan's eldest daughter has long been promised in marriage to the son of the chief of the Ilmakesen clan. They are of the Right pillar, which means they can intermarry with Leshan's Left pillar."

Cecily nodded, although she really didn't follow the nuances. She could only imagine it was a bit like the powerful Vanderbilts intermarrying with the Whitneys.

"Leshan's daughters are the equivalent of princesses in Maasailand. The eldest has come of age now, at thirteen, and of all her sisters, she's considered the most beautiful," Bill continued. "But her father discovered she'd . . . coupled with a *moran*—a warrior—within his own clan and has subsequently become pregnant by him, which is strictly forbidden. If her intended finds out, there could be war between the two clans. At the very least, Leshan would be forced to cast out his daughter and she'd be left to the mercy of the hyenas and jackals."

"Oh, no! That's dreadful! How can these people be so barbaric?"

"It's hard to argue that it's any more barbaric than what is going on in Europe, Cecily, but certainly, the chief loves his daughter, and despite his difficult position he doesn't want to see her harmed."

"Of course not, but what has this got to do with us?"

"He's asked me if I—*we*—would take her in for a while, just until she's had the baby. Once she has, he'll place her back in the clan and hopefully no one will be any the wiser."

Cecily stared blankly at her husband. "You're saying you want this girl to come live *here*? And she's pregnant?"

"That's the long and short of it, yes. Given your recent circumstances, you may think me insensitive to suggest such a thing, but the man has done me a number of favors over the years. Besides, if we don't help, the poor girl has nowhere to go. Out in Maasailand, Leshan can't be seen to help her, but here, where no Maasai would ever think of looking, we *can* help. I've known this girl since she was a baby, and—dare I say it—she is in a similar situation to you when I first met you. Surely you can find it in your heart to offer her shelter on our land?"

"I guess if you put it like that, then I have no choice. How far along is she?"

"Leshan isn't sure; she'd hidden the baby's existence for a while, and it was only when her mother caught her naked while she was washing that it was noticed. Her mother reckons that she has perhaps a couple of months left to go. When she gets close to her time, her mother will be brought here to be with her."

"Do either of these women speak English?"

"No, but Nygasi has some basic English, and it doesn't take long to establish communication—I did. I'd leave him here to guard her and bring her food; he'll find a safe place to make camp somewhere in the woods. You'll hardly even know she's here."

"Okay." Cecily was at least relieved that the girl wouldn't be living in the house with her. "Well, if all we're doing is letting her camp on our land and her mother will be around when it's her time, then I guess that's fine. When will she arrive?"

"She's already here. We hid her under a blanket in the back of the pickup. Nygasi is with her now, scouting for a suitable spot in the woods."

"I see." Cecily realized that this was already a done deal. "I'm sure you'll want to run straight off and help."

"No, but I will go and tell Nygasi that you've agreed to her staying here. Cecily, I implore you again, we cannot tell anyone—I mean, *anyone*—that she's here. Not even Katherine. Now, I'll be back for supper."

As she watched Bill leave the house to head in the direction of the woods, Cecily sighed and walked into the kitchen to put together an evening meal.

"Is it my punishment not only to lose my baby but to be surrounded by pregnant women?" she murmured to herself as she stirred the sauce and placed it on the stove to simmer.

Bill appeared in the kitchen forty minutes later, just as she was taking the curry off the heat.

"That smells good, Cecily. You really are a very good cook, you know."

"Don't butter me up, Bill, just because you want your Maasai girl to stay," Cecily said, half joking because she was secretly pleased at the compliment. "Can you carry the plates through?"

Once they were seated at the dining table, Cecily watched Bill tuck in to his curry. "So is she settled in her . . . camp?" she finally asked.

"Nygasi is building a shelter, and, as I said, I'll leave him with her when I go to Nairobi."

"Oh, my! Are you sure you can cope without him? You never left him behind to look after me when I was pregnant," Cecily remarked, blaming her loose tongue on the gin.

"No, I didn't, and I will always regret it." He eyed her as he put down his knife and fork. "You know there are only so many times that someone can say sorry. Will you ever forgive me for not being there, Cecily?"

"Of course I forgive you. It wasn't your baby in the first place," she said. "Anyway, what is the name of your girl?"

"She isn't 'my girl,' she is simply under my . . . *our* protection until she gives birth. Her name is Njala. It means 'star,'" he murmured. "Every name the Maasai gives has a relevance. And so does everything they do."

Not for the first time, Cecily wondered if Bill wished he'd been born Maasai; he certainly seemed to prefer their company to hers or anyone else's in their group.

"Well, Nygasi must let me know if there is anything she needs."

"Thank you for that. And I will. She's very scared, Cecily."

"I'm not surprised. I can't believe that girls are allowed to get pregnant so young."

"They're considered fair game for the *moran*s as soon as they are fertile," Bill replied. "It's the way of things out on the plains."

"Bill, she is no more than a child, and I think it's obscene."

"I'm sure they think the way we live is equally obscene," he countered.

A silence ensued, which Cecily eventually decided to break. "I saw Katherine a few days ago."

"Did you? How is she?"

"She's fine. And expecting a baby in May."

"I know, Bobby told me. I'm very happy for both of them. Are you?"

"Of course! They'll make wonderful parents. Now, if you're done, I'll clear away."

Cecily stood up abruptly, then collected the plates and marched into the kitchen. As she ran the faucet full blast into the sink, she seethed with anger. Did the man not have an ounce of empathy for her suffering?

Bill left early the next morning, and Cecily went to work on her garden, grasping weeds by the scruffs of their necks and wrenching them from the soil with the force of a child torn from the womb. Even though she had seen neither Nygasi nor the girl now living on their land, it was as if she could feel their presence in the woods nearby.

When she had finished, she sat with Wolfie on the veranda, enjoying her habitual glass of lemonade as she cooled down along with the heat of the day. After fixing a light supper of vegetable soup, Cecily felt unusually restless and couldn't settle to reading as she usually did. She looked out at the sky and saw there was still another hour at least before darkness fell.

"Come on, Wolfie, we're going to pay a visit to our new neighbor."

Arming herself with her flashlight and a bottle of water in a canvas bag, Cecily set off with the dog in the direction of the woods. She'd never entered them before, only skirted around them when she was riding over to visit Katherine. They were set uphill, a good half a mile's walk from the farmhouse, and dusk was already beginning to fall by the time she arrived at the edges.

Wolfie nosed around in front of her as they walked through the shadows of the huge trees. She had never realized that the wood was so dense and only hoped that Wolfie would find the way back home. Darkness had almost descended and Cecily was ready to turn around when Wolfie barked suddenly and gamboled forward. Knowing that this meant he'd picked up a scent—almost certainly of food—Cecily switched on the flashlight and followed him as he set off at full pelt.

"I do hope you know where you're going, Wolfie," she said as she did her best to keep up with him. But soon even she could smell the enticing aroma of meat cooking over a fire, and a few seconds later, the two of them entered a small clearing.

When Cecily shone the flashlight on the small, circular shelter, concocted of smoothly packed mud draped with animal skins, she felt as if she was in a surreal African version of *Hansel and Gretel*. In front of the shelter was a haunch of meat roasting on a spit hanging over a fire pit.

"*Takwena*, Cecily." Nygasi appeared in front of her warily.

"Hello, Nygasi. I—I just came to say hello to—" Cecily indicated the hut. "Is she here?"

"No. She hear dog. Run away. She afraid."

"Oh. Can you tell her that I came here to see her?"

"Yes. You come back with sun." Nygasi pointed upward.

"Okay," she said as Nygasi carved a piece of meat from the spit with a great sharp knife and tossed it to Wolfie.

"*Oldia*. Dog," he said.

"*Oldia*," Cecily repeated, stroking Wolfie.

"*Etaa sere*," he said, then gave her a bow and turned away from her.

Cecily set off back home. Once she had settled down on the veranda with the gas lamp beside her to read her book, she realized it was the first time she'd spoken directly to Nygasi. Having gotten used to him always being with her husband, she admitted to herself that she had always been a little afraid of him; but tonight he'd seemed friendly enough.

As she got into bed an hour later, Cecily decided she would definitely return to the camp tomorrow and meet this Maasai princess for herself.

"Is she here?" she asked Nygasi when she arrived back in the clearing the following morning.

"She there." Nygasi pointed to the shelter.

"Can you tell her I'd like to meet her?"

Nygasi nodded, then walked over to the shelter, peeled back one of the cowhides, and spoke in rapid Maa to the person inside.

"She come. Sit?" he indicated a hide placed on the ground beside the fire pit.

Cecily did so, then watched as the animal-skin door was pulled back slightly and a pair of fearful eyes peered out. Nygasi said what were obviously comforting words, for the hide was peeled back further. Cecily watched in fascination as a young woman unfolded herself from the low shelter. She'd always thought of Nygasi as tall, but the woman who stood next to him was even taller. Cecily drew in her breath at the incredible creature standing in front of her. Her black skin shone ebony in the sunlight that sparkled through the trees, her long limbs were almost impossibly slender, and her neck seemed to go on forever, carrying an exquisitely chiseled face with full lips and high cheekbones below limpid brown eyes. Her hair was shaved neatly down to her scalp, and her chin jutted slightly upward as she stared at Cecily with a certain air of hauteur. She was dressed in a lambskin skirt with a red shawl wrapped around her torso. An assortment of silver earrings hung from her ears, and her neck and wrists were adorned with multicolored beaded bangles and necklaces.

Cecily had been expecting a child, but this thirteen-year-old was every inch a woman, with the noble bearing of the princess that she was. She was so incredibly striking that Cecily could hardly speak for staring at her.

She stood up slowly and walked over to greet the young woman, who towered above her. "I'm Cecily Forsythe, Bill's wife. I'm pleased to meet you, Njala."

She held out her hand and the young woman took it almost regally, giving a nod as she did so.

"No English," Nygasi explained.

"It's okay. I just wanted her to know that if there was any problem, I'm . . . well, I'm there."

Nygasi nodded, then spoke to the girl in Maa. She whispered something back.

"She say thank you for shelter on your land."

"Oh, it's no problem," Cecily stuttered, feeling Njala's amazing eyes upon her. "I love your bangles." Cecily pointed to the woman's wrist. "Very beautiful. Right, then, I'd better be off. Good to meet you, Njala. Bye, now. Come on, Wolfie." Cecily turned away and walked from the clearing. It was only when she was halfway home that she realized she had been so overwhelmed by the woman's beauty, she'd not even taken a glance at Njala's stomach to try to decipher how pregnant she was.

Having spent the day in the garden and after cooking herself another lonely supper, Cecily wandered into the living room, turned on the light, and went over to the bookcase to find one of Bill's books on the Maasai. Lighting a fire in the grate because the evening was chilly, she settled into an armchair and began to read.

It was a white man's account, written by a big-game hunter who'd been captured by a clan while out on their territory. He'd managed to barter his way out of death by offering them his shotgun and had eventually befriended them. The one thing that struck Cecily above all was the barbarous way they treated their women.

She particularly blanched at the descriptions of the female circumcision "ceremony" detailed in the book and occasionally had to put it down to gather herself. She felt light-headed at the thought of her own private parts being abused that way.

As she switched off the light to head for bed, she thought about the proud woman-child sleeping out tonight under her canopy of animal skins—and, for the first time in a while, counted herself lucky to be so privileged.

The next morning, armed with Bill's basic dictionary of Maa words and offerings of potatoes and carrots that could be cooked in the pot over the fire, Cecily made her way through the woods once more. Nygasi gave her an almost imperceptible smile and a small bow as she entered the clearing.

"Hello, Nygasi. Look," Cecily said as she dug in her canvas bag, "I brought some things for Njala to eat and to make her more comfortable. Is she here?"

Nygasi nodded and went to get Njala as Cecily laid out her wares.

"*Takwena*, Njala," she greeted her, once again mesmerized by her beauty as she approached the fire pit. Dragging her eyes away from the young woman's face, she stared at her middle, but it was still covered by the swathes of the long red shawl, so the bump could have been fabric or baby. Whichever it was, it didn't look that large, but then again, Cecily thought, there was more room for a baby inside Njala's six-foot frame than there was in her own at just over five feet.

"Here, I brought you a pillow."

Njala raised her elegant brow in confusion.

"I'll show you." Cecily placed the pillow on the earth beside her and laid her head upon it. "For sleeping. You try?" Cecily offered the pillow to Njala, who accepted it as if Cecily was a maid serving her queen.

"And here are some potatoes and carrots." Cecily took out one of each and showed the girl. Nygasi nodded in approval and came forward to take them.

"Can you ask Njala if there's anything else she needs?" Cecily asked Nygasi.

Nygasi did so, but the girl shook her head.

"Today I get cow." Nygasi indicated the placid animal munching on the grass beneath a tree, tethered on a long piece of rope. "Good for baby," he said.

"Oh yes, it is," said Cecily. "Just let me know if there's anything else either of you needs. *Etaa sere*." Cecily stumbled over the words that meant "Good-bye."

"*Etaa sere*." It was Njala who replied, her childlike tone at odds with her womanly physique.

With a tentative smile and a nod at the two Maasai, Cecily left the clearing.

# 36

In the following month, Cecily found herself drawn to the young woman who lived in the woods. Rather than walking across the open fields that gave such wonderful views of the valley below, once the heat of the day had passed, she and Wolfie would set off to visit their young neighbor. November brought with it sudden heavy downpours that made Cecily worry about Njala's health, but she remained safe and dry within her little shelter, as Nygasi had had the foresight to build it on a raised mound so it would not flood.

At first, Njala would only stand behind Nygasi as Cecily took her daily offerings out of her bag. The chickens Bill had bartered for from a Kikuyu were proving to be wonderful egg layers, so she had plenty to spare.

The first time she'd taken eggs to Njala, Cecily had watched the girl grimace in distaste as she had whispered something to Nygasi.

"She say come from bird bottom," Nygasi had imparted solemnly, and Cecily had had to stifle a giggle.

"Tell her that eggs are good for baby. Look, I'll show you."

Cecily had commandeered the pan that sat beside the fire and mixed two eggs with a little milk, still warm from the cow's udder, adding a little salt and pepper from the twists of paper she'd brought with her.

"There, you try it," she'd said, offering it to Njala once it was cooked. The girl had shaken her head firmly.

"See?" Having no fork or spoon, Cecily had used her fingers to take some of the scrambled egg into her mouth. "Good. *Supat.*"

Njala had looked to Nygasi, who had nodded encouragingly; then she'd stepped forward and dipped her own long fingers into the pan. With an expression that looked as though she was about to eat poison, she'd tasted the concoction.

"See? *Supat.*" Cecily had rubbed her stomach.

Njala had reached for more, so Cecily had offered her the pan, and finally, the girl had knelt down and eaten the remainder contentedly.

After that, Cecily had taken her guest eggs every day and thought that Njala was actually starting to look pleased to see her. She only wished she could communicate better with her and tell her that she understood her plight. So she had begun to take the small chalkboard she kept in the kitchen to mark up reminders of groceries she needed to purchase.

"Can Njala write?" she had asked Nygasi, demonstrating the movement with her chalk.

He had shaken his head.

"Oh. Then perhaps I could help teach her. Here." Cecily had beckoned Njala closer. Then she had written "Njala' in large letters on the board and drawn a star beside the name. She had shown the girl the letters, pointing to them, then to Njala.

"Njala—you." She had gone through the same process for her own name, and finally, after much gesticulating, the girl had seemed to understand.

"Njala." She had pointed at herself. "Cecily." She pointed to Cecily.

"Yes, me!" Cecily had clapped her hands together in delight, and Njala, too, had smiled, showing off her lovely white teeth.

From then on, after Njala had eaten her eggs, Cecily would write basic words such as "Hello" on the board. She would consult the Maa dictionary and ask Nygasi to provide her with the correct pronunciation. As Cecily repeated the Maa word, Njala hesitantly spoke the English word. After a couple of weeks, not only was Njala able to string a basic English sentence together, but Cecily found the girl waiting for her eagerly in the clearing. Cecily didn't quite know how to describe it, but slowly a warmth developed between them. One morning, she saw Njala wince and clutch her stomach.

"Baby kicking?" Cecily mimed the movement with her foot and Njala nodded.

"Can I touch?" She reached out her hand to Njala's stomach. The girl took her hand and placed it on her own belly.

"Oh, my!" Cecily breathed as she felt the movement of a limb beneath the ebony skin. It made her want to weep with joy and sorrow in equal measure. "He or she is strong! Strong!" she repeated, flexing her arm muscle, and both of them giggled.

"You look very bright and breezy tonight," Bill commented as Cecily made supper. He hadn't been home for the past three weeks, unable to get away from his desk at the War Office in Nairobi. What with her newfound friendship with Njala, Cecily had hardly noticed.

"Thanks," she said. "I feel it."

"Then you're probably the only one in Kenya who does," Bill sighed. "Things are pretty grim in Nairobi, I can tell you, especially with the blackouts. The town is heaving with the military."

"There have been no air strikes yet, though?"

"Only one in Malindi down on the coast last month, but since Mussolini declared war, there have been skirmishes between the Allies and the Italian army on Kenyan soil; everyone's preparing for an invasion from the Abyssinian border. You can't move around town without tripping over a sandbag."

"Oh, how awful," Cecily said distractedly as she placed supper on the table and sat down opposite Bill.

"As a matter of fact, I have been asked to take command of a battalion of the King's African Rifles."

That made Cecily look up at him. "Does that mean you'll be fighting?"

"I'll be overseeing recruitment and organizing troop movements at first, but I'll be damned if I don't fight with my men if it comes down to it. Anyway, for now it's good to be home, it really is."

"Want to finish up the last of our gin?" Cecily asked him, suddenly feeling guilty about her lack of thought toward him.

"Why not?" he said as she stood up to get it. "Even old Muthaiga Club is running dry, what with the influx of army personnel. I think you'd better rekindle your relationship with your godmother." He gave her a wan smile as she handed him a glass. "Her cellar never seems to run dry. Tchin tchin."

"Cheers," Cecily toasted.

"So what have you been doing with yourself up here since I saw you last?"

"Oh, the garden, of course—I never realized how demanding rows of carrots and cabbages could be—but I've also been visiting Njala every day."

Bill looked up at her in astonishment. "Have you indeed? Well, now, there's a thing. How is she?"

"She's very well indeed, as a matter of fact. Holy moly, she's a beauty, isn't she?"

"She certainly is, yes."

"I've been taking her eggs and teaching her a little English. And I've even learned to speak some Maa."

"Good for you." Bill studied his wife. "Who would have thought it?"

"Thought what?"

"That you and a Maasai girl would strike up a friendship."

"I don't know why you're looking so surprised, given that you spend half your time with them."

"Sadly, no longer, but I hear what you're saying."

"Bill?"

"Yes?"

"Do you . . . would you know how Njala ended up pregnant?"

"Well, I would assume in the usual way."

"I mean, was she, umm, willing?" Cecily blushed.

"You mean, was this some kind of a mutual relationship or was she taken by force?"

"Yes."

"I can't answer that, but in my experience, the daughter of a chief, especially if she's beautiful, is a precious and well-guarded commodity. So I would imagine that Njala herself must have had something to do with making the necessary . . . arrangements for a tryst."

"She loved someone else who was not her intended?"

"Maybe, but who knows?" Bill sighed. "Sadly, a Maasai woman's path is rarely one she chooses for herself."

"I understand. She makes me feel real blessed," Cecily agreed.

"Exactly. One can always find another whose suffering is far greater. Now, then, given that you seem to be in a more social mood these days, I was wondering if you'd mind if I brought Joss up here for the weekend. He's closed up the Djinn Palace on the lake since his wife, Molly, died. He can't afford to run the damned place and is stuck in his bungalow in town, heavily involved with the war effort like we all are. He's gagging for some fresh air, as you can imagine."

"Okay, why not?" Cecily agreed. "We haven't had guests since . . . well, since we moved in."

"No, and even given my hermit tendencies, it really is time we did. There's also a new couple in town—Jock Delves Broughton and his young wife, Diana. They've moved here from England to escape the war. Not that you can fully escape it at the moment, but at least the weather here is better, I suppose," said Bill with a shrug. "Joss has suggested we could invite them to stay too. Diana isn't much older than you, and it might be good for you to meet someone of your own age."

"All right, though you'll have to find us some meat because there's scarcely any in the butcher's in town."

"Surely you could slaughter one of your chickens?"

"I couldn't do that!" Cecily looked horrified. "They all have names. And besides, they're providing us with eggs every day."

"I knew it." Bill rolled his eyes. "All right, then, I'll ask Nygasi to see what he can arrange and invite Joss and the Broughtons up to Paradise Farm next weekend."

Despite waking up the following morning in a cold sweat, wondering how she could have possibly agreed to having weekend guests, Cecily found she actually enjoyed preparing for them. No one other than Katherine and Bobby had been to the house since they'd moved in—the housewarming party they'd tentatively planned had been put on hold because of Cecily's tragedy. She scrubbed the house until everything gleamed, adding blooms from the burgeoning garden to stand in vases on the polished surfaces. She'd invited Katherine, too—Bobby was unable to get leave, which was convenient as it meant there were even numbers of men and women, something her mother had always deemed important for a dinner party.

On the Friday the guests were due to arrive, Cecily dug out the remaining bottles of champagne from Kiki's hampers, which she hoped would make the party go with a swing, and put them in the refrigerator to cool. Having not seen Njala for the past couple of days, she then set off with Wolfie for the woods. As she approached the clearing and saw the girl appear immediately from her shelter, Cecily thought how full her stomach had grown. No longer was she covering it up, but instead, she wore a piece of fabric fashioned into a skirt beneath the bump. Cecily had the distinct feeling that Njala's time was not far off.

"*Supai*, Nygasi," she said as she approached. "How is she?"

"Baby near," he said as they walked together toward Njala.

"But she is well?"

Nygasi nodded.

"When will you send for her mother?"

"Mother come soon," Nygasi said.

"Hello, Cecily," Njala said with a smile as they arrived by her side. Then she turned to Nygasi and, like a queen dismissing her serf, flicked him away with her hand. Nygasi nodded and wandered off beyond the clearing.

"How are you?"

Njala held her bump and rolled her eyes expressively.

"Yes, I know." Cecily then touched her brow and swept her hand across it to indicate fatigue.

Heading to the side of the clearing and indicating Cecily should follow, Njala led her into the protection of a dense copse of trees. Then she turned and grabbed both Cecily's hands in her own. Her eyes were suddenly filled with fear.

"You," she said, "help." Removing her hands from Cecily's, she indicated her belly, then made a cradling motion with her arms.

"Help? You mean help with the birth?" Cecily then mimed the cradling action, too.

"Yes. Help. Please."

"Njala, your mother is coming to help," she enunciated slowly.

"No! Help baby! Please, Cecily!"

Like a shadow, Nygasi appeared behind Njala. He spoke to her in Maa, indicating she should return to the clearing.

"You go home now," Nygasi told Cecily firmly.

Njala turned toward her, her eyes full of everything she could not say. "Please help baby," she mouthed as Nygasi led her away.

Cecily was still thinking about Njala and trying to interpret what she had meant when Bill arrived home later that afternoon.

"The house looks wonderful, my dear, and so do you." He smiled at her as she emerged from the bedroom in her green dress, ready to make the final preparations for supper. "I like your hair longer." He picked up a ringlet that fell to just below her shoulders and twirled it around a finger.

"It's only long because there's no one around here I trust to cut it."

"Well, I like it, and you should wear it down more often. Now I'm off to have a rare soak in the tub. They're rationing water at Muthaiga Club these days, as we're stuffed to the gills in there—it's two men per room just now, and you remember how small those rooms are," he added as he turned to walk off in the direction of the bathroom.

"Oh, and Bill?"

"Yes?"

"I saw Njala today, and she seemed upset . . . almost frightened. I think she said that she wanted me to help with the birth. I explained that her mother is coming to help her, but I'm not sure she understood. Her time must be real close. You will ask Nygasi to make sure her mother comes soon, won't you? I couldn't bear it if anything"—Cecily gulped—"happened to her."

"Of course I will. Njala knows her mother will arrive when it's time. You probably misunderstood her."

"Probably."

But as Bill closed the door and she heard the sound of the water running, Cecily knew for certain she hadn't mistaken the fear in Njala's eyes.

Cecily and Bill's guests arrived an hour later than expected. Joss Erroll—even though he looked exhausted—was as handsome as ever, and Jock, aka Sir Henry John Delves Broughton, turned out to be a tall elderly Englishman who sported a large paunch and a head of thinning gray hair.

"Please, m'dear, call me Jock. This is m'wife, Diana. Nice for you to have someone of your own age to play with, eh, old girl? Diana's surrounded by octogenarians in Nairobi." Jock chuckled.

"I'm sure that Cecily will agree there aren't many of us under thirty here, are there?" replied his wife.

"Er, no, there sure aren't," she said, unable to stop staring at the striking blond woman standing in front of her. Diana Delves Broughton was definitely what some would call a "looker," and for the life of her, Cecily couldn't understand what such a woman was doing with a man old enough to be her father—or even grandfather.

"This is utterly charming," Diana said as Cecily led the party into the living room, where Katherine was already cracking open the champagne. "We're camping out at Muthaiga Club at the moment."

"Now, m'dear, you know it's only temporary—we'll be moving into the villa in Karen in a few days," Jock reminded her.

"A ghastly dark one in the suburbs of Nairobi," Diana muttered under her breath.

"Diana, this is Katherine Sinclair, my great friend and neighbor," Cecily said quickly.

"Golly! This is obviously where all the bright young things live." Diana turned to her husband. "Can we build a house near here instead, darling? Then I shall have plenty of jolly company."

"Fizz, everyone?" Katherine asked as she poured the champagne into six glasses.

"Rather," said Jock, smiling at the assembled group. "This feels more like the Kenya I used to know. Cheers!"

"Cheers!" everyone chorused.

"And welcome to Happy Valley, Diana," Joss added, his eyes lingering on the new blond recruit.

"Thank you, Joss, I'm pleased to be here," Diana said, holding his gaze.

Even Cecily admitted later that the evening—and Diana—were fun. After dinner, Diana asked if Cecily had a gramophone.

"Why, yes. And Mama sent some of the newest records over from America with it."

"Well, for heaven's sake, let's put them on! The ones at Muthaiga Club might have been popular in the twenties, but they're hardly up to date," Diana drawled.

Cecily did as asked, setting the gramophone up on the veranda, while the men moved the table and chairs out of the way to create a makeshift dance floor.

"Dancing under the stars is just so romantic, don't you think, Cecily?" Diana said dreamily, clasped in the arms of her husband as Glenn Miller's "Moonlight Serenade" played in the background.

"Dance with me, Diana?" asked Joss, holding out his own arms.

"If you insist." Diana smiled, disengaging herself from Jock.

"Then, Cecily, will you afford me the pleasure?" Jock asked.

She had no choice but to agree. Looking over his shoulder as they danced, Cecily saw that Bill had taken to the floor with Katherine, but her attention was mainly caught by Diana and Joss, who were swaying together in a shadowy corner. Jock asked Cecily lots of polite questions, which she duly answered. When the music ended, she excused herself to put another record on the gramophone.

"For goodness' sake, put on something upbeat," whispered Katherine, sifting through the records. "Here, Count Basie will do."

Still Diana and Joss continued to sway languidly together to "Lester Leaps In" as Cecily and Katherine held hands and hopped around the veranda together, giggling as they did so. Bill was now in conversation with Jock at the table, Jock seemingly oblivious to his wife's behavior.

"Bobby says there's already gossip at Muthaiga Club about the two of them," Katherine whispered as, perspiring from their exertions, they sat down on the veranda steps.

"Put on another one, will you, girls?" called Joss. "Do you have 'Blue Orchids'?"

"I'll go and look," said Katherine, getting up. "You stay there, Cecily, you've been on all your feet all night."

"Yes, you have," said Bill, walking over to her with Jock.

"Wonderful party, but I'm rather bushed, what? Think I'll head off to bed. Bill has said he'll take us out with his Maasai chaps on a game drive tomorrow. Good night, m'dear."

Cecily and Bill watched Jock amble rather unsteadily into the house as Glenn Miller's orchestra blared out on the gramophone.

Bill held out his hand to Cecily. "Dance with me?"

"I . . . okay," she agreed, taking Bill's hand and letting him pull her to standing from the steps. She felt a small tingle of desire as Bill's arms went around her, but she pushed it down hastily. She knew Bill would never be interested in her on that level, so she amused herself instead by watching two people who were so obviously *very* interested in each other. One could just tell from the way their bodies moved together and how Diana was looking up into Joss's eyes.

"They make a handsome couple, don't they?" Bill said, lowering his voice.

"They sure do. It's a pity Diana is married."

"That's never stopped Joss before. Even though I love him dearly, his behavior with women . . ." Bill sighed. "Anyway, enough of him. I have to say, you look very lovely tonight, Cecily."

"Why, thank you."

"And now"—Bill released her as the record came to an end—"I must give Katherine a ride home as I promised. I'd go to bed if I were you, leave them to it," Bill whispered, nodding in the direction of Diana and Joss. He kissed her on the forehead. "See you tomorrow."

Cecily was woken by Bill the following morning. He was already dressed in his khaki shirt and pants.

"What time is it?"

"Just after six. Time to rise and shine, we're off on that game drive."

"Do I have to come? You know it's not my thing. I hate watching those beautiful animals die."

"I'd be very grateful if you did. You saw last night what's going on with Joss and Diana, and I need you there to divert attention."

"Whose? Diana's or Jock's? Or, in fact, Joss's?" she pondered out loud as she got out of bed.

"All three of them if possible. Diana and Jock were only married less than a month ago. Even for Joss, this is untenable behavior."

"Diana doesn't seem to mind the attention one bit, so you can't put all the blame on Joss. She's rather beautiful, don't you think?"

"She has a certain allure, I suppose, but her eyes are cold and that red lipstick she insists on wearing all the time is rather vulgar."

"Oh, really?" Cecily was secretly pleased.

"It couldn't be more obvious what's going on, could it?" Bill continued. "A young woman like that marrying a man like Jock—it all smacks of a gold digger. Jock might be a bore, but he doesn't deserve to be treated that way by his wife. No wonder Joss was so eager to bring his 'new friends'—or should I say 'friend'—to stay! Right, I've had Nygasi stock up the pickups with the usual supplies. As soon as you and Diana are ready, we'll leave. I'll see you outside."

"Okay." Cecily went to the closet to retrieve her safari boots, wondering at the fact that her husband didn't seem to have fallen under Diana's spell. Or did he protest too much?

While Nygasi and his fellow Maasai took the pickup stocked with rifles and supplies, Cecily found herself squeezed into the back of the other pickup with Joss and Diana, while Jock sat next to Bill in the front. Cecily turned to look out at the view of the landscape, tactfully attempting to avoid the view to her right, which encompassed Joss's hand snaking up the inside of Diana's thigh. As Joss began openly nuzzling Diana's neck, Cecily sat in an agony of suspense that Jock would turn around at any moment and catch them.

When they arrived at the chosen spot for the day, Nygasi and the Maasai began to set up camp.

"Is Njala okay alone?" Cecily made a beeline for him.

"Njala mother come last night. She okay. Woman's work now," Nygasi said as he unloaded the folding chairs, table, and hampers.

"Which would suit me best?" Diana arrived next to them and picked up one of the rifles. "This one, maybe?" She lifted it into position on her slender shoulder. "Yes, this is perfect. Don't you just love shooting, Cecily?"

"As a matter of fact, I don't. I nearly got eaten by a lion on my first game drive, but Bill saved me."

"How awfully romantic. I've only been out on a couple of safaris since I arrived, and I had to save dear old Jock from a lion myself, didn't I, darling?" She gave a tinkling laugh. "Let's hope we get some sport today."

Cecily was happy to stay in the camp under the shade of the trees with the other Maasai on guard, as Nygasi led the rest of the party into the bush. She saw a large snake slithering along the ground only a few yards from her. Quietly tucking her feet up onto the folding chair, she watched it as it went on its way. She pondered how, only a year ago, she would have screamed in fright at the sight of it, but as it passed her by disinterestedly, she realized how her time in Kenya had changed her. Snakes were commonplace, and she'd learned from Bill and Katherine to spot which ones were benign and which ones weren't.

She gazed at the plain spread out in front of her, the azure sky meeting it on the horizon. A herd of wildebeest loped by in the distance. The rains had brought everything to lush, green life, and the watering holes were bustling with animals, thirsty after a long dry season.

"This is my home," she said in sudden wonder. "I live here in Africa. Who'd have thought it?"

And in that moment, as she took in the sheer magnificence of the natural beauty around her, Cecily felt she was finally beginning to recover.

The others came back for a late lunch of champagne and fresh antelope meat, which Nygasi cooked expertly on a spit.

"How was the game drive?" asked Cecily politely, even though it was obvious by the zebra and the Thomson's gazelles they had dragged back that it had been a success.

"It was a glorious day for it," Bill said as they heard the buzz of a plane circling above them. "One of the reconnaissance lot returning from the border," he remarked. "Just to remind us there's a war on."

"Bally sight better here than it is in Blighty, I can tell you," said Jock, meat juice dribbling from his lips as he spoke. "Doubt we'll get more action today with those buggers frightening the animals. Where have Diana and Joss got to?"

"They went to see if they could spot any elephants," Bill replied smoothly. "Nygasi said a herd was seen around here yesterday."

"They're not looking for ivory, are they?" Cecily asked her husband.

"No, Diana just had a whim to see an elephant; she's not had the luck to spot one before."

"They are magnificent creatures," Cecily agreed as she saw a sudden movement in the bushes.

Diana and Joss were walking back toward them, blatantly holding hands and giggling.

"Spot one, m'dear?" Jock asked her as the pair wandered back into camp.

"Nothing, sadly," she said. "How about we set off back to the ranch? I doubt there'll be further sport this afternoon, will there?"

Cecily watched her as she winked at Joss and refastened her partially unbuttoned shirt.

Back at Paradise Farm, Diana declared that she was desperate to get back to town and dance at Muthaiga Club.

"It's such wonderful fun there on a Saturday night, isn't it? Especially with so many soldiers in town."

"I'm all in for the day after the shoot, but you head off with Joss and I'll see you at the club tomorrow, what?" Jock said.

"Oh, darling, you are sweet to me," Diana gushed as she kissed her husband's ruddy cheek. "Don't rush back to Nairobi on my behalf, will you? I'm sure I won't get eaten by anything in town—well, not by any wild animals, that is." She laughed. "Cecily, may I borrow a mirror to put myself together before I leave?"

"Of course." Cecily led Diana along the hallway. "You'll need to use the one in my bedroom. I keep meaning to put some in the spare rooms, but we haven't had many guests here so far."

"I know. Bill told me you lost your baby last year. Horribly bad luck, you poor thing. Oh, this is delightful!" Diana said as she looked around the bedroom. "You have wonderful taste, which is more than I can say for Jock. The villa in Karen feels like a Victorian mausoleum! I'm dreading moving in—so much brown. I do hate brown, don't you?" Diana sat down at Cecily's dressing table and opened the beauty case she'd carried in with her. "Bill's such a sweetheart and clearly wild about you."

"Oh, I don't think he is, I mean—"

"It's written all over his face. You obviously have a happy marriage—so different from me and dear Jock. He and I have never yet spent a night in the same bed, and I doubt we ever will." She chuckled as she brushed her wavy blond hair and expertly fastened it back with two diamanté clips. "Do you come up to town very often?"

"Not really, no."

"Then you must! I wasn't sure how it would be, but Nairobi is far more fun than London, despite the damned war spilling over to here. I'm having an utter ball," she added as she painted bright red lipstick onto her full lips. "You absolutely must come for race week after Christmas—Joss says it's the most fun to be had here all year. You don't mind if Jock crashes here with you for another night, do you? The drive back is rather arduous, and he does look all in after today's outing."

With a generous spritz of perfume across her neck and décolletage, Diana stood up. "Right, face and hair done, and I'll change into my dress en route. There's so much dust everywhere, isn't there?" She took a last glance at herself in the mirror. "Thank you so much for a wonderful dinner last night, and I do hope I'll be seeing you again soon." She kissed Cecily on both cheeks and walked out of the bedroom, the strong fragrance of her perfume lingering behind her. Cecily sat down on the bed and shook her head. The new Lady Delves Broughton sure was something else.

Having cooked supper for the three of them who remained, Cecily excused herself soon after and left Bill and Jock to chat. In bed, she tried to concentrate on her book, but Diana's comments about it being obvious that Bill was wild about her haunted her mind. Perhaps, she decided eventually, Diana was just being kind, because she was certain that Bill hardly registered her existence as a woman.

Jock and Bill left for Nairobi after lunch the following day. Even if Cecily found Jock rather boring and arrogant, there was a large portion of her that also felt sympathy for him.

"When will you be back?" she asked Bill as she handed him a pile of clean army uniforms.

"I'm not sure, I'm afraid, but I'll let you know as soon as I can. And, my dear, really, it is time for you to get some domestic help." Bill indicated his laundry. "You've been slaving away all weekend."

"I'll think about it," she agreed with a half smile.

"It's not been so bad, having guests here, has it?"

"Not at all."

"Well, take care, won't you?"

"And you," Cecily said as Bill kissed her politely on both cheeks. She followed the men to the veranda and noticed that Nygasi was already in his position at the rear of the pickup. If he was going back with Bill, she presumed that Njala's mother was still in the woods taking care of her.

Cecily waved them off rather wistfully, thinking that it *had* been fun to play hostess for the weekend and to have people admire her house. The week in front of her stretched out like an empty void. Before she became maudlin, she turned back inside and went to the kitchen to tackle the pile of pots and pans waiting to be washed up.

# 37

It took Cecily until Tuesday morning to pluck up the courage to visit Njala. She had no idea about Maasai birthing rituals—or whether Njala had even given birth yet—but a strange instinct had been telling her to stay away. Perhaps it was the fear of arriving to find that something had gone horribly wrong, as it had for her. Finally, curiosity and concern overcame her, and she and Wolfie headed off toward the woods.

It was a beautiful sunny December day, and after thundering rain last night, the air felt crisp and fresh. Cecily even found herself humming "Blue Orchids" and thinking that Bill was right: she should get some domestic help, especially with Christmas on the near horizon. Her mother had telephoned to say that she had sent a Christmas box filled with lots of treats, but what with the war playing havoc with deliveries, Cecily wouldn't be holding her breath for its arrival anytime soon. Still, she was looking forward to the festive season and even thought that she might join Bill for the races in Nairobi during Christmas week.

"You really must be feeling better," she told herself as she entered the clearing and blinked, wondering if Wolfie had taken her the wrong way while she'd been dreaming about the races. The clearing was completely deserted. Cecily walked across to where the shelter used to stand and saw that the only traces left behind were a mound of clay and a few weeds scarred from the fire pit.

"Holy moly!" She looked around in disbelief. "They might have told us they were leaving, Wolfie. What a shame." She sighed. "I'd like to have seen the baby and said good-bye . . . Come on, let's go home."

But Wolfie wasn't listening to his mistress; he'd headed out of the clearing in the opposite direction from home.

"Wolfie! Come back here now!"

The dog continued to run through the trees until he was out of sight.

Cecily turned in the direction of home, knowing he would eventually follow her, when she suddenly heard him bark from some distance away.

"Darned dog!" Cecily muttered as she followed the noise. "Wolfie! Come here!"

The barking continued, and Cecily had no choice but to follow the sound deeper into the woods. It was thick and dark beyond the clearing, and she found herself pushing through brambles that scratched her bare legs.

Eventually, she saw Wolfie's backside—his nose was buried deep in a thicket—and went to see what it was that he was so interested in.

"What is it you've found, boy? Some old bones, most likely. Come on, out of the way, let me take a look."

Cecily pulled the dog away, then plowed into the thicket herself, twigs grazing her arms and face. All she could see on the ground was a pile of dead leaves. Gingerly brushing a few of them aside to see what might be hidden beneath, her fingers touched something warm.

"Agh!" Cecily shrieked as she withdrew her hand abruptly and stepped back, a curl of her hair becoming tangled on a branch as she did so.

It was obviously some kind of animal, but the warmth she had felt told Cecily it was alive. After untangling her hair, she broke off one of the branches behind her and with her heart beating hard tentatively used it to clear more of the leaves away. A small patch of brown skin was revealed.

Then she heard the faintest mewling, like a newborn kitten. Clearing away further leaves, Cecily saw with a start a tiny foot poking up above the diminishing pile.

She swallowed hard, suddenly realizing what the creature in the leafy grave was. And why Wolfie had barked.

"Oh. My. Lord!"

Cecily fell to her knees and used her hands to scrape away the remaining leaves. And there it lay: a tiny but perfectly formed newborn baby girl. Her eyes were closed, and the only visible sign of life was the rosebud lips that were formed into an O as they sucked involuntarily.

Unable to process what might have happened, Cecily reached down and took the baby into her arms. The child was covered in dust and dirt, and the stump of her umbilical cord was seeping yellow pus. Cecily could see the pattern of tiny ribs through the skin; the stomach unnaturally distended, her tiny legs resembling a large frog.

"But she's alive," Cecily whispered. "Oh, Wolfie." Her eyes blurred with tears. "I think you just saved a life. Come on, let's get this little one back to the house as fast as we can."

The baby hardly moved in Cecily's arms on the journey back, and her breathing was so shallow that Cecily could barely detect it. When she arrived at the house, she laid the child on a blanket on the kitchen floor, and Wolfie settled down to guard her.

"Now, you stay there and don't move, okay?" she said before racing back outside and into the barn they used as a storeroom. Bill had packed away all the baby paraphernalia in there before Cecily had arrived home from the hospital. Some of it still lay in its original boxes, and she searched through the pile for feeding bottles and terry-cloth diapers. She also grabbed the shawl that she remembered spending weeks knitting before heading back to the house, thinking she could collect whatever else she might need later. For now, the baby urgently needed milk.

"Heaven only knows how long the poor thing has been lying there," she said breathlessly to Wolfie, who hadn't moved from his spot beside the baby and watched her with mournful eyes. "Let's just hope it's not too late." She grabbed a jug of milk from the refrigerator, warmed some in a saucepan, then washed the bottle in hot water before filling it.

"Come on up here," she said to the baby as she wrapped the shawl around the tiny form, then settled the child into the crook of her arm. She eased the nipple between the baby's lips and wriggled it around.

"Come on, baby, suck for me," she encouraged. "It'll make you feel so much better if you do."

Nothing happened, and then Cecily remembered a tip from one of the books she had read when she was pregnant: "If the baby does not respond to the nipple, attempt to dribble the milk on its lips."

Cecily did so, then waited with bated breath for a reaction. Finally, she noticed the tiniest sucking movement and quickly thrust the nipple back inside the tiny mouth.

"There we go!" Cecily let out the breath she didn't realize she'd been holding.

The suckling was weak at first, and it seemed as though most of the milk was leaking back out of the baby's mouth, but finally it became a little stronger and Cecily could see the movement of swallowing in the child's throat.

"Thank the Lord." Cecily let out a small sob, just as the baby decided to throw up most of the milk she'd managed to take down.

Reaching for a cloth, Cecily wiped herself and the baby down as best she could. The baby emitted small mewling noises that sounded like a pathetic attempt at a cry.

"She must have gotten at least some of that into her little stomach."

And sure enough, a few minutes later, a small trail of green tarlike liquid oozed from her backside.

"At least your system is working. Lord knows how long you were lying there before Wolfie found you."

Eventually, exhausted from the exertion, the baby—who had yet to open her eyes—relaxed her grip on the nipple and exhaled.

"Are you asleep?" Cecily whispered as she bent her head to try to hear the sound of breathing. She could see the baby's chest rising and falling. As she slept, Cecily sat there in an agony of indecision. She knew she should call for Dr. Boyle to come and check the baby over; lying in the woods for however long must have left her dehydrated or perhaps with other medical conditions that Cecily hadn't even heard of. But it had been shady and cool where she'd found her . . . Cecily felt her tiny forehead. There was no fever, and the baby seemed neither too hot nor too cold.

"From the color of those feces, I'd guess she's not much more than a few hours old . . . Besides," she added, looking down at the sleeping child, "Dr. Boyle will just insist he take you with him and he'll place you in some dreadful orphanage like the ones Mama raises funds for."

Cecily must have drifted off herself, exhausted from all the panic, for when she woke, dusk was already falling and the baby was mewling in her arms.

"Okay, okay, let's try a little more milk."

When the baby had finished suckling, Cecily withdrew the bottle and saw that she had drunk over an ounce, and so far it had not come back up.

"Right, I'm sorry, baby, but we need to clean you up. I'm going to put you right there in a bowl in the sink and give you a good wash."

Setting to with a soft clean cloth and a bar of soap, Cecily was wetter than the baby by the time she had cleansed her thoroughly. There was an odd waxy coating on the baby's skin to remove, but Cecily had done her best to keep the umbilical cord dry, remembering that from her baby book. The baby had hollered loudly all the while, flexing her tiny limbs, which gave Cecily confidence that she was healthy.

After swaddling her in a dry towel and laying her gently on the bedroom floor, Cecily went back outside with the flashlight to fill the bassinet—still sheeted in cellophane—with things she might need overnight. Back inside, she tried her best to pin the diaper on the baby correctly, then placed her in the unwrapped bassinet on her bed. The baby had once again fallen asleep, so Cecily took the opportunity to make herself a quick sandwich, then hurried back to the bedroom clutching another bottle of milk as she heard her crying again. The baby took almost two ounces of milk this time, although she was a little sick just after. Then Cecily changed her diaper and dressed her in the tiny cotton nightgown her mother had sent in the parcel from Bloomingdale's over a year ago. Adding a knitted bonnet, Cecily chuckled at what her mother would think of the little black face encased inside it.

"I'd love to see your eyes soon, baby," she said as she lifted her into the bassinet once more. After preparing another bottle just in case the baby woke in the night and storing it in the refrigerator, Cecily locked up the house, turned out the lights, and climbed into bed, having checked the baby was still breathing in the bassinet next to her.

She heard Wolfie whimpering outside the bedroom door, eager to be let in. Cecily could only smile at the thought that he wanted to protect his charge.

"You stay there, boy, the baby's fine in here with me. Good night." Switching off the bedside light, Cecily rested her head on the pillow. She remembered back to that conversation she'd first had with Bill when he'd asked her if Njala could come and stay. And how he'd been somewhat vague about exactly what would happen to the baby once Njala had given birth. When she thought about it rationally, Cecily supposed that there were few alternatives; Njala had been in hiding because it must not be known that she was pregnant, or her marriage would be canceled and she would become an outcast. So had she known that her baby could never return with her?

*Help baby.*

"Oh, Lord!"

Suddenly, it all made sense. That last day she'd gone to the camp, Njala hadn't meant that Cecily should help with the birth, she'd meant exactly what she'd said.

Cecily sat bolt upright in shock. "She *wanted* me and Wolfie to find her."

The baby whimpered in her sleep next to Cecily. Cecily reached for her and tucked her into the crook of her arm. "Hush, little one. You're safe now. Safe here with me."

# 38

Every day for the next week, Cecily told herself she should at least call Bill and let him know what had happened, but each time she went to dial his number at the War Office in Nairobi, she put the receiver down. She was positive he would insist that he take the baby away to an orphanage. As one day rolled into the next and all her bottled-up maternal instincts began to flow out, the thought of anyone harming a hair on the head of the little being who was so dependent on her brought tears to her eyes. Even though she was exhausted from the nighttime feeds—the little newborn who had barely had the energy to suck a few days ago was now a voracious feeder and had a wail that could wake the lions on the plains below—Cecily had never felt quite so happy and content. She had set up a nursery in the room originally designated for her own baby and taken out everything from the barn to furnish it. Now the once empty room smelled deliciously of the talcum powder that she sprinkled over Stella's tiny behind. The baby book had guided her on how to care for the stump of umbilical cord, and it was drying out nicely and should drop off in the next couple of days. There was no time for her garden; she slept when the baby slept, grabbing a slice of toast whenever she could in between feeds.

The name "Stella" had come to her when she'd dozed off and woken to find a pair of huge clear eyes, the irises as dark brown as a coffee bean, staring up at her. She'd thought how like Njala's they were and then remembered Bill telling her that Njala's name meant "star" in English.

"Stella," Cecily had said, remembering from her schoolgirl Latin lessons that it also meant "star." Besides, she couldn't just carry on calling her "Baby."

"So Stella you shall be, at least for now." Cecily had said and sighed.

Two days ago, she'd heard the rumble of a vehicle snaking up the drive. Running to the window, Cecily had seen Katherine's pickup pull up outside. Knowing the front door was locked, Cecily had crouched beneath the window with Stella in her arms as Katherine had proceeded to knock on the door, then shout her name before wandering around the outside of the house to peer in through the windows, obviously confused by Wolfie's loud barking from inside. Katherine knew that the dog either was left outside if Cecily had gone shopping or was somewhere away on the farm with her. When the pickup had finally trundled out of earshot along the drive, Cecily had stood up with the baby in her arms, feeling rather stupid, but just now she wanted nothing to destroy the cozy world that she and Stella and Wolfie had created together.

However, when Cecily woke from yet another disturbed night, she heard the telephone ringing. After debating whether to ignore it, she slipped out of her bed and went to answer the call.

"It's Bill here," he said down a line that was as crackly as the one to New York. "How's tricks?"

"All's well here, Bill, yes. Very well. And how are you?"

"Suffice to say, the situation in Europe—and possibly here, too—gets bleaker by the day. However, I will be home on Christmas Eve."

"When is that?"

"Why, Cecily, it's in three days' time. Are you quite well?"

"Absolutely, never been better, Bill. I . . . went shopping, but there wasn't much meat at the market or much of anything else either," she lied.

"Don't you worry, I shall be barreling home loaded up with festive cheer, even if it costs half my army wages to do so. Are Katherine and Bobby joining us for Christmas Day as they did last year?"

"I haven't asked them. Should I?" Cecily bit her lip, knowing with each word he spoke that the halcyon days alone here with Stella were coming to an end.

"I'll speak to Bobby about it, don't worry, my dear. Are you sure you're all right? Bobby said Katherine called round and you weren't in."

"News travels fast! I was almost certainly in Gilgil, that's all."

"As long as all is well with you," he said. "I shall see you on Christmas Eve. I'll have to travel back the day after Boxing Day to be in the office, but I was rather hoping you'd join me in Nairobi and we could take in the races. You might enjoy them."

"We can talk about it when you get home," she said abruptly, having heard a whimper from the baby. "Bye, Bill."

Cecily put down the receiver with a heavy heart and walked slowly back to the bedroom, where Stella lay in her bassinet. Her arms were sprawled above her head, and with her long eyelashes fluttering against her skin as she dozed, she was the perfect picture of relaxation.

Cecily sat down next to her. "Oh, little one, what on earth are we going to do when Daddy gets home?"

Apart from dashing out while Stella was sleeping to buy jugs of fresh milk from the Maasai woman who had a stall on the road that led to Gilgil, Cecily's preparations for Christmas were virtually nonexistent. Time and again she tried to think what she would say to Bill, but eventually she decided that she would simply have to play it by ear.

On Christmas Eve, she put a record of carols to play on the gramophone, thinking how difficult it was to feel Christmassy when the thermometer was nearing seventy degrees. She bathed in the tub, washed her hair, and left it to dry naturally—Bill had commented that he liked it like that—taming the curls slightly with a couple of bobby pins. She dressed in a fresh blouse and cream skirt, fed and changed Stella, and put her to bed in the bassinet in the nursery. Then she fixed herself a hefty gin with a little vermouth and sat in the living room waiting for her husband to arrive home.

As she heard the sound of tires on the drive, her stomach did a crazy flip.

*It's okay, Cecily, you just have to tell him that you cannot possibly let him take her to an orphanage.*

"Hello," Bill said as he arrived in the hall, carrying a large tree that despite its needlelike leaves didn't much resemble the Christmas trees she remembered from New York. "Look what I dug up en route! I'll put it in a bucket in a jiffy, and maybe you'd like to decorate it."

"I . . . okay."

"I've also managed to purloin a number of delicious things for us to eat. I'll fetch them in a moment," he added, giving her a peck on the cheek. "Merry Christmas, Cecily."

She was rather taken aback by her husband's unusually high spirits. Trying but failing to remember how Bill had been last Christmas—the whole thing had passed in such a blur of misery, the memory had been wiped from her mind—she was glad he seemed so cheerful. It might aid her cause.

"Oh! I almost forgot, there's a hamper from Kiki which Aleeki dropped off at the club for you. It's still in the back of the pickup, and I'm pretty sure from the smell that it includes a side of smoked salmon. It probably needs eating pronto."

"Smoked salmon sandwiches, what riches!" Cecily smiled as Bill bolted out of the door to retrieve it.

She poured them a gin and vermouth each as Bill filled up a bucket with soil and positioned the "Christmas tree" in it so they could decorate it.

"It's all a bit 'make do and mend,' but who cares?" he said. "One should definitely celebrate Christmas as well as one can."

"You like Christmas?" Cecily stated the obvious.

"I love it. Always have, since I was a little boy. It may seem out of character for a man like me, but I just enjoy the fact that everyone is in a good mood. Even my parents didn't fight over Christmas. Now, I'm sure we have some decorations from last year in the barn. I'll go and get them." Bill moved toward the back door.

"Wait! I—"

"What is it?"

"Oh, I'm just a bit weary, that's all. Could we put them up tomorrow?"

"Cecily, tomorrow is Christmas Day, and it'll all nearly be over bar the shouting. It won't take me a minute to get them, and I can put them on the tree myself if you're too tired."

Bill was out of the door, and Cecily was out of excuses to stop him. She hoped against hope that he wouldn't notice the things that were missing from the barn.

He was back in a trice, carrying the box of decorations.

"All the things you gathered for the baby have disappeared. May I ask what you've done with them?"

"Oh . . . I'll tell you later. Now let's get these decorations on the tree," she said, gulping back some gin as she led Bill toward the living room.

"You know, Cecily, the difference in you from this time last year is remarkable. You stayed in bed on Christmas Day, do you remember?" he asked her as they began to hang baubles on the tree.

"I'm ashamed to say that no, I don't."

"You were not yourself, by any means."

A sudden loud screech emanated from beyond the living room.

"Good God! What the deuce is that?"

"I . . . don't know." Cecily felt herself blushing to the roots of her hair.

The screech came again and then turned into a full-scale wail.

Cecily's heart sank; she'd been hoping to tell Bill what had transpired before she introduced him to Stella, but now it was too late.

"It's coming from somewhere inside the house. Have you got a wild animal locked up in here or something?"

"No, I—"

But Bill was already on his way along the hallway to find the source of the caterwauling.

Cecily followed him anxiously as he looked into each of the bedrooms in turn and eventually pulled open the door of the tiny room wedged between them. She watched as Bill leaned over the bassinet, then recoiled in shock.

"Bloody hell! What is this?" he demanded as he turned to her.

She squeezed past him and picked up Stella, just in case Bill was tempted to do something dreadful to her. She walked out of the room with the baby in her arms and into the kitchen, where she retrieved a milk bottle and put it into a pan of water on the stove to warm.

"Cecily! For God's sake, can you at least explain to me what the hell is going on?" Bill was standing at the entrance to the kitchen.

"Let me settle her with a bottle, and then I'll tell you."

"I need another gin."

Cecily watched him retreat to fetch his drink, then sat down with the baby at the kitchen table. The wailing abated and peace descended as Stella suckled heartily.

"Right, then." Bill was back. He took a gulp of his drink and sat down on the chair opposite her.

The baby stopped sucking, and Cecily put a finger to her lips.

"Don't you dare try to silence me," Bill said, and Cecily saw he was shaking with anger. But he did at least lower his voice.

"It's very simple, Bill. Shortly after you last left for Nairobi, I went to visit Njala at her little camp. Even though all trace of it had gone, Wolfie picked up a scent and disappeared into the woods. He started barking and wouldn't come to heel, so I went to fetch him. Wolfie was the one who found her, buried beneath a heap of dead leaves in the forest. I'd guess she'd only been born a few hours before. It was obvious she'd been left to die in the woods, so I did what any Christian would do, or any human being with a heart, for that matter: I picked her up and brought her back home with me. She's been here ever since."

"Oh, God." Bill put one hand on his forehead and rested his elbow on the table.

"Do you think I did the wrong thing?"

"No, of course I don't."

"Did you . . . did you know that they would dump the baby and leave her to die?"

"Of course not. I didn't *want* to know anything." Bill sighed. "I was simply asked if I would provide a safe harbor on our land to my friend's daughter until her time came. I'm sure Leshan told me that the child would be taken to safety. I just can't believe they left her behind in our woods."

"Well, she was buried pretty deep, so it was pure luck that Wolfie found her. A few more hours, and she'd have died. She was so tiny." There were tears in her eyes as she looked down at Stella.

"I must admit, I'm furious that they left their dirty laundry for us to clear up. And—"

"Don't you dare call this baby that! She is not 'dirty laundry,' she's a human being, just like us!"

"Forgive me, Cecily, that was crass and I apologize, but please understand I'm in shock. I've come home on Christmas Eve, looking forward to a couple of days' peace away from the mayhem, to find a black baby in the nursery."

"Is the color of her skin really relevant to you, Bill? You're the one that spends half your life pretending you're a Maasai."

"No, of course it's not relevant in that sense, Cecily, but it obviously means that as soon as Christmas is over, we must take the baby into Nairobi and—"

"*No!* I will not see this child given to a mission or to an orphanage where she won't be adequately cared for. The Lord only knows what her fate would be, and I just couldn't risk letting anything bad happen to her."

"You're not suggesting we should keep her, are you?" Bill said after a pause.

"Why not? We don't have children and never will. Why shouldn't we adopt her?"

Bill stared at Cecily as though she had truly lost her mind. "Are you serious? You would actually entertain the thought of bringing her up here as our child?"

"Yes! We have a home, enough money . . . and besides, Njala obviously knew what was going to happen. She asked me to help her baby in the few words of English I'd taught her. I'm convinced that's why she left the baby close by; she *wanted* me to find her."

"I'm sorry, Cecily, but you're lapsing into fantasy. As you said, it was simply the dog that found her by chance whilst you were taking a walk through the woods—"

"A walk we'd taken every day for the best part of two months. Wolfie knew Njala's scent, which is bound to be similar to Stella's."

"You've named the baby?" Bill looked gray with exhaustion.

"I had to call her something, didn't I? Here, I've winded her and she's sleeping. Would you like to hold her?"

"No, Cecily, I would not." Bill pinched the bridge of his nose between his thumb and forefinger. "I'm sorry, but we simply cannot keep her."

"Why?"

"Because—"

"Yes?"

"She is black. Adoption of such a child just does not happen in our world or anywhere else in the world, for that matter."

"Why, Mr. Forsythe, the great champion of the Maasai, who even has one at his side everywhere he goes. Underneath all that, you're just as prejudiced as everyone else! Well, let me tell you something: if this baby goes, so do I! Because I made a promise to that poor young girl, and I will not send her baby away, you hear me?" Cecily rose with Stella in her arms, marched to the bedroom, then slammed the door behind her and locked it.

Laying the baby down on the bed next to her, Cecily burst into noisy tears. "Don't worry, little one." She hiccupped. "I'll die before I let harm come to you, I swear it."

Cecily was woken by a knock on the door. She looked at the clock and saw it was past midnight. The baby was stirring next to her, stuffing her knuckle into her mouth, which was her way of saying she was hungry.

"Cecily, can I please come in?"

As Stella needed a bottle anyway, Cecily reluctantly unlocked the door with the baby in her arms. She didn't so much as look at Bill as she walked out past him to fetch the bottle. Having warmed it, she sat down on a kitchen chair to feed her charge.

"Forgive me, Cecily," he said as he appeared at the kitchen door. "You've done nothing wrong at all."

"No, I haven't," Cecily retorted. "And anyone who says I have is a despicable human being."

"I agree," Bill said, sitting back down in the chair he'd occupied earlier.

"I mean it. If you suggest again that this baby goes to an orphanage, I will pack my things and leave with her. Do you understand?"

"I hear you loud and clear. But the fact remains that society has not yet been awakened to cross-racial adoption, on either side," he added firmly. "Perhaps someday that won't be the case, and I pray it is so."

"I don't care about what society says, and I didn't think you did either!"

"Cecily, believe me, if I *did* care about the rules of society, I'd never have married you in the first place, and we certainly wouldn't even be having this conversation. I'd have simply grabbed the baby from you and whisked her away to Nairobi. So please give me some credit. Nevertheless, the three of us *do* have to live in society, however much we try to bend the rules. And a white couple adopting a black baby is literally unheard of."

"I—" Cecily opened her mouth to speak, but Bill put up a hand to stop her.

"Hear me out, please. You've obviously become emotionally attached to the baby. Which is understandable, given the loss of your own child. I have only known about this . . . situation for a few hours, so forgive me if I'm struggling to come to terms with it. The fact is, Cecily, that even if you did leave with the baby, you have nowhere to run to."

"Of course I do! Katherine or even Kiki would take us in."

"I'm sure they would initially, but they would say the same as me. You cannot be a mother to a black child. It would not be accepted anywhere in the world. And please don't say you'll go and live with the Maasai, because they wouldn't want you, either," Bill said, making a weak attempt at a joke. "Cecily, do you hear what I'm saying? The fantasy world you've created since I've been away cannot ever be real. You must know that, surely?"

Cecily bit her lip, knowing that to some extent what her husband said was true.

"But I can't give her up, Bill. She was given to me to care for. And besides, this is all your fault to begin with. If you hadn't let Njala come stay here on our land, then we wouldn't be in this situation now."

"I'm aware of that, Cecily, and I now rue the day I said yes. Come, let me hold her," Bill said, reaching his arms across the table.

"You swear you won't make off with her in the night to Nairobi?"

"I promise. Here," he encouraged, and reluctantly Cecily placed Stella in his arms.

"Hello, little one," he said as he stared down at her. "You're just like your mother—absolutely beautiful."

Cecily watched as Bill held out his finger and one of Stella's tiny hands grabbed it and held it tight. The sight brought tears to Cecily's eyes.

"My goodness, Mrs. Forsythe. You've certainly led me a merry dance since I married you." He gave her a weak smile. "And there was me driving home, thinking that we were sailing into calmer waters because you seemed so much better."

Cecily shrugged defensively. "Divorce me if you wish."

"Cecily, in order to sort this situation out, you need to behave like a grown woman, not a petulant child. Can I ask you, does anyone else know of Stella's presence here? Katherine, for example?"

"Nobody—that's why I didn't let Katherine in the other day."

"You're absolutely sure?"

"Totally."

"At least that's something." Bill looked down at the baby. "Let me think calmly about what is best to do for all of us."

"But I—"

Bill put a finger to his lips. "No more tonight, Cecily. I've heard you. Now it's time we all got some sleep. I'm exhausted." He stood up and handed Stella back, then kissed Cecily on the forehead. "Merry Christmas, my dear wife. That's one hell of a present I've come home to."

To her surprise, Cecily wasn't woken by Stella until five. Fearing her cries would wake Bill, she gathered her up and took her into the kitchen to feed her.

"Merry Christmas, darling," she said as a glorious sunrise began to peek above the horizon through the window. "And don't worry, I'll fight for you, whatever it takes."

With Stella fed and asleep in the bassinet, Cecily donned her apron and prepared a fresh batch of bread to accompany the smoked salmon, then used the two-day-old bread from the larder to make stuffing for the chicken Bill had brought home. Preparations made, she put on her favorite green dress, then added some powder to cover the dark circles beneath her eyes and dabbed a little rouge on her pale cheeks. Then she returned to the kitchen to peel some vegetables. Next year, her vegetable garden should be thriving and she could just pick them fresh.

She checked herself. What was she even doing being so jolly? There was every chance that Bill would wake up and say that Stella had to go, which meant that she'd be packing her bags, too.

"Good morning," Bill said as though her thoughts had summoned him to her. "You look bright and breezy. Might I beg a cup of tea?"

"Of course." Cecily put some water on to boil.

"How did you—and *she*—sleep?"

"Very well indeed, thank you. She doesn't fuss much at night."

"But she's obviously up with the lark, eh? Thank you," he said as Cecily passed him his tea. "Right, then, Bobby and Katherine are due round at noon, so I'll complete my morning ablutions and I'll see you in the living room after that. We have to talk, Cecily."

Fifteen minutes later Cecily was sitting in the living room, her heart hammering, when Bill returned fully dressed and sat down in the armchair opposite her.

"I will tell you that I spent a great deal of last night thinking about what was best to do," Bill began. "I realize that I am ultimately responsible for this . . . predicament we find ourselves in. I agreed to have Njala here, after all."

"I know for sure she would have kept her baby if she'd been allowed to, but she wasn't, which was why she wanted me to help her."

"I think, my dear, that we have to deal in hard facts here. I can understand that you feel responsible for the child, but you must know that in reality you should have no such guilt. However, I equally accept that you have become emotionally attached to her and have told me that you will leave with her if I insist she goes."

"I sure will, Bill. I'm sorry, but—"

"Could you spare me any histrionics, Cecily, and simply listen to what I have to say? I told you last night that it is untenable that you, and by association *I*, become the baby's parents. I dread to think what your mother and father would say if you presented Stella to them. So you have to be realistic. Or, in fact, I have to be realistic for you. I've come up with a solution that I hope will keep you—and I and of course Stella herself—happy. Are you prepared to hear me out?"

"Yes."

"Good. So remember I mentioned to you when I left for Nairobi last time that we should employ some domestic help?"

"Yes."

"My suggestion is that we find a woman through Nygasi, who will be told of the situation, who will come into the household to live with us as a cook and housekeeper. I'd already earmarked part of the barn as servants' quarters, and it will take no time to make it habitable. When the woman arrives, we will tell everyone that we have a new maid who has come to us with her baby or, in fact, her granddaughter, depending on her age. That way, Stella can stay with us here at Paradise Farm and grow up under our protection. It's not uncommon for maids to have dependents living with them. It also means that Stella will ostensibly grow up within her own culture. Please remember that's important for her, too."

"Are you saying that Stella will have to live in a barn?" Cecily was horrified.

"To be honest, Cecily, I'm not worried about the details; they can be ironed out later. I'm much more concerned about finding a way for you to know that you fulfilled your promise to Njala, that you did your Christian duty, and that Stella can stay."

"But Bill, I want to bring her up . . . be her mother." Cecily bit her lip.

"And to all intents and purposes, when no one else is around, that's exactly what you can be."

"Won't the maid think it strange that the white lady of the house wishes to spend so much time with the black baby?"

"Maids are not paid to decide what is strange about their employers and what isn't. You can do as you wish, as long as Stella is left with the maid when anyone visits."

Cecily studied her feet silently.

"I understand this is not the perfect outcome," Bill said gently, "but it's the only one I could contemplate. Even I have my limits, Cecily, and trust me, I've certainly been pushed to them in the past year. But I understand that separating you from Stella is as untenable as us bringing her up as our own child. So for your sake and hers, I'm prepared to accept her presence under our roof, as long as you are prepared to accept my compromise. Are you?"

Still, Cecily stared at her feet.

Bill let out a sigh. "I asked you last night not to behave like a petulant child, and I ask you again now. I can do no more. Do you accept?"

Cecily finally raised her eyes to Bill's. "I accept."

"Good. Now, then, perhaps we can get on with having Christmas Day." Bill pointed to the tree. "Look underneath it."

Cecily roused herself and walked over to the tree. Underneath it was a small package.

"Sorry I didn't have time to wrap it properly. I hope you like it."

"Oh, Bill, I feel so bad, my gift to you was in the parcel my parents sent from the States, but it hasn't arrived."

"Really, don't worry, my dear. Go on, open it."

Cecily brought it back to the chair and undid the string and the brown paper to reveal a velvet box. Opening the lid, she saw a delicate gold chain with an exquisite square emerald sitting in the center of a cluster of diamonds.

"Oh, my, Bill! It's so beautiful. You shouldn't have. I . . . I don't deserve it. I don't deserve you."

"Want me to put it on for you? It goes well with that green dress of yours. I've had the stone for years—a South African chap gave it to me when I did him a favor, and rather than it languishing in the drawer, I thought, well . . . it would look beautiful on you. Now, there we go. Why don't you look at it in the mirror?"

Cecily stood up, tears glistening in her eyes, and walked over to glance at her reflection in the mirror set over the fireplace. "It's absolutely perfect. Thank you, Bill, thank you so much. And thank you for allowing Stella to stay."

"Come here, you silly thing." Bill drew Cecily into his arms. "We've had a rough old time of it since we married," he said as she leaned her head on his shoulder. "And what with the war and the new addition to our family, there's almost certainly more to come. But I do hope that this Christmas can at least mark a new era for you and me." He tipped her chin up to look at her. "What do you think, old girl?"

"I think . . . I think I'd like that very much."

"Good." Then Bill leaned down and, for the first time since their wedding day, sought out her lips. It had been so long since she'd been kissed, Cecily had almost forgotten what to do, but an extraordinary rush of warmth filled her body as he teased her lips open with his own.

A screech came from the nursery, and Cecily reluctantly broke away from him.

"Good God! Do you know how long I've been waiting to do that, and now it gets interrupted!" Bill smiled down at her. "Go on, off you go to your new baby," he called after her.

# 39

Cecily knew she would never forget that Christmas Day. She hadn't been happy about Nygasi taking Stella off into the woods and out of sight, especially when she'd seen the look of shock on his face when she and Bill had handed over the baby and enough bottles to keep her going for the next few hours. Bill had assured her that Nygasi would not harm a hair on her head.

"I've told him that if any misfortune comes to her, I will report both him and Njala to the authorities for abandoning a newborn," Bill had comforted her as he'd ushered Cecily back inside the house. "You do understand, don't you, that no one must see her before our new maid arrives?"

"I do, yes. Thank you, Bill, thank you so very much. I promise she won't be any bother, and—"

"You know very well that's not true, but I appreciate the sentiment." Bill shook his head as he closed the front door. "The things I do to make you happy, my dear. Right, I'll go and open the champagne, and you'd better get to the kitchen. Katherine and Bobby will be here any minute."

The day passed in a trance, Cecily hardly able to believe that not only had Bill kissed her earlier but he'd also agreed to give her the best present of all: Stella could stay. No longer did she look at Katherine's growing bump and feel envy, because she, too, had a child to love. It was sad that it could not be in the traditional way, but it was more than she had dared to dream of over the past dreadful year. Her necklace was much admired by Katherine, who followed her into the kitchen to help her serve up lunch.

"You are a miracle, the way that you're prepared to do this all yourself when you could easily afford staff, Cecily," Katherine commented as she flipped the potatoes that were so much part of a traditional English roast.

"As a matter of fact, Bill and I have decided it's time to get some help. We'll be employing a maid as soon as we can."

"Good for you! I'm only hoping there's enough money from Bobby's army wages and from the farm to employ some help for me, too, when the baby comes. I must say, Cecily, you look positively sparkling today," Katherine said as she eyed her friend. "You've finally come out of your funk, and it's wonderful to see you and Bill so happy. I only wish Bobby was so dreamy over me, but we've known each other forever, and I sometimes think he still sees me as that irritating little child who followed him around."

"Katherine, you have one of the happiest marriages I've ever known."

"I'm not sure he'll be after me for my body once I've given birth. Honestly, Cecily, I feel like I've almost doubled in weight already! I'll be the same size as one of his precious heifers by the time I'm due!"

After a very jolly lunch, they played some card games before Katherine said it was time to go home. "I'm utterly shattered, but it's been the most wonderful day. Thank you so much. We'll return the favor next year, promise," she said as she and Bobby hugged their hosts good-bye.

Bill had to hold his wife firmly by the shoulders as the pickup disappeared off along the drive. "Wait for a few minutes, Cecily. You never know, Katherine might have forgotten something and come back for it."

The moment ten minutes was up, Cecily was outside, calling Nygasi's name.

"Do you really have to fetch Stella straight back?" Bill called after her. "I'd have liked to have you to myself for a while."

But Cecily was already out of earshot.

Later that night, when Stella was tucked up in the nursery, seemingly no worse for wear after her day with Uncle Nygasi, Bill lit a fire not just because the evening had grown cool but because it "felt more Christmassy."

"Tell me about your boyhood Christmases," Cecily said, curling up in the chair opposite him.

"Oh, they were frightfully English. Stockings first thing in the morning, then walking through the snow to church . . . I'm sure there wasn't snow every year, but that's how I remember it. So different from here . . ." He sighed and looked at her. "Cecily, I . . . I feel that perhaps we got off on the wrong foot from the start."

"What do you mean?"

"I believe that you presumed I was asking you to marry me merely to save your reputation and to provide me with a wife who would run the home I've never really had. In other words, it was a 'deal' that suited us both."

"Yes, that is what you said, Bill. Did I get it wrong?"

"Not entirely, no. I . . . well, I was certainly drawn to you the minute I met you. You fascinated me because you weren't like the other women round here—you were *real* and didn't worry about what clothes you wore or being seen at the right parties. You were obviously bright and easy on the eye, too." He smiled. "And then we married, and the more I got to know you, I saw your quiet tenacity and the fact you never demanded anything from me but simply accepted who I was. I became, well, more than fond of you. Obviously, I felt it was very inappropriate for us to embark on a . . . physical relationship while you were pregnant, but I want you to know that it wasn't because I didn't want to." A faint blush rose up his neck. "And then, of course, the worst happened and I was not there for you when you needed me. Cecily, it was unforgivable of me to leave you alone here so close to the birth, especially without leaving word of where I was. And when I finally arrived at the hospital and found you sedated, your life hanging in the balance, I realized not only what a completely selfish arse I'd been but also that I . . . that I loved you. Cecily, I sat by your bedside that day and I *cried*. And I hadn't done that since Jenny, the girl who broke my heart, told me our engagement was off."

Bill paused, his face lined with anguish. "By then, of course, it was too late: you were so sick and devastated, and you believed I didn't care a fig for you. And why should you have believed otherwise? I'd married you and then continued with the life I'd lived before you arrived. Then the war came, and although I didn't want to leave you alone here, I had no choice. Besides, I understood that you didn't want me near you. Even though—albeit in my own clumsy way—I did my best to show you I cared, you didn't see it, did you?"

"No, Bill, I didn't think you loved me one bit."

"We were certainly at an impasse, and to be honest, I couldn't see it ever changing. And then, when Njala came here, the gray cloud around you seemed to lift. I saw you smiling occasionally, and on the night that we entertained Joss, Diana, and Jock, you looked utterly lovely. When we danced together, I really began to believe that we could have a future. Do you think we do, Cecily?

"I . . . I think both of us have cut ourselves off from the world in our different ways."

"Agreed. We have. And more importantly, from each other. The burning question is, of course, did you . . . *do* you have any feelings for me?"

"I'm not sure I've dared to, Bill." Cecily shook her head in confusion.

"Like you, I've learned to rely on myself. I . . . I just don't want to be hurt again. After all that's happened, it would break me."

"I understand, of course I do. Perhaps we could go back to the beginning and start again?" Bill's eyes were glassy, and he looked near tears. "I want to try to be a better man for you."

"And for Stella."

He nodded. "And for Stella. Well?" He reached out his hand to her. "Can we give it a go?"

After a short pause, Cecily took it. "We can most certainly try."

"Come here." Bill stood and pulled Cecily to him. Then he took her in his arms and kissed her.

Cecily woke the next morning to a full-scale wailing. She forced her eyes open and saw Bill standing above her, Stella in his arms.

"I think she might be ill. I tried to feed her a bottle, but she kept spitting it out. What do I do?"

Cecily sat up and realized she was naked. "Give her to me," she said, holding out her arms and taking the squalling baby. "Phew, she stinks. You say she wouldn't take her bottle?"

"No, I took it out of the refrigerator, but she refused to countenance it."

"Did you warm it first?"

"No . . . oh, I dare say that's why she wouldn't take it."

"Pass me my robe?"

Bill took it off the hook on the back of the door. Cecily laid Stella on the bed and sat upright to put it on, feeling mighty odd at being unclothed in front of her husband. Bill leaned down and kissed one of her shoulder blades, then nuzzled the back of her neck.

"Last night was wonderful, darling."

"Yes, but I will need to feed the baby so she'll stop hollering." She smiled, tying up her robe and picking the baby up in her arms.

Bill followed her through to the kitchen and watched as she took the bottle and put it into a pan of water to warm.

Once the baby was drinking contentedly, Bill sat down opposite her. He was wearing only a pair of shorts, and the sight of his broad chest made Cecily's nether regions tingle.

"You look utterly gorgeous this morning."

"I'm utterly sure I don't," said Cecily, rolling her eyes. "Why, I haven't even brushed my hair."

"And you never need to again in my book. I love it wild like that, falling over your bare shoulders."

Cecily giggled. "Bill!"

"Anyway, Mrs. Forsythe, I intend to ravish you again as soon as possible, but I wanted to ask you if you wish to come back to Nairobi with me to go to the races. I think it's time you and I showed our faces at Muthaiga Club. Everyone will be there, and with you by my side, I might actually enjoy it."

"Oh, but what on earth do we do with Stella?"

"Nygasi and I think we may have found someone suitable."

"So soon?"

"Yes. I'm sure you've met the woman who sells fresh milk on the road to Gilgil."

"I have, yes."

"Well, it was Nygasi who helped her when she faced the same situation as Njala. She's a cousin of his, and he asked me if I could help out by providing her with a couple of cattle she could milk to sell to people like us. She had her son, who is now ten or so, and she's been staying in that shack by the road with him, scratching a living ever since. Nygasi vouches for her that she's an honest woman, who also has the advantage of speaking limited English, due to her conversing with the white residents when they buy her milk."

Cecily tried to visualize the woman. "How old is she?"

"I'm not sure, probably in her early twenties. And of course, she has brought up her own child, so she knows how to care for a baby."

"Her son would come and live with her here, too?"

"He would, yes. He can help you out in the garden. Nygasi has talked to her already, and she understands the situation with Stella."

"She won't tell anyone, will she?"

"Goodness, no. She already thinks you're a saint for saving the child. And you are, my dear. I'm ashamed and horrified that I may have made you feel anything else."

"Okay, let me get Stella cleaned up and myself dressed and we'll see her," Cecily agreed.

An hour later, she sat in the living room with Bill. Nygasi had led in a painfully thin young woman whom Cecily recognized and a boy whose slight frame marked him out as undernourished for a ten-year-old. Mother and son stood in the living room, looking around in wonder.

"Please"—Cecily pointed to the couch—"sit."

Both looked utterly terrified at the thought, but Nygasi said something to them, and they perched reluctantly on the edge of it.

"This is Lankenua and her son, Kwinet," said Bill. "This is Cecily, my wife," he said in Maa to the pair on the couch.

"Very pleased to meet you. *Takwena*, Lankenua," Cecily added.

"Right, perhaps it's best if Nygasi and I translate the questions you have for Lankenua," Bill suggested.

"I . . . I don't know what to ask."

Cecily was sizing up the young woman in front of her. Her eyes had the look of a frightened deer that would bolt at the slightest noise. She was not particularly comely, her hair shaved close to her scalp, her nose rather large for her face, and her teeth yellowing and uneven. The son was altogether more handsome, with the proud bearing of his Maasai forefathers.

"Lankenua knows what the job entails and is happy—very happy," Bill repeated, "to take it. Perhaps the simplest thing to do is to fetch Stella and see how she interacts with her."

"Okay," said Cecily, standing up. Returning with the baby a few seconds later, she handed her over to Lankenua, whose eyes lit up as she saw Stella. She muttered under her breath and smiled, then cooed at Stella, who lay calmly in her arms.

"What is she saying?" Cecily asked Nygasi.

"That baby is beautiful, like a princess."

"Which, of course, in the world of the Maasai, she is," added Bill.

"Lankenua mother wise woman," put in Nygasi. "Very clever."

Stella began to cry, so Cecily went to fetch her a bottle.

"Let Lankenua feed her, my dear," Bill said.

Cecily did so, and the baby accepted the bottle from Lankenua with no fuss.

"Does she know how to cook?" Cecily asked.

Nygasi duly translated in Maa. "She say not white person food, but she quick learner."

Cecily watched the way that Kwinet, the young boy, was leaning over Stella, his features softening as he smiled down at the baby.

"And there will be laundry, too. And work for the boy in the garden," Cecily said.

"Boy look after cow. He strong," Nygasi explained.

Lankenua said something then to Nygasi, who nodded.

"What did she say?"

"I say you good woman." Lankenua spoke the words slowly as she smiled at Cecily. "I like work you."

Bill looked askance at Cecily. "Well?"

Cecily was still looking at Lankenua. "Okay," she breathed. "I like you work for me, too."

Early that evening, Lankenua, her son, and their two skinny cows were installed in one end of the barn.

"You know, I really don't think there's any need to convert it," Bill commented. "They'll only sleep in there during the rains anyway. They seem as happy as Larry with their new home."

"They must have some sanitary facilities at least, Bill. A lavatory and a faucet. Are you sure we can trust them?"

"Absolutely, and besides, Nygasi will be here to oversee things whilst we're in Nairobi."

"Oh, Bill, I can't go tomorrow. I want to make sure with my own eyes that she'll take care of Stella properly."

"My instinct is that the woman is a trustworthy soul who has had a difficult time of it. I suggest we leave Stella in the nursery with Lankenua now and have an early night." He smiled down at her. "Then see how she's got on in the morning."

"Okay." Cecily took the hint and nodded shyly. With Bill's arm draped across her shoulders, they both walked back toward the house.

# 40

So began a new era for Cecily. Having seen that Lankenua was already in love with Stella, she accompanied Bill to the races in Nairobi. The facts that her clothes were two years out of date and her hair was not cut in the latest fashion didn't matter a damn because Bill told her she looked beautiful anyway. And after long, warm nights of lovemaking in his cell-like room at Muthaiga Club, she felt as gorgeous as Diana, whose affair with Joss was now common knowledge. Cecily and Bill joined them to dine one night, and Jock—the cuckold in the nest, as Bill called him—sat next to her, slowly getting drunker. No one at the club seemed to turn a hair at what was happening.

"They're all used to Joss and his ways, darling," Bill said with a shrug. (Cecily just loved it when he called her "darling.")

She was persuaded to stay on for New Year's Eve and met her godmother at the big party held at the club.

"Why, sweetie! You look positively radiant!" Kiki enveloped her in a cloud of perfume and cigarette smoke. "But you do need to update your wardrobe," she whispered into her ear. "I'll give you the address of a little place I know that sells the most fabulous clothes, copied from the latest Parisian catwalks. And you must meet Prince Paul and Princess Olga of Yugoslavia—they're staying with me while this wretched war continues. Come over one weekend and we'll have a house party!"

Cecily agreed, knowing that Kiki would probably forget all about the invitation. Despite her outward joie de vivre and perfect makeup, her godmother had dark rings under her lovely eyes, and her hand shook as she put her cigarette holder to her lips.

"Must you go home?" Bill asked Cecily as they lay in bed naked, listening to the party still continuing well into the early hours of 1941.

"You know I must, Bill. I haven't seen Stella for days. She might forget who I am."

"As long as babies are fed and their napkins are changed, they don't care who is providing the service," he commented. "Or at least that's what my old nanny used to say."

"I'm sure your nanny was right in a way, but I do believe Stella will be missing me. Besides, you'll be back to work and what will I have to do all day here?"

"True. Well," he said, kissing her on the forehead, "you run back to your baby and your cabbages, and I'll join you as soon as I can."

Cecily left the following morning, the trunk of Katherine's pickup chock-ful of the ready-to-wear clothes Cecily had bought from the boutique Kiki had recommended in Nairobi.

"Wasn't that fun?" Katherine said with a yawn as they headed out of Nairobi, her stomach straining against the steering wheel.

"Do you want me to drive, Katherine?"

"Goodness, no, and most of it isn't the baby, just blubber," she said. "I must say, I'll be glad to get back home; all that partying has quite worn me out. Bill seemed to enjoy himself, too—he's always been such a stick-in-the-mud about such events. Obviously you two are getting along awfully well just now—your husband looks like the cat who got the cream. You walking into his life was the best thing that ever happened to him."

"And I feel the same about him walking into mine." Cecily smiled. "I'll miss him while he's away."

"That's the first time I've heard you say that, and I couldn't be happier for both of you."

And indeed, once Katherine had dropped her and her purchases off at Paradise Farm and had been introduced to Lankenua, Kwinet, and Stella—the last of whom she had cooed over endlessly—Cecily, with the baby in her arms, waved Katherine off and thought that she really couldn't be happier either.

Over the next few weeks, Bill did his best to get home as often as he could, sometimes arriving late at night and leaving again at dawn. During those nights, Cecily installed Lankenua and Stella in one of the spare rooms—she point-blank refused to countenance Stella sleeping in the barn—so that she and Bill wouldn't be disturbed.

The more she got to know Lankenua, who she'd worked out must be around the same age as herself, the more she began to trust and like her. She was a fast learner and after less than a month was already able to present a decent roast chicken dinner and a curry (even though she had mistakenly strangled one of Cecily's precious chickens instead of taking the one from the refrigerator). Kwinet was also proving very useful in the garden, as Cecily taught him how to care for the different varieties of plants and vegetables. She had needed to reprimand him only once, when she had gone out onto the veranda to see the two scrawny cows grazing in the center of her front lawn. On the whole, he was a sweet boy, and the regular nourishment he now received daily was filling out his hollowed cheeks. Lankenua was also end-lessly gentle with Stella, which gave Cecily the confidence to drive down to Nairobi on occasions when Bill couldn't make it home.

In the last week of January, Lankenua woke Cecily with a knock on her bedroom door. "Come, Missus Cecily." Lankenua mimed a telephone re-ceiver held up to her ear. Cecily put on her robe and padded along the hall-way to take the call.

"Hello, darling, it's Bill here," her husband's voice crackled down the line. "I just wanted to warn you that I'll be home late tonight. Something bloody awful has happened."

"What?"

"Joss has had a motoring accident out near Diana and Jock's house in Karen. He's broken his neck, apparently . . . Oh, God, Cecily . . . Joss is dead!"

"Oh, no!" Cecily bit her lip. She knew that Bill adored Joss, despite his friend's appalling antics with women. "I . . . is there anything I can do?"

"No. Obviously I'll have to take over his duties here whilst they sort every-thing out. I'm going to drive over to the mortuary now to . . . see the old chap and say good-bye," Bill added, his voice breaking.

"Oh, darling, I am so very sorry. Perhaps it's better if I come to you?"

"Whatever happens, they'll arrange his funeral pretty quickly. They have to out here, you see. Well, if you're sure you want to come, I'll see you at the club later, then. Take care on the drive, Cecily."

She put down the receiver and went into the kitchen to make herself a strong cup of coffee. Sipping it, she stared out of the window at another glorious morning; a morning that Joss—so full of life and vitality—would not see. She remembered how her father had often used a rather archaic saying, something about if one lived by the sword, one died by it, too. For the first time, Cecily really understood what it meant. Joss had cut a swathe through his own life, hardly pausing for breath. And now he was gone.

Lankenua appeared in the kitchen with Stella in her arms. "Okay, Missus Cecily?"

"I have to go to Nairobi," said Cecily. "You take care of Stella, okay?"

"Okay."

Cecily packed the one black dress and hat she owned and a little after noon set off in Bill's spare pickup for Nairobi. Even though she'd been nervous at first to drive by herself, she'd learned to enjoy the freedom of getting around under her own steam.

The atmosphere at Muthaiga Club was muted, to say the least. She saw through the small window that men were huddled together in the Gentlemen's Bar, drinking whisky and talking in low voices. A few women were sitting out on the terrace, raising their champagne glasses in a toast to Joss. Cecily went to her room, intending to change after the dusty drive, but soon heard the door open behind her.

"Hello, darling, they told me you'd arrived." Bill looked gray and tired, as if he'd aged ten years since the last time she'd seen him. Cecily walked toward him.

"I am so, so sorry. I know what he meant to you."

"Well, despite his faults, life will never be the same around here again. But it gets worse, Cecily. I went to see him in the mortuary and spoke to Superintendent Poppy. This *cannot* become public knowledge until Government House announces it tomorrow, but it looks as if the old boy was murdered."

"Murdered? Oh, my God, Bill. What happened?"

"He was shot in the head. Apparently the bullet had traveled in a straight line from his ear and ended up in his brain. He didn't stand a chance."

"But who would want to murder Joss? Everybody loved him! Didn't they?"

Cecily searched her husband's face for the answer, then thought again. "Oh," she whispered.

"Yes, I'm afraid that's what everyone thinks, especially as it happened very close to Jock and Diana's house. Joss had apparently dropped Diana off there and . . . God only knows what exactly happened, but it's not looking good for Jock Broughton."

"Well, to be frank, Bill, even though I know how fond you were of Joss, I wouldn't entirely blame Jock if he *had* shot him."

"I know, darling, I know." Bill sighed and sat down on the bed. "Obviously this is all top secret—the funeral will go ahead tomorrow, and after that the police will interview Jock."

"Do *you* think he did it?"

"As you say, he certainly had the motive. Anyway, mum's the word for now. I just wanted to tell you. Now I need to get back to the War Office and try and man the ship there. Will you be all right?"

Cecily nodded. "Of course I will."

"I'll be back in time for dinner." With a sad wave, Bill left the room.

The funeral of Josslyn Victor Hay, twenty-second Earl of Erroll, took place the following day at St. Paul's Church in Kiambu, just outside Nairobi. Cecily, sitting with Bill in the front pew, looked behind her and saw that everyone who was anyone was there, but she could not spot Diana. Last night, Bill had told her that only hours before Joss's death, Jock had agreed to divorce Diana so she could marry Joss. He'd toasted to their happiness at Muthaiga Club in full view of the other diners.

"Please remember that only the police authorities know that Joss was murdered; everyone else still believes it was just a tragic car accident," he'd cautioned her before they'd left for the funeral.

Yet it was obvious during the wake at Muthaiga Club afterward that murmurings were already afoot. Both Alice and Idina looked devastated, and there were few kind words for Diana. Jock made an appearance, looking half cut and distressed, and was taken off by his friend June Carberry before he "made a fool of himself," as she explained to Bill.

"It feels like the end of an era," Bill said as he helped Cecily into the pickup later that day. "Happy Valley *was* Joss, and even if I found some of his antics deplorable, the world will be a lesser place without him. Please take care on the journey home, and telephone me when you arrive, won't you?"

"I will."

As she drove off, Cecily fervently hoped that the blow of the death of Bill's closest friend would not put a damper on their own new and wonderful relationship.

Jock Broughton was arrested three weeks later for the murder of Joss Erroll. The scandal made headlines around the world, with even Dorothea calling her for an update.

"So you knew this Joss personally?" Dorothea said breathlessly.

"Yes, he's . . . he was Bill's close friend. He, Diana, and Jock came to stay with us for a weekend in December."

"Oh, my!" There was an enthralled silence. "So you actually met Diana? Is she as beautiful as she looks in the papers?"

"She is very attractive, yes."

"Do you think Sir Jock shot him?"

"Mama, I don't know, but Joss and Diana did nothing to hide their affair in front of him."

"I can't believe you've had them to stay under your roof."

Cecily had to smile, because her mother sounded positively starstruck, however gruesome the situation.

"Were they in love as the papers say?" Dorothea asked.

"Oh, yes." *Or in lust*, Cecily thought. "Anyway, I have to go," she said, hearing Stella's complaints that it was time for a bottle. "Love to everyone."

"Wait, is that a baby I can hear in the background?"

"Yes, it's Stella, my maid's daughter. She's awful cute, Mama."

"Well, if this war ever ends, I'll be straight out on that boat to see you, honey. Kenya sounds like such an interesting place."

"Oh, it is certainly interesting," Cecily said. "Bye, Mama."

News of the war, which had dominated conversations for so long, had been temporarily cast aside in favor of the juicy gossip surrounding the murder investigation. Although Cecily was happily occupied with Stella, her heart ached for her husband, who was spending all his time in Nairobi, not only helping to take on Joss's old job but also sorting out his friend's personal affairs.

Katherine telephoned Paradise Farm regularly. She was spending most of her time with Alice at Wanjohi Farm, doing what she could to ease Alice's grief over Joss.

"I'm worried for her," Katherine had confided to Cecily. "Her father recently died, too, and she is absolutely destroyed by Joss's murder . . . She's not well, Cecily, I don't know what to do."

Jock Broughton's trial finally opened at Nairobi's Central Court at the end of May.

"Honestly, it's like an audience come to see a show, darling," Bill said when he called after the end of the first day. "All of Happy Valley is here, dressed in their best, of course, and there are reporters from all over the world, too. At least Diana's done her bit by hiring her poor husband a gifted barrister. Mind you, she arrived at court this morning dressed in black and ready to play the widow. I hate to speak ill of anyone, but it's almost as if she's enjoying the attention."

*Quelle surprise*, thought Cecily.

"Come up to town if you want, but it is a rather lurid spectacle, especially with the war still on."

"I think I'll stay right here," Cecily said, knowing how disappointed her mother would be that she was missing one of the most sensational murder trials of modern times. She was far more interested in watching Stella—now almost six months old—as she grew. The scrawny baby had developed into a chubby and adorable little thing whose every move delighted Cecily. Stella was fully alert now, and Cecily would lay her on a blanket in the garden under the shade of a fever tree and watch as her huge eyes—so like her mother's—followed the scudding clouds overhead and the birds singing happily from the branches above her. Wolfie adored her and would lie outside the nursery door at night.

"You do seem to spend an awful lot of time minding Stella," Katherine—who was due to give birth any day now and had made an increasingly rare visit—commented as Stella sat on Cecily's knee on the veranda.

"Lankenua is so busy with the house, someone has to care for her. And she's too heavy to be carried around in a carrier," Cecily replied quickly.

Katherine eyed her. "Stella doesn't sound like a very Maasai name, does it?"

"Actually, her name is Njala, which means 'star'; isn't that beautiful? Stella is simply the Latin word for it," Cecily lied easily.

"Just take care you don't become too fond of her and end up looking after her all the time. Otherwise you're just swapping one job for another, aren't you?"

Cecile smiled. "Oh, I don't mind at all. It's better than scrubbing floors, after all."

"So the jury has finally gone away to deliberate on the verdict," Bill said to his wife on the telephone two months later. "To be honest, I'm at the point where I don't much care one way or the other. The whole thing has become a circus, and I'll be very relieved when it's over."

"What do you think they'll come back with?" asked Cecily as she spooned pulped apple into Stella's mouth, holding the receiver at the same time.

"The evidence against him is pretty damning, but Morris, his barrister, gave a spectacular closing speech. He was worth every penny Diana spent. Anyway, I'll call you as soon as the verdict is in. And then perhaps dear old Joss can finally rest in peace."

"I really hope so," Cecily murmured to herself as she replaced the receiver. "And that Bill can begin to find peace, too."

Bill called again at ten o'clock that night. "He's been acquitted! He won't hang after all."

"Holy moly! I thought that most people expected him to be found guilty."

"They did, but . . . to be honest, after hearing all the evidence, I'm not so certain, either. I'm just glad it's over, and darling, I'm so sorry, but I'm afraid I won't be home this weekend; I have to visit an internment camp in Mombasa."

"Oh, gosh, you won't be in any danger there, will you?"

"No, not at all. I just have to check that the POWs are being treated all right. I'll be in touch as soon as I can. Chin up, this simply can't go on much longer."

Cecily hung up, then went out onto the veranda. Although the sky above her was clear, it was an unusually humid evening for July, and the air was heavy with fragrance from the flowers in the garden. She couldn't help but think back to that night when Joss and Diana had danced together right here . . .

Going back inside, she decided she'd call her mother tomorrow with the news. Despite believing in her heart that Jock was guilty, she was glad he hadn't ended up with a noose around his neck. Slipping into bed, she wished fervently that the war would come to an end soon; she'd hardly seen Bill in the past few months. If she hadn't had Stella, she thought, she might have gone mad.

At least Katherine was in the same position and could visit Paradise Farm once again, since her son, Michael, had been born. Together, she and Cecily knitted socks and balaclavas for the soldiers at the front, with Stella and Michael positioned on the rug in front of them. Stella, who could now sit up, would stare solemnly at tiny Michael.

Cecily sighed as she reached to turn off the light. "Roll on the end of the war, so Bill and I can finally be a normal couple."

# 41

*May 1945*

It wasn't for another four years that Cecily got her wish. And it was the longest four years of her life.

When she'd received news that Pearl Harbor had been attacked and that the United States had joined the war, Cecily had clutched Stella tightly to her and sobbed, terrified for her family back in New York. As the food shortages had become more severe, Cecily had only been thankful that her vegetable patch was thriving and that they had eggs and milk from their livestock. Belle, her beautiful mare, had been given over to the war effort, and on the day that Bill had taken the horse away, Cecily hadn't thought she had any tears left to shed.

Although Paradise Farm had not been touched, she had lived in constant fear for Bill's life. In his role as a commander in the King's African Rifles, Bill had been true to his word and had fought with his troops where necessary. The military engagements had been limited at the start of the war, but in 1943, to Cecily's horror, Bill and the 11th Division had shipped out to Burma to fight. Cecily had existed in an agony of suspense as she didn't hear from him for weeks on end, with only a few brief letters telling her of the intense heat and humidity of the jungle and several sentences blacked out by the censors. He had returned briefly to Paradise Farm, gaunt and haunted, only to be shipped out to fight again.

The telephone and the wireless had become her lifelines to the rest of the world, as she'd battened down the hatches, trying at the same time to create a homely atmosphere for Stella, who was growing into a sweet and precociously bright little girl.

During a torrential May downpour in 1945, the telephone rang. It was Bill, imparting news that set Cecily's heart pounding as she put down the receiver.

"It's over, it's really over! Lankenua, it's over!" she cried as she ran down the hallway to the kitchen, where four-year-old Stella was sitting at the table drawing, while Lankenua cleaned. "It's really over!" She laughed, clasping the startled Lankenua in a hug.

"What over, Missus Cecily?"

"War! It's finished for real," she said, going to pick up Stella, who was already a head taller than Michael, even though there were only six months between them. "It's all over." She kissed the top of her beloved child's neatly braided hair. "Now Bill can come home for good and we can finally be a family."

"Why are you crying if you're happy?" Stella asked her.

"Oh, because it's just so wonderful! I can finally take you home and show you New York and . . . oh, a million other things. Now I'm going to Nairobi. There are all sorts of celebrations planned. Lankenua, will you pick out my blue dress with the ribbons on it and give it a steam? Oh, and my old straw hat will have to do."

"Can I come with you?" Stella asked plaintively.

"Not today, town will be far too crowded and you might get lost. But another time, I promise."

"But I like looking at the shops with you and Yeyo."

"I know you do, my darling, but there's nothing left in them. Soon there will be, though, and we'll go and buy you lots of pretty dresses. Here"—Cecily held out her hand—"come and help me get ready."

Stella sat on the bed as Cecily pinned up her curls. "Why do we have different kinds of hair?" she asked.

"Lots of people from different places have different hair."

"But we're both from here," Stella insisted.

"Well, I originally came from the United States of America—remember, I showed you in the atlas? It's all the way across a big ocean. You and Yeyo both come from here in Kenya."

She and Bill had decided that it was best if Stella grew up believing Lankenua to be her mother. Since Stella first began to speak, she had called Lankenua "Yeyo," the Maasai word for "mother," while Cecily had been called "Kuyia," the short form of "Nakuyia," which meant "aunt." Stella spoke in rapid Maa with Lankenua, with her "brother," Kwinet—who had turned into a strapping young man and worked tirelessly for Cecily to keep the gardens in order—and with her Uncle Nygasi. She had also adopted Cecily's Upper East Side accent when she spoke in English, a fact that had made Bill laugh on the few occasions he had been home.

"I hate my hair," Stella said, pulling at her braids, which Lankenua had nimbly put in the day before. "It feels all wiry. Yours is soft and smooth. And why do you paint your face? I look silly if I paint mine," she commented as Cecily smoothed some pink rouge onto each cheek.

"Because I have pasty white skin that needs some help, while yours is so beautiful, it doesn't need anything. Okay," Cecily said, putting her makeup and other odds and ends into the small beauty case. "You can help me by getting my peach nightgown out of the chest of drawers."

Stella opened the top drawer and pulled out one of Cecily's brassieres instead. "Why do you wear this? Yeyo never wears one. Will I wear one when I'm older?"

"If you'd like to, yes. Now, where's that nightgown? I need to get to Nairobi as soon as possible."

Lankenua and Stella waved her off, with Cecily promising she'd be back at home tomorrow. On her way to Nairobi, she joined a line of other cars filled with people who had obviously heard the news and were heading there to celebrate. Cecily thought about the conversation she'd had with Stella that morning. There was no doubt the girl adored her "Yeyo," but she had recently become confused as to why she slept in one of the spare bedrooms (which Cecily had turned into a little girl's paradise), while Yeyo slept outside with Kwinet. Equally, why Lankenua was dressed very plainly, yet Stella always had pretty dresses. Whereas Kwinet had shown no interest in lessons and preferred to work outside, Stella could already read and write—Cecily gave her lessons every morning, and she had proved herself to be an exceptionally quick learner.

"You'll have her going to university by the time she's ten, darling," Bill had said, only half joking one weekend when he was home on leave. "Just be careful you don't give her ideas beyond her station."

That comment had incited one of the worst arguments the two of them had ever had, Cecily accusing Bill of having double standards and assuring him that in the United States, black women were able to go to college.

"That's as may be, but we live in Africa, where there are no such opportunities for Stella."

"Then I'll just have to take her to New York, won't I?" she'd raged at him.

Bill had apologized, but in the past few weeks, Cecily had begun to understand his concern. Stella was confused about her identity—and it was a situation Cecily did not know how to solve.

"That's not for today," she murmured as she drew to a halt just outside Nairobi and joined the line of honking cars, their cheering passengers eager to get into town. The skies had miraculously cleared, and the traffic around Delamere Avenue had come to a standstill. Cecily could hear the sound of the brass band as the victory parade got under way. Giving up all hope of finding Bill, Cecily left her car where it was and went to join the crowds cheering the victorious troops as they marched proudly alongside their comrades.

Bill finally came home for good a month later. Cecily had had Kwinet decorate the front of the house with Union Jack bunting she'd stolen from the victory parade. Katherine, Bobby, and Michael were there, with Stella dancing excitedly around her "Uncle Bill." Bill looked old, Cecily thought, his hair streaked with gray, and there was a haunted look in his eyes that hadn't been there before the war.

"To friends reunited," he toasted, "and to those we miss who are no longer with us."

"To those we miss," they all toasted.

Cecily knew Bill was thinking not only of his fallen comrades but of Joss and also Alice, who had shot herself at home only a few months after Jock Broughton had been acquitted of the murder of her beloved Joss. There had been whispers that perhaps Alice herself was responsible, but then again, so many possible murderers had been suggested. Cecily had learned not to listen to idle gossip and had mourned Alice's death.

"To the start of a new era!" said Bobby, casting a glance down at his wife and pulling her closer. "May we live in peace for the rest of our lives."

"Hear, hear!" chorused everyone.

"My goodness, am I happy to be lying on a soft American mattress," Bill said with a smile as he lay in bed later that night. Cecily joined him, and he put his arms around her.

"Hello, wife."

"Hello, husband," Cecily said as she pushed back a strand of his hair. "I hope you can take some rest in the next week and we can spend some time together," she whispered.

"Rest? Dear girl, I don't know the meaning of such a word, and nor does any man worth his salt. Now the blasted war is finally over, I'm going to have to play hunt the cow. God only knows how many head have gone missing while the boss has been away. I'll be going out there tomorrow to find out."

"Surely you can spare me and Stella a day? She hardly knows who you are—I want you to spend some time with her, and me."

"That's as may be, but there's no point in me sitting here in the house and fretting over my herd."

"How long will you be away?"

"I don't know, but you must understand that I have to go."

*You always have to go somewhere* . . . Cecily bit her lip and swallowed hard. She didn't want to cry on Bill's first night home.

"I was thinking that maybe we could take a trip to visit my parents in America," she said. "You've never been to New York. It might be fun, especially with Stella there to see it, too."

"Cecily, I know you're eager to go, but you must understand that I need to get our farm back under control. It does provide our daily bread. Almost nothing has come into the account for the past few years. What I sold to the government produced very little, and we are at risk of being in debt if I don't sort things out."

"I have some money, Bill, you know I do. We certainly won't starve, that's for sure."

"And I'm equally sure that I don't want to live off my wife." Bill's expression had darkened. "I'm a farmer, not a gentleman of leisure like so many round here. Just because the war has finished doesn't mean that I'm going to retire and sit on my backside drinking gin for the rest of my life. I can't wait to get out on the plains." He turned to her. "Maybe you could join me for a game drive sometime next week?"

"Maybe," Cecily replied without enthusiasm.

"God, I'm bushed," he said as he kissed her on the forehead. "Good night. Sleep well."

Cecily watched him turn over and within seconds heard him snoring. Switching off the lamp on her side of the bed, she let the tears she had stifled roll silently down her face. She could not remember the last time they had made love.

The halcyon days of four years ago, before Joss had died and Bill had left his soul behind in Burma, were only a distant memory.

"Life is so cruel," Cecily whispered as she dashed a hand across her eyes to wipe away her tears. "Thank the Lord for Stella."

During the following year, Cecily felt nothing much had changed since the war. She was alone most of the time and clung to Stella for comfort. This was worse than being alone; she had Bill in her bed again, yet he wasn't really present, nor was he the Bill that she remembered. He was silent and distinctly cold toward her, and his bad moods soured the atmosphere of Paradise Farm. He barely paid attention to Stella.

Her mother called once a month, anxious as to when her daughter would come home, but whenever Cecily broached the subject with Bill, he told her it wasn't the right time and that he couldn't leave until his livestock were thriving again.

"Grant me twelve months to get things back on track; then I can think about it," he'd said.

Cecily realized she had not seen her family in over six years. Her heart longed for home.

# 42

It was November 1946, and the downpours had turned Cecily's garden into a lush tropical paradise. Katherine arrived on Wednesday midmorning as usual with Michael in tow. He was now five years old and adored his best friend, Stella. Cecily had been teaching Stella basic arithmetic at the kitchen table. The little girl loved numbers, and even though Cecily knew there was no genetic link to ascribe it to, she was happy to nurture it. But when Stella had caught sight of Michael, she had squealed and run to hug him.

"Golly," said Katherine with a smile as Michael zoomed around the soaking garden pretending to be an airplane, with Stella screaming as he tried to catch her, "I can barely get my son to sit down at a table to eat, let alone concentrate on mathematics."

"If ever Michael wants to join in the classes, I'd be glad to teach him."

"Maybe I'll take you up on that," Katherine agreed as they both sipped lemonade on the veranda. "You really are terribly fond of Stella, aren't you?"

"Of course I am. She's grown up under my roof," Cecily said defensively.

"Well, it might be very useful for you to take Michael for me occasionally in the next few months. I'm finally pregnant again." Katherine raised an eyebrow.

"Why, that's wonderful news! Are you pleased?"

"Oh, I'm sure I will be when he or she is here, yes. It's just that pregnancy is not my favorite thing."

"Is Bobby pleased?"

"I don't know. He's been so distant since he returned home from the war. To be blunt about it, I'm amazed we even got to the point of making a baby. His interest in that department has been nonexistent for the past few years."

"So has Bill's." Cecily blushed pink at the admission. "And he's awful grumpy most of the time."

Katharine sighed. "I keep hoping that time will heal Bobby. Watching men torn down right in front of your eyes must have affected all of them. But it's been over a year now, and I simply want the Bobby I love back."

"I'm glad it's not just my husband, then."

"Everything feels as though it's changed, doesn't it, Cecily? Even up here in the Valley. I think a lot of the natives who were forced to sign up during the war to serve king and country believed that things would be different when they came back. But of course, nothing has changed for *them*, has it? In fact, given that a lot of the farms weren't cared for the way they should have been, work here is even more scarce than it was before."

"And there was me thinking everything would be better."

"Nothing wrong with being an optimist. It's what got us all through the war. I must admit," Katherine said, "there's part of me that's very tempted to return home to Blighty. The medical facilities there are so much more advanced, and I'd also be able to pursue my career as a vet. Out here, it's almost impossible. The ranchers take one look at the fact I'm a woman and run away with their sickly cows as fast as they can! I've also been dreaming about fog," she chuckled.

"I know exactly how you feel. I want to go home for Christmas, Katherine. I haven't seen my family for more than seven years now."

"Then you must go. Of course you must."

"But what if Bill refuses to come, too?"

"Then leave him behind." Katherine shrugged. "Golly, if I had a chance to get out of Africa for a while and see America, I'd be there like a shot."

"And I'd say come with me, but"—Cecily gave a nod to Katherine's small but noticeable bump—"that isn't going to happen, is it?"

"Not this time, no. But ask me after the baby's born, and it will be a definite yes. Cecily, go and have yourself a proper family Christmas in Manhattan. Take your maid with you if you don't want to go alone."

"And Stella, of course."

Katherine eyed her. "Of course."

When Bill arrived home from the plains a few days later, and knowing a decision had to be made as December was fast approaching, Cecily made him his favorite beef stew with dumplings and uncorked their last bottle of claret.

After he'd eaten and drunk, Cecily plucked up the courage to say the words. "Bill, I'd . . . well, I'd really like to go home and visit my parents for Christmas."

"Would you, now?"

"Yes, I would. And I'd like it even better if you would come with me. I've been patient for a year, as you asked me to be. I know that the farm needs your attention and that you have to rebuild all that was lost in the war. But"—she took a deep breath—"I *need* to see my family. It's been too long. And when it comes to the people we love, we can't waste a second of the precious time that we have left on Earth."

Bill drained his glass and topped it up with more claret. Cecily listened to the rain thumping down on the roof as Bill took a sip and looked at her across the table.

"I do understand completely that you wish to see them, but I absolutely cannot leave the farm just now. However, I don't wish to stop you. So go, by all means."

"Really?"

"Really."

She felt tears pricking the back of her eyes and stood up to give him a kiss. "Thank you, darling. And given that I don't wish to travel unaccompanied, I hope it would be okay if I take Lankenua and Stella with me."

"Is that necessary? Surely there must be someone else returning home who you could travel with?"

"I've asked around, and there isn't. Kiki is already in New York, and there are few Americans left around here these days."

"Well, then, you must take Lankenua, of course."

"I'm sure Nygasi could take care of the house while we're gone. And you have Kwinet for the garden and grounds—"

"Oh, don't worry about me, Cecily. Before you came along, I was perfectly capable of looking after myself."

"Bill." Cecily took his hands in hers. "Please, you've always talked about Christmas and how much you love it. In Manhattan there'd be snow, lights . . . a turkey, even. Won't you come, even for a couple of weeks?"

"Perhaps another time, Cecily. You must also remember that I haven't been out of Africa, socially at least, for many years. I'm not sure I'd be any good in polite company. You go, my dear, and leave your sad, tired husband behind."

Cecily was regretting the fact that she'd opened the claret; it was making

Bill even more maudlin than usual. "Bill, I love you, please don't say that. I'm desperate for my parents to meet their son-in-law."

"I'm sorry, Cecily. Please go, with my blessing. Now"—Bill stood up—"I need some sleep."

Cecily watched him walk away from her, and her eyes filled with tears.

# 43

"Are we nearly in America, Kuyia?" Stella asked as she peered excitedly out of the cabin window.

"Yes, we really are, darling," Cecily replied as Lankenua packed the last of their bits and pieces inside the trunk. Cecily pressed the bell for the steward. "In a moment we'll go up on deck and you can see the Statue of Liberty. It's very famous, and it's there to welcome travelers from all over the world."

The steward duly arrived to take their luggage, and Cecily tipped him, then made sure that their papers were safely stowed in her purse.

It had been a rush to get everything organized; Lankenua and Stella had needed all sorts of paperwork for their entry into the port in New York. Birth certificates, passports, and statements of sponsorships by British officials had had to be issued, and Cecily was only glad of Bill's connections at Government House. After consultation with Nygasi, a suitable surname had been chosen for them both to pass through immigration without a problem.

"We've entered the Hudson River, ma'am, and we'll be alongside the Statue of Liberty in about ten minutes," said the steward.

"Come on," Cecily said to Stella and Lankenua, "let's go up on deck and see her!"

"I stay here." Lankenua shook her head, physically shivering at the thought, even though she was wearing Cecily's thick tweed coat.

"Okay." Cecily held out a hand to Stella. "We'll go."

Up on the first-class deck, there were few who had dared to venture out in the freezing temperatures, though when Cecily looked down, she could see arms stretched out and hear cheers from the lower decks.

"There she is!" she said, pointing to her left as the heavy fog swirled around the bay.

"Where? I can't see her," said Stella.

"There." Cecily pointed at the statue. The sight brought tears to her eyes, which she wiped away quickly before they could freeze to her skin in the frigid air. Lady Liberty's benevolent face welcomed the weary travelers, holding her beacon aloft amid the fog. Cecily had never felt so pleased to see her.

Stella looked up at her. "But she's so small! You told me everything in America was much bigger."

"Well, she's very special, more of a symbol than anything else." Cecily sighed. "Once the fog clears, you'll see the skyscrapers."

"What is this?" Stella put out her small hand as white flakes fell onto her palm.

"Why, it's snow! Remember the pictures I showed you? It's what falls when Santa is due to arrive, and you'll see a lot of it here."

Stella's eyes widened. "Santa Claus lives here in Manhattan?"

"No, but he sends the snow from the North Pole at Christmas so that his sleigh can land on it and leave gifts for good little children."

"Ooh, it's so cold." Stella rubbed her nose. "Can we go inside now?"

"Of course we can, sweetie. But I promise, you are going to love Manhattan," she said as Stella took her hand and they walked back down to their cabin.

Cecily was only thankful for the privilege of traveling first class rather than in steerage. When they docked and she handed their papers to the immigration official, she smiled and fluttered her lashes.

"Oh! I'm so glad to be home, sir. It's been a long seven years," she said as the official studied their documents.

"And how long are you staying, Miss Huntley-Morgan?"

"We're just here for a visit. I'm due to marry my fiancé in Kenya in February," she repeated as she'd been told to, given that her passport still showed her as a single woman.

"So both Mrs. Ankunu and her daughter, Stella, will be traveling back to Africa along with you?"

"Of course. As you can see, our return passage papers are right here. I mean, one wouldn't forget and leave one's maid and her daughter behind, would one?" Cecily giggled girlishly.

"No, of course not, ma'am," the official said, eyeing both Lankenua and Stella. "Do they speak English?"

"Not well, no," said Cecily quickly. "But it'll be fun for them to see Manhattan, won't it?"

"It will." The official stamped Lankenua's and Stella's passports. "Welcome to the United States, and a very merry Christmas to all of you."

Cecily breathed a sigh of relief as she left the hut, briefly looking back and seeing a line of goodness knew how many people stretching from the ship gangplank, standing out in the freezing cold.

"Okay," she said as they emerged into the arrivals area. "We made it! Oh, my! I'm so excited!" She laughed as she saw Mama, Papa, and their chauffeur, Archer, waving at them. "Let's go meet my family!"

Neither her mother nor her father seemed to have aged a bit, and after an emotional reunion on the quayside, Archer ushered the party toward the waiting car.

"Why, who is this?" asked Dorothea, for the first time spotting Stella, who was hiding shyly behind Lankenua.

"This is Stella, my very special friend, aren't you, honey?" Cecily smiled down at her.

"I didn't realize we had an extra body to ferry home," Dorothea said. "The maid can sit up front with Archer, but this child—"

"She can sit on my knee, Mama, there's plenty of room for three and a half of us in the back, after all," Cecily said firmly, taking Stella's hand.

On the ride home, Cecily ignored her mother's bristling disapproval and instead peered out of the window with Stella, pointing out various buildings as the little girl *ooh*-ed and *aah*-ed at the skyscrapers above them.

Back at the house on Fifth Avenue, Cecily was greeted by the whole family, who had assembled in the living room. Priscilla stood beside her husband, Robert, with seven-year-old Christabel, Mamie's daughter, at their side. Hunter had his arm slung around Mamie, who was holding a toddler in her arms, while two more young children were hiding shyly behind their parents. A huge pine tree decorated with candles and baubles stood in pride of place, and the family's cheerful red stockings hung over the fireplace.

"Mary, take the maid and her child up to their room so Miss Cecily can get acquainted with her family," Dorothea ordered their housekeeper.

Reluctantly, Cecily let go of Stella's hand, realizing she should have told her mother that Stella was to sleep on the same floor as her, but she hadn't known how to explain it.

"Cecily!" Mamie and Priscilla came over to shower her in hugs and introduce little Christabel, Adele, "Tricks," and Jimmy. Cecily hugged them all in turn, and while the girls seemed awed at finally meeting their mysterious aunt, three-year-old Jimmy was more focused on his toys which were sprawled all over the rug.

"You look swell, Cecily," Priscilla said approvingly. "You've turned into a real beauty since you've been away."

"Are you saying I wasn't when I left?" Cecily giggled.

"Oh, now, don't you go twisting my words! You never could take a compliment, could she, Mamie?"

"No."

Cecily looked at Mamie, who, with her pale face, deep red lipstick and cropped dark hair, looked ridiculously fashionable. Priscilla was as pretty and wholesome as ever, if a little heavier than when Cecily had last seen her.

"And how are you both?" she asked them.

"Bored to tears with motherhood, but what can a girl do?" Mamie drawled as she lit a cigarette at the end of her holder. "I can't seem to stop having the damned things."

"She's only teasing, Cecily, aren't you?" said Hunter, coming to stand next to his wife.

Mamie sighed dramatically. "Don't you just wish I was?"

"Now, you're to sit down here and tell us absolutely everything about the last seven years of your life," Priscilla said as she steered Cecily to the couch.

"I'm not sure I'll be able to do that tonight," she said. "It's been such a long journey, but I'll do my best to begin."

"Of course she can't," said Dorothea. "I must say, honey, I'm just surprised you haven't returned to us the same color as your maid and that child of hers with all that sun."

Cecily winced inwardly at her mother's words. "I wore a big hat, Mama, that's all."

"Well." Dorothea took a glass of champagne from the tray. "Welcome home, sweetheart. We've all missed you, haven't we?"

"Yes, we have," Walter said with a nod, also taking a glass. "And next time you tell us you're leaving for a few weeks to visit some far-flung place, we simply won't let you go!"

"It was hardly my fault that the war began, was it?" countered Cecily.

"No, of course it wasn't. Were there food shortages out there?" Walter asked.

"Yes, there were, but I had my own vegetable garden, so we ate quite well."

"Vegetable garden?" Priscilla looked at her sister in amazement. "You dug up your own carrots and cabbages?"

"I did indeed, with the help of Lankenua's son, Kwinet. And then, of course, if we got very hungry, I'd just go to the end of the garden, shoot an antelope, and put it on a spit over the fire."

Ten faces looked back at her in astonishment; even Jimmy stopped playing with his toy car.

"You are joking, aren't you?" Priscilla asked.

"Well, maybe not at the bottom of my garden, no, but if Bill and I went out on safari, that's exactly what would happen. Bill's a great hand with a rifle. He once saved me from being eaten by a lion."

"Bang bang!" shouted Jimmy from the rug.

"Yes, Jimmy, that's the right noise, but in real life it's a good deal louder." Cecily smiled, enjoying their rapt expressions.

"You are teasing us, aren't you, Cecily?" Priscilla said.

"As a matter of fact, not much, actually." She chuckled. "And then, of course, there are the snakes, great shiny vipers and cobras who slither into your room at night. I have so many photographs to show you all."

"The good news is, we're not likely to find snakes slithering down Fifth Avenue and dinner will be served without us having to kill the feast first," said Walter dryly.

"We've invited Kiki to join us," said Dorothea. "You heard about the death of her son in action, no doubt?"

"I did, yes. I called around to see her at Mundui House at the time, but Aleeki, her houseboy, said she wasn't seeing anyone," Cecily said soberly. "Is she feeling better?"

"I've only spoken to her on the telephone. She's been staying at the Stanhope with her mother and Lillian, her companion. She doesn't sound too good." Dorothea sighed. "But then, who would, after all the tragedies she's suffered? That friend of hers she was so fond of—Alice—"

"Yes, the two of them went way back, and Kiki was so broken up when Alice killed herself. We all were," said Cecily.

"I read it was because the dashing Earl of Erroll was the love of her life," interjected Priscilla. "Did you really dance with him on your wedding night, Cecily? Was he as much of a dream as the newspapers said?"

"He was certainly very handsome and charming, yes." Cecily was finding her new status—that of being the most interesting person in the room—rather trying. "So come now, tell me what's been happening here."

Later that night, Cecily excused herself from after-dinner coffee and virtually crawled up the stairs to her bedroom. Kiki had not shown up after all, a fact that hadn't surprised Cecily in the least, knowing how unpredictable her godmother was. Stopping on the landing that led to her room, she looked up at the steep set of stairs that led to the attic floor above her.

Taking off her formal high-heeled shoes—she wasn't at all used to wearing them at home in Kenya—Cecily mounted the steps. At the top, she ducked down beneath the eaves of the house as she walked along to the bedroom Lankenua and Stella were sharing.

She heard Lankenua coughing as she knocked on the door. The poor woman had had a cold since they'd boarded the steamer for New York in Southampton.

The room was bitterly cold, and Cecily shivered in her thin silk blouse, which had been perfectly adequate in the heated rooms downstairs.

"Kuyia?" A voice from one of the narrow iron beds whispered. "Is that you?"

"Yes, it's me." Cecily tiptoed across the rough floorboards to reach Stella. Even though the attic window was closed, a chill draft emanated from it. "Are you okay?" Cecily asked. Stella was curled up in a ball with only a thin blanket to keep her warm.

"I'm c-c-cold." The little girl shivered. "It's cold in this New York place, and Yeyo says she doesn't feel so well."

"Here, let me give you a hug," Cecily said as she put her arms around the little girl.

"Where have you been?" Stella asked her.

"Downstairs having dinner with my mama and papa and my sisters."

"Can I come and have some dinner with you tomorrow? We only got a sandwich for our supper, and the bread didn't taste half as good as the bread you make at home."

"Maybe," said Cecily, who realized that Stella was used to eating a full nursery tea with her when Bill wasn't at home—which was most of the time.

"And I don't like it up here in the roof," Stella continued. "It's scary."

"Don't worry, honey, we'll sort out everything tomorrow, I promise. But for now, how about you tiptoe downstairs with me and sleep in my bed? You'll have to be very quiet because Mr. and Mrs. Huntley-Morgan are asleep and will be mad if we wake them up, okay?"

"Okay."

Taking Stella's blanket, she tucked it around Lankenua for extra warmth, then led the girl by the hand back along the narrow hallway and down the stairs, holding her breath in case she bumped into her parents. Once inside her room, she breathed a sigh of relief.

"There now, you climb in and get comfy while I get ready for bed."

"Okay, Kuyia. I like it much better down here," Stella pronounced from the center of the big bed. "It's warm and pretty."

"This is where I slept as a little girl," Cecily said as she got in next to her, then switched off the light. Stella raised her arms for a hug. "Better?" asked Cecily as she folded her arms around the child.

"Better."

"Sleep well, my darling."

"Sleep well, Kuyia."

The following morning, having set her alarm to make sure she was awake so that she could go back upstairs and dress Stella before Evelyn came in with the breakfast tray, Cecily arrived in the attic to find that Lankenua was burning up. She flew downstairs to the kitchen to find some cloths to wet and place on Lankenua's forehead to cool her down.

"Where on earth are you going and what are you doing with those, sweetheart?" Dorothea asked as she passed her daughter in the hall.

"My maid is sick, Mama—she's had a cough since we left England, and this morning she has a high fever. I need to get it down."

"Surely Mary or Evelyn can see to her, Cecily? It's probably just a cold."

"Well, I'm hardly surprised she's sick; it's freezing upstairs in that attic."

"The other servants have never complained about it."

"The other servants haven't just arrived from Africa, Mama. Please get someone to bring a bucket of coal up to the room, and we'll get a fire going in there."

"Will Yeyo be all right?" Stella asked as Cecily wiped Lankenua's sweating, shivering body with the cool cloths. Her cough was deep and rasping, and she was muttering indecipherable words to herself.

"Sure, she will, honey. If she's not better by this evening, I'll call the doctor to come see her. Don't worry," Cecily said as Stella sat on the windowsill looking out at the snow that was falling thickly outside. Cecily had wrapped the girl in one of her own woolen cardigans to keep her warm.

"I hope so, Kuyia. I love her very much."

"So do I, darling. And I swear she'll be better soon. When she is, maybe you'd like to go out shopping with me? We need to buy you some new winter clothes—oh, and of course, there's the toy shop, and we could add in a trip in a horse-drawn carriage around Central Park."

"You mean, like Santa Claus's sleigh pulled by reindeer?" Stella's face lit up. "At least there's snow here for him to land on." She clapped her hands together excitedly as Cecily added more coal to the fire now burning in the small grate. "Only"—Stella counted slowly on her fingers—"five more nights until he's here!"

"Yes, that's right," agreed Cecily, remembering how unhappy Bill had been with her for telling Stella the Santa Claus story. "It simply isn't her culture, and now she'll expect presents to arrive down the chimney for the rest of her childhood," he'd said.

"And what's wrong with that? Africans are allowed to believe in Jesus, aren't they? And more and more of them do."

"Which I don't approve of either," Bill had shot back. "Destroying indigenous cultures that have been in place for hundreds of years is wrong, Cecily. Can't you see that?"

Of course she could, but as this year was the first one that Stella had really been able to understand the concept of Santa Claus, the excitement and anticipation on her face had been enough to wipe out any guilt. It was simply a fairy story like any other, and she couldn't see the harm in it. Besides, Bill was a long way away in Kenya.

"Mama, I need you to call a doctor to come see Lankenua. I can't get her fever down, and I'm worried she has pneumonia," Cecily said that afternoon as she barged into the living room, where Dorothea was taking tea with a friend.

"Excuse me one moment, Maud," she said to the woman as she ushered Cecily out of the living room and into the entrance hall.

"Can you give me the number, and I'll call him," Cecily urged her.

"Honey, we don't call doctors for the servants. If they're sick, they can go to the free clinic and see someone there."

"I *do* call doctors for my staff, Mama, especially given the fact I've brought Lankenua over here. She is my responsibility, can't you see that?"

"Please, Cecily, keep your voice down! Maud is a very rich widow who I'm trying to entice onto our Negro orphans committee."

"Well, Mama, you may very well have an orphan right under your own roof if we don't call a doctor now!"

"Okay, okay . . . the number for Dr. Barnes is in the address book on your father's desk."

"Thanks, and don't worry, I'll pay for it," she called after Dorothea, who was already hurrying back to her rich widow.

On the telephone to Dr. Barnes's secretary, Cecily omitted to mention that it was a black maid she was calling him over to see. When she opened the door to him an hour later, she was relieved to see that he was a younger version of Dr. Barnes—probably his son—and had a far kinder face.

"Thank you so much for coming, Doctor. I'll take you up to see the patient."

Six flights of stairs later, Cecily pushed open the door to the attic room. "Her name is Lankenua, and she arrived just a few days ago from Kenya with me," Cecily said, studying the doctor's face for his reaction.

"All right, then, let's have a look at her, shall we?"

Cecily took Stella's hand, and they both moved out of the way so that Dr. Barnes could examine Lankenua.

"Before I touch her, I must ask you if you think it could be whooping cough? A number of cases have been reported recently, I suspect due to the number of immigrants entering the city."

"Oh, no, it's definitely not whooping cough, Doctor. It's a very bad chest cold that I'm concerned may have turned to pneumonia."

He smiled. "You sure sound as though you know what you're talking about when it comes to sickness, Miss Huntley-Morgan."

"It's Mrs. Forsythe, actually. Well, one has to when one lives miles from the only doctor who serves an area the size of Manhattan," she said. "Lankenua also taught me about the plants her people use for sickness. Her mother was a wise woman, and I reckon her remedies work."

"I'll bet they do, Mrs. Forsythe," Dr. Barnes said as he drew his stethoscope out of his bag and listened to Lankenua's chest. "Could you help me sit her up so I can listen to her back?"

"Of course. When I called, I was expecting your father to arrive here."

"My father has retired, and I've taken over the practice. I'm sorry if you are disappointed."

"Oh! Not at all." Cecily shook her head. "How does her chest sound?"

"Too wheezy for my liking. I think your diagnosis is correct, Mrs. Forsythe. Your maid is on the cusp of developing pneumonia. It's a good job you called me when you did."

"Do you have anything to give her?"

"I do indeed. It's a new wonder drug called penicillin, and it's technically only available in hospitals and administered by injections. I had a couple of patients presenting with much the same symptoms as your maid here and was able to beg some from the hospital. They are both recovering beautifully."

Dr. Barnes dug into his bag once more and produced a small bottle and some syringes. "It has to be administered four times daily over five days. Have you ever given an injection, Mrs. Forsythe?"

"As a matter of fact, I have, yes. My husband, Bill, was deeply clawed by a dying cheetah some years ago, and our doctor prescribed morphine for it. He taught me how to inject it to ease the pain while he recovered."

"You were allowed to administer morphine yourself?" Dr. Barnes looked shocked.

"As I said, when one lives miles from anywhere, one becomes quite self-sufficient," Cecily said. "I'm quite capable of giving an injection."

"That's very helpful," Dr. Barnes said. "The posterior is the best place of entry for such drugs. I'll supervise your administration of the first one, and then it's the same dose four times daily. You should see a change within forty-eight hours. Also, bring up some steaming bowls of water to help with her breathing."

Dr. Barnes helped her measure out the correct dosage, then watched as she gave Lankenua the injection. He nodded in approval.

"Well done, Mrs. Forsythe. You're quite the nurse. Now, I'll be back to check on her tomorrow."

"Goodness, you really don't have to."

"Why, that's what I'm here for, and after all, we'd like it if you could be well for your first Christmas in Manhattan, wouldn't we?" he said to Lankenua, who nodded at him weakly. "Okay, until tomorrow." Dr. Barnes smiled at them all, then left the room.

"Tomorrow I'm going to take Stella out shopping for some warm clothes and to see Santa at Bloomingdale's," said Cecily. "She's bored with her mama sick in bed."

"She can always go to the kitchen and have the staff take care of her. You seem rather attached to that child." Dorothea eyed her daughter. "She is your maid's child, not a relative."

"Maybe things are different in Africa, Dorothea," countered Walter.

"Maybe they are, but I don't think that I have ever seen a white woman wandering around Bloomingdale's with a black child. Have you?"

"Times are changing, dear," said Walter. "I was reading in the *New York Times* only last week that the number of black male entrants to both Yale and Harvard is on the rise."

"What about female students?" Cecily muttered under her breath.

"What was that, honey?" Dorothea asked her.

"Oh, nothing. Has Mary made up the spare room next to mine for Stella? If not, I can do it."

"The spare room is always made up, as you well know, Cecily. Though why it's necessary to move her downstairs, I really don't know."

"Because of the risk of infection, Mama. Dr. Barnes told me I should keep Stella away until her mother is better," Cecily lied. "Anyway, if you'll excuse me, I must go and check on Lankenua." Cecily rose from the table. "Oh, and I thought I'd call the Stanhope Hotel, where Kiki is staying. I want to take her a gift for Christmas."

"I called them today, but her mother said Kiki wasn't seeing visitors."

"Well, I can at least leave my gift at reception for her. Good night, Mama, Papa."

Cecily left the table and went upstairs to the attic, where she was pleased to see that Lankenua was sleeping peacefully and her forehead felt cooler. She'd wake her at ten o'clock for the next dose of medicine.

Stella, whom Cecily had left in her own room while the adults had dinner, was now sitting on Cecily's bed in her nightdress, engrossed in an old picture book called *'Twas the Night Before Christmas.*

Stella looked up anxiously. "How is Yeyo?"

"Oh, she's getting better already, honey. Let's take you to your very own bedroom now." Cecily offered her hand to Stella and led her to the room next to hers, where she had asked Mary to light the fire earlier so it was toasty warm. "Into bed you get," Cecily said, tucking Stella in.

"Can Yeyo come down here when she's better?"

"We'll see. Now, do you want to try reading me a story tonight?" she said, indicating the old book and sitting down on the bed.

Lankenua was definitely better the following morning. Her fever had abated, and even though the cough still sounded vicious, Cecily was pleased that she was able to sip a little water.

Lankenua sighed. "Sorry, Missus Cecily, I big trouble."

"Not at all," Cecily comforted her. "Now, I'll be back to give you your next injection this afternoon. Meantime, I'm taking Stella off shopping."

Lankenua nodded. "I good. You go."

"Rest now," said Cecily, putting some more coal on the fire. "And we'll be back to tell you all about it later."

Cecily and Stella's first port of call was the children's clothes department at Bloomingdale's. Stella's eyes widened at the racks of dresses and pinafores that she could choose from. An assistant—who'd given them a strange look when Cecily had approached her—was following them closely along the aisles as the two of them picked out things for Stella to try on.

"Don't you look a picture," Cecily said with a smild as Stella twirled in front of the mirror wearing a pale orange dress, the skirt made up of layers of net and tulle. "It's perfect for Christmas Day and sets off your coloring to perfection!" Cecily clapped her hands, not caring about the shop assistant's disdainful expression. "Now let's choose some sensible warm clothes, shall we?"

Having arranged for the two large bags of new clothes to be sent down to Archer and the car, Cecily and Stella—now dressed in a red Harris Tweed coat with a velvet collar and shiny brass buttons, complete with a matching beret—left the clothes department to head for the toys. The line to see Santa was a long one; it seemed as though every parent in Manhattan had had the same idea.

"Look, Mama," said the little boy standing in front of them. "She's black like a pickaninny!" He pointed at Stella.

"Jeremy! Please, hush now," the mother reprimanded her son but nonetheless turned to stare at Cecily and Stella.

"And you are white like Kuyia," Stella said, pointing back at him, not in the least perturbed. A few seconds later, mother and son had left the line. Cecily held her breath, waiting for any more comments, while Stella amused herself by pointing out the dolls on the shelves and the life-sized bear that sat against a pillar with a Santa Claus hat on its head.

"Look!" exclaimed Cecily. "It's a lion, like the ones at home!" Stella broke away to run toward the toy. "It won't bite, will it?" she said as she approached it with Cecily following in her wake. "It's only pretend, isn't it?"

"Of course it is," Cecily said as Stella threw her arms around the head of the life-sized lion.

"Oh! I've always wanted to hug a lion." Stella giggled as all the other mothers and children in the line looked on at the display.

"Tell you what, honey, let's not wait in this great long line to see Santa right now. Let's go and buy some gifts for Lankenua and my mama and papa, then go home and put the note to Santa up the chimney as we normally do, okay?"

Stella looked longingly at the man dressed all in red and white, sitting on the dais, and sighed. "I guess the line is kind of long," she agreed.

Cecily did not look back to see all the eyes following their exit.

Back at home later, Stella duly wrote her letter to Santa, with Cecily mentally noting the items she wanted. The big furry lion was at the top of her list.

"But I can't see how he would get it down the chimney, honey," Cecily said as they sat in front of the fire in her bedroom, toasting the s'mores—chocolate and marshmallow melted between graham crackers—which were Stella's new favorite treat.

"True," Stella agreed, taking a sticky marshmallow off the toasting fork that Cecily held out and squashing it like Cecily had shown her between the chocolate and two crackers. "But Michael told me he got a bicycle from Santa last year."

"I'll tell you a secret: I happen to know there's a real-life lion in Central Park," Cecily whispered.

"Really? He must be cold out there in the snow," replied Stella as she stood up and went to the window.

"Oh, he's okay; he has a whole house to himself. Now, why don't you come help me wrap some gifts in this pretty paper?"

After she'd given Stella a bath, Cecily went upstairs to administer another dose of the penicillin to Lankenua. She knew her maid must be better, because she made an awful fuss about the needle and where it had to go.

"There, all done," Cecily said, pulling down Lankenua's nightdress. She then went to fetch Stella and led her up to the attic.

"Honey, I'm just going to head along the block to see a very old friend of mine," Cecily told Stella. "I won't be long, but can you stay here with Yeyo and keep her company while I'm gone? Maybe you'd like to read her your new book about Winnie-the-Pooh?"

Stella nodded eagerly. "That's a good idea. Don't be late, Kuyia," she called as Cecily left the room.

It had finally stopped snowing when Cecily stepped outside and into the back of the family's Chrysler. As the car moved along Fifth Avenue, the sound of traffic was muffled by the thick covering of snow on the sidewalks and streets, the steam from the subway beneath puffing out of the grates and melting the snow atop it. Arriving at the Stanhope Hotel, Cecily asked Archer to wait for her as she stepped out of the car.

"I'll be about thirty minutes or so," she called as she disappeared under the green canopy marking the entrance to the hotel. She could already hear live jazz music coming from the bar as she walked over to the reception and asked them to let Kiki Preston know she was here. Expecting Kiki to be indisposed, she was surprised when the receptionist told her to go on up to the suite. Cecily took the elevator to the fifth floor. After a knock, a woman she didn't recognize answered the door.

"Hello, Cecily, I'm Lillian Turner, a friend of your godmother's. Please come in. Kiki isn't feeling herself tonight, but she said she really wanted to see you," she whispered as she led her into a grand living room, where Kiki was lying on a chaise longue in front of the fire. It was one of the only times she'd ever seen her godmother with her face bare of makeup. Even though Kiki looked dreadfully pale, her dark hair down and scattered with gray, she was still very beautiful.

"My darling Cecily! Excuse me if I don't get up to greet you, but my health has not been robust these past few weeks." Kiki put out one hand to Cecily as she stubbed out her cigarette with the other. "How are you, honey?"

"I'm well, thank you, and excited to be back in Manhattan! It's been so long."

"And there's me pining for Kenya in this dark, depressing city. One simply can't see the sky here." Kiki sighed. "Lillian, do get our guest a drink. What will you have, Cecily? Champagne?"

"I'm fine, I don't want to disturb you if you're sick. I just came to drop off a Christmas gift for you."

"Oh! How terribly sweet of you to think of me. I sometimes feel New York has forgotten all about me. May I open it now?"

"You can, of course, but maybe you should save it for Christmas Day."

"Oh, my angel." Kiki placed an obviously shaking hand onto Cecily's forearm. "The one lesson I've learned is that one should never save special things for another day, because tomorrow may never come." Tears glistened in her eyes. "Now let's see what it is you've brought for me."

"Oh, it's nothing big, I just thought—"

"As you know, it isn't size that counts." Kiki gave Cecily one of her wicked smiles and suddenly looked more like her old self. She took the rectangular box out of its wrapping and opened it.

"It's a photograph of you and me at Mundui House before I left to marry Bill. Aleeki took it with my camera," Cecily explained.

Kiki looked down at the photograph, taken at sunset with Lake Naivasha behind them. "Oh, my! What a beautiful gift you've given me." She stroked the photograph. "And don't we both look so young?" She smiled, tears once again appearing in her eyes. "Thank you so much, Cecily. You're so very sweet, and I am—and always have been—so very fond of you. Here, Lillian, put it on the mantelpiece so I can see it." Lillian did so as Kiki grasped Cecily's hand. "Are you happy, honey?"

"Yes, I am, I think."

"Well, listen to my advice now, and swear you'll act on it: do whatever it takes to make yourself and those you love happy, because before you know it, your life—and theirs—is over and gone. Don't waste it, Cecily, will you? Work out what and who is important to you, and hold fast to them. Promise me?"

"Of course I do, Kiki. Are you sure you're okay? I know a great doctor—"

"Oh, don't worry about me. Now, you come here and give your godmother a big hug."

Cecily bent forward and let Kiki embrace her, her godmother's long red talons sticking into her ribs.

"Merry Christmas," Kiki said as she released her grip, her eyes yet again full of tears. "Be happy, won't you?"

"I will. Merry Christmas, Kiki."

Lillian escorted Cecily to the door.

"Are you sure she's okay?" Cecily spoke in a low voice as she stepped out into the hallway. "She seems . . . out of sorts."

"She's just low about her son," Lillian whispered. "And also she hates Christmas; it reminds her of all the people who are no longer here to celebrate it. Don't worry, I'm sure she'll feel better once it's over. Good-bye, now."

"Good-bye."

# 44

The following morning, Cecily remembered with childish excitement that it was Christmas Eve. She was surprised to find an invitation card addressed to her on a silver salver in the hall.

MRS. TERRENCE JACKSON REQUESTS THE PLEASURE OF
*Mrs. Bill Forsythe*
AT THE VASSAR REUNION
AT HOME ON TUESDAY, JANUARY 3, 1947
RSVP
18 JORALEMON STREET
BROOKLYN, NEW YORK

Cecily was surprised at the invitation; Rosalind had been part of a group of girls who'd shared political and intellectual anecdotes rather than lipsticks in their dorms. Cecily felt Rosalind had always cultivated an air of aloofness, and she'd never quite felt good enough to be a part of her clique.

"Oh, my! You've been honored! Rosalind and her husband's soirees are considered some of the most sought-after tickets in town. Apparently Mrs. Roosevelt herself attended the last one," said Mamie, who had arrived in the hallway with a large bag of presents to drop off. "She's quite the feminist, by all accounts," she added. "You should attend."

"You know what, Mamie? I just might," Cecily smiled at her before she went upstairs to give Lankenua her injection.

Having left Stella in the kitchen with Mary and Essie, the cook, making all sorts of tasty Christmas treats, Cecily shut herself in the bedroom to prepare Lankenua's and Stella's stockings and to wrap up the smaller version of the cuddly Bloomingdale's lion that she'd had delivered to the house yesterday. Reminding herself to put a call through to Bill—who had said he would spend Christmas Eve at Muthaiga Club with some of his army pals—Cecily thought through the knotty problem of how she could persuade her parents that Stella should join them tomorrow for Christmas lunch, rather than eating in the kitchen with the servants.

A sudden rapping on her door brought her out of her reverie. "Who is it?" she asked.

"It's your mother, and I have to speak to you now!"

"Come in!"

Her mother entered the room, utter shock spread across her face.

"What on earth is it, Mama? You look like you've seen a ghost."

"Oh, Lord, oh, Lord, Cecily!" Dorothea drew in a deep breath. "Kiki . . . she's dead!"

"Dead? But she can't be, Mama. I saw her just last night, and she looked fine, if a little low. What's happened?"

Dorothea walked over to an easy chair and slumped into it. "Her mother just called a few minutes ago. Kiki was found lying in a courtyard at the back of the Stanhope. She—" Dorothea gulped. "Apparently, she jumped out of her window. She was wearing her pajamas when they found her."

"Oh, my! Oh, my! Are you sure it was Kiki?"

"Of course I'm sure! Helen would recognize her own daughter, wouldn't she?"

"Forgive me, Mama, I'm just so shocked."

But was she? Cecily thought as she put her arms around her mother and held her as she wept. It was almost as if last night Kiki had been saying good-bye . . .

"They're keeping it quiet over Christmas, but it won't be two minutes before all the newspapers get hold of the story and dig into Kiki's life, so that the whole of America can read about her scandals over their breakfast! Oh, my, Cecily, I adored her; we go back such a long way, and she was so very kind to you, wasn't she?"

"She was, Mama, yes," said Cecily, desperately trying to hold back her own tears.

"And the worst thing is, she wouldn't see *me*, one of her oldest friends. If I'd known how low she was, I'd have done anything—*anything*—to help," Dorothea sobbed.

"Mama, I'm going to ring the bell and get Evelyn to bring us up a little brandy. It will help calm our nerves."

"Oh, Cecily, how can I possibly celebrate Christmas when she's no longer here?"

"Because . . . you know why, Mama? Kiki would want you to. She was one of the most famous party girls in town. And she said to me just last night that I must decide what makes me happy and go for it. So tomorrow we will put on our best dresses for her, and"—Cecily gulped—"celebrate her life. Okay?"

Eventually Dorothea nodded, took Cecily's handkerchief to wipe her tears, then stood up. She walked to the bedroom door as though she was in a dream. "Now," she said with a sigh, "I must go tell your father."

Cecily had gone to bed that night realizing it wasn't the moment to ask her mother whether Stella could join them for lunch. After a restless night full of strange dreams in which Kiki was speaking to her from a cloud in her pajamas and telling her to decide what was really important, she was awake with a start on Christmas morning, feeling tears forming as she remembered the terrible thing that had happened yesterday. Taking a few minutes to gather herself, Cecily got out of bed and donned her robe. Forcing a bright smile on her face, she walked into Stella's bedroom to find the little girl sucking on a candy cane, her lips smeared with the chocolate she had already eaten from her stocking.

"He came, Kuyia!" Stella looked up at her happily and pointed to the toy lion sitting on her lap. "I think Santa must have shrunk him to get him down the chimney. Do you think he'll grow again now he's here?" she asked, her eyes wide.

"I don't know; maybe he's a magic lion."

"I've decided to call him Lucky, because that's what I am!" she giggled, reaching up to hug Cecily, who hugged her back very tightly.

"Ow, Kuyia! You're squashing me!" Stella looked up at Cecily. "Why are you crying? Are you sad?"

"I'm fine, honey. I'm just going to call your Uncle Bill now to wish him a Merry Christmas—I miss him and our home."

"I do, too, but I like it here very much as well," said Stella, who then turned her attention to Lucky.

Still in her robe and suddenly feeling desperate to speak to her husband about Kiki, Cecily went downstairs to her father's study to use the telephone and was put through to Muthaiga Club, where Ali picked up the phone. Cecily smiled as she heard his familiar deep voice.

"Hello, Ali, it's Mrs. Forsythe here. Is Mr. Forsythe there?"

"Happy Christmas, Mrs. Forsythe," said Ali, "although I must offer you my condolences. We have had word here of Mrs. Preston's death."

"Thank you, Ali," said Cecily. She was shocked that the news had traveled so quickly. "I need to speak to Mr. Forsythe. Could you fetch him for me, please?"

"I am afraid I cannot; Mr. Forsythe went out on a game shoot a few hours ago."

Cecily's heart plummeted. "Well, when he gets back, can you please tell him that his wife called and that she really needs to speak to him. He has my telephone number in New York. Thank you, Ali, and Merry Christmas."

She hung up the receiver and sat down in her father's leather chair, trying to collect herself. Once again, when she truly needed her husband, he was nowhere to be found.

At noon, just before her sisters arrived, Cecily took Stella into the kitchen where the servants were busy preparing Christmas lunch.

"Oh, lookie here! Ain't you a picture, baby girl?" said Essie, the cook, who had taken a huge shine to Stella. "Now you come and help your Auntie Essie wiv dem pies."

Stella, who was dressed very inappropriately for the kitchen in her orange tulle dress, happily went to assist Essie.

"Merry Christmas, everyone," Cecily said. "Can someone take some broth up to my maid? She's finally professed herself hungry today."

Essie nodded. "No problem. And don't you be worryin', Miss Cecily, we'll feed her baby girl along with us right here, won't we, Stella?"

"I do hope so, Essie," Stella replied.

Essie laughed. "Gracious me! You done gone and talk like you're as white as they are!"

Despite Cecily's call to her mother to celebrate rather than mourn, Christmas Day was a muted affair. Mamie and Priscilla came over with their families to exchange presents and have lunch, all three sisters doing their best to cheer up the heartbroken Dorothea.

After lunch, Dorothea retired to her room.

"Mama is absolutely devastated," said Mamie to Cecily.

"Kiki was her oldest friend, it's only natural."

"That may be, but she saw her no more than every few years. You *lived* with her when you were first in Africa and saw her the night she died. Are you okay?"

"Obviously I'm real sad, Mamie, but, well . . . I just think that Kiki had run out of hope. And when hope is gone—"

"I know," said Mamie. "There's nothing left. Well, now, time for us to be off and get these little horrors into bed."

Once Cecily had said good-bye to her sisters and their families and Walter had retreated to his study for a nap, Cecily wandered back into the living room. She looked up at the enormous Christmas tree, decorated with so many baubles that there was barely any green to be seen.

She thought of Bill somewhere out on the African plains, the image of him there so at odds with this beautiful Manhattan living room.

*Is this my home,* she wondered, *or do I belong back in Kenya with Bill?* The truth was that she just didn't know.

The day after Christmas, with Dorothea locked upstairs in her bedroom, too distressed to venture out, Cecily decided to take Stella on a tour of New York.

Their first stop was Central Park, where Cecily bought Stella a bag of roasted chestnuts and taught her how to peel and eat the piping hot morsels. At the Central Park Zoo, Stella waved at the lion in its enclosure, speaking to it in Maa. "It is his language, after all," she said as Cecily suppressed a chuckle.

Archer then drove them through the busy city streets, and Stella gasped at the bright lights of Times Square, then listened with rapt attention as Cecily pointed out the Chrysler Building and the Empire State Building. As dusk fell, they indulged in hot chocolate with whipped cream before Cecily took Stella onto the ice rink at Rockefeller Center. Clutching each other for support, they slipped and skidded and giggled their way through the crowds.

Through Stella, Cecily began to see her city anew; she fell in love with it and its magical atmosphere all over again. Perhaps it was because she knew they'd be leaving at the end of January that she felt determined to take in as much of it as possible.

Starved of culture as she had been at Paradise Farm, she and her sisters went out to see the latest Broadway shows. She also enjoyed replenishing her wardrobe and actually wearing it out. Her sisters told her that she had "grown into her looks," and after a haircut by Mamie's stylist, even Cecily began to feel that she wasn't quite the ugly duckling she'd once considered herself to be.

"You're a head turner these days," Priscilla said with just a hint of envy in her voice as a group of good-looking men on Madison Avenue gave Cecily "the eye," as Priscilla called it. After her long years tucked away in Africa, Cecily felt like a lion released from captivity.

The only sad note in a very jolly post-Christmas week was Kiki's funeral. The numbers attending were small—many of the New York elite were out of town for the holidays, and besides, Kiki's life had been lived abroad for years. Cecily helped her father support Dorothea out of the church and on to the wake afterward, where her mother proceeded to get noticeably tipsy. Cecily could not help but feel that Kiki's death was the end of an era—not just for her mother but for her, too.

Cecily returned home one afternoon from a trip to the milliner to replace some of her outdated hats to hear a high-pitched giggle coming from her father's study. Knocking on the door, she found her father with Stella on his lap.

"Good afternoon, Cecily," said Walter. "Stella and I were taking a look at the map of the world in my atlas. I was doing my best lion roar, but then she asked me for the sound a zebra made, so I gave what I thought was a good impression of one, but obviously, you didn't think so, eh, little miss?" Walter smiled at Stella as she slid off his knee and ran toward Cecily.

"You haven't been bothering Mr. Huntley-Morgan, have you, Stella?"

"Not at all," Walter said. "I found her in here looking at the books on the shelves, and we've been having a fine old time. And I've told her to call me Walter, by the way, haven't I?"

Stella nodded shyly.

"She's a bright little kid, Cecily. Will her mother be sending her to school back in Kenya?"

"There aren't any schools there for a child like Stella, but I've been doing my best to teach her to read and write."

"She teaches me sums," Stella added, her little face serious.

"All right, then, let's play the game I used to play with Cecily, shall we? What are two and two?"

"Four."

"Three and four?"

"Seven."

"Eight and five."

"Thirteen," Stella answered without hesitation.

"I'm impressed," Walter smiled. "I think I'll have to make those questions harder, won't I?"

Twenty minutes later, Walter raised his hands as Stella begged him to test her further. "I'm all out of questions, honey, but you're real good at answering them. Exceptionally good," he said, casting a glance at Cecily. "Now, then, both of you run along. I'm expecting a visitor any second."

"I like Walter," said Stella as they walked toward the kitchen to find Lankenua, who was huddled by the stove. "At least I like him better than Mrs. Huntley-Morgan." Stella shrugged as she eyed the chocolate cake sitting on the kitchen table. "But I like that best." She giggled, pointing to it.

"How are you feeling, Lankenua?"

Lankenua nodded. "Okay. When we go home, Missus Cecily?"

"In a few weeks," Cecily replied as she turned to Mary. "Do you think you could bring some coffee up to my room? I'm out again at five, and I should change."

"Of course, Miss Cecily."

Up in her room, Cecily stood in front of the mirror, trying to decide what she should wear for the Vassar reunion. She remembered that Rosalind had never been one for fashion, so she decided on a plain black cocktail dress. Draining her coffee, she asked Mary to call for Archer to bring the car out front. During the drive there, she felt nervous; she still had no idea why Rosalind would think to invite her. She lived in Brooklyn—an address that she'd learned from Priscilla was recently becoming popular with the younger set. Dorothea had commented that it was full of Irish, their families still there after building the Brooklyn Bridge.

"This neighborhood's gotta lot of beautiful old brownstones," Archer said as they drove through the streets. "It's been run-down for a while, but people like your friend are movin' here 'cause they get a lotta house for their dollar. New York's always changing, ain't it, Miss Cecily?"

The car pulled up in front of a neat brownstone set in a row of far shabbier houses, and Cecily stepped out.

"I shouldn't be much longer than an hour," she said to Archer, then walked up the steps to the front door.

"Cecily! How wonderful you could make it." Rosalind, whose dark hair was cut in a sleek bob similar to Mamie's, smiled at her as she led her into a pleasant living room filled with young women, many of them wearing pants. Cecily felt hideously old-fashioned and overdressed.

"Beer or sherry?" Rosalind asked as she steered her over to a drinks cart.

"Oh, sherry, please. Will I know anybody here?"

"Of course you will. Apart from the odd exception, they were all in our year at Vassar. So the New York gossip machine tells me you've been living in Africa?" Rosalind said. "We can't wait to hear all about it, can we, Beatrix?"

A Negro woman with a pair of wide, warm eyes appraised Cecily. "No, we can't, given that's where our forefathers were from, Rosalind."

Cecily looked at the two women in confusion.

"Don't worry, Cecily," Rosalind chuckled. "Most people don't recognize me for the Negro I really am. There was obviously a rogue white man way back when, but my heart is as black as Beatrix's. Vassar didn't know until after I'd received my degree—you know what they're like there, Cecily. If they had their way, we'd be sweeping the floors, not sitting in lecture halls with folks like you. It's changing slowly, mind you. They were embarrassed into taking Beatrix in 1940, as other colleges had a far bigger colored quota. So say hello to our first official Negro Vassar graduate."

"And I hope that I will be the first of many." Beatrix smiled. "I'm at Yale Medical School right now, and the challenge there isn't just the color of my skin but the fact that I'm a woman. Double whammy, eh, Rosalind?"

"You bet," said Rosalind, indicating a quieter corner at the back of the room. "Now, Cecily, come and tell us all about Africa. It's Kenya you live in, isn't it?"

At first Cecily performed her usual party piece about safaris, lions, and deadly snakes, but Rosalind soon stopped her.

"Tell me, in a colonial country, do the Negroes have rights? Are there activist parties?"

"Not to my knowledge."

"So even though Kenya is a predominantly black society, Negroes—in their own country—are still ruled by a few white men in uniform?" asked Beatrix.

"Yes, that's how it is, I'm afraid. Although I know that since the war, when many of them signed up to fight for king and country—"

"Their country but not their king," Beatrix interrupted.

"Yes, of course," Cecily agreed hastily. "They were fed the line that life would improve for them if they did fight. Then they returned, and nothing had changed. In fact, my husband said recently that it's gotten worse."

"Would you say that tension is building there?" Rosalind asked.

"Yes," Cecily replied, thinking back to her conversations with Bill over recent months. "The Kikuyu—that's the largest tribe in Kenya—are no longer simply accepting the appalling conditions and slave labor demanded by their white masters. There is zero health care for any of them—I can only think of one hospital for coloreds nearby, and that's funded by a charity. And as for education—"

"Tell me about it." Rosalind rolled her eyes. "It's not much better for our kids here in the US either, although at least here there is education available for both white and black, and unlike in the South, it isn't segregated. But the white kids outnumber ours, and there's still underlying prejudice, especially from the teaching staff themselves. I know, because I was one of the minority in high school."

"I've done my best to teach my housekeeper's child mathematics and to read and write . . . she's the brightest of buttons."

"Well, well." Rosalind raised an eyebrow at Beatrix, then turned back to Cecily. "I have a five-year-old girl, and I just don't want her to have to face what I went through to complete my education. I want her to learn in a safe and supportive environment where she feels valued and isn't dealing with taunts and jibes from her classmates or being unfairly singled out by her teachers. So . . . I'm in the process of setting up a little school right here in my house. Beatrix and I have chosen a number of bright Negro kids we know who we're planning to educate, with a view to their eventually getting into Ivy League colleges."

"Our kids simply have to have role models they can aspire to. They have to believe they can do it, and it's up to us to show them they can," Beatrix added, her eyes shining with fervor.

"So you say you've been educating your housekeeper's daughter?" said Rosalind.

"I have, yes. Stella—that's her name—soaks up what I teach her like a sponge."

"Would you care to bring her here to meet us?" asked Rosalind. "She might be a good candidate for our school. And if you're interested, I could use an extra pair of teaching hands. Beatrix will be far too busy with medicine at Yale, so I'm pretty much setting this up alone."

"That sounds incredible, Rosalind," breathed Cecily. "I've never thought such a thing might be possible for Stella."

"Well, we'd be mighty glad to have you too. You majored in history, didn't you?"

"I did, but my passion was really economics, and if I do say so myself, I have a good head for figures."

"And Rosalind's all about humanities, so between the two of you and with some help from me when I can spare the time, you could muddle through the sciences." Beatrix chuckled. "You just got to remember that everything's possible in the land of the free—as long as *we* make it happen."

"So when should I bring Stella here to meet you?"

"Just as soon as you like. The semester officially starts next week, so how about this Friday?" Rosalind suggested.

"Perfect."

Beatrix and Rosalind accompanied her to the front door, and as the three of them said good-bye, Rosalind regarded her quizzically. "Say, Cecily, how would you feel about joining us at a protest?"

"I . . . don't know. What exactly are you protesting against?"

"The housing situation in Harlem is abysmal. Negroes are ghettoized—there's just awful overcrowding, not to mention the excessive force used by the police to 'keep things under control.' Mayor O'Dwyer has been a great friend to our community—"

"Only so he can get our votes!" Beatrix cut in.

"That may be, but he's made certain promises, and we're holding him to them. He's due to speak at the Abyssinian Baptist Church next week, and we'll be there to remind him what's at stake," Rosalind continued. "It would be great to have you there, Cecily, you'd be such an asset to our group."

"I . . . Let me think about it, okay?"

"What's there to think about?" said Beatrix. "It's a matter of right and wrong, life or death. You should know that better than anyone, having lived in Africa. Please stand with us, Cecily. We need the whites to support our cause, too."

"All right," she agreed. "I'll be there. And now I really must get home. Bye, now."

"We'll be in touch with where to meet!" called Rosalind.

Archer opened the car door for her, and she slid onto the back seat.

"Sorry I took so long."

"No problem, Miss Cecily. How was your evening?" he asked as they set off back for Manhattan across the Brooklyn Bridge.

"It was . . . well, utterly amazing!" Cecily breathed.

# 45

The following Wednesday, as directed, Cecily dressed in her plainest clothes. Leaving Stella in the care of Lankenua, who was now looking far healthier, she directed Archer to drive her to Harlem.

"Excuse me, Miss Cecily?" he said as he handed her into the rear seat of the Chrysler.

"You heard me, Archer: Harlem, outside the Abyssinian Baptist Church, 132 West 138th Street," Cecily read the address from the note she had written down when on the telephone to Rosalind.

"Do your parents know you're going there?" he said after a pause.

"Of course," Cecily lied, feeling irritated that even as a married woman, Archer still treated her like a child.

"As you wish, Miss Cecily."

Cecily looked out of the window as they made their way uptown toward Harlem, where, despite her bravado when giving Archer the address, she had never been before. As the skyscrapers of Fifth and Madison receded and they drove slowly up Lenox Avenue, she noticed that the faces on the street were various shades of black and brown rather than white. She suddenly felt like a fish out of water in her own city. Black children sat on the stoops of derelict houses watching the Chrysler cruise past, the windows of many of the stores were boarded up, and rusting, overflowing trash cans were gathered on street corners. Despite the fact that it was 1947, it felt as though the Depression hadn't even begun to end here.

Archer brought the car to a halt. Along the street, Cecily could see an imposing gothic church, where a large crowd of protesters had already gathered outside. He stepped out to open the door for her.

"I'll park up at the end of the street, on the corner of Lenox Avenue, just across from here." He pointed. "If there's any trouble, you come a-runnin' and I'll be waitin', okay? You sure you'll be all right?"

"Yes, Archer, thank you, I'm meeting friends," she said with far more confidence than she felt as she walked away from him toward the crowd.

She surveyed the mass of people, many of whom were holding handwritten placards bearing slogans such as EQUAL RIGHTS! and HOUSING FOR ALL! Her heart in her mouth, Cecily walked hesitantly toward the crowd, who were all facing a raised platform that had been set up as a stage on the sidewalk outside the church.

"There you are!" Rosalind's familiar voice cut through the clamor. Cecily turned to see her new friend approaching her, dressed in a pair of slacks and a man's coat. "I'm so glad you came," Rosalind said. "The others were already taking bets on whether you'd turn up or not. This is my husband, Terrence," she said, gesturing to the tall black man beside her.

"Pleasure to meet you, Cecily," he said, shaking her hand and smiling warmly at her. "We appreciate your support."

Cecily wasn't surprised to see that she was one of very few white people present, but she was greeted with smiles as the other protesters stepped out of her way politely. A few were holding flasks of coffee to ward off the cold, and Cecily saw that one woman had a baby strapped to her chest.

"How long will this go on for?" she whispered to Rosalind.

"Oh, just an hour or so," Rosalind replied cheerfully. "It's a great turnout—Beatrix is a marvel at getting people motivated. And look, here she is!"

Beatrix appeared beside them, her eyes shining with excitement, her dark hair braided tightly against her scalp. "Cecily! It's wonderful you came! I—"

Beatrix was drowned out by a roar from the crowd as three men stepped onto the stage. Cecily recognized Mayor O'Dwyer from the photos in the *New York Times*. Two other white men stood beside him, one of whom was dressed in the regalia of a police chief and was glowering at the placards.

"Harlem! 'Tis an honor to be here!" Mayor O'Dwyer began in his strong Irish accent, and the crowd cheered in response. Cecily looked around at the gathered faces and felt suddenly galvanized. Here were people who were passionate about creating a better world; she had not felt such exhilaration and hope around her since the VE Day celebrations in Nairobi. Beatrix handed her a placard that read HARLEM IS NOT A GHETTO! and Cecily proudly held it aloft. She listened to Mayor O'Dwyer's speech, which promised housing reforms and better funding for schools, and blinked as a reporter's flashbulb went off close by.

As people began to jostle forward for a better view, an elbow knocked Cecily from behind, and Rosalind reached out to steady her as she stumbled. Despite the frosty air, Cecily felt sweat gathering at the back of her neck and realized how tightly packed the audience was.

As the police chief stepped up to the microphone, a ripple of unease spread through the crowd, and Cecily shivered. She craned her neck to see how far the crowd extended to either side of her and was shocked to see a ring of police officers surrounding them, their hands on their wooden nightsticks, their faces inscrutable under their blue caps.

"Why are the police here?" she whispered to Rosalind.

"Just stick with me and Terrence, you'll be safe," Rosalind whispered back.

"Murderers!" Beatrix spat. "Those cops attacked Robert Bandy—shot him when he was unarmed and just trying to save a woman's life. Goddamn pigs!"

A wave of anger began to emanate from around them, and Cecily took in a gulp of air as the crowd was pressed further in on itself by the police officers. Cecily could no longer hear the speeches from the stage, only the cries of dismay from the woman near her whose baby began wailing in its sling as she tried to shield it from the crush of bodies.

Screams filled the air. A man pushed her aside to escape a police officer who was coming toward him with his nightstick held aloft. The man raised his placard in self-defense but was struck down until he lay sprawled in the dirty street, protecting his head from the continued blows. Cecily heard a shrill whistle and the whinny of horses and looked up to see that mounted police officers were advancing on the protesters, many of whom were now running away.

"Cecily! Stay close!" Beatrix grabbed her hand and guided her toward a gap in the line of police. Cecily followed Beatrix blindly, her heart thumping as she ran, dodging other protesters who were also seeking safety. She tried to ignore the cries of pain and the sickening thuds of nightsticks colliding with human bodies. With a sudden wrench, she found herself knocked to the ground and looked up to see Beatrix being restrained by two police officers. She was fighting like a wild cat, her curls breaking free from her braids as she was dragged away.

"No! Beatrix!" Cecily shouted, trying to get up as pain shot through her ankle. "Stop! She's done nothing wrong!"

She sat looking around in shock and bewilderment. What had begun as a peaceful, orderly gathering had descended into chaos. "Archer," she murmured as she tried to remember where he'd said he would wait for her. She attempted to stand, but her ankle gave way as a fresh wave of protesters stampeded toward her.

Just as she thought she might be trampled where she sat, she heard a deep male voice from above her.

"Can you walk?" She looked up to see a white man towering over her.

"My ankle—"

"Take my hand."

Cecily did so, and the man pulled her to standing. Then, with his arm supporting her, he began to guide her through the crowd.

"My driver . . . he's waiting for me on Lenox, over there at the end of the street," she managed to gasp as her senses returned to her.

"Then let's get you out of here fast; it looks like things are about to get even uglier."

All around them, violent skirmishes were breaking out as the protesters rallied and began to fight back.

As they neared the intersection of West 138th Street and Lenox Avenue, Cecily spotted the Chrysler and pointed to it. "There's Archer!" she yelled above the melee. The man swept her into his arms and ran with her to the car, wrenching open the rear door as they reached it.

"Thank the Lord you're safe, Miss Cecily!" shouted Archer, starting the engine. "Let's get outta here!"

"You take care, ma'am," the man said as he lowered Cecily into the seat. As he was about to shut the door, Cecily stopped him, seeing two policemen with nightsticks heading toward the car.

"Archer, wait! Get in *now!*" she screamed to the man, mustering her remaining strength as she reached out to grasp his arm and pull him inside, just as the policemen charged forward to grab him. "Go, Archer! Go, go, go!" Archer gunned the engine, and the car sped off.

As the Chrysler pulled away from the nightmare scene they had left behind, the three occupants breathed a collective sigh of relief.

"I can't thank you enough for your help," Cecily ventured.

"It's nothing. I should thank you for yours just then." The man was leaning back in the seat, his eyes half closed.

"Can we take you somewhere? Where do you live?" she asked.

"Just drop me at the nearest subway stop."

"We're just coming to the 110th Street station," Archer interjected.

"That will suit me fine," the man said.

Archer pulled the car over.

"Can I at least take your name?" Cecily said.

The man hesitated for a moment, then reached into his pocket and handed her a card before getting out of the car and slamming the door behind him.

# 46

Cecily woke up two days later, her ankle still throbbing with pain despite the ice packs she had placed on it during the night. On their return from the protest, dirtied and hobbling, she had sworn Archer to absolute secrecy. He had hesitantly promised not to speak of the event to her parents.

"If I'm not oversteppin' my place, Miss Cecily, it might not be a good idea to get involved with those kinda things again," he'd said as they'd sat outside the house while Cecily composed herself, genuine concern in his eyes.

"Thank you, Archer, but I'm old enough to know what I'm doing," she'd replied curtly. "And someone has to stand up to inequality, don't they?"

"So long as you keep safe, Miss Cecily. But that ain't your battle to fight. You're a lady."

Dorothea had been dismayed at the state she was in, and Cecily had quickly fabricated an elaborate lie about tripping on a subway grate before gingerly taking the stairs up to the attic floor to find Stella with Lankenua. Stella had run into her arms, and Cecily had gripped her tightly.

"Why are you so dirty, Kuyia? Where have you been?"

"That's not important, honey," Cecily had said, smiling down at Stella. "I'm simply happy to see you."

There was a tap on her bedroom door, and Evelyn entered with a tray of coffee and toast. She laid it on Cecily's lap, then checked on her ankle, which was propped up on a pillow.

"It's lookin' much better, miss," she said.

"Thank you, Evelyn," Cecily said, regarding her with new eyes. "Evelyn?"

"Yes, miss?"

"Do you like working for my family?"

"Why, what a question, Miss Cecily! I've been doin' it so long now, since you was a little girl."

"Yes, I know, Evelyn, but don't you wish you'd had other opportunities?"

There was a pause, then Evelyn said cheerfully, "I'm very grateful to have *this* opportunity. I've been happy to serve your family, Miss Cecily. Ain't you happy with my work?"

"Of course I am! I'm sorry," Cecily said helplessly. "I just . . . Oh, don't worry, Evelyn, I'm being silly."

"You just ring the bell if you need anythin', Miss Cecily."

Evelyn left the room, and Cecily let her head fall back against her pillows. Since the horrific events of the protest, her entire world view had turned on its axis. She could not stop seeing the terrified faces of the protesters being taken by force by the police and the sheer, outrageous injustice of it all. At least Rosalind had telephoned yesterday to let her know that Beatrix and some dozen other protesters had finally been released from jail.

"It was a hefty bail, but our lawyer spoke to the judge and got them a good deal. It's the second strike against Beatrix, so she has to be more careful in the future."

"That could have been Stella who got attacked, just because of the color of her skin. What kind of world do we live in?" Cecily said softly to herself now.

*A world that benefits you,* her mind replied. And why was that? Simply the fact that she was rich and privileged and *white.*

"Please stand with us," Beatrix had said to her.

Cecily looked out of her bedroom window, where she could see snow covering Central Park in a downy white blanket. Everything looked at peace in this small part of New York, but now that she had been exposed to another side of it—one marred by suffering and oppression—nothing could ever be the same again. She remembered seeing the pictures of German concentration camps liberated by American soldiers at the end of the war, her tears of shock falling onto the newspaper, her mind scrambling to comprehend such cruelty. Yet now she knew that, just like in Kenya, only a short drive from her front door, people's lives were filled daily with similar injustice.

"People believe it's the land of the free, yet we don't do a darned thing about righting the wrongs for them once they're here," she whispered.

As she ate her toast, a bubble of tense energy filled her chest and she felt desperate to speak with Rosalind and Beatrix. She couldn't imagine discussing any of these thoughts with her sisters, let alone her father—or, worse, her mother. If only Dorothea had seen her at the protest, standing shoulder to shoulder with the "Negroes"—whose babies she worked to raise money for but who were no more welcome in her home as guests on an equal footing than the average fat sewer rat.

"But it's true, I'm not one of them," she reminded herself as she drank her coffee. So why did she feel this fire, this need to fight for justice for what she had witnessed in Harlem two days ago?

*Because you love the child you call your daughter,* her senses told her. *And you must fight for her and others like her, because she cannot.*

Later that day, Cecily took a few hesitant steps and found that her ankle could bear weight again. While her mother was taking her afternoon rest, which had grown longer and longer in the weeks since Kiki's death, Cecily dressed Stella in her room and let the little girl admire herself in the full-length mirror.

"Where are we going, Kuyia?" Stella asked as she adjusted the collar on her red coat.

"A school, with lots of other little children just as bright as you. Would you like to meet them?"

"Yes!" Stella squealed. "Can I take Lucky to meet everyone, too?" She gripped the stuffed lion by its mane.

"Of course you can," Cecily said.

Archer brought the car to a halt outside of Rosalind's brownstone. The snow had only recently stopped and had not yet had a chance to turn to slush, so Stella laughed in delight as she made small, perfect footsteps up the stoop to the front door.

"Thank you, Archer."

"No problem, Miss Cecily. I'll be waitin', so whenever you're ready," he said, giving her a wink. It seemed that the secret between them had also forged a bond.

Cecily lifted Stella so she could use the heavy bronze knocker. Rosalind opened the door and greeted Cecily with a warm hug.

"Welcome, sister," she whispered into Cecily's ear. "And you must be Stella," she said, crouching down and extending her hand. Overcome with shyness, Stella hid behind Cecily's legs.

"It's okay, honey," Cecily encouraged her. "Rosalind is a friend of mine, and she'll introduce you to all the other children."

Hesitantly, Stella took Rosalind's hand and allowed her to lead them through to the back of the large house, until they reached an airy room with French doors that opened onto a small patch of garden. It had been converted into a schoolroom of sorts, with a blackboard faced by five small wooden desks. Bookshelves filled with exercise books and primers, stationery and toys lined one side of the room, while another wall was dedicated to times tables, a map of New York, and pictures of animals drawn by childish hands.

"Who's your friend, Stella?" Rosalind asked.

"This is Lucky," Stella said, lifting the lion.

Rosalind petted his fur appreciatively. "He's very beautiful; I'm honored that you brought him. Now, have you been to a school before?"

"No, but Kuyia teaches me." She looked up at Cecily, who nodded encouragingly. " 'Kuyia' means 'Aunt,' " she explained to Rosalind, who then led Stella to a small reading corner, where cushions were strewn on a play mat, and they sat down together. Cecily watched with pride as Stella became animated as Rosalind asked her questions, then reached for one of the picture books on the shelf beside them. Stella began to read aloud the passages that Rosalind pointed to.

Cecily sat at one of the small desks as Rosalind took Stella through some basic arithmetic, then some logic questions, which Stella answered with ease. After thirty minutes, Rosalind suggested that Stella meet the other children, and she jumped up eagerly. They were led downstairs and into a large kitchen, where four children were eating peanut butter and jelly sandwiches at an old oak table.

"Say hello to Stella, everyone!" Rosalind called, and the boys and girls stood up shyly to welcome her. Cecily watched as Stella smiled widely and went to sit at the table next to Rosalind's daughter, who was introduced as Harmony, her hair styled in curly, ribboned ponytails, and gave her half of her sandwich.

"So it would just be you and me teaching at the moment," Rosalind said quietly to Cecily as they watched the children giggling together at the table. "If the school's a success, I hope to expand. My thoughts are that I'd fund it by asking some of my more well-off Negro friends who are hungry to get a decent education for their kids to pay, which would enable us to take on the brighter kids whose parents can't afford to do so."

"That's a great plan. You've really thought this all through," Cecily said, full of admiration for her new friend.

"Well, since I'm home here with Harmony anyway, I might as well put my degree to good use. So tell me more about Stella. It's obvious she's a bright spark and adores you."

Cecily watched to make sure Stella was fully occupied, then indicated that the two of them should move out of earshot. "I actually found her when she was only a few hours old, left for dead in the woods on my farm in Kenya. I took her home, and, well"—Cecily sighed—"it's hard to explain, but it was love at first sight. My husband was shocked when I said I wanted to care for her, to bring her up as our own, but he came around to the idea, and we hatched a plan so that we could."

Cecily explained Lankenua's arrival in their lives and how Stella believed she was her mother. "Of course, no one else knows the truth, Rosalind. My mama would simply die if she got wind of the real state of the relationship, but it's the best we can do."

"I understand," said Rosalind. Cecily saw that there were tears in her eyes. "Can I give you a hug?"

"Why, of course," Cecily said as Rosalind took her into her embrace.

"I just think what you have done for that child is about the most beautiful thing I've ever heard. And I want to help you give Stella everything she deserves and more."

Cecily felt tears in her own eyes, too, because it was the first time since she'd taken Stella into her arms as a newborn that she'd ever been able to share the truth of the situation with anyone but Bill and Lankenua.

"And what about your husband? Is he expecting you back in Kenya anytime soon?" asked Rosalind, her perceptive gaze boring into Cecily's own.

"In truth, yes, but maybe I can delay for a while and see how Stella—and I—settle in here. Like you, I need a purpose—to be able to put my brain to good use. In Kenya, apart from the house and gardens, and Stella, of course, I don't have one. And for her, there is no future in Africa right now."

"All right, kids, who wants to go outside in the snow?" Rosalind turned and asked the children.

"Me! Me!" they all shouted.

Cecily and Rosalind followed them as they trooped out of the kitchen, and the two women helped them don their snow boots and jackets.

"I've never played in the snow before," Stella said quietly to Cecily. "I won't know what to do."

"I'll show you how," piped up Harmony. "We'll make a snowman!"

Stella took her hand, and they ran out into the garden, where they all shrieked and laughed as a snowball fight ensued, then worked together to build a snowman. Watching from the French doors, Cecily had never seen her so confident and happy—in fact, she had never seen Stella play together with so many children. Out of necessity, Stella's world had been small and contained, the only playmate her age being Michael. Here, she could be a normal child among kids just like her. Instinctively, she knew this was absolutely the right place for Stella. And that she would sacrifice just about anything to continue seeing her little girl so happy.

"I would love to have you both join our school," said Rosalind as they stood on the stoop later that afternoon. "But I also know that you've got a big decision to make, right?"

"I do, yes."

"Well, let me know when you've decided, okay?"

"I will."

As she led Stella down the steps to the waiting car, Cecily felt almost tearful as she watched her wave to her new friends.

"Bye-bye, see you soon," Stella called.

As they drove off, Cecily knew that she'd do all she could to make sure her beloved daughter *would*.

The next morning, Cecily woke up, her head and heart aching from a dream of Bill. She dressed quickly and crept downstairs, not wishing to wake the sleeping house. It was still dark outside, with only the first glimmers of dawn touching the sky, and she wrapped herself tightly in her coat and fur muffler and walked toward Central Park. Her ankle still feeling delicate, she cleared some snow off a bench and sat down. The park was quiet, with only a few haggard pigeons pecking fruitlessly at the slush on the ground.

Cecily hugged herself, feeling a little as though she had fallen down a rabbit hole since she had arrived in Manhattan. She watched her breath, visible in the frigid air, now a novelty to her after being so long in the heat of Africa. Here, the Manhattan-Cecily could barely remember the feeling of being too hot and the other Kenya-Cecily felt almost like a dream self, an imposter. She wondered what Bill was doing right now, whether he was still on safari. When she called, he never answered the home telephone, and at Muthaiga Club, Ali said he hadn't seen the *sahib* since Christmas Day.

Stella's destiny lay here; she felt it deep in her bones. Yet if she stayed with her in New York, she would be leaving Bill behind in Kenya. Her home and all it entailed . . . Paradise Farm, Wolfie, Katherine . . . Would Lankenua choose to stay on with her here? She could not ask a mother to leave her son behind.

Perhaps, as she'd said to Rosalind, all she could do was to tell Bill she was delaying her return for a while—he could hardly complain after the years she'd spent trapped in Kenya, and neither was he making any effort to keep in contact with her. At least an extended stay here would give them a chance to try their new life on for size without making any firm decisions.

Back at the house, Cecily ducked into her father's study. She could hear footsteps in the kitchen and the hallways as Evelyn took the morning coffee tray upstairs to her parents and lit the fires. Cecily took a fountain pen and some paper out of her father's desk and began to write.

*Dearest Bill,*

*Happy New Year! I hope you celebrated it wherever you are. I was sorry not to be there with you. How were the Christmas festivities at Muthaiga Club? When I called to speak to you on Christmas Day, Ali mentioned that you had gone out on safari. In fact, I have tried to call you on numerous occasions at the farm and Muthaiga since, so I'm resorting to writing. I am taking your absence as a good sign that you are keeping busy and not consumed in hermit-hood while I'm gone.*

*How are Bobby and Katherine? Is her pregnancy progressing well? Stella misses Michael a great deal.*

*Christmas here in New York was somber, given Kiki's death. I can hardly bear to think of Mundui House standing empty without Kiki in it.*

*I have been taking solace in getting to know my nieces and nephews and growing close to my sisters again. I have also had a wonderful time exploring Manhattan with Stella, and, in truth, the time has gone so fast that I'd like to stay on a little longer. After all, I have been away for seven years! I hope you don't mind, Bill. It's just such a long journey, and I have no idea when I might come back again after I leave. You are, of course, welcome to join me here any time you choose. Mama and Papa would love to meet you, and I would like to show you my city, as you have shown me Kenya.*

*I will let you know when I am booking a passage back.*

*I hope all is going well with the farm, and please send my love to all, and to you especially, of course. I miss you.*

*Please write back or call me. I worry about you!*


*Cecily xx*


As she was addressing the envelope, the door to the study opened and her father walked in.

"Hello, Cecily," he said. "You're up early, honey."

"Yes, I just wanted to write a letter to Bill."

"Ah, of course. You must miss him, but you'll be reunited in a few weeks, won't you?"

"Actually," she said, tapping the envelope against her palm, "I've decided to stay on here in New York for a while longer, if that is okay with you and Mama, of course."

Walter beamed. "You don't even have to ask. That is wonderful news. Now come have breakfast with me, and we can do the *New York Times* crossword together."

Stepping out of the study with her father, Cecily dropped the letter onto the silver dish in the hallway to be mailed.

Stella began school the following Monday, wearing her favorite plaid dress, her hair styled in ponytails like those of her new friend, Harmony. Archer drove them to Brooklyn, and Stella bounded out of the car and up the steps to the front door. Cecily had given Stella her old leather school satchel and had filled it with pencils and erasers, as well as a bag of chocolate cookies Essie had made for her to share with her classmates.

Rosalind ushered them into the classroom, and Stella ran to hug Harmony, who offered the desk beside her. Cecily stood at the back of the room and watched Rosalind begin the class. She saw Stella's eager face listening to every word Rosalind spoke.

From then on, a routine began. Every weekday, Archer would drive Cecily and Stella to Brooklyn to begin the school day at nine o'clock. Cecily and Rosalind took turns to use the schoolroom to teach their different subjects, with the other sitting downstairs preparing lessons and correcting the children's work.

Cecily found she absolutely loved teaching—it took a little time to find her confidence, but once she did, the children responded to her firm but gentle style. After Archer had driven them home, Cecily would walk with Stella through Central Park, where the little girl would chatter happily about all she had learned that day. In the evenings, they would curl up together in Cecily's bed and read a book, and when she fell asleep on her shoulder, Cecily would lift her up and tuck her into her bed in the room next door.

She had also decided to call the number on the card that the man who had rescued her at the protest had given her to thank him. A woman with a French accent had answered and had passed the phone to her husband. Cecily had insisted on buying him and his wife lunch. The three of them had shared an interesting couple of hours at the Waldorf. The Tanits were both well traveled, and it had been inspiring to talk with a couple who had lived through the war in Europe. It made her realize just how inward-looking most Americans in her set were. Sadly, the Tanits had since returned to England, but more and more, Cecily sought out the company of both Beatrix and Rosalind, finding their circle of friends so much more stimulating than the women she knew from her mother's endless charity circuit. The world was changing fast, and Cecily wanted to be part of the future, not stuck in the fast-fading past.

Lankenua had formed a friendship with Evelyn and had recently even begun going to her church on Sunday. Her talk of returning to Kenya had lessened, and Cecily was pleased to see that she was beginning to settle in New York. Now that the Christmas season was over, Walter spent all his days at the bank, retiring to his club at night, and to Cecily's relief, Dorothea had gone on her annual visit to Chicago to see her mother. When he was at home, Walter would pull Stella into his study and play more and more sophisticated math games with her. It was obvious he was fond of the little girl, and on more than one occasion, Cecily had been tempted to tell him the truth about their relationship.

There had been no word from Bill—either by letter or telephone or even when she had sent a telegram to Muthaiga Club. Ali assured her when she called that the *sahib* was well but out on the plains with his cattle, which Katherine also confirmed.

"Maybe he has simply forgotten me already," Cecily muttered as she replaced the receiver after another unanswered call.

Before Cecily knew it, it was the end of March, and spring was forcing out a long New York winter. She was thinking less and less of Paradise Farm, and although she had managed to finally catch Bill on the telephone twice, there had been a distance in his voice that she could not attribute to the long-distance call. Stella, too, had stopped asking when they were going "home." All that marred their happy routine was that Dorothea had returned from Chicago and had brought home a brittle and tense atmosphere.

A final winter blizzard was sweeping through the streets of New York, rattling the windowpanes. Cecily and Stella were tucked up in her bed in their dressing gowns with hot chocolate and *Little House on the Prairie* opened on Stella's lap. Stella read aloud in her high, clear voice but trembled whenever the blizzard buffeted the house.

"I'm scared, Kuyia," she whispered. "What if the wind blows everything away?"

"Everyone is safe and sound inside their homes. This house has been here for a very, very long time and has withstood a hundred blizzards. Now, do you want to read a bit more or go to sleep?"

As every night, Stella stubbornly continued, but Cecily could see her eyes drooping, and eventually she succumbed to sleep. Cecily watched her eyelashes flutter delicately against her dark skin, her features completely at peace. Reaching out to stroke her hair, Cecily allowed her own eyes to close as she joined Stella in a dream world.

There was a knock on the door, and Cecily woke with a jump, disoriented. She saw the morning light streaming in through the bedroom windows, looked at Stella lying next to her, and realized that they must have fallen asleep.

"Come in," she called, expecting Evelyn with her breakfast tray.

It wasn't Evelyn who opened the door but Dorothea. "Cecily, I just wanted to tell you that today I'm going to—"

Her mother stopped dead as she saw Stella's dark little head next to Cecily's on the pillow. She put her hand to her mouth and gave a squeal of horror. "What is *she* doing in bed with you?"

"I . . . Stella was scared of the storm, so she got in with me and we read a story and—"

Dorothea marched across the room and pulled the covers off Stella. Then she grabbed the little girl, who was still half asleep, roughly by the arm and hauled her out of the bed.

"You come with me, miss, right now! Up to the attic where you belong! I've had enough of this ridiculous behavior of yours, Cecily. And this— putting the Negro child of your maid in your *own* bed—just about crowns it!"

"Please!" Stella cried as she tried to wriggle from Dorothea's grasp. "You're hurting me!"

"Let her go *now*, Mama!"

Cecily was also out of bed and tugging at her mother's arm to let Stella free.

"I will do no such thing! I don't care what you do under your own roof in that godforsaken country you call home, but here under mine, dirty little Negroes live up in the attic where they belong!"

"How *dare* you call Stella dirty! She is every bit as clean as I am!" Cecily screamed. "I gave her a bath myself last night!"

"*You* gave her a bath? Dear Lord, Cecily! Has all that sun touched your brain? She is the nigger daughter of your maid!"

"You call her a nigger again, and I swear I will—"

"Ouch!" cried Dorothea as Stella's small white teeth bit into the soft flesh of Dorothea's wrist, and she finally let go of her. Stella ran toward Cecily, who closed her arms about her protectively.

"That child is nothing but a wild savage! Look!" Dorothea proffered her arm. "She's drawn blood! I swear, Cecily, I want her and her mother out of my house as soon as they've packed their things. I need to go call my doctor—she's almost certainly given me some kind of disease!"

"Don't be ridiculous, Mama, Stella is as healthy as you and I."

"I told you, I want her and her mother out of my house today!"

"Fine. Then I will go with them. Besides, I can't stand staying in this house a moment longer anyway, listening to your disgusting prejudices and your racist remarks! Stella is just a child, Mama, the same as any of your beloved grandchildren!"

The racket had attracted Walter, who came out of the master bedroom in his pajamas. "What on earth is going on in here?"

"Your daughter has had a nigger child sleeping in her bed all night," proclaimed Dorothea. "It's obscene!"

"That's it!" Cecily picked Stella up in her arms and calmly carried her to the attic, where Lankenua was hovering nervously at the top of the stairs.

"Could you get yourself and Stella dressed and pack your things quickly, please. We're leaving now."

Lankenua looked from Cecily to Stella in confusion but did as she was bid.

Cecily returned to her bedroom, where she dressed, then threw some clothes into a carry-on. She met Lankenua and Stella in the hallway and then led them downstairs into the entrance hall.

"What on earth are you doing?" Walter said from the top of the stairs, as he watched her bundle Stella into her coat, boots, and hat in the hall.

"Mama has said that Lankenua and Stella must leave the house, so I'm leaving with them, Papa."

For a moment, they looked at each other, Cecily's heart beating fast as she waited to see if he would come to their defense. But as her father made no move to speak, she turned away from him with a sad sigh.

"Mary, fetch Archer now. And please pack up the rest of my things in my trunk. I will send Archer to pick them up for me later," she said to the housekeeper, who was standing, eyes wide with shock, nearby.

"Yes, Miss Cecily."

Donning her own coat, Cecily turned to her parents; her mother's face was still red with anger, one hand nursing her wrist. Her father dropped his eyes away from her gaze.

"Shame on you, Papa," she murmured as Archer appeared by the front door. "Take Stella and put her and my maid in the car, then wait for me outside," she ordered Archer.

"Yes, Miss Cecily." Archer reached out a hand and beckoned Stella toward him. The three of them disappeared through the open front door.

"So this is the choice you are making? Choosing *them* over us?" Dorothea demanded.

"If that is the choice you are giving me, then yes, I choose them."

Brushing away the tears that were flowing down her face, she walked to the front door. Without turning back, Cecily stepped out into the freezing air and left her childhood home behind.

# ELECTRA

*New York*
*June 2008*

# 47

And I never set foot through that front door again."

Stella turned her head toward the New York skyline beyond the windows. Dusk and then night had come at some point, but neither of us had noticed.

"I . . . don't know what to say," I whispered, hauling myself upright. During the long hours of listening, I had placed a cushion beneath my head and lain down on the couch. I could only see the outline of my grandmother in the dim light, her proud profile just visible in the muted multitude of lights cast into the room from the city.

I tried to imagine her as the little girl she had once been, the baby saved by a stranger from certain death and brought here to New York. It was hard to reconcile the two.

"Where did you go when Cecily took you away from the house?"

"To Rosalind's, of course. You know something? Even though I was terrified because of all the shouting and the harsh words I didn't understand at the time, Archer took my hand, led me out into the car, and put me on the back seat. He offered me a lollipop and told me I was to stay there, that it was all going to be okay. And I believed him." Stella gave a glimmer of a smile. "We stayed with Rosalind and her husband, Terrence, for several months. Dorothea revoked Cecily's trust, so for a while, we were penniless. It was Kiki Preston who saved us."

"What do you mean?"

"She left her goddaughter a legacy—some shares and some cash—which eventually allowed us to buy an apartment a street away from Rosalind in Brooklyn. It was nothing like Cecily had been used to, and when I look back now, life must have been very hard for her. That day, she lost her entire family—because of me."

"She must have loved you very much."

Stella nodded. "She did." And I adored her. She proved to be a talented

545

teacher, too, and between her and Rosalind, the little school they'd started went from strength to strength. By the time I was ten, they had managed to gather enough pupils to rent a building of their own. And by the time I left, they had eighty pupils—a few of them white, I might add—and six full-time teachers."

"She found her mission."

"She did, yes. She was one incredible woman, and I miss her to this day."

So many questions that I wanted answers to were jostling for priority in my brain. "What about the maid that you grew up believing was your mother?"

"Lankenua? Oh, she stayed right here in New York with us. She met a man through her church, and they married a year after we left the house on Fifth Avenue. They moved into a small apartment here in Brooklyn, and she continued working for Cecily, caring for me."

"And her son?"

"Kwinet was almost sixteen when we left Kenya. Lankenua asked him if he wanted to come and join her, but he refused. He was happy enough taking care of Paradise Farm."

"Are they dead?"

Stella sighed. "Sadly, yes. Most everyone is, except for Beatrix. She's eighty-five and still going strong. I'd love to introduce her to you one day. Could you turn on a light?"

"Sure." I reached for the lamp on the table next to the couch. The glare of the light somehow broke the spell, and we were both shot back fully into the present.

"Oh, my, it's past two in the morning," Stella commented, looking at her watch. "I must go home."

"I'll call you a cab."

"Thank you, dear. That would be most kind."

I went to the concierge phone and called the cab as Stella stood up and walked rather unsteadily to the bathroom. I went to grab some water from the kitchen and saw that Lizzie's bedroom door was closed. She must have crept back into the apartment at some point during the evening.

Stella came out of the bathroom and went over to the chair to collect her purse. "Are you going to be okay here alone tonight?" she asked me gently. "I can stay."

"I'll be fine. I have a friend here with me, but thanks for the offer."

"Electra, I know there is so much more to talk about . . . that you want and need and have every right to know about your mama. But I hope you understand why it was so important for you to hear about how I came to America. It can't ever excuse what subsequently happened, but—"

"I get it, Stella. You go home and get some rest."

"When would you like me to come back? I have things to do, but you're my priority now, I swear."

"Can I give you a call in the morning once I've had some sleep?"

"Sure. Good night, dear, and I am so very sorry to have upset you."

"That's okay," I said as I opened the front door for her. "At least there's one thing that's cheered me up."

"And what is that?"

"That I really am descended from a line of princesses." I smiled at her. "Good night, Stella."

"You guys were certainly having a long conversation," Lizzie commented as I walked into the kitchen the following morning feeling like I'd done a few lines and a whole bottle of Goose last night.

"We sure were, yes," I agreed as I walked across to the coffee machine to pour myself a strong shot.

"So are you all sorted with your grandmother?"

"I wouldn't put it like that, but I think we're getting somewhere now, yes."

"Good, good. Well, you know I would never want to interfere, but I'm here if you ever want to talk about it, Electra."

"I know, Lizzie, thanks."

"I'm off to the bank this morning—hopefully they'll have found the right forms I need to sign so I can have my funds released to me. Then I can get out of your hair."

"Lizzie, seriously, I absolutely love having you here. In fact, I'd be so upset if you left right now. On my road to self-discovery, I've found I'm not cool living by myself. So how about if you move in permanently?"

"Oh, Electra, I'd jump at the chance, but I simply can't afford what must be an exorbitant rent."

"For one thing, you know money isn't an issue for me, and for another, I've also been thinking that I might like to live elsewhere in the city. My lease is up pretty soon. I went to Harlem with Miles the other day, and it has a real community feel. Up here, you could be just about anywhere, couldn't you?"

"If you mean that it's impersonal, like a hotel, then yes, you'd be right. Harlem with Miles, eh?" Lizzie grinned at me. "I never did get to hear the lowdown on him last night. I mean, it's obvious how *he* feels, but what about you?"

"You've got it wrong, Lizzie. Miles and I are just good friends; we're helping Vanessa and working on a project together. Even though he's had plenty of opportunity, he's never even tried . . . well, anything."

"Maybe he's shy, Electra, or overwhelmed. I mean, you are officially one of the world's most beautiful women. He probably feels he's punching above his weight," Lizzie said as she stood up and went to the counter. "Fancy some avocado on toast? If I can't eat it, I'll enjoy making it for someone who can."

"Yeah, why not?"

"Anyway," she continued, "that's my theory on Miles. He might be a serious piece of man hunk, but he's hardly the kind of brand-name celeb-slash-billionaire you normally date, is he?"

"No, I guess he isn't, thank God. You know what? I never thought about it like that."

"Then maybe you should. Oh, and changing the subject for a minute, when I was in the kitchen last night making myself scarce, I hope you don't mind, but I looked through your sketchbook." Lizzie indicated it lying on the table. "Some of those designs are really, really great."

"Thanks, but they're just doodles. I started drawing again in rehab, remember?"

"You should do something with them, Electra. I'd definitely buy them. I love that whole ethnic look."

"As a matter of fact, I was thinking about that yesterday. Like maybe having the materials ethically sourced and putting the profits from the collection toward the drop-in center. I mean, I don't need the money, do I?"

"Oh, how I wish those words rang true for me, too. I think it's a fabulous idea," she said as she spooned the avocado onto rye toast.

Once Lizzie had left to go to her bank and Mariam had arrived, I took a shower and thought about whether I was up for seeing Stella today. And decided I was. Or at least, I had to be. I just needed to *know*.

*Life can be understood only backward, but it must be lived forward.*

Pa's quote for me on the armillary sphere kept floating into my brain. Perhaps he had chosen it because he'd known that Stella was going to make contact with me and ultimately tell me the story of my heritage. If he felt it was right for me to know, then I really had to trust that it was. After all, he'd loved me more than any other human on the planet . . .

With that thought empowering me, I called Stella, who picked up immediately, and asked her if she could come by later today.

"Of course, or maybe you'd like to come over to me? You could see where Cecily and I lived together."

"You're still in the same apartment?"

"I am, yes, and it hasn't changed much since." Stella chuckled.

"Okay, I'll come to you. What time?"

"Three o'clock would be good. We can drink tea out of Cecily's bone china service."

I wrote down the address, then hung up and went into the kitchen to see Mariam. "Morning." I smiled at her.

"Good morning, Electra. How are you today?"

"I'm good. I'm heading out this afternoon to visit my grandmother and probably won't be back until later."

"Oh, okay."

I looked down at her covered head and her neat little fingers flying across the keyboard as she typed. There was just something about her body language that told me all wasn't well. But it wasn't my business to pry.

"A couple of things," I said as I took a Coke out of the fridge. "Do you think you could look into cotton sourced from Africa? Preferably from Kenya?"

"Of course I could," Mariam said. "May I ask why?"

"Because I'm thinking of designing a collection. I want all the profits to go to the drop-in center that Miles is trying to keep open."

Mariam's reaction, like Lizzie's, was very positive, and we spent an interesting half an hour researching possible sources.

"It would be amazing if you could actually go over there and meet the women who are making these fabrics," commented Mariam.

"Maybe one day I will. My ancestors came from Kenya."

"Did they? Is that what your grandmother told you?"

"Yes, and I'll hear more about everything this afternoon. Can you book me a car to take me over to Brooklyn, arriving at three?"

"Of course I can."

"Great, I'm going to head out for a run now."

Yet again, Tommy wasn't at his post as I jogged across the street. It was weird that someone could play a part in your daily life, yet you had no idea where he lived or how to get in contact with him if he suddenly disappeared.

Lost in my own thoughts, I didn't see the two men until they were on me, one holding me in a headlock from behind as the other tore my Rolex from my wrist, and ripped the tiny diamond and its chain from my throat.

Before I could even shout out or begin to struggle, they were gone, leaving me numb with shock. I bent over, feeling the world spin for a moment. Then I heard a voice beside me. "You okay, ma'am? So sorry I couldn't help, but they had a knife."

I looked up to see an old gray-haired man, who was bent almost as double as I was, but from natural causes.

"There's a bench over there; let me help you to it," he offered.

I felt his arm go around my lower back; it was remarkably firm and comforting as he guided me to the bench. "There we go, you rest for a while," he said as he helped me to sit down.

"S-sorry, it's the shock. I'll be okay in a minute," I panted.

"Here, have some water. It's a fresh bottle—I haven't opened it yet."

"Thanks."

"You shouldn't be running alone in the park. These guys are professionals— they'll have seen you and your jewelry before and planned exactly where to wait for you."

"Yeah, it's my own stupid fault," I agreed. "I normally take my watch off, but—"

The old man chuckled. "That's why I bring Poppet with me; she might look small, but she's got a real fetish for ankles."

I looked down and saw a tiny terrier, complete with a bow on top of its head, sitting by its master's feet and gazing up at me. The sight made me smile.

"You live around here, don't you?" the man continued.

"Yeah, right across the street on Central Park West." I waved an arm in the direction of my apartment.

"Then we're neighbors," he said. "I live right there on Fifth." He pointed to an apartment building. "Have done for eighty-odd years—I was born there."

"My grandmother lived on Fifth for a while, in the pretty house with the curved front."

"No! You don't mean number 925? The house owned by the Huntley-Morgans way back when?"

"I think so, yeah," I said, because my head was still fuzzy from shock.

"Well, well, could I tell you some stories about them. That Dorothea—what a bitter, cranky old witch she was," the man chuckled. "After her husband died, she lived alone there for years. I was only a kid, but she used to terrify me, sitting at the window, all dressed in black staring out like the mother in *Psycho*. I never saw no one come to visit her, not once."

I felt too dazed to reply.

There was a pause before he added, "I know who you are—I've seen you on the billboards. I'm surprised you don't have a bodyguard running with you. If you don't want stuff like that to happen again, you should think about getting one."

"Yeah, I know, but I enjoy the space, and—" I was about to say I could take care of myself, but given the circumstances, it obviously wasn't true. I touched the back of my neck, which was sore from where the necklace had been wrenched away from it. I'd bought it for myself with one of my first big paychecks and hardly ever took it off. I felt oddly naked without it. I saw my fingertips were smeared with blood.

"You better get that cut looked at. Want me to call someone to come get you?"

"No, I'll be okay, it's only a short walk back home," I said as I tentatively stood up.

"I'll walk with you."

So my new guardian angel, his tiny terrier, and I made our way slowly to my apartment building. He even offered his arm to me as we waited for the lights to change so I could cross the street.

"Thanks so much," I said as we walked under the awning of my building.

"Oh, it was nothing, ma'am. It's been a pleasure to talk to you—that doesn't happen too often in this city these days. You oughta call the cops and report it—I'd be happy to be a witness for you."

"For what good the cops will do," I mumbled as the man dug in his trouser pocket and offered me a card.

"That's me, Davey Steinman, at your service. You come see me sometime, and I'll tell you stories about those Huntley-Morgans. My mother hated them—we were Jewish, you see, and even though they were our neighbors for years, they never once passed the time of day with us."

"I will. Thanks for your help, Davey." I smiled as I waved good-bye to him and Poppet, then wobbled inside.

"Oh, my!" Mariam said as I walked into the kitchen and slumped into a chair. "What happened, Electra?"

I shrugged. "I got mugged. But I'm okay. I just need you to take a look at the back of my neck because I can't see the wound."

Mariam was already up and reaching for the first-aid box that was kept in the kitchen cupboard. "I've never been happy with you running alone in that park, Electra. It's just not safe, especially for someone with a high profile like you. Now let's see what we're dealing with."

"Maybe it's only when something happens to you that you realize what you're doing is dangerous. But I enjoy that time alone, you know? Ouch!" I winced as I felt something stinging on the back of my neck.

"Sorry, I just need to clean the cut. It's very small—just where the chain dug into your skin as they whipped it from your neck. You really should call the cops—"

"What's the use? They won't catch them," I muttered.

"So you can get a report to give to your insurance company for the stolen jewelry—and also to make sure it doesn't happen to other people."

"I guess so. I met this sweet old guy who says they'd probably been watching me, which is kind of creepy," I said as Mariam took some gauze and tape to cover the wound.

"Yes, it is," Mariam said vehemently.

"The old guy said I should employ a bodyguard."

"Well, I agree with him, Electra."

"Maybe Tommy wants to apply," I said as I stood up and dug around in the medical box to find a couple of Advil. "Actually, I'm worried about him—I haven't seen him around for a while. Have you?"

"No."

"Do you by any chance have his cell phone number?"

"No, why should I?" Mariam answered abruptly.

"Because I thought you guys were in touch . . . Anyway, let's just hope he turns up in the next few days. Okay, I need to take a shower, grab some lunch, and then head off to Granny's." I smiled at Mariam, whose back was turned to me as she replaced the first-aid kit in the cupboard.

"Okay, there's some sushi in the fridge. I'll take it out for you."

"Thanks."

As I crossed the Brooklyn Bridge on the way to Stella's apartment, I thought again about Mariam and how there had definitely been a subtle shift in her usual calm, composed demeanor. Something was going on with her, I just knew it instinctively, and I decided that tonight I'd ask her what the problem was. If it was me, I really needed to know, because I couldn't bear to lose her.

Arriving at Sidney Place, I stepped out and saw neat brownstones and newer redbricks. The sidewalk was tree-lined and had a calm atmosphere of understated wealth. Walking up the steps of a brownstone with pretty flower boxes in the windows, I pressed the bell that said "Jackson," and within a few seconds, my grandmother was standing at the door.

"Welcome, Electra," she said as she ushered me into an entrance hall and then into a large and airy space, with double-aspect windows that looked out at the front onto the houses opposite and at the back onto a garden below. I noted the dated furniture: there were a couch covered with chintz and two battered leather easy chairs that sat opposite a large fireplace.

"This is lovely," I said and meant it, even if I did feel I'd just stepped back into a different century. There was something comforting about the fact that it looked like everything had been here forever.

"Excuse the decor, I've never been one for interior design," Stella said as she moved a pile of papers from the couch and onto a coffee table already piled high with files. "Can I get you something to drink?"

"A Coke would be great if you've got one."

"I sure do. Want to follow me and see the rest of the apartment?"

"Okay," I agreed. She opened the door at the back of the room, and we took some steps down to the lower ground floor and entered the kitchen. It had double doors leading to the pretty garden beyond it. The walls were a weird yellow color, which I guessed had just gotten that way with age, and cracks zigzagged across the ceiling. There was a big old-fashioned pine table, again covered with papers and folders, and the kind of stove I'd seen recently in a movie set in the 1950s. A dresser sat along one wall with shelves full of colorful earthenware pottery.

"It's pretty much as it was when I was a living here as a kid."

"Did my mom live here with you?"

I watched her pause for a few seconds before she answered. "Yes. Cecily bought the apartment with Kiki's legacy for next to nothing when the area was still cheap. When we first moved in, it was real rough around here, but over the years, she made it into a home for us all, and now, well, the area is called 'desirable' by the realtors. There was a bedroom upstairs for Cecily, one for me, and the other for Lankenua, until she moved out to her own place with her husband. You want to go sit in the garden? At this time of day, it catches the sun."

"Sure," I said as Stella led me out onto the terrace, on which sat an old-fashioned wrought-iron table and two chairs that had once been painted white but were now chipped and turning green from moss.

"I do my best to maintain this," she said, indicating the garden, which was awash with all kinds of flowering plants I couldn't name. "When Cecily was looking after it, it was her pride and joy. She had cuttings shipped over from her friend Katherine in Kenya, but after it fell to me to care for it, the weeds took over. I'm away so often, and I simply don't have the time or the inclination."

"Did Cecily ever go back to Africa? Did you?" I asked.

"Yes to both questions. I understand you have a hundred of them, Electra, but I was thinking before you arrived that it's best to keep telling you the story in chronological order."

"Okay, but just one thing I need to ask you, Stella—is my mom alive? I mean, she can't be that old, and—"

"I'm so sorry, Electra, but no, she isn't. She died many years ago."

"Oh . . . okay."

Stella put out a tentative hand and placed it on mine. "Do you need some time before I tell you what happened after we left the house on Fifth Avenue?"

"No. I mean, you can't really mourn someone that you never knew, can you? I just needed to know."

"You can mourn the thought of her."

I swallowed hard, because my grandmother was right. It was the end of any kind of fantasy I'd ever had of meeting my birth mother. I'd thought about her a lot when I was little and in trouble with Ma for doing something naughty. I'd imagine her (as I was sure most adopted kids did) as an angelic presence who would float in from the skies, wrap her arms around me, and tell me that she loved me unconditionally, however bad I'd been.

I nodded. "I'm fine. I just want to know everything now, so I can move on. When did you find out that Lankenua wasn't your real mother?"

"It was when she wanted to get married. Lankenua was moving on to start a new life and I wasn't going with her, so the two of them told me together."

"Were you upset when you knew the truth?"

"No, because even though I was loved by her, she'd always played a secondary role to Cecily. I suppose you could say she was my nursemaid. It was Kuyia—Cecily—who had brought me up and who I'd always looked to as my mother. The problem was, Cecily suddenly realized that Lankenua and I had come into the United States on a visa that had never been renewed. So we were both technically illegal aliens. Lankenua was okay as she was marrying a US citizen, and in those days, she automatically became one herself. But that left the problem of me. Cecily wanted to adopt me legally, but back then, it wasn't just unheard of but impossible for a white woman to adopt a Negro child. As Lankenua was moving on, it was eventually decided that Rosalind would officially adopt me. Her husband, Terrence, was a lawyer and through their activism, they had friends in high places. At the time, it was the simplest thing to do. So I became Stella Jackson in name and eventually got my citizenship and a US passport, even though I continued to live here with Cecily."

"Jackson . . . of course! I hadn't connected the surnames before. Your Rosalind sounds like she was one hell of a woman."

"Oh, she was, and a huge influence on me throughout my life. It's difficult for you to imagine what it was like growing up as a young black woman in the fifties, which, if you know anything about American history, you'll recognize was the most incredible time for change for black people across America."

"Stella, I gotta be honest here, I know jack shit about any kind of American history. I went to school in Europe, where they just taught us our own."

"I understand, but even you must have heard of Martin Luther King, Jr."

"Yeah, I know of him, of course."

"Well, by the time I won a scholarship to Vassar in 1959 for my bachelor's, just as Cecily and Rosalind had planned, the world here in the States was in turmoil. The Universal Declaration of Human Rights had been passed by the UN in 1948, which was the first step to stopping segregation. I went to college at a moment in time when the protests against it were at their height in the South. And of course, growing up with Rosalind and Beatrix as my mentors, I threw myself into the cause wholeheartedly. I still remember how they and Cecily celebrated in 1954, when the US Supreme Court ruled that racial segregation in public schools was unconstitutional. This meant that segregation . . . You know what that word means, don't you, Electra?" Stella turned to me suddenly.

"Yes, separating the blacks from the whites."

"Exactly. Well, the *Brown v. Board of Education* ruling technically only applied to schools, but it opened the floodgates on protests arguing that segregation in any other place should become illegal, too. That was when Dr. King began his rise to fame. He organized a boycott in the South after a young activist called Rosa Parks had refused to give up her seat on a public bus to a white passenger. The boycott meant that no black person would get on one until segregation was removed, and it brought the bus companies in the South to their knees."

"Wow," I said as I tried to take in what she was telling me.

"Even though this was all happening down South, the students here in the North organized protests to support them." Stella sighed. "Oh, Electra, it's so difficult to explain to a young person such as yourself who takes your rights for granted, but back then, we were all driven by a cause greater than any single one of us."

As Stella paused and her gaze flew across the garden, I could see a light in it that told me she was remembering those glory days.

"Did you ever get arrested when you were protesting?" I asked.

"A couple times, yes, and I'm proud to tell you that your grandmother has a criminal record. I was charged with affray along with six of my college classmates—the police brutality was something else. But I didn't care, nor did my friends, because what we were fighting for—a whole nation's freedom and the right to be treated equally with our fellow white Americans—mattered more. When all this activity culminated in 1963, I was in my last year at Vassar. The atmosphere at that time was amazing; two hundred and fifty thousand of us joined the march on Washington, and we all gathered peacefully to listen to Dr. King make his iconic speech."

"'I have a dream,'" I muttered. Even I had heard of that.

"Yes, that's the one. A quarter of a million of us, and not one of us there showed any violence toward another. It was"—Stella swallowed hard—"a seminal moment in my life, in all sorts of ways."

"I'll bet," I nodded, selfishly eager for the history lesson to be over. "So what did you do then?"

Stella chuckled. "I took the obvious path and took up the place I'd been offered at Columbia Law School, right here in New York, with only one thought in my head: I was going to become the greatest civil rights lawyer and activist that ever lived. I felt that God had sent me to America and given me all these opportunities with only one purpose in mind—to help others like me who hadn't been so fortunate. However, nothing in life ever goes according to plan, does it?"

"What do you mean?"

Stella looked at me for a moment. "You know, I think it's time for that cup of tea I promised you. I also bought some scones; do you like scones?"

"Uh, are they a bit like a muffin with raisins? I think our housekeeper made them sometimes 'cause Pa liked them."

"Kind of. Cecily and her friend Katherine just adored them. Sit here, and I'll set everything out."

So I sat waiting for my grandmother to serve me afternoon tea, with a distinct feeling that she was taking time to gather herself to tell me something. The afternoon sun was quite strong now, and the smell of some exotic pink flower that hung from a trellis in a tangled mass was soporific. I closed my eyes and tried to process what Stella had told me, feeling guilty because I didn't know anything about what women like Stella and Rosalind had done to give me the equality and freedom I enjoyed today.

"History" was something I associated with knights jousting on horses and effigies of ladies lying on top of tombs in the crypts of churches that Pa had made us visit if we stopped off in some medieval town during our summer vacations. The history that Stella was talking about was that of recent times, times *she* had lived through. She and her friends had put their lives at risk so that I could have the liberty to be myself . . .

The thought made me feel very small and very selfish for ever thinking that *I* had problems.

"Here we go," said Stella, bringing out a tray that was fully loaded with a beautiful china teapot, two cups with saucers, and a milk jug.

"Are you okay to pour while I go and get the scones?"

"Yeah, of course."

Even though I wasn't a fan of tea, I picked up what looked like a minisieve and finally worked out that it was to catch the leaves from the pot. Then I added milk.

"This is Darjeeling," Stella said when she returned, "my favorite tea on the planet."

"How come you picked up so many English habits when Cecily was actually American?" I asked, taking a tentative sip of the tea. For the first time, I actually enjoyed the taste.

"Because in those days, Kenya was under British rule, and Cecily's friend Katherine, as you know, was English, not to mention Bill, of course. Here, try a scone; with clotted cream and jam, they're just the best."

I did so, just to please her; the taste was rich and sweet and sticky in my mouth all at once.

"Electra, what I have to tell you next is very difficult. I only hope that you'll understand. I feel ashamed to tell you."

"Given my history, Stella, I'm sure I will understand. I doubt you could do anything more shameful than be completely wasted on booze, drugs, and sleeping pills, then vomit all over yourself."

"Well, this is different, a far worse kind of shame, and I pray you'll forgive me."

"Okay, I promise I will. Now shoot," I said impatiently.

"You know I told you that the march on Washington and Dr. King's speech was a seminal day for me?"

"Yup."

"At the time, I was walking out with—that is, seeing—a young man I'd met at a protest. He'd never had a college education, but he was passionate about the cause and made the most incredible uplifting speeches. Even though he was uneducated, he was so bright and charismatic, and, well . . . I fell for him. And that evening in Washington, after the speeches had ended and everyone was on a high—you just cannot imagine the feeling—I, well, I . . . and he . . . we made love. Under a tree in a park."

"Is that it? Really, Stella, I'm not shocked at all, I promise. You are human after all, and we've all done stuff like that," I reassured her.

"Thank you for that, Electra." Stella looked relieved. "It's just awful embarrassing as a sixty-seven-year-old woman to have to tell your granddaughter something like that."

"I'm cool with it, so don't worry. So what happened then?" I asked, although I'd already guessed the answer.

"I found myself pregnant shortly after," Stella said. "It was a big shock—I mean, I had graduated top of my class at Vassar, and my place at Columbia Law School was confirmed. I remember coming back here to the apartment, knowing I had to tell Cecily what had happened. I don't think I've been more scared in my life than I was at that moment."

"Because you thought she'd disown you?"

"No, not that, it was much more to do with the fact that everything she had worked for and sacrificed to give me had just gone up in smoke. I could hardly bear that I'd let her down."

"How did she react?"

"You know what? She was remarkably calm about it. Which somehow made it worse—I guess I felt I deserved to be ranted and raved at. First she asked me if I loved the father, and as I'd already thought about it a lot since the . . . *event*, I said that I didn't think I did. That I'd just gotten carried away with all the emotion of the night. Then she asked me if I wanted the baby, and I told her truthfully that no, I did not. Is that a terrible thing to admit, Electra?"

"Jeez, no." I shook my head. "I mean, I'm older than you were then, and I'd feel the same. So did you have an abortion?"

"Abortions were illegal in the sixties, even though Cecily said she had made some discreet inquiries and had been told of a good surgeon who did them in secret. So yes, you could say I was offered that choice. But I couldn't take it."

"Why not?"

"Because through Cecily, Rosalind, Terrence, and their kids, I'd been brought up a Christian. I believed in God then, and I still believe in God now. To take another human life, when that life had no say in the matter, and simply throw it away just because the timing didn't suit me was unthinkable. I offered to marry the father, but Kuyia—Cecily—said that I shouldn't if I didn't love him, that we would work it out between us. She suggested that I defer law school for a year and said that she was prepared to take care of the baby for me so I could continue with my education."

"She sounds like an incredible human being," I said, meaning it.

Stella shrugged. "She was my Kuyia; she loved me, and I worshipped her. So that's what happened. I deferred my place at law school, and in due course, I gave birth to your mother."

"So what year was this?"

"Nineteen sixty-four. The year the Civil Rights Act was finally passed."

"I—"

*Finally, I'm going to hear about my mother,* I thought.

"What was her name?"

"I called her Rosa, after Rosa Parks, the woman who began it all. And Rosalind, of course."

"It's a lovely name," I said.

"She was a real cute baby, oh boy, was she cute," Stella smiled, her eyes filling with tears. "Forgive me, Electra, this is your moment to grieve, not mine. I don't know what's come over me; I'm usually not the crying kind."

"Neither am I. But recently, my waterworks have been spouting all over the place. I guess it's good to let it out."

"Yes, it is. And thank you for being so grown up about what I've told you so far."

"Hey, I get the feeling that the worst is yet to come."

"You're right, it is, I'm afraid."

"So?" I asked as I poured myself some more tea just for something to do. The suspense was killing me.

"Well, I completed law school while Cecily cared for Rosa, then got a job in New York working for a housing association and lobbying the mayor's office and anyone I could find for better conditions for the tenants. I'd deal with small disputes, defend women with four kids who were living in one room with no sanitary facilities . . . but what I really wanted to be doing was the big stuff. Then I was offered a chance to join the NAACP—that's the National Association for the Advancement of Colored People—in their legal team. We worked with lawyers across the nation, giving advice on how to address civil rights violations."

"Excuse me? What does that actually mean?"

"Say, if a black man had been arrested and it was obvious the evidence against him had been cooked up by the cops, we would investigate, then sit with the defense in court to advise them. Oh, Electra, it was a job I'd dreamed about for years, and it was all consuming. I had to travel all over the country to brief lawyers in cases."

"Which meant you weren't home often."

"I wasn't, no, but Cecily encouraged me, never once made me feel guilty about the fact she was back home, taking care of Rosa, while I pursued my career. All went well, and I began to make a name for myself in the civil rights world. Then, when Rosa was five, everything changed."

# CECILY

## Brooklyn, New York
## June 1969

Enkang—*settlement. A Maasai family settlement*

# 48

$B$ye-bye, be a good girl, now." Cecily said as she waved at Rosa, then left the airy classroom that she and Rosalind had painted a bright yellow, so it always looked cheerful and welcoming. It wasn't her teaching day today, so she headed straight back to her apartment to catch up on work. When Stella had given birth to Rosa, Cecily had cut back on her teaching days in order to be at home with the new baby. Freelance bookkeeping, which she could do at home, brought in a welcome amount of extra cash.

Cecily arrived home feeling weary. Maybe it was simply that she was getting old—she'd be fifty-three this year—or maybe it was just that Rosa was so very demanding compared to Stella. Everything was a struggle—even the simplest act of putting on her shoes could turn into a fight if Rosa wasn't in the mood to wear them.

"Or maybe I've just forgotten what it's like to have a five-year-old," she sighed as she let herself into the apartment and saw the carnage wreaked by Rosa's earlier temper tantrum visible all over the living room floor.

After collecting the toys into a basket and stowing them away, she made her way downstairs to tackle the dishes. Lankenua had left Brooklyn a couple of years ago on her own fiftieth birthday. Her husband had done well for himself, starting out as a mechanic and eventually saving up enough to open his own shop in New Jersey. Cecily hoped that the reason she'd left was simply because she no longer needed to work and wanted to spend time at home taking care of her husband. She suspected, however, that Lankenua, too, had struggled with Rosa, and besides, the wages she had been able to pay her had been paltry. She knew Lankenua had stayed as long as she had out of love.

"Oh, Lord," Cecily sighed, wondering if she should leave the pots for the housekeeper, who would be in soon, but pride won over sense. Dirty pans were a sign that things were getting out of control. Having finished washing the dishes and opened the door to let the housekeeper in, Cecily made herself a good strong pot of coffee and went into the garden to sit down for a few minutes before she began work. She looked out at the weeds that were springing up with abandon as usual in the warm June weather. She'd get to them later, she thought. Digging in the earth always calmed her, even though this patch was a pathetic postage stamp compared to the magnificent garden she had created back in Kenya.

She heard the doorbell ring upstairs but didn't respond to it—it was almost certainly the mailman and the housekeeper would open the door if it was a package. The sun was so warm, she was almost drifting off when she heard a voice from behind her.

"Hello, Cecily."

It was a deep, familiar voice that she couldn't quite place. She opened her eyes and noticed that something was blocking out the sun.

She looked up at what was causing it and for a moment thought she was hallucinating, because there was her husband, Bill, the sun behind him forming some kind of angelic light around him.

"Oh, my!" she said, because there really wasn't anything else to say. "What on earth are *you* doing here?"

"First and foremost, I believe that technically, you are still my wife. Secondly, over the years, you have issued a number of invitations for me to come and visit you here in New York," Bill said. "I finally decided it was time I took you up on your offer."

"Would you mind awfully stepping out of the sun? I can hardly see your face."

"My apologies," said Bill and moved to pull out the chair on the other side of the wrought-iron table. It was only now that she could see that his hair was still thick but almost completely white. His handsome face was covered in deep lines that told of too much sun and the stresses of a life lived through two world wars. He looked older, yes, Cecily thought, yet as her eyes swept down his still-muscled body, he was as physically strong as he'd always been.

"You don't by any chance have a cold beer, do you?" he asked.

"I don't, no. Just homemade lemonade."

"I'll take some of that, thanks."

Cecily stood up and went inside to fetch the lemonade from the refrigerator. Even though she remained outwardly calm, her heart was pounding hard against her chest. Bill—her husband—was here in New York, sitting on her terrace. The thought was so surreal, she slapped her cheek to make sure she wasn't dreaming.

"There you go," she said as she put a glass in front of him. He picked it up and gulped it down.

"That tastes good." He smiled at her. "I came straight here from the airport. Isn't it amazing how times have moved on? It used to take weeks to travel to New York. Now it's a few stops on an airplane, and Bob's your uncle, here I am. The world becomes smaller every day."

"It sure does," Cecily agreed, feeling his gaze upon her. "What? Do I have a smudge on my cheek?"

"No, I was just thinking how you've hardly changed a jot since I last saw you. Whereas I"—he sighed—"am an old man these days."

"It has been twenty-three years."

"Has it really? How time flies. I'm almost seventy, Cecily."

"And I'm fifty-three years old, Bill."

"You most certainly don't look it."

A long silence passed between them as they stared at the small patch of garden, neither of them sure what to say next.

"Why are you here, Bill?" Cecily said eventually. "You stroll in as cool as a cucumber, like we just said good-bye yesterday. At least you could have called to say you were coming, rather than giving me the shock of my life!"

"I do apologize, my dear. As you might remember, telephones and I have never sat easily together, but you are perfectly right. I should have forewarned you of my arrival first. It's very peaceful here, isn't it?" he commented. "I've always had this vision of New York as a rather frenetic type of a place."

"Walk a few blocks uptown, and you'll find that it is."

"I notice you've brought a little of Africa to Brooklyn." Bill pointed to the hibiscus, growing with abandon up the trellis.

"Yes, Katherine shipped me some seedlings, and, miracle of miracles, a few of them managed to survive the journey and flourish. How is she?"

Bill shrugged. "Back on the farm now and the same as ever. You'll obviously have read about the Mau Mau rebellion?"

"Yes, she wrote to tell me what was happening. She and Bobby left with the kids for safety in Scotland while it was all going on."

"As did thousands of other white settlers; everyone feared the worst, although I did hear that reports of the slaughter of the whites by their former

employees were greatly exaggerated in the newspapers. In total, only thirty-
five of us lot died during the whole bloody awful show. The odd farm was
torched, but most of the bloodshed took place between the Kikuyu themselves. Lord knows how many died as cousin turned on cousin in the struggle
for power. And our government didn't help, either—they were brutal in how
they dealt with suspected Mau Mau perpetrators; many innocent men were
hanged. However, as I'm sure you know, Kenya finally won its independence
in 1963. Colonial rule is no more."

"So you stayed on throughout? I often thought of you and wondered if
you would. I wrote you a couple of times care of Muthaiga Club, but I never
got a reply. To be honest, I had no idea if you were alive or dead."

"Forgive me, Cecily. Even if I did not receive your missives—you can
imagine how chaotic everything was back then—in retrospect, I should have
contacted you to at least tell you that I—and Wolfie at the time, as well as
Kwinet—still breathed and were perfectly safe."

"When did . . . I mean, how did Wolfie die?" The thought of her loyal
companion and the way she had abandoned him brought a guilty surge of
emotion with it.

"Of old age, in his sleep. After you left, he attached himself to Kwinet
and pottered around after him perfectly happily."

"And Paradise Farm?"

"Remains unscathed, although some of your antique furniture could do
with a damned good dust. Never was much of a housewife, as you know."
Bill offered Cecily a weak smile.

"So how are things out there now?"

"As a matter of fact, after the doldrums of the late fifties and early sixties,
Kenya is experiencing rather a boom. President Kenyatta made an impressive speech shortly after independence, urging the white farmers to stay on
and help rebuild the economy—and many of us did. Some, of course, decided to sell up to the newly created Land Bank, but investment is flowing in
at present, and airplanes land every day, bringing tourists on safari."

"Then at least, with some finances available, the new regime must be
providing better health care and education for its own people?"

Bill rolled his eyes. "I wouldn't go that far. The simple fact is, nothing
much has changed for anyone. Seems to me the poor are still as poor as they
always have been, the bloody roads are still as impassable as ever, and as for
education . . . well, now, it's early days yet, and we must all live in hope that

things will improve for the next generation, whose parents were prepared to lay down their lives for the cause."

"Sounds to me like we've both faced revolutions in our different countries," agreed Cecily wryly. "And yes, we must live in hope that the future will be brighter. Otherwise, what is the point of all the suffering?"

"Quite. So tell me what you've been doing in the past twenty years? How's Stella?"

"Oh, she is simply amazing." She smiled. "She's a civil rights lawyer. She works for the NAACP—the National Association for the Advancement of Colored People—in their legal department and spends most of her time flying all over the country to advise lawyers how to fight cases where there is obvious racial prejudice. I'm so very proud of her, and I'm sure you would be, too."

"Good Lord, I take my hat off to you, Cecily. Who would have thought that the little Maasai baby abandoned by her mother would turn into a freedom fighter for the oppressed masses?"

"It was the path she chose and was passionate about, Bill. She always was very bright."

"Yes, she was. And what opportunities you have obviously given her."

"You know how I loved her."

"I do, yes."

They both lapsed into silence again.

"I've often pondered—" said Bill eventually.

"What?"

"Whether you left me or came for her? If you see what I mean."

"I never intended to *leave* you, Bill, but yes, what New York could offer Stella was a big incentive to stay. Especially as you really didn't seem to care one bit whether I came back or not."

"Goodness, Cecily," said Bill hastily. "I did not for one second mean for that to sound as if I was criticizing you. Please don't blame yourself. I freely admit I was hardly an attentive husband. After the war ended, I was far too lost in my own selfish woes to be any good to anybody."

"That wasn't your fault, although I admit that I'd spent five years hoping against hope that once the war was over, we could finally settle down and be a happy family."

"If things—if *I*—had been different, would you have stayed? Even if it had meant that Stella didn't receive the kind of education you wanted for her?"

"Oh, Bill." Cecily sighed, "I can't answer that."

"No, of course you can't. I've often looked back on the two of us and thought that every time we had a shot at happiness, something happened to destroy it. I suppose that's just bad luck and timing, isn't it?"

"I guess it is, yes."

"Cecily, one of the reasons I decided to come and see you is because I thought it was time to bury any hatchets that might be hanging about. I want you to know that I bear you no ill will whatsoever and I never have. And as for deserting me, good God! I spent most of our marriage driving away from Paradise Farm, leaving a trail of dust behind me."

"It was who you were, Bill, and I knew that before I married you."

"Can you believe that we're still married?" Bill chuckled. "Which I rather presume means that you have never had the urge to try again with anyone else, unless of course you're a bigamist?"

"No and no." She smiled.

"Although surely there must have been gentlemen companions over the years?"

"Goodness, no, I've been far too busy with Stella and my teaching and bookkeeping to even think about anything like that."

"Now, that surprises me." He looked at her quizzically. "I was half expecting to be greeted by a great beast of an American male who pronounced himself your boyfriend. Surely now that Stella is all grown up, you must have found time to enjoy yourself?"

"Hardly." Cecily rolled her eyes. "Stella has a child of her own. She lives here with us. Her name is Rosa."

"Well, well," Bill mused, "that makes me feel even older. I suppose I could say that Rosa is the nearest thing to a grandchild either of us will ever have."

"Yes, that's how I see her, anyway. She calls me 'Granny,' as a matter of fact."

"How old is she?"

"Five. And she's cute and bright like her mama but a real handful. I was thinking only this morning that I'm getting too old to care for her."

"Dare I inquire where the daddy is?"

"Neither Stella nor I have any idea. She elected not to tell him—she met him through the protests a few years back. He lived down South, and once everything quieted down, they had no cause to meet."

"Right. So you're back at home holding the baby, so to speak?"

"I am, yes."

"Surely you can get help with that?"

"No, Bill, I'm afraid I can't. I believe I never did tell you the real reason I had to move out of my parents' house on Fifth?"

"No, you just wrote to me with a change of address, if I remember rightly. What happened?"

"My mother came into the bedroom one morning and found me asleep in bed with Stella huddled up next to me. There had been a big storm, and she was frightened. Mama was outraged and disgusted that I could be there in my bed asleep with a Negro child. The words that fell out of her mouth that day, Bill, I don't think I'll ever forget them. She insisted that Lankenua and Stella leave, calling my behavior 'obscene,' so I had no choice but to leave with them. The three of us went to stay with a friend who lives right here in the next street. My mother stopped the allowance I'd received from my trust fund from that day, but thankfully, Kiki, my godmother—do you remember her?"

Bill chuckled. "Why, of course I do! How could one forget Kiki?"

"Well, she left me a generous legacy, which meant I've just about been able to make ends meet over the years and buy this place. I supplement what income I get from Kiki's shares with Stella's contribution from her wages and what I earn from teaching and taking in some bookkeeping."

Bill stared at her open-mouthed. "Good Lord, you silly woman! Why on earth didn't you tell me what had happened? Surely you must have known that I would help!"

"That's very honorable of you to say so, Bill, but if you remember at the time, you were running a big overdraft while you built up your cattle farm again."

"True, but shortly after that things turned around. I began to grow some crops, and I've been quite financially comfortable ever since. You know I would have helped, Cecily, if only you'd asked."

"Bill, to all intents and purposes, I left you," she said gently. "I wasn't going to expect any financial help from you after that, was I?"

"Well, well. I stand—or, in fact, sit—here amazed. There was me in Kenya for all these years, believing that you were living a life of luxury and ease here in New York. I was—*am*—your husband, Cecily, whatever passed between us. You should have come to me."

"I didn't, and that's that. Besides, somehow we survived."

"So the rift between you and your parents has never been resolved?"

"No, never. I heard from my sister Mamie—who left her husband some years back and is the one member of my family who still speaks to me—that Mama tells all her friends I caught a fever in Africa that left me deranged."

"And what about your father? You always described him as being rather a good sort."

"He wasn't—*isn't*—a bad man, no, just a weak one. But that morning, he saw what was happening—he watched the three of us as we left and didn't say a word to Mama in our defense, even though I know he was fond of Stella and of me, too. He wrote me awhile after, saying that I was to come to him if I ever needed help. I'm afraid my pride wouldn't allow it, even at the toughest of financial moments."

"You never thought of coming home to Africa?"

"Time passed, Bill, and I built a life with Stella here."

"Do you ever miss it?" he asked abruptly.

"Kenya, you mean?"

"Yes. I presume that you didn't and still don't. After all, there was no reason why you couldn't have visited during Stella's school holidays."

"Bill, you talk as if we are old friends, as if there was never any feeling between us," Cecily said. "I . . . just needed to move on. To try to forget Africa, *and* you . . . I realized that you'd never really loved me, because if you had, surely you would have come to New York to persuade me to return home. I wrote and asked you to visit often enough. You never did, so for the sake of my sanity, I had to get on with my life."

"Not for a minute did I even *suspect* that you wanted me to do such a thing. If only I'd known . . ."

"Then what, Bill?" said Cecily despairingly. "Wasn't it obvious that I loved you? Those kinds of feelings don't just switch off because you get on a boat or a plane and arrive in another country. After Kiki died, I remember being desperate to speak to you—it was Christmas Day, and I phoned Muthaiga Club, only to be told you'd gone on safari. You had my parents' telephone number in New York. Why didn't you call?"

Bill sighed. "Who knows? At the time, I did feel rather as if you'd deserted me. Pride, perhaps?"

"Or more likely you simply forgot. It's okay to just get real, you know. We are twenty-three years down the track, after all. You can no longer hurt me."

"Oh, God, Cecily, what a mess," Bill groaned and ran a hand through his thick hair. It was such a familiar gesture that Cecily only just restrained herself from reaching out a hand and placing it on his.

"Seriously, Bill, why have you come?"

"Because . . . I felt it was time that I—*we*—formalized our . . . well, mutual arrangements. I'm not getting any younger, as you can see, and the doctor says there's something up with my ticker. Even though it's not life-threatening, I have been told to take life a little more slowly. So I'm thinking of selling Paradise Farm and buying myself something a bit more manageable. As we *are* still married, I felt I should at least ask your permission to do so. After all, Cecily, you made not only the house but also the garden your own, and almost everything in the house is yours. Do you want it back?"

"Oh, Bill, forget the furniture, for goodness' sake! What is it that the doctor has said is wrong with your heart?"

"It's nothing whatsoever to concern yourself with. I was checked over by a Harley Street specialist when I was in England. He's given me this rather revolting medicine to put under my tongue to stop the angina attacks. The good news is, it seems to be working. But that isn't the point, Cecily. I'm asking you how you feel about selling Paradise Farm. As I said, things in Kenya are going through rather a boom, and I have someone who is keen to buy it and run it as a going concern."

Cecily closed her eyes and cast her mind back to her beautiful house and garden. It was rather like opening a book that had sat closed on a shelf for years, its beauty all but forgotten. She heard herself catch her breath as she relived the view of the sunset from the veranda and smiled.

"I loved that house," she breathed. "I was so happy there—if lonely," she added dryly.

"Well, I don't have to sell it, of course, I just rather thought that if you weren't interested in ever coming home again, that I probably would. The other question is, whether we should get a divorce. I'm perfectly prepared to be cited for anything I need to be cited for. Desertion is probably the best, don't you think?"

Cecily turned toward Bill, who, despite his protestations of being old, could pass for younger than any of the balding, pot-bellied Manhattanites around her own age. Tears came unexpectedly to her eyes.

"Good Lord, what have I said now to upset you?"

"I . . . forgive me, it's just the shock of you appearing like a ghost out of the blue. I can't answer those kinds of questions right now. I need time to think, Bill, to adjust to you being here. Okay?"

"Of course. Forgive me, Cecily, I've put my big bloody foot in it again. You civilized me for a while, but I've had all this time to go backward," he said much more gently. "Listen, if you could point me in the direction of a half-decent hotel in the neighborhood, I'll go away and leave you in peace. I haven't slept for the past couple of days, or in fact washed, and I must stink to high heaven."

"It's okay, Bill, I've got a spare room here; it's Stella's, but she's away in Montgomery for the next few days, so you're welcome to it."

"Are you sure? I now feel like a complete rake barging back into your life without any forewarning."

"You never were one to play by the rules, were you, Bill? Where is your luggage?" she asked as she stood up.

"There." Bill indicated a carry-on. "You know me, I travel light."

"Well, I'll show you where the shower is."

Once she had done that, Cecily walked back outside and sat down, feeling utterly wrung out. Despite, well, literally *everything*, that feeling that had taken root inside her when she'd first met Bill and had grown like a tiny sapling as she had gotten to know him better was still there after all these years.

"Darn you, Bill Forsythe!" she muttered as she heard the shower turn on and imagined his firm muscled body naked beneath it . . .

"You're a sad, lonely old woman," she told herself firmly. It had been over twenty-three years since she'd last had any kind of intimate contact with a man. Surely, what she was feeling was just decades of unfulfilled physical longing. Bill was old now and hardly the stuff of dreams on any level. Yet she herself was a dried-up old woman.

Bill appeared behind her, a towel wrapped around his middle. "Which bedroom am I to have?"

"I'll show you," Cecily said, trying to ignore his naked torso, which had endured the passage of time exceptionally well. "Here," she said as she opened a door along the basement hallway. "This is Stella's room."

"And this is Stella?" Bill pointed to a photo of her at her college graduation. "Goodness, what a stunner she is."

"I know, she's the spitting image of her mother."

"And all this"—Bill waved an arm around the pretty room—"stems from my request to give—what was she called?"

"Njala."

"To give Njala safe haven on our land."

"Yes, but I swear, Bill, there's no need to feel guilty about that. Stella is the best thing that ever happened to me. Loving her changed my life, and me," she added. "Now I'll leave you to get some rest. I have to pick up Rosa at three from her school, but if you wake up while I'm gone, please help yourself to anything from the refrigerator."

"Don't worry about me, I can fend for myself," said Bill, throwing back the covers on the bed and tipping Lucky, Stella's beloved cuddly lion, onto the floor.

"I know, but you're in the urban jungle now." Cecily smiled. "Sleep well."

"So this is Rosa," said Bill, who after a shave, some sleep, and a change of clothes was looking far more like himself.

"How do you do, sir?" the little girl said, sticking her hand up toward him.

"I do very well, thank you, Rosa," said Bill.

Rosa turned to Cecily. "Who is this man?" she asked imperiously.

"This man is called Bill. And he's a very old friend of mine."

"Okay. Can I watch TV for a while?"

"Not until you've done your homework, Rosa."

"Oh, but can't I watch TV first—*Mister Rogers* is on soon—then do my homework?"

"Rosa, honey, you know the rules. Now, sit down at the table quietly and get on with your arithmetic."

"No!" Rosa stamped her foot and pouted. "I wanna watch *Mister Rogers!*"

"Well, you can't, and that's that. Sit down now."

"I won't!"

"Rosa, you know what will happen if you carry on like this; you'll be put in your room, and there'll be no dinner until you come out and sit at the table and do your homework."

"But I wanna watch *Mister Rogers*," she whined.

"Okay, let's take you to your room, shall we?" Cecily took the child's hand firmly and marched her down the hallway. Opening the door and steering the squirming child inside, she sat her down on the bed. "So what's it to be?

Sitting in here by yourself or doing your homework and then having peanut butter and jelly sandwiches in front of the TV?"

"I wanna watch *Mister Rogers* now!"

Cecily walked to the door, closed it behind her, and locked it, bracing herself for the screams of protest that would begin immediately from the bedroom. Walking back to the kitchen, she looked at Bill and sighed. "Sorry about the noise; as I mentioned, she's a handful right now."

"Yes, I can hear that," Bill said as the screams penetrated the walls at an ear-piercing level.

"She'll calm down in a minute; she normally does," said Cecily with more confidence than she felt. Sometimes the screaming could go on for hours. "I bought you some beer on the way back home, by the way. It's cooling in the refrigerator."

"Thank you." He went to the refrigerator to pull a bottle out. "You have got your hands full, haven't you?" Bill said as the screams continued.

"I guess I do, but it was either me taking care of her or Stella having to stop everything she'd worked for to bring Rosa up herself. I'm sure she'll meet another man one day, and the three of them will take off to live their own lives."

"Really? I doubt any chap would be keen to take on a child who can make *that* kind of racket."

"Rosa is very sweet underneath it all; she just likes things her own way right now," Cecily replied, suddenly defensive. "I made some beef casserole while you were sleeping. I remembered it was one of your favorites."

"Beef casserole . . ." Bill sniffed the air. "Good Lord, that takes me back. When I'm at home, I live on tinned food, I'm afraid."

"That can't be helping your health, can it, now?" Cecily said as she went to the oven to check on the casserole. "It's ready. Would you like some?"

"Frankly, I'm completely ravenous and could swallow an entire Boran cow down in one."

Eventually, the hollering from the bedroom quietened. As Bill ate his casserole, Cecily went to let Rosa out of her room. "Are you ready to do your homework now?" she asked her.

"Yes, ma'am."

"And what will you say to our poor old guest, who's come all the way from Africa just to hear you screaming?" Cecily asked as she took Rosa's hand and led her back to the kitchen.

"I will say I'm very sorry, Granny," said Rosa. "I'm very sorry, sir," she said as she sat down at the table and Cecily put down the schoolbooks in front of her. "When's Mama coming home?" she asked as she took a pencil out of her case.

"On the weekend, honey."

"Have you met my mama, Bill?" she asked him. "She's real pretty and real clever and has a very important job, which is why she isn't here right now," Rosa said as she painstakingly copied out some numbers, her pencil digging hard into the paper.

"I have, as a matter of fact, young lady. I first met her when she was a tiny baby, didn't I, Cecily?"

"You did, Bill, yes," confirmed Cecily.

"She was born in Africa, you know," Rosa said.

"I do know, because when she was younger, she used to live in my house. In *our* house," Bill checked himself, glancing at Cecily.

"Your house is in Africa?"

"It is, yes."

"Do you get to see any lions?"

"Oh, I do indeed, lots of them."

"Mama loves lions, doesn't she, Granny?"

"She does, yes."

"I'd like to see Africa one day."

"I'm sure you will, young lady."

"Now, Rosa, enough chatter, get on with your homework."

Having wrangled two bedtime stories out of Cecily, then insisting that Bill came to say good night and tell her a story about all the wild animals he'd seen in Africa, Rosa eventually went to sleep. Cecily poured herself a glass of wine—a habit she knew she should probably curb, but she looked forward to it, as it signaled the fact that Rosa was in bed asleep. She suggested to Bill that the two of them go upstairs to the living room.

"How often is Stella home?" Bill asked as he sat down in a chair by the fireplace.

"Oh, it depends on her workweek. She's usually based in Baltimore, which is a three-hour train ride from here, so if she isn't flying off somewhere, she'll leave Sunday after supper and get home late on Friday evening."

"So she doesn't see much of her daughter."

"No, sir, she doesn't," sighed Cecily.

"You really have rather been left to pick up the pieces, haven't you?"

"I'd hardly call Rosa a 'piece,' Bill. To all intents and purposes, she is my grandchild, and I'm only doing what any grandmother would do under the circumstances."

"I can see that, but it could mean you being trapped in this situation for years to come. Surely you want something more?"

"I would have thought that *you* of all people, Bill, have learned, like I have, that life isn't a question of what you *want*. But yes, you're right: lately I have felt a little trapped," she admitted.

"It seems to me that you've sacrificed almost everything for Stella," Bill said quietly. "Your family, your home, money, your marriage, even—and at present, any hope of a life of your own until Rosa has grown up."

"It was a sacrifice worth making," Cecily said defensively. "You do anything you can for those you love, Bill, but I guess you wouldn't understand that."

"Please, Cecily, yet again, forgive me, I've no right to come back here and start telling you what to do with your life. And I . . . well, whatever has passed between us, I still care for you, and I'd like to help if I can."

"That's very kind of you, Bill, but I can't see quite how you could."

"To start with, by giving you some funds so you can get some child care support. Frankly, Cecily, you look utterly exhausted and in desperate need of a holiday."

"I sure haven't had one of those in a long time," she agreed. "But I can't take your money, Bill. It wouldn't be right."

"Please remember, it was I who brought this situation to your door—*our* door—in the first place. The very least I can now do is help out with the consequences of it. You are still my wife, after all, and as it happens, I have plenty of money to spare. Apart from the farm doing well, my older brother died last year and left me the family heap in England. I went to see it on my way to New York—it's near that horrendously ugly hall where you met the original cad and bounder . . . what was his name?"

"Julius," said Cecily with a shudder.

"It might hearten you to know that I heard he left this world some years ago, having gone through countless wives and copious vats of brandy, leaving no progeny. Anyway, the local estate agent says he has an eager buyer for my own far smaller pile. It should bring in a pretty penny—apparently some pop star wants to put a recording studio in the wine cellar. I say, what do you think of these Beatles chaps, then? I heard nothing else on the radio when I was in England, and it seems to be the same here in America."

"Stella adores them, obviously. I guess I like their tunes, too. They're catchy."

"Not exactly smooching music, though, is it? Do you remember that night with Joss and Diana when they were so desperately in love and poor old Jock sat like the eternal cuckold in the corner watching them?" Bill reminisced.

"I do, yes."

"You and I danced to Glenn Miller. I often think back to that night. I remember it being the start of the rehabilitation of you and me after we lost Fleur. If only war hadn't come . . ."

"Well, it did. And here we are now," said Cecily. That night had been seminal for her, and she was amazed that it stuck out in Bill's memory, too.

"Halcyon days," he murmured. "Why is it we only realize that they were in retrospect? Anyway, Cecily, whether you like it or not, I'm going to place an amount into your account and then I'm going to help you find a nursemaid—or whatever one calls them in America—to come and sort Rosa out. And I won't hear another word about it. What are you doing tomorrow?"

"What I always do—taking Rosa to school, then coming home to get on with my bookkeeping, and then—"

"How about instead, tomorrow you take me out and show me the sights of New York? Having finally made it all the way here, I should see what all the fuss is about. What do you say, Cecily?" Bill leaned forward and put a hand on hers.

"I guess so," she agreed, trying to ignore the tingle that shot up her arm at his touch. "Now you'll have to excuse me, but I need to get some sleep."

"Of course. I'll see you in the morning. Thank you again for putting a roof over my head."

"Remember, Bill, you once put a roof over mine. I'm just returning the favor. Good night."

# 49

Despite a sleepless night of tossing and turning and failing to make head or tail out of her thoughts and feelings about Bill's abrupt return to her life, Cecily had a wonderful day out in the city with him. It was a long time since she'd been across to Manhattan, so they started with a carriage ride around Central Park, where she pointed out her family home, dwarfed on either side by huge apartment buildings.

"Does my dragon of a mother-in-law still inhabit the house?" Bill asked her.

"Oh, yes, although Mamie says she constantly moves from one ailment to the next, swearing she's dying and making a fuss."

"And your father?"

"Oh, he just puts up with her like he always has." Cecily gave a small shudder as the carriage clopped away from the house. Then she walked him along Fifth Avenue to where *Breakfast at Tiffany's* had been filmed some years back and was horrified to discover he'd never seen it.

"But, Bill, surely you *have* to have seen it! I doubt there's a person on the planet that hasn't."

"A person on Planet America, maybe, Cecily. Remember, I'm more comfortable in a loincloth with a spear than in this great overwhelming pile of vertical concrete."

Then they went to the Empire State Building, where Bill peered over the edge, only to stumble backward.

"Good God! My head is swimming. I seem to have caught vertigo. And this from the man who climbed Mount Kenya without even pausing for breath. Take me down and plant my feet back on the solid carpet of the earth immediately!"

A trip out on the Hudson to see the Statue of Liberty came next, and Bill pronounced himself extremely disappointed with the whole affair.

"She's so bloody small," he complained, "and I far prefer Lake Naivasha and its hippo population to the murky pond you have here."

"Quit complaining, Bill! You're turning into a grumpy old man."

"You know only too well that I was once a grumpy younger man, so I haven't changed one jot, have I?"

Rosalind had very kindly agreed to take Rosa home with her after school and feed her supper. She knew all about Bill, of course, but when they arrived to pick up Rosa, Cecily felt almost shy when she introduced him to her.

"Well, hi there, Bill," Rosalind said, regarding him with a mixture of suspicion and curiosity.

"I'm awfully glad to make your acquaintance, Rosalind. Cecily has told me that you have been a true friend to her over the years."

Within a few minutes, they were talking like old friends, Bill's British accent winning out over any reservations Rosalind might have had. A drink led to dinner as Terrence arrived home. Rosa was put to bed downstairs, and Terrence and Rosalind listened avidly to everything Bill had to say on the new independent Republic of Kenya.

"I wasn't expecting *him*," Rosalind whispered as she and Cecily cleared the dessert plates away. "He knows his stuff, and he is *hot*, honey, for an older guy." She giggled. "He reminds me a little of Robert Redford, don't you think?"

Both of them had been to see *Butch Cassidy and the Sundance Kid* when it came out and had swooned over Redford and Paul Newman, as had the rest of America.

Rosalind chuckled. "And guess what? Your husband really does know how to wield a gun and ride a horse."

She insisted on having Rosa to stay overnight, so Cecily and Bill walked back to the apartment alone.

"I have to admit that New York is not quite as ghastly as I'd imagined," said Bill as they strolled along the street in the balmy June air.

"Then that makes me very happy."

"I'm not saying I could stay here for long before I ran away screaming for wide-open spaces, but for a few days, it seems to be a most enjoyable city."

"How long *are* you staying, Bill?"

"I haven't actually thought about it—I just made the decision to come here and got on a plane. Why?" He stopped and turned to her. "Are you finding me—*this*—difficult? I can always move into a hotel."

"No, not at all." They walked a bit further in silence before Cecily said,

"Are you telling me the truth about your heart condition, Bill? Or is it more serious than you're saying?"

"For the umpteenth time, my dear Cecily, I swear I am not yet about to shuffle off this mortal coil. However, the presence of a weakness in my formerly titanium-like physique encouraged me to come and see you, yes. We will all die sometime, and my angina attacks simply reminded me that I am indeed mortal, which, as you know, I do occasionally forget. I'm glad I came, Cecily, seriously. It's been a long time since I took a day off and had some fun with a lady. Who also happens to be my wife," he added. "It's reminded me why I liked you in the first place."

"Has it?"

"Yes. You're most definitely a one-off. I knew it then, and I certainly know it now. Beneath that timid veneer lies a tough tiger."

"Remember, there are no tigers in Africa." Cecily smiled.

"Well, now that you've left, there aren't. You have grown into quite a woman, if I may say so. Whereas I have hardly changed at all."

"True," Cecily agreed. "Although you do seem . . . lighter somehow."

"Pray explain."

She chuckled. "I guess you're just not quite so miserable. And of course, at present, you're captive on my territory, whereas in Kenya, I was always captive on yours."

"Good point. Yes, I am in your very capable hands here in Brooklyn. What shall we do tomorrow?"

"I'll be teaching at the school, so you're on your own," she said as they walked up the steps to her apartment and she opened the front door.

"No wonder you're so exhausted. Between bookkeeping, teaching, and taking care of Rosa, you can't have a minute to yourself."

"It's better to be busy. And besides, I love teaching, and a girl's gotta earn a shekel, you know."

"As I told you, if you'll be so good as to give me your account details, I will begin the process of transferring some funds to you. No!" Bill put a finger to Cecily's lips as she opened her mouth to protest. "I will not hear another word about it. You have cost me nothing in the past twenty-three years. Think of it as a back payment for all the past food, clothes, petrol—and, of course, gin—that I haven't had to furnish you with."

Cecily giggled, hardly able to believe she could feel so comfortable with him so quickly after all these years.

"Especially the gin," she agreed. "Talking of which, would you like one? I think I have the dregs of a bottle downstairs."

"You take that, and I'll stick to beer," Bill said. "Now, you stay here and put your feet up and I'll go and fetch the—what is it you call it here?"

"Liquor," Cecily called as he walked down the stairs to the kitchen.

She sat down on the couch, threw off her patent-leather heels, and closed her eyes for a moment, enjoying the fact that someone else was actually making her a drink. Such a simple thing, but she'd forgotten what it felt like to be cared for.

"There you go, madam. One gin laced with something called soda, as there was no tonic or bitter lemon."

"Thanks, I'll try it at least," she said, not really caring what it tasted like, because tonight she felt freer than she had in a very long time.

"By the way, how is Lankenua? I think I recall you telling me many moons ago in a letter that she had married."

"She has, yes, and is very happy, by all accounts."

"I'd like to see her if I can. I have a photograph of Kwinet—and his wife and young child—standing proudly in the garden at Paradise Farm."

"Oh, I'd love to see that photograph. I spent so many hours working with him on it."

"Cecily." Bill took her gin glass, put it down, then grabbed her hands. "Why don't you come back with me to Kenya? Just for a holiday? Kwinet has spent the last two decades tending your precious garden and hoping against hope that one day you would see his handiwork. You could see Katherine, Bobby, and their children, and, of course, Kenya, too."

"Oh, Bill, I'd love to, but how can I? I have Rosa to care for."

"Surely Stella must have some leave owing to her. Maybe she could take a few weeks off?"

"Bill, you don't understand; no one here in the States takes the vacation that they're owed, especially not an ambitious young black female lawyer who is determined to make a name for herself. The work ethic here compared to other countries is just crazy. Life in Happy Valley was all about pleasure; life here these days for someone like Stella is all about working your butt off to get to the top."

"Of course I understand, but that doesn't make it right, Cecily," Bill sighed. "I would like you to think about it. You've told me yourself you haven't taken a holiday since coming here! I think one is long overdue. Please, at least consider it. I'll do what I can to help make it happen, but maybe it's only when you see Paradise Farm again that you can help me decide what I should do. What *we* should do."

"It's a beautiful idea, but there is just no way I can leave Rosa. Anyway"— Cecily yawned—"it's way past my bedtime, and I've drunk far too much. I have a whole classroom of six-year-olds to face tomorrow morning." She stood up and smiled at him. "Thank you for a lovely day. It was like a vacation, and I really enjoyed it. Good night, Bill."

"Good night, Cecily."

When Cecily had left, Bill went downstairs to get another beer from the refrigerator; then he wandered out into the small patch of Kenya Cecily had created in Brooklyn. And began to formulate a plan . . .

Stella arrived home past midnight on Friday, exhausted as usual from a long, hard week down in Alabama. Cecily had sent Bill off to bed while she waited up as she always did for Stella to arrive home. Hot chocolate with cream and homemade cookies were offered as Stella talked about her current case.

"It's just so obvious that the authorities have fabricated evidence—we've discovered the witnesses couldn't possibly have been where they say they were to see Michael Winston shooting this guy . . . We're doing what we can, but I just don't know whether we can save him from death row. The juries in Alabama are notorious for handing out the death penalty."

"All you can do is your best," Cecily said, as she always did, seeing the anger and passion blaze in Stella's eyes and knowing she was partly responsible for putting it there. "Now you need some rest. I'm afraid you're in with Rosa tonight, because I have a guest staying."

"Oh, really? Who?"

"Maybe you won't remember him, because the last time you saw him, you were just five years old. His name is Bill, and when I first found you, I was married to him."

"Bill . . ." Stella scratched her nose. "Yes, I think I do remember him. Did he have light-colored hair and was quite tall?"

"He did, yes, although it's now completely white." Cecily smiled. "It was he who convinced me to let your mother come stay on our farm while she was pregnant with you. He also worked out the plan to have Yeyo come live with us, so you could stay and I could bring you up."

"He actually knew my birth mother?" Stella looked incredulous.

"Yes, he certainly met Njala and was friendly with your grandfather, who was the chief of the clan."

"Then where has he been all this time, Kuyia? Why didn't he come with us to New York?"

"Because he ran a big cattle farm back in Kenya and because . . . Bill just belongs in Africa."

"So you left him behind?"

"I had to, if you were going to have any kind of future. I begged him so many times to come over, but he never wanted to."

"You left him for me?"

"No, Stella, please . . ." Cecily backtracked, realizing what she'd said. "We had—*he* had—all sorts of issues with our marriage at the time. Our future lay here, and his didn't. It's as simple as that."

"Are you still married to him?"

"I am. There never seemed to be any point in getting divorced."

"Jeez! That must feel weird—your husband turning up out of the blue after over twenty years."

"It does and it doesn't, Stella. I'd often wondered what I'd feel if he came to find me, but now it's almost as if the past two decades haven't happened. He bears me no ill will, and I bear him none, either."

"Kuyia!" Stella smiled. "You look kinda dreamy. Do you still love him? It sure looks like you do."

"I don't know. It's just been nice to have some company for a change. And we always did get along well."

"How romantic, him coming to find you after all this time."

"Actually, he came to set things straight. One of the first things he asked me was whether I wanted a divorce! And whether I'd mind if he sold Paradise Farm, where we used to live in Kenya. He's nearly seventy, plus he has a heart condition, so he's hardly Prince Charming riding in on his white charger."

"Well, you sure look like he might be," Stella teased her, then yawned. "I need to get some rest now, I'm so very tired."

"Rosa's on the hideaway, so you can have the bed. Good night, honey."

"Night." Stella gave Cecily a quick hug before she picked up her carry-on and walked wearily down the stairs to bed.

Cecily thought about what Stella had said as the four of them sat at the breakfast table the next morning. Stella and Bill had hit it off immediately, Stella listening fascinated to Bill's stories of the place where she was born and his knowledge of and connections with her ancestral tribe, the Maasai. Even Rosa seemed enraptured, and the sight of the three of them together, looking for all the world like a family, brought a lump to Cecily's throat. That afternoon, they went to a movie theater and watched *The Love Bug*. Rosa was almost doubled up with laughter, which was infectious, and even though Bill fell asleep for half of it, the trip was pronounced a success. They went on to a diner so that Bill could have his first American burger.

"I like the combination of the bun and the cheese, but this beef doesn't hold a candle to the Boran cows of Kenya. And as for that"—Bill pointed at Rosa's hot dog in disgust—"it's full of nothing but maize and bread crumbs."

That evening, Cecily said good night, then left Stella and Bill chatting in the living room and walked to her own bedroom, which sat at the back of the apartment and overlooked the garden below. She undressed, then lay under the cool sheets, marveling at the change Bill's arrival had wrought on the family. Rosa had been far more manageable, Stella had been charmed by Bill, and as for her . . . having coped alone for so long, even the simple fact there was a man about the place was massively comforting. The small things he'd done, like pouring the gin, oiling the kitchen door that squeaked horribly, and even doing the weeding, had been a soothing balm to Cecily's normally self-reliant soul.

"There's no need, Bill," she'd said. "The doctor told you to take it easy."

"I hardly think pulling a few nettles out of this little patch of garden will finish me off. Besides, I am simply not a sitting-down sort of a person, as you well know."

More than anything, Cecily had enjoyed the laughter—when Bill had been on form in the past, he'd always been able to put a smile on her face with his witty comments.

"Oh, how I wish I could go back to Kenya." She sighed as she took out the book she'd just bought by Ernest Hemingway entitled *The Green Hills of Africa*, thinking that it was probably the closest she was likely to get.

On Sunday, with Bill saying he was going stir crazy, Cecily declared that they were all going on a trip to Jones Beach. This was greeted by shrieks of joy from Rosa, whom she'd taken there once before with Stella for her first-ever swim in open water.

The June day was hot and the beach was crowded, but Cecily sat in her deck chair and watched Bill, Stella, and Rosa splashing around in the water. Afterward, they went for a late lunch at the Boardwalk Cafe, which had the most beautiful ocean view.

"Is this good enough for you?" Cecily asked Bill as he stood on the terrace, looking out over the Atlantic.

"I'd hardly say it was the deserted pristine white sands of the beach at Mombasa, but it'll do for now, yes."

That evening, Cecily bathed Rosa and put her to bed.; then Bill told Rosa another story about the meerkats that lived in Africa while Stella packed her carry-on, ready to go to the station and catch the train to Baltimore. None of them was too hungry after the late lunch, so Cecily made a plate of sandwiches and a pot of tea and the three of them sat down to eat before Stella left.

"Kuyia, we have something to talk to you about," said Stella, looking nervously at Bill. "Bill was saying that it's been twenty-three years since you took a vacation. That's far too long a time to never have a day off."

"Honestly"—Cecily eyed them both fiercely—"I'm perfectly happy, thank you very much, and I have lots of time off now that Rosa is at school."

"Hear us out, please," said Stella. "You haven't been to Kenya in all that time, so Bill and I think you should travel back with him and spend some time at Paradise Farm."

"That sounds awful nice in theory," Cecily said, "but what about Rosa?"

"Bill has kindly said he will pay for a nanny to take care of her during the week while you're away. I'm here on weekends, and between us, we'll work the details out."

"But—"

"No buts, Kuyia. Seeing Bill again after all this time has reminded me just how much you've done for me, and if anyone deserves a vacation, it's you. So I'm going to take a few days' leave—I have plenty due to me—and start looking for the right person to be with Rosa while you're away."

"Really, you two, can I not have a say in this?"

"No, I'm afraid you can't. You're not getting any younger. If you don't go back now, maybe you never will. Please, Kuyia," Stella said, reaching her hands across the table and taking Cecily's. "It's your turn now."

"But how long would this vacation be for? I know it's easier to get to Kenya these days, but it's hardly a place one can visit for just a week, is it?"

"We thought a couple of months," said Bill.

"A couple of months? But what about my teaching? My garden?"

"I spoke to Rosalind earlier on the telephone, and she thinks that you should go, too. I know you don't like to think about it, but you are replaceable," said Stella calmly. "Rosalind's got a great new part-timer who's eager to be doing more."

"And as for the garden," piped up Bill, "I've already contacted a domestic agency to find a housekeeper who can keep both the apartment and the garden under control."

Cecily sat back in her chair. "Jeez! You two sure have everything worked out."

"Yes, we do, and for once in your life, you need to let someone else take charge, okay?"

"Okay," Cecily breathed. "But I'd like to meet the person who is going to take care of Rosa. You know how difficult she can be, Stella, but I don't want a witch, and—"

"She's my child! Do you seriously think I'd leave her with a witch?" said Stella. "I'm twenty-eight years old, with a career that relies a lot on character assessment. Please, trust me, okay? Now I must leave, or I'm gonna miss my train." Stella stood up and kissed Cecily on the top of her head. "Remember, we all love you, and it's about time you got a chance to relax and snatch some happiness. See you next Friday," she said as she picked up her carry-on and left the kitchen.

"Gin?" suggested Bill as the front door closed behind Stella. Without waiting for a reply, he stood up. "I went to what they call the liquor store and replenished the stocks," he said, holding aloft a new bottle from the cupboard. "Cheers," he said, after he'd added tonic and ice to the glasses and put one in front of Cecily.

"Cheers, I think," Cecily toasted back and took a large gulp. "So don't I have any say in the matter?"

"Sadly not."

"I feel as though I'm being kidnapped! What if I don't want to go?"

"Oh, but I think you do," Bill said with what Cecily felt was a rather patronizing smile. "I can see it in your eyes every time I talk of Kenya."

"I'm just concerned about Rosa."

"As Stella said, she is a grown woman and ultimately responsible for her daughter. You said that they don't spend enough time together—maybe this will help them bond."

"If I'm not here, you mean."

"Quite." Bill drew Cecily up to standing next to him and held her hands. "Two months, Cecily. That's all. Two months to discover if there is any chance that we could find a way to stay married in ways other than the legal sense, if you know what I mean."

"Yes, I do," said Cecily, feeling the blush travel up her neck to her face.

"I admit, when I arrived here, there was no thought in my mind that there might be a future for us. But, well, I have so enjoyed being with you and find myself dreading the thought of leaving you behind. After all we've been through, surely we owe each other some time together. Unless, of course, these past few days have been utter hell for you and you're just waiting for me to go. If that is the case, then yes, you'd better tell me, but if it isn't—"

Cecily lowered her eyes. "It isn't."

"Good. Then we have a plan. I must say, coming here was just about the best decision I've ever made."

Then Bill bent down toward his wife and kissed her for the first time in twenty-three years.

# ELECTRA

*Brooklyn, New York*
*June 2008*

# 50

So when a suitable nanny and housekeeper had been found, Bill took Cecily back home to Kenya with him," Stella finished.

"Well, that *was* a happy ending, and it sure sounds as though she deserved it," I said. "Especially after having to deal with my mom. I hate to admit it, but she sounds a lot like me when I was a child."

"I can't say, Electra, because I wasn't there to see you grow up, and I will never forgive myself for that. Or for the fact that I wasn't there for Rosa in the ways I should have been, either."

"You were a single working mom, which must have been seriously hard."

"It was, yes, but millions of women around the world manage to do it successfully. Sadly, I didn't."

"Did Bill and Cecily ever come back?" I said, wanting to know the answer before we moved on to what I felt from Stella's expression were far murkier past waters.

"No, they did not."

"Why not?"

"At first it was for all the right reasons; it was obvious from the moment Cecily got back to Kenya that she was as happy as I'd ever heard her. And that she and Bill had finally managed to find the moment in time when they could actually enjoy each other. Sadly, like anything, it didn't last forever."

"Did Bill die from his heart condition?"

"Eventually, yes, but it was my beloved Kuyia I lost first. They extended their stay to six months and went traveling through Africa. They were on their way up through Sudan toward Egypt—Cecily had always wanted to see the pyramids—when she began to feel unwell. Their medical boxes and other supplies were stolen, and they were in the middle of nowhere. By the time Bill managed to get her to a hospital, it was too late. She died a few days later."

"Oh, no." I winced as I watched my grandmother's eyes fill with tears. "What was it?"

"Malaria. If they'd have gotten her treated sooner, there's no doubt she would have lived, but—" Stella swallowed hard. "She died in Bill's arms . . . She asked him to tell me how much she loved me . . . I . . . sorry."

I sat there watching the grief that, even after all these years, was obviously still so raw for my grandmother.

"When I heard the news, all I could think was that I wanted to die, too," Stella continued. "I can't explain to you what that woman was to me. What she did for me, everything she sacrificed for me . . . The only thing that comforted me was that she was with Bill and that they'd at least had six wonderful months together. She died where she wanted to be, with the man she loved."

Even though I'd never known this remarkable woman who had affected both of our lives so dramatically, I felt a lump in my throat, too.

"Bill came back to the States for a while, and we took her ashes and spread them out by the Statue of Liberty. Because she was born in Manhattan and had done so much to give me my own liberty, I thought it was fitting. He stayed with us for a while; he'd aged so much in those few months, but he couldn't make urban Brooklyn his home, so he went back to Kenya, sold Paradise Farm, and bought a cottage near Lake Naivasha. Five years later, I got a telegram to tell me he'd died, too. And that he'd left me everything he had. The will said it was what Cecily would have wanted."

"I think he was right," I agreed. "Can I get you another cup of tea, maybe?"

"No, I'll be fine, thanks, honey."

I sat quietly while Stella composed herself. And as I watched her, I understood the lesson her grief was teaching me: that motherly love did not necessarily have to be biological. So many times I'd railed against Ma—I remembered once when I was in a rage screaming at her that she had no right to tell me I had to go up to my room because she wasn't my real mother, anyway. Yet I understood now that any "real" mother would have reacted in exactly the same way to my unacceptable behavior. I felt a sudden huge burst of love for Ma, who had only ever shown me endless patience and compassion.

"Forgive me, Electra, I'm ready to go on now if you are."

"Sure, but only if you feel up to it. I can always come back."

"I think I'd prefer to keep going, if it's okay with you. We're very close to the end of the story now." Stella took a deep breath. "Nothing much changed in my life during those five years after Cecily died. Rosa had a succession of nannies, all of whom left after a few months. They were unable to deal with such a difficult child. Then, when Bill left me his legacy, it meant that I had the choice to stay home and care for Rosa myself. To my shame, I knew that I just couldn't do that. Coffee mornings and PTA meetings . . . after the kind of stuff I was used to dealing with every day, I knew I couldn't cope with all that. The truth is, Electra, I just wasn't born maternal. Not that I'm using it as an excuse or anything; lots of women aren't, they just have to get on with it, and I did my best to do that."

As Stella paused, I wondered whether *I* was maternal; it was a question I'd never considered up to this very second. I'd certainly never felt the urge to have a baby, but then I thought of my nephew, Bear, and how I'd enjoyed the smell of him and the weight of his body in my arms and thought that I just might be.

"Electra? Are you okay?"

"Yeah, sorry, you lost me for a few seconds then."

"Anytime you just want to stop, please say the word."

"No, I'm good," I said.

"The situation got especially bad when Rosalind told me that they could no longer keep Rosa at the school. She was a disruptive influence, unable to settle down and concentrate on anything. That really burned me. Rosalind was Rosa's godmother, and if she'd lost faith in her, then I knew I had a serious problem on my hands."

"Hey, from what you've said, this was a very academic school. Maybe it just didn't suit my mom," I said, suddenly feeling defensive of Rosa. "I know because I've been there, too."

"That's pretty much what Rosalind said, so I found her another school, one that was run on more holistic, relaxed lines." Stella gave a little chuckle. "Rosa took the lack of rules to an extreme. I remember arriving home one weekend with her new nanny waiting for me in her coat, with her suitcase ready by the door. Apparently, Rosa had spent the entire week at home, watching TV and eating cereal. She'd told the nanny she didn't have to go to school that week, and when the school had called to see where she was, Rosa had recited one of their own guidelines: that the students were there of their own free will to learn and that no penalties were enforced if the child didn't attend class."

I grinned. "My mom sure is sounding more and more like me. I would have done the same."

"The difference is, Electra, that you had a family structure around you and, from what I've heard, a loving mother figure and a father who caught you when you fell. Rosa didn't have that, which was partly to do with circumstances but also a lot to do with me. When Cecily died, I felt even more fire in my belly to become the success she'd always dreamed I'd be. And then, when Bill left me the legacy, I was on a trajectory I just couldn't"— Stella checked herself—"or didn't want to halt. Rosa was ten by then. She had gone through I don't even know how many nannies and four or five schools. To give myself some credit, I did take a month's leave and stayed home with her to organize her tutoring, but I nearly lost my mind, and Rosa was completely out of control. I spoke to Rosalind, and she suggested that maybe the best thing to do was to send Rosa away to boarding school. We found a great place up in Boston that was used to dealing with kids like Rosa."

"You mean, like, rejects?"

"No, Electra, the way they phrased it was 'challenging behavior.' Rosa seemed to like the idea at first—I was going stir crazy, but she had had also enough of being stuck at home with only a tutor and her mama for company. While she was there for her interview, they tested her for all kinds of things, including her IQ. And, of course, it was off the charts. The school told me that often went hand in hand with disruptive children. They developed a program of accelerated learning for her, and off she went to Boston. She seemed happy there for the first three years; the school gave her the stability and security that she needed, and she made some friends. At the same time, I received a call out of the blue from the United Nations. They'd read a paper I'd written on apartheid in South Africa while I'd been at Columbia. They were developing something called the United Nations Centre Against Apartheid. I was called in for an interview—you can imagine my excitement, Electra; the thought of being at the hub of the most powerful human rights organization in the world was the stuff that my dreams were made of. This new department would be collating statistics and factual evidence of the effects of apartheid. They were looking for a team who would write up what they had found into a paper, which would then be published. In one sense, it was a side step from what I'd been doing, but in another, I knew it would open up a whole new world to me. And it sure did. Those years were relatively calm; the UN was based in Manhattan, which meant that when Rosa was home for vacations, I was there every night to cook her supper. All finally felt calmer, until, of course, puberty hit."

"Yeah, that old thing; your cute little girl turns into a bunch of raging hormones." I nodded, remembering how my own had not only rebooted but surpassed any temper tantrums I'd had when I was very young.

"Put it this way: the entire apartment used to shake under the weight of Rosa's stamping and hollering and the slamming of her bedroom door. Next thing I know, I get a call from her school to tell me she's disappeared—a friend of hers said there was a boy in town whom she'd met on an outing. She was found eventually, smoking and drinking bourbon in a park. The boy was almost twenty years old, but your mom was probably even more beautiful than you, if I dare say so. She had these incredible eyes that were simply mesmerizing and obviously contained the kind of witchcraft needed to attract any alley cat in the neighborhood. She looked—and dressed—as if she were eighteen instead of fourteen. It wasn't long until the school wrote me to say they could no longer contain her, so she was sent back home to New York. None of the good day schools would take her because of her track record, so I was reduced to sending her to the local high school. Of course, she got in with the wrong crowd—she always did love bad boys."

I rolled my eyes. "Don't we all?"

"By the time Rosa was sixteen, I'd lost control of her completely—she wasn't attending school and spent most of her time hanging around downtown Brooklyn with her new friends. At first I just thought she was smoking dope when she came home high, but then she started to stay out all night. I had no idea where she went. I began to notice she was losing weight—this was when crack cocaine was beginning to appear on the streets. Electra, I swear, I did everything I possibly could to talk to her about drugs, but she just didn't want to listen."

"I understand," I said quietly. "Look at me, I didn't want to hear, either."

"Anyway, she then got brought home by the cops a few times and was finally charged with petty theft—she'd been shoplifting and selling the stuff on the streets for cash. I paid her bail and found a lawyer to represent her in court. The threat of jail calmed her down for a while, and she stayed home. She drank some, but I think for the time the drugs stopped. The court gave her a caution with the threat of juvenile hall if she got herself back into trouble again. And then—"

I watched Stella as she paused, her hands clasped tightly together, her eyes full of pain as she remembered.

"She disappeared. A week after the court hearing, she went out one night and just never came back. And that was the last time I ever saw her."

"Did you search for her?"

"Of course I searched for her!" Stella turned to me, her eyes blazing with anger. "I turned Brooklyn and Manhattan upside down looking for her! There wasn't a precinct I didn't visit with a photograph, not a neighborhood where I didn't stick a poster on a lamppost. I went to all the ghettos, the crack dens, all the damned places I could find where the lowlifes of the city hung out. I went up to Boston to search for her there, thinking she might have gone back to one of her exes, but nothing. Absolutely nothing. She literally vanished. Over two years I searched for her, working at the UN by day and walking the streets by night. It sounds impossible that someone can truly vanish off the face of the earth, but that is exactly what your mama did. And I swear, Electra, there was no stone I knew of that I left unturned."

"It's okay, Stella, I believe you. So"—I knew we were heading for the denouement of the story and braced myself—"when did you find out she'd died?"

I watched Stella swallow hard. "In truth, only just over a year ago, when your father got in touch with me and asked to meet me in New York. He told me that he'd spent time trying to trace your blood family, because he knew he was dying and he wanted to be able to leave you a letter that would tell you where you'd come from. He'd gone back to Hale House, where he'd found you, and spoken to the daughter of Clara Hale, who'd put him in touch with one of the women who'd worked there at the time. Turned out it was her who took you in that night. She was able to find the register that documented your arrival. As always, there were no details left about your mama, but the woman apparently remembered the man who'd brought you in. She'd seen him around the neighborhood and knew he was a junkie. So your father asked for his name, and the woman said she thought he'd been known as Mickey. Your father scoured the area, and eventually he managed to find him through the Abyssinian Baptist Church in Harlem. He was apparently a reformed man who had found God and was a lay preacher at the church. You must remember, Electra, that I knew nothing of this at the time," Stella clarified. "Anyway, Michael, as he's now called, was able to tell your father what he remembered of your mama."

"Was this Michael my father?" I asked eagerly.

"No, he just happened to live in the same crack den when your mama was pregnant with you. There were constant police raids, so the junkies were always moving on to find different hiding places in abandoned buildings around Manhattan. He was there when she gave birth to you, admittedly out of his mind on crack, but he said that you were starting to scream the place down, which would have alerted the cops. So he scooped you up and took you to Hale House."

"And"—I swallowed—"what happened to my mama?"

"I—" My grandmother reached for my hand and held it fast. "Bear with me, Electra, and forgive me for what I have to tell you. Mickey said he came back to find Rosa bleeding out. It was obvious she was dying, so he and the others just . . . left. He said he went into a phone booth and made an anonymous call to 911 but that he guessed that Rosa would be dead before they found her. God forgive me for having to tell you this . . . and for not being there when I should have been for my beloved daughter."

"But you didn't know where she was, Stella."

"Thank you, Electra, for saying that, but when your father told me the story, I swear, it nearly broke me. The thought of my little girl being left to die alone—"

"Yeah." We both sat in silence for a while. So," I breathed eventually, "I guess there's no happy ending to this story."

"Not for Rosa, no, but I hope—I *really* hope—that the fact that you and I were able to meet because of it can bring us both some comfort. I'm just so sorry I've had to share this terrible story with you at a time when it's the last thing you need."

"But how did Pa find out you were my relative?"

"Because of Michael. He'd lived with Rosa for a few weeks. For a start, he remembered her name, and he also remembered her talking about her mama, who had an important job at the United Nations. He thought that she was called Stella—he remembered because it was his favorite imported beer." She gave me a watery smile. "So, armed with that, your father began to do his research. He knew the year of your birth through Hale House and contacted the UN in New York and asked them to look back through their records to find out if there had been a Stella working for them in 1982. I'll thank Cecily forever for giving me a relatively unusual name—there were only two of us on the records, and one was dead. By that time, he had my surname, looked me up online, and wrote me. The rest you know."

"I—" There was one thing I *didn't* know, but even though I could hardly bear to ask the question, I had to.

"When she was found and"—I gulped—"taken to the place where they take dead people, they must have tried to search for relatives?"

"At the time, Electra, there were bodies of young crack addicts being found all over Manhattan. And legally, the authorities only have to hold on to a body for forty-eight hours. If it's left unclaimed, they can go ahead and bury it."

"Jeez, that's fast," I breathed. "So where *was* she buried?"

"Your father and I visited the Office of Vital Records on Worth Street to find out. We had the date of Rosa's death because it was the same day you were born, which was marked on the register at Hale House. Sure enough, the clerk was able to confirm that the body of an unidentified young black woman had been transferred to the city morgue that night. I was unable to claim her at the time, and it was New York state policy that unidentified bodies be buried on Hart Island in the Bronx. In truth, I haven't been able to bring myself to go there."

"I see." I didn't know whether I wanted to cry or vomit, but I knew I couldn't take any more. "Stella, would you mind if I called for my car to take me home? I need . . . I just need some time to take all of this in."

"Of course," she said as I pulled out my cell and made the call. "Are you going to be okay?"

"Yeah, I have to be, don't I? At least now I know."

"Anything, anything I can do . . . please tell me."

"I will. Just one last thing: you said you were in Africa when I was born and taken to Hale House?"

"I was, yes. I was invited to be part of a secret UN fact-finding mission to South Africa. You have to understand that by then Rosa had been missing for over two years. I swear, Electra, if I had known, I would have been there for her and, of course, for you. But I had to move on with my life, and . . . I went."

"Okay." I nodded as the doorbell rang to tell me my driver had arrived.

"Please keep in contact, and let me know when you're ready to see me. I understand it's so much to take in and you need some time, but I just want to be there for you. It's important you know that," she said as she followed me up the stairs to the front door. "Just let me know when."

"I will."

She reached out her arms to hug me, but I turned away and opened the door. I just needed to breathe some clean air and step back out into the present.

"Good-bye, Stella," I said as I ran down the steps to the waiting car.

# 5 1

W hen I arrived home, I saw Mariam and Lizzie sitting in the kitchen.

"Hi," I said wearily.

"Are you okay, Electra?" Both of them were on their feet immediately, trailing behind me as I walked toward my bedroom.

"Yeah, I'm good, I just need some sleep."

I closed the door in their faces, feeling rude, but I literally couldn't stand up for another second. Just about managing to take off my sneakers and jeans, I fell onto the bed, pressed the control that would bring the blinds down, and closed my eyes.

"Electra?"

I heard a familiar voice calling me, and I groaned as I came to from what felt like the deepest sleep I'd ever had.

"Yup," I murmured.

"It's Lizzie. I was just checking that you're okay."

"I'm fine, just . . . sleepy."

"Okay, good. Just to let you know, it's eleven o'clock."

"At night?"

"No, in the morning. You've slept for something like fourteen hours, and Mariam and I were getting worried about you."

"Really, I'm fine," I emphasized, realizing that maybe they thought I'd been on the hard stuff again.

"Shall I leave you be or get you some coffee? I bought some bagels and smoked salmon at the deli, too."

I lay there and noticed that I was actually starving. "That sounds good, Lizzie, thanks."

I opened the blinds and sat blinking in the bright sunlight. In my entire life, I didn't think I had ever slept as long as I just had. Maybe it was my brain's way of switching me off, giving me rest in order to deal with what I'd heard yesterday. Surprisingly, I thought as I tentatively gauged my brain's reaction, I didn't feel as bad as I'd expected I would. In fact, I felt a weird sense of relief that I finally knew the truth. Even if that truth was crap. I also found myself thinking how lucky I was not to live in a time when the color of my skin would have totally defined my future and that somehow I'd been saved from walking down the same path as my mother.

As I lay there thinking about my heritage and how I'd read that addiction was genetic, I thought of Stella, who had been addicted only to her work: striving to make the world a better place. I thought of her strength and how calm and balanced she was, and I hoped that some of her genes were in me, too. And even though there were bits of my mom that had reminded me of myself, at heart, I'd always wanted to be a good girl, not a bad one. Admittedly, my fiery temper had gotten in the way . . . so maybe I was a mixture of both my mom and my granny, and that suited me just fine.

As for the man who had provided the seed it took to make me . . . I guessed I would never know who he was, but that was all right, too. It was becoming even more obvious that I'd had a pretty amazing father from the beginning, a man who'd apparently spent a lot of time trying to find me some blood family so he could leave them behind for me. And he'd succeeded.

"Here you go, breakfast in bed, madam, and you deserve it," said Lizzie, coming in with a tray on which stood a pot of hot coffee, a cup, and two smoked salmon and cream cheese bagels.

"Really, why?"

"Your granny called about ten times last night and three times this morning. Obviously she didn't give me any details but just said I was to watch out for you. She sounded concerned for you, Electra."

I sighed. "Yeah, she had to tell me some pretty hard-core stuff about my mom. And other ancestors."

"Well," said Lizzie, pouring the coffee into my cup, "you know I'm here if you want to talk about it. Bagel?"

"In a moment, but why don't you take one? I can't eat both."

"No, you might want it; I'm a feeder." She winked at me. "By the way, Mariam was telling me you got mugged in the park yesterday. Have you contacted the cops?"

"What's the point? They don't give a shit if a rich girl's lost her Rolex, do they? It's probably them that are buying it for a hundredth of its value from the perps."

"I definitely think you've got to consider getting yourself some security, Electra. You're a well-known face, a celebrity. In LA, no one like you would ever step out of their gate without some form of protection. I'm sorry to sound like your mum, but I think you have to consider it. Anyway, I'll leave you to eat your breakfast in peace. Anything you need, just give me a call."

I sat there enjoying my coffee and, despite my protestations, managed to down both bagels. I thought how nice it was to have a roommate but also Lizzie had that warm, cozy air of motherliness about her, which made me feel safe and looked after. I so hoped she'd never leave, because I loved having her here. I thought about what she'd said and guessed she was right. Susie had been telling me for years I should have a bodyguard, but the thought of a stranger tracking my every move horrified me. Then I remembered the idea I'd had before, so I showered, dressed in a pair of track pants and a T-shirt, and went into the kitchen. Mariam was at work on her laptop.

"Good morning, Electra, or should I say afternoon?" She smiled at me. "Let me know when you're ready to have a chat. The woman who runs the ethical materials cooperative has gotten back to me. She's very excited at the thought of a possible collaboration with you."

"Great. By the way," I said as Lizzie came into the kitchen with my breakfast tray, "has anyone seen Tommy this morning?"

"No," said Lizzie, "there was no one outside when I popped out to the deli."

"I'm getting worried—it's not like him to disappear. It's got to be a week since I last saw him, and I need to talk to him because I want to offer him a job."

"As what?" Lizzie asked.

"As my bodyguard. I mean, he's, like, sort of doing it now, and I guess he'd quite like to be paid. I mean, he's an army vet, obviously fit, and—"

I stopped talking as Mariam stood up and abruptly ran out of the kitchen into the hall, where she slammed the door to the guest bathroom behind her.

I looked at Lizzie in shock. "Did I say something wrong?"

"Uh . . . maybe." Lizzie was looking shifty and uncomfortable.

"What?"

"Nothing. I mean, I think you'd better talk to Mariam about it. It's none of my business. I'm going into the living room to await the call from the lawyer Miles suggested to me. See you in a bit."

I stared out of the window, confused, but then finally the penny dropped.

"Electra, you're a total moron!" I said to myself as it all began to fall into place. That confession I'd heard at AA that I thought was about me . . . "Miss Ego or what?" I whispered with a roll of my eyes. Then Mariam's abrupt reply when I'd asked for Tommy's cell phone number a few days ago and the way she'd acted in the last few days when I'd just known something was wrong . . .

I walked down the hallway toward the bathroom and tapped gently on the door. "Mariam, it's me, Electra," I said softly. "I'm so sorry if I've been insensitive. You should have said something to me before. Can you come out so we can talk about it?"

Eventually the door opened, and I saw her tear-stained face. "Please forgive me, Electra. My outburst was completely unprofessional. I promise it won't happen again. I am fine now," she said as she passed by me and walked back toward the kitchen.

"It's blatantly obvious you aren't, Mariam. How long has this thing between you and Tommy been going on?" I asked her, sitting down at the table opposite her.

"Oh, it was nothing, and it's over now anyway—" Another tiny sob emanated from her throat, and she swallowed hard. "Sorry."

"Please stop apologizing, it's me who should do that. I've been so wrapped up in Electra world, I didn't see what was right under my nose."

"Honestly, there was nothing to see. It was just after you went into rehab, and, well, the two of us got close," Mariam confessed, pulling a tissue out of her sleeve and blowing her nose. "He's such a kind man and cares for you so much, and even though we come from completely different worlds, we just kind of . . . bonded. I was coming to work at the apartment, and even though you weren't here, he kept appearing on the doorstep. He said he liked his routine. And we started going for walks in Central Park, just sitting on a bench and eating our lunch together. And one thing led to another and . . . we realized that we liked each other a lot."

"But surely that's wonderful, Mariam! I mean, I obviously don't know Tommy as well as you do, but I do know he's a lovely guy and that he's had a rough time."

"No, Electra, it is not wonderful. Tommy is ten years older than me, he has a child and an ex-wife. He's a recovering alcoholic, you know, and he lives off his army pension because he has PTSD and"—Mariam swallowed hard—"besides all that, he isn't of my faith."

"I remember you once telling me that your father had said you must embrace the country in which you were born," I said.

"I did, yes, and he meant it, too. But that sentiment does not go as far as me marrying outside the faith. It is forbidden for any Muslim woman to marry a non-Muslim man."

"Is it? I didn't know that."

"Yes. Even though Muslim men can marry non-Muslim women. Life really isn't fair, is it?"

"My pa always told me that all the old biblical texts were written by men, Mariam, so they could have it all their own way, you know." I shrugged, trying to lighten the atmosphere. "Could you guys not get married in a civil ceremony?"

"I am the eldest daughter in my family, Electra. Our entire life, our community, has been based around our faith since I was young. A civil wedding would not be recognized—I would be going against all the principles that I have been brought up with if I married him."

"Mmph," I said. Not being a believer in organized religion myself, it was difficult for me to have an opinion, apart from the fact that I knew how much it mattered to Mariam. "Could Tommy not convert to your group—I mean, faith?"

"Maybe he could, yes, but remember he was out in Afghanistan, Electra, and even though he has never said this outright, I know he saw some atrocities that were perpetrated by Muslim extremists. He has friends who died at their hands, blown up by mines or bombs . . . Oh, it is just all so complicated!"

"Love always is, isn't it?" I sighed. "I mean, this probably isn't a solution, but could you two just live in sin or something?"

"No, never, Electra. That would be the worst sin of all," Mariam said firmly.

"And what has Tommy said to all this?"

"Nothing. As I told you, I said it was over between us a week or so ago."

*Which must have been around the time I heard him talk at the AA meeting,* I thought.

"So that's why he hasn't been here?"

"Yes."

"And he knows why?"

"Kind of."

"But have you actually asked him whether he would be prepared to convert to Islam? I mean, if that's the only option?"

"Of course I haven't. He hasn't asked me to marry him or anything, but given everything I've just told you, I just can't see a future for us, so I decided that the best thing was simply to end it."

"Well, I get that it's a little complicated," I replied, feeling like the mistress of understatement, "but oh, Mariam, I've known there's something wrong for ages. I also need to tell you—well, I need to break one of the rules of AA confidentiality—and say that I heard him speak at a meeting last week. He stood there and told everyone that he'd fallen in love but the person he was in love with could never be his. I and my overblown ego thought he was talking about me." I smiled. "Of course, he was talking about you. He loves you, Mariam, truly he does. And if you love him, too, I'm sure there's a way that this can be worked out. But you guys have got to speak. You've just got to tell him what you've told me."

Mariam sat there in silence, staring at the kitchen wall in front of her.

"Anyway, I'm worried about him. At least give me his cell phone number so I can check on him."

"Okay," she agreed. "I deleted it from my own cell so I wasn't tempted to call him, but I remember it."

I took down the number and stared at her. "Listen, I'm not you, and from my track record with men, I'm not going to sit here and offer you any advice. But there was something that my grandmother told me that stuck with me. This woman—Kiki Preston was her name—once said to a . . . relative of mine that you have to work out who is important to you and hold fast to them. You have to do whatever it takes to make yourself and those you love happy, because before you know it, your life could be over. And I think she's right. It's what I'm trying to do myself."

"Forgive me, Electra, I feel so terrible burdening you with all my problems when I know what a difficult time you're having just now. Never in my whole career have I had a situation where my personal life has interfered with my professional life. If you wish to employ Tommy as your bodyguard, then I have no right to stop you. I will cope, of course I will," she said.

"Hey, I think we went past keeping our relationship professional when I had my meltdown before I went into rehab. You've been wonderful to me, Mariam, and I wouldn't do anything to jeopardize either your happiness or our future relationship. Promise."

"Well, that is very kind of you to say, but I am a professional and you don't need to take my feelings into account. Now, shall we talk about your design project?" she said, putting on her brightest smile.

Shaken by my experience in the park yesterday, I decided to go to the gym to work out. As I pounded the treadmill, I thought about how my life had changed in the past few weeks. Before, all I'd done was travel from one shoot to the next. Now it was one shoot every ten days or so, yet in between, my life seemed to be overflowing with personal stuff. And however tough some of that might be, I knew I could cope because I had managed to gather a group of great people around me. One of them was my actual blood, and the others seemed to really care about me.

Which immediately brought me to Miles.

I missed him. Not in an "I haven't seen you in a while" kind of missing but in a permanent dragging at my heart—it was a feeling I couldn't quite describe. It was as if I wasn't whole if he wasn't around, which sounded kind of weird *and* serious. Maybe Lizzie was right and he was too intimidated by me to say anything. Or maybe I just hadn't shown him how I felt about him.

But I was scared, too, because I *had* shown Mitch how I felt. In fact, I'd been so needy, I wanted to vomit when I thought about the person I'd been with him. I just couldn't let myself go there again . . .

Later, in the car on the way to my AA meeting, on a whim I redirected the driver to take me by the Flatiron Building to the meeting nearby. If Tommy was in trouble—which I guessed he was—I had a feeling that's where I'd find him.

Sure enough, there he was, sitting a few rows in front of me, his red baseball cap marking him out. He didn't speak this time, and neither did I—after yesterday, if I started, I'd never stop, and I just needed time to process all I'd learned slowly and in my own time. When the meeting was over, I decided to lurk at the back of the room and wait for him to pass by me.

"Hey, Tommy!" I called to him. "Fancy meeting you here."

"Oh, hi, Electra. How are you?"

I saw that his face was pale and his eyes were red, as though he hadn't slept for days. The good news was that I didn't catch any scent of alcohol on his breath as he spoke to me.

"I've missed your presence outside my building," I said cheerily. "Where have you been?"

He shrugged. "Oh, you know, places."

"Want to grab a coffee?" I asked him. "I mean, not that coffee," I said, indicating the urn.

"Really?" He looked at me in surprise.

"Yeah, why not?"

"I . . . okay, then."

We found a place just around the corner and sat down.

"Are you okay, Tommy?" I asked him.

"To be honest," he said and blew on his espresso, "life ain't so great at the moment."

I decided this wasn't the moment to pussyfoot around. "Look, I know what's happened. With Mariam."

"Seriously?" He looked shocked. "How?"

"Long story short, I got mugged in the park yesterday and everyone is telling me I need a bodyguard. So I immediately thought of you and told Mariam, who started crying and went and locked herself in my guest bathroom. Then the whole tale came out."

"Oh, gee, Electra, I'm sorry to put you to any trouble." Then he looked up at me, and I could see the tiniest glint of hope in his eyes. "She locked herself in the bathroom and cried?"

"Yup, she did. She loves you, Tommy, and apparently you love her. I mean, I heard you say it yourself at AA last week. I was at the back. Of course I didn't know you were talking about Mariam, but—"

"Yeah, well, it's all over anyway. She dumped me."

"But do you know why she dumped you?"

"Not really, no. But I can guess. I mean, look at me, Electra, who'd want me? I'm a mess," he said, and then tears came to his eyes.

"Mariam, for one," I said firmly. "This has nothing to do with how she feels about you, Tommy. She thinks you're wonderful. It has everything to do with the fact that she is Muslim. And apparently, a Muslim woman can't marry a man who isn't. It's as simple as that."

"You're kidding me." Tommy looked at me as though I'd landed from another planet and didn't understand humans. "She never even mentioned that to me."

"As she said to me only a couple of hours ago, you hadn't proposed or anything, so she thought it would be kind of weird for her to mention it, but that's the reason, I swear."

"You mean, if I was Muslim, she'd *want* to marry me?"

"Yes, and from the state of her this morning, tomorrow if possible. She ended it because she couldn't see a way forward. You and I can't understand because we're not Muslim, but her entire life—her family, her friends—everything is based around that. She knows you have a kid, too, and, well, what with other things, she felt it was all too complicated."

"Sure, I have my daughter, but my ex-wife's met some guy and wants to take her to California to live with them. Which is another reason why I found myself back at AA. Without my daughter or Mariam . . . Oh, man, Electra, I'm struggling right now."

"Of course you are, Tommy. Okay, I'm gonna cut to the chase: if the deal with Mariam was that you had to convert to her faith in order to be with her, would you?"

"Now, that's a tough one. You're talking to someone who served in Afghanistan. The atrocities I saw that were carried out in the name of Allah . . . I mean, I'd walk across hot coals to be with her, and I understand I was dealing with extremists over there, but to become one of them—" Tommy shook his head. "I just don't know."

"Mariam knows what you went through out there. She's thought all this through, which was why she couldn't bring herself to mention it. Why is life so damned complicated?"

"You tell me, Electra. I mean, I meet a girl that I know is right for me in every way, yet here we are."

"Listen, I'm only the messenger, and now it's down to you two to decide what to do. I understand your dilemma, but isn't love meant to cross boundaries? At the end of the day, she's just a woman and you're just a man. Anyway, at least now you know the real reason why she dumped you. And maybe it is just all too complicated, but that's for you to work out. Now I better head off. And by the way," I said as I stood up, "I'm serious about offering you that job as my bodyguard. But obviously, while things are uncertain between you and Mariam, it just wouldn't be right, would it?"

"No, but thanks anyway."

"Keep in touch, Tommy. I worry about you."

"Thanks for the coffee, Electra. And taking the time to care," he added as I left him sitting there hunched over his cup.

As the car drove me back through New York, I glanced out of the window at the people on the sidewalk, thinking that each one of them had their own dramas playing out that none of us passing by would ever know about. The thought comforted me; it was all too easy to believe that everyone else had a perfect existence (and that certainly seemed to be what the media spewed out every day—I only needed to think of all the endless pictures of me getting into and out of limos dressed to the nines on my way to some celebrity party) when the reality was just sooo different.

*Well,* I thought, *I've done my best to play fairy godmother to two of my favorite people, and now I just have to let them work it out.*

"Electra?"

"Hi, Stella," I said into my cell as I was getting into bed that evening.

"I was just calling to check how you are."

"I'm okay."

"I—I've been so concerned about you since you left. What I told you yesterday was enough to traumatize anyone, let alone a person who recently walked out of rehab. I couldn't bear it if I'd hindered your recovery process in any way."

"As a matter of fact, I kind of feel that knowing about my past is *part* of my recovery process. Of course it was upsetting, but I didn't know my mom, so even though I can't stand the thought of how she died, that makes it easier. Really," I added because I could hear the genuine fear and concern in my grandmother's voice.

"Your attitude is incredible, Electra, and I'm"—Stella's voice cracked and she gulped—"so, so proud of you. I just wanted to tell you that."

"Thanks," I said, knowing I was in danger of welling up, too.

"Would tomorrow be too soon to come visit you? I have something I want to ask you. I can drop by in the evening, at seven, maybe?"

"Okay, I'll see you then."

As I lay in bed, not only did I realize that my cravings for the Goose were definitely lessening but also that, from the sound of her concern, my grandmother truly cared about me. And I was beginning to like her more, too, now that she'd shown her vulnerable side. If I needed a role model, I thought, then I sure had one right there. I'd looked her up earlier on the internet, and it seemed there was no cause she hadn't spoken out for, no country she hadn't visited through her current role with Amnesty International. She'd won all sorts of awards and accolades, and as I began to feel sleepy, I realized that my modeling days were almost certainly coming to an end. I wanted to do something to make a difference, too . . .

I was just dropping off when my cell phone rang.

"Electra?"

"Hi, Miles, everything okay?" I asked sleepily.

"Shit, did I wake you? I only just got in from work, and I wanted to tell you that Vanessa's good for a visit this weekend."

"Fantastic! And how are you?" I asked.

"Oh, snowed under with work . . . I was thinking tonight that maybe it's time for a change. I'm just not enjoying what I do anymore."

"That's weird, 'cause I was just thinking exactly the same thing."

"Well, it's about time I took a break. You doing anything tomorrow night?"

"Nope, apart from getting takeout with Lizzie, maybe."

"You wanna get some dinner with me instead?"

"Yeah, sure, why not?" I said as my heart rate sped up about a hundred thousand beats.

"Great, I'll come collect you around about eight, okay?"

"Sure, perfect, see you tomorrow."

"Good night, Electra."

"Night, Miles."

I closed my eyes and then gave a little wiggle of excitement in my bed before falling asleep with a smile still planted firmly on my face.

# 52

I couldn't remember ever taking so long to choose an outfit for what I wasn't even sure was a date. I had absolutely no idea whether he would take me to the nearest diner or uptown to a smart restaurant. I was sad that the effect of the leather pants had been used up so briefly on his last visit, so in the end, I decided to go vintage with a pair of flared orange Versace pants and a silk blouse that gave the look an air of elegance. Some heavy ethnic orange beads went around my neck, and I was ready for anything.

"You look great, Electra," said Lizzie as she arrived in the bedroom for a viewing. "I just love those trousers, although they'd look hilarious on little old me."

"Hey, tell me what you think about some of the designs I've been playing with this afternoon," I said as I heaped the massive pile of clothes I'd tried on back into the wardrobe for the maid to sort out tomorrow.

"Some of these are great," Lizzie said admiringly. "You're going for it, then?"

"I am. All the profits will be for the drop-in center—I'm gonna get Susie's in-house PR to come visit me in the next few days and get some interviews set up. Mariam's found me a company that can turn my designs into actual clothes, because I wouldn't have the first clue how to do it. We've got the ethical fabric lined up, and I'm really fired up about it."

"A new venture," said Lizzie with a smile. "Well, if you want anyone to do the accounts, I'm good with numbers, so just say the word."

"I might just take you up on that."

"You know what, Electra? Tonight, you're just so full of . . . light. It's lovely to see."

"Yeah, well, it's a new me, and I'm embracing it," I said as the bell rang. "That'll be Stella. Do you mind letting her in?"

Lizzie left, and I went to the bathroom to make one last check of my face.

I felt cool and composed as I walked through to the living room to greet my grandmother. She immediately gave me a hug and reiterated Lizzie's sentiments about my outfit, and somehow, even though I'd been told a million times how beautiful I was, coming from my new best friend and my grandmother, it meant a lot.

"I don't think I need to ask you how you are, Electra," Stella said, sitting down in her usual chair as I poured some water and handed it to her.

"I'm good. As a quote Pa left for me said, life can be understood only backward, but it must be lived forward."

"Even though I only had the pleasure of meeting him briefly, it was obvious that your pa was a very wise man. I truly got the feeling that he'd seen a lot in his life."

"Well, my sisters and I wish we knew just *what* he'd seen. He was a total enigma. We never knew what he did or where he went when he was away or why he collected us girls together from all over the world. And we'll never know now, because he's dead."

"Do you miss him?"

"Yes, I do, badly. Now that the anger has gone."

"Wherever he is, I know he would be so proud of you. Speaking of which, I have something to ask you. Do you remember you saw me on TV that night, speaking about the AIDS crisis in Africa?"

"How could I forget it?"

"They've asked me to go to the Concert for Africa at Madison Square Garden and speak to the audience, tell them what I've seen out there. And . . . well, I'd like you to come onstage with me, talk to the audience—which will be millions of people globally—about the epidemic of drug addiction among the young, both here in New York City and around the world. Dirty needles are one of the major causes of the spread of HIV, and I know Obama is a big supporter of the campaign. Would you? Could you?"

"I—" I was so taken aback, I opened and closed my mouth like a goldfish. "Me? But, Stella, I'm just a model. I mean, I've never given a speech in my life—I'm a clotheshorse, I don't have a voice, I—"

"Oh, but you do, Electra. And your story, and the way drugs nearly destroyed you, would be such a powerful message to the youth around the world, because it would show them that it could happen to anyone, don't you see?"

"Oh, wow." My head was spinning at the thought.

"When I was out in Africa these past few months, I saw the pushers, I saw the pimps with their prostitutes, too drugged up to know what the hell they were doing and with whom. Half of those women—some of them as young as ten or eleven—will end up catching the HIV virus and dying slow and painful deaths. Many of them leave children behind. Electra, do it for your mama, for the terrible end she suffered. I—"

I looked at my grandmother's eyes, which were positively blazing with passion, and realized how she had become such an icon. She was even managing to half convince me that I should stand up there in front of millions of people and talk about my addiction.

"But it's a Concert for Africa, Stella, and besides—"

"Yes, it is! And where are your ancestors from originally, Electra? Where am I from? Those people out there—women in particular—don't have the platform that we do. We're here to speak on their behalf, don't you see?"

"Okay, okay, Stella, whoa." I took some deep breaths. "Let me think about it for a while, will you? I'm just not sure I'm ready to tell the world about my . . . problems, you know? They will follow me forever if I do."

"I get that, Electra, but equally, it might mean that you receive the level of publicity and funds for your drop-in center that you could only dream about. This kind of opportunity only comes once in a blue moon."

Suddenly, my idea of designing a clothing range began to feel very small in comparison to what Stella was suggesting.

"Can I think it over? Please, Stella?"

"Of course you can. And I'm sorry to land this on you today after the trauma of hearing about your mama, but if you're going to do it, I'll have to let them know so they can schedule you in."

"When is it?"

"Saturday night."

"Shit!" I said. "Sorry to swear, but that's real soon."

"Yes, it is, which is why I need an answer from you by tomorrow."

"Well, I'm seeing Miles tonight—the guy who was in rehab with me. I mean, he wasn't actually *in* rehab because he's recovered, but anyway, it's a long story."

"He must be pretty special—you're lit up tonight, honey." Stella smiled as she repeated what Lizzie had said to me earlier.

"Thanks. Hey, Stella, did you never find another man to light you up?"

"Not in the way you mean, but don't worry your head about me, honey, I haven't gone without when I needed some company. Anyway, let's leave that be now, because the other thing I wanted to say to you is that I would like to, in the fullness of time, take you to Kenya, show you the place where I was born and where your forefathers and -mothers, the Maasai, live. I know you've heard me talk about it, Electra, but until you've seen it for yourself, you just can't comprehend the beauty. For years I've thought that when I retire, I'd move back there—I still own Bill's cottage by Lake Naivasha—but my retirement never seems to come. And, of course, I'm not going anywhere until after the election in November. It'll be the proudest moment I ever have if I live to see a black president get into office."

"Yeah, it will be amazing," I agreed, suddenly understanding the resonance and magnitude of such an event for every black person around the world. "I . . . wanted to ask you something."

"What's that, honey?"

"I just bought a house a few weeks ago—it's down in Tucson—and since I started to understand how much suffering and poverty and abuse there is in the world, I've begun to feel guilty that I bought it."

"No, Electra, you really shouldn't. Life can never be fair—there will always be the rich and the poor—even Jesus himself admitted that in the Bible. So enjoy your wealth, but be prepared to use your privilege to help those who haven't been so lucky. It's obvious you're not greedy for material things, anyway."

"Is it?"

"Yes. How much of you is in this apartment, for example?" Stella waved an arm around the room. "I bet you've hardly touched your money, have you?"

"To be honest, no, I haven't, until I bought my house this month."

"There you are, then. It's because its accumulation doesn't interest you."

"Well, it might if I didn't have it," I retorted, and my grandmother laughed.

"True. You really are something, Miss Missy." She smiled as the concierge phone beeped.

I checked my watch and saw that Miles was ten minutes early.

"Who's that?"

"Miles, but he'll just have to wait downstairs until we're finished."

"Invite him up, for heaven's sake. Don't leave the poor guy down there by himself," she ordered me.

With a sigh, I did, knowing I'd have to witness serious fanboying and we might not get out for dinner on time.

"Hi, Miles," I said as he walked in. "How are you?"

"Better, breaking the back of the cases on my desk and—" he stopped midsentence as I led him into the living room and he saw who was sitting there. Stella stood up to greet him.

"Hello, I'm Stella Jackson, Electra's grandmother. And you are Miles—"

"Miles Williamson," he said as his long legs covered the distance of my spacious living room in one and a half paces, and he took Stella's hand. "It's an honor to meet you, ma'am. I heard you speak once at Harvard. You've done amazing things and been an inspiration to me personally."

*Oh God*, I thought, *he looks as though he's about to cry.*

"Why, thank you, Miles, but as I'm sure you're aware, what I do is just a drop in the ocean."

"No, it's more than that, ma'am. You've been a voice for those who don't have one, and you haven't cared who hears it."

"That's true." Stella chuckled. "I've made as many enemies as I've made friends in my lifetime, but you gotta speak out and be heard, don't you?"

"You sure do, and on behalf of me and my generation, I want to take the chance to personally thank you for doing that."

"Electra and I were just talking through an idea I've had for her, haven't we, Electra?" Stella eyeballed me.

"Yeah, we have, but I'm not sure—"

"I don't want to hold you two young things up, but won't you sit down for a moment, Miles? It might be good to hear your opinion on my suggestion."

"Sure." Miles walked to the chair opposite Stella and sat down as I stood there, arms folded, and glared at my grandmother.

"Can't we talk about this another time?"

"Sorry, Electra, but Miles is your friend, and he might have a valid opinion on the subject."

*Yeah, right*, I thought. *He'd fly to the moon for you if you asked him to.*

I stood there as Stella outlined her plan for me to speak at the concert. I braced myself for Miles's enthusiasm and subsequent persuasion to the cause.

"I see," he said when Stella had finished. Then he turned and looked at me. "I can understand why you're reluctant, Electra. You've been through a lot recently, and doing something like that—baring your soul in front of millions—takes real bravery. You need time to think about it, don't you?"

"Yeah, I do," I said with feeling.

"As I said to Electra, we don't have that much time. I have to tell them by tomorrow so she can be put in the program," Stella said.

"I think the last thing Electra needs is that kind of pressure, if you don't mind my saying so, ma'am. Now, I'm gonna take your granddaughter out to dinner, and the two of us can talk it through." Miles stood up. "Ready to go, Electra?"

"Yup."

Then he reached out a hand and offered it to me. I walked across the room to him, took it, and felt him squeeze it tightly. He turned to Stella. "It's been a pleasure to meet you, and I hope we can talk again soon. Good night."

And with that he led me out of the apartment.

Maybe it was the *swoosh* of the elevator going down, but I felt a weird rush of something in my stomach that just might be called love. By the time we reached the lobby, there were tears in my eyes that I couldn't explain.

"Wasn't that rude of us?" I asked him as, still holding my hand, he walked me outside into the warm June night.

"Oh, she'll cope." He grinned at me as he hailed a cab.

"Where are we going?"

"To a special place I know." He gave me a sideways glance. "You couldn't be more suitably dressed if you tried."

We didn't speak much on the journey. We were no longer holding hands, and I wished we were. I could see we were heading uptown toward Harlem. We stepped out in front of a restaurant on the main drag and went inside.

"Welcome to La Savane. Thought it was time you were introduced to some African cuisine."

Over delicious grilled fish, something called plantain, and couscous, I gave him a potted version of what Stella had told me about my mom and her horrible death.

"Wow, Electra, that's all a very big deal. You sure you're coping?"

"Yeah, I am. I was worried that I wouldn't, but it feels like my brain has had this humungous spring cleaning—a clear-out of all the shit that was in it, you know?"

"Sounds like you've been baptized with holy water and you're starting afresh as a new person."

"Yup, if you want to use a religious metaphor, then that just about de-scribes it. I expected to feel more upset about my mom—especially her terrible end—but as I said to Stella, I never knew her, and compared to the way I feel about Pa dying, it hasn't hit me anywhere near as hard. I've decided I don't want to go out to Hart Island—I read about it online, and it sounds like such a miserable place. I mean, they buried unidentified bodies in a mass grave." I shuddered.

"I agree, but maybe you could talk to Stella about marking her passing in some way."

"Yeah, that's a cool idea, I will. I was also thinking whether the sperm, as I call my biological dad, could still be alive."

"He could be, yes, and maybe one day you'll get to find him if you want to. DNA testing is moving on fast, and I'm sure they'll be building up some kind of data bank so that you can find blood relatives. But that's not for now."

"No. Thanks for pulling me out of the apartment the way you did, by the way."

"I could see your grandmother was putting you under pressure, and that's the last thing you need right now. She's a powerhouse, isn't she? Full on when she wants something, but I guess that's how she's managed to achieve all those things. You don't move mountains by not speaking up."

"What do you think about her idea of me telling my story to millions?"

"That's not for me to say, Electra."

"I know it isn't, Miles, but I've got to ask someone their opinion, don't I?"

"I can see why she wants you to do it: you're a public figure and an icon to young people around the world. Stella may be a thousand times more experienced in these things than you are, but any speech she gives won't get the attention that a few words from you would attract."

"But I'm a face, not a voice."

"You are, and if that's the way you prefer to stay, then don't do this. The question has to be, Electra, is it?"

I sighed. "Yes . . . no . . . oh, I don't know, Miles. I mean, I told you last night that I was thinking of making some changes. Modeling just isn't enough for me anymore. And yes, maybe it is in my genes, but I do want to be a force for good and help kids like Vanessa. But there's a big difference between doing a few press interviews about the drop-in center—dipping my toe into the water—and my first gig as an activist being in front of millions of people."

"Yeah, I get that completely."

"I mean, maybe if I was still on the hard stuff, I'd be able to get up the courage to walk out on that stage, but—"

"Don't even say it, Electra. You can't risk doing anything that would jeopardize your recovery."

"Even if I was doing something that could raise millions for the drop-in center and maybe other ones like it across America?" I said, giving him a wry smile.

"That would be cool, admittedly, but not at the risk of your mental health. And if you don't feel you're ready to deal with a big moment like this, then you just keep your powder dry and wait until you are."

"The problem is, I'm not good at waiting for anything, and if I was going to start this campaign—which I was anyway—then wouldn't it be crazy to turn an opportunity like this down?"

"No, because the most important thing is *you* and what you can be in the future. I keep telling you that you've got to remember you're still young."

"Well, at least I think I've found a place to channel all that fire and passion I have inside me. I've got to use it to help others, not dampen it down with the Goose. Like, use my anger issues as a positive force for change and get angry on behalf of others."

"Totally. Excuse me," Miles said as I saw him well up.

"Shit! Did I say the wrong thing?"

"No, just the opposite. I'm just so damned proud of you, that's all."

"Aw, Miles, don't get me going, too." I fanned myself as a young black woman walked up to our table, staring at me shyly. "Hi there." I smiled at her, glad of the distraction.

"Hi, Electra. I . . . I just wanna say that, well, I'm a fan. Like, you bein' black and successful and shit, you inspire me and my friends."

"Hey, thanks, I appreciate that."

"And I really like your new Afro. Maybe I'm gonna give it a go—do the chop, 'cause me and my posse just can't afford the weaves and relaxers and stuff, y'know?"

"Yeah, you go for it, honey, it's the best decision I ever made."

"Can I take a picture with you?"

"Course you can. Come sit by me, and my friend will do the honors."

Miles duly did so, and the girl walked away from the table, smiling from ear to ear.

"Aw, that was cute," I said. "Maybe I could do one last photo shoot with my Afro and it might encourage other kids to escape the tyranny of the hairdresser."

"Well, if you ever wanted proof that you're a role model, Electra, and anything you do is gonna be seen and heard by the youth around the world, I think that was it," said Miles.

"As long as she doesn't tell the paps she's just seen us together; otherwise you're going to end up with your face in the papers."

"Yeah, I don't know how you cope with that stuff. I couldn't."

*If you were with me, then maybe you'd have to . . .*

"Anyway, let's talk about something else, shall we?" I said abruptly. "I have a situation that I wanted to talk through with you. It has to do with my PA, and I wondered if you had any thoughts."

I explained the Mariam/Tommy scenario as Miles listened intently.

"Yeah, that's a tough one," he agreed. "She has her faith, and he's an Afghanistan vet." He shook his head. "What is it with us humans? We always seem to fall in love with somebody who presents us with all kinds of difficult dilemmas."

"But they love each other. They want to be together, and if they could figure it out, selfishly, I'd have the perfect team. Tommy's a great guy, Miles. And you already know how lovely Mariam is. I mean, you're into the religious stuff; if you met, say, a Muslim woman or even a nonbeliever, would it stop you from moving on with the relationship?"

"There's two issues there, Electra. One is the fact there's nothing specific in the Bible to say that women are forbidden from intermarriage. In Mariam's religion, it is forbidden. The second, and to me the most important, thing is the social and cultural issue. Being part of a religion, whatever it may be, provides you with an identity and a community of others who believe in the same moral codes as you. And in a world where morality seems to be slipping away day by day, those communities and that sense of identity become even more important. In my book, anyway. So for Mariam, I would have guessed that the thought of bringing an outsider into her 'club' is just as big an issue as the fact it's technically forbidden for her to marry him. And then you have Tommy and his difficult experience out in Afghanistan, not to mention the Twin Towers and the hatred that's left behind . . . The answer is, I don't know. It's a tough situation. Listen, why don't I talk to him? Maybe I can explain a little bit better where Mariam is coming from. I know some about the Muslim faith—the good bits of it, I mean, of which there are many. He might need to be made aware of those right now."

"Would you, Miles? That would be amazing. Thanks."

Then a weird silence descended on the table, which felt really uncomfortable. Miles was staring at the wall behind me, so I fiddled with my napkin, sensing the change in atmosphere.

"Listen, Electra. Maybe this isn't the moment to talk about it, but—" I saw him swallow hard. "I . . . well . . . I spoke to my pastor before I came over for some advice, and he said I should just spit it out. So here goes: you might have noticed that I enjoy your company a lot. And the truth is that I—despite my best intentions not to—have developed feelings for you. The point is, as I'm sure you learned in rehab, two addicts in a relationship is not usually a cool thing. You're only in the foothills of recovery, too, which makes it even more dangerous. There's always the risk that we will drag each other back down into the shit. Then there's the fact that you're an international superstar and I'm a two-bit lawyer who just about earns enough to keep body and soul together in this crazy expensive city we live in. I'm gonna be honest with you now and say that I am just not sure I could deal with the celebrity lifestyle you have. And even if I told you that the fact you earn a million times more than I do wouldn't affect me, it might, because maybe my sad male ego couldn't cope with it. And then there's the fact that now that I've said all this, you might not be interested in any relationship other than a platonic one, which would make this conversation null and void, anyway."

At that point, he was leaning in toward me so that any listening ears wouldn't be able to hear him. I could see he was waiting for an answer.

"Okay, thanks for sharing, as they say in AA. Yup." I nodded. "I get everything you say."

"And?"

"And what? Oh, come on, Miles, are you going to make me say it out loud or what? Like, surely I've made it obvious I'm interested in you?"

"Well, yeah, I know you like me, but I thought it was just maybe on a friendship level, because of our connection through helping Vanessa."

"Yeah, it's all of that, but it's"—I gulped—"more than that."

"Right, okay, I'm not sure whether that makes me happy or just shit scared." Miles sat back, relief on his face.

"Are you seriously telling me you didn't know? Like, how I felt about you?"

"Yeah, girl, that's what I'm saying." He smiled. "I mean, look at you! You're famous, rich, with the world at your feet. You could have anyone, have had everyone—"

"Hey! I haven't had *every*one," I countered indignantly.

"I meant, superstars like Mitch Duggan and that socialite guy with the stupid name . . ."

"Zed Eszu, you mean."

"Yeah, him. If you'll excuse me for saying it, he looks like a total prick."

"Oh, he is, but that's another story. And it's true, I haven't been a vestal virgin, and if you want one of those, don't come knocking on my door."

"I'm not judging your morality, Electra; you're single and free to do what you want. Though if you were ever with me and you cheated, then that would be the end."

"Good to know." I rolled my eyes at him. "Wow, Miles, you sound like a total lawyer, listing all the possible problems to our hypothetical relationship before we've even begun it! So would you want to drag me into that church of yours and make me take vows of chastity?"

"I sure would, yeah. In an ideal world, that is." He grinned. "Anyway, your telling me about Mariam and Tommy makes everything I've been worrying about seem small and insignificant in comparison. Put simply, I just dig being with you. You brighten up my day, I can't wait to speak to you—"

"Me, too," I said. And we just sat there and smiled at each other.

Then Miles reached out his hand across the table to me, and I took it.

"The point is, despite all my reservations, I think we're good together, Electra, aren't we?"

"Yes," I said. "I know we are."

# 53

I woke up on Saturday morning not knowing whether I wanted to open the blinds and give the world the biggest hug ever for making me feel so happy or run to the bathroom and vomit my guts up. I chose the former, just because it was so dark and the blinds needed to come up so I could actually see something. Thanking the world and a higher power for giving me Miles, I then felt my stomach roll at the thought of what I had agreed to do later today. My hands shook as I grabbed the speech that he and Stella had helped me write yesterday. With the sheet of paper in front of me, I closed my eyes and tried to recite it, but my voice came out as a squeak.

"Shit shit shit!" I pulled the comforter over my face and lay there, contemplating asking Mariam to book me a jet to anywhere that wasn't near New York. In my entire life, I'd never been as terrified as I felt right now.

I got up, feeling my tummy churn and my heart beat hard against my chest, and went in search of coffee. Lizzie was standing in the kitchen, her wonky face devoid of makeup.

"Morning, Electra. Sleep well?"

"Nope. Next question?" I said as I pulled the coffeepot from its stand and poured some coffee into a mug.

"Seriously, you're going to be great, I just know it."

"Lizzie, I am *so* not, and I wish I'd never agreed to it. I'll probably just run offstage in fright—if I ever manage to get my legs to walk me onto it in the first place and—" I then swore loudly and thumped the table. "How did I ever allow myself to get talked into this?" I groaned.

"Because secretly, underneath all that understandable fear, you want to do it. For your mother, your grandmother, and all those kids out there who need you to speak out for them," said Lizzie sagely.

"That's if I *can* speak . . . I tried to go through my speech, and I could barely talk. Shit, Lizzie, what have I done?" I sat down at the table and rested my head on my arms.

"Darling Electra, we're all going to be with you, and I just know you can do it. Now, why don't you go out for a run and clear your head whilst I make breakfast?"

"Because A, you've all banned me from running in the park since my mugging, and B, I'll just puke up any breakfast you offer me."

"Get dressed, Electra, and go downstairs. There's someone waiting for you in the lobby. He'll look after you, okay?"

"Really? Who?"

"You wait and see. Now, off you go," she said in her best maternal voice.

I did so, still trying to work out who it could be that was waiting for me downstairs. Miles, maybe . . . although when he'd kissed me good night yesterday (and it had been a very long and wonderful kind of kiss), he said he'd be around with Stella to pick me up at three this afternoon.

There wasn't anyone in the lobby, so I jogged outside and nearly had a heart attack as someone tapped me on the shoulder. I was obviously still suffering from the aftereffects of the mugging.

"Hi, Electra. Gee, I'm sorry to startle you."

"Tommy! What are you doing here?"

"Well, you did offer me a job as your bodyguard, and I guess I thought I'd better give me a free trial to see if I measure up."

"But—"

"Hey, I know you got a busy day, so let's talk as we run, okay?"

"Okay."

So off we went, Tommy comfortably keeping pace beside me. He told me how Miles had contacted him and they'd met for a coffee a couple of days ago. How Miles had explained to him that the Quran was actually a beautiful book full of wisdom and grace but that, as in any religious or political organization, there would always be extremists who took words out of context and twisted them to suit their own purpose. And that if things were to progress with Mariam, it wouldn't be the worst thing in the world to join her faith.

"I mean, I'm still working on all that," he said, "trying to get my head around it and stuff, but I bought a copy of the book, and Miles is right, it is beautiful. Mind you, it's so long and I ain't the greatest of readers, so my death might come before I get to finish it." He chuckled. And it was good to hear him laugh.

Then he told me how he'd called Mariam and they'd met, after a lot of persuasion from Miles, apparently.

"And I just told her that I knew why she'd ended the relationship and that if it came to the point where any marriage was needed"—he then blushed as he told me she would have to remain chaste until it took place—"then I'd think about converting. So for now, we're just gonna take things slow, you know? See how it all pans out. And if you're still serious about the offer of being your security guy, Mariam and I are gonna be around each other a lot. That'll provide a good test, I think."

"True, and you two had better get along, because I'm not keen on having any 'domestics' on my team," I said, secretly thrilled.

"I swear, Electra, any issues that Mariam and I have to deal with will be done in private and not on your time."

"And how does Mariam feel about this?"

"I think she's happy. I mean, we've got a way to go with this thing first, but you know what? Both of us agreed that, like you said, we might be dead tomorrow and it's pointless looking into the future and being miserable in the present. In the fullness of time, she's gonna introduce me to her family—wow!" He breathed. "That night I'm gonna wish I was back on the juice so I can take a gulp of something before I meet them, you know?"

"Oh, I sure do, Tommy," I said as my own stomach churned at the thought of tonight. "Anyway, I'm thrilled for you. How about I put you on a three-month contract to start off with? I'll get your details across to my financial manager, and we'll get you all set up on the payroll."

"That sounds fantastic. Seriously, Electra, I just can't thank you—or Miles—enough. You guys have saved my life. I was on the brink a few days ago, and now, well, I feel like I might have a future after all," Tommy said as we jogged out of the park and stood waiting to cross the road back to my apartment building.

"I'm just thrilled I'm going to have a running buddy every day from now on. I really need that time."

"No problem. I'll see you later."

"What?" I asked him as he stopped outside the apartment building. "Come up with me, Tommy. For starters, you need a shower, and then I need to officially introduce the newest member of my team to my friend Lizzie."

"You sure, Electra?"

"Of course. And you never know, there might be someone lurking in the elevator, and I'll need you there to protect me." I grinned, as he proudly stepped through the door by my side.

"What a sweet guy," Lizzie said after I'd introduced Tommy to her and he'd gone to use the guest shower.

"I know, he's great, and I'm so happy for him and Mariam. But I need to do something about his wardrobe; I mean, if he's coming with us tonight as my security, he needs a suit or something, doesn't he?"

"I suppose he does, yes."

"So, Lizzie, I wonder if you'd mind taking him shopping for me. He's been wearing that same hoodie since he first turned up outside here months ago. Tell him it's for work purposes, and go buy him something at Sak's or somewhere, will you? He needs a full wardrobe makeover and a decent haircut."

"Okay, boss, happy to help." She saluted me, and I knew she was. Spending a morning on Fifth Avenue buying clothes for Tommy was Lizzie's idea of heaven. And besides, I just wanted—*needed*—some time by myself.

After I'd taken a shower, then gone through the grueling process of deciding what I would wear tonight—I wanted to look professional but also like myself, so in the end, I went for the flared orange trousers and silk blouse I'd worn to dinner with Miles—I went to sit quietly on the terrace.

So much had happened since that terrible night when Tommy had walked me up and down here and helped save my life—and my future—that it was difficult to comprehend. It almost felt as though I'd been on pause for years, alcohol and drugs simply blurring one day into the next. I'd hardly been a human at all, I thought, just a facsimile of one. And even though the pain of getting well again had at some points felt unendurable, somehow, with the help of people who loved me—yes, *loved* me—I'd done it. And now here I was, sitting on the other side, always aware that life could throw me a curveball that could send me crashing backward but confident enough now to know that I would be able to gather all the strength I had to fight it.

"I'm proud of you, Electra," I said suddenly to myself. "Yeah, I am."

Then I stood, walked to the edge of the terrace, and looked up to the heavens. "And I hope, Mama and Pa, wherever you are, that you're both proud of me, too."

"Oh, my God! Shit shit shit!" I muttered under my breath as I heard the roar of the crowd only a few yards away from me. I'd been to concerts before here at Madison Square Garden—sat in the VIP box when Mitch had performed and even been backstage—but I'd never looked out at what felt like the whole of New York stamping and shouting and cheering in front of me. He (yes, *Mitch*) was onstage with his band.

No wonder rock stars need to do stuff, I thought—my undrugged heartbeat was pounding about a million to the dozen right now.

"Hey, look who I just found," said Miles, tapping me on the shoulder as I retreated from my vantage point at the side of the stage.

I turned around and saw Vanessa standing there in my Burberry cap with Ida by her side.

"Oh, my God! I didn't think you were allowed out," I said as I went to give her a hug.

"Well, tonight's special, isn't it?" said Ida. "We thought you'd like Vanessa to be here."

"How are you?" I asked her, noticing that her lovely skin no longer had that pasty color to it and that her eyes—which were as wide as saucers as she stared out beyond the wings and onto the stage—were bright and alert.

"Like, damn, 'Lectra, am I in Kansas or what? I just seen, like, 'bout four of my favorite rappers back there."

"You're not in Kansas, you're right here with me, Vanessa, and I'm so happy you are," I said, looking up at Miles and smiling at him. "Stella?" I shouted to my grandmother over the roar of the crowd. "Come and meet my friend Vanessa. She's the one that started all this, isn't she, Miles?"

He nodded. "She sure is."

Stella turned away from a man with a clipboard who was organizing the proceedings and came over to us. She looked elegant and composed in her black trouser suit with her signature jaunty scarf tied around her neck. She really was the most beautiful woman, even at her age, and I felt very lucky to have inherited her genes.

"Hello, Vanessa, I've heard a lot about you. How are you doing?"

Stella's natural air of authority made Vanessa a little tongue-tied, but she managed a few words.

"Well, everything that's happening here tonight is for you and anyone like you," said Stella.

"Three minutes!" called the guy with the clipboard to Stella as Mitch and his band played out his most famous song, which got the crowd stamping and cheering so hard it felt like the earth was shuddering beneath us.

"You okay?" asked Miles, indicating the rock star onstage.

"You know what? I'm doing just fine," I told him.

"Good, because I don't want any competition for my affections, ya know?"

"I know," I said as he put his arm around my shoulders and drew me in for a hug. I just *loved* the fact that he was taller than me and made me feel all girly and protected.

"Two minutes!" the clipboard man called to Stella as the crowd continued to holler for more at the tops of their voices.

"How are you, Electra?" said Mariam, appearing on the other side of me with Tommy, who was looking smart and handsome with his new haircut and suit.

"Shitting the proverbial, as expected. I just want to get it over with now that I'm here."

"You can do it, Electra, I know you can. And we're all here with you."

"Yes, we are," said Lizzie.

And as Mitch walked offstage toward me and I stood there with Miles's arm around my shoulders, protected by the little family of waifs and strays I seemed to have collected, I really felt they were.

"Oh, hi, Electra," said Mitch, halting right in front of us as he took a towel from one of his roadies and wiped the sweat that was dripping from his face. "How you doin'?"

"I'm real good, thanks, Mitch. You?"

"Yeah, great. Well, good to see you," he said as he gave more than a cursory glance at the handsome guy with his arm around me, who towered over his comparatively small, sweaty presence. "See you around."

"Sure," I said as he passed by, and I gave a little victory wiggle inside.

"Okay, Stella, thirty seconds, then you're on."

Stella turned to me. "So I'll give my spiel and move on to explain that I recently found my long-lost granddaughter. Then you walk onstage—"

"And the place erupts," said clipboard man from behind her. "Okay, ten seconds."

Stella smiled at me. "Good luck. I'm proud of you, Electra."

"Go!" said clipboard man.

Stella got a decent enough reception, even if the crowd was still chanting for Mitch. Then, as she started to speak, you could have heard a pin drop in the audience. Not that I heard the words she spoke, because my brain had turned to mush and every cell in my body was urging me to turn and run.

"I can't do it, I just can't," I said into Miles's ear.

"Yes, you can, Electra. Because your mama and your Pa Salt, not to mention God himself, are all looking down on you. They brought you to this moment because they believe in you and what you can become. Now, go out there and do them proud."

"Okay, okay."

"Thirty seconds, Electra."

My little posse huddled around me, all whispering encouragement to me.

"Ten seconds. She's announcing you."

"Shit!" I whispered.

"Okay, Electra, go!"

"I love you," Miles whispered into my ear. Then, very gently, he pushed me forward and I walked out onto the stage.

# MAIA

*Atlantis, Lake Geneva*
*June 2008*

# 54

*M*on *Dieu!* Ma! Claudia! Ally!" I screamed as I ran out into the hall. "Come here, quickly! Electra's on TV!"

I picked up the remote and pressed the record button, so that at least if they didn't get downstairs in time, we could watch it again. Then I stood there, fascinated and amazed, as my baby sister walked out onto the stage to join the woman who was apparently her grandmother.

A huge roar of surprise went up from the crowd. No one was more surprised than I.

"What is it?" Claudia said as she and Ma came running in.

"Look! It's Electra," I said as Ally and Bear joined us, too.

"Oh, my God!" said Ally. "Isn't this the Concert for Africa thing?"

"Yes, now shush, let's listen to her."

We all watched as the elegant older woman kissed Electra on her cheek, then stepped down from the podium so Electra could step up. Maybe it was because I knew my sister so well, but I could read the fear in her eyes as the camera panned in on her face.

"Good evening, ladies and gentlemen, kids, and everyone watching around the world," she said in a quiet, almost inaudible voice.

"Speak up, Electra!" said Ally.

"As my grandmother just said, I am here because I only just found out that I'm of African heritage. Most of you will only know me by my face; in fact, you've probably never heard me open my mouth before. And I'm not sure that I'm any good at it, but I'm gonna give it a try anyway."

There was a ripple of supportive laughter, and I watched Electra relax a little.

"I want to tell you about a difficult journey I've been on recently. You've heard a lot about drugs tonight and the effect they've had on the people of Africa, but they are not just there, they are everywhere. And . . . addiction happened to me, too. It was only because I had people around me who loved me, but equally importantly, had the finances to get me the help I needed, that I'm standing here in front of you today."

A huge cheer came up from the audience as I gripped Ma's hand and saw tears in her eyes.

"What help I got, I want every young person who is facing addiction to get, too. We—*you*—are the next generation, those who will one day take over the reins and steer our countries into the future. We cannot do that unless, as was mentioned earlier, the governments of the world come together and form a no-tolerance policy to the drug cartels who feed these killer drugs to our kids. And secondarily, we must make sure that if a kid does fall victim to addiction, the facilities are there to provide that child with the support they need."

There was another huge roar of applause. And I felt my heart swell with pride for my little sister's bravery in doing what she had done tonight.

"My standing up here by myself won't fix the problem. It needs every single one of us, in every town and city around the world, to act. In Africa, it's a known cause of the spread of AIDS and other diseases by the use of shared needles, which has to stop. Here on the streets of Manhattan, there's few places for kids like Vanessa, a friend of mine who I met in rehab, to go for help. So tonight, I begin a campaign to open drop-in centers across the nation, places where kids can go to seek help and advice when they feel there is nowhere else to turn. The governments of the world must do their part, too, by providing suitable and free facilities to kids of every social class to help them recover. I recently found out that my mother died alone in a crack den in Harlem—"

At that point, Electra's voice broke, and her grandmother came to stand by her and put an arm around her shoulder. "It was a terrible, undignified, and lonely way to end a life, and I want to make it my mission to make sure that no young person like her suffers in that way again. Please lobby your governments for action, and put your hands in your pockets and pledge money to the Rosa Jackson Drop-in Center Project—that was my mom, by the way," Electra added, as the applause and cheers ratcheted up another notch. "Because it's only by standing together that we can end this growing humanitarian crisis. Thank you."

Ally, Claudia, Ma, and I stood there with tears falling freely down our cheeks. We were so overwhelmed and proud and sad at the same time that none of us had anything to say. We watched as the crowd rose to its feet and cheered my incredibly brave little sister, who had shared her story with the world. Her grandmother took her in her arms and hugged her. I thought I saw her say, "I love you," and I said it with her.

And then a figure walked on from the side of the stage and headed toward Electra and her grandmother.

An almighty cheer went up as the man hugged Electra and shook Stella's hand.

"Isn't that Senator Obama?" said Ally. "Everyone thinks there's a chance he's going to be the next president of America."

"It is," confirmed Ma.

We watched as he continued to talk to Electra and her grandmother off mic, and then they both stood aside to let him speak.

"Thank you," he said, "but most importantly, thank you to Electra, who has so bravely stood here in front of the world and told her story. I reiterate and support everything she has just said to you, and please give generously to her cause."

At that point, we stopped listening and all sat down on the nearest couch or chair, exhausted.

Claudia sensibly handed around a box of tissues, and we blew our noses hard, except Bear, who didn't know what was going on and cooed happily instead.

"Well," said Ally as she set Bear on the floor between her legs and handed him a toy, which he immediately put into his mouth. "That was incredible. I think our little sister might just have got herself a whole new career as an activist."

"If only your father had been here to see that, he would have been so proud," said Ma, who was still very tearful. She was sitting next to me on the couch, so I reached for her hand and squeezed it.

"She's found her voice," I whispered, "and I'm just so proud of her, too."

The whole room nodded in agreement.

"I think we should leave her a message, don't you?" said Ally. "Tell her how amazing she was."

"Good idea," said Ma, who stood up to get the house phone from the kitchen.

"Wasn't that the ex-boyfriend who was performing before she came on?" queried Ally.

"It was," I replied. "I'm so pleased Electra's going to be here with us soon at Atlantis, so we can tell her in person how proud we are. What a turn-around," I said, thinking of the last time I'd seen her in Rio, when she'd been completely out of control. "And she's absolutely right to lobby for more help from the governments," I said with feeling. "I see the drug problem on every street corner as I walk through Rio."

Ma brought in the phone, and we took Electra's number from my cell phone and dialed it. All of us said something on the message, then Ally yawned. "Time for bed, I think. I'm exhausted, even if Bear isn't."

"You go upstairs, Ally. I've got jet lag, so I'm happy to stay up for a bit with him and bring him up later."

"Thanks, Maia," she said as she picked him up and handed him over to me.

I'd arrived at Atlantis from Rio only a couple of hours ago, having de-cided to make the most of my return to Europe after almost a year and spend some time with Ma, Claudia, Ally, and my new nephew. Floriano and Valentina were arriving just before we set sail for the Greek islands to lay Pa's wreath. It was the first time we'd been separated for longer than a couple of nights, and it was feeling very strange.

Just then the doorbell rang, and all four of us women jumped.

"Who on earth can that be at this time of night?" Ma asked nervously. "Christian hasn't taken the boat out tonight, has he?" she asked Claudia.

"I do not think so, no, but I can check."

Then the house phone rang in Ma's hands, making us all jump again.

"*Allo?*" she said in French. "*Ah, bien.*" She ended the call and headed to the front door.

"Who is it?" asked Ally suspiciously.

"It is Georg Hoffman."

Ally and I raised an eyebrow as Ma walked into the hall and unlocked the front door to let him in.

"Sorry to startle everyone," Pa's elegant silver-haired lawyer said as he walked into the living room. "I would have called earlier, but I thought it was simply better to come in person as soon as I could."

"What is it, Georg?" I asked. "Has something happened?"

"Yes, it has, but please, do not be alarmed. It is, well, quite incredible news, which is why I wanted to speak to you as soon as possible. May I sit down?"

"Of course." Ma indicated a chair, and Georg sat down and then drew an envelope out of his jacket pocket.

"I received this email about an hour ago at home. Ally, Maia, I think you should read it."

"Is it to do with Pa? Has something happened to one of our sisters?" asked Ally, eyeing the letter as though it contained dynamite that might blow up at her very touch.

"No, no. Please, believe me, there is nothing wrong."

"Then just tell us," Ally demanded.

"You do not know, girls, but for many, many years, your father and I have conducted a search that has taken both of us around the world. And down countless rabbit holes and dead ends. Then last year, just before your father died, he received some new information, which he passed on to me. Finally tonight, I received some news that I believe is accurate."

"What about?" Ally asked, the voice of all of us.

"Well, you must read the email, but I have reason to believe that, after all this time, we may have found your missing sister . . ."

# Author's Note

I always knew that writing Electra's story would present the biggest challenge of my writing career. Besides her ancestors' story, which takes place during the mid–twentieth century—a momentous time of change for African Americans—Electra herself is definitely the most complex and difficult of the sisters. And because all my plots are written holistically—I know only where I am beginning and ending the stories—the twists and turns of *The Sun Sister* have been as shocking and enlightening for me as they have been for Electra. Never have I found myself so deeply involved or moved as I have been by the bravery, humanity, and sheer determination of the incredible people, both past and present, whom I have encountered during the writing of it.

It is important to remember that *The Sun Sister* is a work of biographical *fiction*, backed up by factual and historical research; many of the characters who appear in the story are real, some are not. Therefore, the information and help that have been so generously shared with me are my own interpretation of fact, plus my imagination, and any mistakes are totally of my own making.

To make sure that I *was* getting my facts as accurate as I could about the issues Electra and her ancestors face in the story, I have many people to thank. Firstly, as always, to my amazing little team: Olivia Riley, who holds the fort so well, and who also runs our Seven Sisters shop site, which sends all proceeds it makes to the charity Mary's Meals, in her spare time. Ella Micheler, my tenacious, passionate editorial and research assistant, who is great at working under pressure (of which there is a lot), and Susan Moss, best friend and shoulder in times of crisis (of which there are also a lot!), who tidies up my dictation and is pedantic to the last on spotting the tiniest of errors. Jacqueline Heslop, who is simply my right- *and* left-hand woman, and Leanne Godsall and Jessica Kearton, who have come on board to ease the chaotic path of my life since the Seven Sisters appeared in it.

In Kenya: Be and Iain Thompson, Chris and Fi Manning, Don Turner, Jackie Ayton, Caro White, and Richard Leakey, all of whom generously shared their time and stories of life in Kenya during the "Happy Valley' era and beyond. High tea with Lieutenant Colin Danvers and his lovely wife, Maria, at the infamous Muthaiga Club, which stands like a time capsule on the outskirts of Nairobi, was a particular highlight. Rodgers Mulwa, our intrepid driver and fount of indigenous Kenyan knowledge, who drove us out into the middle of nowhere on tracks that hardly existed in search of the original Happy Valley, and ended up with us on the middle of Lake Naivasha in a tiny plastic boat surrounded by hippos, without breaking into a sweat once.

In New York: the biggest thanks go to Tracy Allebach Dugan (and her lovely husband, Harry). During the course of this book she has become my unofficial research assistant for all things American, and I can't thank her enough for her help. Doris Lango-Leak at the Schomburg Center for Research in Black Culture, whose tour and insight into Harlem past and present was invaluable, Allen Hassell and the Reverend Alfred Carson at Mother Zion AME Church, whose Sunday-morning service was the highlight of my entire six months of research. Carlos Decamps, our fantastic Manhattan driver, who gave me a wealth of local information, despite getting pulled over by the cops and getting a ticket as we curb crawled around Harlem so I could see what I needed to see. Also for the help I received through Jeannie Lavelle, who explained in detail the pathways Electra needed to follow to recovery at her rehab center. Adonica and Curtis Watkins, who provided so many important insights not only into African American culture but equally the painful and treacherous challenges that young addicts face when they fall foul of the law to pay for their fix. Also, and from the bottom of my heart, I thank the parents who lost their precious children through addiction and were prepared to share their stories with me in the hope that they might help others facing similar circumstances.

As always, to my many fantastic publishers around the world, who have been so incredibly supportive of the mad idea I presented them with six years ago. It's difficult to believe that we are nearing the end of such a huge project.

Julia Brahm, Stefano Guiso, Cathal and Mags Dinneen, and "the lads," Mick Neish and Dom Fahy, Melisse Rose, Lucy Foley, Tracy Rees, Pam Norfolk, Sean Gascoine, Sarah Halstead, Tracy Blackwell, Kate Pickering, James Pascall, Ben Brinsden, Janet Edmonds and Valerie Pennington, Asif

Chaudry and his daughter, Mariam (whose name I was kindly allowed to borrow for one of my characters in the story), who have all in their different ways supported me so stoically in the past year. Jez Trevathan, Claudia Negele, Annalisa Lottini, Antonio Franchini, Alessandro Torrentelli, Knut Gørvell, Pip Hallén, Fernando Mercadante, and Sergio Pinheiro—all of them publishers but, far more important these days, friends. Oh! And a special mention to Sander Knol for somehow managing to convince the whole of the Netherlands to read the Seven Sisters series!

To my family: my husband, agent, and rock, Stephen (somehow we are just about to celebrate twenty years of living, working, fighting, and laughing together!), Harry, Isabella, Leonora, and Kit: for once, I don't have any words to express the love and support they have all offered me during the past year. Nothing would mean anything without you all.

And finally, to *you*, my readers. Even though I would continue to tell my stories to myself if no one else wanted to hear them, the fact that you *do* really is amazing, because I feel part of a "gang." We all go on the journeys together—I laugh, cry (a *lot*!), and get frustrated with the characters, just as you do when they seem to be making terrible mistakes. So thank you for keeping me company on those long writing nights and equally for your support and huge generosity with our Mary's Meals charity: the Seven Sisters shop site will raise enough money this year to sponsor two African schools, providing a lunchtime meal for each child, which therefore encourages both the pupil and the parents to make sure they attend.

Electra's story has left me humbled and horrified as I found myself dealing with issues that I knew existed but that sat safely on the edges of my life. As a novelist, I am aware that as a white European woman of Irish origin (although less than one hundred years ago, I would have been an ethnic minority, too), I currently have an advantage in the sphere of publishing, where so many ethnic voices are underrepresented. I entreat publishers to broaden their author spectrum, so that the world can read more stories from the cultures they represent. In a world whose current political climate feels as if it is edging perilously backward toward the dark days of the past, *never* has it been more important to do so. For now, I can only hope that I've done Electra, and those whose stories she represents, justice.

Lucinda Riley
October 2019

# BIBLIOGRAPHY

Andrews, Munya. *The Seven Sisters of the Pleiades.* (Spinifex Press, 2004).

Barnes, Juliet. *The Ghosts of Happy Valley.* (Aurum, 2013).

Bell, Janet Dewart. *Lighting the Fires of Freedom: African American Women in the Civil Rights Movement.* (New Press, 2018).

Bennett, George. *Kenya: A Political History: The Colonial Period.* (Oxford University Press, 1963).

Bentsen, Cheryl. *Maasai Days.* (Collins, 1990).

Best, Nicholas. *Happy Valley: The Story of the English in Kenya.* (Secker & Warburg, 1979).

Blixen, Karen. *Out of Africa.* (Putnam, 1937).

Chepesiuk, Ron. *Gangsters of Harlem.* (Barricade Books, 2007).

Collier-Thomas, Bettye. *Sisters in the Struggle: African American Women in the Civil Rights-Black Power Movement.* (New York University Press, 2001).

Crawford, Vicky L. *Women in the Civil Rights Movement: Trailblazers and Torchbearers.* (Indiana University Press, 1993).

Fox, James. *White Mischief.* (Jonathan Cape, 1982).

King, Martin Luther, Jr. *A Testament of Hope: The Essential Writings and Speeches.* (HarperOne, 2003).

Mills, Stephen. *The History of the Muthaiga Club,* vol. 1. (Mills Publishing, 2006).

Osborne, Frances. *The Bolter: Idina Sackville.* (Virago, 2008).

Saitoti, Tepilit Ole. *Maasai.* (Abradale Press, 1993).

Spicer, Paul. *The Temptress: The Scandalous Life of Alice, Countess de Janzé.* (Simon & Schuster, 2011).

Thomson, Joseph. *Through Masai Land.* (Frank Cass & Co., 1968).

X, Malcolm. *The Autobiography of Malcolm X.* (Ballantine Books, 1992).

# ABOUT THE AUTHOR

Lucinda Riley was born in Ireland and, after an early career as an actress in film, theater, and television, wrote her first book at age twenty-four. Her books have been translated into thirty-seven languages and sold twenty million copies worldwide. She is a #1 *Sunday Times* and *New York Times* bestseller.

Lucinda is currently writing the Seven Sisters series, which tells the story of adopted sisters and is based allegorically on the mythology of the famous star constellation. It has become a global phenomenon, with each book in the series being a #1 bestseller around the world. The series is currently in development with a major Hollywood production company.

To discover the inspiration behind the series and to read about the real stories, places, and people in this book, please see Lucinda's website:

www.lucindariley.com

Also on this website you can learn more about www.marysmeals.org.uk and how to contribute to its wonderful work.